Stephen White is a clinical psychologist and the author of *The Program*, as well as three *New York Times* bestsellers. He lives in Colorado with his wife and son.

Also by Stephen White

STEVEN WHITE OMNIBUS

Warning Signs
The Best Revenge

STEVEN WHITE

timewarner
paperbacks

A *Time Warner* Paperback

This omnibus edition first published in Great Britain by
Time Warner Paperbacks in 2006

Copyright © Stephen White 2005

First published separately:
Warning Signs first published in the United States in 2002 by
Delacorte Press, a division of Random House, Inc.
First published in Great Britain by Little, Brown in 2002
Copyright © Stephen W. White 2002

The Best Revenge first published in the United States in 2003 by
Delacorte Press, a division of Random House, Inc.
First published in Great Britain by Time Warner Books in 2003
Copyright © Stephen W. White 2003

The moral right of the author has been asserted.

A CIP catalogue record for this book
is available from the British Library.

ISBN-13: 978-0-7515-3788-8
ISBN-10: 0-7515-3788-8

Printed and bound in Great Britain by
Clays Ltd, St Ives plc

Time Warner Paperbacks
An imprint of
Time Warner Book Group UK
Brettenham House
Lancaster Place
London WC2E 7EN

www.twbg.co.uk

Warning Signs

to teachers

ACKNOWLEDGMENTS

In my career as a clinical psychologist, a decade of work was barely enough time for a therapist to be considered seasoned. But in the world of commercial publishing a decade is a long time indeed. Achieving longevity isn't possible without the assistance of many people and my gratitude for all the support I've received seems to grow greater every year.

In order to create *Warning Signs* I relied on guidance and instruction from some dedicated public servants who patiently led me through the specifics of their fields of expertise. My thanks to Jerry Burkhalter, a veteran of the Denver Police Department Bomb Squad, Detective Melissa Kampf of the Boulder Police Department, and Assistant District Attorney Chuck Lepley of Denver County. The responsibility for any damage done to the facts is mine, not theirs.

My wife Rose and my son Xan make all of this possible and worthwhile, and my mother Sara will always be my biggest fan. The Limericks, Patti and Jeff, believed in me at the beginning, and Al Silverman has believed in me ever since. My gratitude to them endures. Adrienne, as always, owes her medical acumen and some of her keenest insights to Dr. Stan Galansky. Elyse Morgan and Judy Pomerantz trained their critical eyes on an early version of the manuscript, and Nancy M. Hall's help was invaluable in assisting me during the difficult task of proofreading. They, too, have my thanks.

Bruce Collamore—the real one, not the fictional one in the first couple of chapters—graciously permitted me to use his name and some of his life story in support of charity. His wisdom might be questioned, but not his goodwill or his generosity. Jane Davis is an unsung hero—with great spirit and unparalleled competence she keeps my Web page humming and insulates me from more daily distractions than I will ever know. Thank you.

Fortunately for all of us, my books don't go directly from my word processor to the bookstore. First, the pages go through the hands of exemplary professionals who tune them, shine them, and prepare them for the light of day. My enduring thanks go to all of those at Bantam Dell and Doubleday whose efforts have been so beneficial to this book—especially Kate Burke Miciak, Nita Taublib, Irwyn Applebaum, Deborah Dwyer, Stephen Rubin, Gail Brussel, and Peter Gethers—and to all the wonderful people who support me year round at Janklow & Nesbit, specifically Lynn Nesbit and Amy Howell.

All women become like their mothers. That is their tragedy. No man does. That is his.

—Oscar Wilde
The Importance of Being Earnest

CHAPTER

1

Hands nipple high, palms up toward the night sky, Bruce Collamore started talking before the cops were even out of their car.

"I almost didn't call you guys. I was thinking that it was all too much like the O.J. thing. Don't you think? I mean, my dog didn't bark like that dog did, but I was walking my dog when I heard the scream. That's pretty close to the O.J. situation, isn't it? Anyway, that's why I almost didn't call. I'm still not sure I should have called. I haven't heard anything since that first scream. Right now, I think maybe it was nothing. That's what I'm beginning to think."

Two Boulder cops had responded to the 911. A coed team. Both were young, handsome, and strong.

The woman was a five-year vet on the Boulder Police force named Kerry VanHorn. She was a devout Christian who kept her religion to herself; she'd once even confided to a girlfriend that she thought prosely-tizing should be a capital offense. She had dirty-blond hair and a friendly Scandinavian face that put people at ease even when she didn't want to put them at ease. Over the years she'd discovered that if she squinted like she was looking into the sun people took her more seriously.

She was the first out of the squad car and the first to speak to the man who apparently remembered way too much about the O.J. case. She tucked her long flashlight under her arm and grabbed a pen before she squinted up at him—the guy was at least six five—and said, "Your name, sir?"

"Collamore, Bruce Collamore." He was wearing a ragged Middlebury College sweatshirt and an accom-modating smile.

"This your house?" She gestured toward the home closest to where they were standing. Jay Street was high on the western edge of Boulder, in territory that the foothills of the Rockies seemed to have yielded only reluctantly to housing. If there was a boundary between urban and rural on the west edge of town, Jay was definitely on the side of the line that was more mountain than burg. The trees and grasses were wild and haphazard, and the curbs cut into the sides of the roadway fooled no one—this was one part of Boulder where the Rockies still reigned.

"This? My house? No. God, no."

"You live on this street, sir?"

"Here? No, I live a couple blocks over on Pleasant.

I was out walking Misty. This is Misty." He reached down and tousled his dog's ears. The yellow Lab dipped her head and wagged her tail. Bruce Collamore and his dog both seemed eager to please.

"So . . . you were out walking your dog and you heard a . . ." While she waited for him to fill in the blank, she briefly lost her focus as she entertained an unbidden association to a crush she'd had on a junior high school teacher she had thought was cute.

Collamore brought her back to the moment as though he were someone who was accustomed to being in conversations where the other party's attention was wandering. He said, "A scream, I heard a scream. A loud one. Long, too. I mean, I haven't heard that many screams in my life but it, you know, seemed longer than . . . well, a normal scream. If there is such a thing? Jeez, 'a normal scream.' Did I really say that? What's wrong with me? Anyway, I think it came from that house. I'm pretty sure it did. That one. There." Collamore pointed at the gray-and-white two-story house directly across from where they stood on the edge of the road. "I had my cell phone with me so I thought I'd go ahead and call 911. Maybe it wasn't the right thing to do. I don't know. I'm a little nervous. You can probably tell I'm nervous."

She could tell. And she wasn't sure that he was nervous only because she was a cop. That suspicion made her a little nervous, too.

His left hand was balled around the dog's leash, so she couldn't see if Collamore was married. When she looked back up at him she squinted, just in case he was thinking what she was worried he was thinking. "What time was that, sir? That you heard the scream?"

"Nine fifty-one."

She wrote down the nine before she looked up from her notepad and lifted an eyebrow. The expression of incredulity interfered with her squint.

"I checked my watch when I heard the scream. You know, the O.J. thing? I thought somebody might want to know what time it happened. It really was that kind of scream—a somebody's-killing-me scream. So I checked my watch when I heard it." He exhaled loudly and ran his fingers through his hair. "God, this is embarrassing. I shouldn't have called, should I?"

She tried to make a neutral face, but wasn't sure she'd succeeded. She said, "No need to be embarrassed. We appreciate help from citizens. Can't do our jobs without it." But she was thinking that in most cities civilians ran and hid after they called 911. In Boulder they stick around on the sidewalk with their cell phones and their yellow Labradors named Misty. And maybe they keep contemporaneous records of their movements on their Palm Pilots. For all she knew this whole situation was already being tracked live on the Net.

Boulder.

Now she looked at the house he'd identified. The dwelling was an oasis of orderliness at the end of the block, the only home that looked like it could be plopped down comfortably in one of Boulder's more sedate neighborhoods. The owners of the surrounding houses—all of which were shabby in the way old cashmere is shabby—were either celebrating their good fortune at having modest homes in such a spectacular location or they were waiting for land values to escalate even more obscenely before they sold their fixer-upper to somebody who'd scrape the lot clear and start all over. She said, "You know who lives in this house, Bruce? May I call you Bruce?"

"Sure. Here? No, I don't. Like I said, I was just walking Misty. We come this way almost every night about this time. Since we walk late, most of the time we don't see anyone. Certainly don't hear many screams. Actually, we don't hear *any* screams. Before tonight, anyway. We heard one tonight, didn't we, girl?" He lowered his tone at least an octave as he addressed the dog.

VanHorn watched Misty's tail sweep the ground. She said, "And that was at nine fifty-one?"

"Yes, nine fifty-one."

"Well, we'll check that out. You don't mind staying here for a few minutes in case we have some more questions? My partner and I are going to speak to whoever is inside the house."

"No, no. We don't mind at all. Misty and I are happy to stick around."

The other cop, Kerry VanHorn's partner, was Colin Carpino. He had two years on the job. He was built like a bulldog but his creamy skin was almost hairless. VanHorn sometimes teased him that she had female relatives who shaved their upper lips more often than he did. She called him Whiskers.

As they moved up the brick walk in single file, she asked, "What do you think, Whiskers?"

"I buy lunch for a week if this is anything other than a waste of time." He shifted his long Mag-Lite from his right hand to his left.

She laughed. "It's your turn to buy. You're getting lunch tomorrow whether this is the Great Train Robbery or the lady of the house freaking out over a spider."

Carpino hit the doorbell button by the front door. They listened as it chimed like a carillon in a cathedral, and they waited.

He knocked. They waited some more.

He hit the bell again. This time he said, "Boulder Police," right after he heard the bells begin to peal inside the house. His tenor carried in the still air. The whole neighborhood of shuttered windows and closed doors had to know now that the cops were here. VanHorn waited for lights to come on, doors to open. It didn't happen. Collamore saw her looking his way and waved at her. She didn't wave back.

Whiskers reached down and tried the latch on the door. It didn't give.

VanHorn responded by touching her holster with her fingertips. The act was a caress, almost sensual in its carelessness—and it was involuntary, like a man checking for the presence of his wallet half a minute after he leaves the automatic teller machine.

The two cops waited for someone to come to the door and tell them everything was just fine.

After most of a minute had leaked into the void between them, VanHorn said, "I'll check the back of the house." She wasn't nervous yet, but she had definitely crossed over the line that separated routine from everything else that existed on a police officer's planet. The feeling was familiar, and not entirely unwelcome. The wariness sharpened her senses. She'd been around long enough to know that wasn't a bad thing.

"I'll take a look at the windows up front here and over on the other side," Carpino said.

The north side of the house was unlit, making it difficult for VanHorn to navigate the uneven path of flagstones. Spreading junipers clotted the open spaces between the window wells. An avid gardener, she hated junipers, especially spreading junipers. She alternated the flashlight beam between the path in front of her and the windows on the side of the house and noticed nothing that alarmed her. She fingered the switch of the radio microphone that was clipped to the left shoulder of her uniform blouse and said, "Nothing unusual on the side of the house. Just some unimaginative landscaping. But even in Boulder I don't think that's a crime."

Carpino replied, "Yet. Hold on, I may have something up here, Kerry." His voice betrayed no alarm. She waited for him to continue. He didn't.

She stepped lightly into the backyard. A streetlight brightened the rear of the house. She reached up and touched the button on her microphone. "What do you have, Whiskers? Open window?"

"No, I'm on the opposite side of the house from you, shining my beam inside into what looks like the living room. I see a lamp lying on the floor and some broken glass. That's all."

After again caressing the flap on her holster with the fingertips of her right hand, Officer VanHorn spent a moment examining the backyard with the beam of her flashlight. Only when she was certain she was alone in the yard did she take determined strides across a pleasant brick patio, past an almost-new gas grill, and up two steps to the door that led to the house. She grabbed the knob of the metal security door and twisted it. The door opened right up. She locked her gaze on the painted French door behind the security panel and fingered her microphone. "Back door's open. Not just unlocked, but open-open. Why don't you call for backup?"

She waited for his response long enough to inhale and exhale twice. Finally, she said, "Colin?"

He said, "Sorry. I may be looking at a person's foot, Kerry, just someone's heel. Like there's somebody lying on the floor. But I can't see past the heel. If it's a foot, then the rest of the body's behind a sofa."

VanHorn sighed. "We'd better go in. Tell dispatch."

"Will do. I'll call for backup and join you back there."

Kerry VanHorn flicked up the flap on her holster and drew her service weapon with her right hand. Her

Mag-Lite was in her left. Before she took another step she squeezed her biceps against her upper torso to convince herself that she'd remembered to wear her vest. She had.

Within seconds, Whiskers joined her at the back door. He, too, had his service weapon ready. He said, "The living room's in the southwest corner. That's where I saw the foot." She nodded and said a silent prayer before she nudged the French door with the toe of her shoe. She winced as the door squeaked open.

She yelled "Boulder Police" as she entered a big kitchen and family room. Shadowed light from the alley street lamp revealed an expensive recent remodel. Cherry cabinets. Granite countertops. Big double stainless-steel sink. Appliances that disappeared into the cabinetry. One appliance she didn't even recognize. She didn't like that kitchens had developed in such a way that people used appliances she couldn't even recognize.

But nothing was out of place. She could hear Whiskers's footsteps on the hardwood floor behind her. The resonant clap was reassuring. There was almost nothing she liked doing less as a cop than walking into dark houses.

The door from the kitchen led to a short hallway. Again she called out, "Boulder Police," and waited for a reply. Nothing. Carpino repeated the announcement. After she waited for a response that never came, she stepped past a powder room and saw a dining room on her right. She played the beam into the room for two or three seconds. It didn't appear that anyone had eaten in there recently; the table was covered with piles of mail. She gestured with her flashlight to reassure her partner before she turned toward the living room. At the bottom of a staircase she flicked the beam up the stairs. She spotted nothing that alarmed her but noticed an odd device on rails attached to the side of the staircase. She also noted a rhythmic *shush-shush, shush-shush, shush-shush* coming down from the second floor. The sound was familiar to her but she couldn't place it. *Shush-shush, shush-shush, shush-shush.* The rhythm wasn't out of place in a house. She was sure of that. But what was it that she was hearing?

Darn. She couldn't place the noise.

She took two steps into the living room and swept her flashlight beam in a wide, slow arc, looking for the foot that Whiskers had seen, praying that he was wrong or, failing that, that there was at least still a person attached to it.

The first thing that caught her attention was the lamp on the floor—she assumed it was the same one that Whiskers had spotted through the window. Then she saw the broken glass, a lot of it. The glass appeared to be some kind of pottery or ceramic; it must have been a big piece before it was busted.

No foot.

Lights flashed outside on the street. VanHorn looked up and was relieved to see a patrol car slide to the curb in front of the house. Her partner whispered,

"Backup's here." She adjusted the grip on her weapon and, for her own benefit, silently mouthed, "I'm doing fine. I'm doing fine."

EEEEHHHHHHHNNNNNN.

A loud, noxious buzzing seemed to fill the house. The sound was bitter and sour, like aural vinegar. It blared for maybe two seconds before it stopped as abruptly as it started. VanHorn's pulse jumped when the noise started and she wheeled around to check behind her. Carpino's eyes were wide as he, too, searched for the source of the sound. VanHorn's service weapon felt heavy in her hand.

She shook her head, announcing she didn't know the source of the sound. Carpino did the same.

The buzzing blared again. *EEEEHHHHHHHNNNNNN.* Once again the sharp sound stopped suddenly.

The noise had seemed to come from everywhere at once.

What was it? What was it? She couldn't place it.

She yelled "Boulder Police" one more time.

Then she noticed that the *shush-shush* had ceased, and the pieces of the puzzle fell into place. VanHorn smiled. She knew what it was. The *shush-shush* had been the refrain of a tumbling clothes dryer. The buzzer was the notification that the cycle was done. Her boyfriend's dryer made the same awful noise. She exhaled and slowly refilled her lungs. "Whiskers? That was a clothes dryer, I think. At the end of its cycle."

He said, "Oh," and definitely sounded relieved.

Someone had recently started a dryer in this house. How long did a load take to dry? Forty-five minutes? An hour?

Through the side windows she watched another black-and-white slide to a stop at the curb.

She stepped around the lamp on the floor so that she could see behind the sofa at the far end of the room. Behind the sofa was an open door. She thought it would lead back to the family room that she'd seen when she first came into the house, the one adjacent to the new kitchen. She swung the beam toward the floor behind the striped couch.

She saw the foot, paused, and then she took another step.

"Oh Jesus. Oh my God. Oh dear Jesus." If she had a free hand she would have crossed herself with it, an affectation of her Catholic past.

At the sight of the blood and the mangled tissue where the person's face should be, VanHorn felt a sour geyser erupting in her esophagus and she swallowed twice to stem the urge to vomit. She took a step back and stumbled over the broken pottery. When she returned her gaze to the body on the floor, she said, "May God rest your soul, whoever you are."

Carpino said, "What?" His voice came from behind her, maybe ten or twelve feet away.

She said, "You were right, there's a body in here, Colin. A lot of blood. Call for an ambulance, okay?"

She counted to three and told herself she was fine. But she didn't feel fine. She felt as though she should sit down to keep from passing out, but she didn't want to disturb what she already knew was a crime scene. Sequentially, she looked everywhere in the room that didn't have a bloody body. She even looked at the ceiling. For her, the act was like looking at the horizon when she was seasick. Finally, the wave of nausea eased and her neurons resumed firing and she carefully checked the room to make triple-sure she and her partner and the guy on the floor didn't have any company.

She dropped to her knees, stooped over the body, and lowered her head to listen for breath sounds. She heard nothing. To feel for a pulse, she needed to put down either her light or her gun. For a moment she weighed her choice, finally deciding to place the torch on the carpet, and, as she'd been taught, she rested three fingers on the underside of the radial bone of the man's right wrist. She was thinking the body was that of a man. The socks were men's socks. She was pretty sure of that. An exposed inch of calf was moderately hairy.

It was a man.

She felt no pulse. She thought, maybe, the body was cooler than it should have been, but only a little, and certainly not cold. She spent a moment trying to remember the speed at which a body gives up its warmth after death—a degree an hour, was that it?— and wondered if it was possible that this man was the same person who had started the dryer upstairs. He couldn't have cooled down that fast, could he? Maybe her own fingers were hot and that's why the body felt cool. That was certainly possible.

Variables, variables.

Bruce Collamore had said he heard the "somebody's-killing-me" scream at 9:51. She looked at her watch. It was 10:17. No, if this were the screamer, he wouldn't have cooled down, yet.

Hot fingers. Had to be her hot fingers.

Still on her knees, she lifted her Mag-Lite again and simultaneously turned her body to address her partner. The beam of the light danced carelessly off the ceiling and the walls. She said, "This guy's dead, and there's a lot of blood. Call for detectives and have the backup team tape off a perimeter out there. Make it a big perimeter. Tell the tall guy with the dog that he's not going anywhere for a while. We have to do the rest of the house. Get some people in here to help out. Tell them to come in the back door and walk straight to the front of the house, then turn left to the living room. And remind them not to touch anything. We have a crime scene and I don't want to be the one to mess it up."

She said a silent prayer and aimed her lamp directly at the body on the floor, trying to discern the details of the man's face through the severe damage and the copious blood.

For a second or two she thought she knew the man and tried to jar an association loose from her memory. It didn't work. VanHorn then decided that she didn't really know him. Again, she repeated her silent prayer and wondered what in heaven God had been thinking at 9:51 that evening.

She decided that He must have been seriously distracted.

CHAPTER

2

The first pair of detectives arrived about twenty minutes before midnight to find a well-delineated perimeter and a crime scene that was barely contaminated. Sam Purdy, the senior detective, was ecstatic. But he kept his joy to himself.

"Who was first officer?" he asked of the patrol cop who was manning the clipboard and controlling access to the scene.

"VanHorn and Carpino."

"RP?" Purdy was asking who had called in the crime—who was the reporting party.

"Still here."

"Wits?"

"Got one, guy named Bruce Collamore. He's the RP, too. That's him sitting in the backseat of my squad. Has a dog with him. Heard a scream a shade before ten. I talked to him a little bit—he's an interesting guy, teaches high school now, math I think. But he played a little pro football when he was younger, if you can believe it."

Purdy grunted. "That's it? That's all you know?"

The officer shrugged. "The Bengals. He was in camp for a few days with the Bengals."

"I should care where he played football?"

"Hey, it's early, Detective. We didn't want to mess with him before you guys got here. Played tight end, if you really want to know. Isn't built like a tight end now, though; he's tall enough, but he's too skinny, more like a Randy Moss type. He's crammed into the back of the squad like an anchovy in a can."

Purdy said, "I might give a shit about any of this if he played for the Vikings, but I certainly don't care about some guy who didn't last a week with the damn Bengals, that's for sure. Whose house is this?"

"Neighbor says it's a family named Peters, but the neighbor didn't hear anything that came down."

Purdy turned to his partner. "You get that? What else do we have, Luce?"

Lucy Tanner looked at her notepad. She knew he was asking her if the detective's log was current. In these circumstances, it was her job to make sure it was. She said, "We were called by dispatch via pager at ten twenty-six, arrived at the scene on Jay Street at eleven thirty-five. Six patrol officers present, all have checked in with the control officer. Medical personnel have come and gone. Photographers present and waiting for clearance to go inside. Ditto CSIs.

Weather? Clear skies, temp near fifty. One wit at the scene, already isolated. Search warrant has been requested from Judge Silverman. We're waiting on it."

"You get snaps? I want a good set of snaps. Who knows what time the photographers will get to go in."

Lucy held up a disposable camera with a built-in flash. "This side of the house is covered."

"Let's go to the back, then."

Kerry VanHorn walked across the front yard of the house, approaching the two detectives. She was squinting. "Detective? I'm Officer VanHorn. I was first officer on the scene, along with Officer Carpino."

"Sam Purdy. This is Lucy Tanner. Where's Carpino?" Purdy thought he recognized VanHorn from a recent altercation he'd investigated between a bicyclist and a pedestrian on Canyon Boulevard. He wasn't sure he'd ever heard of Carpino, didn't think he'd been with VanHorn that day.

VanHorn nodded a greeting to Lucy before she answered. "We entered the home through an open rear door. He's standing watch there."

"Who's been inside?"

"Just Carpino and me initially. After we found the deceased on the main level, two other officers accompanied us on a search of the rest of the premises. Upon further search, we found a disabled person sleeping upstairs in the master bedroom. When we couldn't arouse her enough to take a statement, we called an ambulance. Two paramedics entered the house and removed her. At my request, one of them walked through the section of the house where I found the deceased to confirm that he was, well, deceased. The ambulance left about twenty-five minutes ago. The disabled woman is now at Community Hospital. You may want to dispatch someone to get her statement, Detective. She was not particularly coherent when I tried to talk with her."

"That's it? Got any names?"

"Yes, sir. That's it. And no, sir. The woman was, like I said, incoherent. I think she said her name was Susan, or Suzanne. I had trouble understanding her. She was not able to give a last name. Neighbor a couple of doors down across the street says the family is the Peters. Only wit is the RP, guy named Bruce Collamore. He's waiting in one of the squads. Heard a scream a few minutes before ten. I don't think he's going to be much more help; he's already told us all he knows."

"Yeah, I've already heard all about Collamore. Got cut by the Bengals during training camp, if you can believe that."

"What?" VanHorn asked.

Purdy ignored her question while he went through a mental checklist and reached satisfaction that things were under control. Then he realized he'd missed something. "Coroner here yet?"

"Haven't seen anyone," she said.

Purdy made a note to have Lucy ascertain that Scott Truscott, the coroner's assistant, had been called. He said, "Good job here, VanHorn. You and Carpino managed this scene like you do it every weekend."

Purdy and Lucy followed VanHorn down the path to the backyard. Lucy snapped some photographs of the rear of the house before VanHorn introduced the detectives to Carpino. No one shook hands; Purdy and Lucy were busy pulling latex onto their fingers.

"The yard was like this? Nothing's been touched?"

Whiskers answered, "Just like you see it. No one's been back here but us since we arrived. Only things we touched outside were the doorknobs. We did that before we realized what we had."

The search warrant arrived around twelve-thirty.

The crime scene investigators and the police photographers preceded the two detectives into the house. After about fifteen minutes, the CSIs reported to Purdy that they'd finished clearing and vacuuming the path to the living room and that he could enter.

Everyone pulled coverings onto their shoes. At Purdy's request, VanHorn led the way inside and pointed out the direction she had walked to get to the living room before she discovered the body. On this return visit she went no farther than the foot of the stairs, using the beam of her flashlight to direct the detectives the rest of the way to the deceased. "He's there, behind that couch."

"All the lights were off? Just like this?" Purdy asked

as he carefully crossed the length of the room and lowered himself to a crouch a few feet from the body. The detective's feet were in a little clearing in the center of the pottery debris.

"Yes. We touched nothing in this room. I did feel the victim's wrist for a pulse and I tripped over some of the broken pottery when I got back up. The EMT was careful, too, when he confirmed the death. I watched him. That's it. Nothing else was touched down here. Upstairs was different. We tried to watch what we were doing, but moving that lady to the hospital spilled some milk. Couldn't be avoided. I've started making a list of everything I think was disturbed up there."

"Good. Finish the list and get it to me. We'll take it from here."

"Oh, I almost forgot, the dryer was on. Upstairs? There's a washer and dryer. When I first came in the house, the dryer was on. It finished its cycle just before I found the body. Made a loud buzzing sound."

Purdy took a moment to catch her eyes and smiled at her. "Scared the shit out of you, I bet, didn't it?"

She laughed. "Yeah. Scared the shit out of me." VanHorn didn't generally condone profane language. But the phrase seemed to fit the circumstances.

"That was when?"

"Ten twenty-five, ten-thirty, give or take a couple of minutes."

"Got that, Luce?"

Lucy raised her pen from her notebook but didn't look up. "Yeah, Sam. I got it."

"You can go, Officer. Good work."

Purdy stood up straight, took a flashlight from Lucy's hand, and swept the room with the beam, pausing a few times. While he perused the space, he took note of the temperature in the house, inhaled the aroma of the room, and digested how the shadows played with the darkness. He knew Lucy would be doing the same drill. In a few minutes, they'd compare impressions. When he finally stepped forward, he approached the corpse cautiously, noting the position of the lamp on the floor, treading carefully around the pieces of ceramic.

Lucy hung back; she was at least six feet behind him. Purdy could hear her breathing through her mouth.

"You okay, Luce?" he said.

She said, "Sure." But Purdy didn't quite believe her.

"You need a minute? Or are you ready?"

"I'm right behind you, Sam. I'm fine."

Maybe a stranger would have failed to recognize the catch in her voice. But Purdy heard it. "If you're going to puke, puke outside, okay?"

He expected her to curse at him in reply. Instead, she said, "I told you I'm fine, Sam."

Purdy once again lowered himself to a crouch, this time right beside the body. For a few seconds he focused on the injuries and on the blood, not on the dead person. A gestalt thing—figure, not ground. The head and face wounds that had been inflicted were severe. At least two deep crushing blows. Probably more. Blood pooled around the man's head like a lake on a dark night. The blood loss was copious. With the flashlight beam he traced a fan-shaped splatter that extended up the nearest wall all the way to the crown molding. The conclusion was obvious: The victim had been standing when he was hit and had lived long enough to bleed like a broken dike.

"Is he dead, Sam?" Lucy asked the question as though she didn't quite believe it was true.

Purdy didn't bother feeling for a pulse. He knew dead. "He's really dead, Luce. Bashed in the face and head with something heavy and hard. My money's on the lamp or this broken pottery."

She didn't reply.

Purdy asked, "Can you see outside? Has the coroner's van arrived?"

"I don't see it out there."

He thought she sounded funny.

Sam Purdy was a big man. He lowered one knee to the carpet so he could lean over and examine the undamaged part of the man's face. It took him maybe two seconds of focus to identify the victim.

"Holy shit. You know who this is, Luce?"

She swallowed. Her voice was hollow. "I can't see him from here. Just some blood. All I see is the blood."

Purdy said, "Whose house is this, anyway? Do you know whose house this is? Lucy?"

CHAPTER

3

It should have been my first clue.

For the first time since Grace's birth I put her to bed all by myself. Shortly after nine o'clock on Thursday night Lauren had pulled the satiated baby from her breast and handed her up to me, smiling wanly. She asked if I'd give our daughter a bath. I was delighted to comply.

Grace and I moved swiftly over the familiar territory that led from bath, to diaper, to fresh sleeper, to my favorite part—bedtime stories in the big upholstered rocker in the nursery. I had no illusions that my little girl even knew what a book was, but I could find no reasonable argument for postponing her introduction to the wonders of the written word, and I could find a million reasons for not waiting. Each night we read a few books. Each night both of us loved it.

Lauren never jumped into the ritual that particular

night, even when the usually irresistible trill of Grace's laughter echoed down the hall between the two bedrooms. I enjoyed the independence of it all and assumed that Lauren's request that I put the baby to bed was her way of giving me a vote of confidence. I also knew I'd have to get used to it; the following Monday Lauren was returning to work after half a year of maternity leave.

Once I'd kissed our daughter for the last time and placed her on her back in her crib, I stepped down the hall to the bedroom to find Lauren curled away from the door, asleep. A few minutes later I touched my lips to her inky hair before I crawled into bed beside her.

It wasn't long after Grace's birth six months earlier that we'd developed a family ritual that consisted of breakfast out on Friday or Saturday morning followed by errands and grocery shopping. The morning after my first solo bedtime flight with Grace was one of those Fridays where I'd managed to keep my office calendar clear, and Lauren drove us into town on our way to breakfast. We were planning to eat at Marie's, followed by some grocery shopping at Ideal, bagels from Moe's, bread from Breadworks, and wine from the Boulder Wine Merchant.

All without moving our car. Almost like in a real city.

As we crawled up Balsam past the mini-roundabouts toward Broadway, Lauren cursed at an elderly man in

an impeccably preserved old turquoise Chevy Bel Air
who signaled a left turn and then smoothly pulled right
into the driveway of a modest brick ranch that had held
its value a lot better than his car.

At the sound of Lauren's profanity, I leaned into the
backseat and told Grace to cover her ears.

Lauren didn't laugh.

It should have been my second clue.

The reason I was missing so many clues was, I think,
that I was out of practice. From the moment Lauren
had become pregnant fifteen months before, she'd
enjoyed a sabbatical from her long struggle living with
relapsing-remitting multiple sclerosis. Her neurologist
had told her that the pregnancy might indeed provide
a respite from her chronic symptoms and a brief protection against fresh exacerbations of her illness. It
turned out that he'd been right on both counts.

What were the usual signs that something was brewing with Lauren's health? Withdrawal and distraction.
She'd sense some sign of change in her functioning—
pain, weakness, numbness, vertigo, something—and
she'd pull away from me. She'd also display signs of irri-
tability.

But my radar was rusty and I was out of practice.
For fifteen months I'd floated along on the gentle sea
of denial, buoyed by blind hope that our daughter's
birth would be her mother's ticket to prolonged good
health.

The selection of breads at the bakery didn't include the multigrain that Lauren coveted. Her disappointment at the news was much too keen. The table at Marie's was uneven and Lauren leaned over to fidget with sugar packets until the wobble disappeared. The waitress brought Lauren coffee, not the tea she'd ordered. Lauren tried to sigh away her uncharacteristic annoyance at the mistake. She failed. When she looked over at me and said, "I'm not up for this, Alan. Can we skip breakfast this morning?" I finally realized that something was wrong.

I lowered my coffee mug back to the tabletop and said, "You're not feeling well, are you?"

For a prolonged moment every sound in the crowded coffee shop was muted. No motion blurred anything in my periphery. I followed Lauren's gaze as she looked at Grace, who was asleep in her infant carrier. Tears formed in Lauren's lower lashes.

"What is it?" I asked, even though I already knew.

She didn't answer right away.

"Are you symptomatic?" I said. With Lauren, I didn't need to be any more specific. I didn't need to reference a specific illness. We both knew I was inquiring about her MS.

She nodded, flicked a poignant glance at Grace. At the same moment, she said, "I don't want to be sick anymore, Alan. I don't."

I covered her wrist with my hand—her hand was balled into a fist—and waited almost a full minute for her to continue. When finally she did, she said, "We can talk about this later, okay? I think I'd really like to go home. But we need to stop at the drugstore first. You know?"

I nodded. I already knew about the drugstore stop. She and her neurologist had decided that Lauren would forego prophylactic treatment for her MS during her pregnancy. But by then, Grace and Lauren had each been fortified by six months of breastfeeding and Lauren was planning on resuming her interferon treatments. The prescription for interferon, which was intended to hold fresh exacerbations of Lauren's multiple sclerosis at bay, was waiting for her at the pharmacy. I was suddenly wondering, of course, whether she was restarting the medicine a week or two too late.

Lauren said, "Why don't you take Grace?" and stood. I dropped a couple of bills on the table and lifted our daughter and her baby carrier while Lauren strapped the diaper bag over her shoulder. As she preceded me out the door and headed toward the parking lot, I examined my wife's gait and her balance, looking for signs of what might be ailing her.

I couldn't discern a thing.

Damn disease.

It was like being surrounded by no-see-um bugs. Couldn't find them to swat them away.

Lauren and Grace, Emily, our dog, and Anvil, our foster dog, all slept away much of the afternoon. I was left to spend the day with gutter cleaning, and car washing, and the most noxious of all chores, worrying. Before she retreated to the bedroom for the afternoon, Lauren had revealed that her new symptoms included muscle spasms in three different locations on her left side, some worrisome new tingling in her left hand, and shooting pains in her right foot. The sum of those signs wasn't cause for alarm. She wasn't going blind in one eye, wasn't paralyzed anywhere, wasn't falling over from vertigo. Maybe it wasn't anything major. Not a big storm, I was hoping, just heat lightning flashing on the horizon.

Then she'd added another detail. She was experiencing what she called brain mud, a general fogginess in her sensorium and her thinking. We both knew that she usually experienced the brain mud either as a prelude to or as a result of an exacerbation of her MS.

The presence of the brain mud meant that Lauren and I would be balanced precariously on the edge of a cliff as that day became night and today became tomorrow.

For the second evening in a row I put Grace to sleep by myself. Lauren's fatigue seemed even more pronounced than usual; I sensed that she was asleep before Grace and I finished the last story of our bedtime ritual.

The morning was warm, almost sixty degrees before dawn. Grace and the puppies were still asleep and I was standing in the kitchen tugging on Lycra, hoping to steal an early bicycle ride, when the phone rang. I jumped at the device like a soldier endeavoring to cover a live hand grenade to protect his platoon. I got to the portable after only half a ring, flicking a quick glance at the clock before I punched the talk button and said, "Hello."

It was 5:38. Early.

"Alan? It's Elliot."

I recognized the patrician voice even before he got to his name. Elliot Bellhaven was one of Lauren's colleagues in the Boulder County District Attorney's Office. I'd met him through Lauren years before when he was new in the DA's office, fresh out of Harvard Law. Over the years Elliot had aged, of course, but I still pictured him in my head as the angel-faced, idealistic kid who'd infused the DA's office with a much needed booster of adrenaline. Recently, though, he'd seemed to become part of the establishment he'd once been so eager to jostle.

"Hey, Elliot," I said. I was waiting for him to tell me the bad news. This wasn't a work call. Lauren hadn't been at work in over six months. This wasn't a social call. It was 5:38 on Saturday morning. Elliot's mother had raised him better than that. Much better than that.

"I'm sorry if I woke you, Alan, but I thought Lauren should hear the news from me rather than someone else."

"You didn't wake me; I was up. What news?"

"Is she awake?"

"Not unless the phone woke her." I tucked the phone between my shoulder and my ear and ambled the two steps to the kitchen television and pressed the power button. The set flickered on to Channel 4, the early local news. A female reporter was doing a stand-up in front of a familiar house—a two-story with a wide lawn and a cheery line of bright yellow crocuses near the street. The graphics on the screen read, "LIVE! Boulder." The reporter was dressed in a maroon turtle-neck and looked uncomfortable in the early spring warmth.

Elliot said, "Would you wake Lauren for me, please? I'd very much like to speak with her. Once again, I apologize. I'll hold." He was using a business voice, the kind of tone he might use to an assistant around the office when the boss was around. The tone was polite and respectful, but instantly conveyed the fact that he expected his wishes to be carried out. If I'd been in another mood, I might have humored him and complied.

I eased up the sound on the TV. "*. . . answered a call at about ten-fifteen last night. Apparently, the body was discovered a short time later.*"

I placed the house in my mind. It was over on Jay Street, near the foothills. The house I was looking at on the TV belonged to Royal Peterson, the Boulder County District Attorney—Lauren's boss. Elliot's boss. I'd been to Royal's home for at least three or four staff parties over the years. Had I been there the previous Christmas? No, his wife, Susan, hadn't been well recently. My last visit must have been the Christmas season before.

What body? My heart jumped. I thought about Susan Peterson. Had she been that sick?

"I'd really rather not wake Lauren, Elliot. She's not been feeling well. What's up?" I thought I sounded as normal as anyone would under the circumstances.

"*. . . been able to learn that there are signs of a struggle inside the house. Neighbors reported hearing some shouting—one man we spoke with said 'screaming'—but there are no reports of gunshots.*"

Elliot said, "It's about Royal."

"Yes?"

"*. . . Royal Peterson's body was removed by the Boulder County Coroner at around four o'clock this morning.*"

Instinctively, I reached behind me and found a chair. I tugged it below me and almost fell to the seat.

"He was murdered last night, Alan. In his home."

I tried to say "Royal's dead?" but wasn't sure any sound actually came out of my mouth.

The cameraman pulled his shot back and I saw Elliot Bellhaven standing on the front porch of Royal Peterson's home talking on his cell phone.

He was talking to me.

Elliot was wearing jeans and a T-shirt. The shirt was covered by a tight V-neck sweater. Knowing Elliot, I knew the sweater was cashmere. His left shoulder was to the camera. On the television, the reporter was still talking, but I had stopped listening to her soliloquy.

I inhaled and forced myself to exhale slowly. Royal Peterson murdered? "Jesus, Elliot. What happened?"

"He was beaten to death last night. We think around ten o'clock. We don't know much else."

"How's Susan?"

"An ambulance took her to the hospital. I think she's stable. Haven't heard otherwise." His tone wasn't particularly compassionate. On the TV screen I watched Elliot turn and face the street.

"She's not a sus—"

"Susan? No, no, not at all. I'm sure you know that she's been bedridden lately, not well. So not at this point, no. She was asleep when the police got here and anyway she doesn't have the strength to do what was done to Royal."

Part of me wanted to know what had been done to Royal. Most of me didn't. I knew that Elliot wouldn't tell me the details anyway. But he'd tell Lauren. She'd share them with me in a manner I was more likely to be able to stomach.

I said, "The kids weren't in town?" Royal and Susan had three grown kids. None of them lived in Boulder. I thought one of their two daughters—Amanda? Amelia?—ran a successful decorating business in Durango. She'd been at one of the holiday parties I'd attended, had appeared to worship her father.

"No. No one was here but Roy and Susan. And . . . whoever it was who killed Roy."

On the screen, I watched as my good friend, Boulder Police Department detective Sam Purdy, poked his head out the front door of Royal's house and said something to Elliot. I could hear what he was saying through the phone line, though the sound wasn't quite in sync with Sam's lips as I watched them move on the TV screen. Sam said, "Need you in here, Bellhaven. Now, if you don't mind."

Elliot and Sam weren't friends. I had theories about the animosity between them, but couldn't be sure that I wasn't missing something. If I invested time in trying to understand why Sam didn't like all the people he didn't like, I'd have precious little time left for almost anything else.

Elliot pressed the phone against his chest and said something back to Sam. Reading lips has never been one of my fortes. I watched Elliot lift the phone back to his ear and waited for the sound of him speaking to me. "I'm at Royal's house right now, Alan, and I need to go. The police want me for something inside. Have Lauren page me when she's awake. Why don't you turn on the news? I'm sure you'll learn something interesting from it. This place is crawling with reporters and microwave trucks."

"Yeah, I'll do that. Thanks for calling, Elliot. Were you catching last night? Is this going to be yours?"

"Don't know. Mitchell's on it, too. So's Nora. As far as politics go, this place is drawing potential candidates like an American Legion hall in New Hampshire in primary season. Have Lauren page me. Bye." He was telling me that the posturing to be Royal Peterson's successor was already heating up. As the spouse of an insider, I was privy to the roster of likely candidates: Elliot; Mitchell Crest, Royal's chief trial deputy; and Nora Doyle, the head of sex crimes prosecution. And now all three were already hovering close to the murdered body of their dead boss.

I watched Elliot fold the tiny phone he was carrying and stuff it into the pocket of his trousers. He paused outside the door of the Peterson home while he pushed his hair back from his forehead and snapped a fresh pair of gloves onto his hands. Lucy Tanner, Sam's partner, held the door open for him. He nodded an acknowledgment to her before he squeezed past her and disappeared inside the house. Lucy stepped outside and squatted beside a plastic case that was resting on the lawn. She held her gloved hands out in front of her like a surgeon who had just scrubbed for the OR.

She was searching the case for something a detective might need to deal with evidence at the scene of a homicide.

My attention was drawn back to the sound emanating from the TV. "... *the controversial Boulder DA had been expected to announce that he would not run for re-election. Back to you, Virginia.*"

The next shot was Virginia in the anchor chair. I stripped off my Lycra jersey and walked back toward the bedrooms wearing only my padded biking shorts. Grace was just starting to stir. I lifted her from her crib and as I changed her diaper we chatted about her dreams and I told her about the warm morning. The dogs heard us chatting—that was me—and cooing, which was both of us, and trailed after us as I carried my daughter to the kitchen.

I didn't trouble Grace with the news that her mommy's boss had been murdered. She didn't even know Royal Peterson. He had sent a baby gift, though. I reminded her of that.

I didn't have a clue what the gift had been.

The night before, just before bedtime, Lauren had poked a one-and-a-quarter-inch, 23-gauge needle into the meatiest part of her right thigh. She'd then inject-ed one milliliter of interferon solution into the long muscles of her quad.

Why? To tame the lions of the multiple-sclerosis cir-cus.

To keep the brain mud at bay.

This injection of interferon had been her first dose in fifteen months, and she knew, and I knew, that the interferon beta that she plunged into her thigh would make her sick for the next twenty hours or so. She would feel like she had the flu. She would have mus-cle aches so sharp they brought tears, so deep that she would swear that her bones and her hair hurt. She would have chills. She would have fever.

That's why I was reluctant to wake her when Elliot called. But she woke on her own a few minutes after seven and joined Grace and me in the kitchen. Lauren was wearing a long T-shirt from a Race for the Cure that I knew she hadn't run in. I didn't think I had run in it, either. I embraced her and kissed her on the top of her head.

"Good morning. How are you feeling?" I asked as I handed her the baby. She focused her attention on Grace, shaking her head to tell me she felt pretty much how she looked.

I said, "Let's go sit down someplace comfortable. There's something I need to talk to you about."

She was so intent on Grace that I didn't think she'd heard me. But she turned around and walked toward the living room where she curled up on the sofa with Grace on her lap. The little dog, Anvil, a black miniature poodle whom we'd inherited from a former patient of mine, noodled his way into position on the part of Lauren's lap to which Grace hadn't staked claim. I sat beside them on the sofa and took Lauren's free hand. She tried to smile as she said, "Hey, now that I'm back on interferon and I can't breast-feed anymore, I can have real coffee. With caffeine. That's a good thing, right? So what's up? What did you want to tell me?"

I waited for her to find my gaze. The moment she shifted her attention from the baby to me, I said, "Royal's dead, babe."

"What?" Instantly, her eyes began to fill with tears.

"He was beaten to death in his home last night. That was Elliot who called early this morning."

"Roy?"

Involuntarily, she gripped Grace even tighter and began to kiss her as the first of her tears dripped into the baby's black hair. I suspected that Royal's death would not be uncomplicated news for my wife. During Lauren's time in the DA's office Roy Peterson had been good to her in many ways, but a few years ago he'd also been one of the first to turn his back on her when she'd been mistakenly arrested for murder. She'd never forgiven him for his lack of faith, or his political opportunism, or whatever it was that had motivated him to betray her.

The phone rang. She waved for me to get it. I wasn't surprised when I answered to hear the voice of Mitchell Crest, the chief trial deputy in the DA's office. Mitch had been a close friend of Roy's, and I offered my sympathy to him before I gave the phone over to Lauren. She grabbed it eagerly.

She would learn all about Royal's murder from somebody who actually knew the details.

Lauren insisted on going into the office. I argued with her briefly. I thought I had good arguments. It was the weekend, she was sick from the interferon, she was still officially on pregnancy leave, her body was sending out lots of signs that the MS bears might be stirring from their long hibernation, and she should probably avoid stress.

I made my case.

She went into the office.

CHAPTER
4

Lauren didn't return home until after Grace and I had finished dinner. For the third night in a row I put the baby to bed by myself. Lauren was sound asleep by the time the bedtime ritual was complete. I joined her in our bed shortly after ten and tried to remember the last time we'd made love, but I couldn't.

The next morning the phone rang early again. Unlike the previous morning, this time it did wake me. The night before I'd set my alarm for 5:45, so even in the foggiest recesses of my brain, I knew it was real early. I grabbed the receiver and said, "Hello," trying to make my voice sound like I hadn't been asleep. I don't know why I always did that.

"Sorry, Alan," Sam Purdy said. "And, yeah, I do know what time it is."

I glanced at the clock. Four-twelve, God help me. "You want to talk to Lauren?"

"Eventually, yeah, I do. First, let me tell you

something. You don't talk with anybody but your wife about this, okay?"

"Sure."

"I can't believe I'm saying these words, but I just picked up Lucy for questioning for Royal's murder."

"What? Lucy who? Lucy Tanner? Your Lucy?"

"Yeah. My Lucy." The words sounded heavy, as though they weighed him down like an anchor. He sounded so tired. I guessed that he hadn't slept for more than an hour or two since Royal's body was discovered thirty hours before. If that.

"You think Lucy murdered Roy?" The words felt as oxymoronic as "Congress passed campaign finance reform?"

"That's the way it looks. Witnesses, fingerprints, other stuff. It's a mess. A total damn mess."

My end of the conversation was causing Lauren to stir. When I looked over, she was sitting up next to me, her breasts swollen with milk that Grace was no longer consuming. "What's going on?" she asked.

I covered the microphone on the handset. "It's Sam," I said. "He just picked up Lucy for questioning in Roy's murder."

"What? Give me the phone." She did a much better job of sounding awake than I did.

I gave her the phone. She said, "Sam, what the hell are you talking about?"

As Lauren questioned Sam, I heard the first signs of stirring on the baby monitor. Seconds later, Grace started to cry.

Lauren raised her eyebrow and mouthed, "Do you mind?"

I threw back the comforter and headed down the hall. I was almost to Grace's door when I heard Lauren call, "Wait, Sam wants to talk to you again." Lauren and I—both naked—passed in the hallway and I grabbed the phone from our bed.

I said, "I can't believe Lucy killed Royal, Sam."

"Yeah, I know, I know. Listen, taking Lucy in was my last official act in the investigation of Roy's murder. As you could probably have guessed, they wanted me off the case as soon as I told them where this was headed. I had to sell my soul to even be allowed to bring her in myself."

"Conflict of interest?"

"I'd like to think so. It's certainly the public face they're going to put on it. But part of me thinks that the big boys are actually worried I might have been part of whatever came down at Royal's house on Saturday night."

"You're kidding?"

"I wish I was."

"They said something to you?"

"No. They didn't have to. Hey, I didn't roust you out of bed to bitch at you about my bosses. What the brass thinks about me isn't my immediate problem. I need your advice on something else. Lucy was smart enough not to say a word to me after I went to her house and woke her up and told her what was coming down. I didn't really press her to talk on the drive over. Once I got her to the department, though, she asked me to help her pick a lawyer. Said she'd sit tight until she heard from one. So she's sitting mute in an interrogation room on Thirty-third Street waiting for me to find a lawyer to tell her what to do next."

I waited for Sam to go on.

"Anyway, so here's what I'm thinking: I'm thinking about that guy who helped the Ramseys—what's his name, Hal Haddon? Do I got that right? I always get those Ramsey lawyers mixed up. The one I think is Haddon struck me as a sharp guy. Principled, you know. But I keep wondering whether principles are a good thing in these circumstances, and I'm worried that his profile's too high after all the heat he took over the Ramseys. You think? I want some advice."

I thought for a moment before I replied. I didn't want to get into a political discussion with Sam about legal ethics, and certainly didn't want him to go on yet another vertigo-inducing harangue about the JonBenét case. I said, "That's a realistic concern, Sam. Public opinion could be against someone like Haddon right from the start. That could rub off on Lucy. That wouldn't help."

"My other thought was either Cozier Maitlin or Casey Sparrow. Lucy might like to have a woman involved. I'm wondering how you two felt about the help they gave Lauren that time when she was, you know . . ."

"Arrested?"

"Whatever. What'd you think?"

"You ask Lauren for her opinion?"

"I will. But I thought I'd ask you first. You dealt with them more than she did. So what did you think? Would you go that way again?"

My thought was, *I hope I never have to.* "Cozy and Casey were great. An odd team, but professional, and creative, and sharp. But it's a moot question—Casey's not available. She's defending that woman in Wheat Ridge who's accused of killing her husband and his parents. Goes to trial this week."

"Oh yeah. That case is hers? I didn't know. Can Maitlin handle something like Lucy's situation by himself?"

"Sure."

"Should he?"

"Different question."

I listened to him breathe. "I want to go talk with him before he hears about Lucy's involvement in all this from somebody else. Will you come with me?"

I immediately wondered why he wanted me to accompany him to see Cozy Maitlin. "Lauren and I are going to visit Susan Peterson at the hospital at ten o'clock. We have a babysitter coming then."

"Good," he said, totally missing my point. "If we go now, we'll both be back home by the time she gets there. We had better be—I have to get some sleep soon or I'll be no good to Lucy or Royal or anybody else."

I stared at the clock by the bed. "You want to go to Maitlin's house at four-twenty in the morning?"

"Nah, I wouldn't do that. That would be inconsiderate. The way I'm figuring, by the time we get there it will be almost five. You know where he lives?"

I almost laughed. "Yes. Last year he bought a renovated Victorian on Maxwell, a block or two west of Broadway. Lauren and I were invited there for a housewarming. There were women in tuxedos carrying trays of hors d'oeuvres and champagne. That kind of party."

"Girls in tuxedos? Sounds fun." Sam's sarcasm was way too thick for the predawn darkness. "For some reason I'll never understand, I don't get invited to parties like that. Cross-street?"

"Near Eighth."

"You can find the house?"

"Sure."

"Then I'll see you at Maxwell and Eighth at ten to five." I thought I heard him chuckle as he hung up the phone.

I took a quick shower, shaved with an electric razor, threw on some jeans and a cotton sweater, and still I didn't make it downtown until a couple of minutes before five. The air was cool. Sam was standing on the curb leaning against his old Cherokee, three doors down from Cozier Maitlin's house. I found a spot by the curb in front of Cozy's painted-lady Victorian. Sam headed my way carrying a cardboard tray with three cups of 7-Eleven coffee.

"Thanks for doing this," he said. "How's little Grace?"

"She's great, Sam. I can't believe I waited this long to become a father. Simon?"

"Feels like I haven't seen the kid in a week. Actually had to give up our Avs playoff tickets a few days ago, if you can believe it. We did go snowboarding over spring break. Kid's a maniac, I'll tell you. Boards goofy-footed. Perfect for the kid of an Iron Ranger, don't you think?"

"You boarded, too?"

He shook his head. "You don't want to know." He gestured toward the coffee he was holding. "This is nice of you—I know you aren't that tight with Lucy. I appreciate you agreeing to help me out."

I shrugged. I'd lost count of the number of times Sam had sacrificed to assist Lauren and me. "It's what friends do," I said, and pointed at Cozy's pretty house. "Cozy may not think it's so nice of me."

Sam snorted a short, derisive blast of air through his nose. "Way I look at it, you make over two hundred bucks an hour, you should expect to get rousted out of bed occasionally. A necessary part of staying humble."

"Criminal defense attorneys shouldn't be humble, Sam. You want the same traits in defense attorneys that you want in surgeons and airline pilots. You want confidence bordering on arrogance."

Sam grunted. He couldn't comprehend the concept of admirable traits in members of the defense bar.

I said, "Lucy has family money, right?"

He shifted his weight before he responded. I knew he wasn't comfortable talking about money. "She seems to. We've never talked about it much. She doesn't live like a cop. Nice apartment. Nice clothes. Nice vacations. I'd say she has money. Once said something about her father's mother leaving her something. I'd suspect she has enough to pay Cozy, if that's where you're going."

"That's where I was going."

"Don't worry about money. Maitlin's going to be drooling over this case. A Boulder police detective about to be accused of killing Colorado's best-known and most controversial district attorney? He'd pay me for the chance to take this case, if I put the screws to him." Sam paused for a moment. "Which I'm not planning on doing, by the way."

We reached Cozy's front door. Sam pounded five times with the flat side of his fist, waited ten seconds, and then did it again. He explained, "First time, the noise wakes you up but you're not really sure what the heck it was, so you're tempted to go back to sleep. Second time is like an instant replay to help overcome the short-term cognitive impairment." Sam pounded five more times. "Third time is to make sure his pulse stays high. That's what I like to see when they answer the door—I want them awake, with a little bit of adrenaline flowing."

Less than a minute later I watched lights flick on inside the house and then heard the concussion of heavy steps on the stairs. The door flung open and Cozier Maitlin filled the entire entryway.

I thought that, at that moment, he looked like the apocryphal Rasputin on the Russian's fateful night at the Yusopov Palace.

Cozy stood six feet eight inches tall in his bare feet. And right then, he was, indeed, barefoot. Not to mention bare-chested. The lower half of his body was adorned with pajamas covered with art deco fire trucks. The drawstring was so loose that the pajama bottoms were in danger of falling to the hardwood floor.

I prayed that wouldn't happen.

Cozy's hair looked like a failed do from a punk hair-care training clinic. His mouth hung open like a third eye and the expression in his gaze was as close to homicidal as I hoped it would ever get. A full day's whiskers completed the picture and left me with a graphic representation of what might have driven his ex-wife, first, to divorce him and, second, to become a lesbian.

If I had been alone, I think Cozy would have killed me right there on his front porch. But the fact that a homicide detective accompanied me caused Cozy to pause. He closed his gaping mouth and raised his chin a couple of centimeters. With one hand he tried to tame his unruly hair, with the other hand he, thankfully, grabbed the waistband of his pajama bottoms.

He said, "Gentlemen."

I fought a grin.

"Good morning, Counselor," Sam replied. "May we come in?"

Cozy stepped back. "Of course. Where are my manners? I assume you are here at this . . . *hour*"—he spoke the word as though the very sound of it caused him significant pain—"because we're about to be dealing with a matter of some gravity and some . . . urgency. Would it be appropriate for me to steal a moment or two and pull on a robe? Would that be acceptable under the circumstances?"

Cozy had a knack of communicating condescension and sarcasm without revealing too much malice. I'd always admired that trait in him.

Sam nodded. He raised his cardboard tray full of 7-Eleven cups. "I brought coffee. Didn't think you'd have made any yet. Maybe should have got doughnuts, too, but I wasn't thinking clearly."

"That's quite apparent," Cozy replied. He actually tried to smile before he retreated back up the stairs to his bedroom to find a robe.

After the defense lawyer disappeared up the stairs, Sam said, "That went better than I expected."

Cozy was down about five minutes later. He'd taken a quick shower and was wearing sweats.

"Alan, Sam. I must let you know that the two of you make an odd pair standing at my door in the dark hours before dawn. My initial guess when I saw you, Detective, was that this was about Royal Peterson. But Alan?

I don't figure your part. So, please, Detective—is this about Royal Peterson's murder? You've been working that, haven't you? Is that a fair assumption on my part?"

Sam said, "Yes, Mr. Maitlin. That's a fair assumption." Sam rubbed the back of his hand across the stubble on his chin. The grating sound was audible, and kind of creepy. "Earlier this morning I picked someone up for questioning in Royal's murder. We're here to talk with you about whether or not you'd be interested in representing that person."

Cozy had been ignoring the 7-Eleven coffee. I doubted that he'd consumed anything so plebeian in quite some time. But after Sam disclosed the nature of our errand, Cozy reached down and lifted his cardboard cup, flicked off the plastic lid, and took a long swallow. When he looked back up he was staring at me. I was wearing my psychotherapist's face, disclosing nothing.

"This is irregular," Cozy proclaimed.

"That's an understatement," I said.

"It's not often that I'm approached by the lead detective of a homicide investigation asking me to represent someone he's just . . . fingered. Is that a good description of what is occurring here?"

Sam's shoulders had sunk and he was focusing his attention on the liquid in his cup as though the shimmering surface were the glass of a crystal ball. My impression was that Sam had used all the energy he'd had left just to tell Cozy why we were there.

At that moment, I suspected that was why Sam had

asked me to come along. He needed me to be ready to take over.

I said, "Sam's not part of the investigation any longer, Cozy. He was removed from the case a few hours ago, right after he picked up his partner for questioning for Royal's murder. On his way out she asked him to help her find a lawyer. He asked Lauren and me for advice. Now, Sam wants to talk with you about representing her. Her name is Lucy Tanner. Sam thought it would be better for you and him to talk before the media is all over this."

Cozy shifted his eyes from me to Sam and back. It was as though he was waiting for Sam or me to slap a thigh and tag him with a punch line. Finally, Cozy stood up. He had to duck to avoid hitting his head on the light fixture that hung in the center of the room. For a minute or more he stood at the large window that faced Maxwell Street, his back to us.

Past him, in the distance, I could see the first glimmers of morning light on the eastern horizon.

Sam was still staring into his cup.

Cozy turned around. He said, "I'll do it."

Sam raised his head and his eyes narrowed at Cozy.

"Where is my client?" Cozy asked.

"Sam?" I asked. "Lucy would still be at Thirty-third Street, right? She wouldn't have been moved over to the jail?"

"When I left she was still at the department. They wouldn't take her over to the jail unless they had enough to arrest her." He shifted his gaze to Cozy. "You should be able to find her at Thirty-third Street."

The lawyer asked the detective a lawyer question. "Do they have enough to charge her?"

Sam said, "In my opinion, no. It's not my opinion that counts, though, is it?"

Cozy nodded. "I'd like to ask you a few things. You picked her up this morning? Was that at her home?"

"Yeah. About two-thirty."

"Did she say anything to you at that time?"

Sam buried his lower lip in his mustache and shook his head. "You don't know Lucy Tanner. Let me tell you something about her: Your new client's a very smart lady, Mr. Maitlin. She's not going to be talking to anyone."

"Then why pick her up? What's the upside? Why not wait until more evidence was developed?"

"It wasn't my decision. Once things started playing out the way they started playing out, it was decided to bring her in to talk to her. The department has kind of a bad reputation concerning delaying questioning of witnesses in murder investigations. I think that was a major motivator in the decision. They wanted to talk to Lucy before she figured out that she should be talking to you."

Cozy sat back. "She was there with you on Friday night, right? At the Peterson house?"

"She was."

"The whole time?"

"The whole time. We worked the scene together. She kept the log."

I could tell Cozy adored the image he was forming in his imagination. He was already cross-examining witnesses in his head.

"She's had access to the murder book from the start?"

"From the start."

Cozy nodded. Sipped again at his coffee. He looked at Sam over the rim of the cardboard cup. "You want to tell me what you have on her?"

Sam said, "See . . . this is where it gets dicey, Mr. Maitlin."

"Call me Cozy."

"I'm not comfortable with that, yet. I'll try to work through it, though, I promise."

I wasn't sure Sam's sarcasm even registered on Cozy.

Sam continued. "Anyway, I'm here to help my partner. I'm not here to betray the Boulder Police Department. Even though it's not my case anymore, you know damn well I can't reveal the fruits of the investigation."

"But you had cause to pick her up?"

Sam closed his eyes, grimaced, and added a little headshake. "Bringing her in may not have been my idea, and may not have been a good idea strategically, but it wasn't bogus."

I said, "Cozy? Think about this. Sam just turned in his partner—his close friend—for questioning in a very, very high profile murder. Even though he didn't agree with the decision, he's telling you that he's convinced that the evidence warranted it."

Cozy said, "That's the truth, Sam?"

"Yeah. That's the truth."

Cozy said, "I should make a quick call to the detectives who are chatting with my client and inform them of my involvement."

Sam buried his bottom lip in his mustache and nodded his agreement before he stood to leave. I stood, too.

Cozy said, "I'll do my best for your friend, Sam."

Sam didn't respond until we got to the front door. "I wasn't honest with you before, Mr. Maitlin. She did say something to me when I brought her in. She reached up and grabbed my head and pulled it real close to hers. She stuck her lips next to my ear and she said, 'I didn't do it, Sam. Keep looking.' That's all she said."

Cozy said, "You believe her?"

Sam said, "A thousand percent."

CHAPTER
5

I'd told myself that the media was going to be all over this case, but still I wasn't prepared for the breadth of the invasion that had already occurred. It was all so Ramsey-reminiscent. Microwave trucks were all over town—the Public Safety Building on Thirty-third, the Justice Center on Sixth, and of course, outside the Peterson home—and reporters and producers were tripping over each other trying to discover a virgin angle or finagle a reluctant interview.

Lauren and I tried to pick a route from our home to Community Hospital that would shield us from the press. As I stopped at a red light at Thirtieth, I said, "Are you thinking much about what Lucy is going through?" As a rule, Lauren and I didn't dwell on the episode that had landed her in even worse circumstances than the ones that Lucy currently faced. Lauren had actually been arrested and taken to jail, accused of shooting someone.

At first, Lauren just glanced my way and nodded. Finally, she said, "I'm just praying she doesn't have to go through what comes next—those first few hours at the jail—the body search, the booking—were the worst part of it for me after I was arrested. I have to think it would be even worse for Lucy because she's a cop."

"If they arrest her, they'd have her isolated from the general population, wouldn't they?"

"I'm sure they would."

The light changed and we were quiet until the next red light at Folsom. I asked, "What do you think about Sam's choice of Cozy to defend Lucy?"

"There's a number of people in town who could do it, Alan, and a whole bunch in Denver, but I think . . . Cozy's the right one. His profile is high, but not too high. He has a good relationship with our office, but not too chummy. He's experienced with capital cases." She paused. "He's a good choice."

"Your words are more enthusiastic than your voice."

"Probably. I think I'd feel better about it if Casey Sparrow was available to help him."

"Is it too much for Cozy to do by himself?"

"With all the media? It may be. It all depends whether she's charged. These big cases are so consuming. But I'm thinking more about the perspective Casey would provide. Sometimes Cozy's style requires ballast."

I eased the car straight into the intersection but took a sharp left with the conversation. "How are your symptoms?"

"About the same."

"Not worse?"

"Not much worse."

"Is it an exacerbation?"

"I don't know yet. Could just be a series of reruns. That's what I'm hoping."

Lauren and I walked hand in hand toward Community Hospital, chatting about what it was like to leave Grace with a sitter, what it was going to be like doing it every day now that Lauren's maternity leave was ending. Our guard was down, and neither of us saw the ambush developing as we approached the ER entrance to the hospital. By the time I had started paying attention, a reporter from one of the Denver TV stations had a foam-covered microphone in Lauren's face.

The reporter was a young Asian woman. I'd seen her work; thought she was pretty good. "Ms. Crowder? Ms. Crowder? Are you here to interview Susan Peterson? Is she a suspect in her husband's murder? Have the police interviewed her yet? Ms. Crowder?"

Lauren's balance faltered as the reporter closed in. I tightened my grip on my wife's hand and silently urged her to keep walking. After another step or two, Lauren spoke without turning toward the camera. "I'm here visiting a friend who's hospitalized. That's all."

"Is Susan Peterson a suspect in her husband's murder? Ms. Crowder? Ms. Crowder?"

The reporter's voice faded as the sliding glass doors closed behind us. "I wasn't expecting them here," I said. "You handled yourself well."

"Thanks. They're like grasshoppers. Once they show up in one place, it seems they show up everywhere."

We were alone as we made our way up the elevator. I asked Lauren the same thing the reporter was wondering about. "Is there any chance Susan was involved? What are you hearing in the office?"

"When the police found her in bed she was so heavily medicated that she was almost impossible to arouse. Her neurologist doesn't think she would have had the strength to do what was done to Royal. So, no, even though they'll take a close look, no one's taking that possibility too seriously at this point."

The elevator door opened. We got out and paused at the nursing station to get directions to Susan's room. A nurse pointed out the room and said, "Her doctor's in with her right now. I'm sure it will only be a few more minutes. You can wait in the lounge."

Just then the door to Susan's room opened and her doctor walked out, a Palm Pilot in one hand, a stylus in the other.

I said, "Good morning, Adrienne." Adrienne Arvin, a little fireball of a urologist, was our neighbor and close friend.

She stopped in her tracks, looked up at Lauren and me, then smiled. "Hi, guys. What are you doing here?"

I stepped over to give her a kiss on the cheek, then

Lauren did the same before she responded, "We're here to visit Susan. She's one of yours, I take it?"

"Be silly of me to deny it at this point, I suppose. I'm doing a consult."

"She's okay?" Lauren asked.

Adrienne muttered, "*Oy,*" and made a face that aptly communicated that "okay" was not one of the modifiers she would use to describe Susan Peterson's condition. "MS is a tough disease, Lauren. I don't have to tell you that. Susan's is particularly insidious. The stress of having her husband murdered hasn't made it any easier on her."

I asked, "Can we go in?"

"Be my guest. She'll be pleased to see you, I think. She's quite tired. I wouldn't stay long."

"Of course," Lauren said. Adrienne pocketed her little computer and bounced off down the hall.

Susan Peterson's multiple sclerosis was different from Lauren's. Susan had secondary progressive disease. Although she'd been diagnosed years after Lauren, Susan frequently used a wheelchair, and lately was bedridden more often than not. She was virtually blind in one eye, and Roy had once confided in Lauren that the pain she suffered from spasticity was growing more and more severe. Adrienne's presence on Susan's care-team was a clear indication that she was suffering bladder problems as well.

While Lauren could expect periods of remission

between infrequent exacerbations of her disease, Susan was likely to deteriorate progressively, with little or no respite from the assault of multiple sclerosis.

We found Susan on her side in bed, facing away from the door. Her room was full of floral bouquets and the aroma was a cloying mix of hospital disinfectants and nature's perfume. The television was tuned to religious programming, but the sound was so low I couldn't hear the minister's words.

We took a couple of steps into the room and Lauren said, "Susan? It's Lauren and Alan."

"Oh, oh, good," she said. "You came to see me? Come on over on this side so I can lay my eyes on you."

Lauren and I crossed the room. Immediately, Susan said, "My girls came in early before church and helped me get made up. It's Sunday, and I wanted to look nice. It's not the way I would do it myself, but— Do I look okay?"

Lauren told her, "Your daughters did a great job, Susan. You look wonderful. Lovely."

"Thanks. But I don't know about the eye shadow. It's so, so . . . And my hair after three days in this bed . . . what can you do?"

Despite the fact that Lauren had done all the talking since we'd entered the room, Susan addressed her words to me. I'd always suspected that Susan was uncomfortable with Lauren. I thought it was because Lauren, too, had MS. And I thought perhaps Susan's ambivalence was exacerbated because Lauren had the less malignant form of the disease.

I said, "How are you, Susan?"

"Better, better. The nurses are a little—I don't want to say slow, but—anyway, anyway, let's just say they're not the most prompt. You buzz, you buzz and . . . you know. I wish Matthew could have stayed longer. He came in from Phoenix but he's gone again already. Mothers and sons, right? Thank God I have my girls. They bring food at least." She touched her hair with her hand. "You could starve to death in here waiting for something edible to arrive."

I bit the soft flesh on the inside of my lower lip.

Susan Peterson had probably always been a difficult woman—what her children's generation would have called "high maintenance." According to Royal, when Susan's disease was first diagnosed she actually softened a little, but as the insidious myelin destruction progressed in her central nervous system, the underlying flaws in her character seemed to have become magnified.

If a young psychology graduate student I was supervising asked me to describe a narcissistic character disorder, I would have been tempted to introduce the student to Susan Peterson.

"What you've been-through, Susan . . ." Lauren said. "We're so sorry about what happened to Roy."

"Thank you," she said, and her chin crinkled and began to quiver. "I'm so frightened. So frightened.

"The other night, you know? When it happened? I was asleep. It sounds awful but what can I say? I usually don't sleep well. I have pain that wakes me up. It's in my feet and my back and my left leg . . . sometimes it feels like an electric shock or being stabbed with a sharp knife. So some nights I let Roy give me a sleeping pill so that I sleep through the night. It's mostly for him that I do it, really. It's so I don't wake him during the night with my . . . moaning. Halcion. That's the one he gives me. I don't like it because it knocks me out so much. But sometimes Roy would give it to me in the evening and I'd take it. That's what happened, Friday. He gave it to me and he looked so tired that I took it. I didn't hear anything until these police officers woke me up. They wouldn't tell me what happened to Roy. I didn't find out until the next morning. A policeman told me. A policeman."

She raised a hand to cover her mouth. She looked right at Lauren and started to cry. "Oh, what am I going to do? Who's going to take care of me?"

Ten minutes later as we walked down the corridor outside the door of Susan Peterson's room, I said, "A saint."

Lauren asked, "What are you talking about? What do you mean 'a saint'?"

"She asked who's going to take care of her. Well, that's who's going to take care of her. The answer is, a saint."

"*Alan.* That's so unkind."

"I'm sorry. Her situation is tragic, sweets. But she makes it tough to be purely sympathetic."

"She does. Dear Lord, she does. She's gotten worse, hasn't she? Since she's gone downhill so fast, I mean. I don't complain like that, do I? Tell me I don't. And please tell me I'm not that myopic about my life."

"You don't. You're not. You could never be."

"You don't resent me the way Roy resented her?"

"Roy resented Susan?"

The elevator door opened. Lauren whispered, "He was no saint," as we stepped into the crowded elevator.

"What?" I asked.

"Later."

We exited the hospital through an open delivery door and walked three blocks out of our way to avoid another ambush from the press.

While we were skirting the eastern edge of the park on Ninth Street, the pager we carried so that the babysitter could reach us vibrated on my belt.

I reached for my hip and said, "It might be Viv." Viv was our babysitter/nanny. She was a young Hmong woman with a heart the size of Southeast Asia. With Lauren heading back to work, we were thrilled that Viv had agreed to continue to watch Grace, who seemed to adore her. While Lauren fumbled in her purse for her phone, I glanced at the number on the screen of the pager. I said, "I don't recognize this phone number," and showed it to Lauren.

"Me neither." She punched the number into her cell phone. A moment later she said, "Cozy? Is that you?"

We took about ten more steps as she listened to whatever Cozier Maitlin had to say. Lauren stopped me with a hand on my shoulder and moved off toward a nearby bench. I sat next to her.

Into the phone, Lauren said, "No, I'm technically off leave until tomorrow. . . . That's right, I'm not officially involved with the case at all. I wouldn't be under any circumstances, Cozy. If Roy's murder doesn't go to a special prosecutor, it's going to be run by whichever member of the triad prevails."

Cozy said something. Lauren nodded. "That's right. Mitchell and Nora. The third player in the triad is Elliot." She listened. "Yes, he has that kind of status in the office. Mitch and Nora are wary of him. That's all it takes. Elliot has his supporters, especially among the younger assistants."

I mimed *"What?"* at my wife. She ignored me.

Cozy spoke for almost a full minute before Lauren said, "Are you kidding? Me? Why?" She listened, and looked my way, widened her violet eyes, then raised her eyebrows. Behind her, the park was vibrant with activity. Joggers, bladers, bikers, kids in strollers, couples hand in hand. The mountains loomed immense to the west and the brilliant sky was streaked with wispy clouds. The plums and cherries were in bloom and the air was fragrant with honeysuckle. I catalogued it all while I eavesdropped.

"Yes, I promise I'll think about it. You don't have to worry about that. I'm not sure I'll think about anything else. I'll call you later today. . . . Okay, okay, I'll call you before dinner." Pause. "We eat around six, Cozy. I'll phone you before then. Good-bye."

"Well?" I said.

She folded the phone with uncommon deliberation. "Cozier Maitlin just made me an offer. He'd like me to assist him in representing Lucy."

"You're not kidding?"

"I'm serious."

"Can you do that? I mean can an assistant district attorney just cross over and be a defense attorney?"

"People do it all the time when they leave the office. Cozy used to be an assistant DA himself. With one phone call to Mitchell, I could extend my maternity leave. I haven't gotten the impression that the workload's been killing anyone, so I don't think there'd be any objections. Then I suppose I could do anything I wanted. Once Mitchell learned what my actual plans were, he wouldn't like it one bit, but I don't think there's anything he could do about it."

I sat back on the bench and gave her an appraisal that, had I given it to a stranger, would have probably earned me a whole peck of trouble. I said, "You're interested, aren't you?"

She smiled at me. A soft, natural smile that I hadn't seen in a few days. "You know, hon, I think I am."

CHAPTER

6

Lauren didn't have an answer for Cozy before dinner on Sunday. In fact, she still hadn't arrived at a decision by the time I left the house to drive downtown to see my first patient of the week early on Monday morning. Watching her decision-making process had reminded me of accompanying her to buy a new swimsuit just a few days before. She'd tried on ten different suits but nothing was exactly what she wanted. I tried to stay neutral and supportive as she found a flaw in each and every style she squirmed into, some of which I'd found quite fetching. The problem, I'd decided that day, was that nothing fit the image she had of herself at the beach.

And being a defense attorney didn't fit her image of herself as a lawyer. What she did all day Sunday was the equivalent of twirling in front of the mirror trying to make her ass appear smaller, or larger, or whatever the right size for her ass was.

I'm happy to go on the record as stating that I thought her ass was just fine.

The first patient in my clinical psychology practice that Monday morning was due at 8:45. I had five more scheduled before the end of the day, the last session ending at 5:15. If my patients behaved themselves, it would be a relatively easy day.

By the time I'd finished the earliest appointment, a woman I didn't know had left an urgent message on my voice mail requesting a return call as soon as possible. I phoned her back between sessions. She begged me for my first open appointment. I offered her 11:30.

She wasn't available.

What about 3:15?

Sorry.

We settled—me reluctantly, she enthusiastically— on 5:15. My relatively easy day was deteriorating before my eyes. I left a message for Viv letting her know I'd be home a little later than I'd thought.

The offices that I share with another psychologist named Diane Estevez have a simple system for greeting patients. When a patient arrives in the waiting room, he or she flips a switch marked with either my name or Diane's, which illuminates a tiny red light in the corresponding office. At the appointed time, Diane or I go out and retrieve our patient. Saves a fortune in receptionist expenses.

The light indicating the arrival of my 5:15 wasn't illuminated at 5:15. I walked out to the waiting room just in case the new patient—a woman named Naomi Bigg—hadn't mastered the system, which happened sometimes. But the waiting room was empty. I returned to my office, made the next move in the game of phone tag I'd been playing with Lauren all day long, and wrote some notes, stealing frequent looks at the clock. At 5:25, I decided to give my new patient until 5:30 before I headed home. No-show first appointments were a rarity, but a nuisance nonetheless. My personal rule in life was that fifteen minutes was a reasonable amount of time to wait for anyone, for anything, in almost any circumstances.

The light flashed on at 5:27. I was disappointed; I'd crossed the line and was hoping my new patient had changed her mind and wouldn't show. I reluctantly returned to the waiting room, where I greeted a woman who I guessed was about fifty. She was slender and tall and was dressed in a blue gabardine suit. I assumed she was a businesswoman.

"Hello," she said, stretching out her hand. "I'm so sorry I'm late. It was chaos at the office. I'm sorry, that's not your problem. Oh, I didn't even ask—are you Dr. Gregory? Please say yes."

"I am," I replied, and shook her hand.

"Thank God. I'm Naomi Bigg."

"Please come on back to my office."

Naomi chose the chair opposite mine and surprised me by pulling a compact from her purse and checking her face before she turned her attention to me. The interlude of vanity gave me a chance to observe her.

For some reason, I immediately focused on her eyebrows. They'd been plucked with a ferocity that was impossible to ignore. The remaining arc of hair was so narrow that it appeared to have been drawn into place with a fine-tipped pen.

She snapped the compact shut and returned her gaze to me.

I always started the first session with new patients the same way. I said, "How can I be of help?"

She pulled her hands together in front of her chest as though she were about to pray. "I'm not sure. I'm confused—I guess it would be great if you could help with that." Her eyes were focused out the window. The redbuds in the backyard of the old Victorian were ablaze with the pink of spring. I knew the brilliant blossoms would disappear with the next snowstorm.

I waited for Naomi to continue. She didn't.

Finally, I said, "You're confused?" My words had a singular intent, akin to freeing a stuck CD.

"In the sense that I don't know the right thing to do, yes. I'm that kind of confused."

I waited again, longer this time. It was apparent she wanted to play this like a tennis match. She hit. I hit. I wondered whether it was wise to oblige.

I said, "And you think I can be of help with your decision?"

"Yes. Do you know how I chose you?" She looked my way for the first time since she'd greeted me in the waiting room.

I shook my head.

"I saw you on the news after that thing that happened last fall in Steamboat Springs. You know, with those girls? That's how long I've been thinking about this, about coming to see somebody for . . . help. For therapy, you know? Since at least last fall. I thought because of that work that you did—I mean helping to find who killed those two girls after such a long time—that you might be the right person to help me, too."

She returned her gaze to the redbuds.

I felt like telling her to get on with it, that I had a baby waiting for me at home, a baby who smelled even better than the flowers on those trees. But I didn't.

As I waited for her to resume, my mind drifted back to the previous autumn's events in Steamboat Springs. Lauren and I had accepted an invitation from a private group of forensic specialists called Locard to participate in an investigation of the 1988 murder of two girls outside Steamboat Springs. The outcome of the investigation had garnered a lot of press coverage, both local and national.

"And then I saw you again on the news last night. You were outside Community Hospital? I think you were with your wife. That's when I decided I was going to call, that it was the right time."

Damn news cameras, I thought.

Naomi Bigg said, "You know what anniversary is this week?"

A crack of sunlight burned through my late-day fog. *Aha! Anniversary reaction.* She wanted to talk about a loss she'd suffered at this time last year, or the year before, or . . .

"No," I said, "I don't know what anniversary is this week."

She crossed her long legs, tugged down her skirt. I noticed that her left ankle was bruised. I filed the information.

I was guessing that she'd lost her husband. Divorce or death? I glanced down to check for a wedding ring, but her left hand was covered by her right. My money was on divorce. My second guess was that she'd lost a child. I really hoped not; I knew my heart would resist hearing that story.

"Columbine," she said.

Had Naomi lost a child at Columbine High School? God.

I instantly started considering which colleague I could refer her to, a colleague without a new baby, a colleague who would be able to listen to her grief without terror filling the part of his own heart that cherished a new life.

She was right, of course. That week was the anniversary of the shootings at Columbine High School. Which meant it was also the week of the anniversary of the Oklahoma City bombing. A couple of tragic days in April and a lot of lives for which the beauty of spring would never be the same.

Never.

She gazed at me briefly. "My confusion? I think a lot about the parents, you know?"

"The parents . . . ?"

"The Harrises and the Klebolds."

I'd been wrong, 180 degrees wrong. I thought she'd been talking about the parents of the victims. Instead, she was talking about the parents of the killers.

She went on. "I think about whether they should have known what was going on. Whether they should have known what was in their children's hearts. Even whether they should have turned their own children in to the police. I think about all those things all the time."

The late-day fog in my brain had finally lifted. Suddenly the sunlight was so bright that I couldn't see for the glare.

Sometimes new patients need prompting, and sometimes their stories have such internal force that the words spew forth like fluid from a cut hydraulic hose. The tennis match between us was over and Naomi needed no further prompting. She'd ripped the lid off the Pandora's box that she had carried into my office and snakes were slithering out unfettered.

"Sometimes parents know when their kids are angry, they do. They see it, they feel it. But it doesn't mean they know the depth of the rage, the sense of injustice their children feel, or what awful things their children might do. How could they even have imagined it? The Klebolds and the Harrises? How could they ever, ever have guessed what evil was in their children's hearts? Even with the clues, the term papers, everything. How could they possibly have guessed what their children were going to do that awful day at Columbine?"

The words were so poignant, so potentially revealing, but the tone was impersonal, distant. My new patient was much more comfortable talking about someone else's struggle than she was talking about her own. I glanced again at her left hand. With her thumb she was twirling a platinum wedding band around her ring finger. Good-sized diamond on the matching engagement ring. Married? Separated? I didn't know. But Naomi was about the right age; she could certainly have kids the age of the Columbine assassins.

She lifted her left arm and focused her attention on her fancy watch. "Oh my, the time. We have to stop already, don't we?"

I looked at the small clock on the étagère behind the sofa. We had only two minutes remaining in the session. "In a couple of minutes," I said. "You were talking about how the Harrises and the Klebolds should or shouldn't have known about what their kids were going to do."

Her eyes closed and her breathing became shallow. "It's a hard question to answer from a distance, isn't it? When the tragedy is so terrible, people are so quick to judge."

"Is that how it feels to you?" I asked.

"Can I come back for another session? Now that I've started, I think I'd like to continue talking about all this," she said.

"Of course. We'll find another time before you go." I was rushing my words, husbanding the few remaining seconds. I forced myself to slow down. "Do you have children, Naomi?"

"Work is . . . difficult. I'd need something late in the day. Or maybe I can get away over lunch."

"We still have a minute or so."

"I need to go."

I considered pointing out the resistance she was demonstrating, but it was too early in the process. Anyway, I knew I was being aggressive with my questions. I checked my book. "Thursday at five-thirty?"

"No, not on Thursday. There's a . . . Never mind. I'm sorry, anything else?"

"The only other time I can offer is twelve-thirty tomorrow."

"That's fine. I'll do a late lunch, sure. And yes, I have two children. A boy and a girl."

I couldn't help myself. I asked, "Are you struggling with some of the same questions?"

She was searching her purse for something, perhaps a pen. She said, "Same as . . . what?"

"As the Harrises and the Klebolds? As the parents of Eric and Dylan?"

Once more she focused on her watch. "You know, I think our time is up," she said, stealing my line. She stood and quickly walked toward the door, pausing only long enough to say, "See you tomorrow."

I didn't want her to leave yet. I needed my questions answered. What were her children planning? What did she know? "We have some paperwork to do before you go," I said to her back.

"Tomorrow, okay? We'll do it then. I promise I'll be on time."

CHAPTER

7

I didn't recall locking up my office after Naomi Bigg departed, nor did I remember climbing into my car.

It wasn't the first time in the past few months that the passage of time had escaped my conscious awareness. I feared it wouldn't be the last.

I knew it wouldn't be the last.

See, the previous autumn I'd killed a man.

I'd used a handgun, a silenced .22, and I'd shot him in the head from a distance of about thirty inches. The little slug had entered the man's cranium through his cheek, just below his left eye. The little round of lead had never exited his head.

My own eyes had been closed when I pulled the trigger.

I don't regret pulling the trigger. The man was intent on killing me, my wife, and my then-unborn baby. I don't regret killing him. That's not to say I didn't relive the moment constantly. But every time I replayed it, I once again closed my finger over the metal wand of the trigger, and every time I squeezed gently.

It never changed with the replaying. Every time, I killed him.

It was the right thing to do.

But righteousness failed to quiet the replays. The chaos of the moment still cascaded into my waking thoughts and continued to infiltrate my dreams.

Pieces only. Fragments.

Not the sound of the .22, though. With the suppressor on the barrel, the surprisingly heavy Ruger made just a heartbeat of a sound. Instead, what I still heard during my private nights was the roar of the man's gun as he tried to shoot me. That night the roar had exploded only four times.

But in my relentless dreams the events of the killing continued to explode all night long.

And his grip. The night that I killed the man, I'd felt his hand close around my ankle as though I were his safety line and he was falling off a cliff. When the dreams came, I found myself shaking my leg in my sleep to free myself from his grasp. I'd wake up and he'd be gone. But the next night, or the one after that, his fingers were back on my leg, locked on my skin like leeches.

And Emily, our big dog—I knew she was barking

even though I couldn't hear her. She'd barked furiously at the man I killed that night, her jaws clapping open
and closed, her eyes orange and fierce in the dim,
dusky light. Now she visited in my dreams, too, sounding her clarion all over again. Warning, imploring.
Fierce, silent.

The morning after the dreams, I would wake knowing in my heart that I'd done the right thing and knowing in my soul that I'd never be the same man again.

As I drove home after my first appointment with Naomi
Bigg, I told myself that the intensity I was feeling after
hearing her fears was due to the incessant echoes of that
night the previous autumn.

The night that I shot a man with a silenced .22.

CHAPTER

8

Cozier Maitlin's black BMW was parked in front of our house. Viv's purple Hyundai wasn't.

Our Bouvier, Emily, greeted me at the door. Inside I found Lauren on the couch with Grace and Anvil sharing her lap. Cozy was sitting on what I liked to think of as my chair. In navy suit trousers, a white shirt that had no business looking as crisp as it did this late in the day, and a solid burgundy tie, Cozy offered a much less maniacal portrait than he had the day before when Sam and I had rousted him out of bed before dawn.

A smile to Grace earned me a smile in return. A kiss to my wife did the same. "So I take it you guys are a team?" I asked.

Lauren's grin told me she was happy with the decision she'd made. "Congratulations," I said. "What does Lucy think?"

"She's thrilled," Lauren said. "Or as happy as someone could be in her circumstances."

Cozy said, "I apologize for invading your home. The media doesn't know that Lauren is on board, yet, so for now we're safe up here. They have my house and office staked out, cameras and microphones everywhere. What do they do with all that equipment in between sieges? I was just asking Lauren—you guys control that little road out there?"

"Kind of. We share ownership of the lane with Adrienne."

Cozy said, "Oh."

He and our friend and neighbor, Adrienne, had been in a hot and heavy romance until Cozy made the mistake of introducing her to his ex-wife and Adrienne decided she preferred to navigate the romantic possibilities with Cozy's ex. So the mention of Adrienne's name was not uncomplicated for Cozy. She represented the second woman in a decade who had chosen to leave him for a chance at the fairer sex. Even to someone as pathologically noninsightful as Cozier Maitlin, that fact caused some considerable dis-ease.

He jerked his attention back to the question at hand. "But if you needed to, you could block off the lane? What I'm getting at, of course, is a way of keeping the press at a reasonable distance, should that become necessary."

"That's an oxymoron, Cozy. 'Press' and 'reasonable distance'—it doesn't compute. But the answer to your question is yes. We could block off the lane anytime we wanted. I'm sure Adrienne would happily go along. You know Adrienne; she loves mischief."

He said, "Hopefully it won't be necessary to involve her."

"What are you guys hearing about the case? What's the mood downtown?"

Lauren responded. "Lucy's been on the police force a long time and apparently she has some loyal friends. It looks like the chasm that already existed between the Boulder Police and the DA's office is in danger of growing into the Grand Canyon over this case."

Cozy smiled at the thought. "Tension between the police and the prosecutor's office has been brewing for a long time. You know that Royal's proclivity for pleading out cases has infuriated the cops. And now the DA's office thinks a cop murdered their leader. The rank-and-file cops are already lining up behind Lucy. The brass, not so much. But the lines are drawn. It can only work to our advantage."

"If this doesn't go to a special prosecutor," I said.

Lauren said, "Before I even asked him to extend my maternity leave, Mitchell told me that he's going to try to keep this one in-house. I don't think there's any doubt that he's going to resist the appointment of a special prosecutor even if we ask the court for one."

I took Grace from Lauren's arms. I was wondering about Mitchell Crest's reaction to Lauren's decision to assist Cozy with Lucy's defense. I was taking my lead from my wife, though. She hadn't brought it up, so I assumed that she and I would discuss it later. I said, "And I take it you and your new partner are not going to press for a special prosecutor, are you?"

"Not immediately, no," replied Cozy. "The conflicts within the DA's office and the tension between the district attorney and the cops will work to our advantage. At least in the short term."

"Witness the Ramseys," I said.

"Exactly," he said. "If I'm wrong, Lauren and I can pick and choose the time to demand a special prosecutor. Certainly we'll wait until after Lucy is charged."

"I'll leave you guys to work. It smells like Grace's diaper needs my attention. You want dinner?"

Lauren answered, "Viv left some Asian noodle thing that smells wonderful. Lots of fish sauce. We'll have some of that later on."

Before Grace and I were out of the room, Lauren asked, "How was your day, sweetie?"

I stopped and looked back, recalling how my day had ended with Naomi Bigg. I said, "Fine. Long. I had a new patient this afternoon that was interesting. Nothing like your day, though."

CHAPTER

9

Naomi Bigg wasn't true to her word. She wasn't on time for her second appointment; twelve-thirty on Tuesday came and went and the red light on my office wall never flashed on. Since the appointment wasn't my last of the day I didn't have to ponder how long I'd wait for her. She had me captive for the entire forty-five minutes, whether she was here in person or not.

It's rare, **very** rare, that a patient's story interests me. Don't misunderstand—it's also rare, very rare, that a patient *doesn't* interest me. The distinction is crucial.

After doing psychotherapy for as long as I've done it, I've listened to a lot of stories told in a myriad of different ways by an incredible variety of storytellers. Bad childhoods, wonderful childhoods; tumultuous adolescence, silky adolescence; heavenly marriages, devilish divorces. Isolation, attachments, losses. Health, illness, heartbreak, death after death after death. The stories almost always take a familiar form and the facts almost always lose narrative interest except for what they tell me about the molecular structure of the storyteller.

As I listen to the life tales of most patients, inevitably I'm left with the feeling that I've read this book before.

But as I waited for the red light to flick on announcing her arrival, I suspected that Naomi Bigg's story was going to be one of the exceptions. The prologue to her tale had been so provocative that I'd actually had trouble concentrating on anything else during the time between her first two appointments. Grace's charms could capture me for a few moments, but my thoughts would soon drift back to the long shadows cast by Harris and Klebold and my concern—no, fear—that the shadows were darkening the space where Naomi Bigg was standing.

Lauren's obvious excitement about working with Cozy to defend Lucy Tanner sparked my curiosity and distracted me for a while, but I was soon struggling anew with my trepidation about how I'd handle the news that I expected to hear: that Naomi Bigg suspected that her adolescent children might be planning some unspeakable atrocity à la Columbine.

Ten times I reminded myself that she hadn't said so.

Eleven times I convinced myself that that was exactly where her story was heading.

The light glowed at 12:51. I did the math: Our session would last only twenty-four minutes, a few of which we were going to waste filling out forms.

Naomi didn't bother to apologize. She filled out the forms and signed the state-mandated disclosure statement in record time.

She smoothed the fabric of her pink skirt and straightened the sweater of her twinset. The shell beneath the sweater was cut in a slightly less-than-modest V. The tops of her breasts swelled noticeably as she took a deep breath. "Where were we yesterday? My daughter? Is that what we were talking about? Want to help me here? I don't know if I told you, but her name is Marin. She's nineteen."

I wanted to correct her. I wanted to tell her, *No, we were talking about the Klebolds and the Harrises, and the Columbine anniversary and about how parents couldn't know what evil lurked in their children's hearts.*

I said nothing. Naomi and I had only nineteen minutes left to talk about Marin Bigg. One minute for each year of the young woman's life. I inhaled slowly, tasting stale cigarette smoke, and I reminded myself to be patient, to follow this woman, not to lead her.

She said, "You've been in Boulder a while, haven't you?"

In psychotherapy, few patient queries are uncompli-cated. Was Naomi checking on my experience? My familiarity with the town? Making conversation? What?

I chose an obtuse answer. "I've been practicing in this office since the late eighties."

"I thought so," she said. "Then you may remember what happened to Marin. Four years ago. She was fif-teen." She began spinning her wedding ring with her thumb. "Do you remember?"

I knew that if I said I didn't remember, for Naomi Bigg it would be as if I were failing to recall Pearl Harbor or Kennedy's assassination or . . . the shoot-ings at Columbine.

I said, "No." I said it softly, so that she could uncov-er a covert apology there if she chose.

"She was raped by a CU student. You didn't read about it?" Her tone was slightly incredulous that I had-n't remembered without her prompting.

"I don't recall it specifically, no." During my time in Boulder the local paper had reported way too many rapes. I usually didn't study the stories. The meager details she had provided didn't separate Naomi Bigg's story from the herd.

She looked away from me. "It would be easier if you remembered. I was hoping that you would have." In that moment, I thought I witnessed sadness, and not just the edgy anger that she'd demonstrated thus far.

"That way you wouldn't have to tell me?" I said.

"Yes."

One of the nineteen minutes crept by.

Naomi said, "The details aren't important. She was raped. They called it date rape. Which means what? That she'd agreed to go to a movie first? Anyway, the police arrested the rapist. To make a long story short, the district attorney decided that the rapist deserved a year in jail and cut a deal with him. Without, I might add, the consent of the victim. Or the victim's family."

I noted that Naomi's breathing had grown shallow and rapid. Her eyes had narrowed and the muscles in her face had hardened into something sinewy. I didn't speak.

"He got out of jail in seven months. *Seven* months. He raped my baby and he got out of jail in seven damn months. She didn't get over the rape in seven months. She hasn't gotten over the rape in four years. She won't get over the rape in another forty years."

She pushed her tongue between her front teeth and her upper lip and left it there for a few seconds. "My husband never got over it. He attacked the rapist after he got out of jail. Ringing any bells yet? The man had transferred to Metro. The college in Denver, you know? My husband waited for him to get out of class one night and attacked him in the parking lot at Auraria. I bet the story's ringing those bells now. People forget about rape; they don't forget about assaults on rapists. What does that tell you about this society's priorities?"

Now I remembered what had happened to Marin Bigg. Her father had beaten her rapist to the brink of death with a cut-off baseball bat that big-rig drivers call a tire checker.

"Leo? My husband? His mistake was that he attacked him in Denver. Want to know why that was a mistake? Because they actually hold trials in Denver. The prosecutors in Denver actually prosecute—they don't plead everything out like they do in Boulder. My husband's trial lasted three days. The jury was out for three hours. Three hours. The judge gave Leo six years. The jury foreman phoned me later, after the trial, and he apologized. Said that the jury thought the judge would be lenient, that they never expected him to give my husband six years. Thought that the judge would slap him on the wrist.

"Yeah, the foreman called and said he was sorry. My husband's in Buena Vista. My daughter's scarred for life. My kids don't have a father. I don't have a husband. But the jury foreman was sorry. At least there's that. Right? God, it was such a relief that the man was sorry."

The sarcasm seeped between us like toxic sludge. I was thinking about what to say. I was trying to trace the connection between Marin Bigg's tragedy—the whole Bigg family's tragedy—and the anniversary of the massacre at Columbine. I was trying to fit the Harrises and the Klebolds into the puzzle. I was trying to think of something to say that might be more palliative than "It's apparent how angry you are."

Naomi interrupted my reverie. "But it's Paul I'm worried about. My son. I haven't talked about him. He's seventeen. He's a senior at Fairview."

The clock showed that we had seven minutes left in the session. Fairview was one of Boulder's two high schools. I watched Naomi's discomfort as thirty seconds ticked away before I pulled her back. I said, "You're worried about Paul, Naomi?"

"Yes, I'm worried about Paul. Of course I'm worried about Paul. He's angry. He's young. He's male. He's big. And he thinks that he's been wronged. Wouldn't you be worried about him?"

Her tone was more than sarcastic. It was slightly snide.

I opened my mouth to clarify that the wrong she was alluding to was his sister's rape and its aftermath, but Naomi was quicker than I. "I can't really afford this," she said. Again, I thought I heard some disdain in her tone.

I wondered whether she was talking about money, or whether her complaint was a metaphor for something else. I was about to ask which when she continued.

"Leo's a physician—an oncologist. That gives you some idea of the kind of income we lost when they sent him to prison." She raised her cruelly trimmed eyebrows. "A lot. Now? I'm working as an office manager; I run the practice of one of Leo's old colleagues. How's that for a state of affairs? Let's say things are tight financially in the Bigg household. And it turns out that you're not even a provider with my managed-care plan."

I could've told her that I wasn't a provider with any

managed-care plan, but I didn't. I got lost for a moment as I tried to remember a session with another recent patient where I'd felt so tongue-tied, but I couldn't.

Finally, I said, "Even with the little you've told me, I'm becoming more and more convinced that you can't afford not to do this, Naomi."

She flashed a quick glance at me, sniffed audibly. The sniff wasn't purely derisive, but close. "Go on," she said.

Softly, I said, "I think you might want to tell me more about Paul. Your concerns."

She softened noticeably. "Paul's a good kid. He's my buddy, my friend. He's polite, responsible. He's never been in any kind of trouble at all. If you met him, you'd like him. Everybody does."

"Yes?"

"High school has been tough for him, especially after what happened to his sister and his father. He's been an outsider all through school, very resentful of the popular kids, you know, the athletes. He wasn't treated well. He saw Dr. Haven for a while for help with his . . . impulses. You know her? Dr. Haven? She thought he was depressed, I think. I was never so sure."

Jill Haven was a psychiatrist who specialized in treating adolescents. She was good. "Yes," I said. "I know her."

"Well, it's not important. He doesn't see her any-more. His grades are better, good even. He has a few friends, dates some nice girls. Paul's settled down now. He plays keyboards—that's really his love—and he works at Starbucks. On the Mall? You may have seen him there. He's one of their best baristas. I think he's the best. He makes a killer mocha."

Hearing the word "killer" from Naomi Bigg's mouth gave me a chill. My office was at the west end of downtown, and I didn't get down to the east end of the Downtown Boulder Mall, where Starbucks was, very often, so I doubted that I'd met Paul Bigg. But it was possible.

I found myself fighting off stereotypical visual images of Starbucks's male employees. I wasn't entirely successful. In my mind, Paul suddenly had a persona; he was a tall, distracted kid with a pierced tongue and a sloppy tattoo wearing a filthy green apron.

I allowed Naomi a minute to find the detour she needed to get around her litany of her son's exemplary qualities. She didn't appear to be making a concerted effort to find an alternate route. Finally, I said, "I don't think you've told me why you're worried about him, Naomi."

"I always worry about my children. That's just me. But right now—well, since last fall—I'm worried about him because it seems . . . that he wants to get even. He wants . . . retribution."

"Because of Marin?"

"Sure. And because of Leo."

I should have paused here and allowed her to read the trail ahead, choose her own path, but I didn't. I

said, "Is Paul planning something, some kind of retribution?" I was careful to use her word. My heart was
pounding in my chest. It's rare that I ask a patient a
question when I don't want to hear the answer. But I
didn't want to hear Naomi's answer to my question. I
was thinking of Columbine and a dozen other school
shootings.

But mostly I was thinking about Columbine.

She was silent for longer than I was comfortable
with. Her shoulders sank noticeably. "I don't know for
sure. Okay? I don't know anything for sure, but I think
sometimes he wants to hurt people. As a way of getting
even."

"People?"

"People who he thinks are responsible for what happened. I don't know. He doesn't exactly talk to me
about all this. He's a teenager. We have to remember
that he's only a teenager."

The clock was ticking down toward one-fifteen, the
end of our session. I considered extending the time.
On the opposite wall, the red light was lit. My next
patient was already sitting in the waiting room. "You
think he wants to hurt people? You suspect—"

"I didn't say I suspect anything. I said I'm concerned."

She was right. That's exactly what she had said.

Thirty seconds. Twenty-five. Twenty.

"Naomi?" I said, waiting until she found my eyes
with hers. The moment they locked on, I felt another
chill.

"Yes?"

In other circumstances I would not have pressed her, especially not this early in treatment. She and I had not yet established an alliance, certainly not one that I felt with any assurance could withstand the assault I was contemplating. I questioned my words even before they were out of my mouth.

"Are your concerns about Paul related to the ones you mentioned during yesterday's session?"

She lifted her left wrist and stared at her watch in a manner that left no doubt that she didn't care that I saw her looking. "You mean what I was saying about parental responsibility? About the Harrises and the Klebolds? My sympathy for the position they find themselves in?"

Her tone was provocative. Obviously provocative. I didn't recall Naomi having said anything about sympathy for the position of the Klebolds and Harrises, but I said, "Yes."

She stood up. "Oh my, oh my, look at the time. I'm going to be late getting back to work." She had a package of Salem Slims in her hand before she reached the door. The appearance of the smokes was like magic; I hadn't witnessed the sleight of hand that produced them.

I lifted my book from the table beside my chair. "I think we should set another appointment, Naomi."

She tapped a cigarette into her left hand and fumbled in her purse for a lighter. "Of course, sure. What do you have? Lunch or after work? It's all I can do.

Maybe this time next week? And we have to talk about money. I don't know how I'm going to pay for all this."

Intentionally ignoring the financial question, I said, "Please sit down, I need to say something."

One sigh later she perched on the edge of the chair.

"Unless I'm misreading your concerns—and I don't think I am—the issues you're raising about your son, Paul, are quite serious. Waiting until next week to address those concerns doesn't feel prudent. You decided to come in to see me this week for a reason. You said that you hoped that I could help with your confusion. You mentioned an anniversary that's occurring this week. Are the consequences of putting off our discussion something you want to . . . contemplate?"

She busied herself fingering the long cigarette. "What are you saying, Dr. Gregory?"

"I'm offering you another appointment tonight to give us more time to explore all this. I'm not convinced we should wait."

"Tonight? I can't, I just can't."

"Tomorrow at five forty-five then?"

She considered my offer, finally saying, "All right. Tomorrow at five forty-five."

Over the years, I'd fallen into the habit of taking most Fridays off. Since Grace's birth, I'd promised myself I'd be even more diligent in protecting my Fridays. Occasionally, I knew, I would have to use the time for emergencies. I'd already decided that whatever was going on with Naomi Bigg and her son Paul qualified as an emergency.

"And again Friday at noon?" I said. "If it turns out that it's not necessary, we'll reconsider."

"See you tomorrow, I guess." She didn't even go through the motions of promising to be on time. "I have to think about all this some more. I'll call you if I change my mind."

I have to admit that I was hoping she would almost as much as I was hoping she wouldn't.

Occasionally, I had days at work when I concluded that my patients had spent the previous evening conspiring to find ways to make me crazy. That Tuesday afternoon—after Naomi Bigg had left my office—was one of those. My one-fifteen had just been fired from his new job at Amgen. His résumé for the past twelve months was longer than mine was for my lifetime. I was certain that his parents had been told repeatedly during his preschool years that their son didn't play well with others.

He and I had a lot of work to do.

My two o'clock was a massage therapist with a phobia of gooseflesh. Not the kind of gooseflesh that geese have, but the kind of gooseflesh that people get. How weird was that phobia? So weird that I'd never even been able to find a name for it. The closest I'd been able to get was doraphobia—the fear of the fur or skin of animals. But that wasn't it. Quite simply, this massage therapist was terrified of goose bumps, and although she'd been symptom-free for months, she'd chosen that day to suffer a relapse.

Unfortunately, gooseflesh phobia is a difficult condition for which to design effective behavioral desensitization. Photographs of goose bumps did nothing to instigate my patient's terror, and finding reliable sources of gooseflesh so that I could design progressive exposures for her proved, well, ludicrous. Although medication and psychotherapy had kept her symptoms in remission for almost a year, she explained to me that she had literally run out of a morning hot-stone session in abject panic.

I listened as patiently as I could while I entertained the possibility that she might be better off in a profession where her clients kept their clothes on.

As soon as she'd left my office a woman I'd been seeing for about three months left an urgent message.

The Boulder Police had arrested both her and her husband after a domestic disturbance. He'd been taken to the hospital with a closed head injury. She'd been taken to jail. The fact that she'd been arrested for a domestic disturbance came as no surprise; her marriage was about as stable as an eight-year-old with matches in a fireworks factory. Nor did the fact that she had apparently won the fight; she was tough. What did surprise me was that she chose to use her sole phone call to get in touch with me, and not to call an attorney.

Did I mention that her judgment sucked? It was one of the items we were addressing in the treatment plan.

I was home before Lauren, and Viv seemed eager for some adult company before she left for the day. We sat outside with Grace and the dogs on the deck off the living room and chatted about how school was going for Viv and how cute my baby was. I sipped a beer; Viv drank tea. The sun ducked behind clouds before it plunged behind the Rockies.

As Viv stood to leave she told me that she'd left some shrimp marinating in the refrigerator—she used a word in her native language that I didn't understand before she fumbled for the English word "soaking"— and that she'd already heated up the grill.

I felt blessed that she was watching over my child and my family and I told her so. She blushed.

Lauren came home exhausted. She'd spent much of the day pigeonholed in a conference room in Cozy's Fourteenth Street offices with Lucy Tanner.

Lauren caught up with Grace. I waltzed out to Adrienne's garden and swiped two huge handfuls of spinach that I wilted in a couple of teaspoons of the marinade while shrimp and vegetables sizzled on the grill. When the food was done, Lauren and I sat down to dinner and Grace amused herself in her bouncy chair. Lauren asked about my day before I had a chance to ask about hers.

Her question was polite, conversational, a simple "How was your day? Anything interesting?"

I lifted an asparagus spear with my index finger and thumb—somebody had once told me that the French ate asparagus that way, so I'd convinced myself it was okay—and tried to mimic the casual tone of Lauren's question as I said, "You remember a case from about four years ago, a date rape involving a young Fairview High School girl and a guy from CU?"

Lauren was eating her asparagus by using her silverware to cut it into bite-size pieces. She thought my rationale about the French eating with their fingers was lame. "My case or yours?" she asked.

"Yours. DA's case."

"Four years ago?"

"Yeah."

She sipped some wine. "Yes, I think I do. Why?"

"What do you remember?"

"Bigg. That was the girl, something Bigg. Marina, no . . . Marin Bigg. Her father went nuts after the boy got out of jail and tracked him down and beat him with a baseball bat. That's the case you're talking about, right? My memory is that the father got some hard time. But that was in Denver or somewhere, it wasn't ours."

Grace was cooing and kicking her legs and generally succeeding in stealing more of Lauren's attention than I was getting.

"Yes, that's the case. Since it was a rape prosecution, it would have been Nora's, right?" Nora Doyle had headed the sex crimes unit at the DA's office for as long as I could remember. Instituting the sex crimes unit had been one of Royal's many noteworthy innovations during his tenure.

"Sure, it was Nora's case. But I helped her on it. You don't remember? That was the period where Roy and Nora had just started thinking about expanding the sex crimes office. I did half a dozen cases with Nora before she hired Erica in to pick up the slack. God, this shrimp is good. We should pay Viv something extra if she keeps cooking for us, don't you think? I'm beginning to feel guilty about all the extra work she's doing. And I think I might be getting addicted to her cooking."

"I agree," I said as I set down my fork and picked up my beer. I'd lost my appetite, but I made a conscious effort to sound normal. "You helped Nora? Were you a big part of the case?"

Lauren hadn't even looked at me yet, so she couldn't be aware that I was almost paralyzed with fear by what she'd just told me. Naomi Bigg had said that her son Paul wanted to "hurt people he thinks are responsible."

I'd just realized that list included Lauren.

"We made an early decision to plead it out. Facts are often messy in date rape cases. Dueling witnesses. He says she consented. She says she was forced. Usually no injuries to use as evidence. Rape kit often doesn't tell you much. DNA and blood typing are useless. You know how it goes."

"And you were involved in the decision to do the plea bargain?"

"Sure."

"Was it a clear-cut decision or was it controversial?"

She glanced at me with slightly suspicious eyes. "You know that Royal and Nora always took date rape prosecution seriously. Always. The outcomes weren't always popular, but the cases were always examined carefully. It's been one of our strengths as long as I've been with the DA's office. You know how I feel about all this. We're good on rape, Alan. We're good."

She hadn't answered my question. I said, "Was the family on board?"

"An effort is always made to include the family. But I don't remember specifically. Given what happened later, I'd assume they never signed off on this one. But that's the way it goes sometimes. Given the evidence, I thought it was a good outcome. Still do. In a lot of jurisdictions the offender would have walked given the exact same circumstances."

I knew she was right. "Who defended the boy? The rapist. Do you remember?"

Between bites, she was playing with Grace. Finally, she looked over at me. "Funny you should ask. I think it was Cozy. Why is this so important?"

"Somebody was talking about the case today at work," I said. "That's all. No big deal."

Later, after Grace was down for the night and the dogs were walked, Lauren climbed into bed beside me, and she said, "Lucy was there on Friday night. At Royal's house."

"She was? She admits it?"

"The evidence is pretty compelling that she was there. A witness saw her car around the corner. It's a bright red Volvo. Her prints are in at least two different rooms in the house. None of the police at the scene remember Lucy being inside without gloves during the investigation of the murder. And there's lots of video—all of it shows her wearing gloves.

"So . . . when she heard what they had, Lucy finally admitted to Cozy and me that she was at the Peterson home, but she maintains that it was earlier in the evening. That she left around eight-thirty, quarter to nine. And she said Roy was fine when she left."

I had a hundred questions.

I started with, "Why was she there?"

"She won't tell us. She says that we just have to accept the fact that if we knew why she was there, we'd be convinced she had a reason to kill Roy. She's absolutely certain that talking about why she was at the house will only hurt her. She says she'll reconsider if she's arrested. But not until then."

"She admitted to you that she had a motive to kill Roy?"

"In so many words, I guess she did."

"What could possibly—"

"I don't know. But apparently she's been to his house before."

"She told you that?"

"She's not saying anything about it. But the witness who saw her car remembers the Volvo. Said he's lusted after one forever. He's noticed it parked in front of his house before. He said it's a turbo." She shrugged her shoulders and rolled her violet eyes as though she couldn't imagine being able to tell a turbo from a non-turbo, and certainly couldn't imagine coveting one.

"Had he seen it frequently?"

"A few times, always in the evening."

I asked, "Why did she park on a different street?"

"Obviously she didn't want to be seen going into Royal's house. Maybe she went in through the back. There aren't any fences that would keep her from getting to Royal's back door."

"Does the witness remember what time the Volvo was gone from in front of his house on Friday?"

"We haven't talked to him yet but the police say no. He told them he was out for the evening, got home after eleven. The car was gone when he got home. Cozy and I have an investigator going out to talk to him and to try to corral more neighbors, see if someone saw the car leave before ten o'clock."

"What's Lucy's connection to Royal? Did they have a case together, something they were working on?"

She made a groaning noise to communicate her frustration with my questions. "We don't know. Even if they did have a case, it wouldn't give Lucy cause to have direct contact with the district attorney himself. If it had to do with an investigation, it would be Sam doing the talking, not Lucy, and he'd be talking to someone like me, an assistant DA, not with the district attorney. I can't think of a single reason why someone like Lucy would be dealing with someone like Roy on a direct basis about a case. It just wouldn't happen."

I thought about the details Lauren had shared with me so far. I wasn't a lawyer, but it didn't seem to add up to probable cause. "There must be something else, babe. So she was in the neighborhood—a lot of people were in the neighborhood that night. I don't think Sam would have picked up Lucy based on what you just told me."

"Sam was following orders, that's why he picked her up. But there is more. Murder weapon was a brass lamp. It had been wiped. But Lucy's latents are on pieces of a ceramic dish or something that was found busted on the floor."

"Jesus. What does Lucy say to that?"

"She seemed honestly perplexed. That's all I can say, that she seemed surprised."

We rolled over at the same time and ended up facing each other in the middle of the bed. I rested a hand on her naked hip. "How are you holding up?"

"Okay, I think. I think I'm doing okay."

"No exacerbation?"

"Not so far."

"How's the brain mud?"

"Not so bad. Maybe a little better."

I felt as much relief as multiple sclerosis ever seemed to permit. I said, "So much has happened since last week. I can't believe it's only Tuesday."

She moved my hand to her waist and slid close enough to me that her nipples brushed my skin.

CHAPTER

11

Naomi Bigg was—finally—right on time for the Wednesday session. I let the red light glow on the wall for a good minute before I walked out to the waiting room to invite her back to the office.

She knew exactly where she wanted to start. "Paul has a friend named Ramp. He's older—I don't know for sure, but he's got ID, so I'd say he's twenty-one, maybe twenty-two. Of course, it's possible the ID is fake." She crossed her legs and smiled coyly.

The little grin caught me completely off guard. I didn't know what to make of it. Had it been seductive? Mocking?

"This would be a lot easier if you'd let me smoke."

I didn't say, *It's not my job to make it easier*. I didn't

say, *It's the law in Boulder.* I didn't say, *I can't stand cigarette smoke.*

I said, "Sorry." But I wasn't.

I'd already realized that I didn't especially like Naomi Bigg. I'd tried telling myself that her message was so frightening that I was unable to refrain from blaming the messenger. For whatever good it would do, I was making a conscious effort to monitor the reflexes that my dislike was generating.

Shrinks call this "dealing with the countertransference."

Naomi went on. "I like Ramp. He's pleasant, polite, has a good sense of humor. But I'm not sure he's the best influence in the world on . . . Paul. They've only been friends for a few months, maybe longer than that. Last summer, actually. Paul met Ramp on the Internet, on a bulletin-board-type thing where they were both complaining about the criminal justice system. Ramp has a family situation kind of like ours. His mother was killed by a man who was released on parole after serving four years for murder. The guy got four years for murder, can you believe it?"

"Ramp lives where?" It wasn't like me to demand a fact like this from a therapy patient, but this bit of data seemed important.

"Denver somewhere, I don't know. The truth is that Ramp is even angrier about the justice system's inequities than Paul is. Maybe even more furious than I am."

"You've met him?"

"Oh sure. They hang out at our house a lot, which I encourage. Keeps Paul from driving to Denver so much, and I'd rather have the kids close by, you know, where I can keep an eye on them."

She repeated the coy little smile. I was still unsure what to make of it.

"Every time he comes to the house, Ramp brings papers. Sometimes magazine articles or clippings from the newspaper. But mostly things he's printed off the Net. Stories from around the country about all the things that infuriate him. Plea bargains, mostly. Psychotic parole decisions. Or absurd sentences, like putting murderers on probation. Or giving rapists a few months in jail or no jail at all. He keeps this binder that he calls his 'Hall of Shame.' It's full of pictures of prosecutors, judges, slimy attorneys, expert witnesses who will say anything to get people off. You know what I'm talking about. Everybody knows.

"The stuff Ramp brings keeps Paul stirred up. Now Paul's started collecting stuff on his own, too. They trade it like Paul used to trade baseball cards when he was little."

"Go on," I said. I shouldn't have said anything but I was an impatient audience. I was aware that there was a possibility that my need to hear this story was getting ahead of my patient's need to tell it. In almost all circumstances in psychotherapy, that was a problem.

Naomi said, "Ramp thinks that Leo is a hero."

I tried to remember who Leo was. After half a week of therapy appointments, I sometimes discovered that all the names I'd heard had blended together like the fruit in a smoothie.

"Paul, of course, thinks it's great that there's somebody who understands what his father did."

That Leo. The one who pummeled the rapist with a tire checker. The one doing hard time in a small concrete room in Buena Vista.

"Most of his friends deserted Paul after Leo was arrested for attacking the . . . scum who raped Marin. With Ramp, Paul has a friend who thinks what Leo did is the absolute coolest thing in the world. Ramp actually wants to go up to Buena Vista and visit Leo." She shifted her gaze from the window, to me, and back to the window and the soft light at the end of the day.

"Yes?" I said.

"Ramp's the one who keeps bringing up retribution. 'Wouldn't it be cool?' That's what he says all the time. 'Wouldn't it be cool if somebody raped the judge's daughter? Maybe then he'd know how it feels.' Or 'Wouldn't it be cool if something bad happened to that lawyer's family? Then he'd know the pain.' Or 'Wouldn't it be cool if so-and-so's house blew up?' That's what Ramp always says."

"And Paul plays along?"

"It's like a parlor game. When I ask him about it, he tells me it's just their version of fantasy baseball."

She sounded skeptical. I stated the obvious by saying, "But you're not so sure it's so innocent?"

"I was." For a moment, Naomi appeared uncomfortable. "I didn't like it, that kind of talk. I mean I don't wish tragedy on any family, especially after what we've been through. And then I heard that Royal Peterson had been killed. Since then I haven't been so sure."

There are rare moments in psychotherapy where my practiced façade is tested to the extreme. I think of those moments as slugs that slam into my bulletproof vest. Usually, the lead doesn't pierce the protective shield, but sometimes the bullets rock me back on my heels. This was one of those times.

"What?" I said, as though I was feigning an acute hearing loss. To a casual observer my state could probably just as easily have been mistaken for a brief interim of idiocy.

"Roy Peterson's murder? The boys won't talk about it. Not a word about it since it happened. That alone made me suspicious. The truth was that I half expected them to be celebrating when they heard that Peterson had a dose of the medicine he was dishing out."

"I'm not sure I understand."

"Peterson was like a drug lord. DAs like him all are. With their plea bargains and sentence recommendations they put scum back on the street just like a drug lord ships crack or heroin into town. They think they're doing the right thing but they're really just making things worse. Do you know what percentage of charged crimes went to trial in the last ten years under Peterson? One percent. That's it. One percent."

"I didn't know."

"Do you know that pedophiles, and I mean active

pedophiles—pedophiles who have actually touched children—have received deferred sentences in this county? Do you know that?"

I didn't answer. Part of me knew that it might be true, though. Some cases kept Lauren up at night. They were the ones I heard about at breakfast. I fought an impulse to defend the DA's office.

"Their good-old-boy networks and their political connections—it's disgusting. The excuses, God. When Peterson died, I thought the kids would be celebrating that maybe he choked on some of his own filth."

What did I want to say right then? I wanted to say, *Holy shit! You think your son may have murdered Roy Peterson?* But I kept my mouth shut until I could think of an alternative that might actually keep Naomi talking and not cause her to keep her mouth shut.

"What I talked about that first day? About sympathy for the Klebolds and the Harrises? I think sometimes that I know how they felt in the months before the attack. Maybe even how they feel now. Are you finally beginning to understand what it is I mean?"

I can't say how much time passed before I spoke again. It might have been only a few seconds, but I'd guess it was most of a minute. I broke the silence with a question: "Naomi? Was Royal Peterson ever the focus of any of Paul's wouldn't-it-be-cool games?"

"They were Ramp's games."

The distinction was obviously important to Naomi. Essential, even, as far as our therapeutic alliance was concerned. "Okay—was Roy Peterson ever the focus of any of Ramp's wouldn't-it-be-cool games?"

"I don't really think they did it."

We both recognized that she hadn't responded to my question. I said, "You don't?"

"No." She shook her head for emphasis. "No, I don't think they did it. But, obviously, I'm not sure, not totally sure. So I'm not willing to say anything to anybody about my concerns."

"You just did. You told me you're not convinced that the games the boys are playing are innocent."

"I meant say anything to the police. Or whomever. The question I struggle with all the time is: How much does a parent have to know in order to turn her child in to the police?

"Do you know that before Columbine, Eric Harris's parents failed to notice that their son had an arsenal in their house, for heaven's sake? And that one of them— Eric or Dylan—wrote an essay that predicted what they were going to do? And sometime before the two kids made their assault, Mr. Harris actually took a call for his son from a gun shop? Well, it wasn't enough for him to do anything at all; it certainly wasn't enough for him to turn his son in.

"And the police?" she scoffed. "The sheriff in Jefferson County was informed that Harris had threatened to kill a student a year before the shooting. They even suspected him of detonating a pipe bomb. And they were aware that he had this violent, awful Web site. Some deputies even wrote a request for a search warrant. But the sheriff did nothing with the suspicions. Nothing.

"So I ask you, what does it take to get a parent to believe that her child is planning something evil? What should it take? Believe me, I've thought a lot about it and I don't know the answer to that question. But I do know that it's going to take a hell of a lot more than I know so far."

Softly, I said, "What do you know so far, Naomi?" I didn't say, *Have you found an arsenal, too?* But that's what I wanted to know.

She glared at me as though my question was a trap. "Nothing. I don't know a thing. I haven't found any smoking guns in my house, and I haven't intercepted any calls from gun dealers, and I've checked my child's Web site and it's nothing but the same kind of stuff I hear around the house. I don't know a thing. I know less than the Klebolds and the Harrises knew. I definitely know less than the Jefferson County sheriff knew."

"But don't you think that the Klebolds and the Harrises and the sheriff all should have said something to prevent that tragedy?"

"The sheriff, sure, of course. But the parents? That's easy for us *now*, isn't it? We know what happened. They didn't know what was *going* to happen. Who could've guessed what those two boys were about to do?"

I tried empathy. "It's a tough place for a parent, Naomi."

For a long interval she stared at me, swallowing once or twice, and then she found a place where her composure was more assured. When she spoke again, she took me someplace else I didn't want to be.

We actually spent the rest of the session talking about Naomi's aging parents in Michigan and her fears about the onset of menopause.

I wanted to scream.

The eastern rim of the Boulder Valley was growing dark as I made the final turn onto the lane that led to our house. My headlights immediately illuminated the side of my neighbor Adrienne's big blue Suburban, which was parked at an angle across the narrow width of the gravel lane, just beyond the permanent tin placard that identified the path to our little piece of paradise as a "Private Road." Taped to the side of Adrienne's huge vehicle was a poster-board sign that read NO PRES.

I recognized the artist, and the spelling. The poster was the work of Jonas, Adrienne's son. I was left with an inescapable conclusion: The kid shared not only his mother's aversion to the media but also her spelling challenges.

I pulled around Adrienne's behemoth and drove through the dry grasses until I could ease back up on the lane. In front of our house I found exactly what I was expecting to find, and I also found one surprise. Cozy's BMW was the expectation.

Lucy Tanner's red Volvo turbo was the surprise.

I said quick hellos to everyone, retrieved Grace from her bouncy chair in the center of the coffee table, and retreated from the living room so that Cozy and Lauren could continue to huddle with their client.

Dinner was in a dozen white boxes that were spread all over the kitchen counter, an amazing variety of take-out Chinese, all courtesy of Cozy. But as attractive as the buffet looked, I wasn't hungry. My appetite hadn't recovered from Naomi Bigg's provocative wouldn't-it-be-cool revelations or from her numbing menopause lament.

I stood with Grace in my arms, contemplating a spring roll, but grabbed only a beer on my way to the far end of the house.

The day after Grace was born, Lucy Tanner had stopped by Community Hospital and dropped off a gift, a charming, developmentally appropriate, black-and-white stuffed Gund musical clown with a garish face. Grace loved having the thing hanging above her crib. I didn't think I'd seen Lucy since that day in the hospital.

Although I'd crossed paths with her from time to time over the years during various misadventures I'd had with Sam Purdy, she and I had never grown close. She was a personable, friendly woman with a quick mind, a gentle wit, and an admirable tolerance of her quirky partner. She knew when to let Sam be the boss and she knew when to draw a line across his nose and dare him to cross it. I didn't recall ever seeing her misstep with Sam Purdy, which wasn't easy. I couldn't say the same thing about my own interactions with our mutual friend.

Lucy was uncommonly pretty. Not remarkably pretty, but uncommonly so. With the exception of her glistening blond hair there was nothing conventionally attractive about her features, but the constellation that the individual stars created was alluring, even magnetic. Many men embarrassed themselves when Lucy was in their vicinity, and Lucy was not at all reticent to take advantage of the phenomenon, either personally or professionally.

Over the years, I'd seen her in leather; I'd seen her in a little black dress; I'd seen her in brand-new Donna Karan, but—with the exception of her hours on the job—I'd never seen her dressed to blend in. Lucy always managed to stand off by herself. I suppose that I perceived her as living her life surrounded by a fence. Not chain link topped with razor wire, but more like a good strong wrought-iron barrier with an imposing gate.

Lucy would let you look into her world and its carefully manicured gardens, but she always made it clear that she didn't welcome uninvited visitors.

I was more than a little surprised when I saw Lucy standing in the open doorway to the master bedroom pantomiming a knuckle rap and saying, "Knock, knock." I'd changed into an old pair of shorts and a white T-shirt. Grace was in a fresh diaper and absolutely nothing else.

What do you say to an acquaintance who is suspected of murder? I tried, "I'm so sorry about all this you're going through. It must be like taking a holiday in hell."

"Thanks, Alan. May I come in? Cozy and Lauren are both on the phone. I thought I'd take a little break and was hoping I could sneak another look at the baby. She's wonderful."

Lucy was wearing a starched white shirt and jeans that fit her like hot wax. No jewelry. Black flats. Very little makeup. Given what she'd been through, I expected she would look tired, but she didn't. She somehow managed to slide her hands into the back pockets of her jeans.

"Of course. You want to hold her? She has a fresh diaper—so it's a rare opportunity. Take advantage of it while you can."

She smiled and lifted her arms. "May I?"

I handed Grace over to her. She took the baby with an awkward motion that spoke of unfamiliarity with infants. She said, "Is she always this good?"

"In a word, no. But she's still a wonderful baby. We've been very lucky."

I gestured toward an upholstered chair by the

western window. Lucy sat and made a cute face for Grace's benefit. She said, "Sorry to take over your house. It's been hard to find a place to meet that's not surrounded by the media. My place is impossible. Cozy's office, his house . . ."

"Don't mention it, Lucy. I'm glad there's a place you can go without being harassed."

For a moment she focused all her attention on Grace, whose face was beginning to scrunch up into one of her pre-distress configurations. "Am I doing something wrong?" Lucy asked.

"No, she may be hungry, or she may be cutting a tooth. Those are my current all-purpose explanations for Grace being unhappy. I'm planning to expand the list as necessary as she grows older. But I am hoping those two will suffice at least until her mid-teens."

Lucy laughed gently. "Were life so simple, huh? I wish those were my only two potential problems."

"I do, too, Lucy. I do, too."

Without taking her eyes from the baby, she said, "I told Lauren she could tell you what's been going on. I assume she told you I was there that night? At Royal's house?"

Grace captured and then started sucking on Lucy's pinky. I reached to the bed behind me, grabbed a bottle, and handed it over to Lucy. Grace started eating. "She *was* hungry," Lucy said.

"Yes, she told me you were at the house."

"The press will probably find out soon."

"They usually seem to discover these things."

"I think it was somebody at the department who leaked the fact that I'd been questioned to the media. That still hurts. Sammy picked me up before dawn so nobody would notice."

"Sam's a sweetheart, Lucy. It could have been somebody at the DA's office who was the leak, couldn't it? It might not have been one of your colleagues."

"I suppose," she said before she grew quiet for a moment, apparently fascinated by the simple act of an infant eating. I guessed Lucy was thirty-two, thirty-three years old. She was unmarried and childless, certainly vulnerable to the gravitational pull of maternal yearnings.

I was about to comment about that when she asked, "Alan? You ever do anything . . . ? God . . . you ever do anything that you're so ashamed of . . . ?" She stared out the window at the lights of the city and the silhouette of the mountains. "So ashamed of that you'd do almost anything to undo it?"

"I don't know," I replied, in a moment of stark ineloquence. "Maybe." I tried to guess what was coming next, but was drawing a blank.

"You've probably already figured it out, but I'm talking about the reason I was at Roy Peterson's house."

Moments like these—when acquaintances or friends begin to open up to me as though we were patient and doctor sitting in my office—are always awkward for me. My practiced instinct was to warn Lucy that she enjoyed no confidentiality here in my bedroom, but a friend wouldn't do that, a friend would just listen.

"I wondered," I said, recalling that Lucy had told her attorneys that if people knew why she was at Roy's house it would only support the contention that she had a motive to kill him. Now she was telling me that the reason she was there filled her with shame.

She said, "There's an old saying about good intentions. A proverb, or an aphorism. Are they the same thing, proverbs and aphorisms? Do you know it? Something like the road to hell is paved with good intentions."

I said, "The reason you were at Royal's house— that's still what you're talking about?"

Did she nod in reply? I wasn't quite certain. Finally, she said, "This one was—paved with good intentions, I mean. Not a whole lot of good judgment maybe, but a whole lot of good intentions."

She lowered her head and Grace almost disappeared in the cascade of blond hair. "Grace's done with the bottle. Should she have more? How do you know how much to feed her?"

"We give her what she wants. That seems to work."

Lucy closed her eyes slowly and left them shut. She said, "It's different for adults, I guess."

"What do you mean?"

She opened her eyes and looked up at me. The corners of her mouth turned up in a wry grin. She said, "Giving people what they want, it's more complicated with adults than it is with babies."

"I'm no expert with babies but my initial impression after six months' experience as a father is that almost everything is more complicated with adults than it is with babies." Grace spit out the nipple and started to squirm on Lucy's lap. "She probably needs to be burped, Lucy. Though she sometimes makes that same face in preparation for fouling another diaper. You want to burp her? Don't be surprised if she releases pressure at both ends simultaneously."

"Love to." She moved Grace gingerly up toward her shoulder. "Did Sam tell you that I got engaged a couple of weeks ago?"

"No, Lucy, he didn't. Congratulations. Who's the lucky guy?"

"He's not a cop," she replied.

An interesting prologue, I thought.

"His name is Grant. He's with the Forest Service. I met him last fall when I was out hiking, if you can believe it."

"That's wonderful. When is—"

"Who could guess? Everything's up in the air right now. You know, because of . . . Royal."

I was about to ask Lucy how she'd come to know Royal Peterson when Cozy's huge frame filled the bedroom doorway. He was carrying our foster poodle, Anvil. Anvil looked content in his arms. Against Cozy's huge frame, the sixteen-pound dog also looked like a hamster.

Cozy said, "Hello again, Alan. Did you get some dinner? Wonderful stuff. There's a tart in the refrigerator for later, too. Almonds. No, I didn't bake it. Lucy, want to join us? We're just about ready to get started again."

"Sure." She handed me the baby and said, "Thanks. That was a nice talk. I really appreciate it."

"No problem," I said.

From the other room, Lauren called out, "Sweetie, if you left your pager in the kitchen, it just went off."

I traipsed into the kitchen with Grace in my arms. I didn't recognize the number on my beeper, so I called my office voice mail to see what the emergency page was about. The message was from Naomi Bigg and it was succinct. "Dr. Gregory? There's something more I need to say about what we talked about earlier. Please give me a call."

I asked Grace if she wanted to hazard a guess about Naomi Bigg's pressing problem.

She didn't. Grace had wisdom beyond her months.

I dialed the number off the screen of my pager and heard a smoker's raspy "Hello."

Although I was pretty sure that the voice was Naomi's, I said, "Naomi Bigg, please."

"Dr. Gregory? It's me."

"I'm returning your page." I made certain my tone was as level as a freshly plumbed door.

"You're prompt. Leo always made them wait. He said it was too reinforcing to call right away."

It was becoming clear to me that maybe Leo Bigg was a jerk in more ways than one. Intentionally keeping cancer patients waiting for return phone calls? While I busied myself closing up the cardboard boxes of Chinese food, I let the ball bounce around on Naomi's side of the net.

She took a whack at it after a few seconds. "I was thinking about how we left things today, and what you must be thinking."

"What must I be thinking?"

"That the wouldn't-it-be-cool game I was describing—the one that the boys play—that it might somehow be, I don't know, related to what happened to the district attorney. I assume that I left you with that impression."

Naomi was right on. That was certainly on the list of things that I had been thinking.

She said, "I'm not naive, okay? I can add two and two as well as you can. But, see, none of the wouldn't-it-be-cool games with Ramp and Paul ever—ever—involved someone being assaulted the way that Royal Peterson was assaulted. The news reports all say that he was beaten, you know, hit on the head with something."

I listened as she sucked on a cigarette. She said, "The boys have never joked about doing anything like that—ambushing someone and hitting them on the head, beating them up. You ask me, I think they're too cowardly to do something that confrontational. That's why I don't think they had anything to do with what happened to Peterson."

The argument she was making wasn't particularly compelling. I concluded that the purpose of her call was to reveal to me the foundation for her rationalization. She was eager for me to sign up to support her psychological defenses; she didn't really expect to convince me that her hypothesis was true.

Not feeling particularly cooperative, I assaulted the rationalization I was hearing. "Had the wouldn't-it-be-cool games you overheard ever concerned Royal Peterson in any context?"

"Well, sure. Paul knows the DA's role in the plea-bargain process. Paul and Ramp talked about Peterson all the time. But Roy Peterson was one of ten wouldn't-it-be-cool targets, maybe more. Most of them were people that Ramp was angry at, by the way, not Paul."

"And since Roy Peterson was beaten and not—what?—you think it's evidence that Paul and Ramp weren't involved?"

"Bombs. The boys always joked about using a bomb."

Without any deliberation, I sat down. I had to consciously inhale a breath before I could say, "A bomb? They joked about using a bomb."

"I don't know whether it was a bomb exactly. I don't know about those things. But an explosive of some kind. It's one of Ramp's little hobbies. He talks about blowing things up all the time. He goes out to some ranch out east somewhere, Limon or someplace, and practices. Paul says that once he went out there with Ramp and they actually blew up an old truck. You know, a wreck.

"Ramp's the one who says things like, 'Wouldn't it be cool if the district attorney's house just blew up one day?' Or 'Wouldn't it be cool if so-and-so's car blew up one day?' Like that. All of that stuff comes from Ramp. Paul never talks like that when Ramp's not around."

"Blowing stuff up is a hobby of Ramp's?"

"I don't know, an outside interest, that kind of hobby."

Silently, I counted to ten. Fortunately or unfortunately, the delay didn't change what I was going to say. "I want to make sure I'm understanding you correctly. Because Royal Peterson wasn't killed by an explosive of some kind, you would like to believe that Paul and Ramp weren't involved in whatever happened at his house, even though they'd made overt threats against him."

"They never threatened him. It was just talk about what they wished would happen. When they heard he was dead, it's not like they celebrated or anything."

How nice. "So there's no chance they followed through on their fantasies?"

"Exactly. It was like they felt guilty because they were wishing for someone to die and then it happened. You know what that would be like. You'd feel guilty, responsible. Anybody would."

I considered her argument before I said, "That's a luxurious position for you to have, Naomi."

"What do you mean?"

"I'm thinking of the Klebolds and the Harrises. Over the months before that day at the high school, they probably made the same kinds of judgments about their children. Saw two here, and saw two there, but never allowed themselves to believe that the sum added up to four."

She sputtered as though she couldn't wait to respond to my words. "And, you know what? A thousand other parents—mothers like me—have done the exact same thing. We've seen things and never told the police. And our children never ended up doing a thing wrong. Not a thing. None of them. Two and two never added up. Ever. I thought you would understand."

"Understand what?"

"What it's like for parents. Aren't you a parent? Can you believe that your child is evil? Do you know how hard it is to cross that line?"

I looked down at Grace, asleep in my arms. No, I couldn't believe that my child was evil. Would ever be evil.

Not a chance.

"Not necessarily evil," I said, "but what about flawed? Troubled?" I added a bonus rationalization for Naomi's benefit. "Or what if the child is influenced by the wrong people? That happens."

"Killing someone isn't a flaw, Doctor. It's evil. And evil isn't in the air, you don't just catch it like a virus. It comes from somewhere, some injury deep inside." She paused. "And, although he's certainly been hurt badly by all that's happened, I don't believe my child has ever been to that place. I'd know it if . . . he had— I'm his mother."

I cushioned my voice, foaming the runway with my next words, trying to give her a soft place to land. "But you're not entirely sure, are you, Naomi? That's why we're talking."

She didn't want to come down gently. She said, "Maybe I shouldn't have called you after all. I'll see you on Friday—if I don't reconsider this whole thing."

Hurriedly, I interjected, "The reason you called tonight? Why is it important that I not misinterpret what you said today during our session? It's my impression that you're angry that I'm still able to see both sides of the coin."

"I don't want you to do anything stupid."

"I don't understand."

"I didn't want you to run off and tell anyone what I said. Send the bomb squad to my house or something. That's all."

"I couldn't reveal our conversation to anyone, Naomi. Not without your permission."

"I bet you could find a way around that."

"Are we talking about trust now?"

"I have no damn idea what we're talking about." She hung up as I was trying to figure out a discreet way to inquire about the other nine or so wouldn't-it-be-cool targets that Ramp and Paul had mentioned.

As the line went dead in my ear, I said, "Is my wife on that list, Naomi?"

CHAPTER

13

I went to bed knowing that I needed help. And I woke up the next morning knowing that I needed help.

Although I would've loved to have discussed the whole Naomi Bigg situation with Lauren, and would have welcomed her reasoned counsel, confidentiality concerns and peculiar circumstances made that impossible.

The peculiar circumstance, of course, was the possibility that Lauren was one of the potential targets of Paul and Ramp's wouldn't-it-be-cool games. And the very real possibility that the game was really only a mind game.

The way I looked at it was that my position was simple. I couldn't risk saying anything and I couldn't risk not saying anything.

What **I'd decided** I needed was what psychotherapists call supervision. In another profession, I suppose the same thing might be called consultation. Basically, supervision means that one psychotherapist invites another, hopefully more objective, usually more experienced professional to review and comment upon his or her work.

On those occasions when I decided I needed some objectivity with my practice, I relied on one of three different people, depending on the specifics of the case. When the issues in the case involved ethics, as this one did, my first choice was almost invariably Raymond Farley, Ph.D. Raymond's capacity to detect prevarication and rationalization was finely honed, and I knew I could count on him to help show me which side of the trees the moss was growing on in the forest where I was lost.

I called his home at seven-fifteen on Thursday morning. His youngest daughter was a junior in high school, so I figured the Farley household would already be humming along.

Raymond's wife answered.

"Cyn? It's Alan Gregory, how are you?"

"Alan, hello. How am I? Not quite as awake as you are. You want my sugar, right? I'm trying to get my daughter out the door. Let me find him. Raymond? It's for you."

A moment later I heard Raymond's baritone. "Alan. Long time. How's your new baby?"

"Grace is great, Raymond. How're your kids?"

He answered me at great length and with great patience. There was little hurry in the blood that coursed through Raymond Farley's veins. No one ever, ever took more care while finishing a story, and no one ever finished a meal after Raymond Farley finished his. "You didn't call to get an update on my kids, though, did you? What can I do for you?"

"I've got a case I would love to run by you. It's urgent, unfortunately. I see this woman again tomorrow evening and I should probably talk to you before her next appointment."

"Outpatient?"

"Yes."

"What's the urgency?"

"Columbine issues, Raymond."

"It's that time of year, I guess. What are we talking, grief? Anniversary reaction? Post-traumatic stress?"

"I'm not referring to the last Columbine, Raymond. I'm referring to concerns about the next Columbine."

"Oh," he said. "Oh."

"Can you squeeze me in?"

"I'm going to be at CU in Boulder doing a seminar on suicidal tendencies from one to three today. Meet me outside of Wardenburg—the student health center—at three. If the weather holds we'll find someplace pretty to sit, and we'll talk."

I rescheduled my two forty-five patient, picked up sandwiches and drinks at Alfalfa's on Arapahoe, and started to wait for Ray on the University of Colorado campus.

The campus is over a hundred years old and the founders had had their pick of prime foothills real estate for the location of the university. They'd chosen wisely. The CU campus is far enough from the vaulting mountains to maximize views, close enough to ensure that the Rockies would never cease to be a dominating presence. The flagstone buildings and red tile roofs of the major buildings on the University of Colorado campus are as distinctive an architectural feature as can be found on any campus in the western United States. The feeling is vaguely Italian, and that afternoon, the brilliance of the April sunshine added to the Mediterranean ambience.

Raymond Farley walked out the front door of Wardenburg a few minutes after three. I held up the bag I was carrying. "Grilled chicken on sourdough. I seem to recall you have a fondness. And Dr Pepper? Did I get that right?"

He rewarded me with a welcome embrace and his wide grin. His rich brown skin glowed in the springtime sun. "You recalled correctly, on both counts. I'm afraid I'm responsible for the demise of way too much fowl. Cynthia says that she thinks I'll have to answer to Saint Peter about that."

"If that's all that Saint Peter has to question you about, Raymond, you'll have a fine day at the pearly gates."

We walked in the direction of the planetarium and

found a bench below a small mountain ash that was just beginning to leaf out. Raymond unwrapped his sandwich and popped the top on his Dr Pepper. "You talk while I eat," he said.

"The patient I'm concerned about is a fiftyish female whom I saw for the first time this past Monday. Tomorrow's appointment will be our fourth session this week. That alone should tell you something."

It told him something: Raymond whistled between chews.

It took about five minutes for me to explain Naomi Bigg's situation—her daughter's rape, her husband's jail sentence, her son's friendship with Ramp and their preoccupation with retribution. All the details I could remember about the wouldn't-it-be-cool games.

His first question surprised me. He asked, "Your patient's white?"

Raymond wasn't. I wondered about the question. "Yes, why?"

" 'Cause, for some reason, black kids don't tend to do these things."

Raymond gave me a moment to digest his remark, then asked me to repeat the part that had to do with Royal Peterson's murder.

I did, finally adding, "Lauren was involved in the plea bargain of the kid who raped Naomi Bigg's daughter."

"Ahh," Ray said. "That explains your tone."

"My tone?"

"My impression, listening to you, is that you don't like this woman you're treating. I'm not accustomed to hearing negative countertransference so clearly from you. But now you say that you fear your wife's in danger—that explains your negative feelings."

"I'm pushing her, Ray. Pushing her hard. Her resistance . . . is intense. She desperately wants to believe her son is uninvolved in anything other than some retribution fantasies. I've known her—what?—three days and already I'm pounding away at the resistance, and the reality is that I don't have the alliance to get away with it. She's getting angry at me."

Raymond chewed methodically, appreciating each mouthful of food the way that I imagined Mozart appreciated each note of a concerto. After Ray swallowed, he asked, "Whose idea was the four sessions this week? Yours or hers?"

A simple question. But one that told me that Raymond Farley already understood the crux of why I'd asked him for supervision on this case.

I sighed involuntarily. "Mine."

"You're trying to goad her into taking some action against her son, aren't you? Confront him, turn him in?"

"I suppose I am. That would protect Lauren. And maybe a whole lot of other people, as well."

"Sure it would. But it's not your job. Here's what I'm thinking: Given your concerns about Lauren's safety, you probably shouldn't be treating this patient at all.

You know that you can't be objective as a psychotherapist if you're putting your wife's interests in front of your patient's interests."

"Raymond, that's the dilemma. Given my concerns about Lauren's safety, there's no way in the world I'm *not* going to treat this woman. If Lauren's really at risk, I have to be in a position to know what's coming next. If I refer her to someone else, Lauren could be in danger and I wouldn't even know it."

He kissed the last bit of sauce from the tips of his fingers and wiped his hands with his napkin. He said, "If you've already made your decision, what do you want from me?"

He read my reaction in my expression—I imagined I looked as though I'd been slapped in the face—and he grinned at me kindly. "Step back, Alan. You want from me exactly what she wants from you. She wants you to validate her inaction in regard to her concerns about her son. You? You want me to validate your inaction in regard to your concerns about continuing this treatment. You won't do what your patient wants you to do, and even though I've been bribed with an excellent sandwich, I won't do what you want me to do. I'm not about to tell you that you have a 'get out of jail, free' card on this one."

With some effort, I managed to smile back at him. "I actually didn't think you would, Raymond. Help me with something else then. This kid—her son— how dangerous is he? Because of my anxiety over Lauren, maybe I'm misreading the facts. You work with more young people than I do."

"What do you know about him?"

I told him everything Naomi had revealed about her son, Paul.

When I was through, Raymond leaned back and rested his weight on his hands. "There're some concerns there, no doubt about it. I've been on a committee at Wardenburg trying to help the university develop criteria for identifying kids who might be at risk of violent acting out. Your patient's son has some warning signs, that's for sure."

"What criteria has your committee developed?"

"We started with the criteria the FBI proposed and we're modifying them slightly." He held up one of his big hands, flicking out one finger after another as he ticked off the criteria. "One, kids who are on the outside socially and have verbalized their anger at popular kids, or even bullies. That fits this kid. Two, kids who have made overt threats, especially threats to kill. That fits. Three, kids with a prior mental health history. That fits. Four, kids who feel that they've been wronged, that they're victims. That fits. Five, kids with a history of the troublesome triad—fire setting, bedwetting, cruelty to animals. I'm assuming that you don't know enough about his history to confirm that one, do you?"

"No."

He gave me his wide, all-knowing grin again. "You know what they say? With four out of five, you get egg rolls."

"You're not making me feel any better, Raymond."

"Is that my job? Helping you feel better? How about I just give you a massage. That should help."

"Funny."

He touched his watch. "Couple more minutes, Alan. Then I have to hit the road back to Denver. Damn turnpike, you know?"

I knew all about the damn turnpike. I said, "I'm thinking of leaking some of what my patient told me— the part about the boys' plans to use explosives. I have a friend on the Boulder Police Department, and I'm thinking of suggesting he find a way to sweep Royal Peterson's house for explosives."

Raymond's eyebrows rose like a pair of levitating caterpillars. "You're thinking of what?"

"I know it sounds absurd but hear me out. What if those two boys were in Royal's house to plant an explosive device and Royal discovered them after it was already in place and there was a scuffle and they killed Royal? Then the kids ran. The bomb, or device, or whatever, could still be there, right?"

Raymond gazed at me as though he was wondering what psychotropic medicine I needed.

I pressed on. "When I talk to my detective friend, I wouldn't reveal my patient's name, wouldn't even say that a patient told me. I'd just make an oblique suggestion about my concerns, just enough to get my friend to get the police department to look for explosives at Royal's house."

Raymond's face could hardly have been more

skeptical. "I've heard your rationalization. I'm still wondering about your reasoning."

"What if there is a bomb planted there? Somebody could get killed if it went off. Royal's wife, Susan, Susan's health aide—somebody. If it turns out that nothing's there, I just look a little silly. My cop friend is used to that."

Raymond didn't quite smile and he didn't quite start shaking his head. But it was close. "Say there is something there. And the police find it . . . What if your patient's son's fingerprints are on the device? In effect, you've turned him in to the police, based on confidential information you had no right to divulge."

"Lesser of two evils. *Tarasoff* says I have to give a warning if I feel that someone's in danger based on what a patient tells me."

He opened a palm and held it up like a traffic cop. The pink edges of the soft flesh around his palm surprised me, even though I'd seen Raymond's hands a hundred times before. He said, "Not quite right. The court's *Tarasoff* decision says that you have to provide a warning if your patient makes an overt threat against an identifiable person. Based on what you've told me, your patient hasn't threatened anyone, Alan. No one. And regardless, I've not seen any court decision that extends the *Tarasoff* ruling to include hearsay. This isn't your patient threatening anybody. This is your patient talking about what somebody else might be planning." He removed his eyeglasses and blew at one lens. "If Lauren weren't involved—if you didn't think she was at risk—you wouldn't be considering this kind of action and you know it."

I argued back. "But if it were child abuse that I was hearing about, it wouldn't make any difference. Hearsay or no hearsay, right?"

"The child-abuse exception is handled specifically under Colorado law, Alan. This isn't."

I couldn't argue with the point that Raymond was making, so I moved the argument in a different direction, saying, "What if what's going on is that my patient actually wants me to turn her son in? What if that's her agenda with me? She can't stop him herself, she can't bring herself to turn him in, so she wants me to do it for her. She keeps talking about the Klebolds and the Harrises. There's a message there that I can't ignore."

He didn't respond right away, so I persisted. "The parents of the Columbine murderers may have failed their children and their community with their ignorance or their denial of what their children were planning, Raymond. But the Jefferson County Sheriff's Department had enough information, too. The family of a kid that Klebold and Harris threatened told the sheriff's department all about the threats and about the crap that was on Harris's Web site. The sheriff even linked Harris to a pipe bomb that somebody had exploded and went ahead and drafted an affidavit for a search warrant for his house. That was a year before the killings, but the sheriff didn't follow through with any of it."

"And you don't want to be accused of making the same mistakes as the Jefferson County sheriff?"

"No, I don't, Raymond. I don't. One of those two, Harris or Klebold, was in psychotherapy, too. He was seeing a psychologist. What if he actually told the guy he was planning to kill some students at his high school but didn't mention anyone in particular? Are you saying that the psychologist didn't have an ethical obligation to report that?"

"We don't know what that psychologist knew."

"But I know what I know."

"Do you?"

I said, "I don't want people to die when I might have had enough information to prevent their deaths."

"Especially your wife."

"Of course, especially my wife."

"You're not even certain she's been threatened, are you?"

"I can't risk it, Raymond. I can't."

"I suggest you step back and see the parallel process, my friend."

"What are you talking about, Ray?"

"Your patient is struggling with whether or not she has enough information to do what most parents consider unthinkable—turning her own son in to the authorities because she believes he may be planning an unspeakable atrocity. Go ahead and underline 'may.' Remember Styron? *Sophie's Choice?* This is one of those. You, too, are struggling with whether or not you have enough information to do the unthinkable—breaching your patient's confidentiality and turning this woman's son in to the authorities because you believe he may be planning an unspeakable atrocity. Go ahead and underline 'may' one more time."

I said, "The moral obligations are clear for both of us, Ray. My patient should act. Failing that, I should act."

"Are the moral ambiguities so invisible to you? Are you in any position to make that judgment? I think I've made a damn good case that your objectivity is compromised, Alan. The bottom line is that you shouldn't be treating this woman at all. Your motivation as her therapist is not limited to assisting her with psychological concerns. Not at all. That alone should cause you to excuse yourself. Another therapist, an objective therapist, should make the decision about what to do with these supposed threats."

"How can I turn my back on what I know?"

"You know a mother's fears. That's all that you know. I don't think that's enough."

"She's telling me something, Raymond. She's telling me enough."

Raymond stood. He said, "I've not seen you like this before. You seem to want to believe that the rules don't apply right now."

I could no longer keep the intensity I was feeling out of my voice. "What rules? There aren't any rules that apply to this situation. Ethical standards evolve, Raymond, we both know that. There are always new situations developing that the old rules don't address."

"And this is one?" he asked skeptically. "You're sure of that?"

"Before *Tarasoff,* therapists couldn't even warn potential victims that they'd been threatened. Now we can—we must. That's a change. That's an ethical evolution. Circumstances required it."

"And you want the freedom to decide that this is the foundation for another ethical evolution? *Tarasoff* wasn't the result of a rogue therapist rewriting the rules, Alan. It was a California Supreme Court decision."

I scrambled to my feet. "I've never been in a position like this before. You have to admit these circumstances are unique."

His eyes flaring, he countered, "You have a patient who needs an objective outlet for exploring an issue that is troubling her. What, I ask you, is unique about that circumstance? It happens to both of us every day. The only thing that's unique about this situation is that you've decided to substitute your judgment for your patient's. How long do you think our profession can survive therapists doing *that*?"

"You know exactly what I mean. This is . . . different."

He dabbed at one corner of his mouth with the paper napkin. "Then act like it's different, Alan. The way I see it is that you're trying to straddle a high fence and you can't seem to get either foot on the ground. On one side you're making a case that your concerns are so great that they warrant your violating ethical principles that I know you hold dear. On the other side you're apparently not quite concerned enough about any of it to just go to the police and state your case. You have to get off the damn fence one way or another. Either it's a serious threat and you put your judgment ahead of your patient's, or it's not a serious threat and you shut up and help her with her struggles."

I pressed. "How would you get off the fence? If it were Cynthia in danger? Or one of your kids?"

"Is Lauren really in danger? Is Grace? Are you certain of that?"

"No, I'm not certain."

"Then your question about what I would do if it were Cynthia or one of my kids is too facile. I get to answer your question in the abstract. I get to play 'What if?' You? You have to make your decisions in the here and now when your head is full of nothing but I-don't-knows."

He stared at me while I struggled to reply. Finally, he said, "Where the heck did I leave my car?"

CHAPTER

14

Although I'd seen Royal and Susan Peterson's home plenty of times on the local television news in the days since Roy's murder, I hadn't been there again in person until Friday morning as I was parked across the street sitting in the front passenger seat of Sam Purdy's red Jeep Cherokee. The floor mats of Sam's old car were so caked with dried-on dirt and gravel that I couldn't tell whether they were made of carpet or rubber.

Sam had been quiet since he'd picked me up at my office. Now he'd started humming, never a good sign with Sam.

Out of nervousness as much as anything, I said, "It's just like seeing Plymouth Rock."

Two or three seconds passed before he said, "What the hell are you talking about?"

"Years ago, I drove to Plymouth Rock from Boston—it's a long way. The day I was there it was raining pretty good. You make the long drive, you find a place to park the car, you get out, you walk to the shore, you stand behind a little iron fence, you look down, and what do you see? You see a rock. That's it. A rock. Not a big rock, not an interesting rock. We're not talking Gibraltar. It's just a rock."

"Yeah, your point?"

"That's kind of how I feel right now, seeing Royal and Susan's house. I expected—seeing it in person after the murder, all that's happened there—that it would feel different, somehow, than it used to. More important, more moving. I don't know. But . . . it's just a house."

Sam harrumphed.

I continued, eager for him to understand. "It's like finding out Santa Claus is just a guy in a red suit."

Sam yawned. "I don't know. Lawn needs to be mowed. That never would have happened if Royal were alive. I think he was a keep-the-lawn-mowed-and-the-walkway-edged type of guy. I bet he was a regular Friday-after-work or Saturday-morning-first-thing-type yard guy. So that's different, the lawn not being mowed. In the winter, after a storm, I bet he was the first guy on the block out with his Toro, blowing snow halfway to Nederland."

I looked sideways at him. "Not in a particularly philosophical mood, are you, Sam?"

He laughed. "With what you told me to get me to do

this, you're lucky I'm here at all. Don't hold your breath for Sartre."

I cracked open the car door. "I'm going to get the key. You want to come with or you want to stay here?"

"If it's all the same to you, I'll stay here and ponder the Plymouth Rock thing a little bit more. Maybe I'll get it."

As I walked across the street, I retrieved the yellow sticky note that I'd stuffed in my pocket and checked the address. The number matched the house right next door to the Petersons'. I walked up a flagstone path and rang the bell.

The woman who answered the door was young and harried. She had a toddler perched on one hip and another child, a girl around four, corralled between her legs. "Yes?" she asked. Her tone said, *This had better be good.*

"Ms. Wallace? I'm Alan Gregory; I'm a friend of Susan Peterson's. She said she would call you to authorize you to give me a key to her house. She said she left one with you for emergencies."

"Yeah, right. Hannah! You stay put, you hear me? How is Susan doing?" The little girl tried to squirm away. The woman trapped her with a knee and tried to smile at me. The expression ended up looking more like a grimace. "Such a tragedy what happened to Royal. Have to admit, it's scared the whole neighborhood. Hold on, I'll go get the key." She grabbed Hannah's hand, and mother and children disappeared down the hall.

I heard some insipid children's music playing in the background and reminded myself that my day listening to insipid children's music would soon come. I wondered whether the offensive sound was coming from a CD or a video and whether it involved a purple dinosaur or animated Japanese monsters.

I said a silent prayer that Grace would have good taste.

The woman returned with both children and with the key. She handed the fob out the door, and said, "Here you go. Just slip it back through the mail slot when you're done with it. Nice meeting you."

The door was closed before I said, "Thank you."

Sam met me on the road in front of the house. He said, "You never told me, what did you tell Susan Peterson to get her permission to do this?"

"You may not know this, but your friends at the police department only turned the house back over to her yesterday. Since she got out of the hospital, she's been staying with one of her daughters in Durango. I called down there and made up a story about something Royal and I were working on together, said I knew where the papers were in his study."

"She went for that?"

"She trusts me."

"Fool."

"Your guy is coming, right?"

"My guy is a girl and, yes, she's coming." He glanced at his watch. "We're early. She'll be here."

"She's off duty?"

"Way off duty. She's on disability after getting hurt on the job. Like I told you, she trains K-9s now, earns a little extra money."

Just then, a fifteen- or twenty-year-old Mercedes wagon rounded the corner and slowed as it pulled up to the curb. The paint on the car had oxidized to the point where I couldn't even guess at its original color. One front fender was liberally treated with rubbing compound. A young woman hopped out of the driver's side. She waved hello to Sam and walked to the rear hatch of the car. When she opened it, a medium-sized dog with floppy ears and indeterminate heritage jumped out and heeled beside her. She fixed a lead to the dog's collar and together they joined Sam and me on the sidewalk.

The woman limped noticeably.

Sam said, "Dorsey, this is Alan Gregory. Alan, Dorsey Hamm. Ex–Westminster Police Department, and this is her K-9 friend, uh . . ."

Dorsey was a stocky woman. Her skin showed evidence of a lost battle with adolescent acne. Her hair was cut carelessly. My impression was that she had long ago stopped trying to be attractive and that she was absolutely content with her decision.

She said, "I'm pleased to meet you," and held out her hand. "This here is Shadow." As I drew close enough to her to shake her hand, I thought I caught a whiff of cannabis. Involuntarily, I glanced at Dorsey's eyes. Red trails arced across the whites like lightning bolts.

The dog's tail was in nonstop motion. The rest of him was perfectly still.

"What kind is he?" I asked.

"Lab-shepherd mix. Both breeds tend to be good with explosives." She told him to sit, and he lowered himself without delay. On their best days, my dogs weren't as well-behaved as Shadow.

And they didn't have their best days very often.

Sam said, "I'm not going inside, Dorsey. Wouldn't be appropriate, given Lucy's situation." He handed me a pair of latex gloves and told me to put them on. He said, "Let's not complicate things with your prints, eh?"

Sometimes, especially during the height of hockey season, Sam developed an unconscious tendency to affect a Canadian accent. I think it came from watching too many Canadian athletes and listening to too many Canadian sportscasters on television. The affectation tended to fade a week or so after the league awarded the Stanley Cup.

He offered a pair of gloves to Dorsey. She took them and while she snapped them onto her hands, he said, "I appreciate your willingness to screen this place for me; I owe you one."

Dorsey glanced at the house. "Oh, don't mention it, Sam. Shadow needs the work, and unfamiliar environments are great training tools. We'll be in and out of a place this size in ten minutes, max. Probably not even that long. Don't go out for coffee or anything." She shortened the lead, touched the dog, and leaned down close to his ear. "Come on, boy. Come on. Let's go treasure hunting."

I proceeded up the walk, unlocked the front door of the Peterson home, and held the door for Dorsey and Shadow.

Dorsey reached down and whispered an instruction to Shadow that I couldn't quite hear. Her next message to the dog was a simple hand signal.

The dog charged forward, lowered his head, and started searching the Peterson home for explosives. Dorsey held the lead and stayed within a few feet of him.

My dogs could do that. Either of them.

Right.

Seconds after we were inside, Dorsey led Shadow up the stairs to the second floor. I didn't follow them right away; I was distracted. As soon as we were in the house I'd started looking around, trying to identify the precise place where Royal had been bashed to death. I thought the news reports had mentioned the living room and I was curious whether there would actually be a chalk outline to indicate where the body had been found. By the time I had examined the living room pretty carefully—no chalk—and was ready to start up the stairs, Shadow was already preceding Dorsey back down to the first floor.

Dorsey said, "Upstairs is negative."

I said, "Good."

Shadow moved away from the staircase, lowered his snout to the hardwood, took a few steps, circled a spot just beyond the doorway that led to the dining room, and sat. The dog's head swiveled toward his master and back to the floor. Dorsey looked at the dog, then over to me. "That's an alert—a positive," Dorsey said, her voice suddenly swollen with tension. "Is there a basement below that, or a crawl space? Do you know?"

All I saw was the dog sitting peacefully. I expected something different, though I don't know what. "Basement," I said in reply to Dorsey's question. "My memory is that the stairs are in the kitchen." I added, "What do you mean, 'positive'?" Though I knew what she meant by "positive."

She didn't answer. She found the way to the kitchen and led Shadow down the stairs. I fumbled for a light switch, finally illuminating the dark staircase. The basement was nicely finished, but the ceilings were low and the space felt claustrophobic. The large room at the base of the staircase was set up as a home office for Royal. One long wall was lined with shelves filled with an impressive collection of abstract pottery. I counted fifteen large pieces and a few small ones. A prominent space on a shelf that was near the foot of the stairs was empty.

Royal's collection of ceramics had apparently once included sixteen large pieces.

After no more than ten seconds, Shadow moved from a quick sniff around Royal's office to focus on an adjacent utility room. There he immediately picked a spot near the center of the room, raised his snout in the air, circled once, and sat.

Dorsey said, "Wow. That's another alert. He's confirming."

"Confirming?"

"Watch this," said Dorsey with obvious pride.

She moved a six-foot stepladder from the far wall and set it up on the exact spot where Shadow had been sitting. She released him from his lead and, without a moment's hesitation, the dog climbed the length of the ladder, balancing his front paws on the top platform, his back paws on the second-to-last rung.

"Isn't that cool?" Dorsey said. "I didn't even have to teach him that. He does it all on his own."

"Amazing," I agreed. I could barely breathe. It was as though Shadow were stealing all my air.

"It's another positive," she said, as she lifted the dog off the ladder and placed him on the concrete floor. "I think it's the same spot he smelled from up above. I bet something's been tucked up there between the floor joists."

I leaned in and peered up into the dark recess.

She asked, "What do you think?"

"The floor plan is kind of hard to follow from down here, but, yeah, I think it may be the same spot where he sat upstairs."

She pulled a flashlight from an asspack around her waist and aimed the beam up toward the ceiling. "Holy moly, there it is. Wow, wow, wow. I've never found a real one before. I'm just a trainer, you know?"

I reminded myself to exhale. "Are you going to go up there and look at it?"

"Are you nuts? The device could be booby-trapped. Shadow locates the things; that's where my involvement stops. I sure as hell don't examine them or disarm them. I've already given enough of my body to law enforcement, thank you, and I've gotten as close as I plan to get to that device, whatever it is."

"Of course, I wasn't thinking," I said. I was so nervous, I was barely capable of thinking.

Dorsey said, "What do you say we get the hell out of here as quick as we can? It gives me the willies knowing that there are really explosives here."

"You're sure that we're talking . . . explosives?"

"Me? I don't smell a thing. But Shadow's pretty sure. He's been an A student. Most K-9s work at eighty-five to ninety percent accuracy. Shadow's almost done with his training and he's been near ninety-five percent for the last couple of weeks. The fact that he's sure is plenty good enough for me."

"If that's the case, getting out of here as fast as we can sounds like a perfect plan," I said. My throat was so dry I had trouble getting the words out of my mouth. I held my breath for a moment so I could listen hard for the sound of a clock ticking.

Or my heart pounding.

Nothing.

Dorsey wasted no time herding Shadow back up the basement stairs toward the front door. Seconds later, Dorsey, Shadow, and I were all back outside on the Petersons' front porch. When I looked up, I saw Sam pacing across the street.

Dorsey waved to him while she simultaneously slipped Shadow a treat.

"It's positive, Sam," she called out. "Sorry."

Sam buried his face in his hands. I was pretty certain that if I were any closer to him I would have heard him curse me in some imaginative way.

To Dorsey, I said, "I think I'd feel a whole lot more comfortable if we got off of this porch, maybe joined Sam across the street."

CHAPTER
15

At Sam's suggestion I departed the scene, loitering around the corner while Dorsey loaded Shadow into the back of the old Mercedes. Sam wanted Dorsey and the dog long gone before the Boulder Police Department mobilized its assets to deal with the latest crisis at Royal Peterson's home. Sam had already told me that his plan was to tell his superiors that he'd received an anonymous tip, not that he'd finagled a way to get a bomb-sniffing dog to do the initial reconnaissance of the house.

In the three minutes after Dorsey drove Shadow and the Mercedes away, a half-dozen Boulder Police Department black-and-whites arrived, followed moments later by a big rescue squad truck, a pumper from the Boulder Fire Department, and finally, about ten minutes later, a truck and trailer carrying bomb squad members and their equipment. I thought it was an impressive response for a town the size of Boulder.

The Petersons' block was evacuated in short order; many of the evacuees ended up congregating near my anonymous post around the corner. A lot of people gathered; I assumed that the block behind the house had been evacuated as well. Yellow tape seemed to be stretched everywhere. I kept an eye out for Susan Peterson's neighbor, the one with the two little kids who'd given me the key, but they never came around my corner. I wondered if the police had used Boulder's reverse 911 system to alert the neighbors. The program permitted the authorities to use an automated system to phone residents and inform them of an emergency. I made a mental note to ask Sam.

When the first TV microwave truck arrived, I used it as my cue to begin walking away. On foot, if I ambled, I figured it would take me about fifteen minutes to get to my office downtown. If I pushed the pace a little bit, I thought I might have time to grab a snack before I got to Walnut Street and still have about twenty minutes to prepare myself for Naomi Bigg's noon appointment.

Knowing myself, I knew that I'd spend every one of those twenty minutes second-guessing my decision to alert Sam Purdy that there was a possibility that explosives had been planted in Royal and Susan Peterson's home. Although I couldn't quite convince myself that I'd done what was right, the fact that

Shadow had discovered a cache of explosive material brought me close to convincing myself that I'd done what I had to do.

By twelve o'clock, the scheduled starting time of my appointment with Naomi Bigg, only about an hour had passed since Sam Purdy had called in the threat of explosives at the Peterson home. I decided that the odds were long that Naomi Bigg would have already heard about the arrival of the bomb squad and the fire department. She would have had to be watching TV or listening to the news on the radio. Nonetheless, as I waited for the red light on the wall to flash on, I steeled myself for the possibility.

What would I do if Naomi confronted me? I'd already decided not to lie to her. Instead, my plan was to maintain that by tipping off the police the way I had, I had not breached her confidentiality at all.

My argument? As with most rationalizations I'd heard in my life regarding ethics, my reasoning had a structure as complicated as DNA.

First, I planned to argue that the information that I'd shared with the police was the result of deduction on my part. Naomi had not, in fact, told me that I would find explosives in the Peterson home. Yes, she had obliquely raised the possibility that Ramp and Paul may have been planning to place a bomb, but then she had vociferously argued against it.

I could hardly be accused of breaching confidentiality around a topic that hadn't even been specifically addressed in therapy.

The truth was that I could be so accused, but the argument I was twisting into my personal version of a double helix was comforting, nonetheless.

Second, the information that I'd provided to Sam Purdy could not reasonably lead anyone to discover the identity of my patient. The reality of my profession—for better or for worse—is that psychotherapists share information from psychotherapy sessions all the time. If the information does not provide clues that can be linked back to a specific individual, such leaks are usually treated as harmless indiscretions.

I told myself this was one of those.

Third? The third argument was for my ears only, not for Naomi's. It was this: To whom was Naomi going to complain? She could hardly go to the police with her allegations against me. And a formal petition to the State Board of Psychologist Examiners alleging malfeasance didn't seem likely. She'd have a hard time filing the charge without identifying her son. And I'd actually like to watch the ethics board grapple with the information she would provide about him.

I decided that the worst that could happen is that Naomi would storm out of my office and that I'd never hear from her again.

The trouble was this: Given the danger I feared Lauren might be in, not hearing from Naomi again was my greatest fear.

Naomi Bigg was on time for her appointment. Maybe it was because Dorsey and Shadow and the package above the stepladder were still very much on my mind, but my first thought upon seeing Naomi was that, unlike Dorsey, Naomi would never, ever cease trying to be attractive. Nor, I suspected, would she ever achieve Dorsey's level of contentment with her appearance.

Naomi's black crepe suit was impeccably pressed. Since I was congenitally unable to even bend over without wrinkling my own clothes, I was always amazed when other people could make it through a workday looking as though they had a miniature haberdasher with a steam wand stuffed in their briefcase.

I acknowledged her curt "Hello," and then I waited to discover if she'd learned of the emergency response that was taking place on Jay Street. I rehearsed my arguments while she settled herself on her chair and found a place for the big Vuitton bag. The thing thudded to the floor as though she were transporting dumbbells.

"You know," she said finally, "you never asked me what I thought about Royal Peterson's murder. We talked about the boys, and their reaction, but you never asked about me and my reaction. After I left last time, I found that odd, that you hadn't asked me about it."

No, I thought. *Instead of discussing your reaction to Royal Peterson's murder, we discussed peri-menopause, a topic I find so engrossing that it often distracts me from pursuing more important things, like murder.*

"You would like to talk about—"

"I didn't feel a thing." As she trampled over the end of my sentence, I couldn't tell if my words had been superfluous or if she was just ignoring me. "I didn't feel bad that a man had been killed. I didn't feel particularly good that the man who'd released my daughter's rapist was dead. Hearing that Peterson had been murdered didn't move me at all."

I said, "What do you make of that?"

Like "How does that make you feel?" it was one of those questions that made me feel like a caricature of a psychotherapist. Every time I spoke those or similar words, I was secretly embarrassed. But I asked the questions nonetheless, probably more frequently than I would like to admit.

The reason? Sometimes they worked.

And they always bought me time to think.

Naomi's response sounded rehearsed to me. She said, "Vengeance is a funny thing. If you read the final reports about Klebold and Harris—and believe me, I've read everything—and what they did at Columbine High School, their passion for vengeance had deserted them at the end. After fifteen, twenty minutes they'd lost their energy, they'd stopped hunting down kids, they'd even given up trying to explode their ineffective little bombs, and eventually they just turned their guns on themselves. I think when the adrenaline was finally totally depleted they realized that they'd failed to achieve whatever it was they'd spent a year trying to achieve. I wonder sometimes if vengeance is ever satisfying. I discuss it with Leo all the time. Every visit to prison, it seems we talk about it.

"He maintains that what he did that day in Denver wasn't vengeance. He says it was simply an act of self-respect. In his mind, he did what he had to do as a father. That was all."

"And you, Naomi, what do you think?"

"Leo? He's kidding himself. What he did to the rapist was vengeance, pure and simple."

"But he's satisfied? You just said that you wonder if vengeance is ever satisfying."

"Leo's in prison, for God's sake. He'll rationalize anything to survive that. You would, too. Don't feign ignorance, Doctor; it's not becoming." She flipped her hair off her collar with the fingers of her left hand.

As Naomi's admonition filled the space between us like a bad odor fills an elevator, it finally struck me that she and I had not spoken a single word about the bomb squad's arrival at Royal Peterson's house. We were talking about something else: high school slaughter and an imprisoned husband and father and teenage boys with enough vitriol expanding in their veins to explode their spleens.

I stifled a relieved sigh, not unaware of the irony.

"What?" she demanded.

"You didn't actually answer my question earlier. About your reaction to Royal Peterson's murder."

"You were asking me how I feel about not feeling

anything? It's a preposterous question."

I cautioned myself to portray more patience than I was feeling. "What I'm wondering is . . . how you understand . . . your reaction."

Naomi crossed her legs. The toe of the dangling foot rotated side to side as though she were extinguishing an imaginary cigarette. "Don't talk to me like I'm an idiot. What I'm wondering is why I'm sitting here with you. If I understood my reaction to Roy Peterson's murder, why on earth would I put myself through this? You think sitting here with you is fun?"

Fun? No. How about rewarding, at least. Therapeutic, maybe? I suspected she wasn't done. I waited.

Suddenly, her eyes moistened and I thought she might be near tears. My immediate reaction was to consider the possibility that the sorrow I was witnessing was an act. I cautioned myself to be receptive to the possibility that the emotion was sincere. She leaned over and tugged a tissue from the box on the table by the sofa. The gesture was abrupt and fierce, as though she feared someone might be holding on to the other end of the tissue and she was determined to have it.

She said, "God. I don't want to be this way with you."

"What way?"

"This way. Exasperated. Critical. It's how I am at work. It's how I am at home. I criticized the mailman today for putting two rubber bands around the bundle of mail when one would do fine. What's that about? All the time, I'm irritable, I'm critical . . . I'm bitchy. I swear it's my hormones."

"You know, you have been under a little bit of stress, Naomi." I'd intended the comment to sound slightly sarcastic; Naomi's gentle laughter convinced me that I'd hit my mark.

"Yeah, I guess I have," she said.

From those hopeful words of conciliation my worst fears began to materialize. For the rest of the session I followed Naomi as she led me down the rocky path that took us back into the world of peri-menopause.

My kingdom, I prayed, *for some estrogen.*

I usually had no trouble generating empathy for the plight of women struggling with the assault of unbalanced hormones. But these circumstances were anything but usual. My impulse was to insist that Naomi prioritize. And insist that her number one priority should be helping me figure out what the hell Ramp and Paul were up to.

Any relief I might have been feeling that my patient hadn't mentioned the discovery of an explosive device in Royal's home was simmering away in front of my eyes. Now that I knew that a bomb had indeed been stashed in the house, I needed to discuss it with Naomi, whether she brought it up or not.

I batted the issue back and forth, back and forth, as Naomi tried to numb me with tales of mood changes, body temperature regulation problems, and menstrual irregularities. At one point she said, "And don't even ask me what this has done to my sex life."

I didn't ask. Her husband was in prison. I assumed that fact alone should have greatly impeded her sex life. In my mind, Naomi and I didn't have ten minutes to waste, and I figured any expansive gripes about her sex life could easily devour ten whole sessions.

Nor did I ever decide what to do about Ramp and Paul and the wouldn't-it-be-cool games.

Just peri-menopause.

When our time was up, Naomi and I found a time to meet on the following Monday. She composed herself enough to say thank you. I was surprised to discover that I felt that her sentiment was sincere. As she stood to leave, she picked up her big bag and performed whatever sleight of hand she did to produce her pack of cigarettes, and then she started toward the door to my office.

Halfway there she paused and pivoted on one foot to face me. "By the way," she said. "Did you hear the news this morning? About that bomb?"

By the time I was ready to stammer out a reply, she was out the door.

CHAPTER

16

The neighborhood around South Dahlia Street in Denver is an urban oasis, sequestered in relative privacy between the suburb-mimicking big-box sprawl of University Hills Shopping Center and the always-congested multilane ribbons of concrete that comprise Interstate 25, which bisects southeast Denver like a bypass scar on a cardiac patient. Unlike Washington Park, Highland, University Park, and a dozen other old Denver neighborhoods, the area hugging South Dahlia Street had somehow escaped the infectious gentrification that accompanied Colorado's recent high-tech firestorm of population growth.

The block of Vassar Lane that intersected with South Dahlia from the west was lined with modest, unrenovated houses that rested on decent lots and were shaded by mature trees. The home of Brad and Debbie Levitt was an especially nondescript blond brick ranch with a detached garage, a long driveway, and a crowded grouping of linden trees near the front door.

Debbie Levitt had just returned from dropping off her two children at school and had started to turn her four-year-old Isuzu Trooper into the driveway when she thought she felt a fierce, levitating concussion somewhere below her. She was never able to confirm her suspicions about the acceleration taking place beneath her seat because her awareness of the immense force endured for only a few milliseconds before the brain structures that Debbie Levitt needed to process such simple sensory awareness disappeared in the searing flash that blew up and out through the Trooper.

Right across Vassar Lane, Rosalyn Brae was the only witness to the aftermath of the explosion, which she saw in the rearview mirror of her two-month-old Honda Odyssey. Rosalyn had just strapped her toddler into his child seat and was preparing to back out of her garage to take him to preschool when she felt the force of the explosion as shock waves from the disintegrating Trooper rocked her car. The roar assaulted her ears, the concussion shook her bones, and she looked up at the mirror in time to see metal and plastic flying through the air, a billowing cloud of profuse smoke, and, seconds later, a wall of searing flame.

When she'd recovered from her initial shock, Rosalyn could hear her son screaming from the backseat. She hit the switch that closed her garage door before she grabbed her son from his car seat, and she ran inside to call 911.

She told the emergency dispatcher that something terrible had happened to Debbie Levitt across the street but she didn't know what. The dispatcher pressed her for details.

Rosalyn sobbed, "Her car! Her car! It, it . . . Oh my God!"

"What's wrong with her car, ma'am? Has there been an accident?"

"No, no, it's like—oh God—it's just gone. The noise was so loud."

"The car was stolen?"

"No, no, it's . . . it's still there. But there's a fire. It's on fire."

"A fire? Her car's on fire? Okay, the fire department is on its way, ma'am. Was anyone hurt in the fire?"

"I suppose, I mean, I guess she was driving the car, right? I didn't see her . . . but I guess she was driving. It's still burning. I can see it from where I'm standing right now."

"The fire department is on the way, ma'am. As we speak, they're on their way. Are you close to the car, ma'am? The one that's on fire? Because I would like you to step back."

Rosalyn Brae took two steps back and bumped into her kitchen table.

"Now, you think Debbie Levitt—is that her name?— was driving when the car caught on fire? I'll send the paramedics for her. But you hold on, okay? Keep talking with me, stay on the line until someone gets there."

Rosalyn Brae had a sudden insight and told the dispatcher that she knew what it was that had happened: She thought maybe her neighbor's car had been hit by a meteor.

Two days later, when the audio clips of the 911 call hit the local news, Rosalyn Brae was appropriately humiliated.

By Friday noon, the Denver Police had a pretty good portrait of the victim of the car explosion.

Debbie Levitt was a thirty-one-year-old mother of two. She was someone who introduced herself to strangers as "a wife and mother." But the cops soon learned that, in addition to running her household, Debbie worked part time at The Bookies, a children's bookstore a few miles from her house, volunteered at the Barbara Davis Center for Childhood Diabetes at the University of Colorado Health Sciences Center, ran a Girl Scout troop, and coached her older daughter's soccer team. She also coordinated her local Neighborhood Watch program.

Almost everyone whom the police talked to commented about Debbie's size. She was "a whisper of a woman" according to one neighbor. "Four foot ten, ninety pounds, but as big as a redwood," was how the woman who owned the bookstore where she worked described her.

The thought that Debbie Levitt might have had an enemy who was angry enough to blow up her car was absolutely absurd to every single person interviewed by the Denver Police.

Debbie's husband, Brad, the manager of a retail store in Larimer Square, volunteered to allow the police to search the Levitt home and eagerly provided the family financial records to investigators. By midday police detectives had largely ruled out a drug connection or financial retribution as possible motives for the explosion.

Brad Levitt picked up his two children about an hour before school let out that afternoon. He drove them to his parents' house on the Seventeenth Avenue Parkway in Park Hill. That's where he told the children what had happened to their mother.

CHAPTER
17

Sam Purdy and I hadn't had a chance to talk since I'd left him orchestrating the arrival of the emergency response team at the Peterson home that morning.

I'd called him Friday afternoon after Naomi had departed my office and left him a voice mail asking if he'd meet me after work. He called back and left a message that he'd meet me after he got home from the Avalanche playoff game in Denver, but that he had something he'd promised to do for his wife. He said he'd page me when he got back to Boulder.

When I left home around ten-fifteen and drove toward the King Soopers on Thirtieth Street, Lauren and Grace were both sound asleep.

I spotted Sam over in the produce department. He already had a cart in front of him. It took me three tries to find a cart without a wobbling or stuck wheel. Part of my general karma in life is that I don't have good luck with shopping carts. The wheels all worked on the one I ended up with, but it had something brown and sticky plastered all over the plastic flap that covered the leg holes of the little child seat.

I didn't want to know.

I walked over to join Sam. He was sniffing cantaloupes and tapping the ends of them as though the aromas and echoes told him something important. I said, "Isn't worth buying them before the Texas crop comes in at the beginning of May, Sam." I pointed at the big pile in front of him. "Those are the early season melons from Southern California."

He didn't look up. "Actually, isn't worth buying any of 'em before the Rocky Fords show up at the end of the summer. Now, those Rocky Fords," he said, pausing for emphasis, ". . . now *those* are melons."

A few feet away from us, a tall young woman, her brown hair piled haphazardly on her head, was busy selecting strawberries. As soon as Sam finished speaking, she turned toward him and smiled, her shoulders retreating and her posture straightening just the slightest bit.

Sam Purdy didn't appreciate the irony. I didn't think he'd even noticed the woman's flirtation. He certainly didn't appreciate the fact that in Boulder—after his comment about the melons—she was three times as likely to have hit him over the head with a pineapple as she was to smile at him.

"I didn't want to say anything this morning, but you really look like shit," I told him.

"Avs lost tonight. Sloppy play behind the goal. They gave up two power play goals. Two. There's no excuse for that, none, not in the playoffs. I ever tell you that I hate turnovers?"

"Pastry? You hate those kinds of turnovers?"

He shook his head at me and stepped away from the cantaloupes. "What about kiwis? I like the way they taste but I've never figured out how to get the damn fuzzy stuff off without throwing away half the fruit. How do you do that?"

"You've lost weight, Sam."

"You gonna buy anything or you just gonna yap?"

"I think I'm just gonna yap," I said.

"I don't know why I agreed to do the grocery shopping again. I hate it. Sherry said it would be a growth experience for me. All I'm growing is another hemorrhoid. I keep thinking maybe I shouldn't be a cop in Boulder at all. I should be a cop in some real town where men don't meet their friends on Friday night to do the grocery shopping."

I laughed. "King Soopers is where the girls are, Sam."

"The single ones, yeah. In Boulder, the married ones all send their husbands. This is probably the place where half of the extramarital affairs start in Boulder. I swear we live in a city of wusses. You ever notice that?" He fingered his list, moving his reading glasses down from the top of his head so he could have a prayer of reading the scrap of paper. "Sherry said I should ask you about garlic. She said you'd know how to pick out garlic. I can't believe I have a friend who can't bait a hook but knows how to pick a bunch of garlic."

I couldn't bait a hook. Not a prayer. "A head of garlic, Sam. But that's not important."

"You got that right."

I led him over toward the onions and garlic.

He fumbled with a plastic bag, but his fat fingers couldn't quite get it open. He said, "In case you're wondering, I don't really want to know about garlic. Don't even think about lecturing me about garlic. Just pick one."

"You've lost weight," I said for the second time. "Are you worried about Lucy? Or is something else going on?"

He tried to separate the folds of the bag with his teeth. "You heard the details about the device we recovered at the Peterson home?" he mumbled.

I'd been waiting patiently for him to get around to it. I said, "I heard what's on the news, that's all."

"It was a pipe bomb, rigged to a radio controller. Just needed a signal and it would have gone off."

"Jesus."

"Nothing fancy about it, apparently. X-ray didn't show any booby traps. Guy who made it wasn't trying to hurt anybody who found it."

"How did they disarm it? Did they take it out of the house and put it in that little round trailer you always see on the news?"

He shook his head in disdain at my ignorance. "The little trailer is called a total containment vehicle, and no, they didn't use it. In situations like that they use a robot with a disruptor on it. Blows the thing apart with water. It's like a little water cannon. That way nobody actually has to get close to the device."

"That's it? Couldn't doing that make the bomb go off?"

"There's a risk of sympathetic detonation but it's more theoretical than real. I've never seen it happen."

"How do you know all this?"

Sam ignored me, instead asking, "You done with your questions? Because my supervisors in the department are curious how I knew that there was a bomb in the house."

"First, tell me how you know so much about the bomb squad."

"I took an FBI course. Now, how did you know it was there?"

"What did you tell your supervisors?"

"I told them I got an anonymous tip."

"They believed you?"

He shrugged. "What are they gonna do?"

"How does this all bode for Lucy?"

We'd moved from the produce department to the back of the store. "Is there a right way to do this?" Sam asked. "Should I go all the way across the back and then do each aisle? Or should I just go up and down each aisle and see a little bit of the dairy case each time? How do housewives do this? It seems to me I should do the freezer part last. That makes sense."

"You're free to improvise."

He made a noise. "Don't know if anyone told you but Lucy's prints are on that ceramic thing. The one that was used to bash Royal in the face? We found it in pieces all over the floor in the living room."

"Lauren told me a few hours ago. When I was in the house this morning with Dorsey and Shadow I saw a collection of fancy ceramics downstairs in Royal's office. There was one space empty on the shelves. I was thinking that that's where it came from."

"We reached the same conclusion. Somebody grabbed it downstairs, carried it upstairs to whack Royal."

"Anybody else's fingerprints on the ceramic?"

"Roy's and Susan's."

"The fact that her fingerprints are on it isn't good news for Lucy. But . . . I thought the murder weapon was the brass lamp."

"The coup de grace was from the lamp, yes. Current theory is that the initial blow was from the ceramic thing."

"And Lucy's prints aren't on the lamp?"

"No. Just some partials from Susan and the woman who comes in to help her with the cleaning. That's it. The theory to explain that little discrepancy is that Lucy wiped it where she touched it. She couldn't wipe the ceramic because it was busted all over the floor."

"And now your colleagues are working under the assumption that Lucy planted the bomb we found?"

"Current theory is yes. They searched her place and her car again this afternoon, looking for evidence from the bomb or residue from the explosive. That's something they didn't cover with the initial search warrant. The thinking goes that she planted the bomb, and Peterson discovered her doing it, confronted her. She picked up the ceramic whatever, climbed the stairs, and bashed him in the head with it."

"Why didn't she just use her gun? Shoot him or hit him with it?"

Sam gave me a disgusted look. "Don't go there. She didn't do it. The reason she didn't choose her weapons carefully is because she didn't choose her weapons at all. It's simple."

I knew about the second search warrant at Lucy's place, of course. Lauren and I had discussed some of the day's events at dinner a few hours before. "They find anything at today's search?"

"I don't know yet. God, I told you—of course not. She didn't do it." He waved at the case in front of us. "Are all these eggs the same? Does it make any frigging difference which box of frigging eggs I choose? Never mind, don't answer that."

I pretended to be interested in the fat content of Philadelphia cream cheese as I said, "I'm sure you heard about the explosion in Denver this morning." This was the real reason I'd agreed to meet Sam at the grocery store so late on Friday evening. I wanted to know what he could tell me about the car bomb that I'd heard about from Naomi Bigg and later, on the news.

"Sure. That woman was killed when her car blew up." Sam was still distracted by the eggs. "Denver," he added, shaking his head.

The tone implied that, as far as random explosions went, Denver belonged in the same category as Beirut or Sarajevo or Belfast.

I asked him, "You think it's just a coincidence that a car exploded the same day we found a device in the Petersons' house?"

Sam rolled his eyes, tugged a cell phone from the back pocket of his jeans, and scrolled through the memory until he found the number he wanted. While he was dialing, he said, "The ATF people are way ahead of you. They've been trying all day to see if there's any evidence the two devices were made by the same person. Chemistry takes some time." A few seconds later, he said, "Walter? Sam Purdy in Boulder. How you doing?"

I couldn't tell how Walter was doing, but describing his condition to Sam took quite a bit of time. Sam spent the time examining a rack that displayed single servings of highly processed cheese spread that was packaged with a wide variety of crackers and pretzels. There were some cookies packaged with globs of white goo that looked like frosting, as well. Finally Sam asked Walter what the Denver Police knew about the car explosion earlier that day. Sam apparently wasn't pleased with Walter's response, which caused Sam to remind Walter that Sam was the one who had located the radio-controlled explosive device in Royal Peterson's home that morning.

As I attempted to eavesdrop, I watched the woman with the strawberries from the produce department choose between vanilla and plain soymilk. In her cart she also had a big bag of Cheetos and some Häagen Dazs.

I tried to guess the parameters of her diet. Couldn't. But I guessed that she would go for the vanilla. She did.

Sam flipped his phone closed. "It was definitely a car bomb. They just got a read on the explosive an hour ago. As I said, ATF's involved. They're still filtering debris to try to identify what kind of initiator or timer was used. By the way, the explosive is totally different from what we found in the device in Royal's home this morning. Walter thinks they'll know something specific about the initiator in the Denver bomb the next day or so."

"Motive?"

"Walter says they're not there yet."

"Who's Walter?"

"Somebody I know."

"He's on the Denver Police Department?"

"He's somebody I know. That's all. And his name's not really Walter."

"Really? But you call him Walter? Who is he?"

"Tell me who tipped you off about the bomb in Royal's house and I'll tell you who Walter is. But I won't tell you his real name."

"You know I can't do that."

"It's a patient, isn't it? One of your patients knew that there was a bomb in Royal's house? You know something that will help Lucy and you keep it from me, I swear I'll find a way—"

"You know I can't tell you anything about my patients. Tell me who Walter is or I'm not going to teach you anything else about groceries."

"Promise?"

We walked down the pet food aisle. Sam was perusing the dog treats even though he and Sherry and Simon didn't have any pets. I asked, "Why isn't Lucy in jail? It sure sounds to me as though your colleagues have probable cause."

He pulled a little ball of tissue from his pocket, unfolded it the best he could, and blew his nose. After he stuffed the tissue back into his pocket, he rubbed his eyes with his knuckles before he replied. "Jeez, do you have allergies? What a pain. It's the only thing I don't like about springtime, the only thing. To answer your question: There're a bunch of reasons Lucy hasn't been picked up. One, in Boulder we have a rather well-known history of crossing every *t* and dotting every *i* before we arrest somebody, especially somebody with a high profile, and especially for a high-profile felony. Two, Lucy's no flight risk. Three, the prosecutors don't want to have to deal with Cozy and Lauren about discovery yet, and if we arrest Lucy then they have to start turning stuff over, and four—the real home-run reason—is that nobody has a clue about motive yet. They'd like to have at least a clue about her motive before they lock up a cop for murder. Especially a pretty, blond cop. PR, you know."

He'd let go of the handle of his cart. I pulled it behind me as I continued down the aisle; I still had hopes of finishing the grocery shopping by midnight. Sam trailed absently behind the cart. He was looking for something.

While I waited to find out what, I asked, "Why was Lucy at the Peterson house that night? Has she told you?"

He waved at the incredible variety of dog treats on the upper shelves. "Do your dogs like this crap?"

"Emily will eat anything. Anvil doesn't eat anything. Answer my question about Lucy."

"That little dog is a weird dog. I like him, but he's a weird dog."

"I'm glad you like him, Sam," I said. I didn't argue; Anvil was a weird dog. I loved him anyway.

"I'm in an awkward place here, Alan. I don't mind telling you what I know, but if you go and tell Lauren and Cozy, then the people who are willing to talk to me so far won't be willing to talk to me anymore. Does that make sense? If Lucy gets charged, Cozy and Lauren will get all the investigators' reports. So everybody just needs to be patient."

"I won't tell them anything, Sam."

He stared at me with rheumy eyes. "Okay. I don't know why Lucy was at Royal's house that night. When Susan Peterson was interviewed by our detectives, she confirmed that a female cop had visited Royal 'numerous times' in the past, but she maintains she never met the woman, says she was always upstairs in bed during the visits. Susan figured the woman who was stopping by had something to do with the prosecutor's office, a case Royal was working on, or something like that."

"Susan's sure it was a cop, not a DA?"

"That's what she says."

"Does Susan have a name for the cop?"

"No. Royal never told her or she doesn't remember. Susan says the voice she heard downstairs was female. That's all she knows."

"But she thinks it was the same cop each time?"

"Yeah."

"Multiple visits?"

"Yeah."

"Lucy never mentioned Royal to you, Sam?"

"Not once that I can remember. Not even casually. That's what's so goofy. But she's private, always has been."

I said, "She suggested to me that the reason she was there that night has to do with something she's really ashamed of."

Sam stopped and grabbed his cart back from me. "She said that to you? Recently?"

I nodded.

He checked all around him for the presence of other

shoppers, lowered his voice to a whisper, and said, "You think Lucy was sleeping with Royal? Is that what she was saying?"

I could tell how distasteful the thought was to Sam. I could also tell that this wasn't the first time in the past couple of days that the thought had crossed his mind. I said, "I don't know. She was just talking about things she was ashamed about. Said one of them had to do with the reason she was at Royal's house that night."

"She's engaged, you know," Sam said. "Just got engaged. Wouldn't wear a ring, though, wanted to keep it private."

"She told me that, too. You know the guy?"

"She's talked about him some, but I've never met him." Sam was exceeding the grocery store speed limit now, not even pausing to see whether the shelves he was passing had anything at all to do with the items Sherry had penciled on his grocery list. I caught up with him only because an elderly man was blocking the aisle with his cart while he tried to retrieve a can of guava juice from the top shelf. I helped the man get the can of juice down and he pushed his cart away. I think Sam's driving was scaring him.

Sam argued, "She couldn't have been screwing Peterson. If Lucy loves her fiancé enough to marry him, why would she be having an affair with Royal?"

"We don't know that she was having an affair, Sam. But people do strange things."

"Royal has a reputation. But Lucy?" he muttered. "I

don't get it. She's too smart to get involved with somebody like Royal."

"She was obviously involved with him somehow. She was at his house, right? People don't always do what's smart."

"Tell me about it."

I guided him to a stop in front of the condiments and picked out some ketchup. Sam was shaking his head.

He said, "Don't get that kind. It's runny."

"You're giving me grocery advice?"

"Believe it or not, I know about some things. If it goes on hot dogs or bratwurst, I know about it."

I wasn't ready to digress into discussing meat on buns. "What kind of reputation did Royal Peterson have, Sam? Indefatigable crime fighter? Justice superhero?"

Sam laughed before he said, "Cad."

I raised my eyebrows. "Cad?" I wasn't questioning the concept, just Sam's choice of descriptors.

"It means he screwed around. I think it's a British thing."

"Screwing around is a British thing?" I said.

Sam hit me on the arm. It hurt.

"You know what I mean."

He waited until I looked up and nodded before he spoke again. "It's my nature to chew on you about what you don't tell me, you know that. That doesn't mean that I'm not grateful for what you do tell me. I'm guessing that the tip you gave me about the explosive means you crossed a line that you're not real comfortable crossing. Finding the bomb in Royal's basement will complicate the case against Lucy. I'm grateful to you for that. But"—he smiled in a way that made both of his lips disappear up into his mustache—"I'm not done trying to get you to tell me what else you know. It doesn't stop here, Alan. Friend or no friend, it doesn't stop here."

CHAPTER
18

Ramp flipped among the Denver news channels about a hundred times between the hours of four and six-thirty Friday afternoon. The only breaks he took from thumbing the remote control were to check his computer to see if any of the TV stations had updated their Web sites with fresh information about the explosion in Denver's Dahlia neighborhood.

Two mistakes in one job.

Ramp couldn't figure out what had gone wrong.

When the local news programs were over, he retrieved a Zip disc from its hiding place in a hollowed-out section of the trim that skirted the floor around the perimeter of his small apartment.

He inserted the disc into his computer and retrieved a Microsoft Word document he'd labeled Log 7.

He didn't really need to see the written record; Ramp could have recited the data that was recorded in

Log 7 from memory. But he checked the log anyway. It took him no more than five minutes to review the details of the series of trials he had done at the ranch near Limon.

The device had worked properly all four times that he'd tested it.

All four.

"So what went wrong with number five?" he said out loud. "And why was she driving his car?"

He called Boulder.

"It's me," he said when his call was answered. "You saw the news?"

While he listened to the answer to his question, Ramp stood and moved back to his computer. He linked to the KCNC Web site. It hadn't been updated. He clicked over to KUSA and then to KMGH. Nothing had been added to either site.

You call this news?

Ramp tried to keep the irritation out of his voice when he spoke out loud again. "Like I told you, I followed him twice before I placed it. Both times he was in that car. It was definitely the car he drives to work. I don't know why she was driving it this morning. Bad luck for her is all I can say. I don't feel bad I got her. I only feel bad that I didn't get him and that the message was lost. I'll have to make up for it."

He tucked the phone between his shoulder and his ear as he removed the Zip disc from the drive and tucked it back into its hiding place in the floorboard trim. The trim slid back into place like a hand into a glove.

He shook his head as he said, "No, it was almost all solid state. It shouldn't have shorted. I don't think that's it. I'm thinking it was a rogue radio signal that set it off. The odds are astronomical that another device would be on that frequency in that vicinity, but that's all I can come up with. I've been glued to the news all afternoon. It doesn't look like the police understand the target. And the ATF will waste some time piecing together the device. I'm thinking we're okay. What about the thing at your end? Any fallout from them discovering the bomb in that guy's house?"

Out the front window, Ramp watched a white Denver Police cruiser crawl slowly down the road in front of his Pennsylvania Street apartment. He tracked it with his eyes as it moved south and turned the corner.

"Yeah, I think so, too. Finding the device in Boulder won't point to us at all. I think we're still on track. My guess is that we've had as much bad luck as we're going to get. I say that we both go ahead with tonight's work. You agree? . . . That's right, we should keep the faith."

Ramp pressed the button disconnecting the call. To no one in particular, he said, "Wouldn't it be cool?"

In this phase, Ramp had one more device to place. The schedule called for him to install it that night.

He decided not to alter his plans.

CHAPTER
19

Saturday morning brought Lauren, Grace, and me back to our weekend routine. We left the house early, met our friends Diane and Raoul for breakfast, and did the usual round of errands on North Broadway. During breakfast I tried to maintain a conversation with Raoul, pretending I gave a whit about his newfound passion for fly-fishing while I was simultaneously eavesdropping as Lauren responded to a question about her health from Diane. Raoul was rambling about feathers and string and tying flies; Lauren was saying that she was in less pain and that her brain mud had eased, but that her vertigo was still giving her fits, and, fearing that she might fall, she wouldn't carry Grace more than a few feet. Lauren usually didn't go into such detail about her health with friends.

Or with husbands, for that matter.

When I said "Yes" in answer to a question I didn't really hear from Raoul, he seemed pleased. He said, "Diane didn't think you'd come with me. I told her I thought you would."

I was afraid I'd just agreed to go fly-fishing.

Although April had been warmer and dryer than usual along the Front Range, the weatherpeople were predicting the midday arrival of a cold front from the north preceded by strong winds. It turned out that the meteorologists were wrong by at least a couple of hours. As we were driving home from our errands the winds began to sluice down from Cheyenne with a force that would cause alarm in most places on the North American continent. But not in Boulder. Winds in the fifty- to one-hundred-miles-an-hour range were frequent events in the winter and spring seasons. Only in the upper reaches of the range did the populace seek shelter. In the moderate, fifty- to seventy-five-miles-an-hour range, the primary impact of the winds was inconvenience.

Lauren and I agreed that although these gusts were no stronger than sixty miles an hour, my hopes for a late-morning bicycle ride were shot. As I pulled the car into the garage, Lauren suggested a trip up the turnpike to Flatiron Crossing to buy Grace her first pair of shoes.

"They sell baby shoes in Boulder, don't they?" I asked naively.

"I'd rather go to Flatirons," she replied. Lauren, like many Boulderites, said "Flatirons," not "Flatiron," when referring to the new mall, intentionally refuting all efforts of the huge facility's marketing people to modify the local vernacular. "I want to check out Nordstrom's baby department."

As we entered the house, I was still struggling mightily to find a reason not to go to a suburban shopping mall on a windy weekend morning when everyone else in Boulder County would be looking for an indoor haven to escape the gales. I was actually considering offering to clean the garage when I heard the telephone ringing as we walked in the door.

"I'll get it," I said.

"You're too eager," Lauren said. "If you don't want to go to the Mall, just say so."

I didn't want to go to the Mall. But what I said was "Hello."

"Alan, Sam. Something's come up about Lucy and the bombs. Can you meet me?"

"Now?" I tried to keep the glee out of my voice.

"Yeah, now."

"Sure, where?"

During my drive back downtown to meet Sam, I counted three resounding whacks as the wind lifted rocks and launched them into my windshield. It was one of the reliable melodies of springtime in the Rockies.

The only problem with Sam's plan was that at ten-thirty on Saturday morning the restaurant where we were supposed to meet, the Fourteenth Street Grill on the eastern end of the outdoor Downtown Mall, was closed. I stood for a minute cursing my friend, and had just pulled my cell phone from my pocket to call him when I heard a silky smooth, slightly husky "Thanks for coming."

The voice had no trace of Sam's Minnesota Iron Range accent.

I turned and found myself looking directly into Lucy Tanner's amber eyes. With whatever she was wearing on her feet, she was almost exactly my height. "Lucy," I said, "what a surprise."

"I thought if I called, you'd refuse to meet me, or you'd argue with me or something. Sam said he loved to play around with your head, and he volunteered to make the call."

I was wondering why she thought I would be so resistant to talking with her, when a gust of wind strong enough to cause us both to lean erupted from the north. "Want to get in my car?" I asked. "It's right across the street."

"How about we go someplace and sit down. There's a juice place a couple of doors down from here—it's kind of funky—and there's a Starbucks around the corner. You choose, Alan."

I noted that she hadn't included The Cheesecake Factory, which was right across the street, on her list of possible destinations. I did recall that the Starbucks near the east end of the Mall was the one where Paul Bigg was a barista.

"Starbucks," I said. I hoped there would be someone named Paul behind the counter. I wanted to see if Paul Bigg fit my mental image of the Boulder adolescent Starbucks tender.

Lucy hooked her arm in mine and led me down Pearl Street. Before we made it into the canyon created by the buildings, the wind almost lifted us off our feet. In between gusts, she said, "I'd like a seat that lets me sit with my back to the room, okay? People have been recognizing me."

I led Lucy to a table by the fireplace. She chose the chair facing the wall. "What can I get you?" I asked.

"Chai."

Sometimes I thought I was the last person in Boulder to taste chai—or, considering that Sam Purdy lived in Boulder, too, maybe the second to last. So, although I had no real interest in buying one for myself, I was intrigued at the prospect of at least getting to order one and watch it made. But I was disappointed to see that the baristas at the counter were both young women. One pierced eyebrow and three visible tattoos between the two of them. Impossibly filthy green aprons. No Paul Bigg in sight.

Chai looked to me to be a lot like hot tea and milk. The menu mentioned spices, too. I withheld judgment.

After I paid, I returned to the table with our drinks. Lucy was staring at her hands. Her fingers were long but her nails were trimmed short, and if they were polished, the polish was clear. She looked up and mouthed, "Thank you."

"Why did you think I'd be reluctant to meet with you?" I asked.

She glanced at the occupants of the adjacent tables and leaned into the space between us before she answered. "Sam told me that you were the one who knew about the bomb at Royal's house."

I said, "Shit."

"That's why I thought you'd be reluctant to meet with me."

I shook my head to express my disappointment with Sam. "He shouldn't have told you."

She sat back, narrowed her eyes a little, and she shrugged. "That's one point of view."

"It's mine," I said.

"Is it? You made a decision to tell Sam about the explosives. Are you suggesting that telling one person is okay, but telling two people makes you unprofessional? Sorry, I'm not sure it's a point of view that you can easily defend."

She was right, of course. Pushing Humpty-Dumpty off the wall a second time doesn't make a whole lot of difference to Humpty. It's the first plop that does the irrevocable damage.

"As you can probably guess, Lucy, I can't talk to you about how I suspected that there might be explosives."

Without hesitation she said, "I can help you."

I was taken aback. I expected Lucy to ask for my

assistance, not the other way around. "What do you mean? How can you help me?"

"Sam thinks you've painted yourself into a corner. You know something you'd rather not know. But he says you're someone who can't walk away from what you know. He called it a 'character defect,' by the way." She smiled at me and sipped some of her milky tea. "But he also knows that your problem and my problem may be able to be resolved simultaneously."

"Go ahead."

She lowered her voice to a bedroom whisper. "Whoever planted that bomb probably killed Royal, right?"

"It's likely," I acknowledged.

"I don't think you know who that is. Sam doesn't either. He says you wouldn't leave somebody like that on the street. To me that means only one thing: that you know somebody who may know who planted that bomb. Well, I can help you find the bomber. That's how I can help. Don't forget, I'm a detective, Alan, and right now I have lots and lots of free time on my hands."

"It won't work, Lucy. For you to help me, I'd have to tell you things that I'm not permitted to tell you."

She was prepared for my argument. "And if you don't tell me? Are you ready to live with the conse-quences of that? People who build explosives don't usually build just one and stop. So what if the one at Royal's house isn't the only bomb? What about that? And what about my situation? Are you ready to sit back and watch me go to jail? Cozy thinks that I'll be arrested within the week."

I didn't answer.

Lucy sat back on her chair and said, "I think you're going to let me help you. Want to know why that is?"

"Sure."

"Because, besides Sam, you're the only one who doesn't look at me like they're wondering whether or not I really did it. Even Cozy's not convinced I didn't kill Royal. Your wife—she's very sweet, Alan—but she's not sure about me, either. I can tell. But you seem to be confident that I didn't do it. And that's why I think you're going to let me help you."

I shifted my gaze outside. A plastic trash can was whistling down the Mall, doing, I guessed, about thirty. Way over the speed limit for rubbish containers.

My espresso cup was empty. I tilted it up to my lips anyway and pondered ordering myself a chai. I said, "Let's go someplace else, Lucy. We shouldn't be talking about this here."

CHAPTER

20

Lucy's place wasn't an option. The media was keeping too close an eye on it. My house wasn't an option, either. Neither Lucy nor I wanted Lauren, and therefore Cozy, to know what we were up to.

We were loitering outside Starbucks trying on alternatives when Lucy said, "We could go to Sam's house."

I considered it. "We shouldn't involve him, Lucy. His position is awkward enough as it is."

"You're right. Can we go to your office?"

"I guess that's okay. You know where it is?" She nodded. I'd forgotten that she'd responded to an emergency there with Sam years before. "There's a back door that opens onto the yard. Why don't you come in that way?"

She shifted her blond hair from her face, held it back with one hand, and smiled at me. "How about . . . I'll park my car around the corner and then I'll come

in through the yard, and then come in the back door."
She laughed. "That's always kept me out of trouble in
the past."

I was impressed by her ability to find irony in her
situation.

Lucy and I would be alone at my office. Diane
Estevez, my friend and partner, was as likely to be
working on Saturday as Boulder was to establish a
sister-city relationship with Colorado Springs.

I drove the half-dozen blocks to Walnut Street and
parked in back as I always did. I let myself in the
French door that opened onto the yard, quieted the
alarm system, and waited for Lucy to arrive.

She tapped on one of the glass panels a few minutes
later.

"Nice," she said, looking at my office as though she
were seeing it for the first time.

"Have a seat, Lucy. I can heat some water for tea, if
you'd like. No chai here, I'm afraid."

"No, thank you, I've had enough." She touched the
chair. "Is this where your patients sit?"

"There or on the couch."

Lucy was wearing a suede jacket. She took a
moment to remove it and lay it on the sofa. Beneath it
she was wearing a blue pinstripe shirt that was open
halfway to her navel. Beneath that was a thin cotton
something.

"Where do we start?" she asked.

"I don't know. I should tell you I'm not comfortable
with the position I'm in right now, Lucy."

"I can appreciate that, Alan. I'm not totally comfortable with the position I'm in right now, either."

"Some people—maybe most people—would argue that what I'm about to do is highly unethical."

She sat erect, her hands on her knees. The tendons in her neck had stark definition. For the first time that morning, I got the impression that I was talking with a cop. She said, "Something I've learned working with Sam for so many years is that ethical codes should be written in pencil. Frequently they need revising. When people find new ways to be crooked, that's when it's time to rewrite the rulebook."

The thought sounded like Sam's. The translation was definitely Lucy's. "Maybe that's true, but I've never considered it my job to be the one to do those revisions. I've always been most comfortable with the guidelines that I could read in a book that's already been written."

"But somebody has to rewrite the book. I suspect that none of the authors ever really volunteered. In situations like the one you and I are in, fate determines the authors. Given the predicament, I think you'd have to agree that I'm the lesser of two evils. I'm going to be more discreet with whatever information you give me than the police would be if you called them."

"Lucy, you are the police."

"You know what I mean."

"I've considered going to the police, you know," I said. "Just telling them what I suspect. But realistically, what could they do? Sam might humor me. Maybe he'd go talk to some people. But the people would deny any involvement and say I'm absolutely crazy. I know they would. Nothing would be gained and my professional life would be over for violating confidentiality. That's the only thing that's for sure."

"There are worse things than your professional life being over. Trust me, I know."

I was trying hard not to view Lucy as a cop who was pressuring me to reveal privileged information. "I know that, Lucy. On Friday, I rationalized telling Sam to go look for a bomb at Royal's house. It was highly unlikely that anyone could ever trace that information back to one of my patients. But no matter what I do, I can't think of a way to rationalize what I'm about to tell you."

"Other than that it's the right thing to do?"

"Yeah, other than that." I sighed and said, "There's a guy named Ramp. He lives in Denver. I think he's the key to all of this."

"Ramp? R-a-m-p? Is that what you said?"

"I think that's the spelling. But I don't really know. My experience is that my patients tend to get suspicious when I press them about spelling."

Lucy flashed a grin. "Is that a first name or a last name?"

"Don't know that either."

"What do you know about him?"

"Not much. He's around twenty-one or so, give or take a few years. Like I said, he lives in Denver—city or metro, I don't know—and he's active on the

Internet. He's angry at the criminal justice system because his mother was murdered by somebody who was on probation after an earlier homicide conviction. He apparently talks openly about seeking revenge. He likes explosives. He occasionally hangs out with a high school kid here in Boulder who he met on the Net. The local kid's in a similar situation: feels screwed by the criminal justice system and has all kinds of fantasies about getting even."

"Name of the local kid?"

I hesitated. There was no way around it; I was about to reveal the name of someone I had learned about in psychotherapy, someone whom, maybe, Lucy could track down by checking names in the phone book. "His name is Paul Bigg. He's the one who has the direct beef with Royal Peterson."

Lucy seemed to hesitate a second or two before she asked, "And what do you know about him?"

"He's a senior at Fairview. Actually, he works at that Starbucks we were at this morning, but he wasn't there. From a psychological point of view, he meets just about every one of the criteria the FBI has developed to predict violent acting out by adolescents. These two—Ramp and Paul—have apparently developed a hit list of all the people in the justice system that they feel are responsible for what happened to their families.

"They play this mind game, this 'wouldn't-it-be-cool' game." I explained the game to Lucy in more detail, focusing on the way that Ramp and Paul's game had almost predicted the presence of the bomb in the Peterson home. "Obviously, I concluded that Royal Peterson was definitely on the list of people that these two wanted to harm; that's why I told Sam to figure out a way to search his home for explosives. My problem is that I still don't know who else might be on the would-n't-it-be-cool list." I thought about what I'd just said and concluded, "Unfortunately, that's about all I've learned."

"This Paul Bigg? Is he related to Leo Bigg? That whole mess from a few years ago?"

"Yes. Were you and Sam involved in the original rape investigation? Was it your case?"

Lucy shook her head. "No. But it was one of those cases where the police totally disagreed with the DA's office about the plea. I don't mean we didn't like the plea bargain, I mean we hated it. Everyone who knew anything about the case was convinced that the evidence supported a trial on the charges, or at least a tougher plea bargain. Then when the girl's father ended up doing more time than the rapist . . . Lord. It sucked, what can I say?"

My heart rate was accelerating and my palms were sweaty. I didn't like saying any of this out loud. I forced myself to go on. "There's something else, Lucy. Lauren was involved with the Marin Bigg prosecution. She was helping Nora with the sex crimes unit back then."

Lucy recognized the implication instantly. "Oh, Alan. Oh dear. You haven't told her, have you?"

"No. I keep going back and forth on that. I'm not

sure she's on the list. I'm not sure there really is a list. Her health isn't great right now. I was hoping to learn more from my patient before I brought Lauren in on this."

"And I thought I was the one who was most vulnerable in this situation." Lucy leaned forward, closing the distance between us. She took one of my hands between both of hers. "So Nora's almost definitely on the list. And, maybe, so is Lauren. Who else do you think these two assholes might be targeting?"

"Cozy defended the rapist."

"Great. I take it you haven't said anything to him, either?"

"No. Keep in mind that I don't really know anything, Lucy. I keep weighing the damage I'll do by talking against the damage I'll do by keeping my suspicions to myself. My patient keeps alluding to the Klebolds and the Harrises. Whether they should have known what their kids were up to. Whether they should have talked to the police. That's her big issue. Deciding what her responsibility is. She wants to believe that the kids aren't really planning anything, that this is all just a big fantasy. And they haven't really made any threats that she's heard. Certainly none that I've heard."

Lucy's voice became derisive. "Of course the Klebolds and the Harrises should have known. And they should have talked to the police. There's no doubt about either of those things."

"But at what stage does someone really know enough, Lucy? At what stage do I know enough?

Remember, I still haven't heard any threats. Nothing overt. This is all conjecture."

"The bomb they found yesterday at the Peterson house wasn't conjecture. That was a real bomb, and it was real dangerous. The rest of the people on the hit list are vulnerable, Alan."

"You're right, they are. The problem is that I don't really know the identity of anyone on the list—I'm just guessing at the identity of the people these two might be targeting. I would think it's likely that the list includes the judge who approved the plea agreement. That makes sense, right, that they'd include the judge? But I don't even know who that was."

"That's easy. I'll find out."

I said, "I've given this a lot of thought and I can't think of anyone else who might be targeted in Boulder because of the Bigg case, but I may be missing someone. Ramp apparently has his own list of people who were involved in whatever the situation was with his family in Denver, or wherever it was. I know nothing about that, nothing at all. I think it was his mother's murder. But I don't know the details of the case, where it occurred, even what year it happened."

"That's something I can work on," Lucy said.

I went on. "I am suspicious that the bomb that went off in that car yesterday morning was one of Ramp's. The target doesn't make sense, though. From what I've heard on the news and read in the paper, the woman who was killed in the car bomb has no contact with the criminal justice system. She worked in a children's bookstore. Volunteered at a hospital. She coached her kid's soccer team."

"What about her husband, her family?"

"Her husband works in some store in Larimer Square. Sells some western kitsch or something. Mostly tourist crap." I stood up, walked to the window, and watched the wind whip the last of the beautiful pink flowers from the frail redbud.

"The person who's telling you all of this? Your client? Are you still in touch with that person?"

"Yes."

"So you might learn more?"

"It's possible."

"Let's hope so," Lucy said. "Let's hope so. Tell me who it is, Alan. Who's your client?"

I had a patient once, a man, who routinely visited prostitutes when he was out of town on business trips. He rationalized his trysts as being inconsequential because he never kissed the women. If he actually kissed the prostitutes, he maintained, then the contacts would have been intimate.

I thought of him as I said, "Giving you that name won't help you. I don't want to tell you the name right now. Let's just say it's someone who doesn't want to believe that what they're seeing is true."

Not telling Lucy my patient's name was my way of rationalizing my betrayal of Naomi's confidence. It was my equivalent of not kissing the whore.

Lucy joined me by the window. "What you just said about someone who doesn't want to believe what they're seeing is true? That could be any one of us. It could certainly be me. I think it could be you, too."

I didn't turn to face her. Instead I examined her reflection in the glass. "The biggest reason that I was reluctant to clue Sam in about the bomb and that I'm reluctant to tell Lauren or involve the police—or even to involve you, Lucy—is that I'm terrified that this patient of mine will figure out that I've breached her confidence and then she won't—"

"Come back to see you again."

"Exactly. Then I wouldn't have any way of knowing . . . what kind of danger Lauren might really be in."

Lucy bit her bottom lip, touched me on the shoulder, and said, "You're telling me to be careful?"

"You could say that."

"But you're not going to tell me who your patient is?"

"No."

After a moment, she nodded in resignation. "Then I'll work on discovering who this Ramp guy in Denver is. It's something. Does he use that name online?"

"I don't know."

"I'll also find out what I can about the original Bigg case. See if there are any other potential targets. Maybe somebody in the probation department did an investigation on the rapist and issued a report that the family didn't like. A social worker, someone like that, you never know."

"You never know," I agreed.

CHAPTER

21

That afternoon, while Lauren and Grace napped, I duct-taped a hand mirror to a length of PVC pipe left over from our home remodeling and used the device to check the undercarriage of both of our cars for bombs. I didn't spot anything that didn't match the rather perfect coating of gray-brown grime that was slicked beneath each vehicle, although I did discover a leak in the left front axle boot on my car that I hadn't known about.

When I went back inside the house, I phoned Sam Purdy and asked him for Dorsey's phone number. I could tell that he thought he knew why I wanted it, but he didn't say anything, he just gave it to me. In return for his graciousness, I didn't chew on him about his disclosure to Lucy.

Dorsey couldn't have been kinder when I called. She said that she and Shadow could come by and snoop around that evening around six. I told her that we'd be gone; I didn't want my wife to be home during the search. Before we hung up, I gave Dorsey directions to the house and explained where she could find a key.

When Lauren woke up from her nap, I announced I was treating my girls to an early dinner at Rhumba. Since I didn't want Adrienne wondering why a bomb-sniffing dog was snooping around my house, I invited her and Jonas to come along with us downtown for dinner.

Lauren, of course, wanted to know why I insisted on putting the dogs into the dog run instead of leaving them to roam the house, which is what we would typically do. In response to her question, I said something inane about getting the new litter of fox kits accustomed to the dogs. She looked at me funny but, to my relief, decided not to argue with me. I shushed her out the door ahead of me so that I could lock up the house without setting the burglar alarm.

All the subterfuge and anxiety had left me absolutely exhausted by the time everyone was packed into Adrienne's Suburban for the ride downtown. As she pulled her huge vehicle out onto the lane, Adrienne reminded me, gleefully, that I'd become one of those people who dragged young children along to nice restaurants and ate dinner at five-thirty on weekends.

I smiled at my baby and knew that what my friend was saying was true. Absolutely.

Dorsey had promised me that she would tie something to the front doorknob if Shadow had sensed any explosives on the property. She also said that she would call the bomb squad. Even though I didn't see any emergency vehicles as Adrienne drove back down the lane after dinner, my eyes stayed plastered on the front door.

My relief was palpable as I recognized that the doorknob appeared to be unadorned. The brass handle actually seemed to glow as though Dorsey had polished it.

Adrienne and her son, Jonas, decided to enjoy the sunset and accompany Lauren and Grace and the dogs for a walk through the neighborhood. I pretended that I'd been paged and begged off the evening excursion with the excuse that I had a phone call to return.

I dialed the second I was back in the house. "Dorsey, it's Alan."

"Hi, Alan. Nice house you have, terrific view. And great dogs. What's the big one? Shadow wanted to play with her in the worst way."

"She's a Bouvier des Flandres, a Belgian sheepdog. It's just as well she was in the run—she doesn't always play well with strange dogs." Dorsey may have wanted to chat about the puppies, but I needed to cut to the chase. "The doorknob was empty. I take it you and Shadow didn't find anything?"

"No, your house is clean, so is the garage, so are the cars. I don't know if we were supposed to, but we also did that barn that's a little bit south of your house. It's clean, too."

"The workshop? It actually belongs to our neighbor, but thanks. Can't be too cautious."

"You know," she said, pausing, "Sam didn't really give me much background on all of this."

"I wish I could tell you something, Dorsey. I wish I could."

She paused for a few seconds. I wondered if I heard the wind-whistling-in-the-canyon sound of a deep drag on a joint. "You're a shrink, right?"

"Yeah."

"This has something to do with that?"

"Yeah, it does."

"Okay, well. You let us know if we can be of any more help. Shadow's always looking for training opportunities that involve field trips. She graduates in a couple of weeks and then I'll be dealing with a rookie. If you need help, now's the best time."

CHAPTER
22

Lucy Tanner promised to check in with me on Sunday. She didn't. Grace and I spent the day together as Lauren did her best to cope with the toxic consequences of her weekly interferon injection. She loved the drug almost as much as she hated it. As long as she'd been taking the stuff, it had kept its promise to keep the MS dragons on the other side of the moat. The price for the prophylaxis was that she was sick— sometimes moderately, sometimes severely—for the twenty-four hours after the long needle left her thigh.

Grace and I did what we could to make her comfortable. Whatever it was we did, it felt inadequate. And probably was.

Monday at twelve-fifteen Naomi Bigg showed up right on time for her appointment.

Over the weekend there was virtually no way that she could have avoided the extensive news coverage of the discovery of the explosive device in Royal and Susan Peterson's house. I expected to spend the Monday session dealing with Naomi about my role in the detection of that bomb and rehearsed my arguments as she settled herself on the chair.

Naomi started her session by saying, "What I've been thinking? I've been thinking that there's a big difference between the Klebolds and the Harrises and me—I mean the situation I'm in."

She paused as though she wanted me to ask her what the difference was. I didn't ask. I was too busy trying to spot the ambush that I was sure she was planning about the Peterson bomb.

She went on unprompted. "The difference is that there was no way to defend—to justify—what those two kids were planning. No matter how you look at it, Eric and Dylan were targeting innocent children. They were planning indiscriminate slaughter. They were blaming the world for the way they thought they'd been treated. They wanted blood, they wanted gallons of it, and they wanted it from innocents. If their parents had an inkling of that, there is no excuse for them not acting."

Her words shook me. I stopped plotting my defense to accusations of clueing the police in to look for the bomb. As always, Naomi Bigg had a knack for capturing my attention.

The question that almost jumped out of my

mouth—but didn't—was, *And there is a way to justify what your child and his friend are planning?* I think the reason I didn't actually ask the question out loud was that I feared I was incapable of keeping the incredulousness out of my inflection.

After a few sessions with me, Naomi was growing accustomed to the silences. She didn't hesitate to pick up on her own. "The wouldn't-it-be-cool games that the boys play always target—for want of a better word—perpetrators. People who actually bear responsibility for some serious, serious injustice. That's what's different. So even if Paul and Ramp are actually planning something and not just . . . talking—and I'm not convinced that they are—I think, knowing what I know, that I'm in a different position than the Harrises and the Klebolds. It's a big difference."

What? "It's different because in your circumstances the potential victims . . . deserve what happens to them? Is that it?"

Naomi shrugged. "Want to know what I think? Five years ago, I was somebody who used to think that in this country, justice was equal for everybody. Justice was the courts and the police and the jails. The scales always balanced. What's-her-face never peeked out from beneath her blindfold. But I know now that that's not true. Justice isn't just. Justice isn't like a fresh coat of paint on a wall. It doesn't cover equally. It doesn't spread equally. In our system, justice is more like a line of summer thunderstorms. Some places get soaked. Other places stay bone dry. After going through what

I've been through with my family, can I continue to believe that providing justice should be the sole province of the criminal justice system? For every ten good cops, there's a Royal Peterson. For every office full of passionate prosecutors, there's a rotten cop. And defense attorneys?" She groaned. "Don't even get me started on defense attorneys. Or parole boards? God in heaven. The system is too corrupt to be trusted."

"And the alternative . . . is for people who perceive themselves to be victims of injustice to be free to act on their own?"

She hesitated for only a few seconds. "In certain circumstances, I've concluded that the answer to that might be yes. I couldn't do it myself. But I can understand people doing it."

Was she talking about her husband and his cut-off baseball bat or her son and his friend and their bombs? I couldn't keep myself from asking, "So, if these victims of injustice decide to act as vigilantes based on their own conclusions about events, then their victims deserve what happens to them?"

"Victims?" she scoffed. "Like Royal Peterson? You calling Royal Peterson a victim? Royal Peterson wasn't a victim. He was the poster child of perpetrators. The true victims are the people who suffered because of his plea bargains—and believe me, there are dozens of them that are right now trying to pick up the pieces of their lives all over Boulder County."

As much as I disagreed with some of the prosecutorial decisions that Peterson had made over his long

reign in Boulder, I knew the good he had done far outweighed his mistakes. I could barely contain my
impulse to defend him. I said, "And because you disagree with some of his plea bargains, because of that,
Peterson deserved to die?"

"I've already told you: I don't have any feelings
about that. He's dead. I don't grieve him. I don't celebrate his death."

I struggled to control my breathing. "Let's say,
Naomi, just for the sake of argument, that Ramp and
Paul were involved in Royal Peterson's death. Your current feelings are that murdering Peterson was a reasonable reaction to what he did to your daughter?"

She shrugged. "Who cries when a child molester is
attacked in prison? Huh? Who grieves for that?
Peterson ruined lives, too. Hundreds of them. Take a
look at his record of plea bargains. Go ahead. Well,
let's say someone felt he needed to be punished for
that. If that's the case, then, yes, he paid for his sins.
Some people might call what happened to him a
crime. It feels like justice to me. I'm not going to grieve
for that. I am not."

She paused for an extended period, shifting her
focus to the windows and the yard beyond. Then she
said, "But I don't think they had anything to do with it.
I just don't think they did."

Minutes before the session was scheduled to end,
Naomi abruptly stopped talking about a staffing

problem in her office and said, "The bomb the police found last Friday? At the Petersons'?"

"Yes?" I said, my heart racing.

"Do you wonder how they knew to look for it? Have you wondered about that at all?"

What was I going to say? No? Yes?

"I have," she said, saving me from a lie. "And I'd like to think that you didn't have anything to do with the police deciding to look for it. I'd like to think that I can trust you."

My ensuing silence wasn't strategic. I was absolutely tongue-tied. *Yes, you can trust me, Naomi.*

No, you can't.

"If I can't talk to you about these things, I don't think I'd talk to anyone about them. I certainly wouldn't talk to the police. Even if they knocked at my door, I wouldn't tell them a thing. You know what I mean, don't you? I really need to be able to trust you with all this."

I nodded. I knew exactly what she meant. She was warning me to keep my mouth closed.

Right then I should have heeded her advice. I didn't. I said, "Naomi, it's important that you understand that there are circumstances where I might have an ethical responsibility to reveal certain things that I hear in psychotherapy."

She frowned. "That's obtuse. What are you talking about? What kind of circumstances?"

"If I hear something that indicates to me that someone is being clearly threatened, for instance, I have a responsibility to warn that person or to tell the police about the threat. I have a specific responsibility to protect people from harm."

"So I can't talk to you about these . . . feelings I'm having? About the concerns I have about the boys?"

"Those two questions seem to imply that someone is actually being threatened, Naomi. Is that the case?"

"I've told you already that I don't think anyone's being threatened. I'm trying to understand my feelings. That's all."

"I'm not convinced that's all you're trying to do."

"What do you mean?"

I was ready. "The last few times we've talked, it's felt to me as though you were trying to get me to do something to help you act on your feelings—to get you to do what you know is right. I think you may be trying to back me into the same corner that you feel backed into."

"What corner are you talking about? What is 'right'?"

"The right thing to do would be to protect people from harm. If the boys"—I almost choked as I used her vernacular—"do have a list of people they are thinking of hurting, then those people should be warned. They must be warned. And the boys should be stopped."

"Oh really?"

"Yes."

"Is that what the Boulder DA did with my daughter's case? Putting her rapist in jail for a few months protected the people of Boulder from harm? That was his overriding concern when he made that decision? Protecting people? Innocent girls out on dates? Those kinds of innocent people? I don't think so."

"I think you know what you have to do, Naomi."

"Yeah? What's that?"

"Can you answer that question yourself?"

"Just like a freaking shrink," she scoffed. "Just like a freaking shrink. Ask a question, get a question."

CHAPTER
23

My last session on Monday was over at five-fifteen, so I was surprised when I looked up as the session was ending and noticed that the red light was beaming on the wall.

I gave my patient half a minute to exit the waiting room before I walked out to see whether the light was a mistake or whether I had scheduled another patient and had neglected to note it on my calendar.

I did that sometimes.

The waiting room was empty.

I flicked off the light and moved back to my office to pack up. I walked in to find that Lucy Tanner was sitting in my chair.

"I like this seat better than the other one. This is definitely the power chair in the room."

"Hi, Lucy. How did you get in?" I made a conscious effort to keep my annoyance from my voice. Lucy's presence reminded me of the ethical malignancy that was metastasizing in my treatment of Naomi Bigg. But Lucy also represented my best hope for finding out what Ramp and Paul might be up to.

She tilted her head toward the French door. "That's not much of a lock you have. I can recommend something that's a little harder to pick, if you would like. Sorry. I didn't want to be seen hanging out in your waiting room. How are you holding up?"

I moved to the far end of the sofa and put my feet up. "I'm a wreck. I had a friend of Sam's who trains K-9 dogs come by my house and check for explosives Saturday. I couldn't believe I did it."

"Dorsey? From Westminster?"

I nodded.

"You like her?"

"I do."

I thought Lucy clenched her teeth a little bit. I was about to inquire about her feelings about Dorsey when she distracted me by asking, "She and her dog find anything?"

"Thankfully, no."

"Good. She still smoking dope?"

I swallowed. "I wouldn't know."

"Learn anything new from your 'source'?"

"My *patient,* Lucy. My patient. And no, I didn't learn anything that will help us much. Other than that she is seriously reluctant to believe that her son is plotting anything worrisome. And that if she's approached by the authorities she'll deny everything she told me."

"She's warning you? Does she suspect something?"

"She's suspicious about how the police happened to find the bomb in the Peterson house."

"That's almost like an admission, isn't it?"

"Maybe for a cop, Lucy. It's not enough for me."

She manufactured a small smile. "Sorry I didn't call. I've been pretty busy. When I haven't been with Cozy or his investigator, I've been down in Denver mostly."

"You find Ramp?"

"Not even a trace. I tracked down all sorts of anti-law-enforcement Web sites and scoured the bulletin boards looking for his name. Nothing. Not a first name, not a last name, not a computer name. Asked some friends in the Denver and Aurora PDs if they had anything on anybody with that name, first or last. Nothing. I have a feeler out to someone on the Denver PD bomb squad to see if Ramp's in their database. I'm still waiting to hear.

"Next brainstorm was that I went back ten years and looked at all the murdered women in the Denver metro area. Sorted out all the mothers, then sorted by mothers who had sons, then looked for kids named Ramp.

"I'm working under the assumption that Ramp's a nickname, so I didn't expect to find him on that list, and I didn't. Then I made another list of all the sons of murdered mothers who would be between sixteen and twenty-five years old today. Guess how many that is?"

"Too many. I don't want to know."

"Until I have something else to go on, I'm working

under the assumption that his mother was killed in the metro area. A broader net is just unworkable for me."

"What about the bomb in the Petersons' house? Did that give the bomb squad any clues?"

"Sammy found out what he could for me. But, no. No latents on the bomb. No unusual materials used in the construction. The explosive was commercial dynamite, slightly aged, a little unstable, but not too bad. No recognizable signature. And the architecture of the device didn't draw any hits from the ATF database."

"That's not much."

Lucy said, "I'm left with the phone book."

"Anything there?"

"I've called all the Denver metro Ramps. There aren't that many. I reached two of the listings and ruled them out. A couple more I just got answering machines. Outside Denver metro there are, I think, three more Ramps. I'm going to try them tonight over dinner. It's a good time to reach people."

"So that leaves us where?" I asked.

"We still have the car bomb in Denver. I think—my gut feeling is—that, failing to find Ramp directly, the car bomb in Denver is our best link to him. I have trouble believing that discovering two explosive devices in the metro area on the same day can be isolated events. Sam has a contact with the Denver bomb squad."

"Walter."

"What?"

"Sam's contact's name is Walter. Or at least he calls him Walter."

Lucy laughed. The sound was a refreshing trill. "That means Sam thinks he's reliable. When he doesn't trust sources or snitches, he gives them names that begin with *L*—stands for loser. When he thinks they're reliable, he gives them names that begin with *W*. Those are the winners. So Sam trusts this guy, whoever he is. But until Sam hears more from Walter or something breaks in the news, we're in the dark about the Denver situation."

"That leaves us with Paul or with the mythical Ramp."

"Yes. And the path to Paul leads directly back to your patient, right?"

"Right. But Paul also should eventually lead us to Ramp."

"I agree. That's why Paul is next on my agenda."

I considered the options. If Lucy was discovered following Paul, it would become clear to Naomi that I'd been sharing her information with someone else. That would certainly end the therapy.

"Lucy, I'll follow Paul. If I'm discovered doing it, I have a chance of explaining away my indiscretion. If you get discovered, I'm screwed. My patient would stop talking to me. And I can't risk that."

"You don't know how to do this. This is police work."

"Paul's in school during the day. I know where he works. I know where he lives. I should be able to figure out when he's hanging out with his friend. My patient says they usually get together in Boulder, not Denver."

"And what will you do then?"

"Get a photograph. Get Ramp's license plate number. That should be enough for you to go on, right?"

"Should be," she acknowledged. "Should be."

CHAPTER
24

Cozy's office suite took up a good-sized chunk of the west side—that's the side with the view—of the eighth—that's the top—floor of the Colorado Building on Fourteenth Street near the Pearl Street Mall. After leaving my office, I found a parking place on Walnut, fed the meter, and entered the lobby, which was sized not to impress visitors but rather to maximize leasable square footage for the landlords. One of the building's two elevators was being used for a furniture delivery; the other one—the one I rode in—stopped at five of the eight floors on the way to the top.

I found Cozy and Lauren sitting at each end of a walnut conference table, the surface of which was carpeted with books and papers. Cozy was facing the door and saw me enter. He had a phone to his ear and a file in his other hand. His greeting was a nod.

I walked up behind Lauren and kissed her on her

hair. She reached up and slid her warm fingers across the skin on the back of my neck. I almost asked, "How did you know it was me?" But I didn't. I said, "Hi, how you doing?"

"Tired, but okay."

"You at a place you can stop? We need to get home and rescue Viv. She's had a long day with the baby."

She smiled and said, "Sure."

While she packed up, I examined the overriding reason—hell, the only reason other than its central location—for leasing office space in the Colorado Building: the view.

The streets in downtown Boulder are numbered in ascending order beginning at the base of the foothills of the Rockies. That means that Fourteenth Street is roughly fourteen blocks away from the dramatic incline of the mountains, an almost perfect distance to maximize the view. From Cozy's eighth-floor perch, high above the treetops, Boulder in springtime appeared as a lush landscape of old redbrick and flagstone buildings flanked by gentle rises to the north—Mapleton Hill—to the south—Chautauqua, and barricaded to the west by the vaulting presence of the foothills of the Rockies.

As dusk approached, the vista was glorious.

Lauren and I had almost the same view from our home miles to the east, but ours was wide angle. This was zoom. Every time I saw the close-up perspective from this elevated perch, I was captivated by the difference. Our view from home was mostly sky—the monumental mountains ended up being dwarfed by the infinite western sky. This view was mostly mountains, their sheer mass and grandeur looming over a town that appeared to have been built to the wrong scale.

Lauren took my hand and pulled me away from the windows. We both said good-bye to Cozy. He tucked the phone between his shoulder and his ear and waved good-bye.

In the elevator, Lauren said, "It hasn't been a particularly good afternoon for Lucy, sweets."

I swallowed. "Tell me."

"Over the last hour or so, Cozy and I learned some new things. When Sam and Lucy worked up Royal's house after the murder, one of the pieces of evidence they recovered was unwashed laundry from on top of the washing machine. There was also some laundry in the dryer. Did you know about any of that? I don't remember whether I told you. It hadn't seemed important until today. Anyway, it turns out that a sheet had some stains on it. It now appears that the police suspect that they can link the DNA on the stains to Lucy."

"What kind of stains?"

She sighed. "They think they're vaginal secretions."

"Vaginal secretions?" I said. *Lions and tigers and bears.* "Oh my."

The elevator door opened at the fourth floor. A psychologist, someone I barely knew from some insipid meeting of local psychologists I'd once attended against my better judgment, entered the elevator. I smiled and said, "Hello." She struggled, without apparent success, to place my face before she turned around and stared at the doors. Lauren slid her hand into mine and squeezed. The three of us stood silently and watched the numbers.

It took me only two of the remaining three floors to decide that there weren't very many ways for Lucy Tanner to have left vaginal secretions on sheets in Royal Peterson's house.

In fact, I could only think of one. I wasted a moment considering whether I was being unimaginative.

Outside the building on the Fourteenth Street sidewalk, Lauren asked, "Are you parked nearby?"

"Not too far, over on Walnut. Is your car ready to be picked up?" Her car was in the shop.

She shook her head. "No, they're still waiting for that thing to be delivered. Maybe tomorrow, maybe not." She checked her watch and said, "Let's walk up the Mall for a block or two and circle back to your car. We have time."

The "thing" was a transmission gasket. I took her briefcase and hung it over my shoulder. We held hands. As we turned the corner onto Pearl Street, I said, "Vaginal secretions?"

"Yeah, sorry to say. Apparently the police think they found the whole damn wet spot."

"Semen?"

"No."

"Really?"

"Think condom," she said.

"Oh," I said, feeling stupid. "Did they find that?"

"No."

Wispy clouds hung like smoke above the foothills of the Front Range. The sun was already invisible from our near vantage, though the sky above our heads was still bright. The cloud pattern promised a great finale to sunset, but I knew we wouldn't be home in time to catch it.

Lauren said, "It's too soon to know for sure. But that's the general direction that this is heading. Damned by a wet spot."

While I considered the timelessness of Macbeth, we crossed Thirteenth and moved slowly toward Broadway.

I stated the obvious. "So Lucy and Royal were having an affair?"

"Lucy won't talk about it. She continues to maintain that the details of her relationship to Royal will only serve to solidify the notion that she had a motive to kill him."

I tried to think like a prosecutor. It was not a natural act. "The police think they have means—her fingerprints are on the pottery. They think they have opportunity—a witness places her on the scene. And Lucy basically admits that she had motive. This doesn't look great for your client."

"Tell me about it."

"Lucy was having an affair with Roy and she'd decided to break up with him?" I asked. "Is that what she's saying?"

"She's not saying. But that's what I'm guessing. She's recently engaged, you know?"

"I know, she told me. But the engagement predates the wet spot by a couple of weeks. What's your theory of what happened? One last time with Royal? A good-bye fuck?"

She shook her head. "Nothing fits particularly well, I admit it. Pretty night, isn't it?"

"Lovely. Assume you're right, babe. How do things develop that night so that she ends up whacking him on the head with a lamp?"

"Like I said, nothing fits well."

"Self-defense?"

"Cozy and I would love self-defense. Lucy isn't offering, though. She maintains she had nothing to do with Royal's murder."

"What about Lucy's fiancé? If he found out about the affair, he'd have a motive, too, wouldn't he?"

"We're there already. Cozy's investigator has begun looking into that for us, though Lucy doesn't even know we have an investigator looking at him. I'm sure she'd go nuts if she knew what we were doing."

"And the bomb? What about the bomb? What's the theory as to why Lucy would want to blow up the Peterson house?"

"The bomb is our salvation. It's the only thing keeping Lucy out of jail right now. They can't tie her to it.

If they found a molecule of evidence that put Lucy and that bomb in the same room, she'd be screwed."

I was amazed at how quickly my wife, a lifelong prosecutor, had adopted the vernacular of a defense attorney. People who were her colleagues days before were now "they."

At Broadway, we turned around and traced our steps back down the Mall toward the car. "How do you and Cozy know about the wet spot? There's no required discovery yet, is there? Lucy hasn't been charged."

"No formal discovery, no." She gave my hand a squeeze. "Let's just say that the politics in the DA's office right now are working to our advantage. Everyone's posturing to take Royal's place. Everyone's scrambling to keep this thing from going to a special prosecutor. Keeping us informed is part of . . . someone's strategy."

"Who's feeding you? Mitchell? Elliot? I bet it's not Nora."

She said, "No, of course it's not Nora. And that's all I'm telling you."

On the way home from downtown I slowed to a stop at a red light at the corner of Broadway and University by the Hill. As if to prove to me that Boulder really is a small town, Naomi Bigg pulled up in the lane next to us driving a filthy BMW sedan. She was wearing sunglasses and smoking a cigarette. I don't think she saw me and I said nothing to Lauren about her presence next to us.

Just before the light changed to green, Naomi lowered her window about six inches, took a final deep drag on her cigarette, and tossed the still-lit butt onto the road between our cars.

I didn't get it.

People like Naomi, someone who I suspected wouldn't consider tossing a candy wrapper or a pop can onto the street, thought nothing of discarding cigarette butt after cigarette butt onto public sidewalks and thoroughfares.

Was there some statute I didn't know about that exempted cigarette butts from littering concerns? I suspected that what was more likely was that this was smokers' revenge for society's continuing anticigarette bias.

I also suspected that no matter how successful psychotherapy was, Naomi would still be littering her cigarette butts when we were done.

Later Monday evening I ran into Adrienne while I was taking the dogs outside for them to do their thing at the end of the day. I'd spotted the lights on in her dead husband Peter's old workshop, a barn he'd renovated into a woodworking facility that would leave weekend hobbyists drooling. When the dogs and I walked over we found Adrienne looking futilely for something that she'd put in the workshop in her version of storage, which as far as I'd been able to discern basically involved moving things to a location where she didn't trip over them on a daily basis. So far, nothing she'd moved into the old barn had been labeled, and as far as I could tell, nothing had been organized.

"Hey," she said as I stood in the open doorway. She spoke to me without looking up from the box in which she was rooting around. "You should keep Anvil away from the fields for the foreseeable future. The momma fox just had some new kits, everybody in the family looks hungry, and your poodle, such as he is, looks suspiciously like lunch."

"I know about the kits. They're cute. And Anvil's tough."

She laughed. "Right, and I'm gorgeous." She mumbled a profanity that I think was intended for the box she was trying to open, not for me, before she addressed me again. "I ever tell you that I have a patient who's going through a sex change?"

I raised my eyebrows.

"No, I'm not doing the operation, if that's what you're thinking. Somebody else is actually responsible for remodeling the plumbing."

"Your patient's a guy?" I asked to buy time. The whole topic of sexual transformation made me uncomfortable. Not philosophically, surgically.

"Yeah. You interested?"

"Interested? You mean—"

"Not in trying it, doofus. In helping. You know, professionally. These guys all need psychotherapy. It's part of the protocol. It's required."

"I don't know, Adrienne. How far along is the . . . how do you put it . . . the procedure? Is it like, well—"

"What?"

"Has he, um—"

"You want to know if the hose is still on the fire truck?"

I laughed.

She laughed, too, and returned to rooting in the boxes. She said, "Don't worry, I was just pimping you. I wouldn't send this guy to you. It would make you both crazier than you already are."

"Thanks. I appreciate it more than you know."

She threw a box out of her way and the sound of glass breaking filled the old barn. She ignored the carnage. "So who was the dog snooping around here the other day?"

I'd just recovered from one topic that made me anxious, so I wasn't well prepared for another. "Adrienne," I said. "You know, I disagree with what you said before—you are gorgeous. What, um, dog are you talking about?" Lying isn't one of my best things and I suspected that I'd just succeeded in alerting Adrienne that I was prevaricating.

" 'What, *um*, dog am I talking about?' While we were at dinner the other night, somebody came by with a dog and they walked all around your place, inside and out, and then they came in here."

"What?"

She stood up and faced me. Adrienne was petite. She was holding a folded blanket that she'd pulled from a cardboard box. Next to Emily's bulky mass, she looked like she was a jockey preparing to saddle up for a ride. "Look," she said. "My latest excuse for a nanny came by while we were at dinner and saw some woman and her dog checking out your place like the DEA thinks you're fronting for some drug lord. She said the woman and the dog came in here, too. This place is mine. That makes it my business. So tell me."

Her hands were on her hips.

Adrienne's history with nannies was not illustrious. I tried to distract her with a feint. "You're not happy with your nanny? I didn't know that."

"Let me put it this way: I'll give you ten thousand dollars for the unconditional rights to Viv."

"No way."

"That's what I figured. Now tell me about the drug-sniffing pooch."

I said, "I've been wondering, do you think I'm the right age to start having annual prostate exams?"

"Answer my question or I'll glove up right now and give you one I promise you'll never forget."

I pulled back a dusty canvas tarp and lifted myself up to sit on the edge of one of Peter's old workbenches. I knew that the fact that the shop was pretty much the way Peter had left it when he died had nothing to do with his wife's attempt to create a shrine. Adrienne wasn't exactly preserving Peter's shop in his memory; she just hadn't gotten around to moving any of his stuff, selling it, or giving it away. I suspected that with the exception of continued additions of boxes and assorted household junk from Adrienne, the barn wouldn't change much in the next decade.

I asked, "Did you know Leo Bigg?"

She lowered herself to the top of a box. The dogs immediately decided that she was prey and surrounded her. Emily sniffed her pockets for treats. Anvil tried to crawl onto her lap.

She asked, "Where on earth is that question coming from?"

"Just curious."

She stared at me. "You're often difficult, Alan, but you're not usually this constipated. If you don't answer at least one of my questions, I swear I'm going to kidnap your dogs."

I smiled. "If the threat of a sadistic prostate exam didn't sway me, you think the threat of moving my dogs across the lane and feeding them too many treats is going to unseal my lips?"

"Talk."

"Leo Bigg's story came up in a therapy session. I just thought that you might have known him."

"Leo's not dead, Alan. He's in prison. And, yes, I do know him. He was a good doc—is a good doc. Everything you'd want in an oncologist. But my suspicion is that that's not what you wanted to know. You want to know about his tragedies, don't you? You want to know whether he was the kind of guy who would do what he did?"

"Yes, I do."

"Everyone who knew him was shocked at what he

did. Everyone. He found something most of us, thank God, never find—he found his breaking point. The weight of his heartbreak must have simply overwhelmed him. I can't explain what he did any other way."

I thought about Marin, the rape, and I nodded. "Did you know his family? His wife?"

"I probably met his wife at parties, but I don't remember her well. Those were the days before Jonas was born, and the Biggs already had kids. Plus the Biggs always floated a few social strata above Peter and me. They wouldn't hang with us. It would have been slumming for them."

"Lauren and I hang with you."

"Like I said, slumming."

Anvil had succeeded in curling up on Adrienne's lap. Emily was still nosing around in search of treats, nudging Adrienne in the flanks as though she were reluctant livestock. Adrienne relented and gave each of the dogs a biscuit from her pocket. She rarely went outside unprepared to indulge the dogs.

She said, "Now tell me about Rin Tin Tin."

Instead of answering I asked, "How's Susan Peterson doing?"

She laughed. "You want me to discuss someone else's bladder control with you? Are you psychotic? Tell me— who's Rin Tin Tin?"

"The woman is someone I met recently. She's a disabled police officer who trains K-9 dogs to supplement her income. She likes to take her dogs on what she calls 'field trips' as part of their training. I offered to let her use our place. She came in here by mistake."

"That's the best you can do?"

"Most of it's true."

She laughed loudly.

"The rest I can't tell you."

"Figures. Bet you want me to keep my suspicions from your wife, too, don't you?"

"How'd you guess?"

She stood and returned her attention to the boxes. I asked her if she wanted my help finding something.

She said, "You think I want you to search through my stuff? There're important things in here."

I jumped down from the workbench and started to leave the barn.

Adrienne said, "I ever tell you that being your neighbor is no picnic?"

"Yeah, you've told me. That being the case, it's probably fortunate for me that you love me."

"True. By the by, call my office and set up a time with Phyllis. I think I do want to get a nice slow feel of your prostate."

Under my breath, I said, "Fat chance."

Adrienne said, "I heard that."

CHAPTER
25

Lucy Tanner didn't go home right away after leaving Alan's office.

Shortly after she'd been old enough to drive she'd discovered that nothing she did gave her the succor and peace she felt when she was alone behind the wheel of a car. As a younger woman, she'd required open roads and speed to achieve the contentment she sought from her automobile. During the first few years after she'd graduated from college, she'd thought nothing of driving alone from Colorado to San Diego and back on a long weekend to sneak in a few hours surfing in Encinitas.

The trips were a lark. The surfing was usually a thrill. The driving was a necessity.

Now she could achieve some modicum of solace simply by driving city streets or cruising the narrow canyons that snaked into the foothills above Boulder.

The speed to which she was once addicted was no longer necessary. A dirt lane up Magnolia served her purposes as well as a wide-open interstate on Floyd Hill up I-70. The turbo boost on her cherry-red Volvo was about as essential for her as a box of condoms was to a nun. She was thinking it was time to trade the car in for something else, though she couldn't decide exactly what.

When she left Alan's office, Lucy headed north on Broadway, paralleling the naked hogbacks that ridged Boulder's western rim. Her fiancé, Grant, lived in a townhouse in Niwot, a once-charming rest stop of a village that had grown into an extra bedroom for Boulder's expanding family. She weaved east until she connected with the Diagonal Highway and started the familiar route to her boyfriend's house a few miles down the road. She barely noticed the soft colors that were illuminating the clouds above the hogbacks.

Lucy knew Grant wasn't home. He was in the field, somewhere in central Wyoming, doing a wildlife survey. She'd received an e-mail from him that morning and had sent one back his way, a don't-worry-about-me-I'm-doing-fine pack of lies. Her journey to his home wasn't about seeing him; it was about *driving* to see him. She looped past his house twice, finally parking for a moment in the place beneath the big cottonwood where she usually left her car when she was spending the night.

Her engine running, she listened to Gloria Estefan

sing something in Spanish. The backbeat was invigor-
ating but the tone was lamenting. Gloria obviously
wasn't pleased about something, but Lucy didn't
remember enough of her high school Spanish to know
exactly what. As the song ended and the disc jockey
moved into a commercial for a herbal elixir that he
promised was just as potent as Viagra, Lucy touched a
button to change stations, pulled out from beneath the
cottonwood, and steered her way back onto the
Diagonal, this time heading toward Boulder.

She stayed on the Diagonal until it ended, and then
stayed on Iris until she reached Broadway, where she
turned south. She'd arrived at a decision as she was
stopped at the light at Twenty-eighth Street. Her next
stop was going to be the home of the Bigg family. She'd
already checked their address. They lived south of
Baseline in a cul-de-sac below Chautauqua.

She cruised the cul-de-sac only once. Four houses
on big lots. The garage door was open on one of the
houses on the corner. Somebody was working on an
old motorcycle with a sidecar. A dozen lights were
ablaze in the two-story Bigg home. One car—a six- or
seven-year-old BMW—was parked in the driveway;
two more cars were on the street nearby.

She jotted down the plates on all the vehicles, hoping that she'd happened upon an evening visit by the
man named Ramp. But she didn't think so. Lucy was-
n't feeling particularly lucky.

Sixth took her back toward downtown. But she did-
n't make it all the way downtown. All along she knew

that the Peterson home would be her last stop before heading back to her place.

She cruised Jay Street twice, slowing each time in front of the Peterson house. The lawn had been mowed for the first time that spring. The crime-scene tape was down. The do-not-enter warnings were gone from the front door. The light in one of the upstairs windows was dim, not dark. The ubiquitous flicker of the television screen from Susan Peterson's bedroom, present. She's back home, Lucy thought during her first pass. She felt an urge to park around the corner where she'd always left her car during her prior visits, but resisted, settling instead for permitting herself one more loop past the house.

On her final drive by the house she wondered if she wished things were the same as they always were. As they were a couple of weeks before.

She couldn't decide. She found that interesting, still.

Although she'd promised herself that no matter what she saw in the upstairs window, she absolutely wouldn't stop, she pulled over to the curb and parked her car behind an aging Toyota pickup, killing the engine in the middle of a melancholy ballad by Sinéad O'Connor.

That's one girl, she told herself, who's more confused than I am.

Lucy reached over to the passenger seat and checked her purse to make sure she had everything she might need.

She did.

The air was heavy, the way it is in July when a thunderstorm has just passed. But the April night was dry. A chill permeated her clothing. Lucy kept her head down, counting curb sections, reading the dates imprinted on the borders of the cement work. The oldest section she found had been installed in 1958.

Nineteen fifty-eight must have been a very good year for concrete. The pour was still in good shape. By comparison, some of the newer sections, including one done in 1993, already appeared due for replacement.

She had to cross over Pleasant Street to get to the Peterson home. When she looked up from her reverie to check for traffic, she was almost hit by a bicycle riding on the wrong side of the street.

The walkway that led from the sidewalk to the Petersons' front door was constructed of brick pavers set in a herringbone pattern. The path meandered from start to finish in the elongated shape of a lazy S. Lucy cut the curves, straightening the path into a line.

She had no illusions that she'd find Susan Peterson home alone. She suspected that Susan would have convinced someone—one of her doctors, probably—that her husband's murder had left her in need of a full-time aide. Lucy knew that there was another possibility—that instead of an aide, Susan's caretaker might be one of Susan and Royal's daughters.

Either way, Lucy knew that whomever she discovered in the house would be a woman.

Susan didn't like men close by.

Lucy had never used her key in the front door lock, didn't know if it would even work. Since she'd had the key, she'd always come in through the back door.

She tried the key in the front lock. The thin metal wand slid into the brass slot naturally, as though it belonged. She rotated her hand and the key turned evenly in the lock. She depressed the thumb lever and pushed the heavy door inward. It released with a gentle *whoosh* and Lucy stepped inside the house.

She paused. The living room was to her right. She tried not to think about that night. About Royal.

About Sam.

"You okay, Luce?"

She failed in her attempt to ward off memories of that night; the images flooding her left her feeling a momentary pulse of disorientation. The same almost-vertigo she'd felt when Sam was kneeling over the body.

"Holy shit. You know who this is, Luce?"

She shook her head to clear the slate. Ever since she was a little girl she'd cleared her head the same way she'd erased images from her Etch A Sketch. This time it took two shakes.

The stairs to the second floor were right in front of her.

Lucy heard water running in the kitchen at the rear of the house. That would be the aide or the daughter.

Staying to the far right edge of the staircase because Royal had warned her once that a couple of the treads squeaked, Lucy took the stairs one at a time. She didn't touch the banister.

From the landing at the top of the stairs, she could see that the door to Susan's bedroom was almost closed. Through the narrow opening Lucy could hear the distinct sound of the television.

Martha frigging Stewart.

She paused and thought about Grant.

She was consciously aware that she was looking for a reason to go back down the stairs, back out the door, back into her bright red Volvo. But Grant wasn't going to be that reason. He'd find out everything soon enough and at that point he'd do what he'd do. Lucy thought he'd run like hell, but allowed for the possibility that he might surprise her.

With her left hand Lucy reached into her purse. With her right hand she pushed open the door.

Susan looked up, probably to demand something of the aide.

Lucy said, "Susan. We need to talk."

CHAPTER

26

Lucy e-mailed her fiancé before she scrubbed the makeup from her eyes and slid into bed. She wrote to tell him that she loved him, but she knew in her heart that her words were nothing more than shouting in a canyon.

What she really wanted to hear was the echo.

When the phone rang twenty minutes later, she still wasn't asleep. Wasn't even close to being asleep. She checked the time out of curiosity. The clock read 11:05.

"Hello."

"Lucy Tanner?"

"Yes."

"This is Brett Salomon from the *Daily Camera.*"

In a clear voice, a cop voice, Lucy said, "How the

hell did you get this number? I've told you before, Mr. Salomon, I'm not giving interviews. Good night. Please don't call here again."

"Wait, please. Don't hang up. This call is a courtesy for you, Detective Tanner. Hear me out. In tomorrow morning's edition we will be running a story concerning you and the Petersons, and I wanted to give you an opportunity to comment prior to publication. It's up to you, but I suggest you hear me out."

Lucy's heart felt as though it were a new thing in her chest. The suddenly rapid beating got her attention like a loud knock at the door. She swept her hair off her forehead. "Concerning me how? What's the story about?"

When he started talking again, Lucy thought Salomon's inflection had changed, as though he was reading, or reciting something that he'd rehearsed. He said, "Detective Tanner, we will be reporting in tomorrow morning's paper that Susan Peterson is your mother and we will be characterizing your relationship with her. Feel free to comment. I'd like to print your side of the story, as well."

Lucy pressed the mouthpiece of the phone into her right breast and told herself to breathe. The room was dark and the foot of her bed faced the wall. She thought she saw brilliant flashes of light, like flames, erupt in three or four places where she should be seeing nothing but the familiar shadows of her room at night.

She could still hear Brett Salomon's voice. It

sounded disconnected, hollow, distant. But urgent, pressured. He was saying, "Detective? Detective? This is your chance to comment. Detective Tanner? Detective Tanner?"

Lucy hung up the phone and then she vomited all over the sheets.

CHAPTER
27

I misled my wife in order to get out of the house after midnight. An emergency, I said. Lauren, half asleep, assumed that I meant an emergency with my practice. And now, sometime shortly after midnight, I was sneaking down the street, head down, collar up, hoping no photographers' lenses were pointed my way as I hustled into the old house on Pine Street where Lucy Tanner had a second-floor flat.

I was surprised how cold it was outside.

Lucy had been crying. A pile of spent tissues marked the place on the sofa where she'd been awaiting my arrival.

Her flat was dark, a solitary light from the kitchen spilling shadows into the living room. Even in the muted light I could tell that the room was elegant yet comfortable, a pleasant mixture of the modern and the ancient. An alluring step *tansu* filled much of one wall. A gorgeous old highboy secretary marked off the transition to the kitchen. The sofa where she was sitting was covered in a rich tapestry. It was the kind of room that took either serious bucks or an exceptionally high credit limit from Visa.

"Thanks for coming," she said. "I didn't know who else to call." Lucy was wearing a black robe that reached to mid-thigh. As she sat on her sofa, she had to tug the hem of the robe carefully into place to maintain modesty. She grabbed a wadded tissue from beside her and stretched out one corner of it as though she were about to use it to blow her nose. She didn't. She said, "My fiancé is in Wyoming," as though that explained why she'd called me instead of him.

"Sure," I said.

"After I left your office today, I drove around for a while. I do that sometimes. Just drive around. It helps me relax. You ever do that? Just drive around? Does that make me weird?" The last question informed me that she was aware at that moment that she was talking to a mental health professional.

She pulled on a different corner of the tissue, and it ripped. She slipped a fingertip through the hole.

I shifted my weight so that I was leaning forward, closing the space between the chair where I was sitting and Lucy.

She went on. "During my drive I went, well, I went a lot of places, but one of the places I went was the Peterson house. Susan's moved back home. Did you know that? I saw the lights on upstairs. The TV screen was flickering."

I said, "I didn't know she was back home."

"Me neither. I was kind of surprised, actually."

For a split second she lifted her eyes and looked at me. "I don't have many friends, Alan. Did Sam tell you that about me? That I don't get close to very many people?"

"I think he's told me that you're a private person, Lucy. That's all."

"Sam's nice," she said. Here in the dark with something important on her mind, her voice was almost girlish. "My boyfriend says that I seem to love it when he's intimate with me but that I don't want to be intimate with him."

Almost reflexively, I said, "You say that in a way that makes me wonder whether his words make sense to you." It was a shrink phrase. In that room at that time it was as out of place as a bright red clown nose.

She exchanged the ripped tissue for a fresh one and dabbed at her left nostril. "I've heard it before—things like my boyfriend said—from other men. But I always thought that when they were talking about intimacy, they were really talking about sex. That when they complained that I was too distant, they really meant they were unhappy that I wasn't sleeping with them. Or wasn't sleeping with them as often as they wanted."

I wondered where we were heading. I honestly didn't have a clue. I assumed the reason that I'd been summoned from my bed was weightier than this. Lucy had to be warming up for something.

"But it's not that way with Grant. Grant really wants me to be open—you know, to talk to him." She laughed. "Don't misunderstand. He wants to sleep with me, too. But he says that he wants me to tell him . . . things. What's going on. How I feel about what's going on. You know."

I didn't want to repeat my mistake. I said, "He sounds like quite a find, Lucy." It's something I never would have said in therapy. I know that's why I said it then—to remind myself that I was meeting with Lucy as a friend, not as a therapist. Maybe I wanted to remind her, too.

"He doesn't want me to tell him what's going on right now, I promise you that. Anyway, he's not around."

Here it comes, I thought. *The reason I'm not home in bed.*

She narrowed her eyes and continued. "You know what that means for you and me? It means that tonight, instead of being intimate with my fiancé, I'm going to be intimate with you."

I thought her words carried layers of meaning that weren't readily apparent, and I wasn't sure Lucy was even aware that there were stowaways on board whatever trip she was inviting me on.

Again I said something that I would ordinarily say in

psychotherapy, and almost immediately I regretted it. "Intimacy isn't the same as openness, Lucy. It's not that simple."

She looked at me. Her eyes seemed smaller without makeup. She said, "What? What do you mean?"

I debated whether or not I should answer. Finally, I said, "Let's say you go to Denver and you meet somebody in a bar, and let's say they buy you a drink, and you tell them every deep dark secret in your soul—"

She sighed. "For me that would take more than one drink."

"Well, you do that, you open up like that to a stranger—that's not intimate behavior. That's not what intimacy is."

"I don't get it. It sounds like intimacy to me."

"Let me give you another example. You go to that same bar and meet the same guy and without telling him a thing about yourself, about what's in your heart, about what's dear to you, you go home with him. You sleep with him. Then you leave. You don't even know his name. He doesn't know yours. Well, that's not intimacy, either."

She bit her bottom lip. "Okay, I can buy that."

"But put the two experiences together, and you may—you may—have intimacy."

"You've lost me again, Alan. I'm sorry."

I sat back. "I'm not sure this is that important, Lucy. I'm digressing and you have something you need to talk to me about."

"No, go on, please. This is all part of . . . something."

"Intimacy requires two things to happen. Both are necessary. Neither, alone, is sufficient. One is openness. The other is vulnerability. In the first example I gave you, the openness is there, but there's no vulnerability. The guy you meet in the bar can't hurt you. He knows everything about you—every fact—but he can't really touch you in a way that could cause you any pain.

"In the second example, the vulnerability is there, but there's no openness. You're terribly vulnerable to the guy as you have sex with him. But it's anonymous; you never open up to the guy at all."

"What do you call that?"

"I don't know," I said. "Reckless?"

Lucy pulled both her legs beneath her and crossed her arms. For some reason, I chose that moment to scan the room for a cat. Lucy seemed like the type of woman who would have a cat.

She said, "I need to think about this some more."

"Of course."

It was about this time that I would be glancing at my watch and saying, *I'm afraid our time is up.*

Lucy stood and walked to the other side of the room. I could see her reflection in the glass doors. Her legs were exposed from mid-thigh to the floor; her robe was open from her throat to the middle of her chest.

I hoped the exposure was unintentional. But I wondered about her seductiveness. Could she be so unaware of her behavior with men?

Her lips parted as though she was going to speak, then she pressed them together again. Finally, she said, "It's starting to snow. I didn't even know a storm was coming. Did you?"

"I'd heard a front was coming through. But, no, I didn't know it was going to snow."

"I wonder if it will stick," she said.

I didn't reply. I hadn't left my wife in bed to discuss Boulder's springtime climate.

Lucy shifted her weight and lifted one leg from the floor so that it was bent at the knee at ninety degrees, like a stork. She said, "I don't know exactly how to say this. No, that's not true, I do know exactly how to say this. I just don't want to say it." Once more her mouth opened and closed.

"Take your time, Lucy." It was something I said to patients all the time in psychotherapy. For some reason, it usually made them seem to hurry.

"Susan Peterson is my mother, Alan."

I said, "What?" I knew exactly what she had said. My question expressed my befuddlement, not my failure to hear or comprehend.

Lucy returned her weight to both legs and turned and faced me. She'd pulled the robe closed at her throat with one hand. "Susan Peterson is . . . my mother. Or at least she's the woman who gave birth to me."

At her pronouncement, I stood. I don't know why. "Lucy, Lucy. My God. I had no idea."

"No one did. We are . . . estranged. That's a good word for it. Estranged. In fact, it couldn't be *es-stranger*."

"Royal knew?"

Again, Lucy spun and faced the glass. She'd released the shawl collar of her black robe. The reflection made it clear that it had again fallen open to the middle of her chest. "Of course Royal knew."

"Cozy and Lauren?"

She shook her head. "No one else in town knows." She found her own words humorous, or ironic, or something. "At least no one in town knew. Until tonight. Now that's about to change."

I tried to make sense of the implications of the news that Lucy had just shared. I had to assume that this was the reason she had been in the Peterson home the night that Royal had been murdered. A visit to her mother would explain all the fingerprints the police had found in the house. Lauren and Cozy could create considerable doubt with that revelation.

But Lucy had also told Cozy and Lauren that if the reason she was in the Peterson home that night was known, everyone would be convinced that she had a motive for Royal's murder.

I couldn't make sense of that.

And, of course, I hadn't heard anything yet that would account for the wet spot.

Lucy turned back toward the room. She wasn't holding the collar of her robe this time.

"We're intimate now, aren't we, Alan?"

I thought, *Whoa*. She saw the puzzlement in my face.

"I've certainly been open with you . . . and, God knows, I've never been more vulnerable in my life than I am right now."

CHAPTER

28

Lucy Tanner was the only child of a man named Charles Tanner and a free-spirited woman he'd met at a sit-in in a bank in Ann Arbor, Michigan, in 1969. The woman's name was Susie Pine. Lucy's conception predated Charles and Susie's subsequent marriage by almost six months. Susie's friends were much more surprised that Susie Pine married at all than they were that she never adopted her husband's last name.

The Tanner-Pine marriage endured, at least as far as the state of Michigan was concerned, for seven years. The reason that Susie gave when she initially left her husband and daughter in Ann Arbor was that she felt she had to go to the bedside of her older sister, who was dying of breast cancer in Tucson. Six weeks later, two days after her sister's Arizona funeral, Susie Pine packed up the things she wanted from her sister's house and moved to Boulder. Within days, she filed for divorce from her husband, Charles.

She never returned to Ann Arbor.

The divorce was uncontested, and custody of the minor child, Lucy, was awarded to Charles Tanner. He remarried two years later and his second attempt at marriage was much more successful than his first.

Lucy's adolescence was less tumultuous than her childhood had been, and she considered herself to be a relatively confident, though shy, young person when she graduated high school near the top of her class and moved west to attend Colorado College in Colorado Springs.

Lucy told me that her move west for school had nothing to do with a desire to reconnect with the mother who had abandoned her during her childhood. She maintained that she chose Colorado College solely because of its unique curriculum.

The psychologist in me noted her resistance, but I wasn't in Lucy's flat to give her a boost up on some eventual psychotherapy, I was there to be her friend. I bit my tongue and kept my thoughts about unconscious motivation to myself.

Susie Pine became Susan Peterson a little more than a year after her divorce from Charles Tanner. She and her new husband, an ambitious thirty-year-old prosecuting attorney named Royal, had two children during the first two years of their marriage, and added a third three years later.

One year after the completion of his family Royal Peterson won his first term as district attorney of Boulder County.

When did you find her for the first time?" I asked.

"I didn't even know if she was still in town when I joined the police department. I figured there was as good a chance that she had moved away as there was that she was still here. I never looked for her. That's not true. I checked the phone book once—does that count? Then I went to a reception when they opened the new coroner's offices in the Justice Center. That was about, I'm not sure, four or five years ago. She was there with Royal."

"You recognized her?"

"Sure. Susan had aged well. But I grew up with lots of photographs of her. My father is quite the amateur photographer and he always wanted me to know who my mother was. But she didn't recognize me. And I didn't talk to her that night. Not at all."

A cuckoo clock chirped once. I'd been wondering what time it was. Now I knew. I was also wondering how people survived living with cuckoo clocks. I still didn't know that.

"I finally went and saw her after I heard rumors about her illness. You know, her MS. I don't know why, exactly. Compassion? More likely pity, I guess. That, or it was just a good excuse to see her so I could try to begin to understand how she could leave her daughter so cavalierly. It was probably a combination."

I was uncomfortable with the way Lucy was referring to herself. "Her daughter was you, Lucy."

"Yeah. Her daughter was me. But, let's face it, I'm not the only kid who's ever been left behind by a parent. I remind myself of that a lot. Being left behind by my mother is not an excuse to let myself be damaged for life. My dad raised me well. My stepmother is a sweetheart. Whatever mistakes my father made with women, he got them out of his system by marrying her."

"Does reminding yourself that you're not the only child who's been left behind by a parent help?"

"Not much." She sighed. "I was terrified that first time that I went to her house to see her. Not that she'd slam the door in my face. My biggest fear? My biggest fear was that I was going to adore her, like instantly, the moment I set my eyes on her. As a girl, I'd idealized her after she left. My father was always kind; he never criticized her and I was left to create this image of her that had almost no basis in reality. She was as pretty as a movie star, as kind as the best mother in the world. Anyway, going to see her that day, I felt that some angel was going to answer the door. And I was afraid that the more it turned out that I adored her, the angrier I was going to be that she'd left me behind. Does that make sense?"

"Of course."

Lucy's voice grew small. "But it didn't turn out that way. I didn't like her. I didn't like her at all. She was critical, belittling, selfish. She wasn't this benevolent soul who'd left me to tend to my ill aunt. She was Susan Peterson. You must have gotten to know her through the DA's office. Didn't you? Lauren worked for her husband for years. You had to have known her at least a little bit."

"I've known her socially, yes."

"Do you like her?"

I managed a complete inhale and exhale before I responded, trying to find an alternative way to answer Lucy's question than the one I ended up with: "She can be difficult."

Lucy shook her head. "Please," she said. "You're being diplomatic. Difficult? That's an understatement if I ever heard one. Susan Peterson is a very unpleasant human being. On her best days, she's a bitch."

I forced a small smile. "At least the problem of adoring her never quite materialized."

Lucy didn't crack a smile. "Right," she said bitterly. "At least there was that."

This was the point where Lucy sat all the way back on the sofa, crossed her legs, folded her arms, and told me that the whole story was going to be printed in the next morning's *Daily Camera*.

A good-sized chunk of an hour later Lucy seemed to have run out of words. It was time for me to head home. I told her so.

She nodded.

I said, "One more thing before I go. Lauren and Cozy were trying to get in touch with you tonight. Did they reach you?"

"I got a message from each of them. I wasn't in any mood to call them back. I'll talk to them in the morning. They'll have a lot of questions about the *Daily Camera* article anyway."

I nodded. If I hadn't been so tired, I would have been thinking more clearly, and I think I would have left things alone at that point. I didn't.

"The reason they were calling? Lauren told me when I went to pick her up after you left my office. The police found some laundry, Lucy, in the Peterson home. Some unwashed laundry, including a sheet—a bedsheet—with a stain on it. The lab has identified the stain as being dried vaginal secretions. They're working under the suspicion that when the DNA analysis finally comes back, they're going to discover that the vaginal secretions are yours."

For some reason I found myself contemplating when I'd last used the phrase "vaginal secretions" in a sentence. I decided that it hadn't been recently.

Her eyes widened. "Oh boy," she said. The words almost disappeared in a rapid inhale.

I waited a moment and stated the obvious. "You're not totally surprised, are you, Lucy?"

She was looking off to the side, into the dark room. "What am I supposed to say? That I can't believe it? That there's no way it's true? Okay, I'll say it: I can't believe it. There's no way it's true."

I'm supposed to be good at reading people and I wasn't sure whether or not she even intended for me to believe her.

She grabbed a pillow from the sofa, hugged it to her chest, and began rocking back and forth from the waist, slowly. "Alan, I'm being careful with you. You're not my attorney and you're not my therapist. There're certain lines I can't cross with you. Do you understand?"

"I understand. Maybe I should have just kept my mouth shut about the sheets, Lucy. I thought you'd want to know what the police had found. But this could have waited till tomorrow. I'm sorry I brought it up. I should have left it to Lauren and Cozy. I apologize."

"Don't. I appreciate it, Alan. I appreciate all you've done. Coming over here tonight was kind."

"I'll tell Lauren I was here, Lucy."

"I know. It makes no difference. By this time tomorrow I won't have many secrets left. You know," she added, "I told you I was going to make the rest of the phone calls to the Ramps that are listed in the phone book. I did, reached three more. Two of them I'm not sure I can rule out, so I'm going to go track them down tomorrow in person. With all that's happened tonight . . . I know I'm going to feel like getting out of Boulder. Maybe I'll get lucky and find the kid."

I knew that everything Lucy was suggesting was true. Whatever scrutiny she had received from the media up until then was only a warm-up to the firestorm she could expect after the news of her relationship to Susan Peterson hit the wires in the morning. And, regardless of the press coverage, one of us did have to continue our efforts to try to find Ramp.

"You'll go in the morning?"

She nodded. "Yeah. One of them lives all the way out near Agate."

"Where's Agate?"

"Out east on I-70, just before you get to Limon."

I blurted, "Limon is where Ramp and Paul played around with the explosives."

She cocked her head. "You didn't tell me that."

"I thought I did."

"Well, you didn't."

"My patient told me that Paul went out to some ranch near Limon and he and Ramp blew up a car or something."

"You didn't tell me any of this." The suffix "you idiot" was understood by both of us.

"I'm sorry."

"There's a listing out near Agate for a man named Herbert Ramp. Herbert's dead, but his widow, Ella, answered the phone. When I asked about a son or grandson, she kind of hung up on me."

"So it may be him?"

"You say the two boys played around with bombs out there? Damn right it may be him. I'm definitely going to go talk to her tomorrow."

"Maybe I should do it instead, Lucy. She may be wary of a cop showing up at her door."

"But a shrink from Boulder won't raise her suspicions at all?"

The tendons in the back of my neck felt like rebar. "I'm not sure what's best, which one of us should meet her. Let me think about it overnight, okay? We'll talk in the morning?"

"Yeah. Call me around nine; I think I'm going to try to sleep in a little bit. Use my cell; I'm not going to be answering my phone."

I stood to leave and opened my arms to give Lucy a hug. First, she dropped the pillow, then she leaned into the embrace with a hunger I didn't expect. When she finally released me, I turned toward the door. My hand on the knob, I stopped and asked, "Lucy, were you having an affair with Royal?"

The silence that followed was eerie. For the first few seconds, I suspected that she wasn't going to respond, and I wasn't surprised. I was already questioning my judgment in asking the question. Finally, I turned my head to look at her to examine the impact of my question.

The cuckoo clock chirped twice.

Lucy had spun away from me. Although I couldn't be sure from the reflection she made in the glass doors, I thought she was crying.

Our eyes met in the black glass. She said, "I wish it was that simple, Alan. I wish it was that simple."

Outside, the snow wasn't sticking to the streets, but the sidewalks were wet. The tree buds and flowers looked as though they'd been frosted.

The alarm clock cracked me awake at six-thirty. Lauren was already up with Grace. Before I climbed in the shower, I wasted a minute trying to decide how many hours of sleep I'd had. Before I reached a number that felt correct, I concluded that the answer was simply "not enough."

After a quick shower and shave I joined my family in the kitchen. I was most of the way through a condensed rendition of the previous night's events for Lauren's benefit when my pager went off. Moments later, I was back in the master bedroom closet trying to simultaneously get dressed and maintain a conversation with Naomi Bigg.

She wasted no time. "Can I see you today? Any time at all. I'll leave work. Please."

"Just a second," I said while I zipped up my trousers

and began to thread a belt around my waist. "I have to go get my calendar." I moved from the closet to the bedroom and retrieved my schedule from beside the bed. I was still undecided about trying to run out to Limon or Agate to see Ella Ramp. I didn't know where I could stick an emergency appointment.

She said, "Please, please. What we've been talking about with the kids? It's come to a head, I think. What you've been—what I've been . . . you know. Anyway, this morning, I found a . . . I found something that's convinced me that I need to . . ." Her voice faded away. "Please," she repeated.

Almost impulsively, I said, "Four-thirty this afternoon. I'm afraid that's all I have, Naomi."

"Four-thirty? Is that right? Okay, okay."

I could feel the pressure building. "Can it wait till then? Do you want to take a minute right now, Naomi, and tell me what—"

She hung up.

"I guess not," I said aloud.

"You guess not what?" Lauren asked from the doorway. Grace was asleep in her arms.

"A patient hung up on me in the middle of our conversation."

"Oh," she said, disinterested. She tilted her head back toward the kitchen. "The story about Lucy's mother is on the news. They make it sound awful. As though the fact that Susan is Lucy's mother gives Lucy a reason to murder Royal. It doesn't make any sense."

"They don't know about the wet spot?"

Lauren covered Grace's ears.

"No, they don't know about the wet spot."

"Well, I'm not surprised the press is making it look bad. That seems to be their job," I said. "I'm late—I need to get downtown. You're okay with Grace until Viv gets here?"

"I'm fine," she replied. She kissed the top of the baby's head. "We're great."

The previous night's snow was history. The faintest reminder of the storm still clung as transparent white frosting feathering the highest reaches of the Flatirons, but otherwise the morning was brilliant and warm and the city bore no evidence of the midnight flurries.

Lucy didn't answer her cell when I tried her a few minutes before nine, nor when I tried again at nine forty-five.

I finished with my nine forty-five patient right on time at ten-thirty. As soon as he was out the door, I checked my voice mail and retrieved two messages. One was a cancellation by my one o'clock, the other another call from Naomi.

"It's me again. I'm sorry I'm so scattered. You said four-thirty, didn't you? If that's not right, call me at the office. I can't tell you how much I need to see you. There's another bomb. That lawyer."

That was it.

There's another bomb. That lawyer.

I replayed the message to assure myself that that was what she had said.

There's another bomb. That lawyer.

Shit. I decided that I couldn't wait any longer to find out what Ramp was up to. I called Lucy one more time. Finally, she answered. She was already far from Boulder—at a diner outside Fort Lupton where she'd stopped to have a late breakfast—on her way to the eastern plains. She didn't argue when I told her that I wanted to meet her. I jotted down directions to Ella Ramp's ranch, which was almost precisely halfway between Limon and Agate, and I hustled out the door. From my car I canceled lunch with a colleague and all my remaining therapy appointments until my four-thirty emergency session with Naomi.

It took me almost an hour to plunge through the northern congestion of Denver's metropolitan area and intersect with Interstate 70 on my journey toward Limon, the little town that is the geographic bull's-eye in the center of Colorado's eastern plains.

Many people who have never visited Colorado have a mental image that the state consists predominantly of mountains. Sharp juvenile peaks, high meadows, glacial faces, deep canyons. Travel magazine stuff.

But if a driver heads east away from the Front Range, especially if he's beyond the boundaries of Denver's metropolitan sprawl, and if he doesn't glance back into his rearview mirror, the state of Colorado is hardly distinguishable from Nebraska or Iowa or Kansas. Less corn, more wheat, but mostly mile after mile of mind-numbing Great Plains high prairie. Some people love it, others don't. Either way, the broad expanse of endless horizon and infinite sky takes up roughly half the state.

I'm convinced that if highway planners hadn't chosen the Limon-to-Agate spur for Interstate 70's northwest traverse across the eastern prairie toward Denver, virtually no one would have any reason to be aware exactly where either Agate or Limon is. Nor would anyone care much. In fact, absent the wide ribbon of interstate, Colorado's eastern plains are geographically pretty close to nowhere, and one look at the map confirms that Limon and Agate are about as close to the middle as is theoretically possible.

I made only one wrong turn as I was navigating the grid of county roads east of Agate, and found the Ramp spread on my first try. As I made the last turn, I spotted Lucy's red Volvo parked in the shadow of a huge stack of hay. The lead-gray color of the straw told me that it hadn't been baled or stacked recently. I stopped and got out of my car.

"You been waiting long?" I asked Lucy.

"Half an hour, forty minutes."

"Sorry, I went as fast as I could."

"It's okay, I'm just killing time today anyway. The house is right down there. Why don't we leave your car here, just take mine. I don't want to spook her any more than we already will."

The Ramp home was a sixties-style suburban ranch house that seemed out of place without a few dozen clones crammed around it on six-thousand-square-foot lots. An uninterrupted line of spreading junipers was the only vegetation around the house. A solitary tree— I thought it was a hackberry—stood at the edge of a field about fifty yards to the east.

Lucy drove past the house once before she doubled back toward the driveway. I wasted a moment trying to decide how nearby Ella Ramp's closest neighbor lived. Distances were great out there, and I guessed it was almost a mile between houses.

An impeccably preserved brown Ford pickup—the vintage was late sixties or early seventies—was parked on the dirt drive, not far from the house. Lucy parked behind the truck and we walked to the front door. She knocked. I was already having second thoughts about being out there; a good-sized part of me wished that I'd instead stayed in Boulder and moved up my appointment with Naomi Bigg.

There's another bomb, she'd said. *That lawyer.*

I nearly jumped when I heard somebody say, "Hell!"

Half a minute or so later the door opened. "What?" squealed the woman who stood in the doorway. She was a wiry woman who'd once been of average height, but her frame was beginning to bow to gravity and osteoporosis. Her hair was as gray as slate and her eyes were a blue that glowed like the ocean in the tropics.

"What?" the woman repeated in the same acidic tone. Despite her posture, I pegged her at only about sixty.

Lucy said, "Hello, I'm, um, Lucy Tanner. I—"

"So what?"

Lucy moved back six or eight inches. "We spoke on the phone. I called about your grandson. Do you remember? May I come in?"

"Are you nuts? No, you can't come in. Didn't your mother ever tell you to wait to be invited? Where are your manners? And of course I remember. How many calls like that do you think I get? I'm not feeble."

At the first hollered "Hell!" I'd shifted into clinical mode. This woman—who answered her door by squealing "What?" and who had just called Lucy nuts—was now questioning her manners. I said, "Hello, I, um—"

She stepped right on my words, ignoring me, instead retaining her focus on Lucy. "You a cop?" she asked.

"Excuse me?" Lucy said.

"On TV, the cops always ask to come in. They never wait till they're invited. Something happen to my boy? Are you a cop?"

"I am actually, but I'm not here today as—"

Ella Ramp pushed out the door and shuffled past us. "Come on. I have to check on the chickens. I bet my ass you've never checked on a chicken in your life. I'm right, ain't I? Never mind, I know I'm right. That," she said, pointing at Lucy's Volvo, "ain't no chicken-checker's car."

The henhouse was about thirty yards away, out back. Lucy and I waited while Ella disappeared inside for about three or four minutes. Because she was stooped over, she fit right inside the coop door.

Lucy whispered, "She's . . . interesting, isn't she?"

"Yes," I said. "She is."

Ella shuffled back out and double-checked the clasp on the fence around the henhouse.

I asked, "Has he been out to visit you lately? Your boy?" I was careful to mimic the language she'd used to describe her grandson.

"What's it to you? And who the hell are you, anyway?" Her tone lightened suddenly as she said, "The chickens are fine, by the way, thanks for asking."

"My name is Alan Gregory, and I'm—"

"Well, whoop-dee-do." She turned to Lucy. "You his new girlfriend, missy? He knock you up? Is that why you've come out here? He's got a thing with the girls. And they certainly have a thing with him. But knocking up a cop? Did he? He didn't. Hell's another."

Hell's another? Hell's a mother? I wasn't sure what Ella had said or what on earth it was supposed to mean.

"No, I'm, um, not pregnant."

Ella stopped. She had to crane her neck to look up at Lucy. "Dearest God, you're tall. You're taller than he is. That'd be awkward in my book. But you're not . . . you and he, you're not . . . ?"

"No, we're not."

"That's for the best, I suppose. But you haven't told me why you are here, have you?"

While Lucy sputtered to find a way to reply, I said, "It's about the explosives, Mrs. Ramp."

"Oh, that," Ella replied in a dismissive voice as she shuffled back toward the house. "I thought he was in trouble or something."

Ella busied herself fixing coffee and I agreed to accept a cup even though I would've preferred a glass of water. Lucy, who despised coffee, took one, too. On the way from the front door to the kitchen, I'd tried to spot a collection of framed family photographs, hoping to see a photo of Ella's grandson. But the living room was spare in its decor and the only photographs in sight were of pets. Mostly horses, but also a dog. A huge dog. I thought it was a mastiff, but I wasn't sure.

Ella's kitchen was as spotless as her truck. The pristine room could have been lifted out of the house in one chunk and installed—intact—in some granite edifice as a museum exhibit about life in 1962. Maybe part of a Dwight-and-Mamie-Eisenhower-at-home exhibit at the Smithsonian. The old refrigerator was a Norge and it hummed at a volume that screamed for someone to clean its coils.

The only modern appliance in the kitchen was a little white color television. Ella had it tuned to one of the Denver stations. She turned the sound down all the way before she served the coffee.

Ella said, "Milk? Sugar? I don't use 'em, but I can find 'em if you want 'em."

"No, thank you," I said.

Lucy added, "Black is fine."

"He came by the explosives legal, by the way. They were Herbert's. I told the boy he could experiment with them the way Herbert taught him. The neighbors don't mind; they're used to it by now. It's been going on for at least a quarter century. You know you're getting old when you hear yourself talking in quarter centuries."

I hesitated a moment to see if Lucy was planning to take the lead. She wasn't. I raised the cup to my lips and tried to sound nonchalant as I replied, "The explosives were Herbert's?"

"Who did you say you were? Are you like her lawyer or something?"

"No, I'm Alan Gregory, Dr. Alan Gregory. I'm a psychologist in Boulder."

"Well, what the hell are you doing out here?"

"The explosives," I said. "We came to talk with you about the explosives."

She harrumphed. "You ever been to Las Vegas?" asked Ella.

Lucy said she had driven through, but never stopped. I added, "I've been there a few times."

"Well, I'm proud to say that my Herbert blew up half that damn town. Maybe more than half."

"He did? He blew up half the town?" I didn't have a clue what she was talking about, but was eager to keep her talking about it.

"You know the company called Demolition Specialists? Doesn't matter whether you do or you don't. They're some of the boys who blow up those big buildings all over the place. You always see 'em on the national news, usually on Sunday. They blow most of the big buildings on Sunday on account of there aren't so many people around. People are drawn to explosions for some reason. Like bugs to light, I think. What they do is they implode the buildings actually, so that they fall in on themselves.

"Herbert was a demolition engineer. He worked for Demolition Specialists for most of our marriage. He traveled the world blowing up buildings. Blew up stuff in Japan and Saudi Arabia. Toward the end he was on the team that did all those big demos in Las Vegas. The old casinos? You see those monsters come down on the news? I flew out with him and watched the Sands Hotel come down. That was some week we had, let me tell you. Fireworks, buffets, slot machines, girls dancing around wearin' nothing over their tits. I joked that they'd all lost their shirts gamblin'. Herbert liked that part best, I think, the girls. That was a weekend." Ella smiled at the memory.

It was easy to smile right back at her. "So that's what Herbert did for a living? He blew up buildings? And he took down those old casinos in Vegas?"

"Not just him. He was a team player. You might not think it, but it takes a mess of people to bring down a skyscraper. Takes weeks to get one ready to come down. He was gone half the time, Herbert."

"And he's dead now, Ella?"

"With the Lord." She touched her heart.

"I'm sorry. And the explosives that your grandson

uses for his experiments? They belonged to Herbert?"
I asked.

"Yes, they did. In between jobs, Herbert did
research. His thing was shaped charges. He was always
playing around with shaped charges and the best way
to cut metal. That was his specialty: cutting metal with
shaped charges. Kept material here for his research.
Mostly dynamite, I think. But some other things, too.
I never paid much attention. We got a shed he had
built special. It's more like a vault than a shed, to tell
the truth. Herbert had a thing about security of his
explosives. Wrong hands, you know?"

I wouldn't have known a shaped charge if I was sitting on one, and now I found myself yearning to have
Sam Purdy beside me. Lucy sounded like she was better informed than I when she said, "I always wondered
who did the shaped-charge research. That's remarkable about Herbert. And he taught your grandson what
he knew?"

"A lot of it, he sure did. Always thought that the boy
might follow in his footsteps. Herbert would've loved
to have lived long enough to make the boy an appren-
tice in the company. Can't go to college to learn to do
what Herbert knew about bringing down buildings.
Herbert always said as long as there are bad architects
and worse builders, there'll be a need for people like
him. Can I get you all some more coffee?"

I shook my head and pretended to take another sip
of coffee. Lucy said, "Do you know how I can reach
him? Your grandson? I have some questions for him."

Ella Ramp set her cup on its saucer and stared at her. "You said you're a cop. Now's about the time where you should be getting around to telling me why you want him."

"The truth is, I need to talk with him about the explosives."

Ella stretched her neck from side to side. It appeared that the act caused considerable pain. Midway through the stretch, Ella said, "I'm getting old, I know that. As far as I'm concerned, it's premature, but so be it. Life is what life is. Mine? I live by myself a hundred miles from life as most city people know it. I know more about chickens and horses and dogs than I do about people. I'm stooped over and I'm gray and when I dare myself to look in a mirror I usually conclude that I'm butt ugly. But I'm not particularly stupid. Now stop repeating yourself and tell me what the hell you want with my grandson. What about the damn explosives?"

I took a moment to try to decide how to play this. As a psychologist, I actually adored moments like these. Some of my most memorable conversations with Sam Purdy had been discussions about how to play situations just like this one with Ella.

"Ella," I finally said, "I could bullshit you right now. I could. I'm good at it and despite the fact that I believe you when you say that you are a bright woman, I think I could succeed in bullshitting you. But I won't. So here's the truth: The reason we're trying to find your grandson is that we think he may be responsible for setting some bombs that have hurt some people."

Ella sipped at her coffee. She narrowed her eyes as though she was protecting them from the steam. She asked, "That one in Denver last week? Where that woman died in that car? That's one of 'em?"

"Yes, that's one of them."

She appeared to be puzzled. "Why would he do that? Why would the boy do that?"

Lucy said, "We think he might be angry at law enforcement or the justice system. The courts."

Lucy's words assaulted Ella like a physical blow. Her breath caught in her chest, her eyes closed in a wince, and the fingernails of her right hand cut sharply into the skin of her left arm.

I waited for Ella's next move, which I assumed would be an awkward denial that her grandson was angry at the criminal justice system. But Ella didn't protest. Instead, she narrowed her eyes again and stared at me hard, then glanced over at the TV. "You're that girl who they think killed her momma's husband, aren't you? From up in Boulder? You're the girl from the news this morning?"

Despite her best efforts to maintain her detective's poker face, I could feel Lucy's demeanor change as she tried to process the question.

Ella shook her head in a wide arc. "Well, hell's another. Hell's a—nuh—ther. My own momma always said to wake up looking forward to each day because you never really know what's going to come along with the dawn. But I swear it's been a while since I've had a day quite like this one. A girl from the morning news program sitting right here in my kitchen."

I lifted my cup again but didn't actually get it to my lips before Ella cracked a little smile and said, "So tell me, missy, you have a gun under that jacket? You planning to shoot me if I don't talk?"

Lucy exclaimed, "What?" But she left both hands on the table where Ella could see them. "No, Ella, I'm not going to shoot you."

The tension between the two women was suddenly as thick as butter. I interjected, "But we would like to talk a little bit about how the boy's mother died, Ella. Could we do that?"

Ella burped a tiny burp and covered her mouth. She looked away and closed her eyes, holding them tightly shut.

"Ella?" I said.

"Hell's another," she muttered. "Hell's another."

30

I never used to curse before she died. Not even in anger. Certainly not just for the hell of it like I do now. The man who killed her stuck one knife in her chest and he stuck another one in my soul."

Hell's another.

I was still unsure what relation Ramp's mother was to Ella. I asked, "His mother was your daughter-in-law, Ella?"

"No, no, no. Denise was our daughter. Herbert and me had one daughter, one son. Our son—that's Brian—he died in a Humvee accident in Somalia. He was a medic in the Marines at the time. It was on the news."

Ella sighed quickly—almost a gasp—before she continued. "Then Denise was murdered in Denver. Bang, bang. Strike one, strike two."

"I didn't know. I'm so sorry."

"Brian—that's our son—he was trying to do good when he died. Humanitarian assistance in Somalia. That's in Africa. He was a peacekeeper. A Marine peacekeeper. Herbert always thought it was an oxy— whaddyacallit?"

"Oxymoron."

"Yeah. Oxymoron. Doesn't matter. Fact is, Brian was a peacekeeper at heart. His death was just one of those things that preachers can't explain no matter how hard they try or how long they talk on Sunday mornings about God's mysterious ways. Herbert was philosophical about it, said it could just as easily have been a pickup truck accident on I-70 that killed Brian. If I'd had a bet to place, I would've rather bet my son's life on the pickup and the interstate, you know what I mean?"

I said I did.

Ella required no further prompting. She said, "But Denise?" She shook her head as though trying to cleanse an image of something she'd rather not recall. "It was four years, five months ago. Two weeks before Christmas. She was living with her husband, Patrick, in Denver, in the neighborhood they call Uptown. You know it?"

"Vaguely," I said. Years before during my first marriage, when I'd spent more time in Denver, the neighborhood was called North Capitol Hill. Now dubbed Uptown on the Hill, the compact urban neighborhood just northeast of downtown was an interesting multi-ethnic place with a range of residents who varied widely in financial wherewithal. Despite its new name, though, the neighborhood wasn't on much of a hill. Recently refurbished late-nineteenth-century homes sat adjacent to massive redevelopment projects, vacant lots, and old apartment houses gone to seed.

"Denise was a nurse at one of the hospitals nearby. Presbyterian? She liked the neighborhood because she could walk to work and because there were all kinds of people living there. That was her way of telling us that life there was nothing like being out here in Agate. The whole time she and Pat were there, they didn't even know it but three doors down from their old Denver square was a rooming house that was actually a halfway house, you know, a place for released criminals. The ones who've been, whaddyacallit, paroled?"

"Yes," Lucy said, "paroled."

Ella had already shared enough details that I thought I knew the rest of the story. A Denver woman had been stabbed to death by a guy on parole for a previous murder conviction. I remembered the story from news reports and I recalled discussing it in some detail with Sam over a couple of beers one night.

Sam had been especially irate about the crime. The practice of releasing dangerous felons on early parole was an issue that bugged cops more than it bugged anybody else. Except, maybe, the families of the paroled felon's last victims, or the families of his next victims.

"He'd been in the halfway house for a few months," Ella told us. "Luther Smith is his name. He'd served four years, five months, three days for a manslaughter conviction in Commerce City before he was released into a halfway house in Denver. Why there? Why right down the street from my girl? Who knows? But he was living in that halfway house when he began following my Denise to work and deciding that since she worked at a hospital she might be keeping drugs at her house. That's what he told the police anyway; that's the way he explained breaking into her place and ransacking it and waiting for her to come home from work that day.

"Pat—her husband—worked as a pressman at the *Denver Post*. He was gone evenings. Denise thought she was coming home to an empty house. But she wasn't. Luther Smith was there waiting for her and he was mad as hell because he hadn't found any drugs anywhere in the house."

Ella thrust her chin forward. I could see the effort she was using in her attempt to control the quivering that had erupted.

"He began to try to rape my little girl and she fought him like a banshee. That's what the cops said. She fought him as hard as any woman has ever fought off any man. That's what they told me and Herbert.

"So Luther Smith stabbed her. He did it just once. Sliced right through some big artery at the top of her stomach. And my Denise bled to death right there in her own bedroom. It was Jason who found her when he got home from a football game at his high school that night."

Jason, I said to myself. *He has a name. The bomber has a name. It's Jason, but not Jason Ramp. Ramp's his mother's name. It's Jason what?*

To Ella, I said, "I'm so sorry. You've had so much loss."

Lucy added, "I'm so sorry, too. What happened to your daughter is awful. Inexcusable."

Ella frosted her voice with defeat. "He didn't rape her. Coroner said he didn't rape her. I sometimes find myself wishing that he had. Wishing she hadn't fought him so hard so she might be alive."

Her words covered the contours of the irony of rape like upholstery covers an old sofa. "I'm so sorry, Ella," I said again. There should have been better words, but if there were, I didn't know them.

"I still go to church every Sunday, you know. Despite what God allowed to be done to my children. I made a pledge to keep giving Him a chance to explain Himself until the day that I die."

Lucy said, "It's my understanding that your grandson calls himself Ramp, still. That's in honor of his mother?"

"No, our name—his mother's maiden name—is his middle name. The boy's name is Jason Ramp Bass. His friends started calling him Ramp sometime in high school. Something about skateboarding I never understood. There's a lot about skateboarding I never understood." Ella sighed. "You get to be my age, you realize the list of things you never understood is a hell of a long one."

Lucy and I sat at the kitchen table with Ella for quite a while early that afternoon, learning about Denise and Pat, and the boy his grandmother called Jase.

"Pat couldn't manage Jase after Denise died. Boy gave him no end of trouble. So he came out here to live with me and Herbert. Jase didn't like it out here in the country but he adjusted okay. I give Herbert most of the credit for that. When Herbert was in town between demo jobs, the boy and him were inseparable. Always doing things together. Mostly cutting steel with explosives. Herbert said that the boy had a knack with explosives."

From the corner of my eye, I could see the screen on the television set on the counter. A teaser for the evening news was running. I wasn't sure if Lucy saw it, too, but assuming that Lucy's story was about to be featured, I knew that I didn't want Ella to be reminded of Lucy's recent notoriety.

I stood, carrying dishes toward the sink.

"Don't do that," Ella said. "I'll clean up."

"It's not a bother—it's the way I was brought up," I said. I switched the TV off before I stacked the dishes. "I hope you don't mind that I turned it off. It's distracting me."

"Oh, I don't mind. It's only there for company. And I've already got company, today."

"Where's Jase now? In Denver?" Lucy asked.

"Mmm-hmm. Denver. He works for a welding company. It's something else that Herbert taught him. Herbert was always cutting metal and welding metal for his experiments."

"Shaped charges," Lucy said.

"That's right." One side of Ella's mouth elevated in a smile. "You don't know what they are, do you?"

"No," she admitted. "I don't. I don't have a clue what a shaped charge is."

Ella laughed so hard she started to cough from a place deep in the recesses of her lungs. When she finally controlled the spasm, she said, "You two are going to go talk to him now, aren't you? Once you leave here."

Lucy and I both nodded.

"Figured. Well, I'll save you some time and tell you where to find him, but I want to talk to him first. I should also talk to Pat, his father, let him know what you told me. Once I do those two things, I'll tell you where to find Jase. If he really did what you say, well . . . But I want you to remember something, too. I want you to remember that the boy was hurt by his mother's death. You'll remember that? We've all been hurt by what happened."

I said, "Of course."

Lucy wrote her phone numbers on a sheet of paper and gave it to Ella. She said, "That's fair, Ella. You give me a call after you talk to Jason and his father, okay?"

Ella looked back up at me before she spoke to Lucy. "Right now, you're acting like you're going to wait to talk to Jase until I call you. But you won't wait. You're going to go try to find him as soon as you leave here. You're going to go out to your fancy car and get on your cell phone and call your cop friends or you're going to use some computer whizbang and do some magic thing that the police do on TV and you're going to try and find him. Clear as dew, you'd lie to an old woman."

Lucy said, "To track down whoever has been setting those bombs, Ella, I'd lie to every old woman I could find."

Ella opened a drawer that was recessed into the side of the kitchen table. She reached in and slid out a huge revolver. I thought it might be a .45. It was clean and gleamed with fresh oil. Ella rested the weapon on the table, the barrel pointed only slightly away from Lucy.

My heart galloped.

"I like you both," Ella said. "I do."

I thought, *Hell's another.*

CHAPTER

31

Lucy dropped me off back at my car. I would've loved to have had some time to reflect with her over what we'd just learned—or, at the very least, to hear what she thought about Ella's revolver—but I had to rush to Boulder to have a prayer of getting back for my appointment with Naomi.

I held up my watch and said, "If I make it to my office on time, I'm meeting with her this afternoon." I was still reluctant to use my patient's name in conversation.

Lucy wasn't. She said, "You're seeing Naomi?"

"She said she had some news for me, something important. But what we just learned from Ella can't wait for that—Sam needs to know everything we heard right now. So do the Denver Police."

"I'll do that, don't worry," she said. "I know who to

talk to. And maybe the fact that it comes from me will earn me some redemption."

I spent the long drive back to Boulder watching my mirrors for a State Patrol cruiser and trying to prepare myself for what I expected would be a difficult session with Naomi.

When I got to my office and entered through the rear doors, it was only four-twenty but the red light on the far wall was already beaming. Naomi Bigg wasn't only on time for her extra appointment, she was early. And, given what Lucy and I had discovered about Ramp earlier that afternoon, I was more than ready for the meeting. I took a deep breath and made long strides down the hall to greet her.

But the woman I found standing in the middle of the waiting room wasn't Naomi Bigg.

She heard me open the door and barely threw a glance my way before she demanded, "Where is she? Is she back there? Where is she?"

The voice was frantic and distinctly young. The speaker was, too. When I didn't reply right away, she immediately turned back to scan the street, spying at something through the window.

I guessed that she was in her late teens, early twenties. She was blond and overweight. How overweight was hard to tell; her clothes hung on her like curtains. One eyebrow was pierced and adorned with a thin gold ring. Her hair was cut, well, badly, and dyed even worse, though I suspected that the aesthetic impact of the coiffure was intentional. I thought that there was something unusual about her makeup as well but couldn't decide exactly what. Maybe it was the color around her eyes.

"May I help you?" I asked.

"You're her doctor? My mother's doctor? Is she back there? God, this is important! Is she fucking back there yet? I need to talk to her!"

She'd begun screaming at me.

"No, she's not here yet. You're Marin, aren't you?"

She nodded and returned her attention to the window. I could see her shoulders rise and fall with each rapid breath.

I said, "I expect her any minute. You can talk to her then. In the meantime, is there anything that I can do to help you while—"

She raised her arms up above her head and then dropped them quickly past her waist, as though she were signaling the start of a race. "Oh my God, where is she? I can't believe he'd do this. I never thought he'd do this. It's not what she thinks. It isn't what she thinks."

"Who'd do what?" Her terror was infectious. Naomi's message was still echoing in my ears. I was beginning to become aware of pressure building in my chest, my pulse pounding at the veins in my neck.

There's another bomb. That lawyer.

Marin shook her head, exasperated. "Does she park here? In front? Or do you have a parking lot?"

I stared at her, stammering in an effort to start a sentence.

"When she comes to visit you, goddamn it, where the hell does she park her damn car?"

"Patients usually park on the street. But I've never watched where your mother parks her car."

She looked up. "Is that a siren? Oh my God, oh my God. Do you hear that? In the distance. Is that a siren?"

I listened. I didn't hear a siren. I said so.

"What time is it?" she demanded. She seemed to have totally forgotten about the phantom siren.

I looked at my watch. Employing a voice that tried to reflect a pretense that I wasn't talking to a histrionic stranger, I said, "Four twenty-five. A little after."

"Is she late?"

"No. She's not due here for a few more minutes." I had no right to share that information, but I didn't even consider the possibility of not answering Marin Bigg's question.

Marin pointed outside and screamed, "There she is! There's her car. See it? That's it!"

I looked through the glass and saw the BMW that Naomi had been driving when she'd pulled up next to Lauren and me at the stoplight the day before. She was right out front of my building, backing expertly into a parking space that was only a few feet longer than her car. A cigarette dangled from her lips. Even from this distance I could tell that the ash was precariously long.

Marin ran out the door, waving her arms as though

she were intent on bringing a runaway train to a halt. She started yelling, "Mom! Mom! Don't stop the car! Don't stop the car! Get out and leave it running. Mom! Mom!"

I was totally perplexed. I followed her outside.

Marin leapt off the little porch, still waving her arms. "Mom! Mom! Here! Don't stop the car! *Mom!* Don't—"

Naomi stopped the car. The reassuring BMW purr clicked off.

Marin covered her ears.

I exhaled.

Marin had stopped screaming as suddenly as if someone had pulled the plug on her power source.

Her voice now hollow, she said, "It didn't . . . He didn't . . . Mom, Mom. You're okay, Mom."

She may have actually finished those first two sentences, but I was still on the porch, fifteen or twenty feet behind her, and I couldn't hear her well.

Naomi climbed out of the BMW and stood on the street right beside the still-open door of her car. She took a moment to straighten her clothes, tugging down the bottom of a short-sleeved jacket. Her shoulders were stiff. I thought that she wasn't happy to see her daughter. Shaking her head emphatically, she said, "Not now, Marin. We'll talk later. Go on back home— wait for me there. I'm serious about this—wait there."

Marin held her hands out, palms to the sky. "Mom, I . . . I came to warn you. . . ." Her tone grew plaintive.

"About what? About him?" Naomi's tone was

derisive, cutting. I recognized it instantly; she'd certainly used the same tone often enough with me. "It's a little late for that, isn't it? I just talked to him. He came by the office to plead with me, called upstairs and waited outside by my car. I just left him in the parking lot five minutes ago. So I already know what's going on. All of it. The party the two of you have planned is over as of right now, do you understand? I'll do what I can to help you both, I promise. Now go on home. I can't believe you did this. I just can't believe it."

Marin was frozen in place, standing on the sidewalk ten feet from her mother's car. I couldn't see Marin's face, though I could tell from her posture that the tension wasn't quite gone. She said nothing; she didn't seem to have a response for her mother's words.

Naomi leaned back down and reached into the car, grabbed the big Vuitton bag she always carried with her, and slung it over her shoulder. She slammed the car door. The noise it made was a solid, Bavarian thud. "Go home," she told her daughter. "I'll be there in an hour. We'll decide what to do then."

Either Naomi had not seen me eavesdropping on the porch or she was ignoring me. Either way, I was grateful not to have much of a role in this new act of the Bigg family drama.

For a moment, neither woman took a step. When Naomi finally walked with determined strides toward the sidewalk, I decided that the time had come for me to go back into my office and let this scenario between mother and daughter develop however it was going to develop.

I think I turned my head first.

But I'm not sure.

Maybe I'd even completed turning all the way around so that I was facing the door. But the ragged piece of metal that I caught on the outside of my right thigh argued against that.

Regardless, I remember seeing the flash in the periphery of my vision, and I think I heard the boom. Maybe it was the other way around. I know I felt the concussion. The evidence of that was irrefutable. It threw me against the front door of the old brick house with enough force to crack oak.

When I woke up, or cleared my head, or whatever it was that I did, I could finally hear the sirens. I wanted to tell Marin Bigg that I could finally hear the sirens.

I tried to stand up to go find Marin and Naomi, but a young man with a ring between his nostrils and a tattoo of a black flower on his throat kept a firm grip on my shoulders.

He said, "I don't think you should get up, man. Someone's coming to help you. I don't think you should get up, man. I'm serious, here. Come on, now. Cooperate with me."

"Where's Marin? Tell her I hear the sirens."

"Hey, whatever. I'll tell her. I'll tell her."

Up close, his nasal ring captivated me. I wanted to ask him what it had felt like to get that part of his nose pierced. Did they go through the cartilage with the needle or did they slide the metal in front of it in that soft skin that always got so sore when I had a cold? But it didn't seem like an appropriate question to a stranger, so I kept my musings to myself.

Then I recalled Naomi's message.

There's another bomb. That lawyer.

I tried to sit up. I said, "There's another bomb. That lawyer."

He kept his hands on my shoulders. "What? I don't think you should get up, man. You're not real stable."

That understatement was the last thing I recalled until the ambulance ride.

CHAPTER
32

There's another bomb. That lawyer.

I spilled the beans about the wouldn't-it-be-cool games about five minutes after I arrived at the hospital. It took that long for me to collect my wits. Lauren had been called but she wasn't yet at my side, so Sam Purdy was my first confessor. For some reason, he'd been the one elected by the medical staff to inform me that what little was left of Naomi Bigg was dead.

Come to think of it, it was more likely that Sam's position as town crier was self-appointed. At that moment he'd be more concerned with bomb facts than with my feelings.

I asked him about Marin. The nurses and doctors who'd been treating me had been unwilling to tell me her condition.

Sam, on the other hand, didn't blink at my question. Marin Bigg was on her way to surgery. Her condition wasn't critical, though he didn't know the details. He'd let me know when things changed.

I proceeded to tell Sam about Naomi's message. *There's another bomb. That lawyer.* I tried to put it all in context by telling him everything I remembered about Paul and Ramp and the wouldn't-it-be-cool games. When I got around to mentioning Ella Ramp and Jason Ramp Bass and shaped charges and the explosives vault near Limon, he barked, "What?"

"The things that Lucy called you about a few hours ago. Ramp's grandmother is Ella. Jason Ramp Bass is Ramp's real name. Lucy and I met with the grandmother early this afternoon."

Sam's eyes shimmered with a frightening blend of anger and alarm. "I haven't talked to Lucy today, Alan."

"She didn't call you a few hours ago?"

"No."

"You don't know about our trip to Agate?"

"No."

"Oh, shit," I said. I tried to get up. "Oh . . . shit."

I told Sam that I thought Lucy must be out looking for Ramp on her own, and told him everything that she and I had learned that afternoon in Agate. As I related the story, he used his cell phone to repeat the information almost word for word to someone at the police department.

At his urging I offered him my guesses about the list of people that Paul Bigg might have been targeting in

Boulder. Unfortunately, every one of the potential targets was a lawyer, so my list didn't narrow the realm of potential targets very much. Sam took careful notes and asked good questions. I made him promise to track down Lauren and to get Grace and her babysitter over to Adrienne's house right away. He said to consider it done.

When I was through with my story about the Biggs and Ramp and the Agate ranch, he told me in a soft voice that my judgment was "goofy."

Listening to Sam over the years, I'd learned that "goofy" is an all-purpose Minnesota word that includes connotations ranging from "odd" to "totally fucked up." In these circumstances, I was assuming Sam's intent fell somewhere at the very profane end of the spectrum.

Once he was convinced that he'd accumulated all the salient details about the bombs and the boys, Sam left me to go confirm that protection was in place for all the people who might possibly have been targeted by Paul Bigg in Boulder.

All the lawyers.

I assumed he was also doing whatever had to be done to make sure that every possible stone was being turned in the search for the man named Jason Ramp Bass in Denver.

Adrienne joined me in the ER minutes after Sam departed. When she saw my name on the ER board, she had just finished doing some emergency urological procedure that I was sure would make me cross my legs if she shared the details.

She didn't. She merely shook her head at the sight of me.

"Hi," I said.

She actually laughed. From anyone else the reaction would've struck me as inappropriate. From Adrienne, it was comforting.

She said, "You're alive. That's good. The board outside says 'laceration, shrapnel.' Leaves an awful lot to the imagination. I thought my surgical reconstruction skills might be required."

I shuddered at the thought, then told her about the bomb outside my office.

She had a few questions. I answered them before I asked her if she'd heard from Lauren.

She hadn't.

"Will you page her for me?"

"Right now? Sure." She pulled her cell phone from her pocket and entered a long string of digits while she said, "I'm not supposed to use this in here, you know. Could be short-circuiting a heart monitor or screwing up a CAT scan or something. Anything else you want?"

"Call your nanny and have her go get Grace and Viv and take them back to your place. I don't want them in our house. Sam said he'd call, but could you double-check?"

"And the dogs," she said.

"Yes, and the dogs."

She made that call, too.

"*Mi casa es su casa,* and, even better for me, *su* nanny *es mi* nanny. Now, you want to tell me what's going on?"

I nodded and began to tell her about the Biggs and Ramp. Being in a peculiarly confessional mood, I proceeded to fill her in on almost everything that I'd just told Sam Purdy. I was just about to get to the part of the story where I went to Agate with Lucy when Adrienne raised her hand and extended an index finger straight up. She said, "Alan, what did the neurologist tell you?"

"What do you mean?"

"About your . . . mental status?"

"She said I have a minor concussion. I may have headaches for a while. Told me not to exercise for a few days. Said I was real lucky with the leg wound. The shrapnel almost hit a major vessel. But that wasn't the neurologist. That was the guy who sewed me back up. I think it was an ER guy, a new guy, somebody I don't know."

Adrienne nodded knowingly at my comments even though she didn't really know a thing about my condition. I hate it when doctors do that. My patients probably hate it when I do that.

"What?" I demanded. "Don't just nod your head like I'm some imbecile. What are you thinking?"

"This thing you just told me about Paul Bigg? And his friend—what's his name, Ramp?"

"Yes, Ramp."

"You're sure about it?"

"Yes." Suddenly, I wasn't sure.

She nodded again.

"Adrienne, what?"

"I'm afraid that there's no gentle way to put this. But Paul Bigg is dead, Alan. Very dead."

"Oh God," I said. "They found his body, too? Where was it? At their house? The Bigg house?" For some reason, I immediately suspected suicide. After he'd placed the bomb that killed his mother, he'd gone home and killed himself.

Adrienne shook her head and lowered her voice, making it so soft that her northeast accent almost evaporated. "No, hon. Paul Bigg died playing Little League baseball when he was twelve years old. He got hit in the chest by a ball and died from a heart rhythm abnormality."

I felt as though I'd been punched in the gut.

"What?"

"Paul's been dead for, like, five or six years. I told you the other night that Leo's family has had way too many tragedies, even before he went to prison. Don't you remember?"

I stared at her with my mouth in the classic O sign. It took me a few moments to form my next sentence. "That can't be right. No way. She told me he worked at Starbucks. On the Mall, down near Fifteenth Street. Naomi did." I almost argued that Naomi had said that Paul made the best mocha on the planet. I thought she'd said "on the planet." Maybe it was just that he made a "killer mocha." It bothered me that I couldn't remember exactly what she had said. She certainly hadn't said that her son was long dead and that she'd been making everything up.

"He doesn't work at Starbucks, Alan. He probably died before he ever laid eyes on a Starbucks. Paul Bigg is dead." Adrienne was being uncharacteristically gentle, as though she were speaking to somebody with severe mental instability.

Me.

"Adrienne, that can't be true. Naomi just talked with him. A few minutes before she died. I heard her tell Marin about it. She was mad at him about something. He can't be dead."

Adrienne said, "I think you're mistaken."

I protested. "He has this friend. Ramp."

"Maybe he did, Alan, back then. But not now. Paul's dead. Peter and I went to his funeral. I promise you that he's dead."

"I don't understand. I know all about him. His school, his friends. Everything. I know what psychiatrist he went to, Adrienne. What he was treated for, everything."

Adrienne began to nod again, but she caught herself. In retrospect, I'm sure she was fighting an urge to ask me if I knew my name, knew where I was right then, what day it was, who was the current President of the United States.

She didn't ask. She said, "Well, maybe you don't know quite everything that you think you know."

Duh.

CHAPTER
33

Ramp felt the flash from the bomb the same way he experienced the sun as it broke through a thick cloud cover. The light and heat washed over him and warmed him, licking at his exposed skin all at once. He raised his chin an inch or so to greet the energy as it pulsed and engulfed him. Since it was the first time he would be around to see one of his devices go off in public, he desperately wanted to keep his eyes open to record the visual landscape as it settled in the aftermath of his work, but his reflexes overwhelmed him.

The plastic box with the toggle switch in his jacket pocket was moist from the sweat on his hand. He fingered the slick plastic as impulses flooded him. The energy it consumed to control the urges thwarted his enjoyment of the consequences of the blast. He wanted to thrust his hands into the air and yell, "Yes!" He wanted to pull the transmitter from his pocket and thrust it to his lips and display it to the stunned citizens around him.

He didn't.

He monitored his excited breathing by forcing each deep breath to pass through his nose and go deep into his gut. Despite the chaos that was stirring in the aftermath of the explosion, he could hear himself snort and was afraid he sounded like a horse eager to canter.

Ramp had detonated the bomb from where he'd been standing on Walnut in front of the aging house that old-time Boulderites would probably forever consider to be the second home of Nancy's restaurant. As the echoes of the detonation stilled, Ramp heard people in front of Café Louie, the restaurant that had replaced Nancy's, screaming, "Did you hear that?" "What was that?" "Was that a car that blew up?" and "Oh no, oh my God! I think it was a bomb."

The sounds were all on separate tracks in his consciousness, laid down methodically, distinctly. They were the kinds of details that he knew he'd want to remember later.

As people ran past him toward the location of the blast, he wanted to follow them. He wanted to see for himself what havoc the explosive had wreaked. What carnage the metal splinters had wrought. Did he kill one? Or two? Or even three? But he didn't follow the throngs to the source of the damage.

He was sure he didn't want to see the bodies.

There were bodies. He knew that. The bodies meant

casualties. The casualties were necessary, but he feared that each would remind him of the day he discovered his mother's body.

He turned and walked the opposite direction down Walnut, crossing Ninth and moving at a measured pace to cover the short blocks to the Downtown Mall. The plan called for him to linger for a while with the crowds on the Mall before he returned to his car.

He remembered something his grandfather had said about explosives: *Maniacs destroy maniacally. Engineers destroy scientifically. You are the engineer.*

"I am the engineer," he said, barely moving his lips, hardly making a sound.

"And how was it?" he asked himself, adopting a gravelly, deeper voice. The voice of someone who'd inhaled the poisons of way too many Camels. The voice of his grandfather.

"Better than I would have guessed, Granddad. The best, the absolute best. It's so much better when you're there."

The deeper voice responded, "Wait. They only get better. The better you get, the better they get. I liked the last one I did better than I did the first."

"I wasn't really sure I could do it. The first one went off accidentally, you know. So I wasn't sure I could actually detonate one myself. One that counted, I mean."

"I was sure. I was sure."

At the corner of Eleventh, outside the Walrus, a woman approached him on the sidewalk and Ramp ended the conversation he was having. The last thing he wanted to do was draw attention to himself a block and a half from the crime scene.

Another saying from Granddad: *You don't hurry to meet deadlines. You change deadlines so you don't have to hurry.*

Not this time, Ramp thought as he climbed into the driver's seat of his blue RAV 4. Most of what the old man had said was true. But not that, not this time. Ramp knew he'd have to accelerate the whole timetable. He knew that they'd be looking for him now.

Maybe they even knew who he was already.

He had to act now before it was too late. One quick stop at his apartment and he'd be ready to go.

The sign above the workbench in the explosives shed: *Safety is the product of planning, discipline, and control. If you plan well, deploy with discipline, and control your charges, you will be safe.*

But what if you don't care if you're safe? What if you're willing to go out with the blast?

The old man couldn't have imagined it, so he had never had an aphorism for that.

Ramp started the car.

He tuned the radio to AM and hit the scan button, listening for the sound of breaking news.

Before he made it to the edge of town, he was gripped with a hunger that was as tight as a choke chain. He stopped at the McDonald's on Baseline and ordered a Big Mac Extra Value Meal. As he pulled forward to the pick-up window, a young kid in the required bad clothes and polyester hat asked him if he'd heard about the explosion downtown.

"No," Ramp said. "What happened?"

"Don't know, but somebody got smoked. Did you say you wanted a Coke with that?"

Somebody got smoked. Ramp had trouble finding the skills necessary to continue to breathe. "Yes, I want a Coke with that."

He'd wanted to demand the facts. He'd wanted to ask the kid if only one somebody had been smoked. But he didn't.

Ramp stayed east on Baseline, pulling french fries from their red cardboard sleeve one by one, feeding them into his mouth like severed branches into a shredder, finally turning onto the Foothills Parkway toward the turnpike that would return him to Denver.

He continued to scan the radio stations for news. He was halfway to Denver, driving through a speed trap on Highway 36 in Westminster, before he heard the first bulletin about the explosion. Initial reports listed one victim dead from the explosion in downtown Boulder, three injured.

Three meant at least one innocent bystander.

Ramp shrugged and took a long draw from his Coke.

"Shit!" he said suddenly and yanked the wheel hard to make the exit at Federal Boulevard. He steered with one hand and began patting furiously at the pocket of his jacket with the other.

There it was. He still had it with him. What if he'd been stopped? What if a cop had found an excuse to search him?

He heard the words in his head as clearly as he'd heard them the first time his grandfather had spoken them to him: *Careless is just another word for failure.*

"Shit!" he repeated before silently repeating the old man's mantra over and over again, using it as a way to flog himself back into control.

He drove around the back of the bowling alley that was adjacent to the freeway on the southwest side of the Federal off-ramp and pulled up next to a row of three Dumpsters. He stepped out of the car, pulled the radio controller from his pocket, dropped it to the asphalt, and crushed the plastic box with one sharp thrust of his heel. He divided the shattered electronic remains between the three Dumpsters, saving the tiny joystick as a souvenir.

Ramp spent the next couple of miles on the road trying to devise a way to attach the joystick to his key ring.

Fifteen minutes later he was turning into the alley that ran behind his apartment building. The building had six alley parking spaces for twelve apartments. Ramp was shocked to find one available. He let himself in the back door and climbed the three flights of stairs to his fourth-floor unit.

The first thing he did once inside was to boot up his

computer and check the Internet for fresh news of the
Boulder bombing. Not much had been added to the
radio bulletin. The three living victims had been taken
to Community Hospital; one was in critical condition.
Police weren't commenting on a possible link to the
explosive device that had been found hidden in
District Attorney Royal Peterson's house.

"Let them comment all they want," Ramp said
aloud. "They won't find a single similarity in materials
or design. Signatures are for fools."

Done with the Internet connection, he began the
series of keystrokes that would format the hard drive of
his computer, erasing all his digital tracks. Getting the
process started took him less than a minute. He'd practiced the procedure before. None of it was new to him.

Another sign above the workbench in the explosives
shed: *Novelty creates confusion. Practice eliminates
novelty.*

"Right on, Granddad," Ramp said.

He collected three radio transmitters from the
kitchen cupboard above the dishwasher. The three
devices were dissimilar. One was a garage door opener. One had operated a remote-control children's car.
The third had been designed to operate a model air-
plane. He placed them in a leather dopp kit that was
already provisioned with fresh batteries for the transmitters.

He pried the floorboard away from the wall and
pocketed the Zip disc that he'd stashed there. His work
clothes and the other supplies were already packed in

a duffel bag that he'd used to carry his soccer clothes when he was in high school.

Last, he retrieved a fresh battery for his cell phone, dumped everything into the duffel with his clothes, locked up his apartment, and descended the stairs toward his car.

CHAPTER

34

Before I was allowed to leave the hospital, a lot of people wanted to talk to me. Almost all of them were from law enforcement.

Lauren, I think, wanted only to yell at me. But she didn't. She was overtly kind to me the way that I knew I would someday be overtly kind to Grace after she cut herself or broke a bone solely because of *her* poor judgment and stupidity.

Lauren could afford to be kind to me because she knew that I knew how stupid I'd been. She knew it because I reminded her of it every few minutes.

The first few repetitive apologies took place while I was still at the hospital. The neurologist who was assessing me for closed head injuries actually expressed concern to Lauren that my perseveration might be ample evidence that I'd suffered brain trauma. Soon, however, my wife concluded that my refrain was merely a recurring prayer seeking psychological absolution for my mortal sins against good judgment.

As the shadows were fading and darkness was sealing the end of the day, Lauren drove me home. On the way down North Broadway, I heard birds singing that had probably been singing the evening before and smelled flowers that had certainly smelled just as sweet that morning. But, after surviving the explosion, my senses felt sharper. I wanted to test the hypothesis further and taste my wife's kiss, but she was in no mood to indulge me. As we cruised past the new Bureau of Standards building on South Broadway near Table Mesa, Lauren used an oh-by-the-way tone to caution me that serious discussions were probably ongoing in the district attorney's office about whether or not I could be charged with a crime. Something about withholding evidence.

Like what? I wondered, though not aloud. For some reason, Lauren's warning didn't particularly alarm me. What were they going to do to me?

Maybe I'd be arrested for not blowing the whistle on a kid who had been dead for six years.

I decided that it would almost be worth going to trial just to hear the opening statements on that one.

Prior to making Ella Ramp's acquaintance in Agate that afternoon, the act of rationalizing my willingness to disclose confidential information to the Boulder

Police had taken some significant gymnastics. Because patient privilege survives patient death, even the fact that Naomi was now dead wasn't actually enough to free me from my legal restrictions to keep quiet. What finally liberated me to open my mouth to the authorities about all the things I'd learned from Naomi in psychotherapy was the now undeniable reality that Naomi's fears about bombs and explosives weren't the product of her imagination, and my near one-hundred-percent assurance that the bomber was a kid in Denver named Jason Ramp Bass. My assurance that Jason Bass had set a bomb off in the Louis Vuitton bag that Naomi always carried slung from her shoulder was as close to one hundred percent as it could get.

The leap from those realizations to the acceptance that other people were still in danger from other bombs was all that I needed to free myself from the bounds of confidentiality. Lawyers and practitioners could argue whether the circumstances actually constituted legally enforceable *Tarasoff* conditions, but the truth was that I had lost any remaining interest I'd had in debating the finer legal and ethical threads.

I ran my belated rationalizations by Lauren. She made it clear that she thought I'd jumped through the progression of ethical hoops in a peculiarly tardy fashion. Although it was clear she was admonishing me, I was relieved that she was at least trying to be nice about it.

Sam called around nine o'clock that evening. He had news. The Boulder Police had discovered an "explosive device" during a sweep of the home of the woman who ran the District Attorney's Sex Crimes Unit. The bomb was found in Nora Doyle's garage, well hidden among some gardening supplies that were stored directly opposite the driver's side door of her Honda Accord. Had the bomb gone off, Nora might have been impaled on a hoe.

The bomb squad thought the initiator was radio controlled. Sam promised to tell me more when he knew more.

There's another bomb. That lawyer.

Cozier Maitlin's office, car, and Mapleton Hill home had been swept with extreme care, with negative results. The evacuation of the Colorado Building on Fourteenth Street had apparently been quite an inconvenience for quite a lot of people. Sam reported that at least one passerby voiced her hope that if there was indeed a bomb, she was praying it was big enough to bring the damn ugly place down.

The home and chambers of Superior Court Judge Richard Bates Leventhal, who had approved the plea bargain in Marin Bigg's rape, were swept, too. No bombs were discovered.

Lauren and I already knew, of course, that our property had been re-searched without result before I'd left the hospital that afternoon.

At times of stress, I ride my bike. The more stress I feel, the harder I ride. The amount of stress I was feeling the day Naomi died would have necessitated a fierce climb—a muscle-burning, ass-never-touches-the-saddle ascent that few mountain ranges in the world can offer on paved roads. But the eleven stitches high on the back of my leg near the imaginary line where butt becomes hip and my quasi-concussion conspired to keep me housebound and off my bicycle. My stress relief would have to come from baby Grace, who, bless her heart, handled the job effortlessly, and from the dogs, who, though generally amusing, weren't quite as reliable a tranquilizer as Xanax.

I tried to read. Couldn't concentrate. I tried to nap. Couldn't sleep. Mostly I spent the evening thinking.

Pondering.

Okay, perseverating.

Patients lie to me all the time.

All the time.

Most of the time I accept the mistruths as being part of the process that people go through while they're coming to terms with the myriad of ways that they are lying to themselves. I don't, as a rule, take it personally when I learn that I've been served untruths by patients. And I'm usually not even embarrassed when I discover that I've fallen hook, line, and sinker for the prevarications.

I've heard colleagues say that they know when their

patients are lying to them. I find the contention preposterous. I can't usually tell, and even when I think I can tell, I'm not usually sure. And I'm almost always unconvinced that it matters. I try to make it my job to learn as much from my patients' lies as I do from the truth. Either way, the therapy benefits.

But Naomi Bigg had *lied* to me.

She'd really, really lied to me. And I'd fallen for her creative story like a four-year-old stuffing a tooth beneath his pillow believes in visions of an impending visit from a dental fairy carrying a twinkling wand and dressed in white organza.

Paul Bigg, Naomi's living, breathing, wouldn't-it-be-cool, green-apron-wearing kid, was dead.

Or was he?

I was rapidly approaching a conclusion that Paul hadn't ever really been dead for his mother. Although I'd probably never know for sure, I suspected that Naomi hadn't resurrected Paul solely for my benefit; I suspected that Naomi had never really buried her son at all. In the psychotherapy I'd been doing with Naomi, I wondered if I'd just been hanging out on the bank of the pond, witnessing the ripples of her unsettled grief.

The psychological process Naomi had been engaged in was either crafty as hell or it was delusional as hell. My money was on delusional, on some kind of narrowly defined psychotic process.

If I was right, it meant that, as Naomi's therapist, I'd totally missed the presence of her psychotic symptoms.

There was no escaping the fact that my care of

Naomi Bigg had not been one of my better clinical moments.

Lauren put Grace to bed while I watched the local TV news accounts of the bombing death of Naomi Bigg. Marin, according to all reports, was out of surgery but remained in serious condition.

Reading between the lines, I assumed she was still uncommunicative with the police.

The other big story of the day was the *Daily Camera*'s revelation about Lucy Tanner's parentage. The local legal analysts made it clear that the Boulder prosecutors were getting perilously close to believing that they had a motive that would firmly tie Lucy to the Royal Peterson murder.

Sam called again just as I was about to learn what the weather was going to be the next day in the Carolinas.

"Hey," he said.

"Hi," I replied. "Any word on Lucy?"

"No, not yet. Certain people aren't convinced he's got her. There's a consensus developing that she's just hiding from what was in the paper this morning. Guess where I am."

I wasn't in the mood. "Sam, I'm not in the mood."

"Okay, I'll just tell you. I'm sitting on the stairs that go up to the second floor in Naomi Bigg's house. We're executing a search warrant."

"Oh," I said. I wasn't surprised about anything but

that it had taken so long for the search to begin. I assumed the delay was a paperwork/convince-the-judge kind of problem. I doubted that any evidence of the explosives would be discovered at the Bigg home. Whatever law enforcement personnel ended up searching the Ramp ranch between Agate and Limon were the ones who would find the explosive residue.

"Finding anything?" My feelings about Sam's errand were more than a little confused. Maybe it was the minor concussion. But I wasn't exactly sure whether I wanted Sam to answer my question "Yes" or to answer it "No."

He made a nasal sound that I couldn't interpret. "Who knows? We just got here and we're still looking. I tell you, it's going to take all night to go over this place. Rich people's houses have lots of rooms and they own lots of shit. You ever notice that? This house has a little room that seems to be set aside just for wrapping presents. Like a gift-wrap room. Who has a gift-wrap room? Well, the Biggs do. I look at some of the stuff in this place and I wonder how somebody could be standing in a store somewhere and ever convince themselves that they actually needed one of those. You know the kind of stuff that I mean?"

I did, and I didn't. "You wanted something, Sam?"

"You're okay, right? Just the bump on your head and the cut on your butt?"

"Upper leg, Sam. That, and a dead patient whose daughter is still in serious condition in the hospital. And Lucy." I let the words hang.

He said, "Every cop in the state is looking for Ramp. I'm hoping there's something here that helps us find him. We find him, I think we find her. Anyway, I was telling you what I discovered here. Right at the top of the stairs, first door on the left, is the kid's room. You know, Paul? The one who died playing Little League? The one you thought was busy planning his own little Columbine?"

Regardless of the fact that I'd almost been killed by a bomb earlier that day, my friend Sam wasn't above a well-placed dig. I tried to deflect it. "Paul's room is still there?" I was thinking out loud; I knew that I was still struggling to understand the extent of Naomi's delusions.

Sam, of course, seized on the opportunity to take me literally. "Sure. That happens when kids die. Parents aren't ready to let go. They preserve stuff. Bedroom is often high on the list. This shouldn't be news to you, Alan. It's like your field, you know? Human behavior?"

"Yeah."

"Anyway, I thought I'd call you because I thought it was interesting what's plastered all over the kid's door. Outside of the door, facing the hallway. It's kind of goofy."

"What?"

"Little signs. Maybe fifty of 'em. Maybe more, who knows. I'm sure somebody will end up counting them. They're all lined up in neat rows and columns. The signs are all different designs—no two of 'em match—

but they all say one of two things. Though some are in languages I don't even want to know. Want to guess?"

"No."

"About half of them say 'Do not disturb.' The other half say 'Be right back.' You being a shrink, I thought you'd get a kick out of that."

"Little 'Do not disturb' signs and 'Be right back' signs? All over his door?"

"Yeah, just like the ones you hang from the door-knob when you're staying at a Ramada. Though you probably don't stay at Ramada, do you? Those kinds of signs. The kid must have collected them."

"I don't know about that. I wonder if it was Paul or his mother who put them on the door. What does the room look like?"

"Like a kid's room. It does have a certain time-warp quality. Kid liked the old Dallas Cowboys. Lots of Troy Aikman and Emmett what's-his-face. Good stuff, expensive. Autographed jerseys. Signed pictures. Emmett Smith? Is that it? I think that's right, Smith. I should know that. He sure gave my Vikings enough grief over the years, didn't he?"

I didn't know. "But nothing unusual?"

"Not at first glance. Just the signs. I thought those were unusual, that's why I called."

Although I didn't believe what I was about to say, I said, "They could just be a preadolescent boy putting up a 'No trespassing' sign."

"Doesn't feel that way. I'll get a picture of the door to show you. This is something."

While I was considering the discovery, I said, "Is there someplace in the house where somebody could have made a bomb, Sam?"

"Not at first glance. There's no obvious workshop and we haven't identified any explosives. We'll swab for residue, but I'm betting that we'll come up with jack."

"Then what?"

"Everybody's looking for Ramp. That's where the money is. We're hoping to find an address or phone number here. Other than pointing us toward the Internet and to his grandparents' ranch, you don't know where to send us to find him, right? No recovered memories since this afternoon?"

The "recovered memories" comment was another dig.

"Has anyone talked to Marin, Sam? Is she awake? Maybe she knows something about Ramp."

"Scott Malloy's standing by over at the hospital to talk to her the moment she's able."

"How bad are her injuries?"

"To quote one of the docs, the wounds are uglier than they are serious. Her mom absorbed most of the blast. They think Marin will be fine—if her luck is bad she may lose use of an eye."

"Poor kid."

"Poor kid was mixed up with somebody who made bombs. For all we know right now, she was helping him."

CHAPTER
35

It took Lucy more than a thimbleful of patience, but she'd waited until she was in Agate before she made her next move. She'd allowed Alan to pull out ahead of her and watched him turn onto the interstate as he headed west toward Boulder. She turned into a gas station adjacent to I-70, filled the Volvo's tank, and bought a carton of chocolate milk and a tasteless sandwich filled with milky-white slices of something masquerading as turkey.

She didn't call Sam Purdy.

Instead, she made a phone call to a police department colleague who'd made no secret of the fact that he was eager to get into her pants, and asked him for help tracking down Jason Ramp Bass's current address in Denver. She didn't tell the man why she wanted the address. And he didn't ask.

As she killed the call she figured that she'd know

exactly where to find Ramp before she was done with her sandwich.

She was wrong. The return call with Ramp's address didn't come for almost two and a half hours. Her contact had been yanked into a meeting before he'd been able to get back to her with the information. When he finally did phone, he dangled the address like a carrot at the end of a stick until she agreed to have a drink with him after work. She picked a day for the rendezvous that was almost a week away. It left her plenty of time to cancel.

Once she had the address, she thought once more about calling Sam Purdy with the day's news. If she called him, he'd make her back off, wouldn't even let her close to the case. That wasn't okay.

She reached the same decision she'd reached every other time she'd pondered the problem since Agate. She decided to find Ramp by herself.

Capitol Hill in Denver is just south of the Uptown neighborhood where Jason Ramp Bass once lived with his parents. Although it bears some resemblance to Uptown, Capitol Hill is more densely populated, is even more diverse, and suffers from fewer pockets of acute gentrification than does its northern neighbor.

The apartment building where Lucy thought Ramp lived was in no danger of going condo, and nobody in their right mind was ever going to mistake it for a loft.

It was a postwar brick rectangle that looked as though it had been modeled after a shoebox. It was flanked on each side by gorgeous stone mansions.

She parked her car just down from Ramp's building on Pennsylvania Avenue and walked back toward it. The doorbell to apartment 3B was marked "Bass." Lucy smiled and shook her head. All day long, given the kind of day she'd expected to have, it had all been too easy. It was just about time, she thought, where something should go wrong.

To ring or not to ring, that was the next question.

She rings and he's not home, nothing's lost.

She rings and he's home—that's when things could get complicated. What would she say to him? Sam Purdy had always taught her to walk into any interview she conducted with the cards stacked in her favor. And with at least one ace tucked up her sleeve. Her favorite ace in the hole was her detective shield, and she'd had to give that up when she was suspended.

What else did she have?

Her wits. And her personal handgun. That was about it.

She backed down the concrete steps and started strolling away from the building to give herself time to rethink her options. She considered calling Cozy to see how bad the fallout had been from the *Daily Camera* story about her and Susan Peterson but decided that she could wait to learn about that. No matter how bad it had been, she was sure it had been bad enough. She also second-guessed her decision not to call Sam until she was absolutely certain that Jason Ramp Bass was the man they were looking for.

She reminded herself to think like a cop. There was no way she should approach Jason Bass alone without notifying somebody what she was up to. Ella Ramp may have already called her grandson and warned him that Lucy was on his tail. The young man could be armed.

Lucy stopped and used her cell phone to call Alan. She got his voice mail. "Alan, listen, it's Lucy. I think I found Ramp. He lives in Capitol Hill in Denver." She recited the address on Pennsylvania. "I'm heading up to his apartment to try and talk to him now. If for some reason I don't get back to you later today or this evening, call Sam and tell him what I was up to."

She hung up, squeezed her left triceps against her rib cage to feel the reassuring pressure of her holstered weapon, returned to the front door of the apartment building, and hit the bell marked "Bass."

No answer.

She tried the knob on the front door of the building. Locked.

One more time she tried the bell. As she waited for a response she backed away from the door and stared up at the fourth floor, trying to guess which apartment was Ramp's.

CHAPTER
36

Ramp was halfway to the Water Street location of the welding supply company where he worked when he realized that he'd forgotten his inspiration. He turned his car around and headed back to his apartment.

The elusive alley parking spot was filled. He double-parked and ran up the back stairs. He retrieved the framed photograph of his mother from on top of the bookcase and was just about out the door when the buzzer sounded from downstairs.

Ramp froze momentarily, then slowly walked to his front windows. The buzzer sounded again.

He waited. Half a minute or so later he watched a blond woman back slowly away from the door, looking up toward the fourth floor.

Who is she?

Ramp said, "Shit," and stepped away from the

window. "Here or there?" he asked himself. "Up here
or down there?"

If I let her up here, he thought, whatever happens
will leave evidence. Trace. Can't have that. Out loud,
he said, "The correct answer, therefore, is down there."
He bounded out the door of his apartment and flew
down the stairs like a kid afraid to miss something.
Only slightly winded, he grabbed his bag from his car,
stuffed the photograph of his mother inside, circled his
building, and was on the sidewalk behind the blond
woman before she got all the way back to her car.

The red Volvo had the old, traditional, white-sky-
over-green-mountains style Colorado license plates.
The lettering on the plates read "MST." Ramp knew
that designation meant the car was registered in
Boulder County. The new green-over-white plates
lacked a county code; you couldn't tell where the car
was from.

Who the hell would be visiting him from Boulder?
Nobody he wanted to see, that's who.

He noted the absence of a uniform and the presence of the leather blazer the woman was wearing on
a warm afternoon. If the cops were after him, they
wouldn't send a patrol officer. They'd send a detective,
he thought. Probably two. He wondered about a gun
under the blazer. He wondered about a partner. He
couldn't spot anyone.

If she was a cop, she had a gun. Either under her
blazer or in that purse. But why would they send a solitary cop?

Ramp was five feet behind her when he said, "Detective?"

She turned to face him.

He saw the look of resignation on her face when she realized she'd been duped. He smiled, and he said, "Thank you. That was easy. Go ahead and get in your car, Detective, but slide all the way across to the driver's side. I'll be right behind you. Once you're in the car, put your hands under your thighs. I'll take that purse, now, if you don't mind."

Ramp recognized the woman from the news. She was the Boulder cop who was the prime suspect in killing the Boulder DA. She was on leave from the police force. There'd been something in the news all day long about her mother, too. Ramp hadn't really paid attention.

She didn't seem frightened. Certainly wasn't jumping to obey him.

He said, "Do what I say. Hand me the purse, please, then slide into the car." He lifted the satchel he'd just retrieved from his apartment. "I have a weapon in this bag—actually, it's an explosive device—a bomb—that will kill both of us instantly. Although I'm willing to set it off, I'd really rather not do that."

He watched intently as the cop began to lower herself onto the car seat. When she was seated on the passenger's side, Ramp said, "Stop there for a second." He leaned in toward her and with his left hand pulled back the lapel of her blazer, exposing the butt of her handgun. Careful not to brush her body with his fingers, he removed the weapon and added it to the bag. "Now scoot over to the other side."

She did.

She noted that he wasn't using her weapon against her and asked, "Can I use my hands to raise myself over the console?"

"Sure," he replied. "Thanks for asking. I don't think either of us wants to be surprised right now."

She said, "You're Jason?"

"I am. You're the cop from the news?"

"Yeah, that's me."

"Nice to meet you," he said.

Despite herself, Lucy thought that Jason Ramp Bass was charming. She also thought that the fact that he was charming explained a lot.

CHAPTER
37

Lauren waited until we were in bed to ask me who I thought had killed Naomi Bigg and severely injured Marin. Her question came after I filled her in about my conversation with Sam.

I'd been thinking about that exact question—who had set off the bomb?—all day long, of course. Prior to the moment when Adrienne informed me that Paul Bigg had been dead for six years, I'd been assuming that it was Paul who had placed the bomb that had killed his mother and maimed his sister. I figured that he'd somehow managed to slip the device into Naomi's Vuitton bag during their confrontation in the parking lot outside her office.

I said, "Before my visit to that ranch today I would've thought it was Paul. After I met Ella Ramp, I would've guessed that it could've been either Ramp or Paul."

"But it wasn't Paul." Lauren spoke gently, wary perhaps of the unpredictability of the reaction of someone with closed head trauma. "We know that. Why do you think Naomi did that? Why did she keep Paul alive the way she did?"

"I don't know. I'm not convinced that Naomi actually lied—not in the sense that she was trying to fool me by creating a grown-up version of her son. I think Naomi was just inviting me into her delusions. Maybe she'd split Marin in two and given half her daughter's life to her son in order to keep him alive. I'm not sure. But we know that Ramp is real and that he's connected to Marin in some way that's not clear.

"I am convinced that before Naomi came over to my office, she had just spoken with somebody in her office parking lot."

"Ramp?"

"Yes, has to be."

"And you think he placed the bomb then, right?"

"She carried this big Vuitton bag around with her all the time. It always looked like it weighed a ton. I think he met with her at her office and managed to get the device into her bag."

"Why?"

"I'm not sure. Maybe Ramp wanted to kill her because he found out she was talking to me about her fears about the wouldn't-it-be-cool games. She'd called me and implied that she was about to do just that. So Ramp met her at her office, and he placed the bomb. The alternative is that Naomi was carrying the thing around on her own. I don't see that."

⸱ "Maybe the person who put the bomb in there was trying to kill both Naomi and Marin," Lauren suggested.

"If Marin recovers, maybe we'll know the answer to that. She was terrified that her mother was in danger. She'd come to my office to warn Naomi about something. Marin was frantic, hysterical. She yelled at her mother not to turn off her car. It makes me think that she expected that the car was wired with an explosive."

She asked, "Did Sam say how the bomb was set off?"

"No, he didn't say. Hopefully the police can figure that out from examining the debris. The one they found in Nora's garage had a radio control. They blew it apart with that thing, that—"

"Disruptor. The bomb squad calls it a disruptor. And it will be ATF and CBI doing the figuring, not the police." Lauren gazed at me warily, watching my reaction. I think she was still unconvinced that the condition of my brain would permit me to recognize either the acronym of the Alcohol, Tobacco and Firearms Administration, the federal agency responsible for investigating bombings, or that of the Colorado Bureau of Investigation.

"I know what the letters stand for," I said.

"I heard from Elliot that the ATF is mobilizing a Special Response Team. That means that they're taking this seriously. A forensic chemist deploys as part of the team, so we should know something soon about the explosive residue. I've been thinking, from the way the bomb went off outside your office the fuse had to be connected to either a timer or a radio signal. Do you see it that way?"

I'd considered the options, of course. "That, or some kind of motion switch. She'd just thrown the bag over her shoulder when the explosion happened. Aren't there switches that respond to that kind of thing?"

"I'm sure there are. But it seems like a risky way to set off a bomb to me, don't you think?"

She was right, of course. I shuddered at the thought of the alternative. "If it was a radio switch, whoever set it off had to be close to Naomi. Close enough to see what she was doing, right?"

Lauren said, "Yes."

We both grew quiet as we digested the image of the bomber witnessing the carnage. Finally, I said, "Sam said every cop in the state is looking for Ramp."

She allowed my words to dissipate like smoke and began caressing my neck. The taut muscles that stretched up from my back barely yielded to her touch. She said, "Alan?"

"Mmmm?"

"Did you think Grace and I were in danger?"

"I was never really sure. Naomi hinted at things, but she was never really clear about what she knew. I tried to make decisions . . . as though you were at some risk."

"I don't get it. What do you mean? If you thought we

were in danger, why didn't you tell me what was going on? Why didn't you go to the police?"

There was no mistaking her words. They were an accusation. She was asking how I could put my family at risk.

I made sure she was looking at me. "Like I said, I was reading between the lines. And Naomi warned me that if I told anybody about her concerns, she'd stop talking to me, and then I would have never known whether you were really at risk or not. And I wouldn't have known what the two boys were planning or how to protect you. Or anybody else."

"Even after they found the bomb at Royal's house?"

"While we were at dinner the other night with Adrienne, I had a cop friend of Sam's bring her K-9 over here to check for explosives. She had the dog search the house and your car."

"You did?"

"Yes. She didn't find anything, obviously."

"Why didn't you tell me?"

I didn't want to answer that question, but I did. "One, privilege, which, given what happened today, is lame, I admit. But yesterday, it made some sense. Two, I thought you'd insist on going to the police, and then Naomi would stop talking to me. Three, your health. Although I was afraid, I really didn't know that you were at risk and I didn't want to add stress to your life by alarming you. I've been worried about an exacerbation of your MS."

She digested my words. "And now?"

"I'm still worried about an exacerbation. But now Naomi's dead. She won't be giving me any more clues. The police are all we have."

Silence settled on the room like a comforter snapped over a bed.

I broke the silence. "I didn't have any good choices, Lauren. I did what I thought was best. I thought I was protecting us."

"I know," she said.

"Maybe I blew it. Maybe I made the wrong call," I said.

"Somebody's dead," she said. The words were her way of agreeing that perhaps I had made the wrong call.

"Yes. But I'm still not convinced that things would have been better if I had opened my mouth." I didn't know what else to say. "What exactly would you have wanted me to do, Lauren?"

"I'm not sure. I'll think about it, okay?"

For some reason I thought of Lucy Tanner just then. I was eager to change the subject anyway, so I asked, "Did you and Cozy hear from Lucy today?"

"You mean about Susan?"

"Yes. How she feels about all the news coverage about . . . Susan being her mother."

"Cozy got a message this morning. Lucy said she was planning to spend the day in Denver—I suspected to try to avoid the media—and she was going to get back in touch with him this evening. The last time I spoke with him was a couple of hours ago, and he hadn't heard from her again.

"Before the bomb went off, Alan, I was thinking of calling Susan. Just to see how she was. This has to be terrible for her, too—all the stress. But the day sort of got away from me, you know?"

"Yes," I said. "I know."

The phone beside the bed rang. For the third time that night, Sam Purdy was calling.

CHAPTER
38

Sam picked me up at our house around eleven-thirty. It took me twice as long as it should have to climb into his Cherokee. When we arrived across town at the Peterson house on Jay Street, it took me at least a minute to pull myself back out of the car. The shrapnel wound on my butt had tightened up as though the sutures were contracting like rubber bands, and pain was pulsing across my hindquarters like the backbeat of some hellacious tune.

Watching me, Sam said, "You should really be home in bed."

"Yes, I should be home in bed. But you said this might help find Lucy. There are times you have to play hurt."

A lilt of mirth in his tone, he said, "My, my. You're talking like a hockey player." From Sam, this was the ultimate compliment and expression of appreciation.

I laughed. It hurt, I winced. "Hardly," I said.

Sam arrived at Susan Peterson's threshold long before I did. I was still trying to mount the single step in the walk without having to bend my leg. He turned and looked back down the walk and said, "By the way, I decided not to tell her I was bringing you with me. Thought the surprise factor might work in my favor."

"Whatever."

"Your role inside? In case you're wondering, it's lubricant. That's your job. If the bolt seems stuck, you're the WD-40. Otherwise let me do my thing. Got it? I may be nice to her, I may not. I don't plan these things out. But don't interfere unless things get squeaky."

I nodded. I had a pretty good idea what to expect. In my experience, Sam was almost always the good cop and the bad cop all rolled up into one tasty package.

He waited for me to join him on the landing. "Why don't you ring the bell? She might be happy to see you."

"Sam, the last time I saw her, Susan was bedridden. She's not going to answer her own door. And anyway, it's almost midnight and it's Susan Peterson. She's not going to be happy to see anybody. Go ahead and ring the damn bell."

He did.

Susan's home-health-care worker pulled open the door after twenty or thirty seconds. She was a middle-aged woman with a big smile and bright green eyes. No makeup, wild curly brown hair, peasant blouse. I felt certain she'd been a hippie thirty years earlier.

"I'm Detective Purdy," Sam said, holding out his badge. "I phoned a little while ago."

"Alan Gregory," I added. "I'm a friend of Susan's."

She eyed me suspiciously, as though she was finding it hard to believe that Susan actually had friends. "Hello, hello, we've been expecting you. Come on in. I'm Crystal. Susan's upstairs waiting. Let me show you."

Sam said, "That's not necessary. I know the way." His voice was less than pleasant. I was placing my bet that he was going to start this process in the bad-cop persona.

I said, "The detective has been here before." What I didn't tell Crystal was that Sam's previous visit to this house was the night that Susan's husband was murdered.

My ass throbbing, I gazed longingly at the electric lift that had been installed to assist Susan up and down the staircase. I was tempted to ask Crystal how to use it. I didn't. Sam waited at the top of the stairs while I took the steps one at a time, dragging my wounded leg behind me.

"You're quite a gimp, you know?" He'd lowered his voice to a semblance of a whisper.

"Yeah, I know." After what felt like a technical climb in Eldorado Canyon, I joined him on the upstairs landing.

"You ready? You go first. Go lubricate."

I knocked and walked in. Susan had a hospital bed in her room. Although a bedside lamp was on, she appeared to be sleeping. "Susan? It's Alan Gregory. I came along with that detective who wants to talk with you."

She opened her eyes halfway and said my name. She appeared medicated. I wondered if she was taking something for pain or for sleep.

"Susan, how are you doing?"

"Oh, the pain. I'm having some pain."

"You took something for it?"

"I take things, but they can't find anything that really works. Doctors, doctors. The girl who's here—she's, she's—oh, let's just say she tries to help. I suppose they all try, don't they?" The aroma of her condescension and self-pity filled the room like a tuna sandwich left behind in the trash.

"This is Detective Purdy." I pointed behind me at Sam.

I'd seen Sam interview children before. He had a magical way of folding in on himself to disguise his size and appear less threatening. He managed the same transformation right then with Susan as he approached her bed. He became a big friendly gnome.

"Pleased to meet you," he told her. "I'm so sorry about your husband. I admired his work."

Admired his work? Sam was a private but vocal critic of the dead district attorney's proclivity toward plea bargains—on more than one occasion, I'd heard Sam call Royal Peterson "feckless"—though I didn't think it would be consistent with my role as a can of WD-40 to remind him of that at that moment.

"Yes," she murmured, sighing. "Thank you. It's been a hardship."

The closest chair was across the room. A stack of old newspapers covered the seat. It was apparent that Susan wasn't accustomed to welcoming visitors to her bedside. I cleared off the chair and carried it across the room. I moved an aluminum walker and a fancy carved cane out of the way to make space for Sam before I retreated into the shadows.

"I wish my children were closer," Susan said. "I really shouldn't be alone at a time like this. . . ."

I thought the obvious, that Susan's children had moved from her vicinity as soon as they were able—and that Susan bore some significant responsibility for their migration.

"It has to be hard having them so far away," Sam said. "Especially during a time as difficult as this."

I should have warned Sam to use a light hand when offering sympathy—that Susan was capable of sucking up compassion like a big tornado in Oklahoma sucks up trailer homes.

"I feel like I've been deserted. I'm so alone here."

Her words were weepy. My own compassion reserves were running dry and I didn't plan on using what I had remaining in the tank on Susan Peterson. I wondered if it would be considered rude to go back out the door and check out the operation of the lift on the staircase. But I reminded myself of my role as a can of WD-40.

Sam was searching for words. I chimed in. "Susan? It's funny that you're thinking about your children tonight, because that's what Detective Purdy needs to discuss with you. He has some questions about your first child, your daughter Lucy. From your first marriage."

Susan paled.

She looked away from Sam and me before she spoke again. "All day the phone is ringing. All day. People have questions, questions, questions. They don't even ask how I am. I'm a sick woman who has just lost her husband, lying here in the bed where I'm probably going to die, and everyone has questions about something that happened so long ago. It makes no sense to me. None."

Sam jumped right back in. "The questions I have aren't about long ago, Mrs. Peterson. That's your business. My questions are about the last few days. I'm just wondering if you've spoken to your daughter Lucy recently, if maybe she called you after the story came out in the newspaper."

Susan hesitated before she said, "No. You'd think a daughter would, wouldn't you? I mean call her own mother after something like that shows up in the newspapers." With each word, she sounded older.

Sam straightened up on his chair. The gnome was gone. Sam was now as big as Shaq. "That answer covers today, Mrs. Peterson. What about yesterday? Did you speak to your daughter yesterday?"

"Well, um, let me think. No, no, she didn't call

yesterday either." Susan actually smiled, as though she was proud of her answer. I felt myself cringe. I was riding shotgun with Sam now, and saw the transparency of Susan's protestations. If Susan thought she could play Sam for a fool, she was in for a surprise.

She probably couldn't recognize the signs, but I could. She'd pissed him off. Sam pressed her without mercy. His voice was now as intimidating as his posture. "She didn't call. That means she came by, doesn't it? Lucy came by to see you, Mrs. Peterson? When was that, exactly?"

She lifted a bell from beside her bed and shook it vigorously. I imagined it was an effort to summon Crystal. Susan winced and moaned like an old dog sighs. "The pain . . . I'm not sure, I'm not sure."

Sam stood. "When was she here?"

"I take a lot of medicine."

"And I eat too much food. When was she here?"

Her eyes flashed at Sam, the message behind them volatile. "Last night, about this time. It was the first time I'd seen her in a long time."

Sam ignored her threat. "How long a time?"

She hesitated. I couldn't decide whether she spent the moment trying to remember or whether she used it up manufacturing a lie. "Over a year."

Crystal walked in the door, smiling, and said, "Yes, dear?"

I said, "We'll just be a little while longer, Crystal. Susan will be fine until we leave."

Susan looked as though she wanted to disagree, but

after a glance at Sam she wisely chose not to protest. She just looked pitiful.

Crystal was unsure what to do.

"Really," I told her, "it's fine. I'll let you know when we're leaving. If she needs anything I'll come find you."

Crystal retreated out the door. I closed it behind her.

Sam hadn't turned away from Susan. He asked, "And what did Lucy say when she was here?"

"She warned me."

"Yes?"

"She warned me not to talk to anyone about . . . the family. About her, or me, or Royal. Or her father."

"Did she threaten you?"

"No. Well, kind of. Maybe."

"How did she threaten you?"

Susan considered her answer before she said, "It's not important."

"Then tell me what she didn't want you to tell any-one."

With no hesitation, Susan said, "No." She added, "You can't make me, Detective. I know my rights. My husband was the district attorney."

Sam stepped closer, eliminating the space between him and the edge of the bed. If I'd been the one gaz-ing into his eyes at that moment, I would have told him exactly where the treasure was buried.

Sam said, "Mrs. Peterson, your daughter is missing. I'm trying to find her. I need your help."

"My daughter? You mean Lucy? Sorry, you're going

to have to do better than that, Detective. She's been missing most of my life. She's a worse daughter than I am a mother. Regardless, I don't know anything that will help you find her. She's probably hiding somewhere. I know I would have if I'd done what she did."

"What's that? What did she do?"

Susan smiled. "No, Detective. I'm done talking to you. Alan, please ask that girl to come back in here."

Before Sam had a chance to voice his opinion about Susan Peterson, his cell phone beeped in his pocket. We were standing on the sidewalk in front of the Peterson home as he flipped it open.

"Purdy," he said.

For about a minute he listened, nodding, occasionally saying, "Yeah." Once he said, "They did that?"

He closed up the phone and said, "That was one of my buddies at the department. He just got a call from the Denver Police. They think they found Ramp's car. It was towed out of the alley behind his apartment building after six o'clock tonight. He'd left it double-parked for some reason. They're still busy getting warrants to search his apartment and to search the car, and they're still trying to get one to search that damn ranch out in God-knows-where."

"Agate."

"Yeah. Agate."

"Lucy's car? Anything there?"

"No, no sign of Lucy's car. Thing's as bright as a fire

truck, you'd think it would show up on someone's radar."

"What do you think of Susan's theory that Lucy's just gone into hiding to avoid the press?"

"I don't buy it. She called me this morning, told me she'd be back in touch early this evening. If she went into hiding, she'd call and tell me where she was. I'm sure as hell not going to tell the press. And that message she left for you? Why would she have left that message if she was going into hiding?"

I limped back toward the Cherokee. Sam was next to me. I said, "You guys finish the search at the Bigg home, Sam?"

"Mostly."

"Did you find anything?"

He shrugged. He wasn't sure he wanted to answer my question.

I said, "I don't like this, Sam."

"I don't either. Come on, I'll take you home." He stopped. "Did you know Lucy had visited Susan here?"

"No, Sam, I didn't. She didn't tell me."

He studied my face in a way that left me convinced that he was deciding whether to believe me or not.

I said, "What do you think of Mrs. Peterson?"

"I have trouble believing she's related to Lucy. I now know exactly where I come down on the whole nature/nurture debate. That's what I think. How's your ass holding up?"

"Not too good. I think maybe I should've borrowed some of Susan's pain meds."

"That's a felony. I would've had to take you in for it. Come on, I'll drive you home."

Before he had a chance to fire the car's ignition, Sam's phone sounded again. He flipped it open and said, "Purdy."

I shifted my weight to take the pressure off my wound. It didn't help.

Sam's eyes were open wide as he listened to the phone call. After about a minute, he said, "Be right there."

"Be right where?"

"Marin Bigg is awake and talking. We're going to Community, see if she has any insight into anything."

"Like who murdered her mother?"

"Yeah, like that."

"Drop me off at the Boulderado on the way. I'll get a cab home."

"Sorry, this game has gone into overtime and you're still in the lineup. I want your opinion of her. We're still not sure if she's part of Ramp's crew or if she's a victim."

CHAPTER
39

Lucy spent the night in a filthy construction trailer in Denver's Central Platte Valley, not too far from the REI that had taken over the old Forney Train Museum. A quick glance at the painting on the sign that graced the entrance to the construction site left her thinking that the building that was being framed was going to be some overpriced loft development.

Her hands and ankles were bound by plastic handcuffs that Ramp had discovered in the trunk of her Volvo after he'd parked it in a big shed in an industrial neighborhood on Denver's west side, somewhere between Broadway and Interstate 25. Ramp waited until after dark before he drove them in a gray Ford truck a mile or two to the construction site.

Since they'd arrived he'd only removed the bindings on Lucy's wrists and ankles twice, each time to allow her to use the portable toilet outside the construction trailer. He'd covered her with her own handgun the whole time. When she was done in the toilet, he'd had her rebind her own ankles and then lie prone on her abdomen before he recinched her wrists. Each step he prefaced with "please" and closed with "thank you."

Ramp fed Lucy a dinner of Slim Jims and Dr Pepper. She declined dessert, which was Little Debbie's oatmeal cookies, even though she'd adored their supersweetness when her dad had given them to her as a kid. Ramp allowed Lucy the small sofa that was tucked into one end of the trailer while he curled up on an army-surplus cot ten feet away. The sofa smelled. When Lucy commented on the odor, he told her that he'd smelled it, too, and thought the aroma was from construction adhesive.

Some kind of radio transmitting device—it looked to Lucy like a garage door opener—was taped to the inside of Ramp's left wrist. He demonstrated how he could hit the button with either hand at any time he wanted.

She'd asked him where the bomb was.

"Close by," he'd responded.

"A shaped charge?"

His eyes twinkled. "You've been talking to my grandma," he said. "She's a piece of work. I love that woman to death."

Lucy said, "Yes, I talked to her this morning."

"She tell you where to find me?"

"No. She didn't. I asked, but she wouldn't tell me. She wanted to talk to you and your dad first."

"That sounds like her." He ran the fingers of his right hand through his hair. "She's gotten bitter. It's been hard to watch."

"Your grandmother's had a lot of loss recently. Her husband, your uncle, your mom—it's a lot for someone to deal with."

"I know," he acknowledged. "It's still been hard to watch. When you love somebody, it's hard to watch."

She noted the empathy. Lucy hadn't yet heard a word of malice from Jason Ramp Bass. Not one.

He was a cute kid with tousled blond-brown hair, good skin, and a single silver earring in his right ear. He was also blessed with his grandmother's dazzling blue eyes and the kind of fetching smile that probably opened a lot of doors with girls while he was in high school, which Lucy figured wasn't too long ago.

"What do you like to be called?" she asked him after he told her it was time to get some sleep, that tomorrow was going to be a busy day.

"Jason. I like that best."

"Not Ramp?"

"Nah. My friends hung it on me, but I never loved it."

"Is tomorrow going to be busy for me, or just for you?"

"Both of us. I didn't originally plan on it, but I'm beginning to see how having a hostage might be helpful."

The word sent chills through Lucy. She was the hostage. "What's going to happen? What are your plans, Jason?"

He didn't have to think long before he answered her question. "My plans? I want to get a dialogue going."

"A dialogue?"

"A dialogue. About justice in America. The way it works, the way it doesn't. I have a friend—he's black, a guy I went to high school with—who's doing more time for selling speed than the murderer who killed my mom got for killing his first victim. Is that right? I want a dialogue about stuff like that. I think it's time that we had a dialogue about that. As a society. About sentences and judges and courts and parole. About protecting innocent people. About malpractice in courts the same way we talk about malpractice in hospitals."

"The inequities," Lucy said.

"Yeah, the inequities," he repeated. Lucy thought he seemed pleased at her choice of words.

He stood and moved across the room to the sofa. "I'm going to have to tape you down so I can get some rest without worrying about you trying to get away. What position do you want to be in?"

She thought about it. "On my back, I guess." She could only imagine how sore she would be by morning.

"You want to go to the Super Bowl first?"

"What?"

"The plastic head outside. It's called the Super Bowl. You want to go again before I tie you down?"

"I just went."

"Whatever."

He grabbed a huge roll of duct tape and wound it individually around her ankles and then under and around the sofa. He repeated the procedure twice more and moved up her torso. She could tell that the proximity to her breasts made him uncomfortable. With her manacled hands she held them up and out of the way so that he could wrap her around her rib cage.

"Not too tight, please. I need to breathe."

"I'll be careful," he said.

"Thanks."

He returned to his cot. "Don't know if you noticed, but there was an actual dialogue for a while after the shootings at Columbine, and again for a little while after the thing at Santana, that high school near San Diego. About bullying, and cliques, and jocks and freaks, and insiders and outsiders in high school, how destructive it all is. It got drowned out by all the hoopla because those kids were so angry and so stupid about what they did, so the dialogue didn't do enough or last long enough to accomplish what it could've. The Columbine kids and that boy at Santana were more interested in the killing than the talking. I'm more interested in the talking. I want this dialogue to last longer. And I think it will. I hope it makes a difference, though I doubt I'll be around to see it when it does."

Lucy had a hard time finding a position where she could see her captor across the narrow trailer. But she knew she'd just heard him predict that he wasn't likely to survive whatever was about to happen. "You're sure that you're not just trying to get even? To get some retribution for what happened to your mother?"

His hands were locked behind his head and he was

staring up at the trailer's ceiling. "You ever notice how this country doesn't seem to pay much attention to anything important until somebody dies? It's the funniest thing. Whether it's putting in a traffic light after a kid gets killed on the way to school or something like Columbine or the terrorists who blew up that ship— what was it, the *Cole*? Then it seems we forget about it just as fast as we remembered. Is that human nature, you think? I wonder about that a lot. The more spectacular way somebody dies, though, the longer we seem to talk about it. It's a peculiar thing in this country but I'm willing to take advantage of it. That's for sure.

"Tomorrow's going to be spectacular. There's no doubt about it. People will talk for a while. I just hope it's the right kind of dialogue."

Lucy was aware of parallel instincts. The part of her that was the hostage wanted the captor to fall asleep. The part of her that was a detective wanted to burst from her bonds, overwhelm him, and interrogate the bastard to find out his plans.

Ramp continued. "I don't feel good about what I did today, in case you're wondering. I didn't know how I'd feel if it came to that. But I do, now. I don't feel good about it."

Lucy wondered if he was talking about kidnapping her or if he was talking about something else.

"You mean kidnapping me?"

"No, no, no. I mean, I haven't even thought about how I feel about that. Not yet. I don't know if I will think about it for a while. I'm talking about the bomb in Boulder. Killing Marin's mom."

Lucy's heart felt like it hiccupped. "Marin's mom? You killed Naomi Bigg with a bomb?"

He sat up on his elbows. "You hadn't heard? It's been all over the news since this afternoon."

Her voice was fragile. "I hadn't heard anything about it. I've been avoiding the news because of . . ."

He finished her sentence. "The thing with your mother."

"Yeah, the thing with my mother."

"What is that? I don't understand. What is that thing with your mother? You've been like ignoring her or something? Pretending she wasn't your mom? I can't . . . imagine it. I'd give anything for a chance to spend another day with my mom. Anything."

"I envy you that. That she was so special to you."

"Your mom wasn't?"

"She left me and my dad when I was little."

"She just left?"

"I didn't see her or even hear from her for years, then I tracked her down when I was an adult, hoping for a reconciliation. But it didn't work out the way I wanted. We never got along. The police think that the fact that she and I had such a difficult relationship might have given me a motive to kill her husband. He was the Boulder County district attorney." Lucy suspected that Ramp knew all about the murder of Royal Peterson, but she kept her suspicions to herself.

Ramp lowered himself back down on the cot. "That

doesn't make sense. Why would you kill him for that?"

Lucy sighed. "They think I was sleeping with my mother's husband. That maybe I killed him to shut him up or something, you know, so that she wouldn't find out about the affair."

Ramp was silent for a long stretch before he asked, "Were you? Were you sleeping with him?"

To Lucy, his words sounded reluctant, as though he didn't want to find out that it was true. She wasn't sure how to answer but didn't want to lie. "Yes," Lucy said. "I was. It's funny to say it. I haven't admitted that to anyone before right now. Not even my friends or my lawyers."

"But you didn't kill him."

"No, I didn't kill him."

Lucy recalled the conversation she had recently had with Alan Gregory and what he had said about intimacy. That true intimacy required not only disclosure, but also vulnerability.

Jason had just admitted a murder and she'd just admitted an affair with her mother's husband. That was disclosure.

If she got away, Jason Ramp Bass was on his way to life in prison or even death row in Cañon City. If she didn't get away, Ramp was probably going to kill her.

That was vulnerability.

She looked over at Ramp and thought that they were so intimate at that moment that they may as well have been sleeping naked in the same cot.

Ramp said, "In a way, we both lost our moms."

Lucy felt a flutter in her heart and thought that he'd made the words sound like the lyrics for a song.

He murmured, "Good night, Lucy. Get some sleep."

And she knew she was going to cry. But she wasn't sure why. Just that it had something to do with mothers.

The night before, when Lucy had walked unannounced into the master bedroom of the Peterson house on Jay Street, she'd said, "Susan, we need to talk."

Susan had looked up and greeted her without surprise. She'd said, "What? You think things have changed? Just because Royal's dead?"

"Everything's changed, Susan. You know that."

"You still call me Susan, not Mother. That hasn't changed. I still have this damn disease. That hasn't changed. Royal's not here anymore—that's all that's changed."

Lucy didn't bite. "I haven't told the police that you're my mother, Susan. I came here to talk with you because I think we should leave it that way."

Susan scoffed back. "Why? So your life isn't complicated by the fact that you have a disabled mother? Sorry, if they ask me, I'll tell them. I don't care who knows. I just lost my husband—nobody will care what happened with us, Lucy. They'll forgive me for what I did to you. They might not understand why you're so callous now, but they'll forgive *me*."

"Susan, what do you want from me?"

She straightened the sheets on her bed and hit the mute button on the remote control before she said, "Just do what's right, Lucy. Isn't that what I always taught you?"

CHAPTER

40

I can't sleep. Can you?"

Lucy's eyes had been tracking the linear shadows that were making a picket fence of light appear across the ceiling of the construction trailer. She was wide-awake. In response to Jason Ramp's question, she said, "No."

For a moment both were silent. Lucy finally stammered, "Is it because you killed somebody today?"

"Yeah," Ramp said. "That, and I keep going over what's going to happen tomorrow."

"You want to talk about it?"

"Maybe, I'm not sure. I don't know if I do. More people are going to die tomorrow. I'm sure of that much. So I'm not sure why I'm so weirded out by Marin's mom dying today."

"Maybe that's it—that she was somebody's mom."

"Whoa, I hadn't thought about that. That's something to think about, isn't it?"

"Why did you do it, Jason? Blow her up?"

"She figured out what we were up to. I'm not exactly sure how. I think probably Marin left some stuff around the house or was careless on the Net or something. Doesn't matter now, I suppose. Marin said that her mom was going to tell everything to that shrink she was seeing. I had to keep her from doing that. One more day, that's all we needed. One more day."

Lucy sensed a vulnerability. She tried to exploit it. "You ever kill anyone before?"

"That woman who died in the car bomb in Denver? I caused that. She wasn't the intended victim. Her husband was. I guess you could say I killed her. But the bomb I put under their car went off by accident. I wasn't going to set it off until . . . until the right time came. Her husband should have been driving, not her."

"Why him?"

He ignored her question.

Lucy spoke into the darkness. "Maybe you feel troubled because you knew Marin's mother. I imagine that it makes a difference, killing someone you know."

He parried with his own question. "Have you been angry enough to kill your mother?"

The question felt like a physical blow to Lucy. She had trouble catching her breath. "I've never thought about it."

"Think about it now. Please."

"I don't know, Jason. I don't know. My God, what a question."

"You might be surprised what you can do when you've been hurt enough. You might be surprised."

"Have you been hurt enough?"

"Have you?" he countered.

Lucy looked away from him. "Are the others all going to be strangers?"

"What others?"

"The ones who are going to die tomorrow."

Ramp's voice softened. "I don't know them, not personally, if that's what you mean. I know who they are. I picked them because of who they are, but I don't know them. Others will get hurt or die, too. Unintended victims. No matter how careful you are, bombs tend to be a little indiscriminate when they go off around people. I've accepted that risk."

"So what is it then?" She was trying to feed his self-doubt.

Ramp stood up and crossed the distance between them slowly, his body emerging from the shadows the way a lover might approach the bed. He straddled a metal desk chair three feet from her.

"I'm telling you a lot. You tell me something about you. Something personal, private."

Lucy almost laughed. She looked up at the grimy ceiling before staring into his cool eyes. "I already told you I was sleeping with my mother's husband. How much more private you want me to get?"

She could only see half his face. The eyelid that she

could see was heavy, and a soft beard had emerged on his chin. She thought she recognized something unexpected in his glare.

She double-checked her impressions and decided to take a chance. Lucy said, "My boobs are two different sizes."

He laughed and pounded a boot on the dirty carpet.

She joined him laughing.

"My mom told me that all girls' boobs are two different sizes. That's not a big deal."

"Mine aren't a little different, they're a lot different. More than a whole cup size different."

"That's a lot?"

"Yeah, that's a lot. It made for some tough times in the locker room at school. And it complicates shopping for lingerie." She said the final word wistfully, hoped it hung in the room like perfume.

He crossed his arms on top of the chair back and sprawled his legs out in front of him, smiling to himself. "Which one do you like more?"

She laughed with him again, trying to draw him along. "What kind of question is that?"

"If you could have them both be the same size, which one would you choose?"

"The left one."

He looked down at her chest and laughed again. "That's a good answer."

His appraisal of her chest left her questioning her decision to flirt with him. She said, "Thank you."

"You know," he said, "when I was like nine or ten, I

used to think they had bones in them. Boobs. Breasts. I didn't know they were soft. I thought they had like a cone of little bones holding them in shape. One time I was in a swimming pool playing some game and I accidentally kicked a girl in her chest and her breast just squished underneath my foot. I remember that I thought I'd broken it."

"So how did you find out the truth about boobs?"

"Personal research."

"Seriously."

"My mom. She told me. She'd tell me anything. Never made me feel stupid. Then she died."

Lucy felt the flirtation that was developing between them evaporate like water splashed on a griddle. She knew that the strategic advantage she'd been nurturing evaporated along with the teasing. She said, "I'm so sorry, Jason. About what happened to your mom. It sounds like you two were very close."

He leaned over the edge of the cot and said, "Thanks for saying that. I'm sorry about what happened with you and your mom, too. At least I got a lot of memories with mine. You don't even have that."

"No, I don't even have that."

"Lots of wives and sisters and daughters die because of the stupid way the system works. So this . . . thing I'm doing, it's really about lots of moms. Everyone has to remember that. It's not just about my mom."

"It's about sons and brothers and fathers, too?"

"Yeah."

Lucy said, "What was she like? Your mom?"

"I don't think I want to talk about her."

"You know, I'm no expert on mothers, that's for sure," Lucy said. "But she sounds very special."

Ramp's jaw took on a tight set. He said, "They won't find you here. In case that's what you're hoping. They might be looking for you, but . . ." His voice faded away.

"Oh," Lucy said.

"Nobody knows that I'm here. That we're here, in this trailer. Not even Marin knows where I'm planning to spend the night. The truck I'm using won't be missed for a couple of days. My company thinks it's in the shop with transmission trouble."

Lucy fought a fresh flush of despair. She needed to keep him talking. "How did you know her? Marin?"

"We met on the Web. In a chat room."

"Complaining about the justice system?"

"Yeah."

"You recruit her?"

"I guess. Didn't take much effort. It was more like I invited her. She was as angry as I was. You know what happened to her a few years ago?"

"Yes, I do. I didn't work the case but I knew a lot about it. Are you two like boyfriend and girlfriend?"

"At first, kind of. But no. Not now. I don't stay with girls very long. Not that way, anyway. I'm not ready for a real relationship."

Lucy couldn't tell whether she heard some disappointment or longing lurking in his words.

A siren erupted nearby. Its insistent wail filled the

trailer like a sour stench. Lucy and Jason both waited to discover whether the sound would approach them or recede into the distance.

It faded.

"Told you. They won't find you here."

"Is she part of what's going to happen tomorrow?"

"You mean Marin?"

Lucy nodded.

"She was going to be. Now she's in the hospital, so I guess not. The whole thing was planned so that we would operate independently. Just in case one of us was caught. Either one of us can make our half of the plan work on our own."

Lucy watched Ramp stand and move to the trailer's window. The thick layer of dust on the glass turned the night sky behind him pasty and sick.

"Were you trying to hurt Marin today? Or was that an accident?"

"You know, I'm not really sure. At the moment I touched the button, I wasn't sure whose side she was on. Mine or her mother's."

"Wow," Lucy said. "You're not even sure whether you were trying to hurt her. What a thing to say."

"Yeah."

Lucy pressed. "The bomb at the district attorney's house in Boulder? That was one of yours?"

"Yes. It was. That was going to be part of Marin's route."

"Route?"

"Tomorrow, we each have a route. There will be a

series of bombs. The bombs in Boulder are designed differently from the ones in Denver so that they can't be tied together. And I have something special planned at the end, like a finale at a fireworks show."

"Who's going to die tomorrow?"

The silence that followed her question allowed the hum of I-25 to infiltrate the trailer. An eighteen-wheeler was having trouble with a low gear. The whine of air brakes sounded.

"A lot of people."

"You don't want to tell me who?"

"People who've had a hand in the bullshit. That's all I'll say."

"Regarding your mother? That bullshit?"

"Not just that. Remember, I'm talking about the whole system. I want people to talk about every last place where the system is broken. The problem with Columbine, even with McVeigh in Oklahoma City, was that . . ."

Ramp's words faded into the darkness as he suddenly refocused his attention out the trailer's window.

"Was what, Jason? What was the problem?"

"Shhh." He waved an open hand from his shoulder to near his waist. "Shhh. Don't speak."

She watched the reflexive movement as his fingers curled toward the switch that was taped to his wrist.

Lucy whispered, "Is there someone here?"

Calmly, he said, "I said shut up. I meant it."

Lucy considered the opportunity that was being presented to her. She wasn't gagged. She could scream and maybe get the attention of whomever Ramp was tracking outside the trailer. At this hour, she assumed it would either be a security patrol or a trespasser.

She forced her heart to still so she could hope to hear whatever it was that was going on outside. She heard nothing. No tires on gravel. No voices. No music from a car radio.

Ramp straightened at the window and moved his fingertips away from the switch on his wrist.

Her moment was gone. She felt a tear form in the corner of one eye. "You were telling me what the problem was with McVeigh and with Columbine. What was the problem?"

"Not just one. A few. The main one was their rage. But also the randomness of what they did. And the fact that they targeted innocent people. Those things changed the debate. If the bully steals your lunch and you respond by blowing up the whole damn cafeteria, nobody ends up paying attention to what the bully did to you. They focus on your rage, and on the innocent victims you killed by how you retaliated. That was the problem with Columbine. What they did—killing so many innocent people—changed the debate forever, and their message was diluted to the point that nobody really paid any attention to their motives. Not in the end, anyway. I won't allow that to happen tomorrow."

"You want the debate?"

"I want the debate."

"But you already said that there will be unintended victims from what you're planning."

"Yes, but they're not targets. That's the difference. They will prove one of my points, however."

"I don't understand."

"My mother was the unintended victim of the justice system's decision to free a murderer and put him back on the street. My plan will duplicate that. There's some irony there, I think. The ones who are responsible will suffer losses, and so will some innocent people. The justice system didn't target my mother. But they allowed her to be killed. They were callous to her safety."

"And you'll do the same tomorrow?"

"Yes."

"What gives you the right?"

He laughed, a tight sound that seemed to catch in his throat. "Revolution always begins with an act of anarchy. By definition, no one has the right to be an anarchist. I'm hoping to start a little revolution. So by definition, I'm assuming the right to be an anarchist."

"You can call it anarchy but it sounds like revenge to me. Vengeance. I don't see how what you're doing is any different. You'll be just another pissed-off kid with blood on his hands. You don't have to do this."

"I don't want the blood. I want the dialogue. That's what's different. The blood will get everyone's attention."

She implored him, "Don't do it."

"It's too late."

Lucy felt herself sinking into the sofa. The cogency of Ramp's argument was exhausting her. She wanted to ask him to use his energy differently. To beg him to find another way. But she knew he wasn't remotely interested. Her desperation caused her to play a card she wasn't sure she should play.

"The shrink that Marin's mother was going to see when you killed her today? I know him. His name is Dr. Gregory. He already knows a lot about what you and Marin are planning."

His pale eyes narrowed, the tips of his brows curling down toward the bridge of his nose. "How do you know that?"

"We're friends. He was worried about his wife's safety, so he came to me. I thought he might be able to help me figure out who killed Royal Peterson. We've been helping each other."

"Are you lying?"

"You still have my cell phone?"

"Yeah."

"Hit redial. You'll see his number. He's the last person I called. Or check caller ID. His number's in there."

Ramp retrieved the cell phone from his duffel and hit the redial button. He read the number that came up and then killed the call.

Lucy asked, "You know how to work it? Check the directory and you can match the name and number."

"Yes," he said, touching a series of buttons. "There it is. Alan Gregory."

"See?"

"He could be anybody. You could be playing me right now. How do I know you're not lying?"

Lucy said, "He knows about Paul."

Ramp smiled in a way that seemed full of compassion and something else. She wasn't sure about the something else. "You think Naomi told this Alan Gregory what the plans were?"

"I know he knows some things. I also know he was reluctant to tell me some other things."

"But he knows about the bombs?"

"Yes. And that you're angry at the justice system."

His jaws tightened. "She told him that?"

"Yes."

"What else? Tell me."

"He knows about the wouldn't-it-be-cool games."

"God, really? The man might really know something."

Lucy's phone suddenly came alive, chirping in his hand.

Ramp stared down at the phone. Didn't answer it.

He asked Lucy, "Who do you think was trying to call you?"

She hesitated a heartbeat or two. "My partner. His name is Sam Purdy. He's a detective in Boulder. And he's my friend."

"You were trying to decide whether to lie to me right then, weren't you? What did you decide?"

"I decided to tell you the truth." She paused. "Mostly because you can check for yourself on caller ID."

She waited for him to check the caller ID log. He didn't. "So your friend, this detective, he makes a habit of calling you in the middle of the night?"

"Sam knows I'm missing by now. I told him I'd check in with him when I got back from seeing your grandmother."

"What will he do if he thinks you're missing?"

"Whatever he can think of to find me. Sam's relentless and he's pretty resourceful."

"What does he know?"

"Whatever Alan Gregory knows, Sam knows. They're good friends."

"You making this whole thing up as you go along? You're pretty good if you are."

"It's all true, Jason."

"Do they know about the bombs?"

"For sure? No. But they're the ones who found the bomb at Royal Peterson's house, and Dr. Gregory was so worried that you might have targeted his wife with a bomb that he brought an explosive-sniffing dog into his house and to check his cars."

"Really? You mentioned his wife already. Who is she?"

"She's a deputy DA in Boulder who was tangentially involved in Marin's rape case."

"Her name?"

"Lauren Crowder."

"Doesn't ring a bell. I don't think Marin mentioned her."

Lucy shrugged to hide her sense of relief.

Ramp was flipping the phone into the air, catching it again as it completed one end-to-end rotation.

She said, "The special part you mentioned that would be coming at the end of the day. That's part of your route?"

"It is."

"What good am I in all this?"

"So far you're just good company. I appreciate that. I'm still considering what else you'll do."

"You're going to kill me, aren't you, Jason?" The use of his name was intentional. She even emphasized it.

He stepped back from the window and moved halfway into a shadowed place close to the wall. "I don't think I'll have to. I really hope not."

"I don't understand."

"If I'm still standing at the end of the day, your job is over. I won't have to kill you."

"But if they catch up with you before that?"

"That's up to them, of course. Your presence is to ensure that I get to keep going. To finish what I started."

"But there will be bombs close by all day long. Who knows what will happen? That's what you're saying?"

Ramp's hand flashed toward his right hip as though he'd been stung there by a yellow jacket.

The swift movement of his hand caused Lucy's breath to catch in the middle of her chest as though she'd suddenly been dipped in ice water.

He lifted a beeper from his belt and lit the screen.

"Wow," he said. "What a surprise. I have to go make a call. I'm going to have to gag you. I'm sorry."

"Please, no."

"I said I'm sorry. You want something to drink first?"

CHAPTER
41

They wheeled her to X-ray. She went out a back door when the tech went to get something."

A young detective whom I'd never met was the one doing the I-can't-believe-it-but-we-lost-her shuffle. Even without glancing at his face, I could tell that Sam Purdy wanted to take someone's head off and was considering whether this young man's noggin would be a good place to start.

Sam said, "We were watching her, right?"

"Yeah, we had someone outside her door for her protection. He followed her wheelchair down to X-ray and checked out the room. He thought the other door in the room went to a place for developing the X-ray film or something. Didn't know it led to a hallway."

"So she went out that other door? That's how she got away from him? She just walked away?"

"Yes."

"What's she wearing? One of those hospital gowns?"

"Probably not. There's a supply closet close by where scrubs are stored. We found a gown on the floor by the scrubs. We think it was hers. So she's probably wearing scrubs. Light purple. You know, like lavender."

Sam glared. My guess was that he was reacting to the detective's use of "lavender."

"She's barefoot?"

"She's wearing a pair of those little foam hospital slippers, as far as we know. They weren't with the gown."

"What kind of head start did she get?"

"A few minutes. Maybe five."

"The building get sealed?"

"Not for another five or so minutes after that."

"Maybe ten?"

"Yeah, maybe ten. Seven or eight, you know."

"She's ambulatory?"

"Unfortunately, yeah. Injuries from the bomb were to her upper body. Worst damage is to her left hand, from shrapnel. That's what she was in surgery for earlier. Her face is cut up, too. She has a bandage on her cheek right here, between her ear and her eye." He touched his own face to demonstrate the spot. "Got patched up by a plastic surgeon."

"So she's ambulatory and she has a ten- to fifteen-minute head start. She could be somewhere in this big hospital or she could be out on the street."

"That's the situation."

"What did you get before she ran?"

"Not much. Her surgeon only gave me about five minutes with her at first. She was still pretty groggy from the anesthesia and the painkillers, said she didn't remember anything at all about the bombing. Kept asking me about her mom as though she couldn't believe she was dead."

"But she knew?"

"She knew."

Sam inhaled like he was about to blow up a balloon. Then he sighed. "Nothing at all about this guy Ramp?"

"I asked, Sam. Said she didn't even know him. Didn't know what the hell I was talking about."

A uniformed officer approached us and waited until Sam said, "What do you want, Officer?"

"Sorry to interrupt but we just discovered that a purse is missing. One of the X-ray techs is telling us that her purse is gone along with her denim jacket. The purse was in a little room where the staff hangs out sometimes at the back of radiology. Kind of like a little lounge."

"What was in the purse?"

"What you'd expect. Wallet, ID, about fifty bucks."

"And the denim? Blue, faded, what?"

"Blue, not too old. From The Gap."

"Great," Sam said. "Just fucking great. Now she has money and street clothes. Has anybody called RTD or the taxi companies?"

"We're on that."

Sam stuck his hands in his pockets, probably to

quell his impulse to place them around somebody's neck.

I couldn't see the point in sticking around any longer. I'd been able to convince myself that I might be of some assistance in helping Sam evaluate Marin Bigg. But I didn't see a thing that I could contribute now that the task had evolved into searching for her. Anyway, my ass hurt.

I said, "I'm going to get a cab home, Sam. Call me if there's something else that I can do."

"Yeah," he said.

Reading between the lines, I realized that his words were kind of like "Thanks for your help."

"Wait a second. Before you go, give me your take on all this. She's hurt, she's on the run. Her mother's dead. Her house is surrounded by the good guys. Where would she go? The girl? Where do you think she'd go?"

"That's a tough one. She's young. I'm not sure she'd do anything that you or I might consider predictable."

"Think."

"Assuming that this kid Ramp set off the bomb that killed her mother, she'd try and find him, I think."

"To get even?"

"Possibly. But maybe to join back up with him. It all depends where her allegiance was strongest."

"You mean to him or to her mother?"

"Yes, that's exactly what I mean. She didn't seem that tight with her mother when I saw her yesterday."

"She could forgive Ramp for killing her mother?" Sam looked a little incredulous at the thought.

"Naomi was about to turn her in to the police. Or at least turn her in to me. Marin may be part of this whole conspiracy with Ramp. She may feel that she was betrayed by her mother. Teenagers make strong alliances with their friends, Sam. Stronger than with their families sometimes."

"So you think that if we find her in the next little while, she could lead us to Ramp?"

I knew Sam was thinking that leading him to Ramp meant leading him to Lucy. "I suppose."

"But you're not sure when she finds this Ramp whether she wants to kill him or kiss him?"

"She may not be sure, either." I was so tired that I wanted to sit down, but my butt screamed at the thought of having weight on it. "The only thing we know for sure is that one of them is going to eventually show up at Nora's house," I said. "To set off that bomb that they left there. That's your best bet of finding one of them. Stake out Nora's house and wait."

"It's not going to happen. Those damn Fox News people have the story about the bomb at Nora's house already. They ran with it on their nine o'clock news. If the kids are paying any attention at all, they'll know we found that bomb."

There's another bomb. That lawyer.

As the echo of Naomi's warning sounded in my head, a new question surfaced. Was the bomb at Nora's house the one that Naomi was warning me about? The hospital hallway felt cold in the way that only hospital hallways can. I wished I had a sweater.

"Go ahead and go home," Sam told me. "If you hear from Lucy . . ."

"Of course."

I turned to leave, stopped. "Sam? What if there's another bomb? One that you guys didn't find this afternoon? What if the one at Nora's wasn't even the one that Naomi was telling me about?"

He snapped at me as though he was irritated that I wasn't already gone. "What are you saying?"

"I don't know exactly. It's just that—I'm thinking that maybe there might be someone at risk that we haven't thought about. Maybe there are some people on the wouldn't-it-be-cool list that we haven't even considered."

"More lawyers?"

"I guess. Naomi said, 'That lawyer.' "

There's another bomb. That lawyer.

"You mean besides Nora and Royal?"

"That's what I'm thinking."

Sam's voice took on the timbre of debate. "We checked for bombs around the judge who accepted the plea on Marin's rape. Negative. We checked Cozy Maitlin's house and office. He was the rapist's defense attorney. Negative. We checked everything on Lauren, who was assisting Nora with the prosecution. Negative. We checked and found devices at Nora's and at Royal Peterson's home. So who's left?"

"Maybe Lauren and Nora can answer that. I don't know the system well enough to know who else might have been involved."

He took a step away from me before he stopped and faced me again. "How come every time I think you're going to bring clarity to a process, you end up clouding everything up like a damn fog machine? Why do you think that is?"

CHAPTER
42

She didn't like being bound.

She despised being gagged.

It was obvious that he hadn't planned for this step, either. The gag he fashioned was a clean white sock stuffed partway into her mouth and held in place by a long strip of duct tape.

The ambivalence she was feeling when he left the trailer ambushed her. She found herself wavering back and forth between wishing that Ramp wouldn't be gone long and hoping that the next person she saw walk through the door of the construction trailer would be the job site foreman stumbling in shortly after the eastern sky was streaked with bands of orange and blue. He'd be carrying a cardboard cup of gas station coffee and his brain would be brimming with the assorted headaches that he'd have to solve before lunch. Lucy imagined that he'd drop the coffee at the sight of the woman duct-taped to his sofa.

But Lucy was also hoping that Ramp wouldn't be gone long.

There was a name for what she was feeling. She tried to remember what she'd read about it. It was something Scandinavian. The Copenhagen Effect? No. The Stockholm Syndrome? Yes, that was it. The Stockholm Syndrome. Something about a train hijacking. The psychological phenomenon where hostages begin identifying with their captors.

Was she identifying with him? Lucy didn't think so. His rationalizations for the next day's terror rang hollow for her.

But she liked Jason Ramp Bass. She liked his charm. She liked his respectful manner. She liked the fact that he adored his mother. She even admired the way he'd managed to subvert his rage into something concise and, well, neat.

She wished she could see a clock. She wished she could roll onto her side. She wished she could empty her bladder. Mostly she wished she could call Sam and tell him to send in the cavalry.

People were going to die tomorrow. Nobody knew but her. And she couldn't do a thing about it.

Lucy had dozed off and didn't realize the door to the trailer was opening again. She didn't even hear Ramp enter or approach her.

He touched her gently on the cheek and said, "Hey, gotta get up. Plans have changed. Lucy, Lucy."

When she opened her eyelids, the soft blue of his eyes filled her vision like the sunlight fills the morning sky. Behind him the room was dark but the picket fence shadows still lined the ceiling.

"Hi," she said into the gag. Her heart pounded in her chest and the tape around her body suddenly seemed too tight to allow her to draw a breath.

Part of her response, she knew, was terror about what was going to happen next.

Part of it wasn't.

He removed the duct tape but not the gag and neither the wrist nor the ankle restraints, and he helped her to her feet.

"I'm going to carry you outside to the truck. You want to use the bathroom first?"

She nodded definitively.

She guessed he was only five ten or five eleven, maybe one hundred sixty pounds, but he lifted her effortlessly and carried her out the door the way a new husband lifts his bride over the threshold. She would have hooked an arm around his neck if she could, but she couldn't.

He stood her up outside the chemical toilet and opened the door. She held out her wrists for him to cut her plastic cuffs. Instead, he grabbed her around the waist and lifted her inside the plastic door. "I don't have time to free your restraints. You want help or can you do this yourself?"

She spoke into her gag and nodded her head. He reached up and stretched the sock away from her lips. She spit cotton before she said, "Undo my pants and pull them over my hips."

He hesitated.

"I can do the rest. Do that much." She held up her bound wrists. "I'm not going to slap you, don't worry."

He fumbled with the belt on her pants and had even more trouble with the button. The zipper he mastered quickly.

She wriggled her hips to help him get the tight pants over her butt and hips and stood still while he yanked the waistband all the way down to her upper thighs. Even through the gag, she figured he could tell that at that point she said, "Okay. That's enough."

She thought she saw his gaze focus momentarily on the lime-green triangle of her exposed underwear before he stepped back and gently closed the door of the chemical toilet.

A minute or so later she knocked the door back open with her shoulder. The top of her pants was at mid-thigh, as high as she could get them on her own. "Help me," she said.

She watched as he moved his eyes quickly from her upper legs and crotch to her face, and then back down.

He didn't hesitate this time. As he tugged her pants into place, his fingers grazed the soft skin that was exposed below the hem of her underwear. She felt his knuckles press against her belly as he buttoned her jeans, and she found herself holding her breath as he pulled up the zipper and closed the belt.

With an arm around her waist, he lifted her from the toilet and carried her to a different truck than the one she'd ridden in a few hours before.

This one was a small flatbed with welding supplies strapped into place in the back. The sign on the driver's door read "JT Welding Supplies."

"You're going to have to curl up on the floor. Can you do that? The alternative is that box in the back of the truck. But that will get hot tomorrow, I promise."

Lucy tilted her head at the cab. More despair. Tomorrow seemed like a long way away.

"Good choice," he said.

Once she was curled up on the floor of the cab, Ramp said, "While I was gone, I talked to your doctor friend. I think we're cool. And, for what it's worth, I think he's worried about you."

CHAPTER

43

Cruising taxicabs are rare at any hour in Boulder. Past midnight there was no hope I would find a cab prowling the streets, so I used my cell phone to request that a taxi be sent to the emergency entrance of the hospital. The dispatcher yawned twice before he responded by asking for my phone number and telling me to watch for a car within five minutes, maybe less.

The cell phone rang a few seconds after I ended the call with Yellow Cab. I guessed it was the dispatcher phoning back to ascertain that I was someone who really wanted a ride.

I said, "Hello."

A male voice said, "Is this Alan Gregory?"

I thought the voice was young, and immediately recognized that it wasn't the bored dispatcher with whom I'd just spoken. "Yes, it is. Who's this?"

"Never mind. Tell me what you know about Paul Bigg. I want to hear everything."

My ass suddenly stopped hurting. My ass actually stopped existing. I repeated, "Who is this?"

"Use your imagination and you'll know who this is. Now tell me what you know about Paul Bigg. This is a test, by the way. It's pass/fail. You get one chance. There are no retests."

My mouth felt as though I'd just tried to swallow a dirt clod and failed. I almost coughed out the answer to his question. "He died in a Little League accident about six years ago. A heart rhythm problem, I think."

"Go on."

I assumed I was talking to the infamous Ramp. I couldn't begin to guess what he wanted or how he'd managed to reach me on this number. "His mother, her name is Naomi, acts—acted—as though he were alive sometimes. She talked about him as though he'd never died."

"You passed," Ramp said.

"Good," I said. I suspected my trials weren't complete.

"You have a tall blond friend?"

God. He had Lucy. That's how he got my number. He was holding Lucy. "Yes," I said, "I do. Is she okay?"

Sam, I knew, was going to want to know every word, so I began to chart the conversation in my head to help me remember the details.

"As far as I know, she is."

"Do you have her? Is she with you?"

"I'd prefer to be the one asking the questions, if you don't mind."

"How can I help you?" I said. It was a variation on the line I used to start therapy sessions with new patients. It was similar to the line I'd used with Naomi Bigg only a couple of weeks before. I don't know why I used it right then.

"What have you told the police?"

"I've been talking to them ever since the bomb went off outside my office. I've told them a lot."

"Are they with you right now?"

"No. I'm standing by myself waiting for a taxi to take me home."

"Where?"

"I'm at the hospital in Boulder. Community Hospital."

"Were you hurt today? By the bomb?"

"Yes. I got a piece of shrapnel in my butt and had a minor concussion. I banged my head on the door."

"I'm sorry you were hurt. What do the police know?"

I hesitated. "I'd like to answer your question. But I've told them a lot of things. Do you want me to try to—"

He sighed. "Just tell me about the wouldn't-it-be-cool games. What do they know about those? Before you begin your answer, a reminder: Please don't forget about your tall blond friend."

I hadn't forgotten. "I told them everything Naomi told me about the games. They've put together a list of the people who they think might be on Marin's list and they've already searched all of those people's homes and offices for explosives." I remembered what Sam had said about Fox News letting the cat out of the bag about the bomb at Nora's house. "The police have already found one device. It was in a prosecutor's garage. They've disarmed it."

"They don't actually disarm them. They disrupt them. They blow them apart with water cannons."

"I'm sorry," I said. "I knew that. I'll try to be more specific."

"Did you say 'one device'?"

Did he sound relieved? I wasn't sure. "One," I repeated.

"What about any other wouldn't-it-be-cool lists? Besides Marin's?"

"To the best of my knowledge, they're still working on compiling the . . . other list."

I actually thought I could hear him smile over the phone.

"See you," he said, and the line went dead.

CHAPTER

44

Sam wasn't officially directing the search for Marin Bigg. He wasn't actually officially investigating anything that had to do with any of the Biggs, or anything to do with Ramp, or with the explosion outside my office.

Sam was freelancing.

He was at Community Hospital in the middle of the night because he was looking for Lucy. In his mind, this gave him a platinum-plated invitation to stick his bulbous nose anyplace he felt like sticking it. When I tracked him down inside the hospital, he was in a first-floor corridor pacing on the periphery of a conversation other cops were having about the search of the interior of the hospital that was taking place in an attempt to find Marin.

I caught his eye and mouthed, "Come here."

He apparently saw something in my face that

indicated he should heed my invitation. He walked right over. I led him around the corner into an empty hallway that was lined with closed doors.

"What? I'm busy. I can't give you a ride."

I held up my cell phone. "Ramp just called me, Sam. I was standing outside waiting for a cab and he called me."

Sam grabbed me by the wrist and dragged me down the hall, checking knobs until he found an unlocked door. Once he closed it behind us, he blurted, "Tell me everything."

"He asked me about my 'tall blond friend.' He said it twice. I think he has Lucy."

He leaned his face within six inches of mine and froze me with his glare. "Did he say that?"

"No. But he knows things that I told Lucy. Things about Naomi and Marin and Paul Bigg. And he knew my cell number. Almost no one knows my cell number. But Lucy does."

I watched the tendons at the junctions of Sam's jawbones squirm like fat worms under his skin. "Have you tried her cell phone number?"

"No."

He yanked his phone from his belt and speed-dialed Lucy.

No answer.

He returned his focus to me. "Now tell me every last fucking word of your conversation."

I sat down on a flimsy plastic chair, hanging my wounded buttock over the edge.

I said, "This whole conversation with Ramp is crystal clear in my head. You want to take notes?"

My relating the details of the phone call and Sam's subsequent questions consumed about five minutes. He scribbled details in a notebook for the first sixty seconds or so.

After I was done and he'd asked his last question, he said, "Give me your cell phone."

At moments like this, Sam's intensity overwhelmed his civility, and the rules of polite discourse tended to escape him. I watched as he retrieved the number of the last person who had called me. In this case, that would be Ramp. He then pulled his own phone from a holster on his belt, called the department, and asked somebody to get a reverse listing for the number he'd taken from my phone. He waited for almost a minute before he said, "Figured. Thanks."

"Pay phone?" I said.

"At a 7-Eleven on Speer Boulevard near Federal in Denver. That was a mistake on the kid's part; it's a public place. Maybe there's a wit, somebody who saw him there a few minutes ago."

I couldn't see how that would help us much, unless the witness had thought that the guy talking on the phone had been so suspicious that the witness also decided to scribble down a license plate number or follow Ramp wherever he went after he made the call. I didn't share those thoughts with Sam. Although he was talking out loud, he was really talking to himself, and he was less than not interested in my opinion.

Sam handed me back the phone. "How's the battery on that thing?"

I looked down and checked. "Okay, maybe half charged. Why?"

" 'Cause we have to go to Denver. And when he calls again, I want to make sure the damn phone works."

"Sam, think. Think." I tapped my temple. "What are we going to do in Denver at this hour? We don't know anything."

"For starters, we're going to talk to the guy at the 7-Eleven. See what he can tell us about Ramp."

"What guy? You don't even know that there is a guy. You're guessing about there being a witness. You shouldn't be driving to west Denver on a wild-goose chase, you should be using your time arguing with your colleagues about ways to find Lucy."

With a defeated tone that I wasn't accustomed to hearing in his voice, he said, "I don't expect them to listen to me. There's a search on, but nobody wants to go out on a limb for her right now. Some cops are doing what they can, but to tell you the truth there are more people who believe she's hiding than there are that believe she's been kidnapped."

"You have to try to convince them, then. Tell them about the phone call I got from Ramp."

He stood up, towering over me. "You're right. Even though they're going to think I'm just trying to help Lucy with her defense, I need to try to convince them that Ramp has her." He reached down for the door-knob and added, "There's another bomb hidden some-place here in Boulder, isn't there? That's how you read what Ramp was saying to you?"

"Yeah. That's how I read it. At least one more."

"I agree. Somebody needs to find Marin. She's prob-ably getting into position to set off another bomb."

"The question is, who's the target?"

There's another bomb. That lawyer.

He held the door for me, an act of graciousness that was quite unexpected given the circumstances.

I was a single step past him when it suddenly struck me what Ramp hadn't asked me.

"Sam, Ramp never asked me how Marin's doing."

I turned in time to watch his eyelids drift closed. He said, "Shit."

"That means that when I talked to him on the phone, he either already knew that she'd run from the hospital or he didn't care about her condition. I don't think he doesn't care."

"Shit," Sam repeated. "He's already talked to her." He pounded the doorframe with the blunt side of his closed fist. "What on earth have the two of them got cooked up for us?"

I was about to say, *More bombs,* but I didn't. Sam didn't often wax rhetorical, but I suspected right then that that was exactly what he was doing.

CHAPTER
45

I kissed my sleeping daughter, inhaling her freshness, before I crawled into bed next to Lauren. I accomplished it all without glancing at a clock. It was a conscious effort to avoid learning the time—I didn't want to know how little sleep I was going to get. I did consider waking Lauren and telling her that I thought her one and only client had been kidnapped and was being held hostage by a mad bomber. But I quickly decided that would accomplish nothing.

My wounds and aching head combined to prohibit me from finding a comfortable place in the bed. The telephone conversation with Ramp kept playing in my brain as though it were on an endless loop of tape.

In the shallow water of my dreams the bomb in Naomi's bag didn't explode.

Grace woke up with both nostrils plugged with green snot that appeared to have been mixed with Portland cement before it was spread in a thick layer across both of her rosy cheeks. She was as cranky as I was tired. I changed her diaper while I explained the natural history of colds and generic upper respiratory infections, though it didn't seem to placate her, especially when I used a suction bulb to aspirate the volcanic flows from her tiny nostrils. We moved to the kitchen and I mixed her cereal and warmed her formula while Lauren showered. When Lauren was done getting dressed, we would trade places. In between I gave her the headlines about Lucy, then I showered while Lauren fed the baby.

We were rushing. Though my first patient wasn't until nine, Lauren needed to meet Cozy in his downtown office at eight-thirty. Since her car was still in the shop, I was her ride.

Viv arrived right on time at eight-fifteen. Fortunately, Grace's copious snot didn't faze her. Lauren and I each kissed our baby before we headed downtown. Finding a comfortable way to sit on the driver's seat took some considerable imagination on my part. I was grateful I didn't have to deal with a clutch. On the way to work we finally had a chance to talk about the night before, about Marin leaving the hospital, about the call from Ramp, and my fears about Lucy's safety.

She listened with surprising patience. "God, I hope you're wrong about Lucy."

"Me, too."

"You know, Cozy's going to hate this. This morning's meeting? We're trying to figure out a way to control the damage from the story in the *Camera* about Susan Peterson being Lucy's mother. Now this. God, I hope she's okay. She should never have gone to Denver by herself."

I nodded agreement. "Sam said he'd stay in touch. I'm sure half the Denver Police force is looking for her by now. I promise I'll call if I hear anything." We were stopped at the light on Arapahoe at Twenty-eighth. An ancient Corvair idled in front of us, belching fumes that left me wondering what toxin it was burning for fuel. Lauren was fussing with her eye makeup in the vanity mirror. I decided to risk asking a question that frightened me every time it neared my lips. "You're feeling a little better, aren't you?"

She didn't look over. "Yeah, a little bit. The brain mud is better. I'm hoping it was a false alarm."

I swallowed. "But you're not sure?"

"Am I sure? With this disease? Sorry, sweetie. Hopeful is as optimistic as it gets, I'm afraid. The light's green."

After I'd heard the words I'd been praying for, my heart felt lighter as I ignored the horns honking behind me. A couple of minutes later I pulled into an empty parking space twenty or thirty feet from the lobby door of the Colorado Building.

Lauren kissed me and said, "I wish we had time for coffee. I'd love to talk more about last night."

"I have time for coffee. Starbucks is right around the corner. You know, it's the one where Paul Bigg never worked."

"I don't have time, babe, I'm sorry." She cracked open the door and added, "My car should be ready today."

"I'll give you a ride later to pick it up."

"Don't worry," she told me. "I'll get a ride from Cozy or I'll call a cab."

I spotted Cozy approaching from the north, taking long strides down the sidewalk on Fourteenth from the Pearl Street Mall. He had the kind of chin-in-the-air posture and regal gait that would have looked perfectly natural had he been tapping the sharp end of an umbrella on the sidewalk beside him. I pointed at him. "Cozy's hoofing it today," I told my wife.

We kissed again. "A cab, then. We'll talk later," she said, and hopped out of the car with her briefcase.

She waited for Cozy to join her on the sidewalk.

I checked the time and watched Lauren and Cozy disappear into the front door of the Colorado Building.

I adjusted the volume on the radio and slid the gearshift into reverse. When I looked up to check my rearview mirror again, a bakery truck that had been idling behind me was pulling forward a few feet so that I could get out.

Before I started backing up, I noticed with amazement and wonder that red bricks had begun raining off the side of the Colorado Building, about halfway up its eight-story height.

The glass doors at the lobby entrance blew apart and a muffled roar reached my ears. The car rocked gently as though a passerby had bumped against the fender.

A second or two passed before the thought careened into my head like a drunk turning a corner at high speed:

There's another bomb. That lawyer.

Lauren. Cozy.

Those lawyers.

I threw the gearshift into park and popped out of the car in a single motion.

There's another bomb. That lawyer.

Lauren.

Two steps toward the main doors. Frosty kernels of safety glass sprinkled the sidewalk in front of the building. The brick veneer that had adorned the sheer wall high above the lobby continued to tumble to the concrete alley, falling like bloody hail.

What I noticed from the corner of my eye was the bandage. If it weren't for the bandage, I don't think the fact that a young woman with her head down was walking from the lobby of the building would have registered in my consciousness. The bandaged person climbed into the driver's seat of a white Dodge Neon. She was wearing a floppy hat and sunglasses, and the steel-blue reflection of the lenses mirrored the cold terror I'd begun feeling in my soul.

The fresh white bandage had a tiny stain at the lower edge, close to her nose. The stain was rusty-red and shaped like a crescent moon.

Marin Bigg.

Almost without thinking, I slowed my run to a gentle walk and retreated between the cars toward the street. I climbed into the bakery truck, slid behind the wheel, and dropped it into gear, allowing the big van to roll forward about twenty-five feet until it blocked the rear end of the white Dodge Neon. Pocketing the keys, I climbed down from the truck, and jogged back to the sidewalk.

Sirens had begun to fill the air in downtown Boulder, the shrill squeals reflecting off the faces of the taller buildings until the urgent sounds were squeezed tighter and tighter.

The sirens were apparently Marin's cue to exit the scene. I watched her begin to back up her car. She was still leaning forward on her seat, gazing skyward, watching to see if the fat red bricks would continue to rain from the sky, so she wasn't looking behind her as she backed up. She ran smack into the bakery truck. The impact rocked both vehicles. She'd hit it pretty good.

The impact stunned her. She pulled off her reflective shades and stuffed one of the earpieces between her teeth while she shook her head. Shock and panic bubbled up into her eyes.

Solitary cop cars were approaching down the alley from both the east and the west. The cop coming in from Thirteenth skidded to a stop before his vehicle was directly below the slowing cascade of tumbling bricks. A cop hopped out of the passenger side waving his arms at me. He yelled for me to get farther away from the building.

Marin, too, was climbing out of her car. I walked three steps until I blocked her path to the sidewalk and said, "I don't think you're going anywhere, Marin."

She looked at me as though she didn't quite remember me. I wanted to reintroduce myself by hitting her in the face with my fist. I didn't. She tried to run past me. With malicious intent I grabbed her on her bandaged hand and squeezed until she screamed at a pitch that began to cause me pain.

She stopped running.

The cop approached us with his gun drawn, the barrel pointed at the sky. His eyes betrayed his confusion at the circumstances. Before he could decide what to bark at me, I said, "This woman set off the bomb that just exploded. Her name is Marin Bigg. I think you guys are looking for her."

The cop was busy deciding whether or not to believe me when Marin said, "Fuck you," and spit on the cop.

It ended his indecision. He reached behind his back for his cuffs. As soon as he stepped forward I sprinted toward the lobby of the Colorado Building.

CHAPTER

46

The dust was silky and light, the color of fresh concrete after a rain. It hung in the air like a gentle fog.

Dust or no dust, I'd been in the lobby of the Colorado Building often enough to know where I was heading. The lobby was small, maybe fifteen feet by thirty feet, and it was unfurnished. The only two elevators were side-by-side in the northwest corner, far from the front doors.

One of the mantras of my psych ER training days entered my head as I scanned the space. *The first thing to do during an emergency is to take your own pulse.* Heeding the dictum, I tried to stay calm and was surprised that the chaos in front of me was offering an insistent conclusion about what had occurred.

The two pairs of elevator doors had been blown outward in the center like envelope flaps puffed out by a sharp burst of air. Across the lobby, the glass wall of the brokerage was decimated, the shattered glass fragments blown into the offices, not back into the lobby. The doorway that led to the fire stairs and the lobby's alley exit seemed undamaged.

My conclusion? The direct force of the bomb blast had blown into the lobby from the thick reinforced concrete of the elevator shaft, which focused its explosive intensity like a lens. The bomb had not been placed in the lobby.

I remembered the cascading bricks tumbling from what appeared to be four or five stories up. The bomb had exploded about halfway up the elevator shaft of the eight-story building.

I poked my head through the opening that was created by the damaged elevator doors. One of the two elevator cars, the left one, was below me, in the building's only basement level. The other car had to be somewhere high above me, invisible in the lingering dust. I sniffed the air in the shaft, recognizing nothing but the nasty tang of hot electrical motors. The air was unusually pungent with an odor that wasn't familiar. The explosive?

I glanced down again. The elevator car that was below me sat cockeyed in its concrete channel, the top collapsed on one side, its cable curled on top of it like a sleeping snake.

I listened for motion in the shaft, but heard nothing.

The elevator on the right side was still somewhere high up the concrete cavern.

I yelled down to the damaged car that was in the basement, "Lauren! Cozy!"

I didn't hear a reply.

I yelled up into the darkness.

Nothing.

Behind me someone said, "Hey!" Through the dust I could see a firefighter in full regalia. An ax in one hand, he stood silhouetted against the morning brightness on Fourteenth Street.

The firefighter would soon see what I'd just seen and he would either evacuate the building until the bomb squad checked it out, or he would participate in an immediate effort to rescue anyone caught in the car that had fallen into the basement. I didn't know which option he would choose. If Lauren and Cozy were in the fallen car, I could only pray that the firefighters would get down there as soon as they could. But if Lauren and Cozy were still in the other elevator car, the one high in the shaft, I knew that I had work to do.

I spun and pushed open the door to the stairs. Inside the stairwell, a locked door blocked my path to the basement. Another steel door led directly outside to the alley, and safety.

The firefighter called after me, "Sir? This way out! This way! We need to evacuate the building. Sir!"

Ignoring him and the pain in my butt, I took off up the stairs, taking the treads two at a time. At the landing between the first and second floors, I met two women descending furiously toward the exit. One of them carried her high heels in her right hand while her left was gripping the handrail. The two women were so focused on their retreat from danger that they paid no attention to me as I raced past them.

I passed no one else in the stairwell as I climbed. The other people working in the building must have been using good judgment and exiting the building down the south stairs, as far as possible from the site of the explosion.

At the fifth floor I ran from the stairwell to the elevator lobby. The damage to the elevator doors was much worse than I'd witnessed downstairs. They were peeled back from the center like flower petals seeking the morning sun.

A number of psychologists and social workers I knew and liked had offices down the hall on the fifth floor. I prayed none of them had been arriving at work when the bomb went off.

It took some effort to get close enough to the shaft to try to find the location of the elevator car in the right side of the concrete tower. From that vantage, I spotted the car easily. It was above me, maybe fifteen or twenty feet. I yelled, "Lauren! Cozy!" but heard no reply.

I sprinted back into the stairwell. My destination was the seventh-floor elevator lobby.

From there, it was clearly apparent that the top of the elevator car was about eight or ten feet down the shaft, somewhere between the sixth and seventh floors.

A series of steel treads formed a ladder on the east side of the shaft. I stepped gingerly through the opening in the damaged doors and balanced myself on the narrow stainless-steel threshold above the shaft. Four or six inches at a time I shuffled sideways closer to the steel treads that would lead me down to the car. When I reached the far end of the threshold, with little room for error, I lurched for the closest tread and sealed my fingers around it, allowing my feet to swing down and find purchase below.

It was at that moment that I began to worry what would happen if the elevator suddenly began to rise.

I was down to the roof of the car in seconds. I paused before I left the relative safety of the ladder to check the cable for obvious signs of instability. I couldn't see any, but then, if the thick cable wasn't cut or frayed, I didn't have a clue what I was looking for, nor did I know whether the elevator was operated by counterweights or hydraulics or both.

Gingerly, I stepped to the roof of the car and made my way to the hatch that led to the inside. It took me a moment to free the latch and lift the cover.

A dim light bathed the interior of the car in a glow that reminded me of the lighting inside an aquarium at night. At first all I saw below me was a tableau composed of six legs and five shoes. I counted two wingtips, two New Balance athletic shoes, and one black Cole Haan sandal.

My heart jostled my soul. The sandal was Lauren's.

"Lauren," I said. "Cozy?"

The wingtips had to be Cozy's.

I lowered my head into the hatch.

Cozy was on his back, his head propped unnaturally against the wall of the car, a trail of blood running from one ear down his neck and disappearing below the collar of his perfectly starched shirt.

A woman dressed in cut-off carpenter's pants and a tight sleeveless T-shirt was resting on her side. At first I thought she was covered with blood, but I spotted a pressed cardboard tray and three toppled cups and realized she was covered with spilled coffee.

She squirmed on the floor and a brief grimace spasmed across her face. Her eyes were open and she appeared dazed.

Lauren was against a back corner in a position that approximated sitting, but her left hand and wrist were caught in the elevator's railing at an angle that was painfully unnatural.

None of the three people looked coherent. Only the other woman's eyes were open.

I didn't know what to do.

I heard a faint moan and prayed it was Lauren's.

Fighting every instinct that made me want to drop down into the car to be with my wife, I made my way back to the ladder and climbed away from her. I don't know exactly how I managed to get from the ladder to the elevator lobby. I'm pretty sure I set a world record for descending stairs before I literally ran into three firefighters near the second-floor landing.

I grabbed one of them on his arms and much too

loudly, much too breathlessly, I stammered, "The east elevator—the one on the right—it's caught just below the seventh floor. There are three people in it. They're all hurt. Please help them."

CHAPTER
47

Sam Purdy found me almost instantly after one of the firefighters escorted me from the building.

"You okay?"

I nodded. "I'm fine. Lauren and Cozy are hurt, Sam. They're trapped in an elevator near the seventh floor."

Sam put a hand on my shoulder and nodded. He didn't bother with platitudes. He didn't tell me that he was sure Lauren and Cozy would be fine. I barely noticed the fact that he was leading me down the sidewalk on Fourteenth toward the Mall. We stopped just beyond two parked ambulances, just outside the record store, still well within the confines of the yellow tape that had been stretched far beyond the north side of the Mall.

"Where's Marin?" I asked.

"She's still here. Couple of detectives are putting some pressure on her to find out what's coming next.

We really need to know if there's a secondary in there."

"What's a secondary?"

"A second explosive device. Sometimes these assholes set off one device to draw cops and firefighters close, then they set off a second device to kill them."

I kept looking back at the lobby entrance, hoping to see Lauren emerge through the doorway. I wanted to see her walking out with a firefighter at each of her elbows. I was willing to see her being wheeled out on a stretcher.

But I wanted to see her.

"It's started, Alan. The bomb here. Another one already this morning in Denver. She and Ramp have started their spree."

"What about Lucy?"

"No sign of her yet. Not a trace."

"What happened in Denver this morning?"

"It's kind of baffling. Some ride at Elitch's. Don't see how it has anything to do with the criminal justice system, unless the kid is trying to be metaphorical in some way I'm too tired to comprehend. I don't get it."

I wasn't looking for metaphor. I asked, "Somebody was hurt in the Denver explosion, weren't they?"

"It only happened half an hour ago. They've just started to sift through the mess."

Sam stepped away from me and stopped a patrol officer who was hurrying toward one of the ambulances. I stayed a step behind Sam.

He asked the officer, "What's up?"

"Hey, Detective. One of the elevators had its cable severed by the explosion. They just found a body in the car in the basement."

"Dead?"

"Yeah."

I thought about my friends on the fifth floor.

Sam asked what I was too stunned to ask. "Who is it?"

The officer said, "It's some guy named Bob. He's like the super, the maintenance guy in the building. He fell from fifty, sixty feet up, maybe more. Apparently everybody knows him."

"I don't," I said.

Sam's phone tweeted in his pocket. He pulled it out, hit a button with his fat thumb, and said, "Purdy."

A few seconds later he turned his head away from me and said, "Yeah, of course. What's up, Walter?"

I waited until Sam shut off the call before I asked, "What did Walter have to say?"

He flashed a how-the-hell-do-you-know-about-Walter look until he recalled our conversation wandering the aisles of the grocery store. He said, "The Denver Police just found an apparent explosive device in the center of the stage at Red Rocks. Bomb squad is responding."

I was focusing most of my attention on the lobby entrance to the Colorado Building, waiting for Lauren and Cozy to emerge. What could be taking the rescuers so long? Sam's words registered on the boundaries of my awareness. I said, "What?"

"There's a bomb, or something that looks like a bomb, right in the center of the stage at Red Rocks."

"The amphitheater?" Red Rocks was Denver's world-famous outdoor concert venue. It was set in a gorgeous sandstone bowl in the foothills west of the city. Although totally surrounded by Jefferson County, Red Rocks was technically a Denver city park facility.

"Yeah. The bomb squad's on the way to evaluate it. It doesn't look good; they want to X-ray it."

"Is there a concert or something up there?" I asked.

"On a weekday morning at this hour? Hardly."

A yellow-suited firefighter emerged from the front of the Colorado Building, waving one arm back and forth across his chest to clear a wide path from the lobby to the ambulances waiting nearby. I started toward the doorway as though I were on a moving sidewalk.

The end of a stretcher broke the plane at the front of the building. Thick rubber wheels. Tubular aluminum frame.

I saw sneakers. The woman who had been carrying the coffee.

An eternity passed before a second stretcher breached the doorway.

Wingtips the size of dinghies.

Even from thirty feet away, I could almost count the little holes in the leather.

Cozy.

Sam's fingers curled over my left shoulder. He was

providing comfort. He was also preparing to keep me from rushing the door.

A third stretcher began to emerge from the door as though the building were giving birth to it.

Triplets.

I held my breath and waited to see one black Cole Haan sandal and one elegant, very pretty, bare foot. Lauren's toenails were painted. I tried to recall what color she'd used. I couldn't.

The stretcher came out the door empty.

A sound emerged from somewhere deep in my tissues. Somewhere that knows no sound. It was part groan, part yelp, part plea.

Sam's fingers tightened on my shoulder. He said, "Wait."

It was an order.

I didn't know it at the time, but Sam's eyes were flitting between the doorway and Scott Truscott, the Boulder County coroner's assistant. Scott's vehicle was across the street and Scott was waiting to be invited inside the building to assess the casualties whose injuries were so monumental that they didn't require an ambulance ride to anywhere.

"Where is she?" I said to God.

Another stretcher began to come into view.

I saw black hair and I started to cry.

CHAPTER

48

The long trip from Denver's Platte Valley to the foothills near Morrison perplexed Lucy. She was able to track the journey from her cramped lair on the floor of the welding supply truck by reading the overhead highway signs on the Sixth Avenue Freeway.

When Ramp stopped the truck, he didn't bother to restrain her further. He told her he wouldn't be gone long and that she shouldn't move. She could feel the truck shudder as he did something in the back. The movement stopped; she guessed that Ramp had moved away.

She considered her options. Despite the restraints on her wrists and ankles, she thought that she could manage to get the truck door open, tumble outside, and try to hop away. It was possible that Ramp had parked the truck in a location that would allow a passerby to see her and come to her rescue. Possible, but not likely.

Not at that hour.

She raised herself up from the floor and, bracing her bound wrists on the seat, lifted herself up high enough to look out the back window of the truck. Eight or ten tall green oxygen tanks almost completely blocked her view. She looked out to the side and was thrilled that what she was seeing was slightly familiar.

She couldn't quite place it. The huge rocks. The dust. The flat-roofed building. Wait, wait, wait. Could this be Red Rocks?

"I told you not to move."

Ramp's voice was admonishing but not angry, the kind of tone someone might use to correct a curious puppy.

"Get back down. We're leaving."

Lucy thought, *No explosion?* She fell heavily to the floor of the cab.

As though he'd read her mind, he said, "This one's different from all of the others."

The highway signs told her they were going back into Denver. The noise told her that traffic was starting to accumulate. Ramp played a Dave Matthews CD, not the news, and didn't seem at all concerned about his rearview mirrors.

The light to the east told her it was dawn.

The next place that the truck stopped was somewhere near Sixth and Santa Fe, and Lucy's promise to stay down—the alternative was having her wrists duct-taped to the center console—earned her coffee and an egg-and-chorizo burrito. She wasn't hungry but she forced herself to eat a few bites.

While the gag was still off her mouth, she asked him, "What exactly are you doing?"

"Making this memorable. I want people to talk, remember?"

"Dialogue."

"That's right."

"So you're going to blow up Red Rocks?"

He smiled at her. "That would piss people off, wouldn't it?" She couldn't read his eyes.

He replaced the gag, pausing when he was done to caress the soft skin below her temple. "Don't worry, I don't have enough explosives to blow up Red Rocks. Anyway, I like Red Rocks."

Santa Fe all the way to Speer, Speer north toward I-25. As soon as they were on the freeway, southbound Lucy thought, they exited again. She wished she knew Denver's geography better. She thought that they must have been somewhere near the Children's Museum.

Only thirty seconds or so after they turned off the freeway, they turned again. Soon the truck came to a stop.

Ramp put the truck in park and killed the engine. He said, "I like this view. You want to see it?"

She nodded. He leaned over and helped her pull herself up onto the passenger seat.

She looked out the windshield. Ramp had parked in one of the big lots flanking the banks of the South Platte River just east of Denver's new aquarium, Colorado's Ocean Journey. On the river, a couple of hardy early-season kayakers were slicing across the abbreviated rapids at the confluence of the South Platte and Cherry Creek. On the other side of the river was Six Flags Elitch Gardens, and beyond it, the downtown skyline.

Ramp lifted some binoculars from the floor in front of his seat and raised them to his eyes. To Lucy, it appeared he was examining something in the sky that was just above the jagged profile of the amusement park. In the early-morning light the park looked forlorn and insincere, the way a saloon looks afterhours when the cleaning floods are on bright.

He sighed. "There he is. Right on time. My grandfather loved punctuality more than he loved almost anything in the world other than me and my grandma. He would have loved this guy; he's always on time."

"What guy?" Lucy mumbled into the cotton sock. Lucy thought he was pointing at the Ferris wheel.

Again Ramp reached down to the floor in front of his seat. He raised a complicated black plastic device and extended an antenna from the top. Without looking toward Lucy, he said, "It's for model airplanes. Good range."

He placed the transmitter on his lap and raised the binoculars to his eyes. He held them in place while he studied a narrow slice of the Colorado sky. When he lowered the glasses, he said, "He's getting pretty high up there. It'll be just a couple more minutes."

She wanted to ask, *Till what?* but didn't bother. She knew. Or at least she thought she knew.

He mused, "You know how easy it was to get what I needed for all this? Anything I can't get at Toys 'R' Us, I can get at Radio Shack. Except for the explosives, of course. For that, you need a relative in the demolitions business."

He raised the binoculars once more, held them in place for only a few seconds, and said, "My guy's up there. Here goes. It took me three trips to get all these charges in place. I used more explosives here than everywhere else put together."

He fingered one of the levers on the black plastic box and raised his eyes to a spot just above the horizon. Lucy tried to follow the line of his gaze.

"Three," he whispered, "two . . . one."

At first, Lucy didn't see anything change in her field of vision and wondered if Ramp's device had failed. Then, barely to the right of where she was focusing her attention, she glimpsed a puff of smoke, like a flare from a campfire. It had emerged from a spot close to the ground in the middle of the amusement park.

Rapidly—close by the first—another puff of smoke followed. Lucy's eyes trailed up from the source to the elaborate superstructure of a loop-the-loop thrill ride. The highest part of the metal structure started to lean, she thought, just a little.

Another puff of smoke erupted from the base of the

ride—this one was slightly larger and a little higher off the ground. Lucy thought she could hear the concussion of a blast, too. But she wasn't sure that her mind wasn't just filling in the blanks.

Ramp said, "It's called The Sidewinder. Ever been on it? It's an okay ride. It *was* an okay ride. I don't think it's going to be too much fun anymore."

Lucy watched the single spiral of steel lean farther and farther to the west. Then it steadied and hung in the sky in defiance. She glanced over at Ramp. He touched another switch on the black plastic console.

One more puff exploded near the base of The Sidewinder, and the temporarily reluctant steel structure continued its fall to the west.

"Wow," Ramp said as the structure disappeared into the fabric of the amusement park. "I did it. It fell right where I wanted it to fall."

He stared at the empty sky and the rising cloud of dust for more than a minute before he started the truck and eased away from the bluff above the river. "The guy who was climbing the ride just then? He was the twin brother of the defense attorney who represented the man who killed my mom."

As they circled underneath the viaduct and drove past the big REI store that had been built inside the old Forney Museum, Ramp said, "Things will start to happen fast now. If they go well, you should be free in a couple of hours."

CHAPTER
49

Cozy's injuries were the most severe.

The elevator car had been ascending between the seventh and eighth floors when the explosion rocked the concrete elevator tower. The car came to an abrupt halt, throwing both Lauren and the woman who had been carrying the coffee to the floor. The woman with the coffee broke her right wrist, and Lauren's head slammed against the side of the car. Cozy somehow maintained his balance. The fact that he was still standing made him much more vulnerable when the car dropped precipitously. He flew headfirst up into the ceiling of the car and crashed back to the floor when the car jammed to a stop where I found it in between the sixth and seventh floors.

Lauren's violet eyes were open as I ran to her side

at the rear of the ambulance. She was strapped to a backboard, and huge cushioned cervical braces immobilized her head and upper body.

She asked, "How's Grace?"

What?

"The baby's great," I said. "How are you?"

"I'm okay," she said. They lifted her into the back of the ambulance and closed the doors.

An hour later, Cozy was in surgery. The woman with the coffee had been released from the hospital with her arm in a cast. Lauren was in observation. My own observation was that she was looking pretty good, considering.

During our few minutes together, Lauren had told me what happened.

Bob, the building handyman who'd died in the elevator crash, had been waiting in the lobby when Cozy and Lauren walked in that morning. He'd been puzzling over a sign that had been placed on one elevator declaring it out of service for a furniture delivery. Bob complained to Lauren and Cozy that no one had permission to reserve an elevator without talking to him, certainly not at that hour of the day. He told them to go ahead and use the reserved elevator, which was waiting on the first floor. He'd take the other one and find out who was responsible for the sign.

Lauren said they stopped once on the third floor and the young woman with the coffee joined them.

Moments later the explosion rocked the elevator tower.

Adrienne somehow created enough of a hole in her day to sit with me while I held a cup of hospital coffee in my hand. The coffee was too foul to actually drink, but I got some comfort from holding it. Adrienne was acting unnaturally, saying pacifying things like "You know that you did everything you could." And "It's lucky you told the firefighters where to go." I think I would have actually felt better if she had just lovingly berated me like she usually did.

I said, "Based on my recent experience, I think if you have to be in the emergency room, it's easier being the patient than being the one waiting to hear news about someone you love."

Before she could respond to my comment, the phone in my pocket rang. Initially, the sound meant nothing to me. It simply didn't register. Finally, Adrienne said, "That's your phone. It may be Viv. Let's take it outside. They don't like cells in here."

I followed her out the sliding glass doors of the emergency department, hit a button on the phone, and said, "Alan Gregory." We were standing on the edge of the driveway with three people who were sucking nicotine in smoker's Siberia.

I heard music playing through the phone, a song by Everclear that Lauren liked. I'd never understood how she could like it. I said, "Hello."

The song ended; a commercial jingle started. Something about why I should buy my next car at Burt Chevrolet. Then a man's voice said, "I'm going to try and find the news." The voice was in the background, as though the speaker wasn't talking directly into the microphone.

The voice I'd heard wasn't Viv's, but it was vaguely familiar. I said, "Hello, who is this?"

I was about to hang up when the same voice sounded again. Clearly. "I need to find out if they sent the bomb squad to Red Rocks. I don't think they have two mobile X-ray units. And I don't think they have two robots."

Adrienne asked, "Is it Viv?"

I shook my head. The sound in my ear was of stations changing quickly on a radio. Music, commercial, talk. The channel lottery stopped abruptly with a perky female voice prattling on about the explosion earlier that morning at Elitch's. I wouldn't exactly call what she was doing "news."

Adrienne said, "Who is it?"

I held up a finger, asking for her patience. She squished up one eye and shook her head at me to remind me that patience wasn't one of her best things.

As though I might have forgotten.

I covered the mouthpiece again. "Nobody's talking to me, but I hear a voice talking about the bomb at Red Rocks."

"What?"

That's when I heard a muffled sound of protest.

Oddly, it was the most distinct sound that had yet come through the phone.

Again I covered the mouthpiece. "Adrienne, you have your phone with you?"

It was clear from her expression that it was like asking her whether she had her nose with her.

"Call Sam Purdy. I need to keep this call going." Even Adrienne could recognize the urgency in my voice when I told her the number.

She yanked her phone from her belt and punched at the buttons.

I handed her my phone and took hers. "Adrienne?" I spoke her name to see if she was on my wavelength. She was. "Keep the microphone covered," I told her. "I don't want whoever is on the other end of that call to hear anything from us. Is that clear? If you hear anything interesting, let me know."

She made a face to communicate how unhappy she was about how perplexed she was, but she placed her index finger over the microphone, leaned her head to the side, and slid the phone below her hair.

I waited until I heard Sam's bored voice before I turned my back on Adrienne and spoke. "Sam, it's Alan. Listen—my cell phone just rang. Nobody's actually talking to me but the line is live and I can hear part of a conversation going on in the background. Somebody is talking about the bomb that they found at Red Rocks. I don't know what to make of it."

I counted to three before he responded. "What exactly did you hear?"

"It's a guy talking. He's in a car, I think. He said something to someone about needing to find out whether they sent the bomb squad to Red Rocks. And I'm pretty sure he said that he thought the Denver Bomb Squad only had one mobile X-ray unit and one robot."

"Really? He said that? He talked about mobile X-rays and robots?"

"Yes."

"And this is all just like conversation in the background? He's not talking to you?"

"That's right."

"What else?"

"He's punching buttons on a radio, trying to find the news."

"That's it?"

"And there was a muffled sound like a groan."

"Muffled?"

"Yeah."

"A groan?"

"Yeah."

"The call's still going?"

"Just a sec." I turned to Adrienne. "It's still going?"

She nodded. I saw some magic flicker like a jewel in the corner of her eyes. I knew she wasn't bored.

"Still going, Sam."

"Where are you?"

"Outside the ER entrance at Community."

"I'll be there in three minutes."

I ended the call. When I looked up again, Adrienne's eyes were as big and bright as marbles.

She was almost breathless. "The guy? He just said he would take that off if somebody promised not to scream."

"Take what off?"

"I don't know. There was some funny moaning noise. Then he went, 'I'll take that off if you promise not to scream.' That's all he said. Jesus, Alan, do you really think—"

"Yes," I said. "I really do."

The route into Lower Downtown was familiar to Lucy for two reasons. She was a Rockies fan and she was a young single woman. Being a Rockies fan meant Coors Field. Being a single woman meant way too many regrettable first dates in the clubs and restaurants of LoDo.

After Ramp circled along the Platte past the REI store, he went down Fifteenth Street to Wynkoop, turned left past Union Station, and then made a loop that brought the truck to the corner that was opposite the old Student Movers Building that had been incorporated into the structure of Coors Field. The ground floor of the renovated building was used for the Sandlot Brewery.

"This will work. We can park here for a while," he said. "But you need to stay down." He displayed his wrist, the one with the transmitter button taped to it.

She wondered if he was planning on trying to bring down the baseball stadium and immediately decided that it was impossible. She protested loudly into her gag. He ignored her.

They sat. She couldn't see a clock but she guessed that they sat for at least half an hour.

Finally, he said, "There she is."

Lucy had no idea which woman Ramp was identifying.

He started the truck and turned and circled back around until they came out a block away at the corner of Twentieth and Blake, directly across from the main entrance to the ballpark. Again, Ramp parked the truck on the street. This time, he hopped out of the cab and fed the meter.

When he climbed back into the truck, he said, "I'm going to try and find the news."

Lucy tried to talk into her gag. She couldn't even understand herself. The effort was futile.

Ramp said, "I need to find out if they sent the bomb squad to Red Rocks. I don't think they have two mobile X-ray units. And I don't think they have two robots." He reached out and started punching buttons on the radio.

Lucy tried to understand what was going on. Why did it matter to Ramp what was happening up at Red Rocks? Why was it important how many mobile X-ray units and robots the Denver Bomb Squad had?

She screamed into the gag.

Ramp raised his wrist and lifted an index finger to his lips to warn her to be quiet.

A minute or so passed. He said, "I'll take that off if you promise not to scream."

She nodded urgently.

He reached down and lowered the sock so that it was resting on her chin, not her mouth. Almost involuntarily she said, "Thank you." It came out in a cotton-mouthed whisper.

He was looking out the windshield.

"You're welcome. It's time." He reached down to the floor in front of his seat and lifted a device that looked like a controller for a child's electronic toy. "I thought you wanted to say something."

"Ramp, stop. Please. Don't do it. Don't set off any more bombs."

"That's it? That's all you wanted to say?" He reached over and lifted the sock back into place in Lucy's mouth.

She closed her eyes and shook her head in despair. She tugged at her wrist restraints until the plastic bit into her flesh. It was futile.

"I'll be back in a minute. I need to get closer for this thing to work. It doesn't have great range. Stay down or things will get worse for you. I'll be in sight of you the whole time. Do you understand?"

She didn't look at him.

"I'm telling you that you'll be within range." He raised his arm, the one with the transmitter taped to it.

She nodded.

His voice still even, he said, "I know this isn't any fun. But tell me you understand."

She nodded again.

Twenty or thirty seconds after Ramp exited the car, Lucy heard the reverberation of an explosion. It wasn't loud, or sharp. If she didn't know he was setting off a bomb, she would have believed the sound was caused by something else, something less sinister.

She started to cry.

It wasn't long before Ramp climbed back into the truck. A distant peal of sirens began to pierce through the benign blanket of sounds that covered the city in the morning.

"In case you're wondering, that was for a woman who worked for the Rockies—she was the wife of the judge who approved the sentence of the man who killed my mom. Time to go," he said. "Time to go."

CHAPTER

51

Sam pulled down Balsam from the east. I imagined that he was still at the Colorado Building when I called him, and guessed that he must have come across town on Thirteenth, avoiding Broadway. He was driving his city car, not his old Cherokee, and I didn't recognize him until he turned into the entry drive for the ER. I waved at him, careful to keep one finger planted on the mouthpiece of the phone.

As he pulled into the ambulance-only zone, I ran to his car, pointing to the phone at my ear. "I think I just heard a woman's voice."

"You're sure?"

"The guy said, 'I thought you wanted to say something.' Then the woman's voice said, 'Ramp, stop, please don't do it. Don't set off any more bombs.' Then the guy said, 'That's it?' "

"Anything else?"

"A car door slammed."

"And now?"

"Nothing."

Sam sighed.

Under my breath, I said, "Oh no. Oh my God!"

Sam threw open the door to his car and started to climb out. He barked, "What? What?"

"I think I just heard an explosion, Sam. A bang. No, more like a deep rumble. Now nothing."

"You're not imagining this? You're sure it wasn't like a car backfiring or something?"

"I don't think so."

Sam fell back down onto the seat and pulled his radio to his lips. He asked the dispatcher to check to see if there were any reports of an explosion in Denver in the last couple of minutes.

"Sam? The car door slammed shut again. Then the guy said, 'Time to go. Time to go.'"

Sam nodded at me. Into the radio, he said, "It's okay, I'll wait as long as I have to wait."

Half a minute passed, then a minute. I couldn't understand the reply when it finally squawked back to him through the radio.

"What?" I asked.

"A bomb just went off at Coors Field. There are casualties. The half of the Denver Police force that isn't at Elitch's is responding right now."

"I can hear the sirens," I said, for the first time realizing that I'd heard the explosion live. I pointed at the phone. "I'm listening to Ramp, Sam. He has Lucy with him."

"Let me have the phone."

He listened for maybe fifteen seconds. "I don't hear anything. You sure it's still live?"

I nodded. "It was a few seconds ago."

He handed the phone back to me. "Keep listening. I have to get the location of this call identified somehow. There's no reason to think this kid is done blowing things up."

An out-of-tune diesel delivery truck plowed up Balsam. I turned away from Sam to escape the noise. The call went dead.

I checked the screen of my phone to be sure. I even shook the handset as though that would restore the connection.

"Sam, we lost it."

"Don't tell me that."

"It's gone."

"Check your caller ID. Find out who the hell called you."

I did. Lucy's cell phone number popped up on the little screen. "It was Lucy, Sam."

He buried his lower lip in his mustache and pondered the cards in his hand. "Here's what I think's happening: She speed-dialed you and Ramp doesn't know that her phone is on. She can't risk saying anything but she wants us to hear everything that's going on. When she realizes that the call got dropped, she'll do it all again. Let's be ready."

I asked, "How do we get ready?"

"I don't know." Sam looked exhausted. "How's Lauren doing?"

"It looks like she'll be okay. She sprained her wrist and she banged her head pretty good. They have her in observation now. Cozy broke a bone in his neck. He's in surgery."

"Damn. Fusion?"

"I don't know, maybe."

"The other girl?"

"Broke her wrist, got burned a little from the coffee. She's home already. Is Marin talking?"

"Not yet. She said she'll tell us whatever we want later in the day. Believe it or not, she lawyered up. Is that ironic or what?"

I didn't want to get lost thinking about the Biggs. "What do we do about Lucy, Sam?"

"I'm not sure. I need to call all this in. Why don't you go back inside and check on your wife."

"What's Denver going to do? Evacuate the whole city until this kid runs out of explosives?"

"We have to find them."

"What about the phone?"

"If it rings again, run back out here like someone's life depends on it."

I consciously placed one foot in front of the other and was mildly surprised when the automatic door sensed my presence on my way back inside the hospital.

CHAPTER
52

Sam fiddled with the radio on the dashboard before he asked, "What's the pattern here? Red Rocks is an amphitheater, Elitch Gardens is an amusement park, Coors Field is a baseball stadium. What's the pattern? Where does he go next? The new football stadium? The Pepsi Center? What?" He grunted. "If this asshole does anything to the Pepsi Center and I have to miss any Avalanche games, I swear . . ."

He left the threat unfinished.

We were on the Boulder Turnpike, heading southeast toward Denver, just opposite the Interlocken office park. The morning rush hour was over and the traffic on 36 was merely heavy. Sam was driving his detective mobile. A red beacon on the dash flashed notice of our presence to other cars. I thought the strobe was an inadequate herald, considering our obvious haste. Sam was speeding mercilessly and changing lanes a lot and his driving was making me nervous.

It had been my idea to turn down the offer of a ride to Denver in the Denver Police helicopter. I'd argued that the noise in the chopper would interfere with our ability to hear what was going on if Lucy was able to make another cell phone call. So we were speeding to Denver in Sam's car and I was having second thoughts about not taking the chopper.

I was feeling many things; one of the most prominent was discomfort about leaving Lauren in Boulder.

When I'd told her what was going on with the bombs in Denver and with Lucy and Ramp and the cell phone, she told me to do whatever I had to do, that she'd be fine. I told her Sam wanted me to accompany him to Denver. She encouraged me to go. Adrienne promised to drive Lauren home whenever she was released from the ER, and Viv promised to stay at our house until I got home.

My bases were covered, but my ambivalence was pronounced.

As Sam used the right lane and a good chunk of the shoulder to pass an eighteen-wheeler full of Mercedes SUVs, I said, "I don't think what Ramp's doing is about the buildings, Sam. I think it's about the people. The wouldn't-it-be-cool games that Naomi described were always about people."

Sam scoffed. "He's hit, or tried to hit, three of the most identifiable landmarks in Denver, Alan. You think that's an accident?"

"Not accidental, Sam. But maybe it's incidental."

"I'm too tired. What?"

"He's not after buildings. He's not after body count, either. He could have done any of those buildings when they were full of people, right?"

Sam touched a button on his radio before he replied, "Right. I thought of that, too."

"Well, he didn't. All the venues were basically empty. The bomb he set at Coors Field was actually in an office, not in the stadium itself."

Sam argued, "But people died both times that a bomb went off."

"Exactly. And those are the people we should be paying attention to. I would guess that they were the targets. He's using these bombs to kill specific people, not random people."

Sam looked at his notepad and steered with his knees. I prayed he wasn't going to try to change lanes again, not with his knees. When he looked back up, we were closing on the butt end of a cement mixer. Sam steered around it as though he'd expected it would be in his way. His voice betrayed his skepticism about the hypothesis I was making as he said, "Let's see, three dead so far. And who are they? A couple of ride testers at Elitch Gardens. A bookkeeper for the Rockies and her boyfriend, a . . ." He flipped a page in his notebook. "The boyfriend was an assistant manager in group ticket sales."

"One more, Sam. Don't forget the woman who died in the car explosion last week."

"Okay, four dead. I'll throw in the housewife from last week. I don't care. Look at the list, Alan; these aren't the kind of people that terrorists usually salivate over eliminating."

"Then we're missing something."

Sam rubbed his eye with his knuckle. "There's no doubt about that. How's your phone?"

My cell was resting in my lap. "What do you mean?"

"The battery."

I didn't even have to look. "It's fine."

"Check."

I checked. "It's fine."

Sam said, "You're thinking about something, aren't you?" He made it sound like an accusation.

I said, "Somebody needs to cross-check the list of people involved with letting Ramp's mother's murderer out on parole with the list of the casualties of the explosions so far."

In a monotone, he replied, "Ride checker, bookkeeper, assistant manager, housewife. Those people don't make decisions about sentences and parole. That dog don't hunt."

His argument was academic. He was a professor trying to keep a debate going in a seminar. I was happy to play along. I said, "Look at Marin's list, Sam. The first bomb was found in Royal Peterson's house. He was the DA who signed off on the plea bargain on her rape. Second was in Nora's garage. She was the prosecutor who negotiated the deal. Third was in Cozy's office. He was the defense attorney who represented

Marin's rapist. The progression is purely logical. The wouldn't-it-be-cool games targeted people directly involved with the decision to offer Marin's rapist the plea bargain. Why would Ramp proceed differently? Everything we know tells us that he's the brains behind this thing."

He argued, "It's not that complicated. The brain obviously decided to do landmarks instead of people."

"I don't buy it. It's inconsistent."

Sam shrugged. The shrug said, "Tough." But I surmised he didn't want me to stop arguing with him. I held my breath as we whizzed past a Ford Taurus being driven by someone whose head looked like it was all felt hat and gray hair.

I said, "Humor me. You're already in touch with someone at the Denver Police Department, right? I mean, this morning—whoever it was who offered to send the helicopter for us."

"Yeah."

"Walter?"

"Don't go there."

"Whatever. Call whoever it is and find out where the husband of the woman who was killed in the car bomb last week worked and where he parked his car. Will you do that?"

"Why?"

"Just make the call. You certainly aren't using much of your attention driving this car."

I expected resistance but he flipped open his phone and made the call. I closed my eyes. I didn't want to see how he was going to maneuver the interchange at I-25 one-handed. Or no-handed.

I feared it would involve the steering wheel and Sam's fat knees.

When he was done talking to Denver, he turned to me and said, "Her husband owns a tourist shop in Larimer Square. Sells western shit. He parks right behind his store."

We were merging onto I-25. "See, there you go," I said. "He was the target, not her. That keeps the pattern intact. He was the one who was supposed to get killed in the explosion. It should have gone off this morning while he was parking his car behind his store in Larimer Square."

"Seems to support the landmark theory, not the wouldn't-it-be-cool-to-kill-people theory. We're talking Larimer Square, tourist central. Assuming you're right, and he was the target, and assuming the bomb hadn't gone off prematurely, there would have been one more blown Denver landmark this morning. That's how I read it."

I couldn't believe how fast we were approaching the Mousetrap, the legendary bottleneck interchange of Interstates 70 and 25. I chanced a glance at the speedometer. We were doing over ninety. My pulse was doing twice that, easy. The scariest part was that there were a couple of cars going so fast that we had trouble passing them.

"It's the people, Sam. Don't get distracted by the landmarks. Columbine was about the kids, not the building."

That last comment quieted him. He slowed as we approached the exit that would take us to Coors Field.

He said, "Then why the landmarks?".

"To confuse the situation. To exaggerate the press coverage. I don't know. There could be a dozen reasons. To get the cops to waste time having arguments like the one we're having."

Sam said, "I'll ask them to cross-check the list."

A Denver patrol car was waiting to escort us down the viaduct to the baseball stadium. Sam fell in behind the car while he chatted on the radio with someone about the cross-check. A minute later we pulled to a stop along the curb on Blake Street. We were right in front of the brick walkway beside Coors Field. The Denver Police had established a wide perimeter. The TV stations' microwave trucks were sequestered at least a block away.

Sam threw the phone onto his lap. He said, "The Denver cops are already there. The bomb squad detectives are working under the assumption that the victims were targeted because they were relatives of people involved with Ramp's mother's case. You're smarter than you look."

I said, "One relative worked at Elitch's. Another for the Rockies. What about Red Rocks?"

"No connection they know of. They're still looking."

"And the guy who managed the store in Larimer Square? The one whose wife died in the car bombing?"

"His father is on the parole board. Let's go talk to the people in charge. Compare some notes."

I got out of the car.

Sam asked me, "Why relatives?" This time he seemed genuinely curious about my opinion.

I felt confident about my answer. "Ramp wants the people he believes are responsible to know how it feels to see a loved one killed. It completes the circle for him. The people he wants to hurt now will know exactly what it's like to feel what he felt when his mother died."

"Killing them would be too easy?" Sam was edging close to sarcasm. Close, but not quite there.

"Killing them would spare them the pain they're feeling right now. Ramp doesn't want to do that. He wants them to suffer his pain. The loss he feels."

Sam grunted. This time I translated the grunt to mean that he approved of my argument.

"How's your phone?" he asked.

I glanced down at the battery meter. "It's fine. No problem. It has hours left. Stop worrying."

"You see Lucy sitting pretty anywhere around here? Until you do, I don't stop worrying."

A Denver patrol officer was pointing Sam down the sidewalk, indicating a stocky man with a starched blue shirt and a navy blue tie. The shirt was unbuttoned at the collar, the tie was far from tight, and the shirtsleeves were folded up near the man's elbows. The shoes were polished like a Marine's dress pair.

"You Purdy?" the man asked as we approached.

Sam said, "Yeah. This is Alan Gregory, the guy with the phone."

"That's the phone?" He pointed at my hand.

"Yes," I said.

Without asking permission he took it from my hand and plugged a small tape recorder into it. "It'll kick on automatically. It's a backup in case the phone company doesn't capture the call. Notify me the second it rings.

"I'm Rivera, by the way. You're not going to believe this, but we just took a nonemergency call from somebody warning us about some bombs at East High School."

Sam said, "East High School? Bombs? It's in session, right? The school's full of kids, right?"

"Yeah, it's full of kids. They've started evacuating the buildings. We're sending as many people out there as we can and we've asked the surrounding cities and counties for help from their bomb squads and SWAT teams. The way this morning is developing, we need five bomb squads."

Sam asked, "You getting all the cooperation you want?"

"Anything we need. Except from Boulder. They seem to need help almost as much as we do."

"Did you ID the caller on the warning?"

"The call came in on a nonemergency line, so we didn't get an automatic ID. Anyway, it was blocked, and it was too short a call to trace. We have a tape of the entire call; it's like ten seconds. I'm sure the RP was the kid. They played it for me over the phone. I'm sure it was the same kid. East High School. Damn."

Ramp was "the kid."

My phone rang. I almost dropped it. At first I gaped at it as though it had given me an electrical shock.

Sam stopped in his tracks. He looked at me like he'd just discovered he was standing in the center of a minefield.

Recovering my wits, I hit a button and listened for a count of two before I whispered, "Hello, this is Alan Gregory."

I didn't really expect a reply.

CHAPTER
53

Ramp's gesture as he climbed back into the truck after initiating the explosion at Coors Field was both nonchalant and innocuous, but it was sufficient to fracture the fragile skeleton of hope that Lucy had been constructing.

He removed the windbreaker he'd been wearing and tossed it over the center console of the truck, burying Lucy's cell phone below it.

She wanted to cry. She'd already noticed that her earlier call to Alan Gregory, although live for a while, had been dropped. She'd been waiting for an opportunity to hit the redial button once again. To get a chance, she knew that she'd have to wait for Ramp to make another sojourn from the truck. With the jacket covering the phone, she didn't know how she was going to get her bound hands to the button quickly and she wasn't at all confident that the phone's microphone would pick up sound through the insulation of the jacket's fabric, anyway.

She wondered if Alan had figured out anything from her earlier call. Maybe he hadn't even bothered to listen when he'd discovered that there wasn't anyone at the other end of the line.

Ramp headed down Blake across Broadway into the part of Denver's old warehouse district that hadn't yet been converted into lofts, restaurants, and galleries. He stopped the truck in the middle of a block that was swarming with trucks making pickups and deliveries. He told Lucy, "I have a little time to kill. Try to get some rest."

She watched him lean back in his seat and settle a baseball cap over his eyes. As though he could read her mind, he added, "Don't try anything, Lucy. I'm tense. Try to relax."

She yelled at him into her gag. He slid the hat away from his eyes and glanced down at her. She raised her bound hands as though she were going to remove the gag herself.

He said, "I told you, if you touch that, I'll move your arms behind your back. You won't like that."

She screamed again.

He stared at her for a moment, then lowered the gag so that it rested on her chin. The tape tore at the skin on her jaw. She spit fragments of cotton into the air and tried to speak. The first attempt came out in a rasp.

Finally, she managed, "Why are you blowing up those buildings?"

He didn't answer right away. "I used a lot of explosives to knock down the ride at Elitch's, but the rest of the bombs aren't that powerful. All I'm doing is creating chaos. When the dust settles, hopefully people will wonder why. Dialogue will fill that void. The more people care about the buildings, the more they will wonder why I blew them up. That's why I chose people who work in buildings that people might care about. That's why I didn't do it at their homes. Believe me, that would have been much, much easier."

"You're not just bombing buildings, though. You're killing people, too, aren't you?"

"Yes."

"Why?"

"So that . . . some people, particular people . . . will know how it feels to lose someone they love to stupidity."

"You're not done?"

"No."

"Why?"

"So the people in power will care."

"I don't get it."

"For this to be effective, it has to get personal. People, especially powerful people, have to realize that they are just as vulnerable as I was. They have to believe that in their hearts. Deep in their hearts. There's no other way for me to be certain that I'm getting my message across and that they'll pay attention.

You cause somebody enough pain, you get their attention. Trust me, I know. The people in power have to know that, too."

She fought a swell of compassion for him. She said, "Jason, stop. Please, stop now."

He scoffed. "Why?"

"I'll help you."

"I don't need your help, Lucy. Unless they catch up with me before I'm done, I don't need your help."

"I know a good lawyer."

He laughed. "I know you do. Your lawyer's the one who got Marin's rapist a slap on the wrist. For me, he's part of the problem, not part of the solution. Anyway, it's irrelevant. Your lawyer's dead, too. He was on Marin's list this morning. I set a charge against the counterweight cable in his building's elevator. Marin was supposed to wait until he climbed into the elevator, then she was going to set it off."

She vaulted to her knees. "You little—"

He raised his wrist, curling his fingers so that the tips rested on the switch that was taped to his arm.

She stilled. He pushed the gag back into place. "Why don't you get some rest? Please don't make me sorry I brought you along."

After twenty minutes or so, Ramp exited the truck without a word. Lucy couldn't see which way he went, and didn't know how long he would be gone. She fought the temptation to go for the phone, but suspected that he was testing her, so she remained in place.

He was back in a minute, maybe two. "Just a little diversion," he told her. "I'm sending the bomb squad over to East High School. I have some surprises planted there that should get everyone's attention for a little while. Oh shit, I left the number sitting by the phone. Be right back."

She screamed into her gag and almost choked with the effort. *Not a high school. Please, God, not a high school. Not in Colorado. Not again.*

Ramp climbed out of the truck.

She scrambled to get some balance, threw back the windbreaker, fumbled with the phone until she identified the tiny redial button, and pressed it. She could hear Ramp's footsteps approaching the truck as she tossed the jacket back into place and dropped back onto the floor.

He climbed into the cab and said, "We're off again. Short drive this time. But fasten your seat belt anyway." He looked at her and said, "Just kidding."

She protested into her gag, hoping to create enough noise to alert Alan to what was going on.

He said, "You know, you're cute."

She said, "Fuck you."

He shook his head dismissively, as though he might have actually understood her mumbles.

He started the engine and pulled back onto the street, retracing his route down Blake, crossing Broadway, and heading right back into the heart of LoDo.

CHAPTER

54

I don't think I hear anything, Sam. Maybe some background noise, but I'm not sure. Is there someplace more quiet we could go?"

Rivera led us into the main entrance of the ballpark, near the ticket turnstiles. We were away from the street noise, but I still couldn't make out much on the phone. In my other ear, I heard Rivera tell Sam that the explosion had been right upstairs in the ball club's office suite.

Again, I said, "I don't hear anything."

Sam said, "Give it to me."

I handed him the phone and the attached recorder.

He listened for ten seconds and shook his head. Finally, he said, "Wait, wait. Maybe a voice in the background. Everything's muted. I wonder if she's losing her battery."

He turned to Rivera. He had a phone to his ear, too.

Sam asked, "Can we trace this? Triangulate it?"

"They're trying. The technology's tough apparently. But they're trying. I hope this call doesn't die."

A young woman wearing a bomb squad windbreaker walked toward us and waited until she had Rivera's attention before she said, "Detectives feel confident that the device was under the woman's desk. Or maybe in her desk, in a drawer or something. But she was definitely the target."

Rivera said, "The woman in accounting?"

The young cop nodded. "And we don't think there's a secondary. We did a quick search along with the Rockies people."

"You don't *think* there's a secondary?"

She grinned just the slightest bit. "That's right. In case you haven't noticed, this is a very big building. Your people can go inside anytime. Detective said to remind you that we're handling the detonation investigation."

Rivera said, "I know. We're merely looking for a terrorist who's holding a cop hostage. I'll stay out of your way." They were interrupted by a young black woman who didn't seem to appreciate Rivera's tone. I couldn't hear what she told him but his reply was clear: "What did you say? Dear Jesus."

Sam asked, "What's going on?"

Rivera answered, "The bomb threat at East High School? They just found a device. He wasn't kidding."

Columbine images flooded my consciousness. Everyone's.

Sam was shaking his head slowly. "I'm picking up a siren. Rivera, you recognize it?"

Rivera took the phone from Sam and covered the microphone with his fingers. He closed his eyes as though he were appreciating some good jazz. "I'd say it's the fire department, but I'm not sure. I wonder how fast we can find out where they have trucks running with sirens right now. Shouldn't be that hard to do."

Sam narrowed his eyes and said, "Damn," under his breath. I followed him as he hustled outside onto the wide sidewalk in front of the stadium. He fixed his eyes to the left. A big pumper, lights flashing, siren blaring, was two blocks away, approaching down Blake from the east. He turned to me. "They're here, Alan. I can smell them. Ramp and Lucy. They're right around here."

The truck killed its siren and glided to a stop a hundred feet away. Rivera walked outside to join us. Bomb squad personnel were running past us and jumping into their vehicles to respond to the fresh threat at East High School.

Sam said, "The siren stopped, didn't it?"

Rivera nodded.

Sam pointed at the electric-green pumper. The dirty-yellow-suited firefighters clustered around it, tugging at equipment. Sam said, "That was the truck, Rivera. They're right around here. Damn."

Rivera gave Sam the phone. Immediately, he handed it to me, ordering, "Tell me if you hear anything important."

Sam stared at the streets while he huddled with Rivera. I shuffled close to the building to mute as much traffic noise as I could.

As I listened hard to the tiny speaker at my ear, there were moments when I was convinced that I could hear faint voices, other moments when I was sure that I was hearing nothing more than the desperate pulses of my hope. The whole time, I watched the traffic funneling down the viaduct from I-25 and the traffic being diverted from Blake Street up to Market and Larimer. Did I expect to see Lucy waving to me from the passenger seat of a passing car?

Not really.

But if she was waving, I wanted to be watching. That was the nature of my hope's persistence.

CHAPTER

55

Ramp slowed as a cop waved him away from Blake Street, then he followed the detour up Twenty-second to Larimer, before turning back down Twentieth all the way to Wynkoop.

A little over ten years before, Wynkoop Street had been ground zero for the rejuvenation of Denver's old warehouse district into the trendy center now called LoDo. The very first renovations in the decrepit section of Denver that bordered the railroad tracks of the Santa Fe and the Union Pacific had been in the brick warehouses that faced Denver's 120-year-old Union Station. The arrival of Coors Field in the mid-1990s had cemented the reincarnation, and the new LoDo was crowded with vibrant businesses, overpriced lofts, and the kind of sidewalk bustle that the Chamber of Commerce coveted.

After turning left onto Wynkoop, Ramp passed one

of the most recent renovations, the stately old Beatrice Foods Ice House, and turned into the drive that led to the front entrance of Union Station. The neoclassical railroad hub consisted of a huge stone building that was constructed between the two original 1881 wings after a 1914 fire. From her position on the floor of the truck, Lucy could clearly see the trio of huge arched windows that graced the lobby, and the garish neon "Travel by Train" sign high above the building's stone cornice.

She screamed *"No!"* into her gag.

Ramp turned up the radio in response to her protest, before pulling the truck to a stop on the far left side of the entrance drive. He reached down to the floor in front of his seat and lifted yet another transmitter. The device was bright yellow. "This one's from a model boat. Decent range," he said for Lucy's benefit. "Listen carefully, you might be able to hear it go off. Maybe not—the walls of this place are really thick. You should feel something in your bones, though. Try."

He lowered the volume on the radio. Lucy screamed again.

He looked askance at her. "You want to know who it is?" Ramp asked.

Lucy nodded vociferously.

"A photographer. She has her studio in there. She's the wife of the guy who was head of the parole board when the guy who killed my mom got out of prison."

Lucy's eyes softened and Ramp pressed straight ahead on a lever on the plastic console.

She heard a muted thud that felt like nothing more to her than an extra heartbeat.

Ramp raised an eyebrow as two huge double-hung windows burst outward on the upper floor of the train station and said, "That's it. The cake is baked. All that's left now is the frosting."

I heard some music in my ear. Not clearly enough that I could recognize the artist or the song, but clearly enough to know that the phone call was still alive. I ran over to Sam and Rivera. "I hear music."

Sam said, "That's it? Just music?"

"Yeah. Maybe some voices in the background. I'm not sure."

He turned back to Rivera.

"And I heard a little pop. A little boom."

"An explosion?" Rivera asked.

I said, "I don't know."

"Give me that thing," he said.

I did. Rivera turned his back, pressed the phone against one ear, and stuck an index finger into the other one.

Two bomb squad members came flying out the front door of the Rockies' offices. "Another explosion. This one's at Union Station," one of them said as he passed by. He directed the words at Rivera's back.

Sam said, "What did he say?"

"He said there was just an explosion at Union Station."

Sam grabbed my arm. "Shit. How far away is that?"

"Maybe three blocks."

He released my arm and tapped Rivera on the shoulder. Rivera lowered the phone and took the finger out of his ear. "I don't hear shit," he reported.

Sam pointed at the activity at the curb. "A bomb just went off at Union Station."

The Denver cop shook his head. In disbelief? Disgust? I couldn't tell. He said, "Union Station? Not East High School? Are you sure?"

"That's what they said."

"How bad is it?"

Sam shrugged. His face was the color of the winter sky.

Rivera pointed to a brown sedan at the curb. "That's mine. Let's go."

Ramp exited the drive in front of Union Station and pulled the truck across Wynkoop and then straight down Seventeenth past the Oxford Hotel into Denver's downtown business district. After a few blocks, the wail of sirens began to echo in the canyons between the blunt faces of Denver's skyscrapers. Seventeenth was a one-way street leading away from Union Station, and Ramp's truck was unimpeded by approaching emergency vehicles as it headed toward Broadway.

While he waited for a light to change, he lifted his windbreaker and threw it behind the seat of the truck. He fumbled for some coins on the console. "I'll need some quarters for the parking meter. Don't want to draw any attention prematurely this morning."

Lucy prayed that he wouldn't see the red light that glowed on her phone. To her, it looked as bright as a streetlight on a dark night. She screamed again to distract him.

He looked at her. "What?"

She screamed again. She was trying to say, "Take this off! Take this off!" She kicked at the floor.

The light changed. He said, "I'll take it off in a minute. We're almost at our next stop."

She pounded the console with her closed fists.

He raised his wrist, displaying the transmitter that was taped to his arm. "I said wait."

From the backseat of Rivera's car, I said, "Voices. Sam, I hear voices."

Sam spun on his seat.

I held up my finger, asking for quiet.

"The guy just said, 'What?' Then there were a couple of muffled screams."

Rivera stared at me in the rearview mirror.

"Now the guy said, 'Wait a second. I'll take it off in a minute. We're almost at our next stop.' And then another muffled scream, and . . . and some pounding.

"Wait. It's him talking again. He said, 'I said wait.' " I continued to listen intently. "Silence now, Sam. Just background noise."

I looked up. We'd pulled to a stop in front of Union

Station. Uniformed cops were directing pedestrians and traffic away from the building. By now I knew the drill. The bomb squad would be evacuating the building prior to beginning a search for secondary devices. I couldn't shake the feeling that we were a step behind Ramp and that that was exactly where he wanted us to be.

Rivera ordered me to "Stay put and keep listening." He got out of the car and huddled in front of the train station entrance with a black man in a brown sport coat. Sam nodded his head in their direction. "The guy with Rivera? That's Walter. My friend Walter." For the first time all morning, Sam smiled.

I said, "The one whose name isn't really Walter?"

"Yeah, that Walter."

He pointed at the phone. "Anything?"

I mouthed, "No."

Sam said, "We're wasting our time here. Going from bomb to bomb after they go off isn't going to get us where we need to be."

"I was thinking the same thing." I raised one index finger. "They're talking again. I think I hear Lucy, Sam. I do. She's still alive."

He exhaled as though he'd been holding his breath for most of the morning. "What'd she say? Give me that thing."

Ramp stayed southbound on Broadway until he was just past Fourteenth. He pulled to a stop by the curb opposite the plaza of the block-long complex housing the Colorado History Museum and the Judicial Heritage Center. He hopped out of the cab, fed the parking meter, and jumped right back in.

He stared at Lucy for a few seconds before he reached down and lowered her gag to her chin.

"Stop," she pleaded. "Please, stop. No more bombs, Ramp."

He smiled an ingratiating smile. "Don't worry. This is the last stop. This is where the day ends. If all goes well here, you'll be free."

She couldn't tell where they were parked. The landmarks she could see weren't familiar to her. He placed a nylon windshield screen across the inside of the windshield and pushed a piece of cardboard against the glass of the window above her seat.

"Where are we?"

He chuckled. "We're at the principal's office."

She was amazed at Ramp's calm demeanor. He was like a kid confident that he was about to ace a test. It was as though he already had all the answers.

She said, "What does that mean?"

"One of the many mistakes that Klebold and Harris made is that they failed to target the boss man. They went randomly after kids, and they didn't seem to care who they killed as long as they killed someone. That's unproductive rage. That's not my style. I've identified specific targets, deserving targets. And the final target on my list is the principal, the one who is ultimately responsible for the culture that took my mother from me."

"You're not even in school. Who's the principal? I don't get it."

"My problem is with the judicial system, right? Who makes those rules? Who's the boss?"

He was playing with her. "I don't know—the governor?" Were they parked outside the governor's mansion? From her position on the floor she couldn't tell where they were.

"Wrong. The head of the judiciary in this state is the Colorado Supreme Court. For me, that's the equivalent of the principal's office. That's where it all begins and that's where it will end."

"You're going to kill the Supreme Court justices?"

He reached down between his legs to the floor on the seat in front of him. "I know I won't get them all. But I should be able to get a few."

She had trouble grasping his threat. *Kill the justices?* "Wouldn't you have to kill all the legislators? They make the laws. They write the sentencing statutes."

"No, no. It's too late to change. It's going to be the justices." His hand held a thick roll of duct tape. "I don't trust you not to interfere. I need a few minutes to get set up, and I can't risk you doing anything to draw attention."

She said, "I'll be good. I will."

"Sorry."

Ramp reached down below his seat one more time and came up with a neat package wrapped in brown paper. The package was about the size and shape of a roll of paper towels that had been sliced in half lengthwise. A loop of insulated wire emerged from the package and a slender antenna extended up from the top about three inches.

"What is that?" Lucy demanded. She already knew what it was. She just didn't know what Ramp planned to do with it.

He leaned across the console and placed the flat side of the package against her upper abdomen and chest, pressing down hard, separating her breasts. With economical motions, he affixed the package in place with duct tape, concluding with three quick bands of tape all the way around her back.

He raised his wrist, displaying the switch that was

taped to his arm. With a magician's flourish, he reached behind the switch and touched something. A tiny red light began to glow on the plastic case, a light so small Lucy hadn't even noticed it before.

She knew that he'd just armed the damn thing. And she knew that it hadn't been armed until then.

She mumbled, "Shaped charge?"

"Again?" he said.

"Shaped charge," she repeated. It was no longer a question.

He smiled. "Yes, Lucy. A shaped charge. The energy of the blast is largely directed at your spinal column. But don't worry about paralysis. Before the blast ever gets to your spinal cord, it will liquefy your heart and lungs."

He saw a new level of fear spread across her eyes. It seemed to kill something healthy as it swelled, like a plague.

"I'll be in the back of the truck for a few minutes, getting ready. I'll be able to see you through the rear window the whole time. Do you understand?"

She nodded enthusiastically.

"You get off the floor, you're dead. You try to speak to anyone or get their attention, you're dead. Do you understand me?"

His voice told Lucy that he didn't want to kill her. Not that he wasn't willing to. Only that he didn't want to.

Ramp's eyes moved from Lucy's and rested briefly on the console. She felt certain he could see the status of the cell phone.

He moved his face to within a foot of hers. "Let me tell you something else, okay?" With an awkward motion, he sat back and crossed his left leg over his right knee, exposing the bottom of his hiking boot to Lucy. He pointed a finger at a tiny silver button taped to the sole of the shoe. "See that?"

A thin wire snaked through the treads. The wire was taped to the side of the boot and disappeared under Ramp's trousers.

She nodded. She saw it.

He uncrossed his legs, planting his left foot firmly on the floor of the truck. "It's a pressure switch. A dead-man switch. As long as I have weight on the switch, the circuit's closed. If I don't have weight on the switch for ten seconds, the circuit opens. When the circuit opens, the device on your chest will explode. If the police shoot me before I'm done, and I fall over, you will die ten seconds later. You won't believe how long those ten seconds will last, Lucy. It'll be a whole lifetime."

Involuntarily, she glanced at the cell phone. She regretted the act as soon as she did it.

Without hesitation, he lifted the phone to his face. "You guys get that? I hope so. Now pay attention to this, too. There are a series of explosive devices hidden in the chambers and courtrooms of the Colorado Supreme Court. The staircases and the elevators are wired. So are the fire exits. I want everyone in the building to get ready to come out through the front doors. You have ten minutes to get everyone organized.

But no one leaves until I say so. The justices will come out last. I want them in their robes. No switches. I know exactly what they look like. Got it? Good."

He pressed the "end" button.

57

I was relieved that Sam had the phone. I was terrified by what he was reporting to Rivera.

"Listen to this, listen to this. Ramp's at the Supreme Court Building. He says he's going to kill them, the justices. He says he won't get them all, but that he should get a few. That's his last stand. This is where it's going to end."

Sam made a perplexed face, then nodded to himself as he listened intently to the phone. When he winced, I did, too.

"Jesus. He's taped a shaped charge to Lucy's chest. He says he'll set it off if she does anything. . . . They're in a truck. He's going to the back of the truck to do something. He can see her through the window. He's in a truck, Rivera. Tell them he's in a truck, okay? Do that."

Sam stopped talking for a moment, then his mouth fell open.

"Oh my God. He says he has a dead-man switch on the bottom of one shoe. We shoot him and Lucy dies ten seconds later." He raised his voice. "Ten seconds. Rivera, tell them a cop is wired with explosives. You tell them that, you hear me? Tell them that if they hurt him, a cop dies. You hear me?"

Rivera waved at Sam in a manner even I found dismissive. I assumed that the gesture left Sam homicidal.

Sam's eyes closed in an effort to shut out the chaos that was growing around us. He mumbled, "Oh no, oh *no*. Fuck me. No, no, no." He faced Rivera one more time. "He knows that we're listening to him, Rivera. He's been feeding us all this stuff. Who knows if it's true."

Rivera hustled next to Sam.

Sam went on with his report. "He's talking to us now. He says that the Supreme Court Building's wired. Chambers, courtrooms, elevators, staircases, exits. The whole thing. He wants everyone to evacuate through the front doors. Justices have to come out last, wearing their robes. We have ten minutes to get everybody organized, but nobody comes out until he says so. That's it. Ten minutes."

Rivera stared at Sam. Finally, he said, "Ten minutes?"

"Ten minutes to get everyone organized. Justices have to exit last. In their robes, Rivera."

Five seconds passed. Ten.

Sam's eyes burned into his colleague. "That's a cop in that truck with him, Rivera. You understand? She dies if we shoot him. You understand what I'm saying?"

Rivera's face was impassive.

Sam handed me the phone. "Line's gone dead. Where the hell's the Colorado Supreme Court Building? Anybody know?"

The motorcade of emergency vehicles plowed up Seventeenth Street like the leading edge of an assaulting battalion. Rivera's gray sedan was behind a phalanx of motorcycle officers. I was alone in the backseat; Sam was up front next to Rivera. Traffic cleared in front of us like delicate fish fleeing a school of sharks.

The sirens were deafening. Every sound reflected a thousand times off the glass, aluminum, and stone towers of the central business district. We weren't trying to sneak up on Ramp. That much was certain.

The procession headed south on Broadway before stopping at Fourteenth. Six or seven Denver Police cruisers and at least one fire-rescue vehicle were already in place at the corner. Rivera screeched to a stop and we popped out of the car.

The Colorado Supreme Court was housed in a modern, six-story building at the corner of Fourteenth and Lincoln, across the street from Denver's new main library and a block away from the state capitol. A wide plaza separated the building from the Colorado

History Museum. I'd driven past the complex many times without realizing that the chambers and courtrooms of the Colorado Supreme Court were inside one of the two buildings.

Everyone's attention was locked on a flatbed truck parked against the curb on Broadway. The truck was relatively new. There was an emblem on the door that I couldn't read. A man was standing on the bed in the back. He was partially obscured by a large metal equipment box and a steel rack filled with tall green gas cylinders. The tanks appeared to have been placed into the rack upside down.

The windshield on the truck was screened by a sunshade. I wondered if Lucy was inside the cab.

Someone with binoculars walked up to Rivera and said, "Everyone's concerned that he could have a big device—a fertilizer and fuel-oil type thing—in that equipment box that's on the back of that truck. He may be planning an Oklahoma City rerun. We need to move this perimeter back."

"Do it," snapped Rivera. "And get me somebody from the bomb squad to advise me."

"I'm trying. They're spread all over the city chasing the other bombs. A bunch are on their way to East High School. Some are still at Elitch's and Coors Field. And some are still searching for secondary devices at the train station."

"Damn it," Rivera cursed. "Screw Elitch's and Coors

Field. Screw the train station. Get everybody who's not at the high school back down here. I want the containment vehicle here, everything." Rivera lifted binoculars to his eyes. "It's a kid. Just a kid. The truck is from a company called JT Welding Supplies. Somebody call them. The kid's wired from head to toe. He has something taped to his wrist. Looks like a garage-door opener. And some other switch-type thing at his waist. We have to take him out while we have a chance."

Sam said, "You can't. You shoot him and a cop gets blown to bits. You can't do that, Rivera."

"The alternative? He kills half the justices of the Colorado Supreme Court? It's a tough call, Purdy, but I'm not afraid to make it. Sorry. Columbine taught us all the consequences of waiting too long to go after the bad guys."

Ramp leaned over and briefly disappeared from view. The rack of gas cylinders on the back of the truck slowly pivoted forty-five degrees so that the bottoms of the tanks were directed toward the entrance doors of the Supreme Court Building. I was still wondering why the tanks were upside down.

Sam said, "What the . . . ? What's he doing with that thing? How many tanks are on that rack?"

I counted the blunt ends that were pointing toward the plaza. I said, "Nine."

"What's in them? Anything toxic? Explosive?"

I said, "If they're for welders, they could be a lot of things. Oxygen, acetylene, helium. I don't know. What's weird is that the tanks are loaded into the rack upside down, Sam. Does that mean they're empty?"

"I don't know anything about welding. What's he doing? I need some binoculars."

Rivera handed his field glasses to Sam. Sam stared at the truck. "What the hell is that kid up to?"

"Can you see Lucy?" I asked.

"No. I bet she's in the cab."

Rivera was busy listening to a report on the readiness of his sharpshooters. It sounded to me as though the snipers were ready.

My phone rang.

Sam had the binoculars glued to his eyes. I could tell he was staring at Ramp. Loud enough for everyone to hear, Sam told me, "Answer it, Alan. It's him."

Dr. Gregory," Ramp said to me. I recognized his voice from our conversation the night before.

"Yes. You want to talk to one of the police officers?"

"No, I want you. They'll lie to me without hesitation. You'll hesitate."

Ramp and I were appraising each other over a distance that I guessed was about fifty yards. His body was mostly blocked by the equipment box and the rack of gas cylinders, but I could see him clearly from the chest up. He was holding a phone to his left ear.

The Denver Police helicopter hovered high above him. The *thwack, thwack, thwack* reverberated like the muted pulse of the city's racing heart.

"How's Lucy?" I asked.

"So far, fine. You ready to relay my demands?"

"If that's what you want me to do."

"It is."

"I'm ready."

"Tell them this. If they shoot me, Lucy dies. I'm not kidding about the switch on my boot. In case that's not enough deterrence, have them try this on instead. See this button?" He raised his free hand.

Sam continued to stare through the binoculars. He said, "He's showing us a red box with a button on it."

"Yes," I said. "I can see your hand. And it does appear that there is something in it."

"Every time I touch this button, it resets a time switch for the explosives inside the building. If I don't hit the button, the switch isn't reset, and the explosives go off in ten seconds. Therefore I have to hit the button every ten seconds. If I hold it down for three seconds continuously, the devices in the building will go off instantly. Do you get it?"

"Yes."

"Explain it to those cops. Talk loudly so I can hear what you say. I want to make sure they get it."

I tried to repeat what Ramp had explained to me. It didn't help my concentration to note that Sam was breathing heavily through his nose and that Rivera's dark brow was dotted with sweat, like old macadam after a gentle rain.

When I was through with the explanation, Ramp said, "You did good. I'm going to be sitting down now between the tanks and the equipment box. In about a minute, I'll give the okay to start the evacuation from the building. I want to remind everyone that the justices come out last, wearing their robes. Remind the cops."

I did.

"Now tell them to get the chopper out of here. It's bothering me."

I said, "Rivera? He wants the chopper out of here."

Rivera stared at me malevolently, as though moving the helicopter had been my idea. Within ten seconds, the helicopter departed in the direction of the state capitol building.

Rivera said, "I want a guarantee he's not going to harm the evacuees."

My mouth was as dry as insulation. "The police are concerned that you're planning to hurt the evacuees as they come out of the building. They want your word that you won't."

"They're assholes. Have I spent my day trying to kill innocent people? Let me talk to the cop, the one you keep talking to."

I handed the phone to Rivera. "He wants to talk to you."

Sam asked me, "How does he sound?"

"Less nervous than me."

"Did he say anything about Lucy?"

"No."

Sam said, "He's smart. Where he's sitting now, the sharpshooters would have a hard time hitting him."

"Could they risk it? The way he has the explosives wired it seems too risky to shoot him."

"Rivera thinks he's bluffing."

I tried to swallow that news and ended up almost choking with the effort. "Rivera thinks the kid is bluffing? After all that's happened this morning?"

"I don't envy him; he's in a tough spot. He doesn't want to be accused of waiting to act, the way the sheriff in Jefferson County did during Columbine."

I asked, "What do you think?"

"Lucy's in that truck. That's what I think."

Rivera handed me back the phone. "He wants you again."

"Yes?"

Ramp's voice was harder now. "Change in plans. Let's see if you guys were planning to play fair. I want the justices outside on the plaza within thirty seconds. In their robes. I'm counting, starting now."

I snapped at Rivera: "He's changed his mind. He wants the justices outside on the plaza in their robes within thirty seconds."

"Shit!" Rivera barked a command into his radio. "We can't do it. We can't do it in time. We have state cops in their robes. Buy some time." He began running down the sidewalk to some of his colleagues who were hidden behind patrol cars in front of the library.

Sam and I followed Rivera as I said, "Ramp! Ramp!" into the phone. I was wondering how the hell I was going to buy some time, but when I looked back over to the truck, Ramp was holding the cell phone high in the air, far from his ear. He wasn't prepared to listen to Rivera's excuses.

Sam broke the news. "Rivera, look. He's got the phone in the air. He's not even listening."

The seconds ticked away. I stared at my watch as

three became two became one and then . . . a sharp *craaack* filled the air and glass and stone flew out onto the Broadway sidewalk as at least three windows blew out from the third floor.

In my ear, I heard Ramp's voice. "That one was a warning from an empty office. Thirty more seconds. The next one's going to take some people with it. Tell him."

I did.

Rivera yelled commands into the radio. After twenty-two more seconds leaked away, the justices began to exit the building. One by one they walked to the center of the plaza. Their robes swayed gently in the morning breeze. I couldn't see their faces but I could feel their terror, even from this distance.

Ramp said, "The one in back is not a justice. The tall guy. If he doesn't leave that group in five seconds, you assholes will have some blood on your hands. Tell him that. Do it."

I repeated Ramp's message word for word.

Rivera cursed and spoke into his microphone.

A heartbeat later, one tall, robed figure walked backward away from the clustered judges.

"Tell the cop not to screw with me again. I'm not in the mood."

I held the phone a few inches from my mouth and told Rivera what Ramp had just said.

"Now I want the justices to back up against the wall of the History Museum and get on their knees."

Rivera used a megaphone. The justices moved back

slowly, reluctantly. The building on the other side of the plaza was the Colorado History Museum. Its wall rose from the stone at an unconventional forty-five-degree angle.

"Now, have the people who are still inside the court building begin a single file evacuation. They should exit to Lincoln, then south. No running. No hands in the air. Just have them walk out. The justices stay put."

Rivera eagerly gave those commands.

Sam had the binoculars to his eyes. He said, "He's been moving that rack of tanks on the back of the truck. He's doing it real slowly, but the bottoms of the tanks are pointing directly at the plaza now. The base of the rack is solid metal, not an open grid. That's not usual, is it? What the hell's he doing?"

I said, "The hostages are coming out, Sam."

One by one, stepping quickly, seemingly fighting an urge to run, a steady stream of men and women began walking from the entrance of the building, across the plaza, down to the sidewalk, and then south on Lincoln.

Rivera touched me on the arm. "Cover the microphone on that cell phone."

I did.

He spoke into his radio. "Give me a status report from the sharpshooters. We're taking him out as soon as anyone is ready. On my order."

CHAPTER

59

Without warning, Ramp jumped off the back of the truck and hopped into the cab with Lucy. Within seconds, the driver's-side window was blocked with a sheet of cardboard.

Rivera's order to the sharpshooters had been seconds too late.

I thought he looked like a kid who'd missed Christmas and was trying to figure out how to lure the fat man back down the chimney.

"Shit. Now what?" he asked.

Sam pointed at the plaza. "The justices are moving away. Look."

They were. The whole pack of them was squatting in their robes and edging down the angled wall away from Ramp toward Lincoln Street. From this distance, they looked like a pack of nuns trying to walk away on their knees.

Ramp noticed, too. He barked at me, "Tell them to stop moving. Tell the cop, *now!*"

I said, "Rivera? He wants the justices to stop moving."

Rivera looked to make sure I'd covered the microphone with my finger. "Screw him. They're almost away."

As though he'd read Rivera's lips, Ramp reacted. An audible little boom sounded and a tiny puff of smoke emerged from the steel rack on the back of the truck.

Sam, the binoculars still at his eyes, said, "Oh shit."

One of the tall green tanks began spewing its pressurized contents with an immense hiss and roar. The volume of the noise of the escaping gas was incredible.

As they heard the blast and the subsequent roar, the justices stopped their progression from the plaza and dropped back down to the ground.

Blunt end first, a green tank lifted from the steel rack on the back of the truck like a missile leaving its launcher.

I held my breath.

Another small explosion followed, and then came the roar of additional escaping gases. A second tank immediately lifted from the rack.

Rivera screamed into a megaphone, urging the hostages to run. I'm sure they couldn't hear him. I was five feet from him and I could barely discern his words above the hiss of the ruptured tanks.

Although the first of the tanks launched into the air like a slow-motion rocket, it returned to the ground no more than thirty feet from the truck. It bounced off the stone plaza like a smooth rock on a glass lake, hopping across the wide expanse with a speed and ferocity that should have belonged only to objects launched by the Marines. A stone bench slightly changed the tank's trajectory: It skidded up the angled wall about twenty feet from the huddled Supreme Court justices before it vanished over the top of the roof.

The second tank stayed airborne at least twice as far as the first one had before crashing blunt end first into the plaza. From there it tumbled once end over end like a child's jack, finally bouncing high and disappearing into the second floor of the building, demolishing all the windows in its path. The destruction was only fifteen feet above the huddled hostages.

As the hissing died away, I could hear screams. I could also hear Rivera yelling for someone to take Ramp out.

A third puff of smoke emerged from the back of the truck and a third tank launched into the air with an enormous swoosh. A fourth tank followed two or three seconds later.

My eyes followed the two new hurtling tanks until Sam—Rivera's binoculars still glued to his eyes—screamed into my ear, "He just busted out the back window of the truck. Watch him!"

Ramp dove athletically through the empty space where the window had been and immediately disappeared into the void between the big equipment box and the steel rack full of tanks.

I didn't hear any shots from sharpshooters' rifles.

I looked over in time to see one of the newly fired tanks skittering through the justices like a bowling ball through a fresh stand of pins. Black-robed bodies went flying into the air.

I didn't know where the other tank had gone.

The binoculars still at his eyes, Sam yelled, "He's turning the rack this way. Everybody run!"

The steel rack was now pointing right at us, the blunt end of the remaining tanks shining brightly like polished coins.

Boom! Boom! Boom!

Ramp launched three tanks in rapid succession. Cops, firefighters, and paramedics scattered like ants. I was pinned by two Denver Police patrol cars. My only route to safety was following Sam across the road toward the front end of the parked flatbed truck. Ramp couldn't rotate the rack that far—if he did, the cab would interfere with the launch of any more tanks.

I could feel the impact of one of the newly launched tanks as it crashed into a patrol car behind me. The concussion was so intense that I almost fell to the asphalt as I sprinted after Sam.

The patrol car burst into flames. A second or two later the whole thing ignited like a bomb as the fire reached the fuel in the gas tank.

Sam and I were enveloped in heat; the force of the explosion threw us to the ground. We crawled the rest of the way across the street and crouched out of sight in front of Ramp's truck. I looked back to discover that the other two tanks had made it all the way across Broadway and impaled themselves in the façade of the Philip Johnson-designed Denver Public Library.

I tried to find Rivera in the chaos. I couldn't spot him.

Sam said, "He only has two tanks left."

A new roar filled the air and another rocket left the launcher. Sam held up his index finger and mouthed, "One."

My instinct was to turn my head to follow the trajectory of the missile as it lifted from the back of the truck. But Sam held my face firmly with both his hands, forcing me to stare into his eyes. As the roar of the newly launched tank diminished, he said, "I'm going to shoot him, then I'm going to compress the switch on his foot. You're going to press the button on his hand every five seconds until the bomb squad tells you to stop. You are not going to hold it down. Every five seconds. You got it?"

I nodded.

"You're sure?"

I nodded again.

He moved around to the passenger side of the truck. I followed him.

Ramp turned just as Sam was leveling his weapon. Ramp's eyes were soft and inviting, at once disbelieving and trusting. I sensed that he knew what was about to happen, and that he welcomed it. My ears were so overwhelmed by the hissing gases and the fomenting chaos that I'm not sure I even heard the explosion from Sam's handgun. But I think I saw a dark hole emerge three inches below the collar line and two inches left of center on Ramp's chest.

Ramp's face registered no surprise before he fell.

Sam screamed, "Alan, now! Every five seconds. Count out loud so I can hear you."

Ramp had collapsed into an awkward heap in the confined space between the steel rack that had been full of tanks and the big metal equipment box. Sam and I were bumping into each other, clawing at Ramp's limbs, desperate to find the correct hand and the correct foot.

Sam yelled, "I got his foot! I have the switch."

Ramp's right hand was pinned beneath his body, which seemed to weigh a thousand pounds. I yanked at his elbow. It didn't free his hand.

"You got it?" cried Sam.

I didn't answer. I put all my weight into another tug on Ramp's elbow. In my head I was counting to ten and was already at eleven.

Ramp's hand came free.

I traced down his wrist, turned his hand palm up, and pressed maniacally with my thumb.

The red button was gone.

"It's gone."

"What do you mean it's gone?"

"It's gone."

"Get Lucy and get out of here. Do it! *Now!*"

Sixteen, seventeen, eighteen.

I crawled backward off of Ramp's body and almost fell before I ripped open the door to the truck. Lucy was huddled in the footwell on the passenger side. Her eyes were streaked red and tears stained her cheeks. As she saw me, she pushed herself up onto the seat. I raised her over my shoulder in a fireman's carry and ran north on Broadway, waiting for an explosion to sever Lucy's body and end my life.

I screamed, "Bomb squad! Bomb squad! Over here! Bomb squad!" until Lucy and I were just inside the taped perimeter near Fourteenth Street. But when I arrived at that spot and looked around, I realized we were alone.

The aftermath of the impact of the last few tanks that Ramp had launched and the destruction caused by the exploding patrol car had created enough carnage and confusion to occupy all the emergency personnel on the scene.

I stood Lucy on the sidewalk at Fourteenth and Broadway and stared at her restraints. She was yelling something at me as I tugged at her gag.

She coughed. "That's a shaped charge on my chest. It's not wired to me. It takes a radio signal to set it off. Get it off of me!"

I examined the bulky pack on her chest.

She implored me, "It's just taped on. Take it off! Take it off of me!"

I looked around once again for someone wearing a windbreaker that said "Bomb Squad." No one was coming to help us.

I thought of Sam, contorted in the truck, firmly maintaining pressure on the button on the bottom of Ramp's boot.

Then I began to unwrap the duct tape that secured the package on Lucy's chest. Of course, my fingers shook. Of course, the tape tore where it shouldn't. Of course, I heard ticking even though my head knew that this device wasn't timed.

I could barely see through the images of Grace that were flooding my consciousness and the sweat that was dripping into my eyes.

Finally I had the thing in my hands. It was heavy for its size. My instinct was to twirl into a discus thrower's motion and throw the thing as far away as I could. Instead, I sat it gingerly onto the concrete as though it were a sleeping baby. Then I lifted Lucy into my arms and ran north down Broadway. I put her down in the shadows of the Veteran's Memorial and sprinted back toward Sam, making a wide arc around the shaped charge on the sidewalk.

A hundred feet from him, I yelled, "She's safe, Sam! The bomb is off her chest."

"I can let go?"

"Yeah. The device is back there, on the far corner. But stay down. It's a big thing."

"That's it? There?"

"Yes."

"Nobody's near it?"

"No."

He held his hands high in the air so I could see that he'd released the switch on Ramp's boot.

I counted to ten. When I got to fourteen, the charge on the corner exploded.

CHAPTER

61

The three of us didn't have much to do.

By the time Sam and I had freed Lucy from her restraints and the three of us checked each other for injury and hugged each other about twenty times, the volume of emergency personnel on Broadway made our presence superfluous.

We sat on the lawn in front of the state capitol. Across from us the distant Rockies peeked out above Civic Center Park. Ambulances were streaming from the plaza in front of the Supreme Court Building in the direction of Denver Health Medical Center and Presbyterian St. Luke's Hospital.

A small group of cops hovered around the flatbed truck. They'd found Ramp's body.

"How did Ramp do it?" I asked. "Launch all those tanks? Does either of you know how he did it?"

"He had small charges on the valves," Lucy said. "When he set them off, the valves blew off the tanks and the compressed gases started to escape out the opening. It was just like a rocket nozzle. He modified the rack himself. When he came back inside the truck, he told me all about it."

"The tanks are under that much pressure?"

She shrugged. "He told me that he had them pressurized to almost three thousand pounds per square inch. Think of the air coming out of a balloon."

Sam shook his head at the thought. "Those tanks weigh a ton. It would be like being hit by a truck on the freeway."

I still had my cell phone. I used it to call Lauren to see how she was doing—fine—and to tell her that the three of us were safe. She was near panic, having watched the morning's events unroll on television. Sam asked me to have Lauren call his wife, too.

When Lauren and I were through, I offered the phone to Lucy. "Want to call your fiancé?"

In a quick flash something important transpired in her thinking. In another circumstance I might have asked her about it. But not then. She shook her head. "No, thanks." To Sam, she said, "They probably aren't going to let me go home, are they?"

Sam said, "The Denver cops?"

Lucy nodded.

"No. I doubt it, Luce. I doubt it. They're going to want to talk to you about your time with that kid. Given your circumstances, you should probably have a lawyer with you. They're going to want to talk to us, too, Alan."

Lucy asked, "Why?"

Sam seemed to have trouble forcing his lips apart to say, "I'm the one who shot him over there. The kid."

Lucy said, "Oh." Her eyes widened. "I thought it was a sharpshooter." She lowered her face and rested her chin on her fists. I thought she looked like she was about to cry. "It's kind of crazy, I know, but I . . . liked him. Jason. I liked him. If there was more time, I think I could've talked him out of it. He wasn't evil, Sam. He wasn't crazy, he was . . ."

Sam said, "He killed people, Lucy. He murdered innocent people. What he did was senseless and vicious."

"He had reasons, Sam. He—"

"I don't care about his reasons. He murdered innocent people. That's all we need to know."

"I know what he did, Sam. And I guess that means I should hate him. We're not supposed to have sympathy for kids who do what he did. But I don't hate him. I'm sorry he's dead."

Sam opened his mouth to argue with her some more. She saw it coming and reached out and touched his lips with her index finger. He swallowed his words. I could tell that they didn't go down easily.

She turned toward me and her face fell into shadow. "Is Cozy dead, too, Alan? Ramp told me that the girl set off a bomb at his office this morning."

"Last we heard, he was getting out of surgery," I

said. "Broken bone in his neck. Lauren was there, too, in the building. She's okay, a concussion."

Lucy looked at Sam, not me. "Will Cozy be all right?"

Sam lifted his shoulders and shook his head. He didn't know. I was thinking that he hadn't totally given up arguing with Lucy about Ramp.

Again, I offered the phone to Lucy. I said, "You know, you don't have to cooperate with them. Maybe you should talk to Lauren and get some legal advice before you go over there."

Sam glared at me.

"No," she said. "I don't need a lawyer with me. I'm a cop, right? I was a hostage, right?" She stood up. "I need to pee. Then let's go find somebody in charge. I want to get this over with and go home."

The three of us walked in the direction of the smoldering patrol car. Sam held his shield out in front of him the whole way.

Lucy took my hand. She leaned over and her lips were so close to my ear I could feel the air moving between us as she said, "I liked him a lot."

CHAPTER
62

Over the next couple of days, Sam kept me informed about the progress of the investigation in Denver. I didn't know whether he was getting his information from Rivera or from Walter or from somebody named Lou. I didn't ask, and I didn't really care. I appreciated not having to rely on the reports on the local news.

Ramp, it turned out, had been out of explosives. The explosives vault at his grandmother's ranch near Agate was totally cleaned out.

Much of what he had threatened at the Supreme Court Building was a ruse. The Denver Police Bomb Squad found no additional devices hidden in the building. In fact, the second device that was discovered at Red Rocks turned out to be a fake that was intended to draw bomb disposal resources away from the city. No secondary devices were found at any of the earlier bomb sites. All three devices that were recovered at East High School were dummies.

The gas cylinders that Ramp had launched at the Supreme Court had done a lot of damage. One justice had died, two others had been severely injured. The exploding patrol car had killed one cop and burned three others. A woman watching the drama from a Denver Public Library window had been badly injured by debris sent flying by the tank that had impacted there.

The earlier bombs had mostly hit their marks. Two were dead in the amusement ride at Elitch's; two more were dead in the offices at Coors Field. The target at Union Station had escaped injury because she was down the hall in the bathroom when the bomb went off in her second-floor studio.

It was still unclear whether Ramp would get his wish about public dialogue.

At first, the attention of the media was mostly on the carnage. The seemingly endless news footage of the final conflagration on Broadway proved to be enough of a magnet to attract temporary nonstop national and local coverage of Ramp's Rampage. That's what the event had been nicknamed by the loud blond guy who did *Hardball* on cable, and the moniker had stuck to the events like a bad cold.

Marin's rape, Leo Bigg's retaliation on the rapist, and Ramp's mother's tragic death were all chronicled and rechronicled. Herbert Ramp's role in the demolition of Las Vegas was broadcast and rebroadcast for no other reason, it seemed, than that the tape was available and that it was pretty spectacular to watch the hotels fall down all over again.

CHAPTER
63

Lucy was holding two pine twigs like chopsticks to scratch at the rough granite boulder that we were sitting on. She said, "There are some things in life that Sam can't forgive. I suspect this is one."

"He's a good friend, Lucy. I think you can trust him."

"It's not about trust, Alan," she explained. "You know him. Sammy has a simple view of the world. Simple in a good way. Uncomplicated. He's not an imaginative person. He still gets surprised at what's up on the screen when he goes to the movies. On his own, his mind would never travel down the road where I would have to take him. Not on his own, no way. And the truth is, he doesn't belong there. He'd try to understand what I did, why I did it. He'd try to make sense of it because he's a good guy. But he wouldn't be able to understand, not really. As much as he's been exposed to in life, he's still an innocent in some ways. To forgive me he'd have to find a way to understand what I did. And he could never ever do that."

I still didn't know what it was that Lucy had done, nor was I sure she was planning on telling me. I suspected that her secret had to do with Royal Peterson's murder, but I didn't know whether it was as simple as explaining why she had been at his house that night or whether it was as complicated as explaining why she had killed him. I did know that I was maximally ambivalent about hearing it, whatever it was. My recent experience had taught me that some confidences of this nature, maybe most confidences of this nature, weren't worth knowing. The burden of the knowledge was often greater than any benefit that accrued from harboring the private facts.

Lucy and I had run into each other while visiting Cozy as he was recuperating at his Victorian on Maxwell Street. It was just before noon a couple of days after the morning of bombs in Denver, and Cozy was home from the hospital, though he was still far from agile. His neck was immobilized in a plastic structure that looked as though it had once been part of an architectural model for a single-span suspension bridge.

As we left the house together, Lucy told me she would like to talk and asked if I had a few minutes for her. When I said I did, she led me to her red Volvo and drove us up Flagstaff, taking the sharp curves up the mountainside carefully, as though she was fearful that a tire on her car was about to blow.

The extension of Baseline that twisted up Flagstaff Mountain was the steepest and most curvaceous paved route out of Boulder. Vehicles over thirty feet in length were banned because they couldn't maneuver the curves. The upside was that a minute after passing the Chautauqua complex on Baseline, Lucy and I were afforded the kind of views that in most environs were available only to birds.

"You come up here often?" she asked me.

I shook my head and was going to leave it at that until I realized that Lucy would have to take her eyes from the road to read my head motion. I quickly added, "No, but maybe I should." The truth was that I found the view from the high foothills disconcerting. The perspective from the mountains toward the east was too infinite for my comfort, the Great Plains spreading out like a petrified ocean. I preferred the view from my house toward the west, believing that, visually, Colorado was a place that should be experienced either in the mountains or toward the mountains, but not away from the mountains. This vista, from peaks to plains, was too much like looking at the state from the rear-facing third seat in my parents' old station wagon.

"I do," she said. "Sometimes I like to be above it all." She continued to drive, taking us high above the

Flagstaff House Restaurant. I was beginning to suspect that our destination was the summer 2000 burn near Gross Reservoir until she pulled the car to a stop in a clearing off the shoulder of the narrow road, touched me on the leg, and said, "Come on, this way."

I followed her out of the car and down a dusty path that wound around sharp rock outcroppings and dodged rugged ponderosa pines.

An old-timer had once told me that Boulder had been named by the first pioneer who ever tried to put a shovel into the dirt. The old-timer then laughed and said he knew the story was apocryphal because if it had really happened that way, the town would be called Oh Shit.

He hadn't actually said "apocryphal." He'd said "bullcrap."

I joined Lucy as she scrambled across a rough slab of granite and perched on the edge of a boulder the size of a two-car garage. As she lowered herself to a squat, I examined the position she'd assumed and knew that I hadn't managed that particular posture in about ten years. Maybe fifteen. I sat on my butt and side-by-side we gazed at the oasis that the city of Boulder forms on the border of the endless prairie. We were a little too close to the edge of the cliff for my comfort. My thoughts were rarely far from my daughter anymore, and I was thinking that I wouldn't allow Grace to sit as close to the edge as we were.

That's when Lucy began to tell me about Sam's lack of imagination.

Remember what you told me about intimacy?" she asked me.

"Of course," I said, but my radar was tweaked and I was wary of where we were going.

"There are natural limits, aren't there? With some people, I mean. Like with Sammy, he doesn't really want me to open up to him. He doesn't really want to know my secrets. He gives me lots of signals that tell me when to stop."

I shot a quick glance toward Lucy. She was looking east. A split second before, I'd been looking in the same direction, busy imagining that I could perceive the gentle curvature of the earth on the horizon.

I replied, "In a relationship, intimacy can be restricted, or enhanced, by either person." My words sounded banal. "Sorry, Lucy. That sounds trite. I don't mean it to. What you're saying is true. At least it is about Sam. He draws lines in the sand sometimes. We all do."

She waved a hand, dismissing my apology. "No, it's fine."

Wind whistled through the pines in a short burst. It wasn't a melodic tune—it was more acid than sugar. The sound reminded me of the first gasp of gas escaping the green cylinders on the back of Ramp's truck. Though the day was warm, I felt a chill as the memory hissed at me.

Lucy stood. She towered over me. From our precipice she appeared to be a diver contemplating the degree of difficulty of her next jump. The image troubled me. I didn't stand beside her.

I wondered about Lucy's recklessness, about what despair could have fueled her compulsion to be taunting fate. I knew I wouldn't have let Grace stand there—when she could stand, anyway. I got lost temporarily contemplating how many more weeks that might be and wished I'd paid more attention during the human development class I'd taken as an undergraduate.

"I told Ramp I was sleeping with Royal," she said. "He asked me, so I told him. I spent much of the rest of the time I was with him wondering whether or not it was an act of intimacy on my part."

At Lucy's admission about her relationship with Royal, I felt my breath catch just a little in my chest. The hesitation was not over learning that she'd slept with him, but rather at hearing her admit it. My mind flashed back to Lucy's oddly provocative behavior the night I visited her home, and I tried to put her confession about Royal in that context. Ever since I'd learned about the wet spot, I'd been preparing myself for the likelihood that Lucy had been intimate with the DA. Still, hearing her confirm the fact was far from comforting.

I asked, "Whether what was an act of intimacy? The sex with Royal? Or telling Ramp?"

"Good question. The telling. The sex with Royal wasn't intimacy. I don't have any doubts about that now." She kicked at something on the granite boulder. "How do you do that so easily? You didn't even hiccup when I told you that I'd slept with Royal. Weren't you surprised?"

Although I hadn't really been surprised by Lucy's revelation, at some level I knew that my sensibilities were offended, but years of clinical work had left me practiced at not revealing that kind of reaction. I said, "I suspected, and the truth is, I don't surprise easily anyway. Maybe I'm not as innocent as Sam. Maybe it's the work I do—I hear a lot of things."

"You don't care that I was sleeping with Royal?"

I chose my reply with care. "You mean do I judge you?"

"I guess that's what I mean."

"I'm in no position to do that. Knowing you slept with him is like skipping to the back of a book to find out how it ends. It's dangerous to make assumptions from there. I don't know what came before. What your motivations were."

"Are you curious?"

Good question. "We're both in difficult positions, Lucy."

"Does it make sense why I wouldn't tell Lauren and Cozy?"

"Sure. If you were having an affair with Royal, it wouldn't be hard for someone to extrapolate that maybe you had a motive to kill him." I, for instance, was having no trouble making that precise extrapolation. None. I added, "But they are your lawyers, Lucy."

Almost coyly, she asked, "Do you want to know about it? What happened between Royal and me?"

"I'm not sure. I don't want to be in a position to compromise your position."

"You mean legally?"

"Yes."

"It's not like that. With what I'd like to tell you, you could hurt me, but not legally."

I finally guessed where she was going. "But you would be vulnerable? Psychologically?"

"Yes. I would be very, very vulnerable. To you, certainly." She spread her arms to the side and closed her eyes. She held her position with the assurance of a yogi. "Stand up with me," she said.

Reluctantly, I did. Inches from my toes, the canyon dropped at least a hundred yards—okay, maybe fifty—almost straight down. If I fell, I counted at least two or three sharp outcroppings of rock that would crack my skull and my bones on the way to the bottom.

Lucy looked at me. I turned my head to her slowly, afraid that a more rapid motion would disturb my precarious balance.

She said, "I think Susan wanted me to."

I said, "What?"

"I think she wanted me to be . . . involved with Royal. It served her purposes."

Fortunately, she caught me before I keeled over.

"A little less than a year ago—it was early last summer—she called me one day, out of the blue, and asked me to come over to her house. I thought it was odd, but I did. I went. She said her illness had finally taken its toll on Royal, and that he was planning on leaving her. He wasn't going to run for DA in the next election. He didn't love her anymore and he was going to divorce her and move on with his life.

"She blamed the illness, of course. It never crossed her mind that Royal might have grown to despise her even had she been healthy."

I opened my mouth to speak but reconsidered. I needed to listen, not talk. Lucy had just admitted that she'd been sleeping with her mother's husband, and yet she was choosing to talk not about her own behavior but about her mother's. My antennae were twitching.

Lucy continued. "She said she'd need someone to care for her." I watched as Lucy lifted her right foot from the uneven stone and bent that leg ninety degrees at the knee, finally resting the foot against the inside of her left thigh. "She meant me, of course."

She maintained the position for a count of about twenty. I held my breath until she lowered her leg again. Both feet firmly on the rock, she reached out and grabbed my hand. The breezes were shoving insistently at our backs, nudging us toward something.

"I didn't even let her ask. I told her no, that I wouldn't take care of her. No way. Not a chance."

Lucy grew silent for a while. I was aware that we'd started to sway in unison. I really wanted to sit down.

"She acted surprised, almost offended, that I could think she would ask me to take care of her. But I knew where she was going before she got there. I don't know why, or how, but I just did. Sitting with her then, I felt like you feel right now. On the edge of something dangerous. Unsure of my balance, what I should do next."

She knew I was nervous.

"And she . . . I thought she was kind of threatening me. She was subtle, but I got the message anyway. She told me that she always thought that she could count on her daughters for help if circumstances . . . demanded. Me, I was one of her daughters. What she was doing was she was letting me know she'd be willing to tell people that she was my mother. She actually said she was beyond humiliation. She didn't care if the whole town knew she'd abandoned her daughter."

"She said all that?"

"She didn't have to say it all."

"But it felt like a threat to you?"

"It felt pitiful. It made me despise her more."

"So what do you think she was doing? Why did she invite you over?"

"I don't know. Maybe she was trying to play on my guilt. She knew I didn't want to have anything to do with her. And I'm sure she knew I didn't even want to be associated with her publicly. She was letting me know that she could make living in Boulder uncomfortable for me, and she was offering me an alternative."

"Taking care of her?"

She nodded. The wind stilled temporarily and Lucy seemed to be pondering her next words. I told myself to wait her out. The wait was prolonged. She didn't speak until the wind returned to accompany her tale.

"A week or two later Royal called and asked me to come over to discuss 'things.' That's what he said— 'things.' But I didn't want to go to Susan's house, so I asked him to meet me at my place. It was a Saturday afternoon that he came over. The Broncos were playing a preseason game. I don't even remember against who." Her voice brightened as she asked, "Did you ever get a chance to spend time alone with him?"

"With Royal?"

She nodded.

"I only knew him socially, Lucy. The smallest group I ever saw him in was probably a dinner party."

Her gaze seemed to fall out of focus. "You missed something special. Royal was charming when you got him alone. Truly charming. That day he came over to my house I liked him right away. He was nothing like what I'd expected based on seeing him on the news."

Lucy liked Royal. I tried to process that data.

"Nothing happened that day. We talked about life with Susan. He told me about his plans, what life might bring after he left the DA's office. We talked about the Broncos and cars and being a cop."

And, I wondered, *what bridges to intimacy did you cross?*

"The next move was mine. I called him a week later, asking if we could talk again. Neither of us wanted to be seen out together in public, so he suggested I come by his house after Susan was in bed.

"I did. That's the night we made love for the first time." Her head lolled back and she stared at the sky.

"I almost didn't do it because, in some sick way, I knew right from the start that I was doing it partially for Susan. Like a gift. But I really liked Royal, so I knew I was doing it for me, too. I was having my cake and eating it, too. I can't think of another time when that's been true in my life. Not one."

"I don't think I understand how it was a gift for Susan." Whether or not I understood wasn't particularly relevant. What I was really saying was that I suspected that Lucy didn't truly understand how it was a gift for Susan.

"As long as Royal and I were involved, he wouldn't have a reason to leave her right away. Susan had told me that she thought their youngest daughter could help her out when she got out of school the following spring. My relationship with Royal bought Susan time."

Using my office voice, a voice that sounded foreign to me out here among the rocks and pines, I said, "So you convinced yourself that having sex with Royal was an act of generosity to your mother?"

She registered my change in tone. She stilled and asked, "What do you mean?"

I allowed the vinegar of incredulousness to seep into my words. "By sleeping with her husband you thought you were being generous to her?"

"As long as I was involved with him, I didn't think he'd leave her."

I could hardly believe the level of denial that I was hearing. It bordered on hysteria or dissociation. But if

Lucy's denial were doing its job protecting her ego from the rage she obviously found so intolerable, she would be almost immune to gentle confrontation from me. Part of me felt I should turn and walk away from Lucy's defenses, leaving the thick insulation undisturbed.

Part of me—maybe unfortunately—didn't. I wouldn't put it past Susan to snare Lucy into some kind of evil, but I truly doubted that Susan's motivation would have anything to do with prolonging the Petersons' marriage. I said, "And you believed . . . that what you were doing was . . . uncomplicated? Just a favor to your mother? Like bringing her hot meals occasionally?"

My words were more generous than my thoughts. In my head I was thinking that Lucy had been sticking a dagger into her mother's heart and had somehow convinced herself that the act was bypass surgery.

Could she have performed a similar operation on Royal? I wasn't sure. I just wasn't sure.

"No, of course not. I knew it was weird, that part of it. But the other side of it was that . . . Royal was special to me. I knew that I was getting what I wanted from him. That came first. I'm not blind about all this. If it was just about Susan, I wouldn't have done it."

I sighed involuntarily, and ratcheted up the confrontation. "I think maybe you've been kidding yourself, Lucy." I was eager to be certain that my words had registered, but she didn't look back at me. I continued. "I don't think your decision to sleep with Royal was anywhere near as uncomplicated as you would like to think."

I gave her a chance to reply. She passed on the opportunity. I went on. "If—and it's a big 'if'—Susan was really inviting you to get involved with her husband, what she was really inviting—Look at me please, Lucy." I was mildly surprised that she turned toward me. "What she was really inviting was your hostility, and you fell right into her trap and complied. She held out a noose and you agreed to close it around her neck."

I watched Lucy's jaw tighten, watched her eyes narrow. A gust of wind blew her hair across her face. She threaded it away with her long fingers. "You think that's what I did? I did this to . . . hurt her?"

She looked baffled, almost disoriented, as she recognized with alarm that I'd been busy setting up an ambush on her denial.

I decided to give understatement a chance. "I think you may want to look at it, Lucy."

"She wanted me to punish her?" The question was naive. This was virgin territory for Lucy. I continued to fight astonishment that, despite the events that had transpired since the night Royal was killed, Lucy's defenses were so resilient.

I shrugged. "That's part of it. Assuming she knew what was going on, the other part is that she also wanted to injure you as well. The hostility cut both ways. I'm afraid she accomplished that, too. Didn't she?"

Lucy shook her head as though my words stunned

her, but when she spoke again she ignored my question, returning instead to the issue of her own rage. Her cheeks drained of color as though they'd suddenly been bleached. "That makes me what? Sadistic? To my own mother? Is that what I am—a sadist?"

"I don't think the label is necessary or helpful."

"What, then? What is necessary?"

"The awareness of how furious you've been at her. Maybe that's a good place to start. That's precisely what she took advantage of, Lucy—your anger. She knew all about your anger."

Her shoulders hunched upward and her body began to sway back and forth like a sapling against the breeze.

I put a hand on her upper arm and told her that I needed to sit. She sat with me. Still way too close to the edge for my comfort, but at least we were sitting.

Lucy's sobs were almost drowned out by the gusting wind. I had to struggle to make out her next words. "I could've fallen in love with him. Maybe I did. It wasn't all about Susan."

I weighed her thoughts for further evidence of rationalization. But I knew I'd been witnessing evidence of something else, something more pathological than a garden-variety ego defense. Could it have been possible that her rage at her mother was really as isolated as it appeared? Had she been so incapable of seeing how Susan had been hurting her all over again? So out of touch with her own agony? And so unwilling to see her own vicious response toward her mother?

It seemed like time for me to say something. I said, "This wasn't about Royal, Lucy."

"It wasn't?" The sound of her question was so puerile it was as though I were watching a child move from doubts about immense bunnies to recognition of the fact that Easter morning was a fiction.

I shook my head. "No, it wasn't."

Lucy said, "I wondered if she knew."

I didn't respond.

Lucy went on. "I don't know if she knew. Royal thought she suspected, but I didn't see how she could really know. We met at their house. He'd give her some sleeping medicine before I came over. That was the arrangement. I'd park on the next block and come in through the backyard. Royal and I would get a few hours together." She wiped her eyes with her fingertips and wet her lips with her tongue as she scanned the sky.

Reality was settling the way that dust coats a mirror.

"God, it was hostile, wasn't it? What I did."

I replied, "And what she did. And what Royal did."

In a quick motion she popped to her feet and circled me on the rock. The abyss in front of me felt as though it was pulling at us with the force of a vacuum. For a fleeting moment the image of a bloody confrontation between Royal and Lucy filled my awareness. I considered the possibility that she was intending to jump off the rock, and I wondered if I was strong enough to stop her. I knew I wasn't.

Before I could decide what to do, she stopped wandering around the rock and lowered herself to a squat again. She was slightly in front of me, inches from the edge. "Am I crazy, Alan? How crazy do you have to be to do what I did?"

I thought, *What did you do?* I said, "You're not crazy, Lucy."

"But I have problems, don't I?"

I revisited understatement. "Yes, Lucy. I think you could use some help."

After a few minutes of silence she said, "After I went out with Grant for a while, I decided what I was doing with Royal was crazy and I decided to break it off. The night Royal was killed, I'd told him it was the last time."

"That was it?"

"He wasn't happy about it but I don't think he was surprised. It wasn't like we argued about it or anything. He was . . . rather gracious . . . and he said I didn't have to worry about Susan, that when he moved out he'd make arrangements for her, that he had some long-term-care insurance she didn't know about, and that he'd been looking into assisted-living facilities. He told me that he'd already talked to their kids and none of them was in a position to live with Susan. And that was it.

"I was relieved I wasn't going to have to take care of her. I felt guilty about that, but I was more feeling sad that the thing with Royal was over. We said good-bye and I left."

"Royal was still alive?"

She squeezed my hand. I read no offense in her voice as she murmured, "Of course he was." She squeezed harder. "You know what Royal said right at the end, as I was leaving that last time?"

I shook my head.

"He said, 'I wondered which one of us would come to our senses first. I'm glad it was you.' At the time, I didn't know what he meant."

"And now?"

"Right now? I think he knew what Susan and I were doing. How we were hurting each other."

I added, "But he was willing to participate anyway."

"That's sick, too, isn't it?" she asked.

I didn't have to answer.

She stood up and took a step away from me.

I opened my mouth to ask another question, then closed it. She said, "Go ahead, ask me."

"No, I was going to change the subject."

"Ask."

"Your fingerprints were on the pottery, Lucy. The piece that was used to bash Royal in the head."

She nodded. "The pottery was a new acquisition of Royal's. He was proud of it; it was by some artist he really liked from New York City. He'd found it on eBay and was thrilled that he had won the auction. He showed it to me when I first got there that night."

"That's it?" I asked. "You touched it when he showed it to you?"

She shrugged. "What was it Freud said about cigars?" she asked.

I managed a weak grin for her benefit, but was thinking that Lucy was in no position to make a decision whether or not this cigar was really just a cigar. I also knew that she hadn't shared all her secrets.

CHAPTER
64

Was Ramp there that night, Lucy? Did Royal discover him placing the bomb? Is that what happened?"

She shook her head. "I asked Ramp about it. He said that he and Marin placed the bomb in the Peterson home at least a week before Royal was murdered. He said they were real careful to make sure no one was home. They were in and out of the house in ten minutes and didn't see anyone."

"You believed him?"

"Of course. And I still do. What possible reason would he have had to lie?"

She seemed surprisingly sanguine.

Not really sure why I was asking, I said, "You know who killed Royal, don't you?"

"Any cop will tell you that knowing who did it is sometimes the easy part. Proving who did it, that's the hard part. This town learned that lesson the hardest possible way."

I figured she was alluding to JonBenét Ramsey's murder. The old homicide was a stray dog that followed Boulder cops everywhere they went. No way was I going to comment on that mutt.

She hadn't answered my question. I said, "But you know, don't you?"

"Sure I do. So do you."

She actually smiled.

"What do you mean?" I asked.

She shook her head.

"Sorry," she said. "The hostility has to end somewhere."

CHAPTER

65

Susan Peterson killed herself the next morning.

Sam and I were sitting downstairs at her kitchen table while she did it. I still think that I was more surprised than Sam was, which gives you some idea about how much to rely on a psychologist's ability to predict suicide.

Since Sam wasn't an active part of the investigation of Royal Peterson's murder and had no official reason to visit Susan again, he'd asked if he could accompany me on my next visit to see her.

After my conversation the day before with Lucy about Susan, I wasn't at all certain I would ever choose to see Susan again. When I told Sam that I had absolutely no plans to make another visit to the

Peterson home, he looked at me with mocking condescension and asked me if I was getting thicker with
age.

I replied by wondering aloud if there was any alternative. He said no, that it was important.

I made the necessary calls and we drove to Jay
Street together around eight-thirty the next morning.
Susan's health aide, Crystal, answered the door and
ambushed me by greeting Sam as though they were old
friends, even giving him a little peck on the cheek. She
stepped out onto the porch wearing a cable-knit
sweater. She was carrying a macramé bag over her
shoulder that I guessed functioned as her purse.

To Sam, she said, "An hour, you think?"

He replied, "That should be plenty of time. It's
enough for you?"

"If there's not too bad a line over there, it should be
great for me. You're an angel, Detective, an angel." She
glanced back over her shoulder. "I imagine she'll be
waking up soon enough. Her food's in the fridge all
ready to go."

As Crystal meandered down the walk toward the
street, Sam explained, "She needs to get her driver's
license renewed. I told her we'd keep an eye on things
here for an hour or so."

"You two are tight?"

"We had a beer last night. She likes hockey, actually
knows what she's talking about. I told her if this works
out I might be able to get her some Avs tickets. She's
from Wisconsin, but Crystal's okay."

I'd never understood the nature of the relationship between the residents of Wisconsin and Minnesota, but decided not to pursue an explanation at that moment. "If what works out? What did she tell you?"

I thought he almost grinned as he said, "You'll see."

I followed Sam inside the Peterson home and watched as he squatted down and opened the housing on the underside of the electric lift that Susan used to get up and down the stairs. I was instantly suspicious—if Susan was upstairs sleeping, as Crystal had just implied, the chair should have been at the top of the stairs, not the bottom. Sam flicked a red switch before he shut the cover back tight onto the housing.

A large oval piece of pottery sat smack in the middle of the third step on the staircase. Sam touched it to make sure it wasn't balanced too precariously. He whispered, "Recognize it? This is from Royal's collection downstairs. With that hole in it, though, I don't know what you'd actually use it for, but it's kind of nice to look at."

I assumed he wasn't planning on telling me what he was up to, so, sotto voce, I asked, "You turned the lift off?"

He nodded. "Crystal promised to leave some coffee and things for us. Come on."

We walked into the kitchen. Sam poured us each a mug of coffee and dragged a plate of muffins across the table so that it was smack in front of him. I smelled apples and spice. Morning light drenched the kitchen and from our perch on the sloping foothills of the Front Range the budding leaves on the trees in the Boulder Valley gave the beautiful view a lime-green aura.

I could have pressed him to divulge his strategy, but it would have been futile. Sam was directing this play and act two would come after act one. That was the natural order of things. Sam liked natural order.

After ten minutes or so talking about our kids and hockey, Sam said, without segue, "Lucy says that Royal told her that he was going to leave Susan. Was thinking about putting her in a nursing home. Did you know that? He had some insurance or something that would help pay."

"Lucy told me the same thing, Sam. Just yesterday." I didn't tell Sam what else Lucy had told me the day before.

He nodded as though he knew exactly what Lucy had revealed to me. But I knew he didn't know. Lucy would never tell Sam what she'd told me on Flagstaff Mountain.

Never.

With the fat edge of his hand, Sam scraped muffin crumbs into a little pile in front of him and then pressed them into a tiny orb that he tossed into his mouth. He said, "Even though I really shouldn't be here, I can't sit and wait around for this investigation to go on any longer. I don't ever want to know what the lab says about the stain on the sheet, you know? Not today, not tomorrow." He began to break apart another muffin. "Remember a cop named Manes? Brian Manes?"

I shook my head.

"Couple of years back, he was accused of coercing women to have sex with him on traffic stops?"

"I remember now."

"He went to my church. Has a kid Simon's age. He coached the kids' soccer team. His wife is a sweetheart. And, until the first woman filed a complaint against him, he had a perfect record as a cop."

I sensed where he was going. "Sometimes you just can't see what's going on below the surface with people, can you?"

"I could never figure out why, what was going on in his head, how he could risk so much for so little."

Were we talking about Brian Manes or were we talking about Lucy? I decided Sam didn't really want me to know for sure. "Sometimes people don't even recognize what they're doing, let alone why they're doing it."

"That's what keeps you in business? The fact that people fuck up their lives and don't have a clue what the hell they were doing or why the hell they were doing it?"

"What do they say, Sam? Denial's not a river in Egypt."

Sam adjusted his ample weight on the chair. He didn't move any of the crumbled muffin pieces toward his mouth. "Anyway, I don't want to know how the stain on the sheet got there. Not a bit. And I don't really want anybody else to know, either." He forced his chin forward. "I suspect there's a good possibility that it wouldn't be good news for Lucy. All in all, I'd rather not confront that possibility."

Sam was wrapping himself in his denial as though he were bundling up in a parka to go out in a blizzard. I wondered if the gesture was intended to be an ironic charade on his part. I said, "I can understand that, Sam. But remember, Brian Manes abused his office. If Lucy screwed anything up, it was only her personal life."

"That's what I tell myself, too, that everybody has dirty laundry." He smiled at the inadvertent allusion. "But there's something else," he said. "Something that doesn't really have to do with my deep level of disappointment in my fellow man. I've had trouble with the whole laundry thing right from the beginning. Not the sheet with the stain on it so much. That wakes me up in the middle of the night, sure, but that's not what I mean. I mean the laundry that was already in the dryer. You may remember that the first officer in the house heard the dryer running when she went in. I asked Lucy about it. She says that Royal was as likely to do a load of laundry as he was to change the oil on the space shuttle. So I wondered who it was who put that load in the dryer."

"It wasn't Lucy?"

"She says not."

The intercom erupted across the room, Susan's voice emerging from the speaker. I found the sound irritating, like the grainy feeling in my sinuses when I'm warding off a sneeze.

She said, "Crystal, I'm awake. I'm ready anytime."

To me, Sam whispered, "Crystal says that despite how it appears, Susan's strong enough to do laundry. So I'm doing a little experiment. You know me, I like to be empirical."

I wondered how Sam was planning on tricking Susan into doing a load of whites. But I didn't say anything. Sam had asked for an hour or two. I had time.

A minute later, after the plumbing announced the flush of a toilet, Susan repeated her entreaty to Crystal, her voice a decibel or two higher.

Sam asked me if I wanted more coffee.

I didn't.

Susan's patience was diminishing. When she called for Crystal again, she sounded closer. She seemed to be screaming down from the top of the stairs, apparently suspicious that the problem she was experiencing might be with the intercom and not with her health aide.

She finished her little tirade with, "I can smell the coffee down there, Crystal, damn it."

Sam raised his index finger to his lips to keep me silent. Seconds later we could hear Susan fumbling with the switch that, had Sam not disabled it, would have called the seat of the lift from the bottom of the stairs to the top. Susan cursed at the machinery when it didn't budge.

Sam raised his eyebrows in mock surprise and mouthed, "Such language."

We listened to two or three minutes of shuffling and

huffing and puffing and cursing and mumbling before Susan muttered, "Who left this thing on the stairs?" More profanity, then a final, "Crystal, did you turn this off? Crystal! Where are you, woman?"

A few seconds later, Susan Peterson walked into the kitchen looking like she'd spent the last eight hours sleeping with the devil. Her pajamas were creased. Her hair was a mess, her face was devoid of makeup, and her eyes had the glaze of someone with a narcotic hangover. She supported herself with one hand on a cane that was carved to resemble a stack of tiny turtles.

In the other hand she held the large oval ceramic that had been on the stairs. She held it up easily, naturally, as though she were about to waggle it at Crystal and demand to know what it had been doing on the stairs.

Her mouth hung open when she saw us sitting at the kitchen table.

The silence in the room was stunning.

Susan's eyes darted from Sam to me and then back to Sam before they came to rest on the heavy piece of pottery that she was holding in her hand. Finally, she said, "Oh."

Sam said, "Crystal will be back in a bit. She had an errand to run. I see you made it down the stairs all right. I wondered how you'd manage with the lift not working. It seems I needn't have worried; you managed just fine."

Susan shook her head, as though she were disagreeing with something Sam had said. Or perhaps she was trying to clear her thoughts. The gesture caused me to have an uncomfortable association to Lucy.

Sam went on. "Crystal said your arms are stronger than your legs. The way you're holding that heavy piece of pottery, it looks like she was right. But apparently your legs are strong enough to get down the stairs."

"And . . . what's your point?" Susan asked defiantly, but I could tell that her heart wasn't really in her protest.

Sam placed his hands palm-down on the smooth surface of the table. He said, "Why don't you go get dressed, Susan? I'd like you to come with me over to Thirty-third Street."

Her voice cracked as she asked, "Why?"

He paused, inhaling a thin stream of air through pursed lips, tasting his words the way my friend Peter used to taste wine before he pronounced it palatable. "I think you killed your husband. The detectives who are investigating his murder will have some questions for you." He somehow managed to make the declaration sound mundane.

His words reeled me back to a recollection of my recent afternoon visit up Flagstaff Mountain with Lucy. I thought of her almost intractable denial about her strange ménage à trois, and about the way she was able to wall off her hostility toward her mother. And then I realized that perhaps she wasn't alone—that my own denial of the events that had taken place in this house had been as impenetrable as blackout curtains.

I wasn't in denial that Susan might have killed

Royal—at some suburb of my awareness I'd been entertaining that possibility for a while. No, my denial had been about Susan Peterson's ultimate expression of hostility. As I sat watching Sam's production I was finally beginning to accept the obvious: *From the moment she descended the stairs to kill her husband, Susan had been setting up her own daughter to take the fall.*

Evil, I realized, had many faces. It was becoming increasingly obvious that Susan Peterson wore most of them.

Susan made a noise. It seemed to come from deep in her throat, but it wasn't exactly a groan. I thought that she appeared to be weighing Sam's directive that they head across town to the police department. As though she'd reached a conclusion, her eyelids closed slowly, like a curtain descending at the end of an evening at the theater.

There was no applause.

I watched as she shifted the bulk of her weight onto the arm supported by the cane. She mumbled, "I'm not well."

I didn't think the words were intended for Sam or me. I think she spoke them because she found them palliative.

Sam said, "Mrs. Peterson? Susan?" When she didn't respond, he repeated her name twice more until she reopened her eyes. The moment she did, he recited Miranda to her, the familiar words somehow as lyrical as Whitman.

I was still thinking about the faces of evil as I heard the hum of the lift carrying her up the stairs.

The roar of the gunshot came about three or four minutes later. I jumped up at the sharp clap, knocking my coffee mug off the edge of the table.

Sam winced and shook his head. He said, "I wondered if she'd do that. Actually thought she might take some pills. Didn't really think about Royal having a gun in the house, but I have to admit that I wondered whether she'd do something." He stood up and sighed. "I guess I have to go upstairs and see how good a shot she is. Or was."

I intertwined my fingers to quiet the tremor that had erupted in my hands.

"Want to come with?" Sam asked.

The Best Revenge

This one's in memory of Peter Barton

ACKNOWLEDGMENTS

Writing is an individual endeavor. In my case, it's me, maybe one or two dogs, and an otherwise empty room. Publishing, however, is a team sport, and I'm lucky to have a team of all-stars behind me. Kate Miciak and Nita Taublib edit the old-fashioned way, and I'm a better writer because of it. Irwyn Applebaum, in his inimitable fashion, asked a simple question at the beginning of this project that sharpened its focus. Others at Bantam Dell — Susan Corcoran, Elizabeth Hulsebosch, Deborah Dwyer — do their job as well as or better than anybody in this industry. Thanks so much to you all.

I'm not naïve enough to think that it stops there. Every player has his or her own team. Some of them I know well (thanks to Loyale Coles and Samantha Bruce-Benjamin), others I barely know, or have never met. But I know that they've left their mark on this book. My gratitude goes out to them.

My agent, Lynn Nesbit, is backed up by a great team, too. Specific thanks to Amy Howell and Richard Morris. And I don't want to forget Eileen Hutton and her staff at Brilliance Audio.

In the early summer of 1997, I was invited by Paula Woodward of KUSA-TV in Denver to witness an interview she was conducting on Death Row at the Colorado State Penitentiary with a condemned prisoner named Gary Davis. In many ways the seeds of *The Best Revenge* were planted that day. I thank Paula for the unique opportunity she afforded me.

Early readers of this manuscript helped me polish it. Elyse Morgan and Al Silverman continue to honor me with their critiques and their friendships. Jane Davis is the webmaster behind www.authorstephenwhite.com. She's as good as they come, both as webmistress and human being. Nancy M. Hall's astute eyes eliminated many errors in the final book. And, although this career of mine is extending into its second decade, I try not to lose sight of the beginning, when Patti and Jeff Limerick kicked open the first door for me.

A delightful trend in fiction publishing is the practice of authors donating naming rights for a character to a worthy charity that in turn auctions off the opportunity to have a character named after a real live person. This time the process resulted in a strange outcome. The high bidders at the auction were Mark Reese and his wife Martha Graves Reese, who is the sister of Kansas Governor Bill Graves. She asked me to create a character using her brother's name. I did my part (I actually included the real governor *and* a fictional counterpart, in addition to finding a role for Martha) and I thank Martha and Mark Reese and Governor Bill Graves for their graciousness and generosity.

Special thanks to some other writers. Candice DeLong (*Special Agent*), Christopher Whitcomb (*Cold Zero*), and David Fisher (*Hard Evidence*). Their nonfiction books were especially helpful for background research and – for any readers interested in learning more about the unique culture of the FBI – the books were illuminating and entertaining, as well. Any damage done to the facts should be blamed on me, not them.

Finally, I thank my friends and my family. To say this work wouldn't be possible without them is trite, but true. My mother, Sara, is more excited about each new book than even I am. And my wife, Rose, and my son, Xan, inspire and energize me in ways that are as essential as oxygen.

There are two tragedies in life.
One is not to get your heart's desire.
The other is to get it.
– George Bernard Shaw

If the desire to kill and the opportunity
to kill came always together,
who would escape hanging?
– Mark Twain

PROLOGUE

1997

If Kelda James hadn't been wearing inch-and-a-half heels and the toilet paper roll hadn't been empty, Rosa Alija would probably be dead.

At about ten-twenty that morning Kelda had excused herself from her fellow FBI agents and followed directions to the rest room – down the long hall, go left, last door on the right. The bathroom was a step up from what she had expected to find, given the tacky condition of the rest of the building. She was relieved to see that the sink was reasonably clean and the toilet seat wasn't stained with yellow coins of urine. The only problem was that there was no toilet paper on the cardboard roll.

Kelda stepped back out into the hall to retrace her route and retrieve her shoulder bag and its stash of tissues, but noticed a closet marked 'Utility' adjacent to the bathroom. The knob on the door wasn't locked and she found herself staring into a space about six feet square. A window was mounted high on the wall, dividing the small room in half. A jumble of brooms and mops leaned against a cracked porcelain sink on one side; the opposite side was stacked with particleboard shelves piled high with what appeared to be a lifetime supply of paper towels, soap, disinfectants, and toilet paper. Kelda reached onto an upper shelf for a fresh roll of toilet tissue and reflexively glanced over the sill and out the window as she rotated back toward the door.

The window overlooked the alley behind the building. Across the alley was the back of a single-story light-industrial building not noticeably different from the one that Kelda and her FBI colleagues had just raided.

Except for the hand.

Kelda was sure that for a split second she had glimpsed a hand in a window of the building across the alley. In her mind she was already considering it to have been a tiny hand, a child's hand.

She approached the utility closet window, stood on her toes, and peered again at the building across the alley. No hand. She raised her fingers to the sill to hold herself up and examined the distant window in detail. The bottom edge of the cloudy pane was streaked with parallel vertical lines that could have been made by fingers.

Tiny fingers. Child's fingers.

'Oh my God,' she said.

Fresh out of the FBI Academy, Special Agent Kelda James had been in the Denver, Colorado, field office for all of five weeks. Her initial assignment was to a squad that investigated white-collar crime, and that morning she had been ordered to accompany three other agents – all male, all senior to her, all somewhere between significantly and maximally apprehensive of her skills – to serve a federal warrant and raid a company called Account Assistants, Inc., on Delaware Street in Denver's Golden Triangle neighborhood. The company did contract billing for medical practices, and the raid was intended to collect evidence of suspected Medicare fraud.

For an FBI white-collar crime squad, this was routine stuff.

Prior to entering the FBI Academy, Kelda had earned her credentials as a certified public accountant and had spent a few years investigating fraud for an international insurance company. Her role in the raid of Account Assistants, Inc., was to cover the back door as the raid started and, later, to use her forensic accounting background to help make certain that the agents didn't fail to retrieve any records that they might ultimately need to press their case against the firm.

Most important, though, she knew that her primary responsibility was to remember at all times that she was the new guy, or in FBI parlance, 'the fucking new guy.' Her primary responsibility was not to screw up.

Later in the day, after she and the other agents had finished collecting the evidence and had transported the boxes back to the Denver Field Office, Kelda figured that she – the fucking new guy – would be the one who would be assigned to spend the next few weeks sitting at her Bureau desk examining the mind-numbing details of the service and billing records, trying to use Account Assistants, Inc.'s own numbers to prove the fraud case that had spawned the warrant and the raid.

It's what she did. And she knew she did it well.

That was what she was contemplating when she saw the hand flash across the window a second time. But as swiftly as it appeared in the window, the little hand disappeared again.

A more experienced agent might have gone back to her squad, reported what she'd seen, and asked one of her colleagues to accompany her across the alley to investigate the fleeting hand. A more experienced agent – one who wasn't a bookish young woman with an accounting degree whose colleagues called her Clarice behind her back – would have been less concerned about the scorn she would suffer if she pulled a fellow agent – or two, or three – away from important work to search the back of an adjacent building because she *thought that maybe* she had seen a child's hand in the bottom of a window.

Kelda could only imagine the relentless ridicule she would endure from her fellow agents after word spread in the field office that she had begged for assistance in checking out what would probably turn out to be nothing more nefarious than an unlicensed day-care facility.

Kelda moved out of the utility closet, closed the door, and took three steps farther down the hall to a door that was marked 'Exit.' An hour and a half earlier she'd stood in the alley on the other side of this very door in case any of the principals of Account Assistants, Inc., tried to flee out the back as the FBI team announced the raid and the warrant was served by the agents who entered the building through the door at the front.

She checked the inside of the exit door for an alarm: She couldn't spot any electronic devices attached to the heavy door that would announce that she had opened it. She stepped outside, propped the door open with a softball-sized piece of concrete, and then jogged across the alley to the window with the streaky glass and the disappearing tiny hand.

Two days before, six-year-old Rosa Alija had vanished from the playground of her elementary school's summer day camp near Thirty-second and Federal on Denver's near west side. The other children on the playground told police conflicting tales of a van or truck that was gray or brown and one man who was white or two men who were black or two men and a woman who were all kinds of different combinations of races and colors who had waited for a child to chase a ball into the field adjacent to the school and then, when Rosa Alija had been that child, had scooped her up, covered her mouth, and carried her away in the van or truck.

Some of the child witnesses reported that Rosa had kicked her legs and cried. Others maintained she was already dead by the time she got to the van.

No adult reported seeing a thing.

And no one had seen Rosa since. The girl's frantic parents, an independent landscaper named José Alija and his receptionist wife, Maria, waited in vain for a ransom demand. But neither the police nor the local FBI office expected to hear from Rosa's abductors. The Alijas weren't the type of family who were chosen for a kidnapping for ransom.

Rosa Alija had been taken for some other purpose.

Denver mobilized in an unprecedented fashion to find the girl. Hundreds of citizens – Hispanic, white, black, Native American, Asian – searched the city for little Rosa. Posses of private citizens scoured the banks of the South Platte River and Cherry Creek. The huge expanse of rail yard between her school and Lower Downtown was searched, and the interior of every last boxcar in the yard was examined. Her picture was featured on the front page of both daily papers, and the quest to find her dominated the local TV and radio news.

Bloodhounds tracked her route away from the school. The dogs seemed confident that her abductor had taken her down Speer Boulevard after the kidnapping, but the hounds lost the scent near the spot where Speer intersected with Interstate 25. The cops knew that once Rosa's abductors had her on Denver's main freeway, they could have taken her anywhere.

Anywhere. The Rocky Mountains, the Great Plains, the Great Basin. North to Wyoming, south to New Mexico. Anywhere.

Even into the back room of a light-industrial building in one of Denver's transitional urban neighborhoods.

The bottom of the window in the building across the alley was level with the top of Kelda's head. She listened for the sounds of children playing, but all she heard was the sough of distant traffic on Speer Boulevard; she heard nothing to convince herself that she'd stumbled onto a day-care facility. A moment's contemplation failed to suggest any other good reason that a small child would be scratching at the glass in a back room in a building in this neighborhood.

Kelda grabbed a discarded plastic milk crate from the alley and carried it back toward the window to check and see what was inside the building.

Before she had a chance to step onto the crate, she saw the hand again. It was reaching, groping, the fingers extended against the bottom edge of the pane, but they could only stay there for a second or two. Kelda imagined that every time the girl lifted her hand someone else was yanking it right back down.

Most of the doubt about what she had discovered evaporated from Kelda's mind. *Rosa Alija*, she was hoping. *It's Rosa Alija.* But even in her head, the thought was only a whisper. If hope was the balloon, reality was the ballast.

What if it's not?

For the first time since Kelda had graduated from the Academy, she withdrew her handgun from its holster with the clear understanding that she might be about to fire it. The Sig Sauer felt almost weightless in her hand as she stepped up onto the crate. Her confidence grew; Kelda's best days in training at Quantico were the days that her Sig weighed about as much as a glove. She knew instantly that this was going to be one of those days.

The filth on the glass and the dark interior of the room kept Kelda from peering inside. For a split second she considered returning to Account Assistants to collect her colleagues, but she was already fearing what would happen if she left the little girl alone for another minute. She decided that she would use her radio to summon the other agents the moment she was absolutely certain that she had indeed found the abducted child.

The building had a small loading dock that faced the alley. She pulled herself onto the narrow cement shelf of the dock and tried the big door. It was locked tight. She hopped back down and moved to the side of the building. The long cinder-block wall was interrupted by a solitary steel door that was secured by a hasp and padlock. Around the front, two old newspapers still in their delivery bags littered the sidewalk at the main entrance. A big 'For Lease' sign hung in the window, and three or four flyers were stuffed in the mail slot. Kelda put pressure on the handle of the glass entrance door. It didn't give.

Whatever this place once was, it wasn't in business anymore.

She returned to the side door. The bolt on the lock was in place, but the hasp seemed to be beginning to break free of whatever was holding it to the cinder block. She searched the weeds behind her and found a rusty length of angle iron, jammed it behind the hasp, and began to pry the steel hasp away from the wall.

After two minutes of constant pressure, the fasteners securing the hasp gave way and the door creaked inward half an inch.

Kelda had made a hundred armed entries into buildings during her training at Quantico. Maybe two hundred. She knew the drill. She knew where to look, what to say, how to hold her weapon.

She also knew not to do it alone.

In one minute, she promised herself, she'd call for help. Right after she was sure that Rosa Alija was safe and that her kidnapper couldn't spirit her away to some new location before the cavalry arrived.

Once inside the door, Kelda turned left toward the back of the building and stopped. Her gun was in her hand. It was not pointed at the ceiling; it was pointed in front of her. Why? Because that's what the FBI had taught her. Why? Because, as one instructor had shouted at a classmate during a drill, 'very few fucking UNSUBs are going to be waiting on the ceiling.'

She listened for any indication that the building was occupied. She heard nothing, and the stale air she was breathing confirmed her impression that the building was probably not being used.

She paced silently across the empty loading area until she confronted a closed door. The door, she figured, should lead to the room with the window. With the same gentle squeeze she would use to compress a trigger, she put pressure on the knob. It was locked.

She thought she heard a whimper.

Kelda's heart was cleaving. *She thinks he's coming back, that's why she's crying.* Kelda swallowed, checked her breathing.

He could come back any second.

Any second.

Her breathing grew faster, shallower. She realized there was a possibility she hadn't considered: *Maybe he's already in there with her.*

Kelda retreated across the loading area and backed into the hallway. She keyed her handheld radio. She'd decided not to communicate any doubt about her discovery: she'd already wasted too much time – she couldn't afford to give the other agents a reason to delay.

'Gary?' Gary Cross was the supervising agent of her squad. He was a fifty-year-old black man who seemed sincerely interested in helping her adjust to the curious culture of the FBI. He also seemed sincerely interested in making certain that no one else recognized how helpful he was being to her.

'Gary?' she repeated.

'Yeah? Where the hell are you? Get back here. We need you to look at something.'

In a throaty whisper she said, 'I've just stumbled on Rosa Alija. You know, the little girl who was kidnapped? I'm in the building directly across the back alley from you. The door on the west side is open. The girl's in a room that faces the alley. I need backup. Hot.'

'What? You found Rosa Alija?'

His reply had been too loud. Cursing silently, Kelda fumbled with the volume on the radio. 'Gary, please confirm. I have a feeling I'm not alone here.'

She actually heard a clatter of footsteps before she heard him say, 'We're on our way.'

The door that led from the loading area to the adjacent room opened slowly. Kelda could hear it squeak. She couldn't see the doorway, though, from where she was standing; she had melded herself against the cheap walnut paneling that lined the hallway.

A male voice called out, 'Who is it? Who's there?' He was breathing loudly through his mouth. She listened to his footfalls and knew that the man had taken two steps before he repeated, 'Who is it? Is somebody there?'

She tried to analyze the accent. *What is it? A little bit of East Texas? Or is that more Louisiana?*

The man took another step. One more, she figured, and he'd be able to see her where she was standing in the hall.

Kelda turned to face where he'd be after his next step, slid her left foot forward into an ideal shooting stance, and said, crisply, 'Federal agent! Get down! Drop your weapon!' Before the last words had passed her lips, a gunshot pierced the seam of the paneling across the hall from her. The hole in the wood was at chest height. After a half-a-heartbeat delay, two more shots followed. One was higher, the other was lower, inches from her waist. The shooter was covering his bases, bracketing his shots like a photographer unsure of the light.

She heard a shuffled step; she interpreted the noise to mean that he'd moved away from her, not toward her.

Intuitively, she was sure that he was retreating now, intent on barricading himself in the room with little Rosa. Kelda knew she couldn't permit that. The situation she'd walked into would be exponentially more difficult if the UNSUB could use the little girl as a hostage.

Staying low, she sprang forward, dove, and rolled across the loading area, finally coming to rest in a prone position eight feet away from where she'd been hiding in the hall. As she moved she heard more shots – two, three, four. She wasn't sure exactly how many. She did feel confident that none of them had entered her body.

Rolling to a stop, Kelda jammed her elbows against the floor, the 9mm poised and ready. Within a fraction of a second she fixed the man's torso in her sight and in rapid succession fired three times into the black and white target that she imagined was pinned to the center of his chest.

Each impact caused him to jerk a little, as though he'd hiccupped. He didn't drop his gun right away. She released a fourth round and kept light pressure on the trigger until he fell. It took every bit of discipline she'd acquired in her training to refrain from emptying her clip into him.

The room, she thought, smelled like the range at Quantico.

It was as comforting as the aroma of a lover's sweat.

Two or three seconds passed. Through the haze of what she had just done she saw the silhouettes of two of her colleagues as they entered the building through the side door. She held up her left hand to them to tell them to wait where they were. 'I'm okay, Gary,' she called. 'The UNSUB is down. Let me go in and get the girl.' The reverberation of the gunshots still echoed in her head, so she couldn't hear her own words as she spoke, and wondered if she'd said them loudly enough for Gary to hear her.

Kelda stood and stepped over to the man she'd shot, keeping the Sig pointed at his head until she was able to kick his weapon farther away from his hand. The handgun the man had fired at her was a monstrous .45; she shuddered at the thought of being hit by one of the gun's slugs.

The UNSUB on the floor was slight. He wore new Adidas, a clean pair of jeans, and a white shirt with the sleeves rolled up to his elbows. His shirt was untucked and his belt was undone.

The man had fallen on his side, facing away from her, and she couldn't detect any sign that he was still breathing.

His rimless eyeglasses sat cockeyed on his head. She didn't see much blood, just three dark circles on the back of his shirt. She wondered if she'd somehow lost the fourth round that she'd fired, though she couldn't imagine how that could have happened.

Her Sig at the ready, she crouched beside him and checked his pulse.

Nothing.

Standing erect over him, she said, 'Damn you. Don't die, asshole. Don't you dare die.'

In order to control an impulse to kick him in the face, she stepped back away from the man. Then she inhaled twice to quiet the echo of the exact same impulse. In her peripheral vision she saw Gary move into the room like a bishop striking from the corner of a chessboard.

'Get the girl,' he said. His voice competed unsuccessfully with the echoes of the gunshot; he sounded as though he was trying to get her attention across a crowded bar. But she knew what he had said.

Three quick steps forward took her into the room with the window that faced the alley.

Rosa was kneeling sideways on a mattress, wearing only a pink T-shirt with a filthy picture of Big Bird on it. The little girl's face was wound with duct tape. One of her skinny arms was manacled to a chain that was bolted to a D-ring that was anchored to the wall.

She was weeping.

'Hi, baby,' Kelda said. 'I'm here to take you home.'

Kelda was weeping, too.

13

PART ONE

Taunting the Hangman

1

'I can just walk out that door? That's what you're saying?'
The warden held back a smile and said, 'You can stay here if you'd like. But if you do, I'll have to start charging you room and board. I can pretty much guarantee you won't like the rates.'

The two men were standing in the sterile public lobby of the Colorado State Penitentiary. The spacious front room of the modern prison was all concrete and light. Some tile. It only hinted at what was inside – 'inside' meaning the other side of the security doors.

Just hinted.

A dozen steps away, near the guards who acted as the gatekeepers/receptionists for the public, one of the warden's assistants leaned against the wall.

From where the warden stood near the front doors, the tall, electrified chain-link fences were visible through the glass, and above them coiled rows of concertina sparkled

17

with the earliest indication of a summer dawn. Beyond the fences, miles of high prairie loomed. Beyond that, the Rocky Mountains hovered ominously.

Tom Clone's mind wasn't on the far horizon yet. He found himself examining the details of the room. He was uncomfortable with its unfamiliarity, and with its spaciousness. He said, 'How do I get somewhere? I mean somewhere else besides here?'

'Your lawyer's sending someone to get you. I would guess they should be here anytime now.'

'So that's it?' Clone asked the warden. He fingered the collar of his new knit shirt with his left hand and touched the money in his pants pocket with the fingers of his right. 'After thirteen years here, I sign some papers, get a hundred bucks and some clothes from Kmart, and then I'm . . . gone? That's it?'

'You want a brass band maybe? Some dancing girls? With a little more notice, maybe . . .'

'That's not what I mean.'

'Most guys don't get the ride from their lawyer, Tom. All they get is a cold seat in a big bus to Pueblo or Denver.' *Usually get themselves a round-trip ticket, too,* the warden thought, but he didn't say it. He was pondering the question of whether – no, when – he'd be welcoming Tom Clone back again.

'Most guys who leave here aren't innocent, Warden.'

The warden shrugged. 'You ask them, they'll tell you they are. Don't ask them, most of them will tell you they are anyway.'

'But most guys who walk out that door don't have DNA tests on the murder weapon to back up their contention.'

The warden considered his reply before he said, 'I suppose they don't, Tom. I suppose they don't.'

The inmate's sharp eyes read the time on the warden's Timex. 'Why is this happening at five o'clock in the morning? Why not during the day?'

Completely deadpan, the warden said, 'What? You wanted to sleep in? Damn, I hate it when the guests don't make their requests clear. We try so hard to please.' He made a compassionate face. 'Other than this one early wake-up call, you weren't disappointed with anything else during your stay, were you?'

'It's a serious question, Warden. I've never been released from prison before, but I'd be surprised to learn that it usually involves a personal visit with the warden and an opportunity to watch the sun rise.'

'Well, if it's a serious question, then here's a serious answer. Once I actually received the order from the judge in Park County last night, I knew you were going elsewhere. Getting you out of here at dawn was my idea. Why? Because I don't want to give the press a chance to get themselves organized for your release, which they still think is scheduled for sometime this afternoon. As far as I'm concerned you can have your dog-and-pony show with the ACLU and the Innocence Project someplace else besides in my prison.'

Tom didn't expect the honesty. He lifted his eyebrows involuntarily.

'As a general rule,' the warden continued, 'I'm not a big fan of commotion. You may have noticed over the years that we don't hold too many unnecessary group functions around here.'

Tom Clone's eyes swept the big room again before they settled back on the warden. There was a time when Clone might have appreciated the sardonic nature of the man. But thirteen years living alone in a concrete room on death row had dulled his sense of irony. Anyway, the warden was a stranger to him, and Tom wasn't sure what to make of him. He'd noticed that the entire time they'd been talking the big man's tongue was busy in his mouth, as though maybe he had a poppy seed stuck someplace he'd rather not have one, and he'd really like to have a toothpick.

The warden looked away for a second or two before he returned his gaze to Clone. 'Tom? You don't mind that I call you Tom, do you? Good. Listen, if you're waiting for an apology from me – and I'm beginning to suspect that you are – don't waste your energy. You won't get one. The courts told me to lock you up, and I did that. And now the courts have told me to let you go, so I'm doing that. I make it a practice not to apologize for doing my job.'

Tom said, 'How'd you know that's what I was thinking?'

'It's what I'd be thinking if I was standing in your boots.' Both men looked down. 'Or your cheap sneakers, as the case may be.'

Tom Clone laughed. He heard the noise as though it had come from someone else. He thought, *That was my first laughter as a free man,* and said, 'So what else might I be thinking?'

'Scared thoughts. Unless you're a fool, if you're not scared already, you'll be scared soon. Something tells me you're not a fool. You'll be scared soon. You can bet on it.'

'I've been watching my back for thirteen years, Warden. Fear is nothing new for me.'

'Not that kind of scared. Though that kind won't go away for a while, either. I'm talking scared that life's passed you by. Thirteen years is a long time to be institutionalized. Back then, you still had a life ahead of you; you were a hotshot kid who was about to become a doctor. Now you're an old-timer. You're used to this place. To us, to our ways. To being a small man in a small world.'

The warden pointed out the door. 'You don't know shit about what's outside that door anymore, and people on the outside are going to hear where you've been all this time and they're going to treat you like a con. That's scary to you already, or it damn well should be.'

The words made him nervous, but Tom shook his head stubbornly. 'I'm leaving here an innocent man. It's going to be different for me out there than it is for other people who walk out that door.'

'Maybe. Maybe not. Some people may believe you're innocent, but most won't. Sorry, but that's just the way it is. Look, that there's your ride, I bet.' He pointed at a green Buick sedan that was pulling into the otherwise empty visitors' lot half a football field away. 'Good luck, son. You'll need it more than you know.' He pushed the door open. 'Now grab your duffel and get out of here before somebody up in Park County comes to their senses.'

Tom hesitated as though he didn't trust what the man had said. Finally, he leaned down, picked up the blue canvas bag that was filled with his few personal belongings, and began to walk away. As Tom Clone cleared the front door and took his first steps outside as a free man, the warden's assistant sauntered forward and stood beside his boss. 'How about twenty bucks?'

The warden replied, 'I said I'll do up to fifty. But it's your call, Hank. If I were you, I'd save my money.'

'Twenty's fine, Warden.'

The concrete path that led through the gate in the fence ran about fifty yards to the parking lot. Almost exactly halfway down the path, Tom Clone tossed his duffel far ahead of him and immediately sprang forward. He took a little hop, picked up some speed, and launched himself into a cartwheel. When he completed the cartwheel – which he accomplished with some skill – he leaned backward and then, with an additional little push of his strong legs and a fluid thrust of his arms, he finished with a nicely executed back flip.

He planted the landing well. Only one little extraneous hop.

The warden held out his hand; the assistant warden carpeted his boss's palm with a twenty-dollar bill. 'How did you know he'd do that?'

'For the last month, since the rumors started about him getting out, that's how he's been spending his hour a week in the yard. Cartwheels and back flips. Cartwheels and back flips. Over and over again. I figured we were going to have a little recital as he left.'

The assistant shook his head and said, 'Damn. I think these guys can't surprise me anymore and then . . .' He let the morning breeze carry the thought across the high prairie.

Eyes still on Tom Clone, the warden said, 'I can't tell you how glad I am that there weren't any news cameras here to see him do that. I would have had to watch his gymnastics twenty more times on the news. There would have been a thousand e-mails and everybody including the governor would have been calling wondering how we could have allowed him to do that.'

'That's why we were up at four o'clock in the morning? So the press wouldn't see him play Olga Korbut?'

'Nadia Comaneci. But yeah, that's the only damn reason.'

Tom Clone finished his back flip and pumped both fists into the air. Before he could shriek in exaltation, he heard a woman's voice behind him.

'Tom Clone? Mr. Clone?'

Even before he turned toward the sound, he was drinking in the novelty of the melody of a female voice that didn't belong to a guard. He reflexively inhaled, hoping the woman was wearing perfume. The morning breeze carried her scent. He wasn't disappointed.

The woman he faced was lovely. She was silhouetted against the mountains but he could tell that her dark hair was tied back behind her head and that her face was adorned with little makeup. She wore white jeans and had on a claret-colored leather jacket that was zipped up to her throat.

He inhaled her perfume again.

'Mr. Clone?' she said once more.

He nodded and thrust out his hand. She didn't touch it. She kept her free hand by her side, while the other stayed atop the leather bag that hung from her shoulder.

Finally, he spoke. He said, 'Yes, I'm Tom Clone.'

'Hello,' the woman said. 'I'm Special Agent Kelda James of the FBI. Your attorney asked me to come to get you this morning. I'm your ride out of here. Welcome back to freedom.'

Upon hearing her name, his impulse was to rush in and hug her, but he sensed her reticence and held himself back. He'd had a lot of recent practice with restraint. 'Kelda James. My God, you're the one who . . . who –'

'Yes,' she said. 'I am that one.'

He stepped forward and hugged her. Despite her stiffness at the embrace, the contour of a female body against his was almost overwhelming to him.

'Thank you,' he said into her hair. 'Thank you, thank you.'

'Please let go of me, Mr. Clone. Please.'

He did, and took a step back from her as well. Her voice carried that kind of authority.

'Those are all your things?' she asked.

'Yes,' he said. 'I donated everything else to Goodwill.'

The lines of her mouth softened into the slightest grin. 'Let's go, then,' she said.

2

1989

Martha Reese was red-eyed and her lime green apron was stained with cherry juice and almost perfectly parallel drools of her own vomit. She was shaking so badly that water was sloshing out of the cup she tried to hold in her hands. The cup was decorated with pictures of the Car Guys from NPR. The guys were laughing.

'I came over here for a cup of sugar, I swear. I know it sounds like a cliché but it's true. I bought a bucket of sour cherries this morning from a roadside stand out on the highway – you know the one by the turnoff to town? – and I was busy making pies and I totally misjudged how much sugar I'd need, and I just flat ran out. It happens, it does, even to experienced bakers.

'I knew the Greens were visiting their kids in California, but the lights were on at their place and the house sitter's car was out front, so I walked down the road to try to borrow some sugar. Nancy doesn't bake, but I'm sure she has sugar. I mean everybody has sugar. Maybe not diabetics, I suppose, but that's not the Greens. They're not diabetics. I'm telling the truth. I promise.'

A young sheriff's deputy sat across from her on a hard teak chair on the front porch of the Greens' house. It didn't even cross the young cop's mind that Mrs. Reese wasn't telling the truth about the cup of sugar and the Greens not being diabetics.

Only a couple of hundred yards or so separated the cabin that Martha Reese shared with her husband – 'It's really a house. I don't know why everybody calls them cabins' – and the Greens' home. The evergreen forest was sparse on the county road between the homes, and a dry spring had left the lane especially dusty. Summer hadn't even officially arrived, yet Park County was already a tinderbox. The neighbors were talking about what they could do to make sure that illegal campers or kids with fireworks didn't set the whole mountainside ablaze by the Fourth of July.

Martha was a few pounds overweight – 'Okay, maybe twenty' – and regretted not driving up the hill for the sugar. As she climbed up to the Greens' place she was struggling to keep her breathing even and was more than a little embarrassed about the sweat that was dotting her upper lip and dripping in a rivulet down her spine. The sun had sunk behind the Divide but the early evening temperature was still in the seventies. 'Some people might not consider that warm, but I do. For us up here, that's a little warm for the evening.'

She and Nancy Green weren't close – 'They're more modern people than us. But we get along, you know?' The Greens and the Reeses were good mountain neighbors. They shared plowing expenses in the winter and pooled their resources to get deadwood cleared from the land around their homes in the summer. Nancy Green was comfortable stopping by to borrow Italian parsley – 'I probably shouldn't admit this, but I didn't even know what it was. Why can't the Italians just use regular parsley?' – and Martha was comfortable going up the hill for sugar when she ran out while baking sour cherry pies.

Martha dreaded the final steep climb from the road up the driveway to the Greens' house. At the base of the driveway she actually considered going all the way back to her house and getting her car. But she didn't.

The Greens didn't have a regular doorbell; they had one of those speakerphone systems attached to their telephone. The apparatus made Martha uncomfortable. She was never quite sure what to do – 'Am I supposed to lean over and speak into the little box or can they hear me if I speak regular?' She just didn't know. Nor did she understand why someone would want something like that living up in the mountains. It wasn't as though anybody but neighbors ever knocked on anybody's doors up in Park County. 'You know as well as I do that we don't get too many Mormons or Jehovah's Witnesses walking around up here trying to get you to read their funny books. It just doesn't happen. I suppose we aren't worth the effort, or something.'

Martha hit the button on the speakerphone but no one answered. She hit it one more time, but again, no reply. She wondered, of course, if maybe she was operating the thing incorrectly, so she went ahead and knocked, using the heavy brass knocker that said 'The Greens' in raised letters that looked a little Gothic. After waiting a few minutes for a reply, she decided to check out behind the house. The Greens had a spa – 'We call them hot tubs around here. But Nancy calls theirs a "spa." Who can figure, right?' – on the big deck behind their house, and Martha wondered if the house sitter might be using it, though lolling around in a swirling pool of hot water was about the last thing that Martha could have imagined doing right then. Martha had met the house sitter, a nice enough girl named Ivy, a couple of times but didn't know whether she was a hot-tub-on-a-blistering-summer-evening type of person.

Martha followed the path on the south side of the house – 'I've been here before and that's the best way to get to the back' – and climbed the cedar stairs to the big deck. She paused at the top of the stairs and admired the view to the east – 'It's a much nicer view than ours. You wouldn't think a couple of hundred yards would make such a difference, but it does. We see mostly treetops from our cabin, but the Greens have a view with a capital V.'

The spa wasn't being used, though. Without a breeze to mask the sound, Martha could tell that the water wasn't even gurgling beneath the fancy gazebo-type thing on the far corner of the deck. She peered through the wall of windows that led outside from the back of the house.

'I knew right away something was wrong. Why? Simple. The water was running in the kitchen sink. I could see it from the window. It was just running right down the drain.

28

Nobody was standing there using it; it was just running. The sliding glass door was open, so . . .'

Martha kicked her favorite Merrell clogs off her feet – 'Nancy has a thing about shoes in her house, like she is part Japanese or something. Not that I have anything against the Japanese, believe me, I don't' – and hustled over to the sink to shut off the water.

'I didn't see Ivy at first; my eyes were on the sink. Yours would have been, too. They would have. The water was just running and running. It gets your attention, something like that does.'

What happened on the way from the back door to the sink was that Martha stepped in Ivy's blood.

'It was still just the slightest bit warm and it just squished right up through my toes. I didn't know it was blood, of course. If I'd known that . . .' She didn't finish the thought. 'I thought something warm was spilled on the floor, like hot chocolate or soup or something like that. I did think soup for some reason, I don't know why, but I kept going for the sink. I really wanted to turn off that running water. None of us have enough faith in our wells that we'll waste water like that, especially when it's been so dry out like it has been this spring. Every time one of us has to drill a new well, we have to drill deeper than the last one did. The well we dug summer before last had to be drilled 262 feet deep. I don't have to tell you how much that cost us, do I? I didn't think so.'

The Greens' sink was on the other side of their kitchen island – 'We don't have an island in our house. Just a sink built into the counter below the kitchen window. The regular way, you know.' Martha shut off the water and grabbed a big handful of paper towels to wipe up the hot chocolate or soup or whatever it was that Ivy had spilled on the floor. She was guessing that Ivy must have been taking a shower or something. 'That's when I saw the footprints – turned out they were my own footprints – across the kitchen tile. I realized right then and there that I'd stepped in blood. I don't know of one single kind of soup that would leave footprints that color. Maybe beet soup. But beets and I don't get along, if you know what I mean. Who makes beet soup, anyway? Russians do, right?'

Martha reported that when she recognized exactly what it was that she had stepped in, she tried to scream but couldn't get the sound to escape her throat. She thought about going for the phone to call 911. She thought about running back out the door. Then she looked up and saw Ivy and she fell backward against the island. 'That's when I knocked that big bowl on the floor. It's where Nancy kept her fresh fruit. In that bowl. That's why there are plums all over the floor. I did that. The plums, I mean. I'm so sorry.'

She had to make herself look at Ivy again. 'She was sitting in the corner behind the kitchen table on one of those big chrome chairs that Nancy has in her breakfast nook. Her head was hanging off to the side because somebody had cut right through her neck all the way to the bone. I could see the bone.'

Martha was surprised that she didn't faint. 'I should have fainted, don't you think? Seeing something like that? I'll probably have nightmares for the rest of my life. The whole rest of my life.'

The young deputy who had been first to arrive at the Greens' house in response to Martha's frantic call to 911 just let her talk and talk. He didn't know when the detectives would arrive to take over, but he wasn't at all eager to go back inside the house anyway. He'd already seen all he wanted to see. He held his hat in his hand and he nodded almost the whole time that the woman spoke.

Martha sipped from the water she held in her hands and asked, 'Is it all right if I clean between my toes, Officer? Or is that considered evidence?'

3

June 1989

A girlfriend of Ivy Campbell's who was in nursing school at the medical center had told her about the deal: twenty dollars to sit through an interview with a medical student who was practicing basic interviewing skills during his senior psychiatry rotation. She'd spend sixty to ninety minutes answering questions about her life – that was it. Math wasn't her strong suit, but Ivy figured she would be making at least thirteen or fourteen dollars an hour, way more than the seven-thirty she was making at the new mall in Cherry Creek. The medical school interview would be videotaped, but the tape would be destroyed at the end of the semester. Her confidentiality, she was promised, was assured.

For Ivy, twenty bucks meant a night out drinking with her girlfriends or a concert ticket at Red Rocks or, if she went early enough in the season, a lift ticket at Copper or Winter Park. She could spare a couple of hours for that.

She arrived at the Health Sciences Center at Ninth and Colorado in Denver a few minutes early for her two o'clock appointment and found her way to a sterile classroom on the third floor of a brick building that didn't seem anywhere near as close to the library as she'd been told.

A woman greeted her in the classroom, checked her in, and explained that her interviewer hadn't arrived quite yet.

Ivy smiled, pointed to the clock on the wall above the blackboard, and said, 'In two minutes the meter starts running, right?'

The woman who had checked her in was a skinny black woman in a horizontally striped dress and black-framed glasses. She shook her head disdainfully. 'These med students, let me tell you, I think one of the first things they learn in medical school is how to keep people waiting for them. They go through life like everybody's sitting reading an old *People* magazine with nothing better to do than wait for them to show up.'

Ivy liked the woman immediately. She smiled again. 'I don't mind the waiting as long as I'm being paid. You're on the clock, too, I bet. Hi, I'm Ivy,' she said.

'Bertha.' She bowed about thirty degrees from the waist. 'I'm a department secretary. Trust me, this isn't my normal gig. I'm filling in for a friend who talked an ob-gyn resident into a free ultrasound of her baby.'

'Cool. What department do you work in?'

'Psychiatry.'

Ivy lifted her eyebrows.

33

Bertha said, 'Yeah. Exactly. Oooh, I hear footsteps. It may be our young doctor, only a few minutes late.'

The young 'doctor' – white lab coat and all – walked right past the open door of the classroom before he doubled back, poked his head inside the door, and said, 'Is this where I'm supposed to be?'

Bertha sighed.

Ivy replied. 'Cosmically speaking, the answer to that question, I think, is always yes.'

Bertha almost choked as she swallowed her laughter. She covered herself by looking down at her list. She asked, 'You Clone?'

One hand went to the stethoscope that was hanging around his neck. He didn't seem to know how to respond. Ivy feared for a moment that he was going to need to check his white plastic nametag before he answered Bertha's question. Instead, he nodded.

Bertha said, 'Good. This is Ivy Campbell. She's your interview. Ivy Campbell, this is Thomas Clone. He's your senior medical student.' Ivy noted that Bertha emphasized the word 'senior.'

Bertha faced Thomas Clone. 'A/V promises me the camera's all ready to go. Just hit "record" when you're ready to start the interview. I'll be back in about an hour to get the tape. Any questions?'

Ivy said, 'You promise you'll send me a check?'

Bertha shook the paperwork in her hand. 'We will, Ivy, you have my word. You call me yourself if there are any problems. Anything else? Dr Clone? No? Fine then. You two be good, now. You promise?'

Ivy said, 'Later, Bertha.'

'You too, girl.'

Clone's hand flew to his hip. 'That's my pager. I have to get that.' His eyes flitted around the room. 'There's no phone in here.'

Ivy walked over to the video camera, hit the 'record' button, and held her watch up to the lens for about five seconds. She said, 'Do whatever you would like, Dr. Clone. As of now, we're on the clock.' She sat on the chair that she guessed was intended for her and pulled a copy of *Entertainment Weekly* from her backpack. 'I'll be here whenever you're ready for me.'

Three or four minutes later Tom Clone rushed back into the classroom. He stopped just inside the door, composed himself, which included stuffing his stethoscope into a pocket of the lab coat, and walked over to Ivy. 'Hello,' he said. 'I'm Dr. Clone. How do you do?' He offered her his hand.

'Hi, I'm Ivy Campbell.' She didn't release his hand. After about ten seconds he realized that he was going to have to yank it away from her. He did and sat down on a chair five feet away.

'We're, uh, just going to talk a little bit about your life here, uh, today, Ms. Campbell.'

Tom Clone was handsome enough, Ivy thought, in a my-God-he's-too-young-to-be-a-doctor kind of way. Nice shoulders. Good hair. Really, really nice eyes. 'You can call me Ivy.'

'Thank you, Ivy.' He still hadn't actually looked at her for more than a few seconds.

'This is an unusual situation, isn't it?' she asked.

'I'm not sure what you mean.'

'Usually when I go to the doctor – when anyone goes to the doctor, probably – I'm kind of nervous, certainly more nervous than the doctor. But today, you're more nervous. Way more nervous. That's what's unusual.'

'Um, yes, well. That may, um, be true.' He flicked a glance her way. 'Today, anyway. Now, would you like to tell me something about yourself?'

'Do you think I'm pretty?' She knew she wasn't giving him a chance. Nor did she intend to.

The trouble was, Tom didn't just think Ivy was pretty; Tom Clone thought she was gorgeous. Her fine hair was such a glistening mahogany color that it seemed to be radiating. Her eyes were so bright and deep, he felt as though he were looking into them the way he'd examine tropical fish in an aquarium. Her legs were so long – he didn't finish the thought. 'Yes, um, well – why don't you tell me about yourself?'

'Do you like hamburgers and beer?' Ivy asked.

'Excuse me?'

'Ever been to the Cherry Cricket? It's in Cherry Creek, behind Sears? They have great burgers. Awesome, actually. Almost perfect burgers.'

'Um. I, uh . . .'

'Are you allowed to ask me out to dinner? Like on a date? Even though we've done this interview thing?'

'I suppose. I'm—'

'Good. I was hoping you could. How about the Cherry Cricket this weekend? Saturday? Is nine okay?'

'Um, yes. Yes, nine's okay. I'm not . . . I'm not really sure it's something I should do but, yes, nine's okay.'

'And then maybe we'll do a movie? But I pick, okay? I have a thing about movies. I get nervous.'

'Sure. A movie. Yes.'

'Great. My address is on the sheet that Bertha has. Pick me up. And don't be late, Doctor.'

He looked puzzled.

'Bertha's the secretary who was here. You know, the black woman?' Ivy stood up and walked over to the video camera. She rewound the tape. 'We're going to start all over, now, Dr. Clone. If you want to go back out the door and pretend you're just walking in again to start the interview, that would probably look best to your teachers. Don't you think?'

'Okay.'

After he'd gone out the door and walked back into the room and repeated his introduction for the camera, she replied, 'Hello, Dr. Clone, it's very nice to meet you.'

Tom Clone continued, 'We're going to spend a little while talking about your life here today, Ms. Campbell. Why don't you tell me about yourself?'

So she did, figuring that it would save them both some time on their first date.

'You have to put on your seat belt. It's the law now.'

Tom Clone was flummoxed, totally flummoxed. The woman, the car, the perfume, the light. So much space everywhere. No guards, no shackles. No pale paint on concrete walls. He said, 'What? Excuse me?'

'Your seat belt? Everybody has to wear them now. It's the law.'

Now.

The word floored him. He was living *now.*

Not *then. Now.*

Tom looked down toward Kelda James's waist, saw the nylon strap stretched low across her abdomen, and noted the location of the latch beside the seat. He reached down between his own seat and the door and fumbled for his belt. It wasn't there. He felt like a fool. His last car had been a '77 Rabbit. He couldn't remember if it even had shoulder belts. He certainly couldn't remember wearing them.

'It's behind you. It comes across your shoulder. Here, like this.' She removed her own belt and let it retract to its starting position before she reattached the buckle.

He mimicked her actions. 'Thanks. There's so much I guess I don't know about . . .'

'Yes,' she said, confirming the thought, and started the car.

He stared back at the prison. 'I wasn't even sure what the place actually looked like from the outside. When they brought me here after it opened in 1990, they did it at night. I barely remember seeing the building.'

She glanced over at the shadowy complex and said, 'Take away the fences, if you didn't know what it really was, it wouldn't look like much. Some kind of industrial complex.'

He felt a chill crawl up his spine. 'I know what it really is.'

Kelda flipped open a device that was no bigger than a jumbo pack of Juicy Fruit and hit a solitary button with her thumb. He guessed the thing she was holding was a phone. Damn, they'd gotten small.

Seconds later she said, 'Tony? Hope I didn't wake you but I thought you'd want to know that Tom Clone and I are driving away from the penitentiary as we speak.' She paused and steered the car from the parking lot onto the street. 'I think he's okay. Maybe a little overwhelmed by the suddenness of it all. You want to say hi?' She handed Tom the phone. 'It's your lawyer. I think he'll be happy to hear your voice.'

She saw him hesitate. 'Hold the top part up by your ear. Don't worry about the other part. It won't actually reach your lips.'

'Hello, Mr. Loving,' Tom said. 'I'm a free man, thanks to you.'

The high prairie that fills the gap between the Front Range peaks of the Pike National Forest and those of the San Isabel National Forest is a desolate expanse that hasn't changed much since Native Americans were the only humans traversing the valleys. Late in June the landscape already reflected the aridity of summer, and the wind that gusted continually seemed designed by nature to suck whatever moisture it could from any living thing that had any water remaining in it. Despite the altitude, nobody of sound mind would mistake this land for mountain meadow. As a rule, meadows were green and lush. This long spread between Cañon City and Colorado Springs on the front porch of the Rocky Mountains wasn't.

With the exception of the tiny metropolis of Penrose – which isn't much of an exception at all – for the thirty-plus miles of Highway 115 that connect the prison towns of Cañon City and Florence with Colorado Springs, people reading maps don't have to check the key for any symbols at all. No towns, no cities, no tourist attractions. Nothing. The only highway signs by the side of the road are the ones that tell drivers how far it is to someplace else.

ROYAL GORGE 15 MILES.

The only things that seem to grow naturally on that high prairie are sagebrush and prisons. The years have proven that it's a hospitable environment for both.

Tom Clone finished his call with Anthony Loving as the Buick was approaching the edge of Florence. Kelda said,

40

'Just fold it up. That shuts it off.' He did and handed it back to her.

'I couldn't help overhearing,' she said. 'You don't want me to take you back to Cripple Creek?'

'No, there's nothing up there for me. Nothing but bad memories and injustice. Until I get settled into something and can afford my own place, I'm going to be staying with my grandfather. He lives in Boulder. Mr. Loving said he'd move the press meetings and interviews he has set up for later today up there. He said he thought you wouldn't mind dropping me at the bus station in Denver.'

'I don't mind. It's actually more convenient for me than going over to Cripple Creek.'

They were quiet until about five miles past Penrose, where the boundary of Fort Carson first rubs along the eastern shoulder of Highway 115. Then Tom said, 'I can't get over the fact that anytime I want I can open the door to the car and just walk away. You don't know what that feels like.'

She said, 'If you decide to exercise that option, I hope you'll let me bring the car to a stop first.'

He laughed. 'I promise. You know I don't know how to thank you for what you did for me.'

'Tony wanted to stay close to the courthouse, in case something came up at the last minute. The wheelchair makes it a struggle for him, anyway. When the warden called about the predawn release, Tony asked me if I was available. Thought I might be interested. I was. It's no big deal.'

'I'm not talking about the ride this morning, although I'm grateful for that. I'm talking about what you did . . . for

41

my case. Mr. Loving told me what you did to help me. I know that I wouldn't be . . . free . . . without you.'

Kelda didn't respond at first – in the mirror she'd noticed the headlights of a car far behind her and then watched as they suddenly disappeared. She replied, 'What you just said? That's thanks enough. Let's leave it at that.'

Tom couldn't let it go. 'Why did you do it?'

She squirmed and changed the position of her hands on the wheel. 'I didn't do it for you, Tom. I was doing my job and it turned out that you were the beneficiary. I did it because it was the right thing to do.'

'It wasn't the right thing for an FBI agent to do. You jeopardized your career for me.'

She shrugged. 'No, I didn't. I think the Bureau will get over it. Besides, I'm a little more bulletproof than most agents.' She was making a reference to the insulation she had in the Bureau because of Rosa Alija, though she assumed that Tom Clone didn't know about Rosa Alija.

'What does that mean?' he asked.

'Nothing,' she said.

'You helped a convicted murderer get off of death row? You think the FBI will forgive that? If that's true, then things have really changed since I got locked up.' He paused. 'I was running out of appeals, you know.'

She shook her head in disagreement, but her eyes stayed focused on the rearview mirror. In the distance the pair of headlights reappeared, then flashed off again. 'I don't know about that. Tony Loving seemed to think he still had a few appellate tricks up his sleeve. He wasn't convinced you were ever going to be executed. So it wasn't exactly like I had to rush right in there and pull the IV out of your arm.'

Tom Clone shuddered at the image. 'Mr. Loving's an optimist. Appellate lawyers have to be, I think. But appeals run out. They would have executed me, maybe later this year. Maybe next. Look what happened to Gary Davis. There were a lot of people who said he'd never actually be executed. Well, he was. Me? I thought I was running out of hope. But I didn't know about you.'

'I did my job. I followed a lead. The evidence supported your release. That's all it was.'

'Mr. Loving says there are a lot of people who are disappointed that I'm out.'

Kelda said, 'That may be true. But here's what I believe, Tom: For the death penalty to survive in this society, we have to stop using it on the wrong people. If I ended up helping you, that was my motivation. To try to protect part of our justice system. It wasn't about you.'

'You support it? The death penalty?'

'I don't really want to go into that right now, if you don't mind.'

He exhaled and said, 'Okay.'

Neither spoke for about a minute. Finally, Tom asked, 'You're not working this morning, are you? I mean, it isn't actually the FBI that's giving me a ride home from prison, is it?'

'FBI agents are always working. We're just not always on duty. And I don't go back on duty until tomorrow. The Bureau has nothing to do with this, I assure you. If my SAC knew I was giving you a ride home from prison, he'd . . .' She let the thought slide away and checked the mirror again. The speck behind them was now definitely a car, and the car was closing on them so fast that Kelda glanced at her speedometer to assure herself that her Buick was actually maintaining its speed.

It was.

Kelda became concerned that the car behind her – she pegged it to be a Chevy Suburban, an old one – was going to ram her Buick from the rear, and she tensed to prepare to take an evasive maneuver onto the shoulder. But as the Suburban closed to about two hundred yards it switched into the other lane and shot past Kelda and Tom at a speed that she guessed was close to a hundred miles an hour.

Tom said, 'Damn, what the hell was that?'

'I don't know,' Kelda said. 'Just some jerk.' In half a minute the Suburban was once again a speck in the distance, this time in front of them, not behind them.

Thirty seconds later things started happening so fast that she wasn't sure whether she first lost control of the steering or whether she first heard the pop. Maybe the two events happened simultaneously. Regardless, her instincts took over. She turned the wheel in the direction she wanted the car to go, but the car had already begun fishtailing on the thin layer of sand and gravel on the highway. Within seconds the Buick had spun 180 degrees and Kelda busied herself trying to get control of the car. She found herself checking the road that had been behind her through the windshield, while in the rearview mirror she eyed the second approach of the Chevy Suburban that had zoomed past her only seconds before.

The Buick continued to skid until its two passenger-side

wheels plopped off the shoulder onto the dirt. She braced herself – she feared that the car was going to flip.

Abruptly, the sideways movement stopped and the Buick came to rest on the dirt shoulder.

Tom Clone said, 'Shit. That was some driving. Did we get a flat, or what?'

Kelda asked, 'Are you all right?'

He nodded.

The Chevy Suburban was right on their tail now. It had crossed the road and stopped about a hundred feet away from the trunk of the Buick. As she had suspected, the grill identified it as an older model. It had once been blue, but the paint had oxidized to something that was closer to gray. The sun reflected off the windshield, obscuring the identity of the occupants. Kelda thought she saw the silhouettes of at least two people inside.

As the driver-side door opened, she reached for her handgun.

She had a feeling this wasn't a Samaritan.

5

Fred Prehost was the lead Park County detective who showed up at the Greens' house the evening in 1989 that Ivy Campbell was murdered.

If you caught Prehost in a confessional mood over a beer some evening in one of his hangouts in Cripple Creek, he'd probably admit that the crime scene wasn't handled perfectly – not according-to-the-book perfectly – but he'd argue that, given the department's general lack of experience in dealing with violent crimes of that nature, the Park County Sheriff's Office had done a pretty darn good job of working up the murder of Ivy Campbell.

He'd tell you proudly that the neighbors who lived within a half-mile radius of the house were all interviewed before midnight the day of the crime. He wouldn't admit that given the density of the residential area in question, the canvass covered a grand total of nine families, nor would he mention that three of the nine weren't even using their Park County residences the night of the murder.

He'd boast that the land around the crime scene — a total of almost two acres — was scoured carefully for evidence by noon the next day, though he might not admit that the sheriff's deputies who walked the perimeter that had been delineated by Prehost and another detective named George Bonnet — whom everybody called Hoppy — didn't really know exactly what they were looking for while they were walking, and that they didn't collect a single piece of evidence that would ultimately be used at the trial.

Prehost would argue that the .house itself was left largely undisturbed for the crime scene specialists from the Colorado Bureau of Investigation, who, he would point out repeatedly, didn't show up until *the next morning*. He certainly wouldn't specify what exceptions were included in the phrase 'largely undisturbed.' But he would emphasize the fact that the state criminalists seemed to take their sweet time getting themselves and their equipment to the scene.

Maybe by the time a couple of pitchers of Stroh's were empty, Fred Prehost might admit what he and the other Park County investigators didn't do correctly, and what they failed to find. One of the things they didn't do correctly was protect the dirt road and gravel driveway leading up to the Greens' home. At least a dozen different law enforcement and rescue vehicles had traveled the path up to the Greens' door by the time somebody considered that the road itself might be concealing some evidence.

What the Park County Sheriff failed to find was the murder weapon, whatever sharp object it was that had been used to almost decapitate Ivy Campbell. The coroner who did the post on Ivy Campbell's body narrowed the murder weapon down to a 'large-bladed, sharp object.'

Fred Prehost was confident that the 'large-bladed, sharp object' was the Chicago Cutlery knife missing from the butcher-block set in the Greens' kitchen. But despite everything the detectives did to find it, the knife was never discovered.

CHAPTER

6

Kelda had her Bureau wallet ready in her lap when the man who climbed down from the cab of the Suburban arrived at the door of the Buick. The first thing she noticed were the big rings he wore on the pinkies of both hands. She noted that he was dressed in worn dress trousers and scuffed black cowboy boots and a white T-shirt that had only recently been in a plastic bag that said 'Fruit of the Loom.' His rolling biceps more than filled the sleeves of the T-shirt. A brimmed hat like the stupid one her brother wore to go fly-fishing shaded his face. She took a second glance at the biceps and wondered about steroids.

She muttered to Tom, 'We have company – that car that sped past us a minute ago. Don't say anything. Not a word. I don't trust this. I think this guy may have spiked the road. That's why we got the flat.'

'Why? What's going on?' he asked.

'Not a word, you hear me? I'm handling this.'

Tom twisted around to look back at the Suburban. He said, 'It's not just the driver. There's somebody else in that car. In the passenger seat.'

She was staring at the rearview mirror. 'I know. I see him, too. Now shut up.'

She lowered the window in the door beside her seat. The morning air that blew inside the car bore only the slightest chill. After a moment's hesitation she decided to leave the engine of the Buick running. She was considering the likelihood that she might have to take off quickly and wondered how badly the car would handle with a flat front tire. Pretty badly, she concluded. Certainly not well enough to outrun an old Chevy Suburban that she had just seen cruising at close to a hundred.

The man leaned down and peered into the front seat. 'You folks having a bit of car trouble?'

'Just a flat,' Kelda replied in an even voice. 'We'll take care of it. I have a jack and a spare. No problem.' The man was so close to the door she couldn't see down to where he was holding his hands. That concerned her.

'Why don't you get on out of the car?' he said. 'I'll see what I can do to help.'

Kelda replied the same way she'd replied before. 'I said we'd take care of it. Thanks.'

The man leaned down a little farther and looked across the front seat at Tom Clone. Kelda thought the stranger's eyes hardened.

Without warning, the man thrust his hand toward her face. In the instant she prepared herself for the impact of his fist, she scolded herself for letting him get so close to her.

Those biceps.

But his hand stopped inches from her face.

He was holding a badge. But he was holding it so close to her eyes that she couldn't read it.

The man said, 'Like I said before, ma'am, why don't you get out of the car. I'll see what I can do to help.' Kelda didn't move. The man raised his voice. The menace in it, she thought, was practiced. 'Do it now! In case you can't read, I'm a peace officer and I'm giving you an order.'

She spun sideways on her seat and shoved her open ID wallet into his face before he could complete his smirk.

She barked right back at him. 'And I'm a federal agent. My name is Special Agent Kelda James and I'm with the Federal Bureau of Investigation. Get the hell out of my face, Officer. I told you I don't want your help with my goddamned flat. Now, back off.'

His chin dropped down half an inch and he stepped back, not in compliance, but so he could focus his middle-aged eyes to be able to read her ID.

He sneered, 'It's "Detective," not "Officer." And I don't give a damn who you work for, I want you out of the car, now. As I said, that's an order. I've identified myself as a peace officer and I expect my order to be o-beyed.'

She didn't budge. Her voice still even, she said, 'I'm sorry but I missed it. Your wallet. I'd like to see your badge again, Detective.' To Tom, she muttered, 'Let me know if the car door opens up back there.'

The man who had identified himself as a detective stepped another half step away from the Buick. With his left hand he reached behind his back.

51

Kelda knew he wasn't going for his badge. Her voice suddenly sharp enough to leave a paper cut, she rasped, 'Don't touch that gun. It would be a big mistake.'

He looked back at her to discover that a 9mm Sig Sauer was aimed at the center of his chest. 'Hands on top of your head,' she ordered. 'Don't screw around with me. I promise I don't miss from this distance. And it's quite obvious you're not wearing a vest.'

After a moment's deliberation he moved his hands slowly until his fingers came together on top of his head.

'So how many times have you fired from this distance?' he asked. His tone mocked her.

She thought about the little girl. About Rosa Alija. About the man she had killed that day. She said, 'Exactly enough times to know that you're well within my range. I guarantee that from this distance I can empty this clip faster than you can belch, and still place every slug within three inches of your goddamned aorta.'

A hint of recognition crept across his face. She thought he mouthed a profanity in reply.

She said, 'Now take another half step back and lower your right hand so I can see that badge of yours again.'

He did. His eyes were cold and the same dirty, gray-brown color as the snow that freezes into ice in the gutters in winter. His chest rose rhythmically, each inhale inflating the front of his T-shirt. He was menacing without even trying to be.

Kelda said, 'Call back to your friend or whoever that is and tell him to get out of the car.'

The man glanced back at the Suburban. 'He's a cop, too. I think you're making a big mistake.'

'Do I look like I care what you think?'

The man beside Kelda's Buick tucked his lower lip below his upper teeth, slotted the tip of his tongue between them and whistled, then gestured with his head. The second man climbed from the Suburban to join the roadside drama. He was slight and thin but almost as tall as the first man. His shirt was a dress shirt buttoned all the way to his neck, and he wore jeans that needed a few more washings to even approach a state where they were soft enough to wear comfortably. Even from that distance Kelda thought it was creepy the way the man's eyes bulged from his face.

When he was halfway between the two vehicles, Kelda said, 'Tell him to stop right there. Not another step.'

'That's far enough, Hoppy.'

'I want his hands behind his head, too. I'm sure he knows exactly how to do it.'

'The lady wants your hands up, Hoppy. She's kind of agitated. Go ahead and do what she says. In case you can't see from where you are, she has a cute little semiautomatic pointed at my chest.'

Kelda said, 'I think you're a little lost, Detective, aren't you? This part of the road is Fremont County, hell, maybe even El Paso County – I haven't really been paying attention to the road signs. But it sure as hell isn't Park County, which is what I read on your badge. You're a little out of your jurisdiction, aren't you?'

He seemed momentarily at a loss for words.

'Talk to me,' she cooed.

'Makes no difference what county I'm in, 'cause I'm not working. I saw a motorist in trouble. I stopped to help.'

'That was going to be your rationalization for rousting me out of my car? Flimsy, Detective. Real flimsy. You want to stick with that? I have a witness sitting next to me, remember?'

She immediately regretted focusing any attention on her passenger.

The detective scoffed, 'A witness, huh? Well hell, let's talk about your little witness. I'm taking my hands down now and I'm going to put them on my knees. When I do I'd like you to point that little pistol of yours someplace else. You're beginning to make me nervous with it.'

Kelda didn't respond as he lowered his hands, and she kept the Sig focused on an imaginary X over his heart. His eyes were now level with hers but he was looking past her, at Tom Clone.

Kelda couldn't tell, but Tom wasn't returning the cop's gaze; his attention was focused straight ahead out the windshield, back in the general direction of the Colorado State Pen.

The Park County detective flicked off his silly hat with his right hand. 'Hey, Tom,' he said. 'Fancy meeting you here.'

Tom Clone looked over. When he saw the red hair, his eyes closed to block out the memories.

CHAPTER

7

It was Alice Graham who initially led Detective Prehost to Tom Clone. Alice was a waitress at the Fossil Bed Café in Florissant who recognized the picture of Ivy Campbell in the *Rocky Mountain News* the day after she was murdered.

Alice had recognized the victim immediately. She was certain that she had waited on Ivy and a young man eight or nine days before. They had arrived in the café for a late breakfast, and the man had decided to use the opportunity of having her in a public place to break up with Ivy. Alice recalled that the girl didn't eat a thing during the meal. Her untouched breakfast consisted of two poached eggs, a toasted English muffin, and half a grapefruit.

Alice related to Detective Prehost that she thought the man had been unnecessarily cruel to the murdered girl, reciting the reasons he was dumping Ivy in great detail and repeating himself unmercifully in a manner that Alice considered belittling. The Fossil Bed is not a big restaurant, and even though Alice maintained that she wasn't eavesdropping, it was hard for her not to hear what was going on between the couple. She remembered thinking that if there were indeed fifty ways to leave your lover, this guy had chosen one of the worst. Maybe number forty-seven or forty-eight.

The man who broke up with Ivy Campbell was also one of only a handful of customers at the Fossil Bed Café to pay his bill that morning with a credit card. Alice remembered that, too, because after taking up her best booth for a couple of hours in prime time in the middle of tourist season, the guy at least had the decency to tip her well. It was her only fifty percent tip of the week.

The credit card voucher provided to the sheriff's office by Alice's boss at the Fossil Bed Café led Detective Prehost directly to Thomas Clone, a fourth-year medical student at the University of Colorado Health Sciences Center in Denver.

The case against Clone developed with surprising speed.

Although he denied even being in Park County the day that Ivy was murdered, a woman selling early sweet corn and apricots at a roadside stand a half mile from the house where Ivy died recalled seeing a man driving a car similar to Clone's Honda Civic stop on the shoulder opposite her stand to examine a map. She was closing up for the day when he stopped, so she knew that the time was about two-thirty, no later than a quarter to three.

Three days after the murder she called a local tip line to report what she had seen.

A day after that she picked a photo of Tom Clone out of a photo lineup. 'That's the guy with the map,' she told Detective Hoppy Bonnet. 'Yep, that's him.'

Clone's alibi for the time of the murder wasn't without flaws. He maintained that he'd attended a book signing at the Tattered Cover in Denver the evening of the murder. He even had a copy of the book *The Charm School*, by Nelson DeMille, that was inscribed to him, 'To Tom, Best wishes, Nelson DeMille.' The date was written below the signature. But the El Paso County medical examiner, who'd done the post on Ivy Campbell's body, had placed the time of death as early as five-thirty that afternoon, which would have allowed Tom Clone plenty of time to get back to Denver for a seven-thirty book signing in Cherry Creek.

Clone maintained that he'd broken up with Ivy over a week before – he admitted that he'd done it over breakfast at the Fossil Bed Café, but he insisted that he hadn't seen her since she'd asked him to come over to talk about their relationship three nights later. She wanted to try to work things out; his version was that she had begged him for another chance. He said he'd driven back up and they had talked in the Greens' cabin, but that nothing had changed and Tom had decided not to see her again.

'That was the last time you saw her?' Prehost had asked.

'Yes.'

During that first interview with Detective Prehost, who was accompanied by a detective from the local police department, Tom said he'd spent the afternoon of the murder studying at his little apartment in Cherry Hills, but he didn't think anyone had seen him there. His memory was that he hadn't left his home that day until the book signing at the Tattered Cover.

Tom's home in Cherry Hills was a one-bedroom caretaker's unit attached to a decrepit barn on a three-acre spread near the end of Vista Road, which sits on a high bluff above University Boulevard in suburban, rural Denver. Now that their kids were gone, the couple who owned the place spent twice as much time at their second home in Carmel as they did in their place in Cherry Hills, so they no longer kept horses in the barn. Tom's rent for the caretaker's cottage was negligible. In return for a great deal on his tacky apartment, he agreed to keep an eye on the main house and make sure that the various service people who were supposed to show up to do maintenance – the gardeners, the guys who plowed the snow off the long driveway, the woman who cleaned the pool – did indeed show up. He also collected mail and kept an eye on the front porch for packages.

Although his apartment was only fifteen minutes from the medical center, Tom felt as though he lived in the heart of the country. He knew he was the envy of his med student friends and considered the setup perfect. The way he looked at it, by living in Cherry Hills he was getting a taste of the life he'd have once he finished his radiology residency and set up shop reading MRIs at two hundred dollars a pop.

As laboratory analysis proceeded on the fruits of the crime scene search, the local media dogged the Park County cops, and the Park County cops focused more and more of their attention on Tom Clone. The forensics lab at the

Colorado Bureau of Investigation identified hair similar to Tom's hairs in the guest room bed where Ivy had been sleeping. Semen from a secretor with Tom's blood type was discovered dried on the sheets. His fingerprints were picked up in a dozen locations around the house, including on three different items in the refrigerator.

During a subsequent interview with the medical student, Prehost, the young, agitated, redheaded detective, said, 'So you were there?'

'I told you I was there. Not that day, that week. I spent the night there earlier in the week.'

'Did you sleep with her?'

'Not that it's any of your business, but yes, I did.'

'That was three nights after you took her out to breakfast and told her that you didn't want to see her again?'

'Something like that.'

'Something like that? Or that exactly? Which is it?'

'Three or four nights.'

Prehost snorted.

'What difference does that make, Detective?'

'I'm asking the questions.'

'The hell with this. I think I'd like a lawyer present if we're going to continue this conversation.'

'Just like that?' Prehost said. 'I ask a tough question or two and you want a lawyer.'

'Just like that. I guess we're done unless I'm advised otherwise.'

'We're not done, sonny. We're not done by any means.'

Two days later Hoppy Bonnet had a brainstorm about the contents of the refrigerator in the Greens' kitchen. He'd taken the expiration date from the milk carton in the refrigerator – one of the three items that was marked with Tom Clone's fingerprints – to the local grocery store and asked what the earliest date was that the store had sold milk with that particular expiration date.

Bonnet had then confirmed the date with the dairy that had packaged the milk. The first date that the milk had been delivered for retail sale, it turned out, was the day after the last day that Tom Clone claimed he was in the Greens' house.

'How,' Hoppy had asked Fred Prehost, 'are his fingerprints on a carton of milk that didn't arrive in the stores until the day after he said he was last up in Park County?'

'Good question.'

'The man is lying, Fred. Why is he lying?'

Three days later, three weeks after Ivy Campbell's murder, Prehost and Hoppy Bonnet arrested Tom Clone outside the auditorium where Grand Rounds was being held at the Health Sciences Center and charged him with first-degree murder.

Prehost wasn't quite smiling as he looked past Kelda at Tom Clone, but she thought that his eyes were twinkling like an evil version of Santa Claus.

'Remember us, Tom? Me and Hoppy?'

Tom didn't answer.

Prehost said, 'Just in case you're confused about what it means that you're off death row, here's what it means and here's all that it means: It means we're not done, Tom, you and me and Hoppy. I want you to know that. I have some advice for you. You want to hear it?'

Tom had resumed staring out the windshield.

'Cat got your tongue? Too bad. I'll offer my advice anyway. Here's what I think you should do: Check for us every day when you wake up. That's right, as soon as you open your eyes, and long before you begin to appreciate that you're not living in a cement room anymore, I want you to take a look around and make sure that we're not there watching you, waiting.

'And if I were you, I'd check my back all day long, and then do a real careful check every night before you go to sleep. Why? Because one time I'll be there, or Hoppy'll be there, right where you least want to find us. See, we're not going to rest until justice is done. And in my mind, justice won't be done until they take that IV needle out of your arm and they slide your miserable dead body into a big plastic bag. Sometime before that happens, me and Hoppy'll be there with a fresh warrant and an ice-cold pair of handcuffs.'

Kelda said, 'What the hell are you talking about?'

Tom answered her. 'This is Detective Fred Prehost of the Park County Sheriff's office. He's the detective who led the investigation of the murder of Ivy Campbell. He's the one who arrested me. And out there?' He pointed at the skinny man standing on the shoulder of the road. 'That's his sidekick, a man named Hoppy Bonnet. Mr. Bonnet thinks he's a genius.'

Prehost said, 'Yes, Special Agent, ma'am, I'm proud to say that I'm the one who put this man away back in 1989.'

Kelda said, 'And now you're threatening him?'

'No, no, no. Dear me, no. I don't make threats. Never felt much of a need to. I'm just telling him the way things are.' She thought Prehost puffed up his chest just a little bit for her benefit.

'And how are things, Detective?' Kelda asked.

'Things are fucked up, Ms. Special Agent. That's how things are. When convicted killers get set free, in my book things aren't good. Especially when they get help they shouldn't have from people who should know better.'

She knew that he was talking about her.

Tom said, 'The DNA says I didn't do it. I'm innocent, like I always told you I was.'

'The DNA is fucked.'

'DNA doesn't lie, Detective.'

'The eyewitnesses say you were there, Tom. Your fingerprints say you were there. Your lies say you were there.'

Tom said, 'Eyewitness testimony is unreliable. You know that.'

Prehost countered, 'Ivy's friends said she was frightened of you. Then you went ahead and proved she had a reason to be.'

'And I told my mother the tooth fairy was going to come. Then the next morning there was a buck under my pillow. Is that evidence that she actually showed up, Detective?'

The detective shook his head. 'The fat lady hasn't sung, Tom. You've been released pending a new trial, that's all. For now, the Park County DA has chosen not to retry the case. That means nothing is settled. Nothing. Given some time, who knows, I'm confident that I'll be able to change the district attorney's mind and you and me will get to do the same dance all over again.'

Kelda asked, 'Why don't you just let it go, Detective? Let the courts do what they're going to do?'

'You want to know why? Here's why: Because Ivy Campbell was a sweet kid. A really sweet kid. I only got to know her after she died. But I got to know her well enough to know that she didn't deserve what she got from this asshole. Why do I care? Because my heart says that someone needs to be concerned about jerks like this who prey on sweet young women who don't have a clue what they're up against.'

'I'm innocent, Prehost. Get used to it.'

'Ivy Campbell is still dead,' Prehost told him. 'I've been trying for over a decade and I haven't gotten used to that. So don't count on me suddenly getting comfortable with you being off death row. What girl's next, Tom? You picked out your next victim yet?'

'Someone else killed Ivy Campbell. Go find him. Leave me alone.'

Prehost laughed. 'We're not done, Tom. You and me. We're not done. The only finish line I'll recognize is the flat line on a monitor attached to your heart.'

Kelda said, 'That sounds like a threat to me.'

'Really? Why don't you take it up with your FBI supervisors then, Ms. Special Agent. See if they want to investigate me for harassing this asshole. Maybe we can do a whole civil-rights-violation song and dance. I'm sure you're their very favorite special agent right now and your word about what happened out here today will carry just a ton of weight with the U.S. Attorney.' He laughed again, turned, and took leisurely strides back toward Detective Bonnet, whose hands were still on top of his head.

'Come on, Hoppy,' Prehost said, walking away. 'And get your hands down, goddamn it.'

Tom didn't take his eyes off Prehost.

A half dozen steps away, Prehost stopped and turned. He pointed a finger at Kelda. 'You hang with this guy, you better watch your back. That's free advice. And that's good advice.'

Beside her, Kelda thought Clone mumbled, 'I could kill that fuck. I swear.' But she wasn't a hundred percent sure.

Less than an hour later the Buick was motoring up a tree-lined residential street on the southwestern side of Colorado Springs. 'Is this area familiar at all?' Kelda asked.

Tom said, 'No. It's sure pretty, but it's not familiar. I don't think I've ever been here.' He took note of the elegant homes and big lots. 'A lot of rich people in this neighborhood. Really rich people.'

'That's the truth.'

'Where are we going?'

Kelda said, 'I need some breakfast. After all these years locked up, I'm sure you could use some real food. And after that little run-in with your cop friends from Park County, we could both use what some say are the finest Bloody Marys in the state of Colorado.'

Suddenly, the patrician outline of the stucco front of the main building of the Broadmoor Hotel was visible through the trees. Tom said, 'We're going to the Broadmoor for breakfast? I can't believe it.'

'Believe it. It's what free people do. They eat when they want to, where they want to. Don't worry, it's my treat.'

'Am I dressed okay?'

'You're dressed fine. This is still Colorado, people tolerate just about anything.'

The hour hand on the clock in the lobby wasn't quite pointing due south when they walked into the hotel. At that early hour they were only the second couple in the restaurant, and the view from their choice window table extended from the placid lake in the center of the resort, to the emerald contours of the golf course, to the vaulting leap of Cheyenne Mountain, which seemed close enough to the hotel that Kelda thought she could hit it with a strong seven iron, and finally to the uncluttered morning sky.

The waitress was pretty, pleasant, and efficient. With Kelda's encouragement, Tom ordered a full breakfast – eggs, bacon, toast, potatoes, juice, and coffee. Kelda added waffles with fresh berries to his order and ordered a complete spread for herself – fruit, oatmeal, and an egg-white omelette. When the waitress asked, 'Anything else?' Kelda said, 'Yes, two Bloody Marys, please.'

'Of course.'

Tom sat back and fingered the silver cutlery. 'It feels better than I'd dreamed. Being out.'

'Blame it on the Broadmoor. This place has been known to distort reality a little bit.'

'How about I blame it on you, instead? I'm just so happy to be free. I owe you so much for what you did.'

'You can still say that even after our little visit from Detective Prehost?'

Tom nodded. 'I half expected to see him sometime soon. I thought it would be later on at the news conference, actually. Didn't think he'd get in my face so quickly after I left . . . but I've prepared myself for the fact that there are going to be some people who are unwilling to accept my innocence. Prehost is definitely at the top of the list.'

'You think that's all that was? He was expressing his unwillingness to accept your innocence?'

Tom managed a pinched smile. 'No, that's not all it was. Prehost wants me dead. He won't be happy until I take the needle.'

Kelda swallowed and looked away from him. Her eyes were focused on the lake as she said, 'It's hard for me to imagine that he could find that outcome so . . . satisfying.'

'For people like Prehost, it completes the circle, I guess. Things aren't complete for him yet.'

'What about for you? How do you right the wrong that's been done to you? How do you complete the circle?'

'How do I get even with Prehost?'

'Yes. I guess that's what I'm asking.'

'I don't know. Maybe some lawsuits. I don't know. I'm tempted to go there sometimes but . . .' He sighed. 'I probably don't get even. I think I probably just move on.'

'You can turn the other cheek? Just like that? Before, in the car, you said you could kill him.'

'What? I didn't say that. Time will tell whether I can turn the other cheek, won't it? I am surprised that Prehost pulled this in front of you, though. That surprised me. It doesn't show much discipline. I thought he was disciplined.'

'Well, he didn't waste any time getting in your face.'

'His act didn't seem to faze you much. Weren't you . . . scared? The guy terrifies me.'

'For some reason, people like him don't intimidate me. If they did, I never would have made it out of the FBI Academy. Female agents have to have especially thick skins. God knows that the Bureau has its share of self-righteous bullies. Fortunately, people like Prehost just get me riled.'

'Won't he turn you in to somebody for pointing your gun at him?'

'No. He'd have to admit to spiking the road and harassing you. What just happened out there will become a story he embellishes for his cop buddies the next time he's at his favorite saloon. But he'll change it a little bit – in his version the girl won't get the draw on him, I can promise you that.'

Tom sat back on his chair. 'So what *does* scare you?'

Kelda found it an interesting question. She pondered it a moment before she said, 'Bees. Some spiders. Failing. Mice, a little, but not so much.'

'But not bullies with badges and guns?'

'Not them, no. I've never had a problem with them.'

The Bloody Marys arrived. Tom lifted his glass. 'To freedom, and freedom fighters.'

Kelda acknowledged the compliment and touched her glass to his. The celery stalk and the tomato juice caused her to think about Christmas and long, white flannel nightgowns at dawn. As she sipped at the drink the fire from a healthy dose of peppers lit the back of her tongue.

They both looked at the mountains.

'God, this is good,' he said.

'The Bloody Mary?'

'Everything. This moment. You, the drink, this place, the mountains. Everything is good. I haven't felt that for a long, long time.'

Silence took over the space between them. 'The dark, sometimes,' Kelda finally said.

'What? '

'You asked what scared me. The dark does sometimes.'

Her admission caused his breathing to pause and he wondered if his heart had added an extra beat to its routine.

The waitress arrived with their food. He was momentarily transfixed by the bounty that was placed before him. When he looked up from the table, Kelda was smiling at him.

Tom said, 'You don't smile much. You should. It makes you even more attractive.'

'Maybe,' she said, 'that's why I don't do it.'

CHAPTER

9

Kelda and Tom had finally made it past the madness of T-Rex, the 'transportation expansion' that was decimating seventeen miles of Denver's primary interstate corridor in honor of the vanity that building more lanes of highway might somehow result in less traffic, and they were skirting downtown on I-25 near the new football stadium.

Kelda said, 'I think I'll take you to Boulder myself. It'll save you a bus ride on your first day out.'

'You don't have to do that.' He was trying to decide whether he liked the new stadium better than he'd liked Mile High.

'I know I don't. Look, I actually live in Lafayette. Going a little farther down the turnpike to Boulder is not that big a deal for me. I can run some errands while I'm there.'

'Great, then, thanks,' Tom said. A moment later he added, 'You just decided, didn't you? To take me to Boulder.

You were originally planning on taking me to the bus station, weren't you?'

'Just decided? No. I actually made up my mind back near Park Meadows.'

She realized that Tom wouldn't know what, or where, Park Meadows was. The huge mall had been conceived long after his incarceration began.

He asked, 'Why?'

'Why what?'

'Why did you decide to pick me up today?'

She checked her mirrors for Prehost's Suburban, something she'd done regularly since fixing the flat. 'Just so you understand ... What I did over the past few months in Park County? With the evidence in your case? That wasn't about you. That was about justice. I was doing my job. There's no benefit to any of us in this country when we convict the wrong man, let alone when we execute him.

'Picking you up this morning? That was a combination of simple curiosity and me agreeing to do a favor for Tony Loving. And breakfast at the Broadmoor? To be honest, that was selfish; I wanted to treat myself. I really enjoy having breakfast at the Broadmoor, and I don't get down that way very often. Let's face it, asking you to wait in the car wouldn't have been exactly polite. But since we sat down to eat, I've begun to come to the conclusion that you may be a decent enough guy, so I've decided to do you a small kindness by driving you to your grandfather's house.'

'Thank you for your honesty.'

'You're welcome.'

'What kind of name is Kelda?'

She shook her head and made a disappointed face. 'Maybe some other time, Tom. The question is, like, so first-date-ish, you know what I mean?'

Tom Clone's grandfather lived on High Street, just off Fourteenth, at the end of the cul-de-sac that extended up from Casey School north of the Downtown Mall. The few blocks of High Street in Boulder hadn't been named on a whim by some pioneer who'd enjoyed a little too much whiskey. The precious strip of land enjoyed prime territory on the front shelf of a bluff above downtown, and the views to the south were special. The red brick of the old city, the vaulting faces of the Flatirons, the miles of greenbelt around Chautauqua. The Rockies.

The location was convenient, too. The charm of the Downtown Mall was within walking distance. Tom's grandfather lived mere blocks from the offices of the doctors who cared for his myriad health problems, and he could buy groceries, his favorite brandy, and fresh bread minutes from his front door.

Despite all that, the house that Tom's mother had grown up in on High Street was almost worthless.

But Tom's grandfather slept well at night knowing that the land on which it rested was worth a fortune.

'You want to come in?' Tom asked Kelda.

'No, thanks. You and your grandfather need some time together. And I have to get back home to my cat.' She didn't have a cat, but the imaginary pet came in handy when she was in need of an excuse.

They stood in front of the house. Tom's duffel was at his feet. 'Will you be at the press conference later?'

Kelda said, 'No, I won't be there. Tony thinks that word is leaking out about my role in your release. Now that you're out of prison I think it's prudent for me to try to reduce my profile a little. This is a story I'd rather not become part of.'

'Yeah. Tony told me that on the phone. I'm cool with that.'

A whining drone increased in volume as a cherry red Vespa came into view from down the street.

Tom said, 'There he is. He said he got a new scooter. I like it. Do you like it?'

'That's your grandfather on that scooter?'

Long gray hair flowed out from beneath a helmet that matched the bike. The driver raised a hand to wave before turning up toward the house.

'That's Grandpa. He's had a bum hip for years, so he's been getting around on a scooter since I was a kid. He's always been kind of a legend in the neighborhood. Gave us all rides when we were kids, let us drive it around parking lots on Sundays. He's a good guy.'

'God bless him,' Kelda said.

'Yeah,' Tom said.

'What about the winter?'

'Snowy days cramp his style.'

'I bet they do.' She turned to leave. 'Hey, good luck, Tom.'

'Thank you. Thanks for everything.'

Kelda stepped away from the awkwardness of their good-bye, slid back into the Buick, and watched through the windshield as an elderly man hobbled from the garage with the aid of a cane. His grandson saw him, too. Tom took a little skip and a hop before launching himself into the cartwheel/back flip combination that Kelda had first witnessed that morning just before dawn on the walkway leading up to the public entrance of the Colorado State Penitentiary.

She circled the end of the cul-de-sac on High Street and chanced a final glance in the mirror.

Tom was two steps from his grandfather, his arms outstretched. As Tom closed on him, the thin, frail man actually took a clear step back, away from his grandson. Their eventual embrace was cordial, but not exuberant. A pat on the back, good-to-see-you kind of hug. As a child, Kelda got warmer greetings than that after she returned from a sleepover at a friend's house. What did it mean that Tom Clone only got a pat on the back after thirteen years on death row?

She wasn't sure. Probably nothing.

When she finally returned her attention to the road, she thought she saw the tail end of an old Chevy Suburban descending Fourteenth toward downtown Boulder.

But she wasn't quite sure about that either.

Kelda didn't bother to watch the news coverage of Tom and Tony's press conference that afternoon.

The drive from High Street in Boulder to her old farmhouse in Lafayette took her only about twenty minutes. Recently she'd been getting the uneasy feeling that new tract homes were filling the fallow fields near her two acres so fast that they were literally going up overnight. She told herself that it couldn't be true.

Couldn't be. But she knew that it wasn't going to be long before she was going to have neighbors who were close enough to peer through her windows.

She parked the Buick in the shade cast by the two elms that were closest to her home, walked in the side door, and shut off her alarm. She flicked on the swamp cooler and began stripping off her clothes, sparing a moment to return the Sig Sauer to its temporary resting place on top of the highboy in her bedroom. She took a quick shower and pulled on a long T-shirt that was one of her few remaining mementos from the FBI Academy.

Kelda was ready to begin her ritual.

From the freezer in the kitchen she pulled six bags of frozen peas and carried them into her bedroom. The blinds on the window were closed against the relentless heat, and she left the light muted in the little room, though she did flick on the ceiling fan. On her bed she spread two bath towels and carefully aligned three bags of peas on each before folding the towels over to cover the plastic bags. She fluffed the pillows at the head of the bed before she propped herself against them, slowly lowering her legs onto the parallel rows of frozen vegetables.

Beneath each leg, one bag of peas pressed against the meatiest part of her calf, another against the underside of her knee. The final bag pressed against the terrain where Kelda's buttocks became her thigh.

She slowed her breathing, forcing herself to inhale more deeply than usual. At first she felt no temperature change on her legs; the insulation of the terry cloth temporarily prevented the peas from yielding their chill. But as the seconds became minutes the cold began escaping the cotton, and she thought maybe she knew how addicts felt as the tip of the needle pierced their skin.

Usually she thought she felt the pain most intensely at the instant when she was on the threshold of relief. This was one of those times. She tried not to cry but soon the tears were tracking down her cheeks. She captured one salty drop with the tip of her tongue and realized she was thirsty. Getting something to drink meant getting up and going to the kitchen. The act felt impossible to her.

Impossible.

Instead, she cried some more and used her tongue to steal each tear as it meandered toward her chin.

She didn't think she'd be able to nap but she did. Her last remembered thought was about Tom's grandfather's red Vespa. She wondered if maybe she should get one – if they were as helpful for bad legs as they were for bad hips. And she wondered if they came in green.

When she awoke, the afternoon sun had just begun its descent toward the mountains. The air along the Front Range was calm, and the billowing clouds that could provide a canopy of relief were still tantalizing miles away over the Divide. The swamp cooler was losing its battle to make the tiny house temperate, and the rhythmic pulse of breeze from the ceiling fan washing over her bare skin offered the only respite from the heat.

Beneath Kelda's legs the peas had softened, and the thunder and lightning in her lower body had diminished its burn and roar. She stood and carried the flaccid bags of peas to the freezer, carefully hanging the damp towels over the backs of kitchen chairs to dry. The clock above the door that led out to the service pantry told her it was just after four in the afternoon.

She mouthed a profanity at her forgetfulness and took quick steps toward the tiny bathroom. She crossed her arms in front of her and lifted the T-shirt over her head. She immediately turned her back to the mirror, looking over her left shoulder at a spot high above her scapula.

The patch wasn't there. Her heart skipped a beat and then she remembered she'd chosen a new location for the one she'd put on three days before. Kelda spun back around and without checking her reflection touched a spot on her right side, level with her navel. She slid a fingernail beneath the edge of the clear rectangular patch, grabbed the edge of the plastic, and ripped it off her skin. She dropped the solitary square inch of material into the toilet, and she flushed it away.

The telephone rang.

Kelda mouthed another profanity and half ran to the side of the bed. She sat on top of the comforter and crossed her legs before lifting the receiver.

'Hello,' she said. It was her Bureau voice. She feared that the call was from somebody at the office wanting to harass her about what she'd been doing to help Tom Clone.

The line went dead. She hit *69 and waited to hear the number of the last telephone that had been used to call her home. But the phone company's system couldn't – or wouldn't – identify it. She logged the call in a notebook she kept beside the phone. It was the third hangup she'd received in the past six days, since the rumors began surfacing about what she'd done to help Tom Clone.

Before she had a chance to stand up, the phone rang again.

She grimaced, cursing silently. 'Hello,' she said, again using her Special Agent intonation.

'Kelda? It's Tom, Tom Clone.'

She mouthed yet another profanity.

'How did you get my number?'

'I asked Mr. Loving for it. He gave it to me. I'm sorry. I shouldn't have called, should I?'

Damn, Tony, she thought. *How about a little discretion? We had a deal, right? Jesus.*

'It's okay. What can I do for you?'

'Um, if this is a bad time . . . Look, I'm sorry. This was a mistake, obviously. I shouldn't have bothered you again. You've been so great already. I'll—'

She sighed. 'What is it you want? Just tell me, please.'

'My grandfather? He and I have been talking. He's come up with some conditions for me to live with him. They're okay, they're reasonable. I understand where he's coming from. Basic things. He wants me to start looking for work within a week or so, which is fine – I was going to do it anyway.'

'Yes?'

'He wants me to talk to a lawyer friend of his about my options. I'd planned to do that anyway, too. And . . . he wants me to get some psychotherapy. Thinks I might have some issues to work through for some reason.'

She ignored his attempt at humor. She said, 'Your grandfather wants you to go into psychotherapy?' A fly landed on her knee and immediately jumped up to her left breast. She flicked it away with the back of her hand.

'As you may have gathered earlier, my grandfather is not your typical eighty-year-old. He's real bright, real sharp, and he tries to keep up with the world. He says he's serious about the psychotherapy – that he doesn't want me to carry around any baggage from what I went through in prison. It's a pain, but he's doing me a favor, right? I'll humor him for a while. But I don't know who to go see. I wondered, since you live close to Boulder, if you know of anybody here, or even out your way in Lafayette. I'd rather have a recommendation than just go to somebody cold, you know.'

'Tony doesn't know anyone you could see?'

'Mr. Loving said he doesn't know anything about anyone north of Denver.'

Kelda said, 'I know one guy, in Boulder. His name is Dr. Alan Gregory. He's good. Try him.'

'You know his number?'

'Check the phone book. I'm sure he's there.'

'Thanks,' Tom said. 'That's all I ever seem to say to you. I'd like to make it up to you at some point.'

'That's not necessary. Low profile, remember? No grand gestures, please.'

'I understand.'

'Listen, I need to run. Good-bye, Tom. Good luck.'

After hanging up the phone, Kelda opened her closet and punched in the code that unlocked the heavy door on her little gun safe. From inside the safe she pinched a small foil-lined pouch out of a flimsy cardboard box. She clenched the edge of the pouch between her teeth while she retrieved her Sig Sauer from the top of the highboy and returned it to its home in the safe.

The fly flew in with it.

She said, 'Stupid fly,' closed the door on the insect, and walked back to the bathroom. She ripped the pouch open, withdrew the solitary patch from inside, peeled the lining from the adhesive, and stuck the plastic square onto the firm skin of her abdomen six inches or so from her navel. This time the patch went on her left side.

After keeping pressure on the patch for half a minute with the palm of her hand, she pulled the FBI Academy T-shirt back over her head and ran her fingers through her hair. The narcotics in the patch were absorbed slowly; the fentanyl wouldn't make it through the membrane of the patch into her skin and from her skin into her bloodstream until sometime during the middle of the night.

Which meant that if she wanted to dull the pain, she'd go through a lot of frozen peas and Percocet by bedtime.

Out loud, she said, 'Why the hell did I give him Alan's name? God, Kelda. Think, think.'

She thought about the fly inside the safe, and noticed that the light that was seeping into the room through the cracks in the blinds was slightly gray. She concluded that the clouds that had been building above the Divide must have finally blown down from the mountains.

Maybe there'd be some rain. Maybe there would be an early beginning of the summer monsoons.

Maybe Tom Clone wouldn't call him. Or maybe Dr. Alan Gregory and Tom Clone wouldn't hit it off.

Right.

And maybe her pain would be gone by morning.

She walked over to the gun safe and punched in the

combination. The fly burst out and immediately landed on the side of her highboy.

She swatted at it with her open palm and missed. It took off toward the window and crashed into the glass.

'Stupid fly,' she said again.

The sky had darkened and the swamp cooler was finally beginning to catch up with the heat in the house by the time someone knocked on Kelda's door. She glanced at her laptop monitor and noted the time at the bottom right corner of the screen: 8:47.

Kelda lifted her legs from the bath towels and checked the condition of the peas. Definitely thawed, on the way to mushy. She yelled, 'Coming,' picked up the half-dozen bags, and returned them to the freezer. She opened the front door without bothering to check the peephole first.

She smiled. 'God, I was hoping it was you.'

The man who stood on her porch wore a faded yellow T-shirt with the sleeves cut off and a pair of Billabong board shorts that looked as old as he did. Even though his feet were adorned with flipflops, he towered over her. He said, 'Who else was it going to be? You shouldn't be on your feet, Kelda. You know that. Come on, find a place to lie down and I'll rub your legs.'

She stood on her tiptoes and kissed him on the scruff on his chin. 'Okay, I'll let you. Come on in, Ira.'

Ira switched on Kelda's little stereo and slipped in a CD he'd burned for her. Mostly jazz, some electronic synthesized stuff he was trying to sell her on. They sat on the sofa in the living room, and she rested one of her legs on his lap. He reached across her body for the remote control and flicked on the TV across the room, which he tuned to ESPN. He muted the volume before he began his practiced ministrations on her thigh.

'That hurts so good,' she said. '*SportsCenter*'s coming on?'

'Yeah.'

'If you want to listen, too, it's okay with me. Maybe Mike Hampton pitched today. I think he's cute. Did you work this late?'

Ira was a veterinarian.

'I was done about six, six-thirty. I had to do an emergency operation on a—'

'I'm sorry, I don't want to hear about surgery on animals today. What have you been doing since you left the clinic?'

He touched the line of dew that was visible on his brow right below his hairline. 'I've been doing what everybody in the state is doing. I'm waiting on the thunderstorms. God, we need rain, don't we? What's this – eleven straight days above ninety? It's too hot, even for me.'

'I don't think the storms are coming early this year. Maybe by mid-July if we're lucky. But, I agree . . . it does feel some days like it's never going to rain here again.'

'I'm still hopeful. One of those storms will blow out of the mountains and drench us. You have to have faith, darling.'

Kelda lifted the T-shirt away from her sticky chest. 'Please, please, please. I don't want to talk about the heat, either.'

'How about we talk about Tom? I saw a little bit of the news earlier. He's really out of prison.'

As he spoke Ira's cheeks rose along with his eyebrows and Kelda thought, not for the first time, that he looked a little like Stan Laurel. 'Yeah, he really is. I saw him in the flesh. There was a change in plans this morning. I was the one who picked him up at the penitentiary and drove him to Boulder.' She didn't tell Ira about stopping for breakfast at the Broadmoor.

Ira paused the ministrations to her legs. 'Seriously? Do you think that was a good idea? How did that happen?'

She slapped him lightly. 'Don't stop rubbing when you ask questions – it interrupts the flow. His lawyer called late last night and told me that the judge in Park County had just issued the order for the release. He kind of asked me to help out. The prison warden wanted to get Clone out the door before dawn so the press couldn't make a fuss about the release. His lawyer's in a wheelchair, he figured I might be curious about the guy, so I made some suggestions and he asked me if I would pick him up.'

'Yeah?'

'Then it got interesting. The detective who originally arrested Clone followed us away from the penitentiary. He spread some spikes or something on the road to give me a flat tire and then tried to intimidate Clone.'

'What did you do?'

'I had my gun on him before he knew who he was dealing with.'

'No?' Ira stopped rubbing.

'Yeah. Don't stop.'

'Is he going to be trouble? The detective?'

She shrugged. 'He's the least of my concerns. I'm much more worried about the reaction I'm going to face at work.'

'Your boss knows that you helped the lawyer?'

'All he knows is that somebody leaked that lab report to the lawyer. I'm on the short list of suspects. I don't think he can prove anything, but . . .'

Ira was using his thumbs to circle the bone on her left ankle. 'So why did you take Clone to Boulder? I thought he would be going to Cripple Creek to sue everybody he could find down there or that he'd be moving back to Denver. That's where he was, right, Denver? In medical school?'

'Yes. For whatever reason, he's going to stay with his grandfather in Boulder for a while until he adjusts to life outside.'

Ira nodded. 'Where in Boulder?'

'A little house on High Street. You know it? It's right above downtown. Terrific views of the Mall and Chautauqua.'

Ira didn't respond. His skilled fingers moved from Kelda's feet up toward the territory where her quads closed in on her knee. 'You still feeling okay about . . . everything you did, love?'

She smiled with her eyes. 'Yes, I am. I still feel good about it. It was the right thing to do.'

'Justice?'

'Yes, Ira. It is about justice. It's all about justice.'

'Even if it ends up causing you problems at work? You'll still think it was worth it?'

'If I don't get a handle on this pain, Ira, my days in the Bureau are numbered anyway. I can't take any more medicine than I'm taking without being sedated. I'm just hoping that Rosa Alija will continue to protect me until I decide it's time to leave. Fortunately for me, the Bureau doesn't want to be perceived as mistreating one of its heroes.'

'I hope you're right.'

She winced and said, 'That's a bit too hard.'

He lightened up on the pressure and said, 'You and I are still okay?'

'What do you mean?'

'Nothing's changed?'

'No, nothing's changed. We'll give things another month or so to cool off. Then we'll go. Everything's the same.'

Her arms were crossed across her chest, the fingers of each hand curled over the opposite shoulder.

He noted the posture and jumped at an interpretation. He asked, 'You're in between pain patches, aren't you?'

'They're not lasting the full three days anymore. And I changed this one a little late, anyway. The new patch will kick in soon. Before morning for sure. I'll be okay by the time I go back on duty.'

He allowed his hand to migrate up the inside of her thigh.

Her breath caught in her throat. After a moment of indecision, she responded to him by sliding her toes inside his shirt.

'Why is it,' she asked, 'that there are only two things that totally distract me from my pain, and one of them is hot, and the other is cold?'

'Me and the ice?' Ira asked.

'Yes,' she murmured.

'The thing about me and ice is, we're both hard,' he said. 'Maybe that's it.'

'Maybe,' she agreed. 'Maybe.'

PART TWO

Necessary Lies

CHAPTER

10

The sign on the bricks beside the front door of our offices in the old Victorian on Walnut Street in downtown Boulder is simple. On top it reads 'Alan Gregory, Ph.D.' On the bottom it reads 'Diane Estevez, Ph.D.' Diane and I had toyed with the idea of putting 'Clinical Psychology' on a third line below our names, but had gotten so caught up in an alpha dog argument about whose name should be on top that we neglected to resolve the question of whether we should list our profession on the sign.

The sign maker had resolved it for us. The result was that to someone strolling by on the street, our offices could easily be mistaken for the habitat of a couple of petroleum geologists.

A coin toss – actually, since this was Diane I was dealing with, it was best two out of three – had placed my name at the top of the sign. It was a contest she's made sure I've wished I'd lost ever since.

My four o'clock patient that summer afternoon was a woman whom I'd been treating for much too long who thought that there was actually a correct way to load a dishwasher. Not a preferred way to load a dishwasher, but a correct way. My private name for her was 'the Kitchen Aid Lady.' The details of her argument, I admit, had numbed me right from the moment she'd first revealed them many, many sessions before, but one of her more passionate protests had to do with an arcane concept she called silverware nesting.

We revisited the concept at regular intervals. I can't tell you how much I looked forward to it each time.

My patient adamantly believed that anyone who didn't load the dishwasher the correct way was ill informed or, more likely, an idiot. The idiot in question during our session that day was, of course, the Kitchen Aid Lady's husband. But she did not consider her spouse to be mentally challenged; in fact she considered his intellectual acumen one of his more attractive features. His failure to load the dishwasher correctly was therefore – no surprise here – an unmistakable sign that he didn't really love her.

His position, I gleaned from her newly refined comments that afternoon, was that there were many ways to load a dishwasher and that reasonable people could disagree on which method was best. He also seemed intent on not compromising on the issue, refusing to allow the measure of his love to be determined by what he considered to be a spurious dishwasher-loading assay.

My patient wrapped up her soliloquy that hot summer afternoon by asking me to cast my lot on the dishwasher-loading question. She didn't exactly ask; what she did was insist that I validate her position. Was I a proponent of her method – the correct one that took into account such issues as silverware nesting? Or was I a proponent of some radical or haphazard alternative method – like her idiot spouse?

Dodging the question adroitly – I admit that I hadn't paid enough attention during any of her previous recitations of the specifics of dishwasher-loading etiquette to make a rational choice between the various methodologies – I suggested that it appeared that she was, right then and there, doing the same thing with me that she was doing with her husband.

'What?' she asked. 'What on earth are you talking about?' She was stupefied. She couldn't see the point I was making.

I repeated my gentle confrontation. That worked sometimes.

Not this time. She still didn't get it.

I spelled it out for her. 'It seems to me that you've decided to equate your husband's love for you with his willingness to load the dishwasher according to your desires. Now, apparently, you've decided to equate my capacity to be a helpful psychotherapist with my position on the same question.'

When I finished my interpretation I sat back and awaited the reward of her *Aha, you are so brilliant*.

It didn't come. Instead, she made a short guttural sound deep in her throat and appraised me as though I had just peed on the carpet. Finally, she asked, 'Are you saying that if you load the dishwasher right, I'll think you love me?'

Despite my commitment to helping my patient with her problems, at that moment I couldn't help but empathize with her idiot husband.

I made a few notes, returned a couple of phone calls – including one to schedule an initial appointment the next day for a new patient, and packed up to leave. My quasi partner in my clinical psychology practice, Diane Estevez, walked out to her car a few moments after I walked out to mine. Diane and I had been friends and colleagues for enough years that I no longer remembered precisely how many years it had been. That was a very nice feeling.

Although our clinical practices were separate entities, she and I co-owned the little Victorian house on Walnut Street in downtown Boulder that housed both of our offices and that of our tenant, a gnomic man of Pakistani ancestry who for the past fifteen months or so had used the upstairs attic/alcove for a business that had something to do with security on the Internet. For the first fortnight or so of his tenancy, Diane and I had both tried to understand his business strategy, but his broken English and our intact technological ignorance combined to make it clear we weren't ever going to get it.

The early summer heat was stifling. A big tacky thermometer with an oxymoronic enticement for cigarettes – 'Lucky Strike Means Fine Tobacco' – was nailed up on the ramshackle garage at the rear of the property, a structure that by all rights should have already been blown over by any number of recent winter Chinook windstorms. I walked halfway over to the garage – it was as close as I liked to get to the thing – and eyed the temperature. The gauge maintained that the air that was currently enveloping me was ninety-six degrees. And that was in the shade.

Diane opened the door to her Saab and stood outside to allow the thermal waves to escape from her leather seats. I did the same with my car, although my seats were cloth. 'Hey,' she said. 'Haven't seen you much lately.'

'Yeah, I've missed you,' I replied. 'My hours have been weird. Lauren and I have been juggling our schedules to try to spend more time with the baby. You and Raoul doing okay?'

'Yeah, yeah. He's traveling a lot for his new business. But we're fine. Grace is good?'

'Terrific. She's getting big. She's walking, talking—'

'Peeing, pooping.' Diane's vision of parenthood had never been quite the same as mine. The bottom line was that she focused more on diapers than I did.

'That, too,' I said. I threw my canvas briefcase into the car. 'Diane, does the work get to you sometimes?'

'Therapy? That work?'

'Yes.'

She flicked a glance at her watch, then spent a moment examining my face. She ordered, 'Take off your sunglasses.' I raised them obediently to my forehead and held them there. She said, 'Just what I thought. You have time for a drink?'

I looked at my watch and considered her offer for a second or two while I wondered what she had seen in my eyes. 'Yeah, that would be great. Let me call Viv and tell her I'll be a while.'

'She's your nanny, right? I don't want to be interfering with a tryst with some mistress.'

'Lauren and I consider Viv our goddess. But to outsiders, "nanny" seems to be less controversial.'

'You want to get something to eat? I've been fantasizing all day about eating my entire next meal at Emiliana and you can save me from myself. What do you say we walk over to Triana? Although it's not going to be as satisfying as the six-course dessert indulgence at Emiliana, I think I could go for some tapas and sherry as a consolation prize.' She fanned herself. 'Anyway, it's too hot for a full meal.'

The full name of Emiliana was Emiliana Dessert House and Restaurant. My wife, Lauren, liked to say that they put last things first, right where they belong. To Diane, I said, 'You like sherry?'

'No. I like beer. But it sounds better to say tapas and sherry. Don't you think it sounds better?'

'Is that what Raoul says?' Diane's husband's family was from somewhere close to Barcelona.

'No, he says snacks and beer. But I know he does it just to annoy me.'

Triana was a couple of doors west of the Downtown Boulder Mall. Only a few years old, the restaurant consumed the century-old space of what for years had been Boulder's iconic used-book store, Stage House Books.

The bar was almost full when Diane and I arrived. She found a couple of seats at a tiny table that was in the precise location where in the building's Stage House days I'd once discovered a treasure trove of nineteenth-century political cartoons. Diane waved across the room at a waitress who couldn't have been old enough to serve us. She couldn't have been. To me, Diane said, 'I think it's too hot for sherry, so I'm going to get a beer.'

She said it with a straight face. I was impressed. 'Make it two.'

She'd grabbed the little bar menu from the table. 'Do you mind if I order the tapas?'

'Would it make any difference if I minded? Go ahead and order enough for both of us. And remember I don't like olives.'

'I forgot. With you it's olive oil, *si*, olives, *no*. I don't get it. What do you have against olives?'

'Do you really want to go there?'

'Probably not. So, what, are you burned out, Alan? Or are you just a precocious marcher in the midlife crisis parade?'

I'd had enough practice conversing with Diane over the years that I could usually follow the uneven terrain of the progression of her thinking without tripping over my feet. 'Maybe. I don't know. I hadn't been thinking about it that way, but, shoot, it's a possibility.' I'd never considered myself one of those people who were vulnerable to professional burnout, but I spent a few minutes recounting the story of my four o'clock appointment and the dishwasher-loading dilemma as a way of trying to elucidate for Diane whatever it was that I was vulnerable to.

'Raoul would agree with your patient. Sometimes I catch him rearranging the dirty dishes after I load the dishwasher.'

'No, no, no,' I protested. 'The difference is that Raoul doesn't consider you flawed because of it and he doesn't consider your failure to learn different dishwasher-loading techniques to be a measure of your love for him.'

'Wrong,' Diane replied. 'Raoul definitely considers me flawed, but he would consider me flawed no matter how the hell I loaded the damn dishwasher. He loves me anyway. Why does he love me anyway? Because I am much more lovable than I am flawed. That's what Freud said mental health was, by the way – the ability to feel worthwhile despite your flaws.'

'No, Diane, Freud didn't say that. Freud said mental health was the capacity to love and to work. But otherwise, my point exactly. Good try.'

She frowned at me. Diane didn't like being corrected, especially when she'd been caught fabricating quotes from dead people.

The waitress had arrived tableside in time to listen politely to the last few back-and-forths between Diane and me. She pretended to be unfazed by our interchange, however, took our order from Diane, and strolled away into what I still thought of as the nonfiction section of the restaurant.

'We both know it's not the dishwasher princess that's bothering you,' Diane told me. 'So what is it?'

'I prefer to think of her as the Kitchen Aid Lady. But the answer to your question is "I don't know,"' I replied.

She laughed at me. 'Boy, you sure gave that a lot of thought. Are you always this contemplative these days?'

I smiled at her. 'I don't know what it is, Diane. I just don't.' From experience, I knew that even if I didn't know, Diane probably had an opinion or two that she could spare.

'The diagnosis you blew last year maybe?'

'What?' I said.

The waitress returned with our beer. I drank a third of mine in one long draw. There is nothing like the first drink of cold beer on a hot day. Nothing. Unfortunately, that includes the second drink of cold beer on a hot day, so I made the first drink last as long as I could.

Diane drank half of her beer before she clarified her accusation. 'The woman who got blown up on the street outside our office – remember her? Your, um, shall we say "miscalculations" – is that too strong a word? – in that case allowed a few people to die, as I recall.'

I sat back on my chair. 'Well,' I said, removing the knife from my chest and preparing to defend myself with it.

She reached across and rested one hand on my wrist and sipped at her beer with her free hand. 'Do I have your attention, now?'

'You bet, Diane.'

'You've had some tough cases, dearest. That whole situation last year with the kids and the bombs, the whole witness protection thing you got mixed up with before that. Your practice has not exactly been something to envy. I sometimes think that there should be some kind of government-mandated caution sign on your office door. All of it has to have taken its toll on you.'

I shook my head. Her argument didn't taste right. 'I don't regret those cases. They're not what I think about when I have doubts about what I'm doing every day in my office. I end up thinking about cases like this woman and her dishwasher.'

'What?'

'The one-step-forward, two-steps-back cases. You know, the depression that won't crack. The abused woman who keeps going back to her husband. The therapy that should last six months that isn't any better after a year. Those are the cases that make me nuts. The people who come into the office and dare you to help them change. They're the ones. It seems most days go by and I don't think I've done anything to help anyone get better.'

'So? Me neither.'

'And it doesn't bother you?'

'No, it doesn't. Okay, maybe a little, but I get over it.' She wiped her lips with her cocktail napkin. 'You know, I used to think it was my job to help people get better. Now I know I was wrong. My job is to help them get better equipped. The whole give-a-man-a-fish-and-he-eats-for-a-day routine, you know? And I bet you do that every day whether you give yourself credit for it or not.'

'I don't know if sitting in that room listening to people is the best way to help them do that.'

'But that's what we do, sweetheart.' She had softened her tone in a way that was disarming. 'Those are the bricks we lay. If you've started hating the bricks, maybe it's time to reconsider being a bricklayer.'

'What?' I laughed.

She laughed, too. 'I thought that was pretty good. I didn't even know it was coming, it just rolled right out of my brain.'

'It was cute, I'll give you that. But seriously? I wonder if I'm making a difference, if what I do is truly important. I worry that I'm beginning to lack compassion. This woman, today, I had no empathy for what she's struggling with. I just wanted to take her by the shoulders, and . . . and . . .'

'Throttle her?'

We laughed together and finished our beers just in time for the arrival of the tapas. Diane had ordered so much food that it didn't all fit on the table. She yanked a free chair from an adjoining table and moved a platter of something onto it. She did it so quickly that I didn't get a clear look at what was on the platter. Before the waitress disappeared, Diane ordered another beer. I shook my head, declining.

Diane lurched first for the trout, which had made a not-so-seamless transition from swimming in a river with its head attached to swimming in a pool of olive oil, herbs, and white wine without its head attached. She swallowed a big mouthful before she said, 'I could send you some custody work and court referrals. That would break the tedium for you.'

'Ugh. Please, don't do me any favors. And leave some of that trout, if you don't mind.'

She reluctantly shifted her attention from the trout to the eggplant and baby leeks. 'You and Lauren have any vacations scheduled? Maybe getting out of town would help. Raoul and I found this great place where we stay sometimes outside of Sedona.' She paused. 'That's in Arizona.'

I shook my head. 'Diane, I know where Sedona is. But no, that's not a solution. We got away last month.'

'And look at you now,' she said, making a dubious face.

'Yeah, and look at me now.'

'Well,' she said as she sat back on her chair with a cute little drool of olive oil on her chin. 'Then I think you'll just have to suck it up, Alan. I don't have a clue what you should do.'

I eyed her for a moment before I said, 'I really have missed you. We should do this more often. We really should.'

She'd already returned her attention to the food. 'I know. This problem-solving stuff? It's my forte. If we come back here and do this come autumn, I'll really truly order sherry and make it even more authentic.'

We attacked the food with gusto for a couple of silent minutes. Diane broke the spell by saying, 'Alan, you know I'll do anything to help you. Anything. A few years ago – after that patient was killed by her husband in my office – I had a rough time. I'm sure you remember what a disaster I was. Nothing really seemed to matter to me for a while after the shooting. Nothing. But I muddled through it. I kept working at it. Raoul helped, you helped, my other friends helped, and things, well, they just got better. That'll happen for you, too. Things will get better.'

CHAPTER

11

My wife, Lauren, must have recognized my growing malaise before I did.

Diane and I returned to our cars after stuffing ourselves with tapas at Triana. I drove straight home.

Lauren, Grace – our baby – Emily, our dog, and Anvil, our foster dog, and I lived in a renovated caretaker's house that shared the few remaining acres of a ranch that was high on the slope of the western-facing hills of the Boulder Valley in a neighborhood called Spanish Hills. My happy-hour respite with Diane had spared me most of the after-work traffic, and I was home twenty minutes after leaving downtown.

Although it wasn't totally dark outside, the night was almost moonless and my headlights were necessary in order to navigate the way down the dirt and gravel lane that led to our house. The beams illuminated the door to the garage just as I was fumbling on the console for the button that would activate the automatic opener. When I spotted the decorations plastered on the door, I immediately stopped the car. I was parked fifty feet or so shy of the garage, which left me just opposite the front of the house.

The front door opened and Lauren stepped out. She was dressed in a little cotton sundress that she called a rag and that I adored. She was barefoot. Grace was in her arms, waving, saying, 'Daddy, Daddy,' or more precisely, the toddler equivalent. The dogs were both on leashes and I could tell that it was taking most of Lauren's energy to keep them beside her.

The word 'bucolic' came to mind.

Domestic visions like that one almost allowed me the luxury of denying the reality that my wife struggled with relapsing/remitting MS. Not quite, but almost.

I shut off the radio, lowered the window, and said, 'Hi, sweets,' as I gestured toward the garage door, which was crisscrossed with yellow ribbons and adorned with a huge bow that had been fashioned to look like a giant rose. I knew that my wife, who wasn't particularly craft-oriented, had received some significant help with the bow. I asked, 'What's going on?'

Simultaneously, I was silently reviewing the gift-giving occasions of which I had apparently lost track – anniversary, no; her birthday, no; Valentine's Day, no. Christmas? Hardly.

Lauren smiled. Her anthracite hair had grown long enough that she could hook it behind her ears. Her violet eyes sparkled in the light reflected from my headlamps as she shook her head a little and said, 'Open your present. Don't worry, you didn't forget anything.'

'Open the garage?' I asked.

She nodded in one grand motion and said, 'Yes.'

I touched the button on the transmitter and waited as the garage door began to roll up its tracks. The huge bow was decimated just as the interior lights kicked on, and I saw that an unfamiliar vehicle had been backed into the place in the garage where I usually parked my car.

I recognized it, but I didn't. And then I did.

My first car had been a very used red-with-white-top 1964 Mini Cooper. I'd loved her. Absolutely loved her.

She hadn't loved me back, though.

In retrospect, I'd made the same mistake with the Mini that I would make years later with my first wife, the one who shared my bed before Lauren. I went for the flash and the feel and let the passion of love-at-first-sight overwhelm any objectivity I should have been able to muster.

I called my Mini Sadie. She was every bit as gorgeous and high-maintenance as my first wife had been. And just like my first wife, Sadie was an adorable girl who responded to a firm touch, but who, alas, had an aversion to rough roads.

I poured money into Sadie. Money I didn't have back then. Her weakness wasn't old Persian rugs – that was one of Merideth's, my ex's, many indulgences. Sadie's weakness was her electrical system. The wiring in my old Mini was inhabited with more gremlins and spooks than the tackiest B movie I'd ever taken her to the drive-in to see. No matter how much I invested in making Sadie content with the flow of her electrons, she was never satisfied. She consumed generators, alternators, solenoids, and wiring harnesses the way Madonna consumed lingerie. Where electrical components were involved, Sadie always seemed to be going for a good poker hand: One of something wasn't enough – she wanted two, three, four of a kind. Her house was never full, though. Never.

I left Sadie after three tough, expensive years. I sold her to an ex-Army Ranger, someone I hoped could find the fortitude to discipline her and make her toe the line. But I never forgot her.

Apparently Lauren had never forgotten my lame stories about my love affair with Sadie. Because sitting in the garage in front of me was the distinctive front-end grill of a brand-new, red-with-white-top BMW Mini, the incredibly-difficult-to-find, even-more-difficult-to-purchase, recently reincarnated version of my once-beloved.

I hopped out of my old car, took one step, and then I stalled. I wanted to move in two directions at once. I wanted to rush to the Mini and I wanted to rush over and hug my family. To Lauren I said, 'You . . . you . . . how did you . . . they're so hard to . . . Is this mine? Is this really mine?'

She smiled.

'Why? What did I do to . . .?'

'I thought you would like it. Do you? Do you like it?' she asked, and I made my decision, running toward her, not the car.

The dogs broke free of Lauren. My instincts told me to watch out for Emily, our big Bouvier des Flandres. I knew from experience that Emily could take me down at the knees with one exuberant sweep of her solid flank. But I should have kept an eye out for Anvil, too. Sixteen pounds dripping wet, Anvil was a miniature poodle currently groomed to resemble a small sheep. He was without an aggressive gene lurking anywhere on his strands of DNA. But Anvil was tricky the way ferrets are tricky.

I dodged Emily's playful greeting, shifted my weight, rolled my ankle a little – just enough to compromise my balance – and then I tripped trying to avoid Anvil. The crack I heard as I extended my arm to cushion my fall on the gravel warned me that something bad had happened as I hit the dirt.

The pain that exploded up my right arm confirmed it.

The humerus is the big bone that runs from the elbow up to the shoulder. Breaking it makes a lot of noise and causes a lot of pain. Trust me. The crack sounded like a gunshot in a closed room and the pain was enough to make me wish for my mother's shoulder to cry on.

In my case the treatment for a supracondylar humerus fracture involved immobilizing my arm in a cast that locked my elbow at a roughly sixty-degree angle. Over the next twenty-four hours I would learn that sixty degrees is the incorrect angle for almost everything that a human being might choose to do over the course of a typical day.

Think about it.

The ER doc who evaluated me at Community Hospital was a friend of mine named Marty Klein. After the orthopod he'd called in for a consultation had left the hospital to return to his family, Marty supervised the construction of the cast on my arm. Finishing up his project with the application of a bright red outer coat – based on the flimsiest of evidence, Lauren and I were both of the opinion that red was Grace's favorite color – he commented that the cast was going to severely hinder my participation in the summer bicycling season.

I nodded silently. I was already lamenting that fact. Bicycling was my Xanax. And summer was high season for my habit.

Dr. Marty added, 'But there're two good things. One, you're lucky you don't play golf, and two, you're lucky that piece-of-shit car of yours is an automatic. If it was a stick, you wouldn't be able to drive it for a while.'

I thought of O. Henry and launched into a maudlin, self-pitying explanation about the brand-new – I stressed the 'yet-to-be-driven' – BMW Mini that was sitting in my garage. As I completed the story, Marty seemed almost as bummed as I was. He was a car nut; I didn't even have to point out to him that the Mini came with a standard shift.

He eagerly offered to come over and take me for a ride, though.

I wanted to cry.

CHAPTER

12

I dread displaying visible injuries to my patients. Even a simple Band-Aid on my cheek from a razor injury was likely to require an hourly – or more accurately, every-forty-five-minute – recounting of whatever had caused the defacement. One patient out of three or four would be sure to express doubt about my explanation that I'd cut myself shaving, and we'd end up going back and forth about my denials that I didn't really have malignant melanoma.

There was always a subset of patients who would not notice whatever damage I was displaying on my body. These were the patients whose own maladies or characterological predilections had left them so self-involved that they were either unable or unwilling to register the Band-Aid that was on my face, or the jaw that was swollen from my just completed root canal, or the cherry red cast that was holding my right arm at an impossibly inconvenient angle.

Despite the fact that Lauren had encouraged me to take some time off work, I drove myself to the office the day after my poodle-induced tumble. The hours would pass more quickly, I was surmising, if I was occupied with other people's problems than if I was focusing solely on my own.

My schedule those days had me working late on Thursdays, so my initial appointment wasn't until ten. While I awaited my first patient's arrival my arm was still throbbing and the ibuprofen I'd been downing like Altoids after a tuna and onion sandwich was turning out to be an inadequate defense against my agony. It was going to be a long day.

Lauren had called Diane, told her about my humerus, and warned her that I was in the process of making some testosterone-induced masochistic statement by showing up at the office. Diane was actually sweet about it. She brought me coffee and a bagel and apologized profusely for filling me with the beer that she was certain had led to my accident. I reminded her that I'd only had one beer at Triana and assured her that I didn't hold her responsible for the tumble.

Good, she replied. Because she didn't either. She had just been acting polite.

I was already truly tired of having a broken arm by the time I welcomed my new patient at two forty-five that afternoon. We shook hands awkwardly in the waiting room – his right hand, my left – and I led him down the hall to my office, a walk that typically takes only about ten seconds. I spent the entire ten seconds berating myself for the slight mistake I'd made when I'd recorded my new patient's name in my appointment book the day before.

The man who took the seat opposite me wasn't Thomas Cone, which is the name that I'd written in on the 2:45 line in my book. He was actually Tom Clone, the man who'd just been released from the Colorado State Penitentiary after DNA testing had cast considerable doubt upon his conviction for a brutal murder that had taken place in Park County in the late eighties.

During our brief phone conversation the day before, had I even asked how he'd gotten my name?

I didn't think I had. Which meant I hadn't.

The previous day I definitely hadn't been on top of my game.

'How can I be of help?' I said after Tom Clone seemed settled on the chair across from me. It was my stock opening line.

'Do you know who I am?' he asked. His voice was hopeful. It was apparent he didn't want to have to tell me.

'Yes, I do, Mr. Clone.' *I didn't yesterday when you called, but I do now.* 'I saw some coverage in the news.'

'Then you can probably guess how you can be of help.'

'I could make a guess,' I said, 'but my experience tells me that I'd probably be wrong.'

He pursed his lips and exhaled through them. 'This isn't exactly my idea. Coming here.'

I waited, immediately concerned that Mr. Clone's presence in my office was court-mandated, though I couldn't imagine under what legal circumstances that might have occurred. I took the opportunity to observe him. He was wearing what I guessed were new clothes. His shorts had cargo pockets on the legs, a fashion statement that wasn't being made when Tom had entered the Colorado penal system. His feet were clad in Tevas. Ditto.

I thought his body looked slightly puffy, as though he were still coming off an extended period on steroids. Something I'd learned during a consultation I'd done years earlier at Camp George West, a minimum-security facility in nearby Golden, was that inmates often grew pudgy during their time inside. The culprit was lack of exercise coupled with a less-than-ideal diet. An analogy came to mind and it felt right: Tom Clone looked like a frat boy who occasionally lifted some weights but had otherwise started to go to seed.

'I'm staying with my grandfather. As part of the bargain, he's insisting that I see somebody for therapy. He's a good guy, but he's stubborn sometimes. Hey, listen, I'm not saying it's not a good idea, but I thought you should know the circumstances of my being here.'

I waited some more, wondered if I knew his grandfather, and wondered whether he might be the source of the referral.

'I guess since I have to do it, I'd like to make use of the time and get some help adjusting,' he said. 'It's so weird being here. Out of prison, I mean. I don't want to screw it up. There're a lot of people who would like me to screw it up.'

I heard what might have been the rustling winds of paranoia, but reminded myself to allow the possibility that my new patient's concerns were absolutely justified. 'That sounds like a reasonable goal, Tom. Where would you like to begin?'

Tom said, 'You broke your arm.'

'I tripped over my dog.' After four prior attempts at explaining my malady to patients that day, I'd distilled it down to its essence.

He appeared to be about to say something else about my arm, or my dog, or my klutziness, but he didn't. He said, 'Thirteen years. That's what they took from me. They took thirteen years that I'll never get back.'

The throbbing in my arm probably hadn't stopped. But I suddenly wasn't noticing it. I was confident that I was about to get a chance to do something that might renew my faith in the value of this work I did. I was anticipating that I was about to hear something that I hadn't heard in all my years in practice. I was about to learn what it was like for a man to be incarcerated for a crime he didn't commit, what it was like for him to sacrifice, involuntarily, a huge chunk of the prime of his life to a miscarriage of our justice system.

I was about to learn firsthand what it was like for him to watch his appeals dwindle like a winter's supply of firewood while he waited for the final chill to arrive.

What it was like to sit on death row waiting for someone to tell him 'It's time.'

But that's not exactly what Tom Clone began telling me about. Instead, he began telling me about his ride home from prison. More specifically, he began telling me about his conversation with the warden and about the woman who picked him up and drove him to Boulder.

He went into great detail telling me about an FBI agent named Kelda James and the perfume she wore and the white jeans that hugged her ass and the run-in that they'd had with sheriff's detectives from Park County and how fast she had filled her hand and the cop's face with the barrel of a Sig Sauer, whatever that was.

'When she pulled the gun on that asshole, I thought – sweet Jesus, I can say anything here, right? You can't tell anybody? Good. This isn't being taped, is it?' He twisted his head left and right as though he half expected to see a camera sitting on a tripod across the room.

I opened my mouth to explain the limits of confidentiality, but my explanation was quickly overrun by the continuation of his narration.

'When she had that gun pointed at his nuts, I was scared, sure, but I was also thinking this woman was the hottest female on the planet Earth. The way she took him down, stood him up, backed him down. Oh man! She never wavered, I swear. He tried to act tough but she had him pissing his boots.

'Sexy? Oh, let me tell you. After where I've been and what I've been through, that barely begins to describe the way she was. I swear my single goal right now is to find some way to get back in touch with that woman.'

I wondered when he would stop to take a breath. I hadn't detected an inhalation from him for a while.

'First, she's gorgeous. I mean hotter-than-hot gorgeous with a body that shows no sign of her years – I mean, she's not exactly twenty-five anymore – and then she sends this guy packing and then the next minute she's down on her knees changing the tire on her car like she practices doing it every night when she gets home from work. I swear I've never seen a woman do something like that in my life.

'And then? And then – you'll love this part – she takes me to the damn Broadmoor Hotel for breakfast. She's the sexiest thing in the world and she's driving me up to the front door of this great hotel. I'm thinking I'm dreaming, this can't be happening. I'm an hour out of the damn penitentiary and this fox is taking me to a five-star crib.

'I can tell you honestly that breakfast was the furthest thing from my mind as we walked into that hotel lobby. Have you ever been there? It's like, oh my God, I just wanted to reach into my wallet, pull out my credit card, and get us a big suite overlooking that damn lake and those mountains. That's what I wanted to do. I didn't care what it cost.' Abruptly, he slowed his soliloquy. 'Problem was I didn't have a wallet, and I sure as hell didn't have a credit card. I'm stuck wearing these crap clothes they give you to leave the damn pen, and I don't even have a fucking wallet to stick my damn hundred dollars in.'

He grew silent and for a few seconds his mind seemed to go somewhere I wasn't supposed to accompany him. I was about to point that out when he brightened and started talking again.

'Did I tell you about the cartwheels? I didn't, did I? Okay, okay. Here's that part. This is good.'

He told me about the cartwheels. And the back flips.

And then he returned to his plans for getting back in touch with Kelda James.

The whole time, I remained oblivious to the pulsing pain in my arm. I was too busy casting aside all my assumptions about who Tom Clone might be. Caution was imperative, I knew; I couldn't begin to fathom what this man had endured over the last baker's-dozen years. I was certainly prepared to discover that the man sitting across from me was a poster boy for post-traumatic stress disorder.

Before the time was up, Tom and I agreed to meet again the following Wednesday.

'Do you know,' Tom asked just as the final moments of our session were approaching, 'that I actually made it through all that time inside without a single tattoo? I'm proud of that.' He held out his arms for my inspection, then rotated them so that I could examine both sides.

'Congratulations,' I said. I don't know why I said it. Maybe it was because he seemed so sincere.

'Yep,' he replied cheerfully.

CHAPTER

13

Kelda James was one of the reasons that I had started to work late on Thursday evenings. A month before, when she'd called me seeking an initial appointment, my Thursday schedule ended at five forty-five. But I'd agreed to see Kelda James at six o'clock. So now my Thursdays ended at six forty-five. Why did I agree to stay late for her? I figured that I had three reasons.

One: At some level, I suspected she wasn't going to be wasting much of my time lecturing me on the vicissitudes of dishwasher loading.

Two: She was an FBI agent and I thought it would be interesting to hear about her life. Number two was, admittedly, a rotten reason for agreeing to see a new patient. But there it was. I couldn't deny it. The truth was that, had Kelda James been a produce manager at Whole Foods or a marketing consultant at IBM, or spent her days disinfecting laboratories out at Amgen in Longmont, I might have referred her on to another therapist rather than agreeing to extend my workday.

Reason number three for agreeing to treat her even though it meant staying late? Reason number three was complicated.

If Lauren had spotted Kelda in my waiting room, she would have argued that reason number three was even more pathetic than reason number two. She would have maintained that reason number three I was seeing Kelda was that she was more than pleasant to look at.

I didn't even want to approach the entrance to that cave, so I didn't. I was self-aware enough that I knew I was at a stage in my career and my life where I could barely tolerate an increase in professional self-doubt.

So what was *my* reason number three for agreeing to treat Kelda so late in the day? Call it rationalization – Lauren probably would; Diane definitely would – but I had a suspicion that I was the right person to help Kelda James.

However burned out I was feeling, I wasn't burned out enough that I'd stopped caring about that.

The day after I broke my arm, Kelda was late for her appointment, not arriving until ten minutes after six.

During our very first session she'd warned me that she wasn't going to be punctual for therapy, that sometimes she'd cancel sessions at the last minute, and that at other times she would not even be able to cancel – she'd just not show up. Her work was like that. She didn't ask whether it was okay with me. She just wanted my consent that I'd live with it.

I'd thought about it for a moment that day and finally explained to her that I'd wait for twenty-five minutes for her to show up for her sessions. If she didn't arrive, during her next appointment we'd discuss her rationale for not showing up. If her excuse didn't involve FBI business, I would charge her anyway.

'Deal,' she'd said.

Patients come in to see a clinical psychologist for a lot of reasons. Some are sent by others: Husbands by their wives. Teenagers by their parents. Employees by their bosses.

Or, as I'd recently learned, exonerated murderers are sent by their grandfathers.

But mostly people come to see people like me because they are in pain. The pain is usually not new. Typically it is pain that the patient has lived with and endured for months or years or even decades. The patients come in to see a psychotherapist like me because something has changed that has caused their tolerance of their pain to crumble. The pain has gotten just *that much* worse. Or they've decided they can't live with it anymore.

Something.

Kelda's motivation was a combination of the two categories. First, she was certainly in pain. There was no doubt about it. And second, she'd been sent to see me by someone else. Her referral to me was made by her Boulder neurologist, Larry Arbuthnot. What was unusual about treating Kelda was that her experience of her pain was more corporal than psychological. Larry was treating Kelda for chronic pain in her legs, and part of his willingness to continue to treat her while he searched for a diagnosis that would explain the agony she suffered was his insistence that she see someone like me to assess possible concomitant psychological components of her condition.

Patients being treated for what they consider to be purely physical illnesses usually don't like to hear that their physicians are thinking that there might be a psychological component present. Kelda was no different. She'd spent much of her first three sessions with me displaying resistance to the idea. I was already prepared to spend a fourth, and fifth, and a ninth and tenth session doing the exact same thing. It hadn't taken long for me to recognize that Kelda James's will was something to behold.

The only topic other than Kelda's physical pain that we'd covered in any detail during those initial sessions was the story of Rosa Alija. I remembered the little girl's name, of course, from the blanket news coverage of her kidnapping and rescue, and could have related the gist of her story myself. Rosa was the Denver child who'd been rescued by Kelda in dramatic fashion a few years earlier. I still recalled that one of my more cynical friends had commented, after her rescue, that Rosa Alija was 'the metropolitan area's antidote to JonBenét Ramsey.'

For some reason, people do tend to forget the names of heroes sooner than they forget the names of villains or their victims. But Kelda James had proven to be different. I think half the population of the metro area could still have identified her as the person who had rescued Rosa Alija.

Along Colorado's Front Range, Kelda James was a certified hero.

Not surprisingly, her impression of herself was different. She'd informed me, 'I'm not a hero. I'm just an average person who was lucky enough to save a little girl. Some days I'm not even sure I qualify as an average person.'

'How so?' I'd said.

'I'm sorry about how things happened that day. I'm sorry that I had to kill the guy. I wish I could do it all over again, and do it differently.'

'How would you do it differently?'

She didn't blink. 'I wish he wasn't dead.'

I made a puzzled face. I was eager for her to keep talking.

She still didn't blink.

After all the years I'd been doing psychotherapy, sometimes I actually knew when to shut up. This was one of those times.

A few seconds later Kelda finally said, 'Rosa still suffers. She'll probably suffer until she dies. Her parents still suffer. Their agony will never end. So why should that monster rest in peace?'

Oh.

Although the possibility of a psychological connection seemed so seductive, I reminded myself that the pain in Kelda's legs had developed years before she'd saved Rosa Alija. There couldn't be a connection, right?

I was almost convinced.

I asked, 'And you?'

'What? '

'Do you still suffer, too?'

She blinked and looked away from me.

'It's not about me,' she said.

'No? Well, this is,' I replied, waving my hand between us.

119

I thought she shook her head, but the movement she made was so constricted that I wasn't totally sure. I thought at the time that she was daring me to start digging, and I admit that I was tempted to put a shovel in the dirt right then and there.

I didn't. I made a judgment that the alliance between this patient and this therapist wasn't secure enough yet.

Was my failure to heft the shovel evidence of clinical acumen? Or was it clinical cowardice?

As she left the office that day, I generously decided that the jury was still out on that.

It would turn out to be one of many things I would be guilty of misjudging regarding Kelda James.

The first words from Kelda's mouth in the waiting room the day after my run-in with my poodle were, 'Oh my God, Alan! What on earth did you do to your arm?'

I tried the Cliffs Notes version. 'I tripped.'

'Are you okay? Does it hurt? When did you do it? How did it happen?'

'I just did it yesterday, Kelda. It's still a little achy, but I'll be okay when I get used to the cast. Come on back to the office.'

Less than a minute later she settled onto the chair opposite mine and watched me struggle to lower myself into position. 'We can cancel. Why don't you go home and take care of yourself? You must be miserable.'

'Thank you for your concern, but I'm okay.' My reply was intended to acknowledge her compassion and to redirect her to focus on to the reason she was in my office.

'You're sure you're all right?' The fact that Kelda couldn't distract herself from my broken arm was every bit as meaningful as was the fact that Tom Clone had barely noticed it.

'What happened?'

I told her about tripping over my dog. The story sounded sillier every time I told it.

She wanted to know if the dog was okay.

I decided to try being more direct with Kelda. 'Yes, the dog is fine. What about you?'

She sighed and adjusted her position on the chair while the fingers of her left hand kneaded the muscles on the outside of her thigh. I wasn't certain she was even aware she was doing it.

'You asked me to try to remember when the pain started. What was going on in my life?'

'Yes,' I said, although I hadn't actually asked her to remember. I'd suggested that it might be helpful for her to remember. I noted the slight translation she had made.

'You're sure you're okay?'

I said I was.

'I think, looking back, that the pain started when I was in Australia, living in Sydney. It may have been earlier but I think it was then. I think I told you about Australia. Didn't I?'

I shook my head.

'The insurance company I worked for when I first got out of college had an office in New South Wales. One of my bosses in the accounting department was sent over to supervise an internal investigation of some fraud they suspected was going on in the Australian office. He asked me to come with him to Sydney to help with the investigation.

'At some level I knew he asked me to go only because he figured he could get me to sleep with him, but I was fresh out of school, I was twenty-four years old, and I thought, hey, what a great opportunity to get to see some of the world. So I went to Sydney, and ended up being there for almost six months. I loved Australia – just had a terrific time – and I learned most of what I know about forensic accounting while I was there. It was a wonderful period in my life.'

Her affect didn't reflect her words. No joy sparkled in her eyes, and her wide mouth was set flat. Her right hand was doing the kneading now, higher on her leg, near her hip. She pushed her dark hair away from her face with her other hand before she rested the tip of her index finger on her upper lip.

'And that's when the pain began?' I asked.

'Yes, I think it was right around then. At first I thought it was just because I was doing so much. You know, activity-wise. The people I was hanging around with in Sydney lived for the water, and I wanted to try every single activity they were involved in. I was learning to surf and trying to learn to windsurf and I met a guy who had a boat and he was teaching me to wakeboard. When I wasn't in the water, it seemed I was out bushwalking with friends in the Blue Mountains. I assumed the pain in my legs was just because I was so active.'

'Did you see a doctor while you were there?'

She shook her head. 'I *dated* a doctor a couple of times while I was there. He was interesting. But no, I didn't go to see anybody for the pain in my legs. I thought it would go away.'

I could have asked another question. A few came to mind. But my scorecard showed that I'd already asked one too many, and I was curious where Kelda was going to wander next if I didn't get in her way.

'When I was in Sydney I met another Kelda, too. A girl from Queensland. Her grandmother was from County Cork, just like mine. She's the only other Kelda I've ever met.' She smiled self-consciously. 'She reminded me of Jones. Same blond hair, same fair skin, same green eyes. Almost as skinny.'

'Jones?' I asked.

Kelda's face softened. 'Yeah, Jones. I haven't talked about Jones, have I? A friend from college. My best friend, really. My best friend ever. Joan Samantha Winslett.' She crossed her legs. 'The day we met I saw her name written on a class roster at DU. It said "Winslett, JoanS." The space was missing between the *n* of Joan and her middle initial S. When I saw it I read it out loud as "Winslett, Jones." She was standing next to me and thought it was hilarious. We became great friends; we were even roommates the last couple of years at school.

'Right from that first day I always called her Jones. No one else did. It was just our thing, part of our bond, I think. Anyway, the Kelda I met in Sydney reminded me of Jones.'

Intuition, I've decided, is a combination of experience and attentiveness and maybe some other magical things that I haven't yet isolated. The amalgam, whatever its actual components, was shouting at me that Jones wasn't just some old friend of Kelda's.

'Was?' I asked. 'You said it *was* your thing.'

'I did say that. Jones is dead. She died that same year while she was living in Hawaii. She was an artist.'

The non sequitur *she was living in Hawaii/she was an artist* hung in the air between us like a mist that refused to settle.

I compared the time periods in my head. 'Jones died while you were in Australia?'

Kelda looked back up at me, her eyes moist with tears. 'I'm not ready to talk about Jones yet. Okay?'

The statement was poignant for many reasons. The most important was that it told me that Kelda was aware that talking about Jones was one of the crucial things that she and I needed to do.

'Of course,' I said. 'I'd just like to point out that when you started talking about the beginning of your pain, it didn't take very long for your mind to go to your friend, Jones.'

The look she gave me was steely – some alloy of *You want to make something of it?* and *Please don't make me talk about her.*

It wasn't the first admonition that Kelda had communicated to me. The first had come during our initial session and had to do with the fact that she wasn't using her government health insurance to pay for her treatment; she was paying for the psychotherapy herself. She admitted that the FBI wasn't aware that she was seeing a neurologist for chronic pain, nor were they aware that she relied on narcotics to function, and she certainly wasn't planning to make them aware that she was seeing a psychotherapist for issues that might be related to her pain.

She'd even admitted to me that she had devised a few different ingenious systems – including an old IV bag taped to her back with a tube down the crack of her ass – that had, so far, successfully allowed her to thwart the FBI's best efforts to discover the morphine derivatives in her urine.

She'd made clear to me that I wasn't to divulge either the fact of, or the nature of, her treatment to anyone. It could cost her her job if the FBI learned that she was taking narcotics on a regular basis.

I had assured her that I had no wish, and certainly no obligation, to inform the FBI about anything having to do with her psychotherapy.

Despite some gentle encouragement on my part, we didn't talk any more about Jones that day.

As the session came to a close, Kelda collected her things to leave the office, stood, and said, 'I gave somebody your name. As a therapist, I mean. That guy who was just released from death row? Tom Clone.' She stood. 'You may have heard that the press has been speculating that it was an FBI agent who helped discover the evidence that got him freed from prison. Well, they're right, it was. I'm that FBI agent. I'm the one who found the knife you might have been reading about.'

She took a step toward the door, then turned. 'Hope your arm feels better, Alan. Next time try to step over the dog. I'll see you in a week.'

I was halfway home, caught in traffic on South Boulder Road, when I stopped wondering about Jones and my arm began to hurt again.

It made me think about the Mini.

I didn't know at the time, of course, that it was the wrong association.

But it's the one that I made.

CHAPTER

14

Kelda's route back to Lafayette would take her down Arapahoe Road, on a path parallel to the one that her therapist, Alan Gregory, was taking to his house. Before she headed home, though, she decided to run a couple of errands in Boulder – Liquor Mart to pick up some beer from Crested Butte that Ira liked, and McGuckin Hardware to get some material to fix the screen on her bathroom window. There was no sense heading east before she allowed some time for the local roads to lose some of their rush-hour inflammation.

Other than to notice that it pulled in just as she was walking into the store, she didn't actually pay much attention to the burgundy Toyota pickup that followed her into the Liquor Mart parking lot. After she bought Ira's favorite beer and left the store, she noted that the Toyota pickup turned from the lot onto Canyon Boulevard about ten seconds after she did.

Could be a coincidence, she thought. *Probably is.*

A few blocks east she turned right on Folsom and then immediately got into the far lane to turn left into the McGuckin lot. The pickup followed her onto Folsom but continued past her as she waited to turn. As the vehicle passed her she tried to get a look at the driver, but the sun visor blocked her view through the windshield, and the window tint kept her from looking into the pickup from the side. She thought that the driver of the truck was a man. The front license plate on the truck was missing. The one on the rear was obscured by a convenient splash of dried mud.

A half block farther ahead the truck eased into the left-hand turn lane at Arapahoe Road.

Had she been trying to do a one-vehicle tail – which she wouldn't: any experienced agent would argue that they're almost impossible to pull off unless the target is oblivious – she would have made the exact same maneuver that the pickup made before finding another route into the parking lot. She parked her car and ambled to the entrance to the hardware store, waiting just inside the door for the truck to reappear. A minute later she spied it as it pulled into the lot from the direction of Arapahoe.

This is no coincidence.

Errand accomplished, screen repair supplies in hand, she returned to her car and snaked through the lot until she could turn onto Arapahoe. When she pulled to a stop at the red light at Twenty-eighth Street, the truck followed her onto Arapahoe. After the light changed she lost sight of the tail for a couple of miles but spotted it again thirty blocks later. The Toyota was a dozen cars behind her.

Kelda lifted her Sig from her shoulder holster and set it on her lap. She edged her Buick into the right lane and slowed, hoping the driver of the Toyota pickup wouldn't notice the speed change. But the tactic didn't work. The truck stayed a few hundred feet back.

Three miles farther east, Kelda approached the left-hand turn onto 111th Street that would take her to her tiny ranch. She knew she didn't want to lead whoever was driving the truck back to her home, so she made a decision to bypass 111th and proceed up to 119th. She'd turn right instead of left and do some maneuvers to lose the tail in the residential clutter of the last decade's orgy of suburban excess as she doubled back between Baseline and Arapahoe. Then she would head home and try to sort out what was going on.

She accelerated gently as she approached 111th, keeping her eyes glued to her mirror as the distance increased between herself and the Toyota. Her impression was that the distance between the two vehicles was increasing much faster than she was accelerating.

Kelda was a couple of hundred yards past 111th, staring into her mirror, trying to make sense of the rapidly increasing gap between her Buick and the tailing Toyota, when the Toyota slowed and turned onto the road that led toward her home. Absently she touched the handgun on her lap and returned her attention from the mirror to the road just in time to see the blunt yellow end of a school bus light up in bright red orbs a hundred feet in front of her.

She slammed on her brakes but knew instinctively that she wasn't going to be able to stop in time to avoid colliding with the back end of the bus. Escaping to the right shoulder was out of the question – that's where the kids would be exiting the bus. Her only choice was to swerve into the oncoming lane of traffic. She tried to process the data that was screaming at her: at least three pairs of headlights were approaching in the opposite lane. She would somehow have to swerve between two of the oncoming cars in the instant before she impacted the bus full of children.

The first car passed. Kelda's heart pounded as she recognized that an Impala full of teenagers had just driven past her. The last two pairs of headlights appeared tightly spaced, but she determined that the gap would have to be large enough.

The yellow wall grew closer. The red lights on the back of the bus flashed so brightly that Kelda could feel them as though they were pounding hard at her flesh.

Kelda's eyes locked onto the two child restraints she saw poking up in the rear seat of a Dodge minivan, and she began the sudden maneuvers she hoped would help her avoid an impact with the back of the bus.

The bus was only feet away when Kelda yanked the wheel of her Buick to the left and simultaneously lightened the pressure on her brakes. Instantly, her car bolted into the oncoming traffic, eluding the back of the school bus by inches and heading at a sharp angle across the lane of oncoming traffic.

The car hurtling at her was a new VW Bug that was painted a shade of yellow that nature reserved for bananas, birds, and tropical fish. The expression on the driver's face was one of complete incredulity. Kelda's appearance in the lane in front of her was so sudden that the young woman driving the VW didn't even process the danger she was in – only shock was apparent on her face.

In the next instant, Kelda recalled seeing the flash of yellow swim past her. But she wasn't immediately sure whether it was the mustard yellow of the school bus or the neon yellow of the VW that flowed by in her periphery. She didn't know for sure that she had escaped colliding with the onrushing vehicles until the left wheels of her Buick plopped off the macadam shoulder on the far side of Arapahoe Road.

She said, 'Shit,' and skidded her car to a stop, two wheels in the dust, two on the asphalt shoulder. Traffic continued to surge by in both directions as though nothing had happened. The flow of the road returned to normal long before Kelda's breathing did.

Kelda retrieved her handgun from the floor below the steering wheel and slid it back into her holster. She waited what felt like forever for a break in the traffic that was sufficient to allow her to pull back onto Arapahoe again.

She slowed after she completed the turn onto 111th, her eyes peeled for the burgundy Toyota truck. It wasn't there. As she accelerated toward the speed limit, an uneven ribbon of pink grays hugged the fractured tops of the mountains of the Divide to her left. Sunset was in its final moments. High above the horizon in front of her, stars had begun to pop into the black sky.

But there was no sign of the arrival of the monsoons.

Unlike Arapahoe, 111th Street wasn't a busy street. That night, traffic was even more muted than normal. Few cars passed Kelda as she covered the final mile that would take her to the lane that led to her house. No headlights appeared in her rearview mirror. She checked every few seconds to be sure.

She tapped her brakes as she approached her lane. A car was coming her way from the north; she decided to wait until it passed to complete the turn. The car – a big SUV – zoomed past and she eased into a wide arc that would take her to the bank of mailboxes at the end of the lane. She moved the shift lever to 'park' and pulled herself from the car to retrieve her mail. The adrenaline that had pumped into her veins was dissipating almost as rapidly as it had arrived, and as the hormone disappeared, the pain was returning to her legs. She felt deep aches in her calves and thighs as she walked up to the post that was topped with her galvanized mailbox.

A loud click pierced the night.

Kelda froze.

A heartbeat later her right hand snaked inside her jacket. A starter motor whirred and in a split second she heard the roar of an engine revving much faster than any manufacturer would have recommended. She looked down the lane and then back out on 111th but she couldn't tell where the vehicle was parked.

A pair of lights flashed into her eyes from down the lane. Seconds later the glare boosted to bright and the roar of the motor began to quiet. She heard the crackling of tires on gravel as the car moved at a measured pace in her direction. She stepped behind the Buick and crouched down. Her Bureau training was almost instinctive; she was putting the engine compartment and the tire between her body and whoever was coming down the lane.

The burgundy front end of the Toyota pickup emerged from the illuminated dust that was hanging above the lane. The visor was still down on the driver's side of the pickup, and the tint on the glass was no more transparent than it had been earlier. The truck pulled even with her Buick and stopped. Kelda stayed low and held the Sig just out of sight.

Ten seconds passed. Fifteen. Finally, the window cracked open about two inches.

Kelda thought she smelled cigarette smoke emerge from the cab.

A voice that Kelda was certain was male said, 'Evening, darlin'.'

Prehost?

The window rolled back up and the truck turned south, back toward Arapahoe Road. Kelda watched it go until the two red tail-lights merged into a solitary pink dot.

From her car, she grabbed her big flashlight and a few plastic bags and paced down the lane toward the spot where the Toyota had been parked. She held the big light in her left hand and her 9mm Sig Sauer in her right. She swept the dirt path with the beam of her torch, trying to determine exactly where the truck had stopped. Twice she paused and crouched to examine cigarette butts in the brush by the near side of the lane. In each case the butts had already started to disintegrate.

A hundred yards down the lane a pair of headlights flashed on. An engine rumbled to life. Kelda skipped off the lane and hopped the little fence that lined her property. The Sig felt weightless in her hand.

The car approached. She could see the driver lean his head out the window. She crouched behind a fence post, and the Sig floated into firing position as though her arm were being lifted by a helium-filled balloon.

'It's me, baby. Ira.'

She said, 'Shit, Ira. You almost gave me a heart attack. A few more seconds and I would have shot you.'

He pulled up opposite her and killed the engine.

She said, 'What the hell were you doing down there?'

He shook his head in disbelief. 'I came over to see you a while ago, and your car wasn't here but someone else's was. Some guy sitting in a truck seemed to be watching your house. I decided to see what he was up to, so I drove past him down the lane, parked my car, and pretended to go into Lucas's place. Then I watched the truck. Do you know that guy?'

'No. I was in Boulder seeing that shrink. I thought I saw this truck following me home but I thought I lost him. Apparently, I didn't. Did you get a plate or a clear look at the guy?'

'Negative on both counts. Obviously he knows where you live, Kelda. That can't be good.'

'Tell me about it.'

'What did he want?'

'He drove by real slowly and said, "Hi, darlin'."'

'That's it?'

'That's it. I think somebody was just letting me know that he can find me.'

'Why? Does this have to do with Tom Clone?'

She shrugged. 'I don't know. Maybe. Probably. Right now, I assume everything does.'

'Was it one of the guys who hassled you on the way home from the penitentiary?'

'I don't think so. It could have been one of them, but if I had to guess, I'd guess not. The voice wasn't right.'

'You want some company tonight?'

'I don't think so, Ira. I'm tired. I just want to freeze my legs and try to get some sleep.'

'At least let me come in while you check the house.'

'Ira? What are you going to do? You would faint if it turned out that there was someone in there. I'm better off doing it by myself. I'll be fine. Call me tomorrow, okay?'

After a moment, he answered, 'Whatever you want.'

She watched Ira drive away before she continued her search. She walked on until she was at least a hundred feet past her own driveway and spotted two more cigarette butts, one in the dirt, the other floating on top of some dried grass like a golf ball perched on a tee. Both were the same brand and both had filters. These two butts – one burnt all the way down to the filter, the other almost – weren't disintegrating from exposure to the elements. These were fresh. She stuck her right hand inside one plastic bag and used her protected fingers to lift the butts from the lane and drop them in a second bag.

Methodically, she walked a wide perimeter around where she was guessing that the Toyota truck had been parked. She crisscrossed the space in between the perimeter lines, her eyes on the lookout for any clue as to who might have been in the truck. But she ended her search after finding nothing but the two cigarette butts and some tire prints in the dust.

Flashlight in hand, she walked around the outside of her house, examining every opening for signs of forced entry. She flashed the beam on the entire length of the electrical line as it snaked from the post on the lane to her house. She did the same with the phone line and even examined the natural gas pipe that led into and out of her gas meter. She didn't see a thing that would indicate that whoever had been in that truck had approached her house or tampered with anything.

Kelda retraced her steps down the lane and retrieved her car. She parked it in the usual place beneath the twin elms.

Her legs were on fire by the time she slid the key into her back door and entered her house. The alarm sounded as it always did. Her Sig still at the ready, she shut the alarm down and searched the interior of her home as though she was certain that it had been invaded.

Ten minutes later she felt confident that there was no one there. And that no one had been there.

She stripped off her clothes, pulled on some short cotton pajamas, flicked on the swamp cooler and the ceiling fan, and shut all the window coverings before she grabbed two bath towels and six bags of frozen peas. She was only halfway done arranging the peas and towels on her bed when the phone rang. Caller ID said 'Private.'

'Hello,' she said.

'Kelda? It's Tom Clone.'

'Yes?' Her shoulders slumped.

'Is this a bad time?'

She mouthed a profanity, but said, 'What's up, Tom?' She tucked the phone between her ear and shoulder while she completed the placement of the peas and the careful folding of the towels on her bed.

'I think somebody broke into my grandfather's house.'

'What?'

'There's been some weird stuff going on since I got here. The past day or so especially. I'm thinking somebody's been in the house.'

'Why don't you call the Boulder Police? I'm sure they'll be happy to help you out. Just dial 911.'

'I don't really want to get involved with the police. I hope you can understand why.'

The subtext of Tom's call was suddenly clear to Kelda. Involuntarily, her mind formed a picture of Ira. It developed slowly in her head, like an old Polaroid bubbling to life.

'I can't help you, Tom. I'm a federal agent. What you're describing is not an FBI problem, it's a local one.'

'I'm not asking for your official help, Kelda. I'm just, I don't know, I guess I'm kind of paranoid. Wondered if you'd look around, unofficially. Let me know if you think I'm being crazy. I don't know who else to call.'

Wistfully, she stared at the towels. Imagined the peas releasing their chill into her legs.

Ira.

She shook her head and sighed. 'It'll take me at least twenty minutes to get there.'

'I really appreciate it.'

'See you soon,' she said. With the same reluctance that an alcoholic feels when recorking a bottle, she returned the six bags of peas to the freezer, leaving the bath towels in place on the bed.

Agony twanged in her legs as though the devil himself were playing the cello on her tendons. Before she pulled on some jeans and a soft gray T-shirt, she swallowed a couple of Percocet and wondered how the hell she'd make it through the night, let alone through her week.

As she walked out the door, she was careful to reset the alarm. She used the thirty-second delay to grab two bags of peas and a couple of kitchen towels. On the drive to Boulder she'd do what she could to freeze away the pain.

15

The trip back to Boulder didn't take Kelda long. She'd given herself a headache trying to track the headlights that appeared behind her. She didn't think she'd been followed, but she really wasn't sure.

As Kelda parked her Buick by the curb near the end of High Street, the clock on the dashboard clock read 9:06.

Tom Clone was waiting on the front porch of his grandfather's house.

She hooked her purse over her shoulder and began to walk across the narrow lawn. She paused a moment to watch heat lightning illuminate the dark skies of the southeastern horizon like the last gasp of giant sparklers. The sky was clear to the west, which everyone but recent transplants knew meant that this would be another summer night without rain. One of the DJs she'd been listening to on the drive over said that there had apparently been a pretty good hailstorm up north around Greeley, but nothing near Boulder County.

'Thanks for coming, Kelda,' Tom said. He stood, took a couple of steps forward, and extended a hand to her.

She stopped five feet from him, at the foot of a couple of flagstone steps. 'Hi. So how's life outside?'

As he moved into the light, she could see that his hair was wet and concluded that he'd just stepped out of the shower. She made a conscious decision not to take it personally; she didn't want to think he'd showered just for her visit.

'Better than life inside.' He touched his clothes – a pair of cargo shorts and a T-shirt – and swept an arm up toward the sky. 'I can't get enough of all this. Do you know I'd forgotten what the night sky looked like? Or how a summer peach smelled. Or what beer tastes like. I'm serious; I'd forgotten what beer tastes like. But the high point so far was that ride home with you. I won't forget that for a while. I can still remember the way you looked and smelled when I walked out of that prison.'

At his words, Kelda felt a chill in the base of her spine.

'That's nice,' she said. 'Listen, it's late. I have to get back home; I have a full day tomorrow. Why don't you go ahead and show me what it is that you're so worried about?'

'My manners,' he said, ignoring her question. 'Can I offer you something? A beer? My grandfather drinks Bud. There's plenty of that. Some orange juice, too, I think. Maybe something else.'

'Nothing, thank you. Let's just get started.'

'Of course, whatever you would like. Come on out around back. I'll show you what's going on.' He led her around the west side of the house and through the gate of a chain-link fence. 'I'm not accustomed to a world where

I can open and close gates whenever I want to,' he said. 'But I think I'm going to like it.'

Although the lights of downtown sparkled right below them, the back corner of the house was dark, dark enough that she couldn't see her feet. Kelda's mind wasn't far from the burgundy Toyota, and the darkness made her feel especially wary. 'Will I need my flashlight back here?' she asked. 'I have one in the car.'

'No,' he replied. 'Wait.'

She adjusted her shoulder bag and checked the slit that allowed her access to her handgun.

He reached up the wall and slid his fingers into a light fixture. The bulb suddenly flashed on and a harsh yellow light bathed both of them. 'That's exactly how I found it tonight. With the bulb loose. Exact same thing on the other side of the house. Last night these lights were on. Grandpa grilled pork chops and sweet corn for us out here. The lights were both on. I remember.'

'What else?'

'This way.' The rear of the house had a cracked concrete patio and some lawn furniture that had somehow managed to get coated with rust despite Colorado's minuscule humidity. Tom crossed the patio and stood in front of a window that was a double-hung design, maybe two feet by three feet. 'This goes to Grandpa's laundry room, just a little alcove off the kitchen. The screen's been cut. Look.'

She stood next to him and could smell his scent. She thought that he might actually be wearing cologne. She shuddered.

The screen had been sliced so that it could be peeled away from one corner. The cut was too straight to have

141

been accidental. She guessed a razor knife. 'Is the window locked from inside?' she asked.

'Kind of. There's one of those hook catches on it, but I was able to get it to give by sliding a putty knife in between the two sashes from out here. It would be easy to get inside if you wanted to.'

Kelda stared at the window for half a minute more before she asked, 'Anything else? Anything missing inside?'

'Not that my grandfather noticed. He's in bed now. He really wanted to stay up to meet you, but he gets too tired. He said he wanted to shake your hand and give you a kiss and say thanks.'

Kelda smiled politely. 'That's nice. Tell him thank you for me, but that it's not necessary. So it's just the loosened lightbulbs and the cut screen? That's it?' She tried not to sound dismissive, but she was pretty sure that what her words had ended up saying to Tom was *You brought me all the way to Boulder for this?*

'Yes, I guess that's it. I thought it was important. It looked like somebody had tried to get in and couldn't, or . . . maybe somebody had done the preparations so that they could get in tonight, or sometime soon.'

'And why would someone want to get in, Tom?'

A sharp *craaack* snapped behind them, followed by the sound of running through the bushes at the back of the property.

Tom spun to the noise even faster than Kelda did. After staring into the night for a couple of seconds, he said, 'The stupid raccoons are back.' When he turned back to face Kelda, she had her handgun pointed into the darkness.

'Damn,' he said. 'You're quick with that thing. Where

the hell did that come from?' With his eyes he checked her outfit for a holster and didn't find one. 'Did you get that out of your bag that fast?'

'Raccoons?' she replied.

He couldn't take his eyes off the gun. 'Do you always draw your gun this much? I'm with you twice and both times you're like Wyatt Earp or John Dillinger with that thing.'

'Raccoons?' she repeated.

'Yeah. Grandpa said that he's only seen them come all the way up here two or three times in all the years he's lived here, but with the dry spring they've been wandering farther and farther from the creek looking for food. They're scavengers. They knock over trash cans and eat garbage.'

She slipped the Sig back into her bag. 'Is there a reason why someone would want to get into your grandfather's house? Does he have valuables? Collectibles? Antiques? Anything like that?'

Tom considered the question for a moment. She felt that he was taking advantage of the opportunity to stare at her. 'He likes marbles. There's a whole section of wall in his den that's covered with marbles.'

'But that's it? Just marbles?'

'Pretty much. I don't think whoever is doing this is after my grandfather's money.'

She raised an eyebrow. She meant for her face to ask, *Then what the hell are they after?*

'There are people who don't like that I'm out of prison. Who don't like that I'm off death row. We've gotten phone calls. My attorney has received threats against me and him.'

Again, Kelda thought about the burgundy Toyota that had followed her home.

'I'm sure that's true, that there are people who don't agree with the decision to let you out of prison,' she said.

'I think I have to consider the possibility that there may be someone who might try to break in here to get at me.'

After a moment she said, 'That can't feel too good.'

'It feels like prison all over again. I'm out. I'm free, but I still have to watch my back.'

'Well, I'd say you probably do have something to worry about then. I agree with your impression that someone's been tampering with the house in a way that is consistent with planning an intrusion. I'll repeat what I said to you on the phone: This is something to take up with the local police. I would guess that Tony Loving would be able to arrange some extra attention for the house in terms of patrols.'

'Kelda? Look. Like I said, not everybody is happy about me getting out of prison. I'm including the local cops on that list. For right now, I'd rather fly below their radar, you know?'

She didn't want to debate police attitudes with Tom Clone. 'Does the house have an alarm system?'

'No.'

'You might consider it.'

'My grandfather doesn't have that kind of money. He's worried about having enough to pay his property taxes. And I don't have a job yet.'

'Then you might want to nail or pin the windows shut. That's the only way to really secure those old double-hungs.' Kelda knew about double-hung windows. Her little house in Lafayette had them, too. 'How are the locks on the doors?'

'They're shitty. Only one out of three even has a dead bolt.'

'That's your first priority, Tom. Better locks on those doors.'

'So I should go ahead and build myself a little prison? That's what you're suggesting?'

'That's not what I meant.' Her legs were on fire. She wanted to leave Boulder and drive home to more frozen peas. 'I changed my mind. I will take some of that orange juice, if you don't mind,' she said as she lowered herself to sit on one of the old patio chairs. Sitting didn't eliminate her pain, but it changed it. Sometimes, when relief wasn't possible, the novelty of a fresh perspective on her discomfort was all she could hope for.

She didn't tell Tom that she needed the juice to wash down another Percocet. Or two.

'You okay?' he asked when he returned with the juice.

She cursed to herself. She didn't like it when people noticed her pain.

From someone else, the question might have sounded sympathetic, but for some reason, from Tom Clone, Kelda was left doubting the depth of his compassion. She was wondering if his sensitivity to her pain was something like the radar a bull elephant has for an injured foe or that a shark has for blood.

She tried to keep the wariness out of her voice as she asked, 'What do you mean? I'm fine.' She took the glass from his hand and held it to her lips. She'd swallowed a pill dry while he was gone, and it felt as if it was caught in her throat. She allowed the cool drink to flush it down.

'Do you know the last thing I did every night when I was inside?' Tom asked.

She suspected the question was rhetorical. She glanced at him over the rim of her glass, relieved that they were no longer talking about her pain.

'I tied my cell door shut. When I could steal one, a shoelace worked well. But mostly I used little ropes that I braided out of threads from my blankets or my clothes. But every night, I had to tie the cell door shut or I couldn't sleep.' He stared at her eyes and nodded slowly. 'That's right, believe it. I locked myself into my very own cell every night.'

She wondered where he was going with his story.

'I'm confined in a fucking maximum-security penitentiary and my last act each night is the exact same one that almost every suburban homeowner does. I locked my doors to keep out the bad guys. Except in my case the bad guys weren't nickel-and-dime burglars; they were killers and rapists. The people who wanted into my cell at night were mad dogs.'

She watched him, but didn't reply.

'You're having trouble being sympathetic, aren't you?' he asked.

'Um, no.'

'My point is that I'm accustomed to going to bed scared. I did it every night I was inside. Every single night for thirteen years. And I don't want to do it anymore. I just don't want to.'

'That's why this is so hard?' She gestured toward the back of the house. 'The lightbulbs and the cut screen? Because it means you're still going to bed scared?'

'Yeah. I feel like I'm hoarding shoelaces again. Weaving ropes. Tying my cell door shut.'

'Was that the worst part inside? The fear?' Kelda surprised herself with the question, surprised herself how sincerely she wanted to know the answer.

'The worst part?' He pointed to the sky. 'That's like asking which part of the night is the blackest. Black is black.'

Almost involuntarily a tear formed in the corner of her eye. She turned away from him.

'What did I say? Did I upset you?'

She turned back. 'No. I'm sorry. What you said reminded me of something.' Kelda was thinking about Jones. Thinking about Jones talking about her fears.

'You're very pretty.'

She shook her head in a narrow arc to try to make the compliment go away. She wouldn't admit it to him, but he still felt like an inmate to her, his flattery like a profanity shouted between the bars.

He took a step away from her before he spoke again. 'I hated the sound the cell doors made when they were shut. I never got used to it. And I hated the footsteps in the halls. The echoes. Everything inside echoed. Everything. And meals? It was just slop in a trough.

'But it was all black. There was no worst part. No darkest part. All of it was black. I was on death row for a murder I didn't commit. How could there be a worst part?'

This was when she was supposed to say, 'I'm so sorry.' She didn't. She struggled to keep her fingertips away from the long muscles in her legs. She thought, *We all have our prisons.*

He was staring at her, waiting for her to say something.

She stammered out a reply. 'You, uh, don't babble on about it, about the injustice, I mean. Not with me. Considering what you've been put through, I would think that you wouldn't be able to talk about anything else. Where's your rage?'

He looked away from her for a second.

Kelda opened her mouth to say something more, but Tom turned back, locked his eyes on hers, and spoke first. 'I saw that Dr. Gregory today. How do you know him?'

Kelda hesitated, moistened her lips with the tip of her tongue. She thought she'd succeeded in keeping her expression neutral. 'A friend sees him,' she said. She stood, and repositioned her shoulder bag to better handle the weight of the Sig. She added, 'You really should call the police, Tom. For your grandfather's sake, if not for your own. What's going on here at the house, this could be a serious problem.'

'I'll think about it. I promise.'

He followed her out to the curb.

'I've been wondering,' he said abruptly. 'The call that you got about where to find the murder weapon? The knife? That just came out of the blue one day?'

'Yes,' she said. Tom was silhouetted against the front porch light of his grandfather's house. She couldn't see his eyes. 'Maybe someday I'll tell you the whole story.'

'I'd like that,' he said.

On the ride back to Lafayette, Kelda began to wonder about how the possible had become the inevitable and how justice and science had somehow become Siamese twins.

The whole way home she kept checking her mirror for the burgundy Toyota. She tracked a hundred pairs of headlights, but none of them followed her down 111th toward her little house.

She half expected to see Ira's car in front of her house or to find him sitting by her door with his daypack over his shoulder. She didn't want to explain about her trip back to Boulder.

She wouldn't have to; he wasn't there.

16

Kelda had taken the phone call ten months before. It had come, just as Tom Clone had suggested, seemingly out of the blue.

She recalled that the morning was cold for September and the evidence of the season's always-surprising first snow was lingering on the still-green lawns of Denver. The thin coating of fat flakes that coated the grass felt like an affront to everyone who adored summer.

When the phone rang on her desk, Kelda was standing across the big office she shared with other agents. She'd been talking with a friend of hers, an agent named Bill Graves, whose desk was ten feet away. She interrupted the conversation with Graves to take the call.

She said, 'Special Agent James.' After listening for a few seconds, she added, 'Yes, this is Special Agent Kelda James. How can I help you?'

That was how it all began. She'd taken a phone call while standing beside her desk.

Three or four minutes later she turned to Bill Graves and said, 'That was odd. Someone just called and told me that he knows where I can find the weapon that was used in an old murder.'

Bill had returned his attention to a file on his desk. He looked up and said, 'Really? Just like that?'

'Yes, just like that. Guy says there was some old murder up in Park County in 1989 and he says he knows where the murder weapon is hidden. Said he saw the murderer hide it.'

'You get a name?'

'No, not from the guy who was on the telephone. He wouldn't say, but he gave me the victim's name. Dead woman was named . . .' Kelda glanced down at the notes she'd scribbled while on the phone. 'She was named Ivy Campbell. Does it ring a bell? You weren't here in '89, were you?'

Bill shook his head. 'No, I was still in Topeka. Why did this person call you? Why didn't he just call the local cops and tell them about the weapon?'

Kelda looked away from the other agent. Even though she trusted Bill, she was embarrassed about the implications of what she was about to say. 'He says he doesn't trust the local cops, and that's why he called the FBI. He said he asked for me, specifically, because of . . . you know, the girl.'

Rosa Alija. The girl.

Bill Graves nodded and sighed, as though he was disheartened by her reply. He knew precisely what girl Kelda was referring to. With half a smile on his face he said, 'That little girl is like an annuity for you, isn't she? She just keeps paying dividends year after year. Who would have guessed what those few minutes in that warehouse would do for you?'

Kelda heard the echoes of envy in his voice. She'd heard them before from other agents, but never from Bill Graves. She said, 'Yes. It seems that way sometimes.'

'Why did he call after all these years?'

'He said that he thinks the cops may have the wrong guy in prison for murdering this Ivy Campbell and he can't live with that anymore.'

'You going to check out his story?'

'I don't think I should ignore it. I'll run it by the SAC. The guy was clear that he wants us to deal with the information he provides by ourselves. He said if we involve the local cops, he won't tell me where to find the weapon. I told him I had to get clearance before I could investigate anything. He's going to call back in a couple of hours to hear the decision.'

Bill said, 'It's a no-brainer, Kelda. The SAC' – Bill always broke convention and put the emphasis on the A. For him, the Special Agent in Charge was the s-A-c – 'loves stuff like this, stuff that makes the locals look bad and us look good. Especially given all the bad press we've gotten lately. He'll tell you to check it out. Bet your lunch on it.'

'If he tells me to check it out, then I'll check it out, won't I?'

'You said Park County, right?'

She nodded.

'Get me in on it, Kelda. I could use a day in the mountains.'

Kelda picked up the phone, called the switchboard operator, and asked for an origination number for the call that had just been forwarded to her extension.

She took a call back in about a minute with the not unexpected news that the call had come from a pay phone. The phone was in Colorado Springs, not too far from Park County.

Kelda spent about an hour on her telephone and on her computer getting her facts straight before she sent the SAC a concise e-mail about the chronology of Ivy Campbell's murder and the subsequent response of the criminal justice system. She highlighted the convicted murderer's recent efforts to gain a new trial. At the end of the e-mail, she described the anonymous phone call from the man who offered the tip about where the FBI could recover the weapon that had, purportedly, been used to slice Ivy Campbell's throat all the way to the bone.

The SAC's reply came back to her in about ten minutes. It was as cryptic as he was. *Do it.*

She e-mailed back asking if Bill Graves could accompany her.

The reply was almost instantaneous. *Yeah, take Graves. He has more experience collecting evidence than you do. Get a video record of everything you do while you're there. And I want to know exactly what you two find before any calls are placed to the locals.*

Almost exactly an hour after Kelda read the SAC's e-mail, the anonymous man called back. The agents were ready this time. A simple caller ID machine identified the source of the call as a pay phone in Woodland Park, about twenty miles east of Park County. The man on the phone listened to Kelda's assurances that the local police wouldn't be involved until after the search for the weapon, then gave her detailed directions to a rusted drainage pipe that was near a culvert about a hundred yards or so from Highway 24, not too far from Lake George.

The chill was still in the air at three-thirty in the afternoon as Kelda and Bill Graves drove from Denver to a location that the *Pierson Guides* map indicated hugged the boundary between Park and Teller Counties. Bill was thrilled at the chance to get out of the city and up into the mountains and was eager to drive. He chose to avoid the interstate, taking 67 out of Sedalia, passing up through Deckers, and coming within sight of the intersection with Highway 24 a few minutes after five.

'God, I love it in the mountains in the fall,' Kelda said as they neared their destination.

Bill shot back, 'Check the calendar, my friend. It's still summer. It's not fall. Fall means winter's coming soon, and I'm not ready for winter.'

'It snowed last night, Bill. Calling it summer doesn't make it summer.'

'A few flakes. That's nothing. It's going to be in the eighties tomorrow.'

'How about Indian summer, then? I love it up here during Indian summer. Can you live with that?'

'Yeah, as long as Indian summer lasts three months, or even better, six. Do I go left or do I go right at the intersection?'

Kelda checked her notes. 'If this is Highway 24 coming up, go right. Then we go nineteen miles and start watching for a dirt road on the left-hand side of the road.'

A while later they both saw the dirt lane. 'I turn here, right?' Bill asked.

'You turn here, *left*. Apparently there's a little clearing about fifty yards in. We park there.'

The forests along most of Colorado's Front Range are commonly pine or fir. This one was mostly pine. Although no visible signs of the previous night's snow remained, the storm had left an unfamiliar moistness in the woods. After standing outside the car for ten seconds to gauge the temperature, Kelda shed her blazer and pulled a fleece jacket out of the backseat.

Bill collected an evidence kit and a video camera and tripod from the trunk of the car. Kelda grabbed a big flashlight and hung a 35mm Canon around her neck. He said, 'We look like a couple of tourists from Kansas.'

She laughed. 'You are from Kansas, aren't you?'

'Yeah.' Bill said it proudly, with the kind of conceit that usually accompanied people announcing their allegiance to Texas.

'Tell me something. Is your cousin really the governor, or is that just one of the stories you tell around the office?'

'No, my cousin is really the governor. Second-term Republican. Elected first back in 1994.'

'Are you guys close?'

'We were as kids. He's a little bit older than me. I followed him to Kansas Wesleyan for college. After I got my CPA, I worked with him for a while in the family trucking business in a little town called Salina.'

'Yeah?'

'Yeah. We have the same name. When we were little, everybody called him Bill and they called me Billy.'

'Billy? You? People called you Billy?' She had trouble seeing anyone calling Special Agent Graves 'Billy.' He stood six-two and was a chiseled 210 pounds.

'Yes. Me.'

'Can I call you Billy?'

'I wouldn't recommend it.'

'I'm still not sure if you're making this up.'

He held up three fingers. 'Scout's honor.'

'Were you a scout?'

'No. But he was. The governor.'

'Jerk.'

Bill asked, 'This is National Forest, right? Federal land? This whole area around here?'

'That's what the map says.'

'I just wanted to be sure we have jurisdiction to do what we're about to do.' He looked down the road. 'So now what?'

Kelda shrugged and looked at her notes. 'We walk up the road a little bit until we see a drainage culvert coming in from the west. He said that the culvert is really just a big galvanized pipe that goes under the road. He said all we'll really see from a distance is a dry creek bed.'

Bill spotted the creek first. It was nothing more than a smooth contour of recessed barren ground. 'That must be it, Kelda. It probably only has water in it during the thunderstorm season.'

She glanced up briefly, nodded in agreement, and then continued reading from her notes. 'Ten, twelve feet farther down the road there should be an old drainpipe that was part of the system that the culvert replaced. The guy on the phone said the pipe was small and that the entrance sticks up out of the ground only a few inches. It's bent now, and rusty.'

Bill walked a few paces farther along the road and announced, 'Here it is. Here's the rusty pipe, just like the man said.'

Kelda was still examining her notes. 'How big is it?'

'I don't know, four inches in diameter, maybe five.'

'Big enough for a knife?'

He tilted his head to change the angle of his vision. 'Sure, big enough for a whole set of knives.'

Kelda said, 'We should probably slow down and take some pictures before we go any farther.'

Bill said, 'Yeah.' He pulled the lens cap from the video camera. 'Did it cross your mind that this could be a setup?'

'You mean a wild-goose chase? Of course.'

'No, that's not what I mean. I've been thinking that . . . this is a great way to get a couple of FBI agents out in the middle of nowhere. Let's make sure we're alone out here. That's all.'

Dusk had just begun seeping into the forest, and the approaching night seemed to highlight the discomfort in Kelda's legs. The pain was reaching all the way from her toes to her hips. The tingling in her feet had degenerated into a burn. 'I don't see anybody, Bill. I don't think it's really necessary.'

'Humor me, Kelda. Give me the flashlight.'

Five minutes later Kelda greeted him on his return from his trek through the woods. He'd covered a perimeter that led away from the culvert at a radius of about a hundred feet. 'See anything?'

'Beer cans. Couple of old illegal campfires. Condoms, empty pint of tequila. What is this place, party central?'

She shuddered. 'Not my idea of a great place for a romantic interlude. Come on, it's getting cold, Bill. Let's get this over with. I got pictures of everything while you were pretending you'd been a Boy Scout. Why don't I set up lights and do the video camera and you can decide how you want to proceed with the evidence collection.'

Bill used the flashlight to peer down into the pipe. 'If there's anything in there, it's probably more than a foot down the pipe. I'm not convinced we'll get anything. It may turn out that we're going to need to get some help getting anything out. Maybe it would even be best to excavate the whole pipe and take it back to Denver. The search would be cleaner that way.'

'May I look?'

'Yeah.'

Kelda took the flashlight and stared into the pipe. 'There's something down there, I think. Look.'

Bill leaned over the opening.

Kelda moved her head out of his way. They were so close that she could smell whatever it was he used on his hair. She said, 'Move the flashlight around. See that shadow on the left-hand side? A foot down, maybe a little more? Well, something is causing that shadow.'

'Yeah. Maybe.'

'I think I can get my hand into the pipe.'

Bill laughed. 'Yeah, maybe you can. The question, of course, is whether you can get your hand back out of the pipe. If you don't, there will be a whole new Kelda James legend for the boys back at the office.'

She scoffed, 'Give me a glove. Let me try.'

He handed her a glove. She pulled the latex onto her fingers and snapped it tightly around her wrist.

Bill stepped away, hit the 'record' button on the video camera, and checked the composition of the framing of the shot. 'We're rolling. Go for it anytime, Houdini.'

Kelda paused, pulled off her fleece jacket, and rolled up the right sleeve of her shirt. Bringing her fingers together to make her hand as narrow as possible, she inserted it into the pipe. Her hand had disappeared almost to her wrist when she suddenly yanked it back out. She blurted, 'Do me a big favor? Check again for bugs.'

'Bugs?'

'Spiders. I don't like spiders. That pipe is a great place for a black widow or even' – she shuddered – 'a brown recluse.'

'A brown what?'

'Check for spiders, please.'

He laughed, but he picked up a stick and used it and the flashlight to probe the opening for spiders.

'Not even a web, Kelda. Now go on, go fish.'

She took a deep breath and reinserted her hand. It was almost twelve inches into the pipe when she felt the metal of the opening tighten on her forearm, near her elbow. She tried not to think about the creatures whose home she was invading. 'I'm not sure I can get it in any farther,' she said.

As the words left her mouth she prayed that Bill was too much of a gentleman to take advantage of the fat serve that she'd just hit over the net. Sardonically, he said, 'That's too bad. I guess we'll have to come back out here tomorrow when we're better prepared. I still like the idea of excavating the whole pipe and cutting off a section. We'll use power tools. Or acetylene torches. That would be even better.'

'Wait, wait,' she whispered. 'I feel something.'

'What is it?'

'How the hell would I know what it is? My arm is stuck down a pipe full of spiders.'

'You know, Kelda, my brother's a gastroenterologist in Topeka. Maybe we could get a flexible camera and a light like he uses for sigmoidoscopies and see what it is that's down there.'

'This isn't somebody's rectum, Bill. It's a damn drainage pipe and I've got something hard between my fingers. I'm going to try and bring it up. Do you have gloves on? I'm going to need some help grabbing it if I am able to get this thing to come out. My fingers are going to cramp up in this position and I'm afraid I'll drop it.'

'Two seconds,' he said. He went back to the evidence kit and pulled gloves on both of his hands. 'Kelda?'

'What?'

'You know, your butt is perfectly framed for the camera right now.'

She cursed at him. There were maybe two men in the Denver field office that she would permit to get away with that comment. Bill Graves was one of them. She turned half a step so her body was in profile to the camera.

He walked back to stand beside her. Slowly, she pulled her arm straight up from the pipe. She'd managed only about two inches when a dull thud sounded.

'Damn it,' Kelda muttered. 'Lost it.'

'It's okay. We'll come back tomorrow with the right equipment. We'll get whatever it is. I'm thinking torches, maybe. That'd be fun.'

'I'm going to try once more.' Again, she lowered her hand all the way into the pipe. 'I think I've got it. Yes, yes, I do. And I have a better grip this time. Here it comes. Here she comes.' Slowly, her arm emerged from the pipe. 'One second,' she said, 'get ready to grab it!'

'Got it,' he said. 'Good work, Kelda. Bravo.'

Kelda shook her arm from the exertion of having clamped down so hard with her fingertips on the wooden handle of what turned out to be an eight-inch kitchen knife. Even through the crusted dirt it was apparent that the engraved handle read 'Chicago Cutlery.'

'Wow,' Bill said. He was holding the knife by its wooden grip between his index finger and his thumb. The blade of the knife, which was pointing straight at the ground, was stainless steel and didn't appear to be rusted, but the whole knife was coated in an uneven red-brown layer of grime.

Kelda said, 'Damn. Maybe Ivy Campbell *is* back from the grave. Is that dried blood, do you think?'

Bill leaned over, moving his eyes to within six inches of the knife. But he didn't respond to her question.

She said, 'I bet it is. We'll know within a day or two.'

'This won't get examined locally, Kelda. The SAC is going to want to send this to the big lab in the sky. And since the crime in question has already been solved, and the perpetrator is on death row, I don't think it's going to be the highest of priorities for them.'

Kelda knew that Bill was talking about the laboratory at FBI Headquarters. 'Yes,' she concurred. 'You're right. The SAC will want to send it east. I'll get a bag for it. Then let's see if we can get anything else out of that pipe.'

Bill said, 'Want to get some dinner on the way back to town? Celebrate our find? There used to be a great bar in Morrison. And . . . if you promise to fill out the FD-620, I'll spring for dinner.'

'You hang out in bars in Morrison?'

'Not hang out, exactly. But I've been once or twice. I have a Harley. I like to ride up there.'

Bill placed the knife into a bag that Kelda was holding open.

'You have a Harley?' she said.

'I do.'

'Is your cousin really the governor of Kansas?'

He laughed.

17

I ndian summer was in rare form the September that Kelda and Bill found the knife.

But by the time that Kelda received the first report with the analyses of the weapon that she'd sent to the FBI laboratory in D.C., the daytime temperature was still hovering in the sixties, the glory of the annual metamorphosis of the aspen trees from emerald to gold in the Colorado Rockies was complete, Halloween had passed, and the stores were screaming, 'Thanksgiving's almost here!'

She'd collected case records and laboratory samples from the original case files and evidence records from the original prosecution and shipped them along with the knife to the attention of the DNA Analysis Unit in Washington, but her FD-620 had specifically requested that the laboratory provide 'all appropriate analyses.'

The agent-examiner in the DNA Unit had reviewed the circumstances involved in recovering the knife and determined that it should also make the rounds of many of the other forensic laboratories on the third floor of the FBI Headquarters building at Ninth and Pennsylvania in Washington, D.C. Ultimately, Fingerprints, Toolmarks, Chemistry, and Hair and Fibers had taken turns examining the knife.

The report the lab provided back to the FBI's Denver Field Office was packed with insights about the weapon.

An attempt had been made to wipe the handle of the knife clean of prints but two partials were recovered. A cursory attempt had also been made to wipe the blade clean of blood. No useful hairs or fibers were recovered from the weapon. Chemistry of residue from the surface of the knife was not remarkable. The toolmarks analysts found nothing idiosyncratic about the blade that could identify it as anything more than a likely weapon in the Ivy Campbell murder.

The first surprise in the report? The partial fingerprints were not consistent with the exemplars from Tom Clone.

The report saved the blood and DNA analysis for last.

Despite the UNSUB's efforts to wipe the blade clean of blood, traces remained on the knife blade. Modern forensic techniques permitted a wealth of analyses to be performed on the limited blood residue that was recovered.

Kelda and Bill weren't surprised to learn that the lab wizards had managed to isolate the DNA from the blood.

But they were surprised to learn that the DNA of two individuals was discovered in the blood residue on the knife. The analysis revealed that some of the blood was, indeed, Ivy Campbell's. The identity of the person whose blood ended up on the knife along with Ivy Campbell's was, of course, unknown to the FBI examiner.

But Kelda and Bill assumed it might belong to Ivy's killer.

'Bill, look,' Kelda said. She'd copied some pages from the records of the initial investigation of Ivy Campbell's murder. The page that she shoved in front of Bill Graves's eyes was the write-up of an interview that Detective Prehost had conducted with Tom Clone two days after the girl's murder.

'What?'

'You have a minute? I want to talk about the knife.'

He marked a spot on a column of figures with his fingertip. 'Huh?'

'Stay with me, here, okay? We have blood from an UNSUB on the knife along with the victim's blood, right?'

'This is about the Ivy Campbell knife, right?'

'Right. The one we found? Remember? Hello. The big lab in the sky found the victim's blood and they found blood from an UNSUB on the knife.'

'Yeah, I saw the report, too, Kelda. I've moved on. You should think about doing the same.'

'Well, I've been doing a little more investigating. Just a little – come on, Bill. Anyway, here's what I know today that I didn't know yesterday: Two days after Ivy's murder, the detective from Park County who was investigating the murder – his name was Prehost, in case you don't remember—'

'I remember.'

She put a second page in front of him. 'Good. Two days after the murder, Prehost observed a cut on the heel of the thumb on Tom Clone's left hand. Look at the next page – Prehost even traced his own hand and drew in the precise location of the cut. I kind of like this guy, Prehost, the way he thinks, you know. In case you don't recall, Clone's the guy sitting on death row for the murder.'

She was teasing him. He knew that, and she thought he liked it. 'Yeah.'

'At the time of the interview, Clone's explanation for the wound was that he cut himself at work. At the time, he was a med student who worked in various clinics at the Health Sciences Center.' She placed another sheet of paper in front of Bill. 'Now look at the third page.'

Bill lifted the second sheet off his desk.

'Well, it turns out that Detective Prehost was thorough; he followed up on Clone's story. He interviewed the nurse who Clone said witnessed the accident at the hospital.'

Bill made a 'go on, go on' motion with his right hand.

'The quote-accident-unquote happened in a treatment room in the orthopedic clinic the day after Campbell was murdered. The nurse told Prehost that she helped Tom Clone clean and dress the wound on his hand, but she didn't actually see the incident occur. She remembered he told her he'd slipped with an instrument or something. A scalpel, maybe.'

Bill looked up at Kelda and smiled warmly. 'This is sure a fun story but we're getting near the punch line, I hope.'

She slapped a final sheet of paper on Bill's desk. 'Prehost also talked to one of Clone's classmates who thought he'd seen a Band-Aid on Clone's hand the morning before the accident in the treatment room, but the witness wasn't one hundred percent sure. Now, what do you think of that?'

'You're thinking that Clone cut himself on the murder weapon and then tried to cover up the wound by faking an accident at the hospital?'

'Exactly. Watch this.' Kelda turned and lifted a long, thin box from the top of her desk. She raised the lid off and exposed an eight-inch Chicago Cutlery French knife. 'This is the same model as the one we found in the pipe. I found it at a garage sale. And it's the same model as the one missing from the kitchen where the murder occurred.'

He sat back on his chair, finally acknowledging to himself that Kelda's intrusion was going to last a while.

'Clone's right-handed, by the way. But let's say he's getting ready to wipe the blood off the knife – he'd hold it in his left hand and use his right hand to do the wiping, right? I'm right-handed and I would.' She demonstrated, first holding the knife by the handle and wiping the blade with an imaginary cloth, and then by the blade and wiping the handle the exact same way. 'See, if he held it like this, blade down, the base of his thumb is exactly where the butt of the blade would be. If he wasn't careful, he could cut himself.'

'That's what you think happened?'

'Yes. That's why his blood's not at the murder scene. He didn't cut himself until later, when he was trying to clean the knife. Maybe he even did it right where we were a few weeks ago, at that pipe.'

'What's the point of all this? This Clone guy is already on death row, Kelda. How much worse can we make it for the guy?'

'He still has appeals left. Anything can happen in these cases, you know that. He's trying to get his lawyer to get him a new trial as we speak.'

'So what do you want to do? See if Clone will volunteer a DNA sample so we can hang him with it? Something tells me that there are some Fourth Amendment issues that we should be considering here.'

She sat on the corner of Bill's desk. Across from her a hinged frame held a picture of his daughter on one side; the other side – the side where his ex-wife's portrait had been – was empty. His wife Cynthia's affair was still an open wound for Bill.

'Kelda, we have a lot of unsolved cases.' He gestured toward the top of his desk, which was cluttered with paperwork. 'More than we have time for. I don't see any reason to waste any more time on one that's already been solved. I don't think the SAC will authorize another minute for you to waste forging yet another nail that's going to serve no other purpose than to secure this guy's coffin.'

'Maybe Clone gave some blood or tissue samples during the initial investigation. We could send those back to the lab for comparison.'

'Why? What's to be gained? The right guy has been convicted. He's on death row.'

'We could short-circuit his appeals.'

Bill raised his eyebrows. 'Again, why? My experience is that the courts will do what the courts will do. If his appeals get out of hand, we can always play the trump card. Keep it up your sleeve for now. There're lots of bad guys out there who deserve our attention more than Tom Clone does.'

'What he did was vicious, Bill. He sliced that girl all the way to the bone. You've seen the pictures.'

'So that means we should convict him twice? That means we should kill him twice? Come on, Kelda. It's not like you to spin your wheels.' He lifted a file from his desk. 'Pull up a chair – we have money-launderers to catch.'

She didn't move.

'Anyway,' he said, 'there's always the possibility that the blood on the knife isn't Clone's. The partial prints on that knife aren't Clone's. What are we going to do then?'

'What do you mean?'

'What if we go for a DNA match with the UNSUB's blood on the knife and it doesn't match Tom Clone? What then?'

'I hadn't thought of that.'

'Well, I have.'

'Look at the evidence against this guy, Bill. It's overwhelming. Everything points to Clone. Everything.'

'If the prints on the murder weapon don't match and the DNA of that blood doesn't match, the rest of the evidence is crap. You know it and I know it. We already have a conviction. We already have a death sentence. Everybody involved thinks it's the right guy. We should be patient and let his appeals evaporate.'

'What? You think running the DNA is just a roll of the dice?'

'No, of course not. I think there's a ninety-nine percent chance the UNSUB blood on the knife will match Clone's. But if I told you that there was a ninety-nine percent chance that you wouldn't be killed in the elevator as you left work today, I bet you'd take the stairs.'

CHAPTER

18

I eyed Tom Clone. He was slumped on the chair across
from me in my office. The cocky energy that I'd
witnessed during the previous week's session as he'd talked
about his ride home from the penitentiary with Kelda
James was absent. He appeared weary, and frustrated. I
suspected that he was going to be one of those patients
who offered the promise of surprise every time he walked
through my office door.

'It's not going as well as I'd hoped. Being out of prison, I
mean. People are more suspicious, less forgiving than I'd
anticipated. I thought people would seem happier for me,
you know? But everybody acts wary, like they're not really
sure I should have gotten out at all. I'm not sure that all the
news coverage my lawyer arranged was that good an idea.'

Although nothing that Tom said particularly surprised
me, I still didn't know what to make of him. That alone
made him interesting to me. I used my silence as bait.

He took it.

'The first few days were real exciting. I did lots of news interviews. But that gets old fast, you know? Talking to those people, answering the same questions over and over and over. It's okay with me that they're gone. Anyway, my lawyer wants me to keep a low profile now while he's making decisions about the lawsuit we're going to file. Hopefully there will be a lot of money coming my way. I want somebody to pay for what they did to my life.'

Since he'd walked through the door I didn't think a minute had passed that he hadn't stolen a look behind him. He did it again right then. I tried to imagine what life was like when the ghost of somebody with a shank was always in your rearview mirror.

'I may take a job working as a pharmacy aide at the Kaiser clinic. You know the one. It doesn't pay much but I can walk there from my grandfather's house. It would give me something to do while my lawyer twiddles his thumbs and I decide about applying to finish med school.

'I think they'd have to take me back into school, don't you think? I mean how could they not? They'd probably make me repeat some coursework; I mean, I would have to catch up on thirteen years of medical progress. There have been lots of developments. AIDS, biotechnology, this whole Internet thing, too. Who would have thought?' He nodded to himself, as though he appreciated the cogency of his own argument.

He looked around my office again as though he was seeing it for the first time. I watched his eyes scan the corners where the walls met the ceilings. 'I thought of doing this years ago, you know that? When I was still at the

172

Health Sciences Center, one of my supervisors suggested I consider therapy, and I really did think about it. But . . .' His voice trailed away.

'But?' I repeated after him. It was my first word of the session. I'd been tempted to query him about the supervisor's rationale for suggesting psychotherapy, but I decided instead to follow Tom's lead. Early on in treatment, the path of least resistance was sometimes the best path to take.

'I didn't want to get into all that shit with someone who worked at the same place I did. It didn't feel safe.'

'What shit was that?' I asked, my voice absent of inflection. I often thought that if psychotherapists had been in the California gold rush, a strike into the mother lode would have been greeted, not with 'Eureka!' but with a carefully modulated version of 'I wonder if this is what we've been looking for.'

'The stuff when I was growing up,' he replied. 'I'm sure you've read all about it. Or at least the public version of it. People like to make a big deal out of shit they really don't understand.'

'No,' I said. 'I haven't read about it.'

I actually hadn't. My tolerance of what the modern media considered 'news' had been diminishing as I aged. O.J. had been the first straw, Chandra Levy one of the last. JonBenét had come somewhere in between. Perhaps the Gulf War and the September 11 travesties had deserved nonstop cable TV coverage. It was hard for me to believe that so many other things did. But I did find it interesting that Tom Clone assumed I was learning about his life through the media.

I said, 'Tell me.'

173

'My mom was bipolar.' Tom put a big, fat period at the end of the sentence. It was his way of exclaiming, 'Enough said.'

When a patient turns the traffic signals in therapy from green to yellow, few therapists can resist the urge to put the pedal to the floor and run the light. I leaned forward on my chair just a little bit as I prepared to gun the engine. The gesture caused me to have to readjust the position of the arm with the cast on it: 'Wow, that must have been something. What was that like for you, Tom? Growing up with a manic-depressive mother?'

I could tell that my questions had disarmed him a little. They didn't shake him; they just surprised him. I don't know what he had expected me to say, but I guessed it was probably some version of 'Really? What was her disease like?' or 'Really? Was she stable on lithium?'

'It wasn't all bad,' is how he replied. 'She and I had some great times when she was "feeling good." That's what she used to call her manic phases when I was little, you know. She'd say, "I'm starting to feel good, Tom," and all of a sudden she'd rush into my room and put both her hands on my face and tell me, "You have two minutes to grab your stuff and get in the car," and before I knew it we were off on a road trip to visit relatives in Illinois or we were going to the Grand Canyon or we were going to Las Vegas. That was one of her favorite places when she was "feeling good." She loved Las Vegas. But when I climbed in the front seat with her, I knew we could be going anywhere.

'I felt like the little kids in *Peter Pan*. I was off on an adventure to a land where my mother loved me.'

*

I moved my arm into my lap, sat back on my chair, and said, 'So when you were little, you liked the eggs?'

He looked at me as though I were nuts. 'What?'

As my partner Diane would say, I had his attention. In explanation, I walked him through the penultimate scene in *Annie Hall*, where Woody Allen's character is explaining to a psychiatrist that when he was growing up he had a brother who thought he was a chicken, but that the family tolerated the pathology because 'We liked the eggs.'

Tom laughed. 'Yeah, when I was little, there were times when I liked the eggs.' He smiled at some memory. 'When Mom was "feeling good" we had a lot of fun. I didn't know she was sick back then. I just knew that this sad, quiet woman would suddenly become the most fun friend I had in the whole world. And I was the one in the center of her universe. Especially on those road trips. We had an old VW station wagon we used to take. I loved those times. I really did. It was so great to be with her – it was like she chose me to be her kid all over again. "You're my best buddy, Tommy – my best buddy in the whole wide world!" she'd scream out the window of the car.' Suddenly, Tom's smile diminished. 'Yeah, I think you could say that I liked the eggs.'

I said, 'But at some point she would crash?'

The natural history of bipolar disease is loosely governed by the rules of gravity. What goes up with mania eventually comes down with depression. Usually the descent from euphoria into despair, like the crash of Newton's apple, leaves someone feeling bruised. Without the cushion of appropriate medication, bipolar phasing isn't a graceful process for the patient or anyone in close proximity to the patient.

'At some point she would crash. When I was older – what, sixth grade maybe? – I could feel the crash coming a day or two or three before it happened. Her batteries would start to wear down, the sound around her would get quieter like the tornado was running out of steam, you know, and the frantic energy would slow, and then finally . . . finally she would start to weep, and she would start to see sadness in everything. She wouldn't talk as much. She'd cry at flowers. At traffic signs. I remember once that a "Yield" sign left her weeping for hours. I thought that was all the sickness was – the sadness and the tears. I never considered that the good times were part of it, too, that everything was all tied up together.

'I thought that when she was "feeling good" she was her true self. But then she'd crash.

'We'd get home somehow – but it was always an adventure. Broken-down cars, out of money, skipping on motel bills, caught shoplifting – you name it, it happened to us on those trips. By the time we got home she'd have lost whatever job she had and she'd disappear into her room. One of her sisters or brothers would show up to take care of her. Sometimes my grandfather would come, but not too often. Usually it was one of my aunts.'

The old house creaked and Tom spun in his chair to track the source of the sound.

'And you?' I asked.

He returned his attention to me. 'I went back to my life. My life as I knew it stopped when she was "feeling good" and it started up again when we got back home. She got worse as I got older. The manic periods weren't that different, maybe they were a little shorter and more intense. But the time before and after – the depression times – those were worse. Those were definitely worse.'

I noted that he had said that the relatives arrived 'to take care of her,' not 'to take care of me.'

'Did it get harder for you, too, as you got older?' I asked.

Tom, I thought, wanted to talk about his mother. I was much more interested in hearing about the little boy who lived with her, but I doubted that was going to happen, at least not that day. I suspected that I was going to lose him soon. He would drift off into some area that was less tender for him than his memories of living with his mother's mental illness, and given that we were only in our second session, I would be inclined to allow whatever drift he required without attempting to reel him back in.

That was my supposition on what was about to happen. But that's not what happened.

Almost as though he was intent on proving me wrong, Tom said, 'She killed herself when I was fourteen.'

Reflexively, I replied, 'I'm sorry.'

Yes, for his loss. But I was also lamenting my assumption that talking about his mother was misdirection, not direction. I prepared to move from probing mode to some stance that would permit this man who had lost so much to explore whatever residual grief remained from his mother's suicide.

But Tom had other ideas. He shrugged and said, 'I was relieved when she died. The craziness of living with her ups and downs was really starting to get to me. When she killed herself, it let me get off the roller coaster. The thing about roller coasters is that they're fun to ride for a while, but it's no fun when you don't have any control about getting on and getting off. Imagine living a life where someone can at any second yank you away from whatever you're doing and plop you into the front seat of the Twister? You know what that's like?'.

He took a quick glance over his left shoulder to check for a shadow with a shank. Then he looked back at me.

My face was impassive.

He said, 'I expected you to ask me how she killed herself. Everybody does. Everybody seems to want to know that.'

'Do you want to tell me?'

He put an I-don't-care expression on his face and started picking at a scab on the back of his left hand. 'She sliced her own throat, if you can believe it. My mother was really crazy. I think you'd have to be really crazy to slice your own throat. Don't you agree?'

I had a question at that point. I asked, 'Were you the one who found her after she killed herself, Tom?' The image of a fourteen-year-old boy discovering his mother's body after she killed herself by cutting her own throat flashed across my consciousness and then vanished in a microsecond, as though someone had quickly changed the channel with a remote control.

He nodded. 'Yeah. What a mess.'

The scab popped off his hand and the wound began to bleed. A full red drop hovered above where the scab had been. He stared at the blood as he might gaze at an insect that had landed on his hand. He told me, 'This is where you should be making the connection between my mother and Ivy Campbell.'

'Pardon me?' I said.

'They both had their throats cut. That's quite a coincidence, or so I'm told. Plenty of people have used it as evidence that my mother's suicide drove me to repeat the act with Ivy. The shrinks who interviewed me before my trial sure thought it was important. What about you? You don't find some psychological diamonds to mine in those facts, Doctor?'

I found the challenge that Tom was making interesting. 'I'm more than a little perplexed. The DNA testing says you didn't have anything to do with Ivy Campbell's murder, Tom. Right? So how could there be a psychological connection between that and your mother's suicide?'

My eyes found the clock that was on a table behind his chair. Our time was almost up.

He smiled at me in a way that made me uncomfortable. 'She was crazy, too. Ivy was. Not like my mom. Ivy had panic attacks. Ever been around somebody while they had a panic attack? It's not a pretty thing.'

I didn't answer his question. Tom had just traversed the ground between telling me that he'd grown up with a mother with a severe mood disorder and telling me that he'd once been romantically drawn to a woman with another serious mental illness, so I encouraged him to keep talking. 'Ivy Campbell had panic attacks?'

'Yeah. Suddenly she'd freak for no reason. She'd actually hide in closets, pull all the clothes around her. She'd yell, she'd cry. She'd think she was dying.'

'Would she want you around to soothe her?' I already suspected that I knew the answer.

'Are you kidding? The way I knew the panic attacks

were coming is that she'd kick me out. She wouldn't want me around.'

'What was she like in between panic episodes?'

'She was terrific. She was exciting. She was a truly passionate girl.' He smiled at some memory. 'Ivy always made me want to dance.'

I pondered my next move for the time it took me to inhale and exhale twice. Then I said, 'You suggested that I might be interested in the parallel between how Ivy died and how your mother died. I find that I'm actually interested in a different parallel. It sounds as though, at least in this instance, you found yourself attracted to a woman with a mental disorder.'

I paused solely for effect. But Tom didn't wait for me to resume.

'Like my momma?' he said. I suspected that he'd been waiting for me to say what I did. He pounced on my reflection and whacked it right back over the net like Andre Agassi slamming a perfect overhand.

'Yes, Tom. Like your mother.'

His eyes lit up. 'Well, that's something, isn't it?'

As I suspected at the beginning of the session, Tom Clone was going to offer me the promise of constant surprise.

19

My best friend was a cop. That was easily as astounding to me as it was to Sam Purdy that his best friend was a shrink.

Although we'd talked on the phone once, Sam hadn't seen me in the days since I'd lost the tussle with my poodle. I wasn't anticipating a whole lot of sympathy from him; it wasn't his nature to fuss over illness and injury. And the fact that a sixteen-pound miniature poodle was responsible for keeping me from driving my dream car for at least six weeks would amuse him no end.

He'd come over to our house after dinner. The rationalization for the visit was that Simon, his son, wanted to see Grace, our daughter. I knew that it was a ruse; the truth was that Sam missed me.

He and I were standing in the open door of the garage. Sam was holding a bottle of Odell's. I kept his favorite local beer in the house just for him.

I was admiring the Mini. Sam wasn't.

'Lauren was right about this? You really wanted one of these?' he asked. He was leaning over way too far, as though he needed to demonstrate that he couldn't see inside the diminutive car without almost getting down on his knees.

'I didn't know that I did but . . . yeah, I guess I really did want one, Sam. Lauren must have read my mind. I think she may be trying to preempt an incipient midlife crisis.'

He grunted.

I took a few moments to explain to Sam about my first car.

He wasn't moved by the story of my adolescent fling with a British import named Sadie. He said, 'Simon has a skateboard with bigger wheels than this thing. Maybe his scooter has bigger wheels, too. Shoot, you know what, I think I have a suitcase with bigger wheels than this thing.'

'You're not an aficionado, I take it?'

Sam laughed. 'My first car was a Pontiac GTO, Alan. Hurst shifter, twin carbs. My current dream car is a Lincoln Town Car or one of those Buick whatever-they're-calleds. The big ones.' He gestured at the Mini. 'If I sneezed inside this thing, I'd blow out the windows.' Sam was a large man. When he was ignoring his diet, which was usually, he outweighed me by most of a hundred pounds.

'Want to know what's ironic?' I said. 'I haven't even driven it. I broke my arm the night Lauren gave it to me. It's been sitting in the garage the whole time.'

'Why am I not surprised?' Sam asked.

Sam carried Emily's retractable leash in one hand and a fresh beer in the other as we walked down the dirt lanes that laced the hillsides adjacent to the house. Emily wasn't attached to the leash; she ran free in the dry grasses, following the scent of the red foxes or some of the other critters that roamed the undeveloped parts of the eastern rim of the Boulder Valley. The night was as dry as the day had been. I'd heard weather reports of thunderstorms full of hail near Pueblo, down south, but a high-pressure ridge that was parked in just the wrong place was still responsible for pushing the main channel of the monsoonal flow into Texas and Oklahoma.

What that meant in the real world was that it wasn't going to rain in Boulder County.

Sam was working on a task force that was trying to reduce the number of assaults that were disrupting the peace on the Hill, the student-dominated neighborhood west of the University of Colorado. Although he wouldn't say he was seeking my professional opinion – hell, when he was in certain moods, he wouldn't even acknowledge that what I did for a living constituted a profession – he was seeking my professional opinion. We talked about young kids away from home and drugs and alcohol and how best to influence the mix. I told him what I thought, but the truth was that the conversation didn't leave me feeling like a wizard.

After we paused to watch the sun make its final descent behind the Divide, we started back up the hill to the house. Sam wanted to corral Lauren and the kids and go out someplace for ice cream. He thought his wife might drive someplace and meet us.

We walked a few more steps and Sam said, 'Simon told me that his friends say I have a unibrow.'

'What on earth are you talking about?'

He leaned toward me and tapped the bridge of his nose. 'See, my eyebrows run together above my nose. Simon says it's called a unibrow. I didn't even know there was a name for it.'

'A unibrow, huh? And that's a bad thing?' I gazed at the shrub of hair that seemed to connect his eyebrows. I'd never noticed it before, but sure enough, there it was.

'I guess. His friends are telling him he's going to have one, too. He's kind of worried about it.'

'Given the rest of the genetic bounty he's getting from you, I think it's a small price to pay.'

He raised half his unibrow. 'That was sarcastic, right?'

'So what did you tell him, Sam?'

'I told him that he'd inherited Sherry's eyebrows, not mine. It seemed to satisfy him for now.'

'I assume he doesn't know about plucking?'

'Nope. He's blissfully ignorant about plucking.'

'Well,' I said, 'I suppose that's one of the good things about being under ten.'

'He asked me if I have a six-pack, too.'

'Like beer?'

'No, like abs. He wanted to know whether I'm, you know, buffed.'

I choked and ended up in a paroxysmal spasm trying to swallow my laughter.

'What did you tell him?'

Sam rubbed one hand over his rounded abdomen. His voice grew slightly defensive. 'I told him what I have is better than a six-pack.'

'Yeah? How's that?'

'I told him I have a whole keg. He seemed impressed.'

'You're quick on your feet, Sam.'

'That I am. That, I am.'

We continued walking. I used the ensuing silence as an excuse to change the subject. 'What do you guys think about having Tom Clone living in Boulder?'

Two steps, then, 'What guys? Are you talking about me and Sherry? Or me and the rest of the cops?'

'You and the rest of the cops. I'm wondering how the police feel about having Tom Clone in town.'

'Why are you asking?' Sam was a detective; he couldn't keep himself from exploring questions like that. His job, like mine, was one that often left residue after hours.

'Just wondering.'

'Yeah, right. You have a broken arm and a brand-new widget of a car that you can't drive, a gorgeous wife and a daughter who's cute as they come, and you're wasting your time wondering about Tom Clone? I'm not stupid. You're involved with him somehow. Don't tell me he's one of your, you know, your—'

'Sam, stop. Stop right there. Would I tell you if he was?'

Emily raced to within ten feet of us before plowing back into the fields. I think she just wanted to make certain that we hadn't been attacked by foxes. Sam shook his head in disdain at my question and said, 'I don't care that Clone is here. I just care that he's not there.'

'"There"? What does that mean?'

'I don't care that he's in Boulder. If he stays out of trouble, he's just another civilian as far as I'm concerned. I'm just not convinced he should have been let out of the penitentiary in the first place.'

'I thought you were a proponent of DNA testing. Even if it means going back after conviction. It's one of your more progressive public-policy positions.'

He glanced over at me to gauge my intent with the little dig I'd just sent his way before replying. 'I am. But leave the DNA out of the case and this guy looks as guilty as they come, Alan. I can't think of a way he didn't kill that girl.'

'So someone else got ahold of the knife after her murder and bled all over it? That's a stretch, Sam.'

He eyed me suspiciously. 'It's possible. Why are you defending him? The cops had eyewitnesses that put him there – that's plural – and they had enough circumstantial evidence to construct a skyscraper. They had motive. It's all there. The guy was just dripping guilt.'

'I'm not defending him, Sam. I'm . . . I don't know what I'm doing. Barry Scheck has a book full of stories about people who were convicted with the same kinds of evidence. They were all wrongly convicted. If it weren't for DNA, they'd either be dead or still on death row.'

'I'm trying to enjoy myself here and you want to talk about Barry Scheck? Why don't I just tell you about the last catheter your friend Adrienne shoved up my . . .'

Thankfully, he let the image of my urologist neighbor, Adrienne, evaporate in the dry air. I was about to change the subject when he continued. 'Well, I can't explain it. I just can't find a single hole in the case that they put together against this guy. Some of Scheck's cases? I've read his book. They were flimsy to start with. There were holes. But not this murder they had Clone for. I only know what I've heard from other cops, but Clone sure looks guilty to me.'

'Didn't the prosecutors rely on a lot of eyewitnesses to make their case against Clone in court?'

'Yeah, they did. So what? Personally, I like eyewitnesses.'

'But you know the data, Sam. Eyewitnesses are terribly unreliable informants about what actually happened.'

'I don't really care about "the data." Want to know why I like eyewitnesses? Because juries like eyewitnesses. And that's good enough for me, because it's how our system works. Those cops nailed Tom Clone, Alan. They played by the rules and it was a good collar.'

'Except for the DNA. And those partial prints that don't match. The DNA says someone else's blood is on the murder weapon.'

'Yeah,' Sam said while he kicked at the dirt. 'Except for that. The DNA is a problem, I admit it. I don't pretend to understand it, but I admit it.'

'And you're still not convinced about his innocence?'

His response was some dismissive sound that involved expelling air rapidly in a single burst from between his lips.

I asked, 'Given what you know about the case, would you have been okay with him being executed?'

He shot a suspicious glance my way. 'You sure you wouldn't rather talk about hockey or even, God forbid, the Rockies? Or how dry it's been this summer? I'll even talk about your funny little car some more if you want.'

'I'll take that as a yes,' I said.

Sam and I saw eye to eye on virtually nothing, politically speaking. We had an unspoken agreement to avoid discussing most public controversies. The pact had served us well over the years.

'Don't make assumptions about me, Alan.'

I tried to spot Emily's dark mass mowing over the prairie grasses on the hill beside us. When I did see her, the appearance was more apparition than anything else. It reminded me of reports of sightings of the Loch Ness Monster. Emily was there – or was she? – and then she was gone.

'Really?' I said to Sam. 'On some things, you're pretty predictable.'

'Stop walking for a second,' Sam said. I did. He looked me in the eyes. 'What I'm about to say goes nowhere, you understand?'

'Sure.'

He pulled a wrapped toothpick from his pocket – I guessed he'd lifted it from the last restaurant he'd visited – poked it through the paper sleeve, and stuck it in the corner of his mouth. Most of the wooden stick vanished under the umbrella of his mustache. 'Fucking McVeigh,' he said, finally. 'God forgive me, but I hate him and I hate what he did.'

I thought of responding. I didn't. I couldn't begin to guess where the 'Fucking McVeigh' segue was taking us, and I didn't want to be responsible for altering the course Sam was plotting.

Sam continued. 'At the end – during the last few months before he was finally executed – once McVeigh finally started talking about his crime, he said he blew up that building in Oklahoma City in order to punish those people he considered responsible for committing the quote-unquote reprehensible murders at Waco and Ruby Ridge. He felt that the responsible parties were the Feds and that the Feds worked in the Murrow Building, so that's why he blew it up.'

'The kids in the day-care center, too?' I asked. 'They were responsible for something?'

He glared at me but when he replied his tone was gently admonishing, not angry. 'Don't get sidetracked there, Alan. Don't. It's an easy detour. But it's a dead end. The truth is that we would have tracked McVeigh down, convicted him, and executed him even if there were no children and no civilians in that building. The fact that he killed kids and innocent civilians gives us an excuse to hate him even more than we do – and I'm as guilty of that as the next guy – but we didn't turn the world upside down to arrest and convict this guy only because of the kids he killed. Take the children out of the equation and he's still a monster. Take the kids out of that building – and God, I wish I could go back and do just that – and McVeigh is still going to lie down on a cold table and take the needle.'

Sam paused long enough to give me a chance to make the mistake of saying something in reply. I didn't.

'When it came time to rationalize his execution, the powers that be said that he needed to die because it was the only appropriate punishment for the quote-unquote reprehensible murders he committed in Oklahoma City.'

Across from me, to the north, Emily suddenly popped up above the grass, twisted 180 degrees in midair, landed, and took off in the opposite direction. Her herding instincts were firing but some creature out there had her snookered. It was great fun to watch.

Sam let his words hang in the dry air for a few

moments. I wondered if they were going to spin and do a one-eighty, too.

'It got me thinking,' he went on, finally. 'We, the people, used the exact same argument to kill McVeigh that he was using to justify killing a building full of federal employees. Is that just some great cosmic irony? Or are we, as a society, teaching the exact kind of retribution that we say is so reprehensible? What gives us the right to decide who lives and dies? We killed McVeigh for making the exact same decision that we as a society want the freedom to make.'

He made an I-don't-get-it face and said, 'Huh? What?' while he kicked again at the dust. 'McVeigh thought that what those federal employees in the Murrow Building did was reprehensible enough that they deserved to die. So he killed them. We thought that what McVeigh did was reprehensible enough that he deserved to die. So we killed him. Right?

'Well, what gives? Are we writing the rules and just don't like the fact that other people have decided to play by them, too? Or are the terrorists and murderers writing the rules and now we've decided to stoop low enough to play at their level? I'm no longer sure, no longer sure at all.'

I found myself entranced by my friend's soliloquy.

He asked, 'How do I teach this distinction to my kid? I can't figure it out. It's like telling Simon it's okay for a teacher to hit a kid but not for a kid to hit another kid. Well, I don't want him to think that. So do I tell him the government knows best? That because the government has said capital punishment is the law and the government is doing the killing, that somehow the Ten Commandments don't apply? I'm a conservative Republican, Alan. There's not a bone in my body that believes that the government always knows best. Not about taxes, not about religion, not about much of anything that comes anywhere close to my home or my family. Certainly not about who should live and who should die.'

He started walking. I whistled for Emily and followed Sam back up the lane. As far as I knew, we were on our way to get ice cream.

He looked at me over his right shoulder and, in a voice that was stunning for its normalcy, he said, 'I know you, Alan. I know where your mind is going. If you're even thinking about mentioning the World Trade Center to me, don't. Our response to the events of that day was self-defense. That was war. War is a different story, and . . . war has a different ending.'

I took a step. He didn't; he'd stopped walking. I wasn't about to say anything about September 11 or the World Trade Center or the Pentagon. What happened that day *was* different. We were painfully learning all the ways that it was different.

In the same everyday voice, he continued. 'Once we put him in jail and dragged him to court and convicted McVeigh, it wasn't war. It was justice. The same thing never happened with bin Laden because from moment one that was war. We can't mix them up, war and justice.'

I knew he wasn't done.

Finally, he said softly, 'I don't think our society could survive that.'

CHAPTER

20

Kelda was on time for her appointment for the first time since I'd started seeing her for psychotherapy.

I started by rescheduling the following week's session from Thursday to Tuesday. Kelda agreed to a late afternoon time. She didn't ask, so I didn't explain that I had to take Grace to the pediatrician for a checkup late in the day on Thursday.

Kelda used a minute or two of the remaining time to ask about my arm and my adjustment to my injury. I deflected her inquiries as well as I could without becoming rude. When it was clear that I wasn't inviting any further attention on my condition, she crossed her legs, ran her teeth over her bottom lip, and said, 'I imagine that you want me to talk about Jones.'

The only neutral response was no response. If I said I did, Jones would become my topic, not Kelda's. If I said I didn't, I ran the risk of dismissing something that might be important to her. I could have been obvious and told Kelda that we would talk about whatever she wanted to talk about. My silence said the same thing.

She uncrossed her legs, untied her hair, and threaded through it with her fingers before she sat back and recrossed her right leg over her left. Then she smiled, laughed out loud, and said, 'Jones was the first person I ever knew who shaped her pubic hair. She said it was an artistic statement.' She shook her head in amusement. 'We'd be out somewhere and she'd pull me aside into a room or just off by ourselves and all of a sudden she'd drop her pants or lift her skirt and point to her crotch and say, "What do you think, Kelda? Is this my best work, or what?"'

I was enamored as Kelda's eyes sparkled. The memory of Jones's shaved pubes lit her like stage lights. Something about her friend was the electricity.

'I don't know why I told you that, but that . . . that was Jones. She was always a step ahead of the world, always . . . out there a little bit. Have you ever been with one of those people whose face seemed to be in a never-ending smile? You know, someone who was like the opposite of the rest of us. Most of us have a normal face, and sometimes we smile, right? Not Jones. Jones's normal face was this big half-moon smile and sometimes she would have to force herself to close her mouth and *not* smile. No matter how you were feeling, you ended up smiling back at her when you were with Jones. If things seemed dark, she always managed to light a different path for you.'

Kelda uncrossed her legs and crossed her arms across her chest, curling her fingers around her biceps. I didn't think I was observing a strategy to cope with physical pain.

She was embracing herself in preparation for something she was about to tell me.

What? I didn't know. So I waited.

'And then she died,' Kelda said. 'And then Jones went and died. I don't think I've been the same since.'

'We lost touch a little bit when I went to Australia. I think she was kind of hurt that I would just pack up and leave Denver. Leave her. I thought she was being silly about the whole thing. For me, Australia was a lark, a chance to go exploring and see a piece of the world. Because of her fears, Jones couldn't do that, just pick someplace and go. But it wasn't like we were fighting or anything. We exchanged a couple of letters during the first few weeks, and I called her once and woke her up because I misjudged the time difference. I didn't think much about her and me while I was there. I always thought that when I got back to Denver we'd be the same great friends we'd always been.'

Kelda grew silent.

I said, 'And then she went and died.'

She sighed. 'I didn't even know she was dead until I got home. After I'd been in Australia for a few months she sent me a letter, more of a change of address really, just a note letting me know that she was moving to Hawaii, to Maui, to be part of some co-op gallery. She had an opportunity to do art full-time. I was surprised – shocked is more like it – I didn't think that Jones could make that big a change in her life. But I thought, great, that I'd stop and see her on my way back to the States when I was done with my work in Sydney. I sent her a postcard or something telling her to watch for me one day soon on her doorstep, and I waited to hear back from her. But I never did hear back from her, and I didn't stop in Hawaii.

'I tried to reach her once more before I came home, but the letter was returned to me. When I finally got back to Denver, I called her parents in New Hampshire to try to find out where I could find her. That's when I learned that she'd died a couple of months before on Maui.'

'What happened?' I asked.

'Do you know Maui?'

'No,' I said. I'd been to Hawaii once years before, but hadn't spent much time on Maui.

'The island is shaped like a peanut, and she was living in the hills outside a little town called Paia that's on the side of the isthmus where the tourists don't tend to stay. Paia's an old cowboy town that's kind of been taken over by aging hippies and young hippies and windsurfers. A lot of artists have congregated there, too. It was a real little town, not a tourist place. She could find real people there; it was the kind of place where Jones could thrive.'

I waited, wondering why the geography lesson had been important.

'Anyway, Jones fell – that's how she died. She went hiking one day by herself near some cliffs above the ocean outside of Paia on the road to Hana. It was low tide and somehow she fell about sixty feet onto some rocks, and she died. She crushed her head on the rocks.'

I was still wondering why the geography lesson had been important. I was about to ask when Kelda continued. 'There's a wonderful old cemetery outside of Paia on this sloping hillside above the Pacific. It's a tiny graveyard, just a little wispy place below some sugarcane fields that's dotted with gravestones and a few crosses. She's buried there.

'The wind blows hard on that part of Maui almost all the time; it's this constant, strong force that comes off the ocean. Not a breeze, but a real wind. A few years after she died – after I came back to Denver from the FBI Academy – I went there, to Hawaii, and I spent a few days in Paia and I visited her grave three or four times. On a clear day you can see the shoreline where she was hiking right from the cemetery.

'I was moved by it all. The cemetery, the cliffs, the ocean, the wind. The wind reminded me of Jones. Its power. Its energy. Since then I've thought about her every time I've felt a breeze wash over my skin. It's like a sign that she's visiting me, looking over me.'

'You went to Hawaii to say good-bye?' I almost immediately regretted the presumptiveness of my words.

'Yes,' she said. 'To say good-bye. To say I'm sorry. And to make sure she was resting in the right place.'

'Is she?'

Kelda nodded. 'Yes, yes, yes.' Her words were a hoarse whisper.

'You said that you went to say that you're sorry?'

'Yes. For losing touch with her, for not being as good a friend as I could have been, for not being with her when she went for that hike.'

'I don't understand that last part, Kelda. You were sorry for not being with her when she went on the hike?'

'You had to know Jones, Alan. If I had been living in Denver when she decided to move, she would have begged me to go to Hawaii with her. And if I'd said no, she wouldn't have gone by herself. Jones had fears. Serious fears, phobia fears. They ruled her life sometimes. She was afraid of heights, of fire, of loud noises. She was always worried about someone breaking into her apartment. Even in Denver, she had more locks on her doors than anybody I knew. She had this weird thing about electrical wiring – she was always checking for electrical shorts and worrying about the wiring in the walls. She used to crawl around and sniff the electrical sockets to see if she could smell fire. And lightning? God, you didn't want to be outside with Jones on a summer afternoon.

'She told me once that if it wasn't for her fears – and the fact that she had one or two freckles too many – she'd be an almost perfect person. I don't think she was speaking from conceit – I know she wasn't – I think she was telling me that at some level her phobias and her fears kept her humble.'

I didn't know which strand of the story to tug. I tried one almost at random. 'But even though she was afraid of flying, she somehow got the nerve to get on a plane to go to Hawaii – a place she'd never been – by herself?'

'Yes, she did.'

'Did that surprise you?'

'The whole thing surprised me. Jones wasn't an independent person. Sometimes I thought that her demeanor was so magnetic because she constantly needed to attract new people to be around her. People got fed up with her fears, and they got fed up fast. She wouldn't do *this* because of that fear. She wouldn't do *that* because of this fear. It was always something with Jones. Her friendships started quickly and they ended quickly. She burned through friends and she really burned through boyfriends.' She shook her head. 'Packing up and moving someplace where she didn't know anyone? That wasn't Jones. It just wasn't. Her fears were like anchors. They kept her from moving, they kept her from going anywhere.

'And she definitely wouldn't have made the move if I was in Denver instead of Australia. I would have talked her out of it.'

'You would have talked her out of it?'

'Yes. That's sounds funny, doesn't it? I wouldn't convince her not to go. That's not what I mean. I'd simply point out alternatives, and help her see what she'd have to confront if she did go. That's all.'

'In terms of her fears?'

'Yes.'

I asked, 'You mentioned something about regretting not being with Jones when she went hiking. What's that about?'

'Jones didn't tolerate her fears passively. She was constantly confronting them, you know, like inching up to things that terrified her. She thought if she desensitized herself that maybe the fears would go away. She'd light candles in her room and try to read by candlelight. The whole time she'd be sure her hair was on fire. She'd use an extension cord when she didn't have to, and every thirty seconds she'd feel it to see how hot it was.

'And my role? She'd count on me to tell her when she'd gone too far. Where things she was afraid of were concerned, she didn't have a sense of what was reasonable for her to do.'

'Like walking too close to a cliff?'

'Exactly. Like getting too close to a cliff. I would have been the one who would have said, 'People who aren't afraid of heights wouldn't get any closer than this, Jones. It's not safe – this is as close as you need to get to the edge.' She wouldn't have a natural sense of that. She would think that she needed to get right to the edge and curl her toes over the rocks – that that was the only way to confront her fear, that that's what other people would do. Normal people.

'I have an image in my head of the last few seconds of her life. Of her approaching that cliff edge and that big strong wind blowing off the Pacific into her face. What I think Jones would have been doing is she would have been leaning into the wind. She would have had her arms out like the wings of a bird, letting the wind hold her up as she tried to look down over the rocks and the water. Her heart would have been pounding and the fear would have almost paralyzed her but she would have forced herself to do it, to get all the way to the edge. The picture in my head is that the wind . . .' Kelda exhaled in a little burst. 'What happened is that the wind paused, just for a second, the way it does sometimes, and in that instant it stopped holding her up and she lost her balance and she toppled over and she fell.'

I asked, 'But if you had been there, you would have warned her that she was close enough, and she would have backed off from the edge of the cliff? That's what you think?'

'I should have been the one to tell her she was too close to the edge or that the wind wouldn't really hold her up. It was one of the things that I did. It was my job as her friend.'

'And you think it would have made a difference?'

She didn't answer.

'Do you think it's reasonable for you to feel responsible for her falling off that cliff?'

'Reasonable? God, no. But you wanted to talk about my pain, right? Well, the pain in my legs started right around the time that Jones moved to Maui. Maybe even the exact same week that she moved to Maui. I didn't even know that she'd moved, of course, but . . .'

'Are you suggesting a relationship between Jones's decision and the onset of your pain?'

Kelda's voice turned slightly mocking. 'Are you going to allow me to get away without taking a look at that possibility, Doctor?'

I smiled.

Kelda said, 'Are you wondering if she got help for her anxieties? Professional help?'

I nodded, although what I had actually been considering was the likelihood that Kelda really didn't understand the magnitude of her friend's anxiety. Kelda was describing a level of fearfulness that left me wondering about a significant underlying paranoia, and not just a strange pattern of multiple phobias. If Jones had been my patient, I would have tuned my antennae to the frequencies that were most sensitive to a complex presentation of post-traumatic stress disorder.

'Your friend had some serious problems,' I said.

Kelda's eyes were unblinking as she responded, 'The fears were definitely a problem.'

'Not just the fears, Kelda. The way she reacted to you going to Australia. I suspect that other things might have been going on with Jones, too. Was she ever worried about things that weren't inherently dangerous?'

'What do you mean?'

'The things you describe – her fears of fire, electricity, lightning, airplanes – are all exaggerated responses to everyday things that have the potential to be dangerous but usually aren't. I'm wondering whether she was ever fearful of things that aren't usually considered potentially dangerous.'

'You're talking about paranoia? People after her? Like that?'

'Sure,' I said, grateful that Kelda had made the last hop on her own.

'Sometimes she would worry that people didn't understand her. That they were . . . trying to undermine her. There were some people she didn't trust, wouldn't want to be around. Like that.'

I waited. *Go on*, I thought, *go on*.

'But that wasn't often. Mostly, it was the fears that we dealt with. Just the fears,' she insisted.

'Phobias don't usually come in bunches like hers did. It's an atypical presentation.'

'Funny. That's what my neurologist says about my pain. It's atypical. I don't care. It's still real.'

I debated proceeding with my psychopathology lesson. Before I was even aware I'd reached a decision, I said, 'Even if the phobias were all that Jones was dealing with, there are some medications that might have helped her, and there are a few therapeutic approaches – desensitization and even traditional psychotherapy, for example – that work for a lot of people. But yes, to get back to your original question, I was thinking that maybe she didn't have to suffer so much. That someone could have eased her pain.'

'She sought help. She went to see different therapists at least twice while I knew her. In my opinion, she saw a couple of flakes, unfortunately. One guy she saw hit on her during their second session – asked her to go skiing with him for a weekend at his condo in Winter Park. And a woman therapist she went to see took her fire walking with a bunch of her friends out on some ranch near Parker.'

I would have liked to say I was surprised. I wasn't. Anybody with an inclination could hang out a shingle as a psychotherapist in Colorado. Most consumers didn't seem to understand the distinction between a licensed and an unlicensed therapist, between a psychologist and a psychiatrist and a clinical social worker, between a competent professional and an unskilled quack. My impulse with Kelda was to apologize for the behavior of people I sometimes abhorred having to consider colleagues. Instead, I said, 'Fire walking?'

Kelda said, 'Yes. Fire walking. She aced it. It turned out Jones didn't have any phobias about prancing down a bed of hot coals.'

CHAPTER

21

Kelda called Rosa Alija *'hermanita'* – little sister. The girl, a shy child, called Kelda *'hermana.'*

Since Kelda had rescued Rosa, the two had never gone more than eight weeks without visiting, and they talked frequently by phone in between encounters. Kelda could rely on receiving an e-mail message from the girl at least a couple of times a week.

Rosa enjoyed all the visits. Kelda had taken the girl to Broncos and Rockies games, to the ballet, had even endured a trip to the Pepsi Center to see some boy band. But the visits that Rosa seemed to enjoy most were the weekend afternoons at Kelda's little piece of property in Lafayette. Rosa's mother or father would drop her by sometime during the late morning on a Saturday or after church on Sunday, always bringing something special along for Kelda. José would pull a shrub from the back of his pickup to plant in the long bed near the highway, or he'd spend twenty minutes lining the walkway with a tantalizing border of annuals, or he'd dig a hole for a sapling that would someday grow to replace one of the aging elms on the property.

When it was Maria who drove Rosa to Lafayette, she would offer a covered dish full of *tamales* or, Kelda's favorite, a basket of homemade *churros*. Once she took over Kelda's kitchen to make a huge platter of *chilaquiles*, which she said was her daughter's favorite meal.

Kelda ate more than Rosa did.

Rosa would spend the long afternoons in Lafayette exploring the fallow fields and repeatedly acting out some homesteading fantasy that Kelda never really understood. The girl was a natural athlete who was fearless in the trees. She would climb to limbs high in the elms. The dangerous heights made Kelda crazy. Rosa could spend hours on the swing that Kelda had hung from the big branch on the elm that was closest to the lane. The swing faced the mountains, and Rosa would swing higher and higher, kicking hard at the top of the arc as though she was certain she could reach out and tickle the glaciers on the northern slopes of Mount Evans.

Rosa was on the swing and Kelda was watching her from the kitchen window when Kelda spotted the microwave truck lumbering down the street near her home. Involuntarily the muscles in her jaw tightened. The familiar logo on the side of the rig identified it as being from Denver's Fox News affiliate.

A few summers before, all of Denver's television stations had done anniversary pieces on Kelda's rescue of Rosa.

Two of the stations had sent crews to Lafayette during one of Rosa's visits to Kelda's home and had ultimately agreed to Kelda's restriction that they film the little girl only from the rear. Kelda, after consultation with the Denver SAC and with the Alijas, had agreed in return to brief interviews. But she set firm ground rules: She would answer questions about her current relationship with Rosa, but wouldn't discuss anything about the rescue.

She would say nothing about the shooting.

Nothing.

What she would talk about on camera was the man who had kidnapped Rosa. After years of delving into his background on her own time, Kelda knew more about the kidnapper than Boswell knew about Johnson. 'Why is it so important to know him so well?' the reporters would ask her.

'Because it is,' she would reply. 'We have to know our enemy.'

Each summer since, Kelda had been forced to deal with at least one TV station eager to reminisce about the dramatic rescue as the anniversary date approached. The truck on 111th Street meant to Kelda that this summer would be no different than the others.

'*Hermanita*,' Kelda called from the side door of her house. 'Inside for a few minutes, please.'

'Why?'

Kelda nodded at the microwave truck and the little girl immediately understood what was happening. Kelda said, 'Don't worry, I'll go talk to them. I just made fresh lemonade. It's in the fridge. You help yourself, okay?'

'Can I pick some fresh mint to put in it first?'

Rosa was already running to the thick patch of mint on the south side of the house. 'You bet,' Kelda yelled after her.

It took Kelda almost ten minutes to negotiate to a stalemate with the reporter who got out of the truck. The reporter ultimately used her cell phone to reach her producer, who asked to speak with Kelda.

Kelda took the phone and walked away from the reporter before she said anything to the producer. Once she was fifty feet or so down the lane, she said, 'We're okay, right? No changes from what we agreed?'

The producer was a young man whom Kelda had dealt with twice before on Rosa Alija stories. He wore his ambition on his sleeve and because he was so brash about it Kelda found that she trusted him as much as she trusted anybody in the media.

He said, 'We're okay on this, Kelda. Just tape, no audio. We'll only show the kid from behind. But . . .'

He let the word hang between them. 'But what?' she asked.

'But . . . I'm running down a story that you might have had something to do with Clone's release from death row. Is that true? Were you really the one who found the knife that got him sprung from the pen?'

'Rafe, you know I can't comment on reports like that. Rosa Alija is human interest. Tom Clone is law enforcement business. If you have questions about that old case, take them up with Park County or with the FBI information officer.'

'So the FBI is involved?'

'Uh-uh. I'm not going there with you.'

'I'm doing you a favor here, with this shoot. I want you to remember me if this Tom Clone thing breaks open. Is that a deal?'

She said, 'I know you're doing me a favor.'

'Is that a deal?' he pressed.

'I said I know you're doing me a favor.' She started retracing her steps back down the lane.

The producer said, 'I'm going to take that as a yes.'

'No comment. Hold on. I want to say all this out loud in front of your talent.' Kelda approached the reporter, a pretty woman whose skirt was too short for a Sunday afternoon in Lafayette. Almost too short for a Sunday afternoon in Denver. Kelda held the cell phone out between them.

'Your producer and I have reached an understanding. Here it is: You can tape me outside the house, and you can tape Rosa from behind, but no audio and no interview. Not with me. Not with Rosa. No interview. And no copy and no shots that would identify the location of my house.'

The reporter took the phone from Kelda. She had trouble finding a comfortable way to get it close to her ear over her big earring. Finally, she said, 'That's the deal, Rafe?'

She listened for a moment to her producer, then folded up the cell phone and reluctantly gave instructions to the woman who was handling the camera. When Kelda asked, the reporter said that the piece should be ready to air by the following night at nine.

The news truck pulled away from her house about forty-five minutes later. Kelda sat on a lawn chair and watched the dust settle in the lane. Rosa crawled onto her lap and pressed her face into Kelda's breast. '*Hermana?*' she said.

'Yes.'

'You killed him? The bad man? My father said you killed him.'

In all the years that had passed, Rosa had never asked about that day. Kelda hoped she would have forgotten.

She hoped for peace in the Middle East, too.

'Yes, *hermanita*, I did. You don't have to worry about him ever again. I killed him.'

The little girl pressed harder against her chest. 'I'm glad he's dead, *hermana*.'

Kelda said, 'I'm glad, too.'

The fentanyl patches were designed to provide relief for Kelda's pain for seventy-two hours. After she'd kissed Rosa good-bye and tucked her into José's truck and yanked on her seat belt at least a couple of times, she walked inside and checked the calendar by the phone and read the notation she'd penciled in the previous Thursday at bedtime. It read 'F – 11:30pm.' The clock on the microwave told her it was only 3:31. That meant that the patch she'd put on Thursday night had been on her skin for only sixty-four hours. Yet she could already feel it failing. A fresh patch, even if she put it on right then, wouldn't provide relief until almost morning.

She popped a Percocet and washed it down with the rest of the lemonade from the refrigerator. There was enough mint floating in the pitcher to flavor the contents of a bathtub. Rosa's excess made her smile.

Kelda left a message on Ira's voicemail, suggesting he

stop and pick up some Thai takeout for dinner before he came over. She set up her bath towels and her frozen peas, and spread out on the bed to take a nap.

When the rumble of thunder woke her, she glanced at the clock by the bed; it was a little after four-thirty. The light that was filtering into her room was grayer than usual. She listened for the melody of raindrops on the roof but wasn't sure if she heard a faint pattering or not. *Had the monsoons finally arrived?* Hopeful, she eased herself from the bed and walked to the western window. Between the trees, she could see a curtain of virga silhouetted against the sky between Lafayette and Boulder. But virga was to weather watchers what fool's gold was to a miner: Kelda could tell at a glance that the mirage of moisture would all evaporate before it reached the soil of Boulder County.

She picked up the phone and tried Ira again. When he didn't answer, she hung up without leaving another message and collected the bags of peas from the bed to return them to the freezer.

She was still craving *pad Thai*.

She took another Percocet instead.

Twenty minutes later she reached for the phone to try Ira one more time. But the phone rang before she got the receiver out of the cradle.

'Hello,' she said.

The line was silent. With her free hand she depressed the button on the phone that would kill the call, and then hit *69. Once again, the phone company failed to identify the location of the caller. She noted the date and time of the call in the log she kept beside the phone.

After saying 'What the hell,' she picked up the local phone book and checked for a number. Finding it, she dialed. After two rings, a man answered. She thought she recognized his voice. 'Have dinner with me,' she said.

'Is this Kelda?'

'How many women do you have calling you out of the blue asking you out for dinner?'

'Not enough.'

'How many would be enough?'

Tom Clone said, 'If you're the woman doing the calling, one is enough. The answer is absolutely, you bet – yes! But I can't come to wherever you are; I don't have a car, Kelda.'

'I'll come by and get you. We'll walk over to the Mall or something. I'll be there around six-thirty.'

Days in Boulder are a little more compressed than they are in the nearby towns on the eastern plains of Colorado. Boulder's elevation above sea level is a tad more than a mile, while the nearby sun-shielding peaks of the highest reaches of the Continental Divide rise to over fourteen thousand feet. The difference in altitude between Boulder and the highest mountaintops, which are less than twenty miles away, is a fraction under two miles. As the summer sun sets in clear skies behind that two-mile-high wall of mountains, it casts quite a shadow. That's why day disappears early in Boulder and night seems to be in a hurry to impose its presence.

But on hot summer days spent waiting for the monsoons, the early nightfall and cooling shadows are a blessing to almost everyone. Even if the dry air holds no prayer of rain, as the evening sky above the Front Range glows in grays and pastels, in the high desert of Colorado there is always the promise of an overnight chill.

It was a few minutes before seven when Tom and Kelda walked down the hill from Tom's grandfather's house on High Street toward the nightlife of the Downtown Boulder Mall.

Boulder's Downtown Mall is a mall in the manner Americans thought of malls before the last quarter of the twentieth century. The Downtown Mall is a brick-paved, tree-lined promenade that traverses four blocks of lovely public spaces, with shops and restaurants in century-old buildings. Motor vehicles are prohibited — along with bicycles, dogs, skateboards, scooters, in-line skates, and anything else that the City Council's current whims determine are impediments to public enjoyment. On a warm evening in early summer the Mall and its adjacent streets are packed with people. The sounds of street musicians or buskers and their audiences overlap on the short blocks, and the outdoor seats at the Mall's cafés and restaurants are temporarily the hottest real estate in town.

Tom and Kelda scored a table at Mateo, a Mediterranean restaurant just off the east end of the Mall. She never told him that she was craving *pad Thai*.

As they sat down she said, 'Don't worry. I'm paying.'

He said, 'Thank you, I'm not working yet. But I got a job. I start Tuesday.' He told her about the job in the Kaiser pharmacy.

'That sounds good, Tom. Congratulations. It's hard for me to tell, though — are you pleased with it?'

He was studying the menu. 'I'm still having trouble getting used to the prices of everything,' he said. 'Hey, I have a question for you.'

'Yes?' She was wondering why he'd ignored her question.

'Is this a date, Kelda?'

She let his words hang in the air. 'I'll let you know when I take you back home, Tom. How's that?' She offered him a smile.

'I'll take that. You know, when you smile at me, I can feel it all the way into my bones.' He smiled back at her.

She looked away.

'But why?' he asked.

'Why what?'

'Why me? You could have any guy you wanted, Kelda. Why are you sitting here with me tonight? Some guy who just got out of prison?'

'I don't know. And I don't think what you said is true. I'll turn it around on you – why did you say yes when I asked?'

'That's easy. Because you're gorgeous. Because you've been wonderful to me.' He sighed and leaned back in his chair. 'And because you're hot.'

'Hot?' She exaggerated the query in her inflection as she tried not to choke on the word.

'What? Are you playing with me? Have you looked in a mirror lately? You're as hot as they come.'

She blushed. 'I think maybe you've been in prison too long.'

'Kelda, I've definitely been in prison too long. One day was too long. But you . . . you . . . you make me want to dance.'

A chill traveled the length of her spine and she felt goose bumps cause the tiny hairs on her arms to become erect. She smiled again. 'I've never heard that before,' she said. 'No one has ever told me that.'

'Well, then, they're crazy. As great as it is to be out of prison, the most alive I've felt since I got out has been the little bit of time I've spent with you.'

'You're sweet, Tom. But I think you probably just have a thing for women who are constantly drawing their handguns.'

He looked around. She wondered if her response had made him nervous.

'Have you seen our waitress?' he asked.

'This is Boulder. She's probably still at home getting dressed for work. Or is still up in the canyon stowing her climbing gear into her SUV. Don't worry, someone will come by before we starve.' She leaned forward and lowered her voice. 'And nobody really says "waitress" much anymore. It's "waiter" or "server," regardless of gender.'

'I'm sorry,' he said, frowning. 'I bet that I make a lot of mistakes like that. The last few days I've felt like Rip van Winkle. People use words I've never heard, talk about things I don't know anything about. And TV? My God, what's on—'

'Where's your anger?' she asked abruptly.

He tucked his chin. 'What do you mean?'

'You've lost a lot of years, Tom. They're just gone. You'll never get them back. Where's your anger? You just seem like this mild-mannered guy, not like someone who's just been let out of prison for a murder that he didn't commit.'

He shrugged. 'What can I do? I'll try to get even in court.

Tony Loving's optimistic. But whatever happens, I'll try to live my life well. As they say, that'll be the best revenge.'

Again she tried not to react visibly to his words. She said, 'I read the trial record, you know. You didn't even say anything when the verdict was read against you.'

'What good would it have done?'

'You're always that rational?'

'I have a high boiling point. People used to tell me they thought I'd be great in the ER because I stay calm under pressure.'

'You can put up with a lot?'

'In most circumstances, yes. It's served me well, I think. Impulsiveness doesn't go over well when you're inside.' He checked behind him. Kelda thought he was looking for the waiter again.

She asked, 'What does it take to get you angry?'

'I don't know. It happens. I certainly got angry a few times when I was in the penitentiary.'

'You want to tell me?'

He thought about it for a moment before he said, 'No.'

'What about fear? What frightens you?'

'That's easy. Going back to prison. Being locked up. What about you?'

'What do you mean?'

'You. Anger. On our ride home. Did you really mean what you said to Prehost that day?'

'He was pushing me around. I told you I don't like to be intimidated. So I pushed back. That's who I am.'

'Did you mean what you said to him, though? About shooting someone? Did you really do that?'

Before she could figure out how to respond, Tom went

on. 'You told him that you knew you wouldn't miss from that distance. He asked you how many times you'd fired from that distance. You said you'd done it before. Is that true? Have you?'

'Yes, I have.' She touched the daisy that was in a small white vase on the table, wondering if it was real. It was. 'When you were . . . in the penitentiary, did you ever hear about a little girl named Rosa Alija?'

He shook his head. 'For some reason I had constant trouble with the delivery of the newspaper. I complained and complained, but it was never on the porch where it was supposed to be.'

She smiled.

'Who was she? The girl?' Tom asked.

Without looking at him once, Kelda told him about being a rookie FBI agent and accidentally finding a little kidnapped girl in an industrial building in Denver's Golden Triangle and about rolling along a dirty floor and coming up firing and clustering three slugs in the center of a child molester's chest while he was trying to blow her to shreds with a gigantic .45.

'Wow. You weren't kidding.'

'No, I wasn't kidding.'

'What's an UNSUB?' he asked.

'It stands for "unknown subject." It's FBI lingo for a suspect.'

'And you shot him?'

'I did.'

'You killed him?'

'Unfortunately.'

'Why unfortunately? It sounds like he deserved it.'

She flattened her palms on the table. 'Because he deserved worse. He was dead in seconds. That's why it was unfortunate.'

'Gotcha,' he said.

She thought his eyes said something else entirely. She said, 'Can we change the subject?'

He reached across the table and with the tips of his fingers he touched her hand. 'Okay, how about this? Back last fall, how come you were so sure that the knife you found was really the one used to kill Ivy Campbell?'

She had trouble keeping her surprise from showing. 'What?'

'When the guy called you that day with directions on how to find the knife, why were you sure it was really the one? After all those years, why would somebody suddenly call the FBI about the murder weapon in a case that was all settled?'

She stammered, 'I wasn't sure. I wasn't sure about anything until the laboratory results came back.'

He closed his hand over hers and lowered his voice. Given his sultry tone, the words he spoke seemed bizarre. 'Until that moment – until the lab results came back – did you think I did it? That I killed Ivy?'

'Yes, Tom. I did. There was a lot of evidence that said you did. And I didn't know you then.'

He sat back a little, but kept his hand on hers. 'Thanks. For being honest about that.'

'You're welcome.'

She watched him take a few deeper breaths before he asked, 'Are you a hundred percent sure right now – right this minute – that I didn't do it? That I didn't kill her?'

'If this is a first date, Tom, I swear it's the strangest conversation I've ever had on one.'

'Please. I need to know. It's important that I know that at least one person believes that I'm innocent.'

'What about your grandfather?'

'He'd like to believe it. Maybe he'll get there. Maybe he won't. He loves me. Right now that's all I can ask of him, I think. Please answer me.'

He surprised her with his insight. She said, 'The answer to your question is yes, Tom, I'm a hundred percent sure you didn't kill Ivy Campbell. Is there anything else?'

'Yes, there is.' He raised an eyebrow. 'Is this ... a first date?'

She held her breath and nodded once.

His face broke into a wide grin. 'Well, hallelujah. Since this is a first date, you said you were going to tell me how you came to be named Kelda.'

She looked down at his hand touching hers. 'Okay,' she said. 'Have you ever heard of the Book of Kells?'

'Something else I missed when I was inside? Like you saving that kid?'

'No, hardly. It's an old book, an old Irish book. It's a beautiful hand-drawn manuscript of the four gospels that was written around 800 AD. The book is in Ireland, in the library at Trinity College in Dublin. My grandparents are from there and my grandfather was an amateur scholar who was always interested in the manuscript. The name was their idea. Kelda — it's in honor of the Book of Kells.'

'That's certainly more interesting than "Tom."'

She closed her eyes and imagined jumping off a cliff. At

the same moment, she turned her hand over so that her fingertips touched his.

'I guess,' she said.

'A hundred percent sure?'

'Yes.'

'Good.'

'And I make you want to dance?'

'Yeah, and I'm not talking a waltz, either.'

CHAPTER

23

Sam Purdy called my home a few minutes after nine. I knew immediately that he was on his cell phone and that he was attempting the call from one of the canyons of crappy reception that dot Boulder.

'Hey, Alan,' he said after I answered. 'It's Sam.'

Sam was from northern Minnesota, a little town in the Iron Range called Hibbing. His accent had emigrated to Colorado along with him. Anytime he called, once I'd heard his voice on the phone, I had no need for further identification. 'I know who it is,' I said. 'How are you doing?'

'I'm working.' He said something else but all I heard was some crackling and the word 'goofy.'

'You're breaking up.'

'What?'

'You're breaking up.'

In a few seconds he said, 'Is that better?'

'Yeah, a little bit. I didn't hear a thing you said before other than the word "goofy."'

'I'm with Lucy. We're finishing up working a home intrusion and assault in an old house on High Street. You know High Street? It's a little bit east of Casey Park. Nice street. I don't think I've ever answered a call up here before. Anyway, an old man was beat up. It's ugly.'

Lucy was Sam's partner. I wasn't sure what to say about the news of the home intrusion and assault. I tried, 'I'm sorry.'

'I'm not asking for your sympathy. I'm calling to tell you that the victim is the grandfather of Tom Clone. I thought that, given the interest you showed when I was at your house the other night, you might be curious about it. Turns out that Clone is living here with his grandfather, but something tells me you already knew that.'

'Huh,' I muttered.

'What?'

'Nothing. What's goofy about it?'

'Goofy? What? I don't even remember what I was saying before. You have any thoughts that might make my evening any shorter? I'd like to get home before Simon graduates from high school.'

Simon was, maybe, in the third grade. 'You mean . . . thoughts about the assault?'

'Yes, I mean about the assault.' Sam's patience, never exemplary, was fading with the cell signal.

'No, Sam. I don't know a thing that would help you. Why would I? Are you suspecting Tom Clone?'

'Now, why would you think that?'

'Don't be cute. You guys always suspect the family in domestic assaults. How is the grandfather?'

'He's unconscious. They took him by ambulance to Community. Tom Clone called this in himself, by the way. Believe it or not, he says that an FBI agent – a woman – was with him when he got here.'

'Really?'

'Yeah, she's his alibi. He says they were on a date or something. Clone and this Fed. Go figure. Guy gets a free pass off death row and a week later he's dating a Fed.'

'Really?'

'That's what he says. Haven't talked to her yet – he says she drove away before he went inside and found his grandfather – but I'll track her down.' He paused as though he was expecting me to say something. When I didn't, he said, 'Listen, you've been terribly helpful and all, but I think maybe I should get back to work.'

Trying hard not to sound sarcastic in reply, I said, 'Thanks for calling, Sam. I appreciate the heads-up. I do.'

'Whatever. Tell Lauren I said not to get mixed up in this one. I'm already dodging microphones and cameras, and the media leeches don't even know who the victim is yet. Once they know it was Clone's grandfather, this one's going to be a real circus. But . . .' He paused. 'Hey, since circuses are now illegal in Boulder, I'll have to think of another metaphor, won't I?'

Sam had been exceedingly amused when the Boulder City Council voted to ban circuses with animals from performing in the city. He told me he'd had a lifelong ambition to collar an elephant sometime in his career and it looked like he was finally going to get his chance.

Lauren was a prosecutor for Boulder County. As far as I knew, she wasn't carrying the beeper to catch cases that night for the district attorney's office, so odds were that she wouldn't end up prosecuting the assault on Tom Clone's grandfather.

That was the only good news I could glean from the events. Still, I told Sam I would pass along his advice.

After I hung up the phone, I checked to see what the local news channels had to say about the crime. The nine o'clock news programs had crews at the scene already, but the reporters didn't know much; in fact, as Sam had said, they weren't yet reporting Tom Clone's involvement in the incident. I clicked off the TV set and ambled into the nursery to kiss Grace's sleeping face.

The phone rang once more a few minutes before eleven. I'd just crawled into bed. Figuring it was Sam again, I answered by saying, simply, 'Yeah.'

After I listened to the greeting on the other end of the line, I replied, 'Hold on. I need to change phones.'

Lauren rolled my way and said, 'What is it?'

'It's a patient. I'll get it in the other room. Go back to sleep.'

'Okay,' she murmured and rolled over the other way.

I picked up the portable in the kitchen and carried it into the living room. The sky was surprisingly black, with few stars, but below me the Boulder Valley was carpeted with twinkling lights. I was wondering how one of my patients had gotten my home phone number. In an emergency, patients were instructed to call a number that activated my beeper. My home phone was unlisted.

'Yes, Tom,' I said after taking a few seconds to capture my composure.

'My grandfather was assaulted tonight. Somebody broke into his house and beat him up.'

As his words registered, the circumstance I found myself in perplexed me. I tried to decide whether I should pretend that I didn't already know about the assault. If I revealed to Tom that I'd received an early heads-up about his grandfather from a police detective, he would be suspicious about why I'd been called and might question whether I'd been indiscreet with Sam about his confidentiality. Impulsively, I chose to try to adopt a middle ground. But I knew my path was paved with banana peels.

'How is he?' I asked.

'Not good. I'm calling you from the hospital. He's in the ICU. They hit the poor guy in the head. There's blood all over the hallway. It looks like he was trying to get down the hall to his room or the bathroom or something when they caught up with him and hit him. He doesn't move very fast.'

'I'm so sorry.'

The sound I was hearing suddenly changed. I thought he might have covered the phone with his cupped palm. 'I think the police think I did it.'

'Go on,' I said.

Tom went into great detail about his interview with Sam Purdy. It did sound as though Sam thought that Tom might have done it. But with Sam you never knew; his whole posture could be a ruse. I'd once been on the receiving end of his interrogation skills. It wasn't a pleasant experience.

'Did you call your lawyer?' I asked.

'Yeah, sure. What? You think I'd call you first? Of course I called my lawyer. As soon as I started getting a weird vibe from that detective, I called him, got one of the other lawyers in his office. She talked to the detective on the phone and asked if I was under arrest. When the detective said no, I got back on the phone and this lawyer told me to shut up. Then she told me to tell the cops to get out of my house and to get a search warrant.'

'Tom, what can I do for you tonight?'

'I don't know. I'm upset. I feel vulnerable, you know. I don't know why someone was in the house. Why they would beat up an old man like that, whether they might have been gunning for me. I'm afraid that the police are looking for an excuse to put me back in jail. I'm vulnerable. I feel like a fish in a barrel.'

'I can only imagine.'

'Maybe I should set up another appointment. Something sooner than the one we have scheduled. I need some advice on how to handle myself so that I don't get in any deeper.'

'A big chunk of that advice will need to come from your lawyer, Tom. The part that has to do with the stress you're feeling – you and I can do that. But first things first: Are you okay tonight?'

'Yeah, I guess. I need to find someplace to stay. The police won't let me back in the house until they're done. I may just sleep here at the hospital. I don't have any money with me.'

Was he suggesting that I offer him a bed? My reaction to the prospect troubled me almost as much as did the image of Tom sleeping downstairs from my daughter. I knew there was no way I would invite this man into my home. Not only because he was a patient, but also because I now reluctantly realized that I wasn't one hundred percent convinced about the events that had landed him in prison in the first place. I got lost for a moment considering the implications of my musings before I said, 'I'm sure that your grandfather would be grateful that you stayed with him at the hospital. It will mean a lot to him to see the face of a loved one by his side when he wakes up.'

Tom said, 'Yeah, I guess.'

I couldn't tell whether or not he was at all convinced. I said, 'I'm curious about something. How did you get my home number, Tom? Although this certainly qualifies as an emergency, as I explained to you during our first session I usually hear from patients on my beeper.'

Without hesitation, he said, 'I called Information. You know, four-one-one. They gave me the number.'

'Oh,' I replied. 'So you want to set up that extra appointment?'

A moment later, as I hung up the phone, I entertained the possibility that it was Kelda who had given Tom my home number. I had no illusions that phone numbers that were unlisted to the rest of us were actually unavailable to curious FBI agents. I also considered the possibility that Sam Purdy had scribbled the number on the back of one of his business cards and given it to Tom.

When he was in certain moods, Sam would have thought that such a prank was pretty funny.

What I wasn't entertaining was the possibility that

Tom Clone had told me the truth about calling directory assistance.

There was a time early in my career when I might have marched straight to my closet, changed my clothes, and driven across town to Community Hospital to check personally on Tom Clone's emotional state. Most of the motivation for making such a humanitarian trip would have been the result of a grandiose sense of the psychotherapist's purview – early in my career I actually functioned under the mistaken belief that part of my job was to provide comfort in its purest form.

But two minutes after I'd hung up the phone, I wasn't pulling on a pair of jeans and preparing to drive across town. No, I was back in my bed, focusing more of my mental energy on the violation I felt at having my home phone number compromised than I was directing it toward compassion for Tom Clone's personal tragedy, or toward curiosity at the revelation that Tom Clone and Kelda James were developing a social relationship.

I didn't want to admit it to myself, but I was beginning to regret picking up Tom Clone's case at all. Why?

I was no longer at all certain that he was the victim of the justice system that I originally thought he was. At first, I'd been willing, even eager, to offer him the benefit of the doubt.

Now, no.

But that wasn't all. An honest appraisal would reveal that I was ambivalent about Tom Clone because he was tugging at me in ways that threatened my complacency. He needed me in ways that I didn't want to be needed.

What had Diane said to me? *If you've started hating the bricks, maybe it's time to reconsider being a bricklayer.*

Maybe it is time, I thought. Maybe it is.

I fell asleep pondering the reality that, other than my therapeutic abilities, I possessed absolutely no marketable skills.

CHAPTER

24

After they finished their dinner on the Mall, Kelda and Tom had walked down Pearl Street and Tom had tried to recall what buildings had been demolished and identify what buildings were new in all the redevelopment that had taken place during the nineties in the blocks adjacent to the east end of the Mall. She thought it was an interesting exercise for someone trying to make sense of what had happened in the world during all his missing years. They had coffee at Penny Lane because it was one of the few businesses that Tom remembered from the years before he'd been arrested and incarcerated.

While he stood at the counter picking up their drinks, Kelda turned her back to him and popped another Percocet into her mouth.

A little bit after nine, at Kelda's suggestion, they strolled back up the hill to High Street. She stopped when they reached her Buick, which was parked on the street, one door down from Tom's grandfather's house.

He asked her, 'Have you been limping?'

'Maybe,' she said. 'I worked out hard this morning. My muscles get a little sore sometimes.'

'That's it? You're sure? You got quiet, too, when you started to limp. After we had coffee and started walking, you got quiet.'

She opened her purse and reached inside for her car keys. She was surprised that he'd noticed the connection between her pain and her distraction. She liked to think she made it invisible to others, especially to people who didn't know her well. She replied, 'I think you're imagining that, Tom. It's no big deal. My leg gets a little sore sometimes. That's all.'

He shook his head. 'I don't think that's all that's going on. Whatever, why don't you come on inside? Maybe my grandfather will be awake. He really wants to meet you.'

'No, thank you, I don't think so. I'm going to head home. Maybe some other time.'

He asked, 'Why not?' and the resentful undertow in his tone caused her to step back involuntarily.

'What do you mean, "Why not?"' She tried to force some playfulness into her voice. 'I don't need a reason. I just don't feel like going inside with you. I'm tired, and I want to get home.'

'I thought we were having a good time.'

'We were.' She stressed the second word.

'Is it whatever's going on with your limp? Is that it?'

'Tom, I said no. I don't know what things were like for you when you went to prison, but in the twenty-first century when women say no – especially this woman – you would be wise to heed them.'

'Because you have a gun?'

She couldn't tell if he was joking, but hoped he was. 'I had a nice time, Tom. Good night.' She pressed the button on her key ring that unlocked her car door. She had to wait for him to step back before she had room to swing the door open. Her impression was that he forced her to wait an additional second or two. When he finally moved away, she lowered herself into the car.

Her breathing was rapid. His wasn't. She lowered the window and placed her left hand on the ledge of the door. 'This was fun,' she said, hoping to defuse the tension she was feeling.

'Yeah,' he replied, and leaned down so that his face was opposite hers.

Don't, she thought. *Don't try it.*

He lowered his head and brushed her fingers lightly with his lips. His touch was like an electric shock. She repressed a flinch. 'See you,' he said, looking at her dashboard. 'Hey, what time do you have?'

She glanced at the clock. 'It's nine-twenty.'

'Thanks. Good night,' he said. 'I'll call you. Assuming that's still okay in the twenty-first century?'

'Yeah,' she said. 'That's okay. Good night, Tom.'

She made a U-turn in the cul-de-sac at the end of High Street and headed back toward Fourteenth. Her headlights were illuminating the silhouette of a Chevy Suburban that was parked along the curb on High opposite the grounds of Casey School. A man was sitting in the driver's seat, but she couldn't make out his features. As she turned the corner she decided that the Suburban was an older model and that the paint was dull blue or gray.

'Prehost,' she said aloud. She hit her brakes hard and brought the Buick to a stop. She hadn't planned her next move. One option was to get out of the car and have a chat with the Park County detective, but she quickly decided against it. She wasn't sure what a confrontation would accomplish. Instead, she took a moment to memorize the license plates on the Suburban, then she glided down the hill toward Mapleton.

Four minutes later, as she turned onto Arapahoe to head home, Kelda used her cell phone to call Ira. 'Hey, you,' she said when Ira answered his phone.

'Hello, girl. I tried to get back to you earlier, but I kept getting your machine. I thought you might not be answering because you were freezing your legs. Hope I didn't wake you.'

'No, I've been out, I had some things I had to do.'

'Is the pain okay?'

'It's been better. If you're free now, I could sure use a massage.'

He laughed. 'Is that all I am to you? A good pair of hands? I'm not doing anything. Are you home? You sound like you're on your cell.'

'I am, but I'm on my way home. Give me twenty minutes.'

'You got it.'

Ira was sitting on the wooden steps that led up to her side door when she pulled her car under the elms. He had his ratty daypack beside him. That meant he was planning to spend the night.

The next morning she parked her Buick in its usual spot at work and took the elevator up to the FBI offices. Bill Graves spotted her as soon as she stepped off the elevator. He took her by the arm and hustled her away from the reception desk. 'Come with me,' he murmured.

'What?'

He checked the hallway around them before he asked, 'What did you get yourself into last night, Kelda? The SAC is ready to take your head off.'

She thought, *Oh shit, he's probably having a fit about the Rosa Alija anniversary piece on Fox.* She'd forgotten all about it and wondered how it could have aired already. She quickly decided to deny everything. 'I didn't do anything last night, Bill. I don't know what on earth you're talking about.'

'Well, apparently there's some Boulder police detective who wants to talk to you about an assault on Tom Clone's grandfather that happened last night. He called the SAC at home and told him that Clone's using you for an alibi. The detective wants permission to interview you.'

She shook her head slowly and said, 'Damn.'

Bill took half a step back and asked, incredulously, 'It's true? You were with Clone last night?'

'Not last night. A couple of hours yesterday evening. We had dinner. That's all. That's it.' She grimaced. 'Shit.'

'The SAC is going to string you up if you really did this. He doesn't need this kind of public attention right now. The Bureau doesn't need this kind of public attention right now. Everybody's under orders to make sure that the only publicity we get is good publicity. And everybody includes you, Kelda.' Then, with obvious disdain in his voice, he added, 'You had a date with Tom Clone? What the hell were you thinking? Haven't you jeopardized enough with what you've done for that guy?'

She didn't answer. She said, 'Thanks for the warning about the SAC, Bill. You're a good friend.' And she walked away from him.

A message in the middle of her blotter directed her to go to the SAC's office as soon as she arrived. She mumbled another profanity and tried to figure out how she was going to finesse this with him.

One word came to mind.

Prehost.

Ten minutes later she returned to her desk and grabbed her shoulder bag. She gestured to Bill Graves with a slight movement of her head. He stood and followed her to the elevator.

'Let's get some coffee,' she said.

'Is it a good career move for me to be seen with you right now?'

'Ha, that's funny.' The elevator arrived and they stepped in. An Asian woman with an infant in a baby carrier was already in the car.

'So?' he said.

'Patience, Mr. Governor's Cousin.' She lowered her voice to a whisper. 'We're not alone.'

'I don't want coffee, Kelda.'

'Then at least wait until we get outside the building, okay?'

'I don't have much time. I have calls I'm waiting for.'

'Shush, we won't be long.' As the elevator opened she grabbed his hand and led him outside onto Stout Street. The Federal Building was on the edge of Denver's downtown business district, and she turned toward the I. M. Pei-designed pedestrian mall that bisected downtown on Sixteenth Street.

'I've never seen him so angry,' she said as they reached a red light at the corner of Eighteenth and Stout.

Bill laughed and said, 'The SAC? That's because you weren't involved the day that Smith and Jorgensen dropped that surveillance on the—'

'No, you're right, I wasn't part of that. Listen, Bill, I need to ask you something. Has anyone been following you?'

'What?'

'Any strange phone calls? Hang-ups at your house? I'm talking basically since about the time that the press seemed to get wind of Tom Clone's impending release from prison.'

'Kelda, what on earth—'

The light changed. Bill's feet seemed permanently affixed to the sidewalk. She almost had to yank him off the curb to get him to cross Eighteenth Street. She lowered her voice. 'I've been seeing this car, this old blue Suburban, and another car, a burgundy Toyota pickup, around me for the last few days. Since Clone's release, maybe even a few days before. Thursday, the Toyota was on the lane by my house in Lafayette when I got home.'

'Yeah? Anybody do anything threatening?'

She thought of Prehost and the flat he caused on her Buick in the middle of nowhere. His badge in her face.

The size of his biceps. 'No, no. Nothing like that. What about you?'

'No. But I haven't exactly been watching for tails, either. Maybe I should.' He grunted. 'And you've been getting phone calls, too?'

'Hang-ups. A few. I've star-six-nined all of them. Nothing ever comes up. I've been guessing that this all has to do with what we did with the Tom Clone case.'

'Why you and not me?'

'I don't know. My profile's higher because of . . . you know, Rosa. Maybe that's it. Or maybe it's just because I'm a woman and they think that makes me more vulnerable.'

'Why didn't you tell me before this?'

'I thought it was just crank stuff. Some of the same sort of thing happened to me after I found Rosa. In addition to a million wonderful notes I got from people thanking me, I also got some calls and a few letters that I'd prefer not to have received. It comes with the notoriety. It all faded after a while; I figured that this would fade, too.'

'But?'

'The Suburban was parked down the street from Tom Clone's house last night. I saw it when I was pulling away.'

'So you really did alibi Clone?'

She nodded and said, 'Yes, I was with him. I don't really know any details of what happened to his grandfather – certainly couldn't tell you what time the assault occurred – but I told the SAC that I was with Tom for almost three hours last evening. We had dinner, coffee. Went for a walk.'

'And what time did you see the Suburban?'

'Nine-twenty. I left his house at nine-twenty. I

remember looking at the clock on my dashboard just before I drove away.' She also remembered that she'd looked at the clock because Tom Clone had asked her to. Kelda didn't tell Bill that part. She noticed the pedestrian light change to 'Walk' a hundred feet in front of them, and tugged Bill along with her so that they would have a chance to make the light at the corner.

'Did you tell the SAC all this?'

'Yes, I did. I even gave him a license plate number for the Suburban.'

Bill raised an eyebrow. 'You got the license plate? You're always thinking, Kelda. I like that.'

They rushed across the intersection at Seventeenth Street.

Bill said, 'Why are we hurrying? Do you have plate numbers on the Toyota that followed you, too?'

'We're not hurrying, I'm just trying to be sensitive to your schedule. You said that you had stuff to do. And no, the guy in the Toyota had his plates conveniently caked with mud.'

'Did you tell the SAC about the other times you saw the Suburban? And about the Toyota and the phone calls?'

She took two more steps before she said, 'Kind of.'

He suddenly stopped walking, planting his feet so that she couldn't pull him along. 'What does that mean?'

'What? What does what mean?'

'You didn't tell the SAC that you think you're being followed?'

'I . . . alluded to it. You know how he reacts to stuff like this, Bill. I can handle it myself. I'm being vigilant. I spotted the tails, didn't I?'

'Are you nuts? He reacts to "stuff like this" because he doesn't want any of his agents ambushed, Kelda. Jesus, I can't believe you would . . . In case you haven't looked at a calendar lately, it's after September 2001. Way after.'

'Bill, I—'

'You spotted the tails, Kelda? And how do you know what tails you might have missed? You could be putting other agents at risk by keeping this to yourself. You could . . .' The expression on his face went from concern laced with annoyance to something decidedly less sympathetic. He leaned back against the wall behind him and placed the sole of one shoe flat against the granite face of the building and shook his head.

'What?' she asked.

'Are you dating this guy, Kelda? Do you have feelings for this . . . this accused murderer, this, this—'

'Bill, it's . . .' She looked away from him. Her weak protest hung awkwardly between them.

'It's what?'

'It's complicated.'

'Complicated? You bet it's complicated. Tom Clone is not an innocent man, Kelda. His conviction was thrown out. Thrown out, that's all. He wasn't suddenly found not guilty. He certainly wasn't exonerated. There's no evidence that he didn't kill that girl. You know the book in that murder case in Park County better than anyone but the detective who ran Clone down. One little break for the local cops and Clone could be rearrested at any time. You're putting a lot at risk personally and professionally by even being seen with the guy, let alone getting involved with him. And now, now look what's happened – the SAC knows that you're up to something and . . . it appears that somebody's following you . . . and you're Clone's alibi for—'

She stepped back from him. She told herself not to get defensive. The admonition didn't work. 'Have you forgotten about the knife we found? You know, the one with somebody else's blood on it? Have you forgotten about that?'

'No,' he replied. 'I think about it every day.'

The chill in his words slapped at her. 'I know what I'm doing, Bill. I'm not sure why, but I have this need to understand him, to know how people could think him capable of what they think he did to—'

'It's not our job to understand them, Kelda. It's our job to catch them and convict them.'

'I don't think I agree. Anyway, it's none of your business whom I'm seeing socially.'

He turned his head away from her toward the Sixteenth Street Mall. 'That little girl can't protect you from everything, Kelda. One of these times you're going to go to make a withdrawal from that account and you're going to find out that it's busted. Totally empty.'

'What are you implying?' But she knew exactly what he was implying. He was reminding Kelda that her public heroics in rescuing Rosa Alija wouldn't insulate her forever.

'You know exactly what I mean,' he said.

'Screw you, Graves. I do not need Rosa Alija to keep me out of trouble with the SAC.'

'You don't? Tell me that after you get your ass reassigned to Billings. But please don't drag me up there with you. Denver's as cold as I ever want to get.'

He stared at her for about ten seconds, pivoted, and started walking. His long strides were taking him away from the Sixteenth Street Mall, back in the direction of the Federal Building.

'Wait,' Kelda called after him.

Bill Graves didn't slow. He broke into a jog and cut into a cloud of diesel exhaust hanging behind an RTD bus that was holding up traffic on Seventeenth.

I woke feeling guilty about how I'd handled the phone call with Tom Clone the previous evening. Doubt about my own clinical judgment had once been a rare emotional state for me, but over the past year I'd begun to question my therapeutic decisions with increasing frequency and, unfortunately, I could argue, with increasing justification. The previous year my clinical missteps had cost some people their lives, and I was already beginning to suspect that the cavalier method with which I'd handled the emergency the night before might end up having similarly grave consequences.

While I was showering I tried to convince myself that my self-flagellation was nothing more than mindless catastrophizing. My behavior the night before might not have been an ideal clinical intervention, but it was hardly lethal. But my rationalization wasn't sufficient; the guilt and regret that I was feeling didn't wash right off and disappear down the drain.

Lauren didn't know I was treating Tom Clone. That wasn't surprising – typically she didn't know any of my patients' names. It was therefore coincidence that she initiated a discussion over breakfast regarding the story in the *Daily Camera* about the assault on his grandfather. I made small talk in reply and succeeded in nudging our conversation away from Tom Clone and on to the ongoing dilemma of juggling our workdays and Grace's care, and negotiating which of us was going to be home first to rescue Viv, our daytime nanny.

The answer that day was Lauren.

She asked if my telephone emergency had turned out okay the night before. I told her it had.

And that was it.

I didn't tell her that the emergency patient was Tom Clone and that he had probably slept on a couch in the ICU waiting room at Community Hospital, but that he would have been much happier in our guest room. Nor did I mention that Sam Purdy was acting as though he suspected Tom of involvement in the assault on his grandfather. I didn't tell her that the heroic FBI agent who had rescued Rosa Alija was one of my patients and that she was apparently now dating the controversial man who had once been convicted of almost beheading his ex-girlfriend in Park County, and who was now – miraculously, it seemed – out of prison.

I didn't tell her that I was full of doubts about whether I was still capable of doing work that left people trusting me for insight into their lives.

What I told her was that I wished that the cast was off my arm and that I yearned to take her and Grace and both dogs and drive the Mini the whole length of the Peak to Peak Highway and maybe take it over Trail Ridge Road into Rocky Mountain National Park.

She told me that I was a good father and that she loved me, and I left for work with just enough warmth coursing through my veins to suspect that I would make it through another day as a psychologist.

Tom Clone's emergency appointment was that afternoon at three. He showed up right on time.

He and I were alone in the waiting room, so I greeted him by saying, 'How's your grandfather doing, Tom?'

'A little better, they think. He's resting better anyway. But I'm worried. His EEG is showing some anomalies, he lost more blood than anybody his age can really afford to lose, and his kidney functions are screwy. I'm afraid his kidneys are going to shut down. That would kill him, for sure.'

As I processed the technical sophistication of his remarks, I reminded myself that Tom Clone had been only months away from completing medical school when he was incarcerated for almost decapitating his girlfriend in Park County.

I consciously reminded myself that he hadn't done it. He hadn't killed that girl. The DNA said so.

'Come on back to the office,' I said.

After we settled on our chairs, I waited for him to choose a place to start.

He scanned the perimeter of the office once before he

said, 'I was with that FBI agent last night. The one I told you about who picked me up from prison. The one who found the knife.'

That FBI agent. Kelda.

I said, 'When your grandfather was assaulted? That's who you were with? The FBI agent?'

'Yeah. She called out of the blue and asked me out, bought me dinner. We were down on the Mall most of the evening. We were having a great time – I thought we were, anyway – but once we got back to my place she was, I don't know, gone. Cold. You know, distant.'

I waited.

'She said she was tired. That her leg was sore. Why would she drive to town, take me to dinner, and then suddenly go cold on me? The night just . . . ended. I don't get it. Maybe I'm just out of practice, but I think it's bullshit.'

I thought a little reality testing might be in order. 'Maybe, Tom, she was tired and her leg was sore.'

He scowled at me. 'No, you weren't there. It wasn't like that. Everything was great, perfect, and then suddenly, everything wasn't. She just said she was leaving, got in her car, and left. I don't know why I bothered.'

His voice had sharpened and I realized that the events of the previous evening with Kelda had become over-determined for Tom – they'd taken on meaning beyond the simple progression of events. Along with that aware-ness, a thought one-hopped through my consciousness like a hard shot across the infield: If I hadn't mentioned Tom's grandfather in the waiting room, would Tom have brought up the old man's condition on his own? There was no way to answer that question and I kicked myself for putting my compassion in front of my clinical obligations.

I said, 'And that left you feeling . . . how?'

At first blush his response was pure non sequitur. He said, 'I'm starting work tomorrow at Kaiser. In the pharmacy? The lady in their personnel department knew my story, feels I've been screwed, and says I'm perfect for the job. To tell you the truth, I think I got lucky that I ran into somebody who feels that way. She's in the minority, believe me.'

'Congratulations.'

'Yeah. Anyway, their insurance won't pay for me to come here to see you. If I want to see somebody, I have to see somebody on the Kaiser staff. I don't know if my attorney will continue to pay for therapy if I can see somebody on my insurance plan for free. So I don't know what's going to happen.'

I could have gone into a harangue about how long the waiting list was going to be to see a psychotherapist at Kaiser, or how restrictive the mental health treatment options were going to be. It would have made me feel better, but I didn't. I said, 'You don't know what's going to happen about what?'

'What's the point?' His words were perilously close to a whine. 'Why should I get something started with you when I'll just have to stop? What good is that going to do?'

Lightbulb time.

Duh. Remember a concept called transference, Dr. Gregory?

I said, 'Tom?' and waited until he was focused on my words. 'What you're describing right now? It's similar to what you're feeling with that FBI agent, isn't it?' I almost said 'with Kelda,' but I caught myself just as the back of my tongue was curling toward the roof of my mouth to form the *K*. I didn't think Tom Clone had ever used her name with me.

He replied, 'What do you mean?'

If I dissected his reply, I thought I would find about an equal blend of 'I don't understand' and 'What the fuck are you talking about?'

In the face of an interpretation similar to the one I'd just made to Tom, the response of 'What do you mean?' wasn't an uncommon one, especially in the early stages of psychotherapy. A major goal of insight-oriented psycho-therapy is to increase self-awareness so that similarities between emotional reactions to prior events and emo-tional reactions to current ones, like the circumstance I was pointing out to Tom, become self-evident to the patient.

Responding to his innocuous-sounding 'What do you mean?' meant that I had a clinical judgment to make: How far should I stretch the interpretation that I was making? I decided to go for broke. The worst that would happen is that he would consider the connections I was suggesting to be totally inane. The best that would happen is that he would begin to see himself as vulnerable to the gravity of emotional and historical forces that he hadn't previously recognized.

In other words, as human.

'Tom, you haven't been out of prison long. And you haven't been coming to see me for long. Yet in the brief time that you've been here, you've focused most of our time together on events where people become very meaningful to you and then seem to turn their backs on you.'

He made a perplexed face. It wasn't just confusion, though. A healthy dose of skepticism was mixed with something I was interpreting as aggravation. He said, 'I don't know . . . I don't know what you're talking about.'

I caught enough hesitation in his voice that I thought he was at least curious about the point I was making.

'Your mother?' I continued. 'When you were young and she'd get manic, she'd take you on these terrific E-ticket rides, on these grand adventures she concocted, and then suddenly her mania would crash into depression and she'd leave you stranded and alone.'

He was staring at me.

I asked, 'Still with me?'

'So far.'

The two words carried a surprising modicum of warning.

I felt the caution – it was milder than my reaction to a dog baring its teeth, though not much – and I pressed on. 'Then there's this FBI agent who shows up in your life. First she finds the evidence that gets you out of jail, then she picks you up to take you home from prison, and she takes you out for a wonderful meal in a romantic hotel. The next time you try to reach her, she acts as though you're nothing but a bother. Then . . . she calls out of the blue and takes you out to dinner. The evening is terrific. But when you try to extend your time together, she just disappears like the night had meant nothing to her.' I thought I'd explained enough. I waited for Tom to reply.

He didn't oblige.

I asked, 'Do you see a pattern?'

He snorted at me through his nose. 'I don't know what the fuck you're talking about.'

I nodded once, slowly. I'd swung for the fences and failed to make contact. It wasn't the first time I'd gone down swinging, and it certainly wouldn't be the last. At least, I consoled myself, I didn't get called out on strikes.

I said, 'Okay.'

As I figuratively made the stroll back to the dugout, I was recalling what Tom had said to me the previous night when he'd called and requested the extra appointment. He'd told me that he was feeling vulnerable, both in terms of his physical safety and in terms of his legal status. I wondered if he would get around to talking about either concern during this session.

He said, 'You done with that other thing?'

I said, 'Yes.' I thought, *You bet*.

'Here's something weird for you. The last couple of times I slept in my grandfather's house, I heard doors clanging shut. It sounded just like when I was inside when the cell doors slammed.'

'You were awake or asleep?'

'The first night I was asleep. The sound woke me up. I thought it was just a bad dream. The next night I was asleep the first time I heard it, but the next time was maybe an hour later and I was still awake. It made me jump. It sounded just like a cell door slamming. Exactly.'

'What do you think it was?' I asked.

'I don't know. I'm jumpy. I have a lot on my mind. Maybe I'm just hearing things. But that never happened to me before, even when I was on death row.' He sat forward on the edge of his chair with his elbows on his knees. 'I was also wondering about post-traumatic stress. Wondered if you thought that was possible.'

I'd been watching for signs of post-traumatic stress disorder since Tom Clone had stepped into my office for the first time. Like combat veterans, or abused spouses, or the tens of thousands of people trapped in lower Manhattan on September 11, or hundreds of other categories of trauma-tized people, Tom's experiences in prison had left him vulnerable for symptoms of post-traumatic stress.

'It's certainly possible, Tom. PTSD could certainly cause flashbacks like the ones you're describing. And your experiences in the criminal justice system were certainly severe enough stressors to place you at risk. Did you have any other . . . sensations associated with hearing the doors slam?'

'Like what? You mean anxiety symptoms, like that? What else would I look for – rapid breathing, heart palps, sweaty palms? That sort of thing?'

I nodded, although I was reluctant to provide a shopping list of symptoms. The list was longer than the one Tom had asked about, of course, but I didn't enumerate any of the alternatives. I generally wasn't eager to suggest to Tom, or to any patient, that there were symptomatic targets at which to take aim.

'No. Nothing like that. Just the damn doors slamming.' He shivered. 'Once you've heard it a few times for real – and, believe me, it's real when you're the one that they're locking up – you'll never, ever forget it. You don't know what it's like, that sound.'

I watched, eerily fascinated, as his eyes told me he'd gone someplace else.

No, I thought, *I don't know what it's like*.

I asked, 'Are you having any other experiences that remind you of the time that you spent in prison?'

'Like what?'

'Flashbacks.'

'What would they be like?'

'I wasn't there, Tom. I can only imagine what you went through. You haven't told me much about what life was like for you inside, so I don't know specifically what to ask.'

'I don't like to think about it. I don't think I'm ever going to want to think about it.'

I waited thirty seconds or so for Tom to exit my office before I made the stroll to the waiting room for my next patient. As I greeted her, I could see through the front window that Tom was climbing on a bright red Vespa parked at a bike rack in front of my office.

I followed my new patient back down the hall to my office wondering how a man just released from the penitentiary could afford to have a motor scooter that looked brand-new.

CHAPTER

26

Kelda didn't comment about my cast at the beginning of her rescheduled session the following week. And she didn't ask about the condition of my arm.

She was almost fifteen minutes late and seemed intent on using the remaining minutes of her allotted time efficiently. She sat on her chair, released her hair from confinement behind her head, and said, 'That trip to Hawaii I told you about? I didn't go on my own. Jones's family was going over to get some closure after her death. I went with them. They wanted to collect some of her things that someone had found at the gallery where she'd worked and meet the people who knew her at the end. They invited me to go along. So when I went, I went over with her mother and her brother.'

I didn't know what parable I had just heard the preamble to. So I waited patiently to hear the fable.

'She'd hadn't been in Maui long, you know, when she

died. Jones hadn't. Yet she'd already done about a dozen paintings – acrylics – and twice that many watercolors. That was a remarkable output for her. Three dozen pieces would have been a year's work for her in Denver, maybe more. To me that meant that something was stimulating her there, driving her.

'I didn't get it at first – I told you I didn't understand why she'd gone to Hawaii at all. But when I walked into that co-op, that gallery where they'd found some of her old things, I think I finally began to understand what was going on with her.

'The gallery had found five pieces in this upstairs storage room they have. The pictures weren't even framed. Two acrylics, three watercolors. The watercolors were small, maybe each about the size of a book. The two acrylics were larger – they were square, maybe thirty inches on a side. Something like that.' She exhaled audibly. The sound was almost a sigh.

'In each of the five paintings in that storage room, there was an "Oh my God, I'm in Hawaii" quality to it. You know, ocean vistas, palm trees, old churches, Haleakala – that's the name of the volcano on Maui. The person who showed us her pictures at the gallery said that painting that stuff was like a rite of passage for newly arrived artists in Hawaii. The good ones, she said, are the ones who get past it. The artists who don't get past it end up smoking weed and selling thirty-dollar prints to tourists. She said that Jones – she called her Joan, of course – she said that it was clear from the start that Jones was technically good – you know, that she had talent – but that these early pieces never sold in the gallery because they were just Hawaiian clichés – the sort of thing you could find at every souvenir shop on the island.'

Kelda laughed. 'I remember thinking during the conversation, *The early pieces? What are we talking? The first week? Ten days?*' She shook her head. 'The woman in the gallery said that once Jones started putting herself – her feelings, her life, her spirit, whatever Oprah's calling it these days – into her work, she'd immediately started selling paintings. At first the other artists at the gallery thought it was just because Jones was pricing her stuff for less than they were, but soon it was clear to everybody in the co-op that Jones was doing something special, and that the customers were responding to it.'

I watched Kelda dab at the corner of her left eye with the tip of her finger. Evidence of a tear? It would have been the first I'd seen from her. But it was a speck of something less poignant than a tear that she was clearing from her eye.

'The woman said that once word got around that Jones had died, the remaining paintings sold within days, but that everybody had forgotten about the five that were in storage because Jones had pulled them from the gallery and hadn't wanted them displayed.

'I asked her if there was any way that I could see any of the paintings that the gallery had sold. Any of the later ones. The ones with Jones's spirit.' Kelda smiled as she said 'spirit.' I couldn't read the grin and wondered whether she was being sardonic or sarcastic. 'The woman said she didn't know, excused herself to go check some records, and joined us again in a few minutes. "The invoices show that they went to people from the mainland, mostly," she said. "A couple of large ones went to a designer who was decorating a condo at Ka'anapali. We have the designer's name, but not the clients'. Mainlanders are our typical customers. And there is a local collector who lives in Makawao" – that's a little cowboy town up on the side of the volcano – "who has two paintings. And Joan traded one to her landlord for rent. So if M'loo – that's her landlord – didn't sell it, she has one." She told us how to find M'loo, and Jones's mother made arrangements to have the five remaining pictures shipped to her home. We thanked the woman in the gallery and we turned to leave.

'The woman touched Jones's mother on her shoulder and said, "I almost forgot. I have her kit, too. It has her sketchpad in it and some paints and brushes. A little journal she kept. Should I include those when I ship the paintings?"

'Mrs. Winslett said she would like that, and we started to go.

'"And I have one," the woman in the gallery called after us. "I have one of the chasing pictures, too. I didn't want to tell you because I was afraid you'd ask to take it with you and I don't think . . . I can give it up."

'Jones's mother – Mrs. Winslett – went back to New Hampshire a couple of days later. Jones's brother and I decided to stay and try to see if we could find some of the paintings that Jones had sold. He wanted to see if he could get somebody to sell one to him. It was really important to him.'

I spoke for the first time since I had greeted Kelda that day. 'The woman in the gallery called them the "chasing pictures"? Did you and Jones's brother discover what that meant?'

Kelda nodded. 'Over the next few days we ended up seeing some of the paintings. Jones's old landlord turned out to be an absolutely obese Indonesian woman with this huge smile and a laugh that made your eyes quiver. She still had the painting that she'd traded for rent for the little shack where Jones had been living. And the woman at the gallery let us see the one she had. And . . . the collector she told us about, a guy who owns a protea farm on the side of the volcano up near Makawao, he had two. The ones in the condo in Ka'anapali we never got to see. We tracked down the designer who'd bought them, but the owners of the condo weren't on the island while we were there.'

Kelda crossed her legs. 'The paintings were very different from the ones we'd seen in the storeroom at the gallery. The Hawaiian landscape aspects were more abstract – more impressionistic is probably a better way to put it – than in the first paintings we saw. I'm no art critic, but that's the way it seemed to me.

'But the main difference was that in the later pictures there was always a figure, you know, a person. The paintings weren't just landscapes, but the person wasn't the focus, either. The person was secondary, not front and center, and in each painting there is always some force at her back. In every painting, it's always a woman. The force in one is the wind, almost blowing her over. In another, she's on a beach and the force is a big wave crashing unevenly against some rocks behind her. You know that the water is about to wash over her. In another one that's set on one of the two main roads in Paia, it's a car that's after her as she's trying to cross a street. It's clear she's not going to make it out of the way.'

Stating the obvious, I said, 'Something is always after her? The woman in the pictures? Chasing her?'

'Yes. The last one we saw? It's the one that her landlord has. It's the most disturbing of all of them. In that one it's the darkness that's chasing her. The woman in the painting is facing west at sunset in a field near the ocean. M'loo said the plants in the field are pineapples; she even offered to take us to see the field where Jones had painted it. It's outside of Paia on the road to Hana. The darkness is creeping up on the woman from behind. It's sneaking right out of the sugarcane fields like a thief.'

Words entered my head an instant before Kelda spoke again. It turned out that the words that came out of her mouth were the exact same ones that had just materialized in my head.

She said, 'Or a killer.'

I felt as though I were mouthing the words as she spoke them, and I wondered what that meant.

'A killer?' I repeated.

'The painting felt . . . dangerous. They all did. The darkness wasn't going to surround her. It was going to consume her. That's how it looked to me.'

'What are you saying, Kelda?'

'I'm not sure. She wasn't feeling safe. I know she wasn't feeling safe. I could see it in her art.'

'Were the Hawaii paintings that different from the work she did in Colorado?'

'They were better, that's for sure. But the biggest difference was the tone. Her work here was light, energetic. The chasing pictures are dark, ominous. She was frightened.'

I stated the obvious. It was my job. 'Jones never felt safe, though, did she?'

'Of course she didn't, but . . . this was different. The Hawaii paintings told us she was in danger.'

'From what?'

'I don't know. I just know she felt she was in danger.'

'She suffered from multiple phobias, Kelda. She spent a good chunk of her life frightened.'

'I have her journal, Alan. The one that she left in the gallery? I have it. She was afraid. That's what the darkness represents in the painting that M'loo has. That's what all the chasing pictures are about. Her fear of someone.'

'Not something?'

'She was always afraid of something. But never someone. Jones loved people. That's not how her fears worked.'

A suspicion was developing in my mind. It came into shape slowly, erratically, like a web page loading from a recalcitrant server. When I had enough pieces to identify it, I followed the hunch. 'How do you feel about darkness, Kelda?'

'No,' she said immediately. She swallowed and shook her head, looking down at her hands in her lap. 'I've covered enough rough ground today, Alan. That will have to wait for another time.'

Kelda sat in that same position for a minute or two after finishing her tale about Jones and the chasing pictures and evading my question about the darkness. The silence wasn't awkward. It wasn't even particularly poignant. Kelda seemed to be like a runner catching her breath, surprised that she was still standing after a race she hadn't been sure she could even complete.

Typically, I wouldn't end a protracted silence like that one – I would leave that choice up to my patient. But in this case, the stillness of Kelda's posture was a clue about something I felt was worth a little exploration. Finally, I asked, 'How's your pain right now?'

Her eyes brightened a little. 'Aren't you supposed to call it "my discomfort," Alan? Isn't that what shrinks are supposed to say? You don't want to be guilty of suggestion, do you?'

Kelda wasn't usually playful with me.

Rather than get sidetracked by her remark, which is what I suspected she intended and what would have been most comfortable for her, I rephrased my question. 'So how is your discomfort right now?'

Her features softened. The little wrinkles in her forehead and at the corners of her eyes disappeared as though some recent Botox injections had just magically kicked in.

She said, 'I don't hurt right now.'

'What do you make of that?'

She closed her eyes. I could see her eyeballs moving below her eyelids. It reminded me of watching Lauren while she was dreaming.

'I don't see what this has to do with Jones.' She opened her eyes.

'Neither do I. Together we may be able to find out, though. I think that's the point.'

'Usually by this time of day, I'm in a lot of pain.'

I nodded.

'I don't see what this has to do with Jones, Alan.'

I repeated, 'Neither do I.'

I really didn't. I didn't have a clue.

She stood to leave a minute later. I was very aware that she hadn't mentioned Tom Clone or the assault on his grandfather or the fact that she and Tom had been spending time together.

Usually, as I proceed in psychotherapy with my patients I remain ignorant of their omissions. During the course of treatment I am able to observe the continuity of their thoughts and even recognize the nature of the associations that they make, consciously or unconsciously, as they move from one topic to another. I can chart the process of their behavior as though I'm taking notes on a piece of music. But I typically have no way to observe the exclusionary choices that they make.

That means that I have no way to know the important topics that they are *not* discussing.

With Kelda, because of Tom Clone's revelations and because of Sam Purdy's updates, I had a narrow channel by which to chance a look in the rearview mirror of Kelda's life. And in that narrow tunnel of vision I could see what she'd chosen to drive right on by.

I reminded myself, however, that Tom Clone, not Kelda James, was holding the mirror I was looking in, and that Tom was undoubtedly pointing it precisely where he wished.

Still.

Kelda stopped at the door and turned. Her eyes were aimed down near my abdomen. 'How's your arm?' she asked.

'Good,' I said. 'Fine.'

'Great. I'm glad. Next week regular time then?'

'Yes.'

27

I was out the door less than a minute after Kelda left my office. I considered it propitious that the sky was mottled gray and that I could hear the rumble of distant thunder. Maybe the monsoons were finally coming. But a moment's reflection told me that the early evening air was still quite warm and it was obvious that it didn't contain enough humidity to allow me the luxury of forgetting my lip balm.

A glance confirmed that no raindrops dotted the dust that coated the surface of my car.

So maybe the monsoons weren't arriving after all.

I climbed into my car, opened all the windows to air it out, and checked my rearview mirror a second time when I was about halfway down the driveway. I looked just in time to see Sam Purdy pulling into the driveway from Walnut Street. He saw me coming, stopped, and got out of his car. I shut off the engine and got out of mine.

I wondered if he'd seen Kelda leaving my office, wondered if he knew what Kelda looked like. Then I thought, *Of course he does. Everyone knows what Kelda looks like. They know because of Rosa Alija.*

'Your arm's still broken,' he said.

'Imagine that. Hey, Sam, how are you doing?'

'You don't want to know how I'm doing. And a few seconds from now you're not going to be happy to see me.'

'What makes you think I'm happy to see you now?'

'Cute.'

He closed the distance between us until he was close enough that I could examine the stains from food he'd spilled on his tie. The spots weren't recent; as far as I knew, Sam owned only three ties and this one was the oldest in the collection. One particular spot had been there as long as we'd been friends. The stain was shaped like Idaho and was about the size of a healthy fava bean.

'Why won't I be happy to see you?'

Lowering his voice to a melodramatic whisper, he said, 'Because I need to talk to you about Tom Clone.'

I winced. 'I can't. You know that.'

'By telling me you can't, you're already telling me something you're not supposed to tell me. So why don't you just go ahead and tell me one or two other things that you're not supposed to tell me. That way I don't have to make threats and impugn your character and we can still be friends.'

Damn. I consoled myself with the fact that Sam's tone was civil, so far. I held out hope he was willing to be playful. Otherwise this was going to degenerate into confrontation as quickly as Grace's naptime whimpers became tears. I said, 'I don't know what you mean.'

He sighed. 'Okay, I'll explain it to you then. You just told me you can't talk about Clone. If you can't talk about him, that means he's your patient or your client or whatever the hell you're calling the unfortunate schmucks you work with these days. Well, the fact is you weren't even supposed to tell me *that*. So we've already crossed the line about you not telling me things. You've lost your confidentiality virginity, so to speak.'

His deduction was, as always, sound. I smiled at him as a boom of thunder shook the air all around us.

Sam ducked. Why did he duck? I don't know. I would guess that he felt as though the heavens were getting ready to swat him upside the head. I wasn't at all sure he didn't deserve it.

I asked, 'And in your mind that means I should just become a confidentiality slut?'

'Yeah, exactly. That would sure make my life easier.' He turned and gazed at the western sky. 'Why don't you come get in my car with me before we get fried by lightning?'

'No, you come down here and get in mine. If I get in your car, you'll take me hostage until I agree to sacrifice my chastity.'

'It's not your chastity I'm after.'

'We've been down this road before, Sam. You know I'm not going to tell you what you want to know.'

'We'll see. Just sit with me for a minute.'

He followed me back down the driveway to my car. As he settled on the seat he said, 'I don't think it's really going to rain. The air is too dry. It'll just be thunder and more virga. The lightning will probably start a fire up there somewhere.' He gestured to the west, up toward the mountains.

'You're probably right.' I had enough things to argue with Sam about. I didn't need to argue with him about the weather.

'I can't find Tom Clone,' he said.

'Really?' At his unexpected change of focus, I switched over to my parent voice. 'Do you remember if you put him back where he belonged the last time you used him?'

He didn't bite. 'He's gone missing. He hasn't been by the hospital to visit his grandfather for over twenty-four hours, and he's not at home. Neighbors haven't seen him. He's vanished. What I need to know from you is whether he has a job and if he does, where he works.'

'That's it?'

Sam laughed. 'No, but it's all I'm allowing myself to hope for.'

'Have you tried his attorney?'

'Yeah, as a matter of fact, I have. He's in Kenya. I wish I were in Kenya. I could do a month or two in Kenya communing with the animals without a problem. But it'll never happen. Want to know why? Fancy attorneys go to Kenya; cops go to Disneyland, if we're lucky. And then we spend two years making payments on our Visa to cover the trip. By the time we're done with the interest payments, we've paid enough that we realize we should have just gone to Kenya after all.'

'Why do you want to talk with Tom Clone?'

'Come on, Alan, don't ask me stuff like that. Don't take advantage of the fact that I pretend to like you.'

I sighed. 'Just tell me if you want to arrest him or just want to talk to him.'

Sam looked out the car window at the house that contained my office. 'You own this place or do you rent?'

'I own it with Diane and Raoul and General Electric.'

He continued to gaze on the little brick Victorian wistfully. Diane and I had been prescient enough, or savvy enough, or, most likely, just damn lucky enough, to buy a building that was in the center of downtown on a good-sized piece of land with enviable zoning just before Boulder's property values went through the roof.

'Mortgage?' he asked.

'Yeah, that's the GE part. But we bought the place when the market was soft, so we're doing okay. I consider the place my retirement plan or Grace's college fund, whichever comes first.'

'Doing better than okay with it, I bet,' Sam said.

'Yeah, better than okay.'

'I never told you, but Sherry and I own the shop where she sells her flowers. It's a retail/condo-type thing. We have a mortgage, too, but over the years, we've made more money on the real estate than she's made selling flowers.'

'Sometimes,' I said, 'being lucky is much more lucrative than being smart.'

I watched him as he reached into his shirt pocket and held up a flimsy piece of paper with a few rows of Powerball picks on them. He said, 'Amen to that,' and laughed. After he stuffed the lottery ticket back into his pocket, he raised his chin and yanked at the knot in his tie. Then he spent an inordinate amount of time undoing the top button of his shirt. I thought the difficulty could have had something to do with the fact that he appeared to be wearing a size-sixteen shirt on his size-seventeen-and-a-half neck.

My sense of self-preservation caused me to withhold comment on my observation.

'Here's the thing – if Clone walked up that sidewalk over there and climbed the stairs to your office door right this minute, I'd just want to talk to him. But the truth is that if he didn't answer some of my questions just right, I'm not too far away from arresting him. I'm trying to be honest with you here.'

'For his grandfather's assault?'

Sam sighed. 'I'm afraid so.'

I felt sweat on my temple and started the engine so that the air conditioner would kick on. 'Close your door,' I said.

'We going somewhere?' Sam asked.

I said, 'No, I'm not anyway. I just want to get the AC running. You think he did it?'

'What's "it"? That murder in Park County? Or the assault on the grandfather?'

I'd already heard Sam's thoughts on Ivy Campbell's murder. 'I'm talking about his grandfather.'

'I think there are things he's not explaining adequately. Time-frame things, mostly.'

'What happened to his alibi? When you called me the other night, you said he has an alibi.'

'His alibi held up okay – actually pretty good – but it turns out that there're some outstanding questions about the time of the actual assault. It may have happened before his alibi kicks in. We're not sure.'

I moved my hands to my face and rubbed my eyes. I suddenly felt tired. 'I can't tell you where he works. I wish I could. I know you'll find out eventually anyway and I'd love to save you the hassle.'

'Who else might know where he works?'

'His grandfather?'

'The old guy is still gorked.'

Gork: God only really knows. Sam was using the hospital staff acronym to tell me that Tom Clone's grandfather was in no neurological position to reveal his grandson's employer. I felt even more tired than I had.

'I don't know who else might know. What about a parole officer?'

'Clone's not on parole, Alan. He's a free man.'

Of course he was. I knew that.

Sam reached for the door handle. 'For the record,' he said, 'I'm worried about him.'

'Huh? You're worried about him? Why?'

'I don't like it when people go missing.'

'Are you worried about what he's up to? Or are you worried that he may be in danger? Which is it?'

'Maybe both. Certainly the latter. I have to consider the possibility that it wasn't a stranger who assaulted the grandfather and that the grandfather wasn't the intended victim.' He cracked open the door.

'Wait,' I said. I forced a deep breath and asked, 'Sam, is anyone else in danger in this situation? From Tom Clone? Are you keeping anything from me? Has he threatened anyone?'

Sam chuckled. 'Of course I'm keeping things from you. But no, Clone hasn't threatened anyone that we know of.'

He opened his mouth to say something more but only said, 'Oh,' and winced before he closed it again. Finally, he added, 'Danger? Yeah, maybe. Maybe someone else is in danger.'

'Imminent danger?'

'Yeah, imminent danger. That's possible.'

'But no specific threat that you're aware of?'

'No, no threat.'

'Possible's not good enough.' I took another deliberate breath. At some level of my awareness, I knew I was pausing to give Sam a chance to catch up with me. 'But you think he might be in danger, Sam? Clone? Say he didn't assault his grandfather, but someone else did. Tom Clone might still be in danger from the same person who broke into the house and beat up his grandfather?'

Sam was beginning to get a feel for the melody of the tune I was humming, and finally started tapping his foot to the music.

'Yeah, absolutely,' he said. 'No doubt about it. Until we get this thing solved, you have to figure that anyone else who lived in that house with the grandfather is in danger. If Clone didn't do the assault, he could even be somewhere injured right now – hell, maybe that's why we can't find him. We're talking definite imminent danger.' He paused. 'Definite.'

I wasn't looking at Sam. Yes, I was concerned for Tom Clone's safety, but I knew I'd been dangling clues that invited Sam to conspire with me to rationalize an indiscretion I absolutely shouldn't commit. Sam was a quick study and he'd read his lines just right. I said, 'Kaiser pharmacy over on Thirteenth. You know it?'

Sam said, 'It's where the clinic is? By Casey School?'

'Yeah.'

'We take Simon there,' he said. He opened the door and stepped out of the car. Slamming the door, he leaned down and looked across at me. 'You'll take me for a ride in that funny little car of yours, right? Once your arm's okay?'

'Maybe, if you promise not to sneeze.'

He said, 'Thanks, Alan.'

I said nothing. I watched Sam walk away, not feeling good about what I'd done. And I knew I wouldn't have felt good if I had done nothing. I also knew that a year before, I wouldn't have revealed what I'd just revealed.

So why did I do it? Here was my rationalization: I did it because the cost of my silence the last time a cop asked me to talk still weighed on me like wet shoes. I had stayed silent that time and one of my patients had ended up dying less than a hundred feet away from me.

Was what I just did with Sam ethical? Probably not.

Hell, definitely not.

Was it right?

I'd once thought that the question was one of blacks and whites, occasionally charcoal grays and off-whites. Now? Sometimes I couldn't tell at all any longer.

Was I growing more experienced? Or just more jaded?

I didn't know. That was the nature of the funk I was in those days.

Grace was squirming on the changing table in front of me. The little changing-table dance was something she often did just as I released the second taped tab from the diaper that was destined for the bin. Keeping her on the table while I fumbled to keep the contents of the old diaper inside the diaper was a significant challenge to my dexterity when I had two unbroken arms. With one arm encased in fiberglass, the task had become a bad vaudeville routine. That's why I didn't turn my head when I heard Lauren enter the room behind me and say, 'Sam's on the phone.'

I thought – okay, I hoped – that my wife would offer to take over the diapering operation, but a whiff of what awaited her had apparently made it across the room before she had a chance to be so magnanimous.

She tucked the cordless phone between my shoulder and my ear and whispered, 'That looks like a two-hander you got there. Say hi to Sammy for me.'

'What does she mean, "a two-hander"?' Sam asked.

'I'm in the middle of changing Grace's diaper. That kind of two-hander.'

'Oh, bad memories, I can call back.'

'No, just give me a minute or two to finish up here.' I set the phone down and gave Grace's hygiene a hundred percent of my attention until she smelled as fresh as a baby can smell. After I snapped her into a fresh pair of jammies, I handed her off to Lauren and returned to the phone.

'What's up, Sam?' I was afraid, of course, that he was about to remind me of my newly earned confidentiality-slut status and demand some fresh Tom Clone information from me.

His agenda, it turned out, was more generous than that. 'I thought you deserved an update about what we discussed earlier. Well, here's the latest scoop from inside the halls of the Boulder Public Safety Building: Mr. Clone is officially still missing. A crack detective learned from unidentified sources that today was supposed to be his first day of work at Kaiser, but he didn't show up for his new job and he didn't call in. They don't know where he is and, by the way, they don't really care, because he no longer has a job.'

I was too cynical to be surprised. I did feel a flush of unease over Tom Clone's well-being. Almost immediately, I started blathering. 'There seem to be only a few possible explanations, Sam. One is that for some reason he doesn't want to be found. Two—'

'Wait,' Sam interrupted. 'If he doesn't want to be found, I say it's because he's guilty of something. For argument's sake, something like beating the shit out of his grandfather. That's just my nature. But go on.'

'Two is that something has happened to him – you know, like an accident – and he's incapacitated in some way and that's why he can't be found.'

Sam grunted. The grunt did not indicate his assent to my speculation.

I pressed on. 'Three, it turns out that he has been in jeopardy all along and somebody has . . . hurt him.'

'Because I like you; I'm not even going to comment on the odds of number two. He's been hurt and he can't get to a telephone? Come on. And I'll trade you my winning Powerball ticket if you can help me come up with a motive for number three. Why would somebody want to hurt Clone?'

'Sorry, Sam. That would require speculation based on privileged information, and this slut is going into recovery. I've changed my evil ways.'

He laughed. 'Figured as much. You have a minute for a little story?'

'Like a parable? From you?' I sat down on the upholstered chair in the nursery. Instantly I could smell the aromas of my baby – the good smells – and my wife. I felt my blood pressure drop.

'Last week a neighbor knocked on my door late, maybe nine o'clock. Simon was in bed already. I know this guy to see him, but I don't know him personally at all – we're not even on a wave-to-each-other-when-you're-driving-by-and-the-other-guy's-mowing-the-lawn kind of basis. He's a stockbroker.'

Sam said 'He's a stockbroker' as though the man's choice of professions should have been an adequate explanation for why Sam and the neighbor weren't more friendly. I knew better. Sam was characterologically cranky and generally mistrustful of civilians. That was the reason he kept his neighbors – probably every last one of them – at arm's length. His wife, on the other hand, could probably quote chapter and verse of the first couple of branches of each of her neighbors' family trees.

'Guy is kind of nervous, says he doesn't want to bother me but he's had this client for years, some sweet old man who lives over in Martin Acres. The guy – the old guy – has a small portfolio of bonds and uses the income to supplement his Social Security.

'"Small," by the way, turns out to be two hundred and eleven thousand dollars. Was I away when two hundred and eleven thousand dollars stopped being considered real money? Anyway, over the last couple of months, the old guy has started to sell off some of his bonds, one by one. Tell me something, is it "sell" or "redeem"? I know from bad guys and I know from bratwurst; I don't know from bonds.'

I said, 'I'm not sure.'

'Figures. Where was I? Oh yeah, this old guy who never does anything without his broker's advice apparently won't tell the broker why he's suddenly so interested in divesting himself of double-A sewer-improvement notes for the City of Thornton, even though it's jeopardizing his retirement income.

'And this neighbor of mine – did I mention *whom I hardly know* – wondered if I'd check it out.'

'Check what out?'

'Exactly. That's what I asked. Last time I looked, it was still legal for people to sell their bonds and not tell their broker why they're doing it. I say that and the guy stuffs his hands in the pockets of his Bermuda shorts and sighs and backpedals on my little front porch until he finally – finally – tells me that the old guy's daughter moved back in with him a few months back and he – the broker – thinks that she might be mistreating him, maybe even shaking him down for the money. The one time the broker saw the old guy recently, he had bruises up and down one arm and seemed very uncomfortable talking about his daughter.'

'Abuse of the elderly,' I said.

'Yeah, bingo. Well, from a public safety point of view, that's a rib with some significant meat on it – that's something I can check out. So the next day I get a few minutes free and I drive out to Martin Acres. I hang my shield on my coat pocket and puff up my chest, and I knock on the guy's front door.'

I savored the image.

'The old guy came to the door himself. I introduce myself right through the screen. He stares at my shield for maybe ten seconds, then he says, "Are you here to arrest Dorothy?"'

'Wow,' I said. 'Just like that, Sam? You're good. God, you're good. I ever tell you that?'

'Yeah, your sarcasm aside, I know I'm good. But to get back to my story, just like that the old guy says, "Are you here to arrest Dorothy?" When I don't reply to the man's question right away, he starts to cry. I figure it's tears of relief, you know, so I'm standing there feeling pretty good about myself and my neighbor the stockbroker.'

'Did you arrest Dorothy?'

'Yeah. Dorothy and I sat down and chatted at her daddy's kitchen table and she spilled the beans and I arrested her right then and there. I did.'

Sam stopped talking. I waited for something else. It didn't come.

'I give up, Sam. I'm missing the parable. It just sounds like another sad story to me.'

'Were you always this concrete? I used to think that you had a more abstract side to your personality. Isn't that like a requirement for people in your profession?'

'You going to tell me the point?'

'My neighbor, the broker? He had no right to tell me what he told me about this guy selling his bonds.'

'Ah,' I said. 'So your neighbor is yet another confidentiality slut. But because of his indiscretion, an old man is safe. That's the message that's supposed to help me sleep better tonight? Thank you, Aesop.'

'Close but not quite, Doc. This is where the parable gets even more heuristic.'

It was at moments when Sam used words like 'heuristic' that I was reminded about his master's degree in literature.

'See, the truth is the old man's life has turned to shit. He'd already sold off over half the bonds that he needed to supplement his Social Security income' – Sam's pronunciation of the words made them sound like 'so-so security' – 'and he'll never get that money back. None of it. What's worse, as far as I can tell, it all went up Dorothy's nose. If you can believe it, the old man even sold off two more bonds to pay for a lawyer for the bitch daughter after I arrested her.

'And that's not the worst. The worst is that now what's left of his family is fractured so badly that it will never recover. The man lost his money and his family turned to crap.'

I said, 'It would have been worse if Dorothy had been permitted to continue to abuse him, Sam.'

'You never know that, though, do you? She managed to ruin things for him no matter what we did to try to help. That's the parable. In court the day she was arraigned, he told me that he wished she had just gone ahead and killed him. You just never know about these things.'

I tried to be palliative. 'You did what you thought was best.'

'Did I? I go back to that day that I'm standing at his door, and I'm no longer sure that the tears I saw on his cheek were from relief. I think the guy realized that whatever good cards he'd been holding in his hand up until that point in his life, fate had just figured out how to trump him. He'd gone from king of the old retired guys at the Senior Center to being some beat-up old chump who knows bitterness like he knows the gap in his mouth where the tooth is missing.'

I inhaled deeply, trying to recapture the aroma of my family. 'This Tom Clone thing you're looking into isn't going to have a pretty ending either, is it, Sam?'

'Nope. Not a prayer.'

'Good night, Sam. Thanks for the update.'

'Yeah. Hey, one more thing.'

I wasn't surprised there was one more thing.

'You know anything you can tell me about this female FBI agent? The one who alibied him that night? You never even commented on the fact that they were together. The other night, I told you that Clone's alibi was a female FBI agent and you didn't even say a single word about it. Not even a flinch from you. The detective part of me finds that just the slightest bit goofy.'

I know a lot about the FBI agent, I thought. *Or I may only know a little; I'm not quite sure which*. But whichever it was, I couldn't tell Sam a thing about Kelda James and anything she might have to do with Tom Clone.

I don't like being trapped. With both his parable and his question, Sam had me trapped. I scrambled for a way out of the snare. Injecting my tone full of mock indignation for his benefit, I said, 'What do you think I am?'

It was his turn to laugh. 'We've already established that, haven't we?'

I didn't want to wake Sam's wife and son, so I used his pager number when I tried to reach him much later that night.

I held Lauren's little phone in my hand as I stood outside on the narrow deck off the living room listening to the sounds of the night. The usual nocturnal symphony was being poisoned by an eruption of noise that was something like a duel between a gasoline-powered leaf blower and a violin being played by a baboon. Just for the record, the sound of a cantankerous fox almost succeeds in causing the caterwaul of a feline in heat to sound like Mozart.

The phone vibrated in my hand. It was a good thing that it was set to vibrate. Had it only chirped, I might not have heard it over the fox's screeching and moaning. I flipped it open. 'Hi, Sam. It's Alan.'

He wasn't happy that I'd called. 'Whose number is this?'

'Lauren's cell. I didn't want your call to wake her, so I'm out on the deck listening to a pissed-off fox.'

'You woke me. What does a pissed-off fox sound like?'

I held the phone out into the night for about fifteen seconds before I returned it to my face and said, 'Like that.'

'It's awful. You guys have to listen to that every night? Is that the price of living in the country?'

'This is a rare treat. Listen, has Tom Clone been seen since Monday afternoon? Like midafternoon?'

I felt a brief hesitation from Sam before he said, 'No.'

'Then I may have been the last one to see him. I saw him climbing onto a red Vespa on Walnut Street at about three forty-five Monday afternoon.'

My rationalization? Technically, this bit of news about my patient wasn't privileged information. Given the media coverage his release from prison had generated recently, Tom was, whether he liked it or not, a public figure, and I could tell Sam what I'd observed him doing outside the confines of my office. If I hadn't been worried about Tom's welfare, however, I never would have shared with Sam the fact that I'd watched Tom climb onto a Vespa.

Even though Sam knew very well that my office was on Walnut Street and he also knew exactly where I spent my weekday afternoons, he was wise enough not to editorialize on either fact.

He wasn't wise enough, however, to know what a Vespa was.

'A red Vespa? What the hell is a Vespa?'

'It's an Italian scooter.'

'Like my kid's Razor? That kind of scooter?'

'No, not a kid's scooter. A motor scooter, the kind that cool people in Rome use to get around the city. That kind of scooter. Like a little motorcycle. I'm sure you've seen them.'

'I haven't been to Rome lately. Why didn't you just say motorcycle?'

I didn't answer that. I silently counted to three before I said, 'I thought you might want to know that Clone was on a . . . vehicle.'

'You called because of my parable, didn't you? It got to you, my goofy little story about the old guy with the bonds got to you.'

'No, I didn't call because of your parable. I haven't thought about your parable once since you told it to me.'

After a delay of a few seconds, Sam asked, 'This has kept you from sleeping, hasn't it? All this guilty knowledge you have about Clone?' His voice was uncommonly compassionate.

'Yes, it has.'

'Well, go on back to bed. This should help us. Sometimes it's easier to find a motorcycle – excuse me, a Vespa – than it is to find a person.'

When I pressed the button to end the call, all I could hear were the incessant chirps of a few dozen crickets. The fox had stopped its caterwauling.

PART THREE

Praying for Monsoons

CHAPTER
29

'What the . . .' Tom Clone mumbled as he realized he was waking up outdoors. The air tasted different and his nose was assaulted by a sharp scent of pine. A metallic taste coated his tongue. He raised his head and lowered it immediately, trying to quell the flash of pain that was connecting his temples as though a hot spike had been inserted between the two sides of his skull. 'Shit,' he said aloud, grimacing.

Grimacing hurt so much that he grimaced again.

He attempted to move his feet but they would only slide laterally a few inches. He felt the slick surface of ripstop nylon against the skin on his arms and realized that he was in a sleeping bag. *There's an explanation*, he assured himself. *There's a way to explain this. Where was I last night?*

Tom Clone wasn't one of those Colorado natives who were more comfortable waking up in a mummy bag with his sleep-crusted eyes focused on the streaky skies of morning. Prior to his incarceration, his idea of roughing it involved staying in motels without air-conditioning.

His memory of the previous night was a black hole. Groaning, he rolled his head to the left and then ever so slowly to the right, half expecting to discover that he was sleeping next to someone, some girl he'd picked up and who'd convinced him against his better judgment to go camping.

Camping?

After so long, he thought, he'd have done anything to get laid. Even gone camping. But he didn't remember getting laid.

There wasn't another sleeping bag beside him. He was alone. Oddly, a chain-link fence rose from the ground parallel to the sleeping bag not ten feet from his right side. 'God, I must have been drunk to even think about sleeping here,' he mumbled. His tongue felt as though it had been lacquered during the night.

His brain was trying to answer the simple question of where 'here' was. It failed.

He raised his arms out of the sleeping bag and noticed a pinprick and bruise on the inside of his left wrist. 'I don't know,' he said, as though he was trying to answer his next question. 'What the hell did I do to myself?'

His eyes focused past the evidence of injury on his wrist, and he saw another fence. This one was on his left.

'What the . . .?'

Tom sat up abruptly. Pain radiated out from his spine. 'Damn,' he moaned. 'Shit,' he added as he rotated at his waist and looked back in the opposite direction.

The fence surrounded him, creating a square of about twenty feet on a side. He scrambled out of the sleeping bag and yanked himself to his feet. He paced backward around the rumpled sack. The walls around him rose eight feet.

'What the fuck?' he said. 'What the hell is going on? Where's the damn gate?'

He approached the links and then jogged all four sides of the interior perimeter. 'There's no gate,' he said. 'There's no gate.' He heard the panic in his voice.

He realized suddenly that his feet were in dirty white socks. He wasn't wearing shoes.

He dove down onto the bag and rooted around to find his shoes inside. They weren't there. He lowered himself so that he was sitting on the bag, raised his knees, and wrapped his arms around his legs.

'Think,' he said. 'Think, think, think.'

He was in the mountains, and he was below timberline. A thick pine forest grew in all directions just beyond the fence. Not too far to the west – on the darker side of the dawn sky – a line of snow-capped peaks seemed close enough to touch. He knew there were plenty of Coloradans who would have been able to recognize the vista from memory. He wasn't one of them.

Had he been more experienced in the wilderness, the stunted height of the nearby pines would have been a clue that he was somewhere very high in the mountains. But he wasn't experienced.

Where was he?

He didn't know. It could be anywhere from Cortez to Steamboat Springs as far as he could tell. He could even be in Wyoming or Utah.

He tried to remember the night before.

Nothing. Not a thing.

Damn.

He hopped to his feet, moved toward the fence, and looked up to the top. From his years in prison, he was so accustomed to the glint of concertina that he expected to see endless coils of razor-sharp stainless steel above this fence, too. But the coils weren't there. This was just a fence.

Was this some kind of sick joke?

He allowed himself a sardonic smile and reached out with one hand to begin to scale the fence.

'*I wouldn't do that,*' an amplified voice said.

Tom froze, then spun a full 360 degrees to try to find the person who was speaking to him. He didn't see anyone. He took a deep, raspy breath and scanned the adjacent forest more carefully. Still nothing.

He reached again for the fence.

'*I wouldn't—*'

Tom crumpled in agony at the foot of the fence. He was temporarily paralyzed by the jolt of electricity that had ratcheted through his body. The bottoms of his feet burned like they were on fire.

He watched with surprise as a dark stain spread on the inside thigh of his trousers. The discoloration spread for at least ten seconds before he felt the warm moisture from his own urine against his skin.

'*Next time, listen to my suggestions. They are valuable. In the meantime, stay away from the fence. It's uncomfortable to touch it. But I guess you know that by now, don't you?*'

Tom rolled away from the fence. The voice was

obviously male. But he had no associations to it in his memory. He demanded, 'Who the fuck are you?'

'I'm not surprised you don't recognize me, actually. You don't have much experience with people like me.'

'What? You're my jailer. I know all about jailers.'

'No, Tom, I'm your conscience. And you don't know a damn thing about having a conscience.'

Tom felt suddenly sick. 'Where are you?' he asked.

'I'm right here. Where are you?'

'Fuck you. What are you doing to me? How did I get here? What the fuck do you want?'

'I'll answer a couple of your questions. How did you get here? I drugged you and brought you up here. What do I want? Satisfaction. Now, no more questions. No more answers.'

'Fuck you!'

'You know, I've been told that thirst tends to improve attitude. I think we'll do a little empirical study and see if that turns out to be true. In case your internal altimeter isn't working, we're well over nine thousand feet above sea level right now, Tom. The weather forecast is for another hot and dry day. Even way up here, it'll be in the eighties by midafternoon. Humidity should be hovering around twenty percent. That's dry. Real dry. You enjoy your morning.'

'Wait!' Tom yelled.

No reply.

'Come back!' he tried.

Nothing.

'Shit!'

He was back in prison. He felt it in every cell in his body.

CHAPTER

30

Kelda called Tom Clone at his grandfather's house over her lunch hour on Wednesday. She used a pay phone one block away from the Federal Building. Only after the phone rang six or seven times did she remember that he'd told her that he was starting work that week.

She called directory assistance and got the number for the pharmacy at Boulder's Kaiser clinic and dialed. After punching menu choices for about two minutes, she finally reached a human being, and asked the woman who answered if she could speak to Tom Clone.

'I'm sorry. We don't have anyone here by that name,' was the reply. Kelda thought the woman sounded as if she was twelve years old.

'This is the pharmacy?'

'Yes.'

Kelda explained, 'I'm looking for the new guy. He just started yesterday, I think. He's, um—'

'Oh, him? He didn't show up yesterday. So, well,' the woman giggled, 'he doesn't, like, even work here. Somebody else has been hired. The new new guy is a friend of Jack's, I think.'

'The first new guy didn't show up today?'

'No, he didn't; he didn't show up at all. Not yesterday, not today. So I can't help you, I guess. Would you like the extension for Human Resources? Maybe they know something.'

'No. Thank you.'

Kelda hung up and tried Tom's grandfather's house again. This time she listened to the drone of the phone for fifteen rings before she hung up. She fought a flush of dread. A beige haze masked the western horizon. In the distance, white clouds billowed high above the Divide. The pastiche looked like meringue on top of dirt.

She dug around in her purse for more coins and a business card and punched a number, another Boulder number, into her phone.

A distracted voice answered, 'Detective Purdy.'

'Detective? This is Special Agent Kelda James. You and I spoke about Tom Clone.'

'Yeah, I remember,' Purdy said. 'Almost like it was yesterday.'

Which it had been.

'Have you arrested him?' Kelda asked.

She could hear Purdy breathing, and wondered whether he was intentionally exhaling directly into the telephone. 'Is this a request for professional courtesy, Agent James? If it is, I respectfully decline.'

In her well-practiced I'm-a-federal-agent-don't-give-me-any-shit voice, Kelda said, 'Look, Detective. I can't find Tom Clone. I'll stop looking for him if I know that you have him behind bars. It's a simple question.'

In the silence that followed, Kelda assumed that the Boulder detective was considering the advantage she had just offered him. If Tom Clone had been arrested, the detective could play Kelda any number of different ways. If Tom Clone hadn't been arrested, Purdy was probably playing out the possibilities of why Kelda James wasn't able to find him.

One distinct possibility, she knew – and she knew that Purdy knew – was that Tom didn't want to be found. She tried to consider the ramifications if Tom had gone on the run.

'If he was under arrest, that would be public record,' Purdy said.

'Yes.'

'But he's not.'

'Thank you,' she sighed. She didn't even try to keep the exasperation out of her voice.

'Not at all. If you do find Clone, I'd like to talk with him. Would you tell him that for me?'

'Yes, I'll pass that along. You should probably tell his attorney that, you know.'

'His office already knows,' Purdy replied. 'But the attorney has just left on a safari in Kenya.'

'Oh.'

While she was considering Tony Loving's trip to Africa, Purdy asked her, 'You wouldn't happen to know anything about a red Vespa, would you? It's apparently like a motor scooter. Maybe it belongs to Clone?'

She momentarily toyed with being as much of an asshole as Purdy was being. Instead, she decided to answer his question civilly in hopes of getting some cooperation in return. 'Yes, I do know something about it, actually. It belongs to his grandfather, not to Tom. His grandfather has a bad hip, uses the scooter to get around town. Apparently, he finds using it more comfortable than getting in and out of cars.'

'Grandfather probably isn't using it much right now. Don't think they allow Vespas in the ICU.'

The bolus of sarcasm from Purdy was disappointing but not totally unexpected to Kelda. The legendary tension between federal agents and local cops wasn't just myth. 'I imagine not,' she said, intentionally trying not to aggravate the situation.

'Does Tom ever use it?' Purdy asked.

'I don't know. Why don't you ask him?'

'For the same reason you can't ask him whatever you want to ask him. Because I can't find him either.'

'Since when?'

'He was last seen Monday afternoon. Midafternoon, to be specific. Did you hear from him after that?'

Without hesitation, she said, 'No, I didn't. And why do you want to know about the Vespa anyway? What does that have to do with it? Did you find the Vespa someplace?' She gave him a couple of seconds to respond. When he didn't, she prodded, 'Come on. I've been up-front with you.'

She felt another echoing exhale in her earpiece before Purdy said evenly, 'It's just a loose end. I'm sure even FBI agents get them sometimes. Loose ends, I mean. Not as often as someone like me investigating assaults and minor crap like that in Boulder might get them. But sometimes.'

She wanted to scream at him. 'Can we be frank, Detective?'

'That would be refreshing, Special Agent James. Dear God, that would be refreshing.'

She had been about to divulge to Purdy that Tom Clone had been concerned about his safety, but suddenly her mouth hung open, she blinked her eyes twice, and she completely reconsidered what she had been about to say.

'Never mind,' she said. 'Good-bye, Detective.'

She hung up the phone and shook her head. Nearby, she saw a couple of support personnel from the Bureau walking along the sidewalk. If she had been alone, she would have thrown something or slammed the receiver against the phone – or something – and she would have screamed, 'You goddamn shit!'

Instead, she adjusted her shoulder bag and pulled her sunglasses down in front of her eyes and crossed the street just as the light changed. The pace she took to the lobby of the Hotel Monaco would have forced almost anybody trying to stay with her to jog.

She dropped two coins into the lobby pay phone and punched in a familiar number.

No answer.

She retrieved the two coins and punched in another familiar number.

After only one ring, she heard the beginning of a recording from the veterinary practice of Dr. Ira Winslett. The practice, she learned, was temporarily closed due to a family emergency. The doctor's calls were being taken by – Kelda slammed the phone down before she learned what other vet was covering for Ira. She didn't really care.

She cursed under her breath, stepped away from the phone, and closed her eyes, trying to compose herself.

When she opened her eyes again, she saw the fleeting image of a man in a dark suit moving rapidly along the sidewalk in front of the hotel.

She thought it might have been Bill Graves.

'Oh damn,' she whispered.

CHAPTER

31

The amplified voice said, *'In case you're wondering, it's one o'clock. How's your attitude?'*

Tom Clone was sitting with his legs crossed. He was holding the sleeping bag above his head as a shelter against the sun, but the heat was almost intolerable. In reply to the voice, he lifted his right hand out from beneath the bag and raised his middle finger to the sky.

'Thirsty?' the voice inquired.

Tom lifted his left hand so he could flip his captor the bird with both hands. The sleeping bag slipped to the ground behind him. A few clouds were forming above the Divide, but to him the sky didn't portend rain. He thought wistfully that he'd settle for some cloud cover and a little shade.

'Now catch!' The quality of the voice had changed dramatically. It was no longer amplified.

'What?'

'Turn around.'

Tom did.

'I said, "Catch!"' A figure wearing a bulky canvas suit with fat gloves and a helmet with a screen over the face stood on the edge of the pine forest. In one hand the person held a wooden box about eighteen inches square with a handle on the top. In the other hand he carried a shopping bag with a flat bottom.

Tom perused the disguise and had to admit it was pretty good camouflage. He couldn't identify whoever was wearing the suit. He still thought the voice had been a man's.

'Catch what?' Tom asked.

The man took a half-dozen steps forward until he stood only ten feet from the fence. He set the box down on the dirt, reached into the bag, and removed a half-liter bottle of water. He tossed it over the fence.

Tom jumped back a yard or so and caught it.

His ears picked up a droning noise, as though someone was operating a lawn mower a hundred yards away. *Were they that close to civilization?*

The thought gave him hope.

'Now put down the bottle and catch this.' The man in the canvas suit reached back into the bag and lifted an orb about the size of a softball. He held it up above his head so that Tom could examine it. Then, with an exaggerated underhanded motion, he tossed it high over the fence.

Tom dropped the bottle and braced to catch the orb. It was coming straight at him. The second it hit his hands the ball disintegrated and he found himself instantly enveloped in a cloud of fine yellow powder. All that remained of the ball in his hands was a crumpled pile of cheesecloth, flat toothpicks, and a little bit of tape.

He coughed and tried to spit the yellow dust out of his mouth. 'What the fuck was that?'

'Pollen.'

'Pollen?'

'Yes, Tom, pollen. You like pollen?'

'Not particularly. I'd rather have a sandwich.'

'You know who likes pollen?'

'Mary Poppins?'

'Bees like pollen, Tom. And to make them like it even more, I chopped up a few queen bees and mixed them up with the pollen. The scent of the queen bees draws the worker bees like naked girls draw adolescent boys. And these particular bees are a tad on the aggressive side, anyway.'

Tom's heartbeat accelerated and, without thinking, he brushed at his bare arms. The dust, as fine as cake flour, coated him like paint. Brushing it only seemed to force the yellow pigment into his skin.

He stared at the man. With monumental alarm, his mind recognized the purpose of the canvas suit the man was wearing.

It wasn't a disguise.

It was a beekeeper's outfit.

'No!' Tom screamed. He started a frantic dance, flailing his legs, maniacally rubbing his hands over his skin and clothing. 'Are they killer bees? Are they going to kill me?'

The man reached down and grabbed the handle on the wooden box.

'No, you can't!' Tom yelled, still swiping at the yellow powder that covered his body.

The man lifted the box and began to swing it front to back.

The droning noise grew louder.

'Wait! Tell me what you want! You can't do that!' Tom implored.

The length of the arc of the box increased a little bit each time the man swung it. It reminded Tom of a child climbing progressively higher on a swing.

The humming sound permeated the clearing.

Tom ran to the farthest corner of the enclosure. It felt futile, but he didn't know what else to do.

Near the top of its forward arc, the man released the wooden box from his hand. It accelerated as it shot into the air, easily clearing the top of the fence before falling and crashing to the dust about five feet into the pen.

The wooden box collapsed upon impact and the sound of the furious swarm of bees escaping their confinement was the scariest thing Tom had heard since the night in prison when . . .

The bees were upon him before he could complete the thought.

'No, they're not killer bees,' the man said. 'And I do hope you're not allergic.' He didn't think Tom Clone heard him.

The funny thing was, his words were totally sincere.

32

Kelda almost didn't have to fake it. Ten minutes after she'd left the lobby of the Hotel Monaco, she felt almost as sick as she was pretending to be when she took the elevator back up to the FBI Field Office and told the young guy at the reception desk that she had just thrown up her lunch and was going to take the rest of the day off.

Bill Graves watched her collect her things and stuff them into her shoulder bag. 'Where are you going?' he finally asked.

'Home. I'm not feeling well. I just puked up my lunch.'

'Oh,' he said. 'I hope you feel better. Anything I can do? Do you need a ride someplace?'

She forced a smile. 'Thanks, but no. I'm sure I'll be fine. It's just a stomach bug, probably.'

'Please don't tell me you ate at that Italian place at the Hotel Monaco? Panzano? I really like that place, wouldn't want to think it made you sick.'

His words caused her to hold her breath. Bill had seen her in the lobby of the Hotel Monaco. And he wanted her to know that he'd seen her. The question was: Why did he want her to know?

Was he warning her about something?

'No, no. There was too long a wait at the restaurant, and I didn't have time. I just ended up grabbing something from a street vendor. Just my luck, it came right back up.' She regretted the lie even as she was telling it. If Bill had been following her, he would know that she hadn't really stopped at any of the sidewalk stands for lunch.

He'd know she was lying. And he'd conclude she had a reason to lie.

After a moment's contemplation, he said, 'Well, I do hope you feel better. Take care.'

'Thanks, Bill. You're a sweetheart, you know that?'

'I keep telling you that, Kelda.'

She slipped her bag over her left shoulder and headed toward the bank of elevators.

When the car arrived, Kelda stepped in, moved to the back corner of the elevator, and leaned against the wall. The sudden swoosh of the rapid descent flipped her empty stomach, and she wondered if she really was going to throw up. As the car stopped about halfway down the building to pick up additional passengers, she suddenly realized why Bill Graves had told her that he'd seen her standing in the lobby at the Hotel Monaco.

He wanted her to know she was being followed.

Kelda bolted out of the elevator just before the door closed on the eleventh floor, and hustled down the hall to the staircase. Descending the stairs to the building's lobby, she used a delivery door that a UPS driver had left propped open and made her way out to the alley.

The tail that Bill Graves was warning her about could have been unofficial – it could have been nothing more than Bill being curious or intrusive. That was worrisome, but Kelda was confident she could lose any tail Bill put on her if he was acting alone. But . . . if the tail was something that had been mounted by the SAC with full Bureau resources, that was something else altogether. If that was the case, Kelda couldn't risk using her car to leave downtown. She couldn't even risk renting a car with her own ID.

The air was hot and still. A block from the Federal Building, she checked her wallet and counted her cash. Thirty-seven dollars. She backtracked half a block and withdrew four hundred dollars from an ATM. If her colleagues wanted to know she'd collected money from her account, she knew that they could get the information easily. But it wouldn't tell them anything important about her location. She was exactly where they thought she would be, less than a block from the field office.

Kelda convinced herself that no helicopters – they couldn't want to know what she was up to *that* badly – were involved in tracking her, and she flagged down a cab. She told the driver to drop her at the corner of Thirty-second and Speer, just across Federal Boulevard on the other side of Interstate 25. At the conclusion of the ten-minute ride, she gave the driver one of the fresh bills that she'd just gotten out of the ATM and told him to keep the change. She waited on the corner until the cab was out of sight. After carefully examining the area for signs that her colleagues had managed to track her – she didn't notice a thing – she headed on foot toward Highland Park.

It only took her two minutes to get to the address she was seeking on Grove Street, less than a block from the park. The home was a bungalow with a tiny lawn and impeccably maintained landscaping. Kelda climbed three wooden steps to the front porch and touched the bell.

'Please be home, please be home,' Kelda murmured as she fished in her change purse for a couple of Percocet. Still waiting, she popped them into her mouth and swallowed them dry.

Seconds later, Maria Alija answered the door. She was dressed in a simple print dress and open-toed shoes.

Kelda asked, 'May I come in, Maria?'

A storm of alarm rose in Maria's eyes. 'Is my baby okay?'

Kelda raised both palms. 'Rosa's fine. She's fine.' The panic in Maria's eyes didn't ebb. Kelda said, 'You believe me, don't you, Maria?'

'*Si.*'

'I need a favor from you, *por favor.* Can I borrow your car? It's kind of an emergency.'

Without hesitation, Maria Alija reached into her purse and held out her keys to Kelda. 'I was just heading back to work. You can have it as long as you want. Overnight, whatever you need. Anything for you. You are family.'

'And you are a saint, Maria. I'll drop you off at your work,' Kelda said. 'How's that?'

Maria worked in a dentist's office that was about a mile north of her home. A couple of minutes later, as Kelda pulled Maria's old Ford Contour into the lot, she asked, 'One more favor, Maria? Another big one.'

'*Si*.'

'Do you carry a cell phone?'

'*Si*, for Rosa. She worries.'

'May I borrow it?'

Maria smiled. 'Kelda, I would give you a kidney, gladly.'

33

'*You shouldn't have swatted at them. It only pisses them off. If you had just stayed still, I don't think you would have been stung so often. Maybe not even at all. But, although I wouldn't know, I bet that's hard to do when a thousand bees are buzzing around your head.*'

The voice was once again amplified.

Tom could hear it, clearly. As far as he could tell, he hadn't been stung on his ears. He would have said, 'Fuck you,' but his lips were already so swollen he didn't think it was worth the agony it would cause to try to speak.

'*The point wasn't the stinging. It was the fear. Did you experience the fear, Tom? Did you?*'

Tom nodded. A few bees still buzzed around the enclosure. The faint noise they made sounded to Tom like a dentist's drill hovering above his unanesthetized molar.

'*What? Did you say something?*'

'I could ha'e gone into shock and died. You could ha'e killed 'e.'

'That's true. I took that risk.'

Tom had already poured half the bottle of water that the man had thrown to him over his skin. The other half he'd poured down his throat, trying not to touch the rim of the bottle to his lips. 'It really 'ucking hurts. The stings. They 'ucking 'urn and they 'ucking sting.'

'I bet they do.'

'One got inside 'y 'outh. I even ha'e a sting in 'y arm'it.'

'Really? One stung you inside your mouth? That's why you're talking so funny. And you have one in your armpit? Ouch.'

'Why?' Tom pleaded.

'Why? Why am I doing this? You tell me. Why? Why would someone do this to you? Terrify you half to death? Why?'

Tom was fighting tears. 'I don't know. Why?'

'You don't know yet? I guess we're not done, then. The lessons will just have to continue. You keep working on an answer, okay? Tom? It's important. I hope you get this right, because if you don't understand the lessons, I promise that you won't want to take the final.'

'No 'ore 'ees. No 'ore 'ees. 'ease.' Tom Clone had made it through all his years in the penitentiary without begging. But he was begging.

'Just tell me then, why would someone do this to you? Just tell me and we'll move on to another lesson.'

Tom could barely create a coherent thought through the volume of agony he was suffering from the plethora of fresh bee stings. *Another lesson? Oh God.* He shook his head, mute and helpless.

'*Hey,*' the voice coaxed, '*listen to this.*'

For almost a minute, Tom heard nothing. What he was listening for was the drone of the distant lawn mower, which to him would mean the advent of another swarm of bees and more agony. What he finally heard was even more frightening: the unforgettable sound of steel doors slamming.

Prison doors.

'Oh '*an.* You '*ucker,*' Tom said. 'It was you. You 'ade those 'oises in 'y house.'

'*Yes, I did. I actually recorded them right off the DVD of* The Green Mile. *You probably missed it, but it was a pretty good Tom Hanks movie about death row. Then I cleaned them up digitally a bit. It's a cassette recorder on a timer up in the attic. I think the effects sound pretty good. Do you agree?*'

Tom didn't reply.

'*Good. I'm just going to keep playing that loop for a while. I have it set up so that the doors seem to close at random. Just like it must have been for you when you were inside. You just never know what's coming. That can't be pleasant. Could make you fearful.*'

Tom felt his heart pop in his chest, and his mind flashed on a lesson from his senior psychiatry rotation. *Learned Helplessness*, maybe. An orange book. Someone named Seligman – or something like that – wrote it.

It was about the connection between despair and the inability to control negative consequences in life. *This is what life was like for those rats and dogs*, he thought. *I'm helpless. There's nothing I can do to stop this madman.*

'I'm behind you now, Tom.' The voice was natural again, lacking amplification. 'You should turn around.'

Tom crawled to his knees. Slowly, he rotated to face his captor.

The man was ten feet from the fence. He was wearing faded blue jeans, a polo shirt, and lightweight hiking boots. A motorcycle helmet – a full one, with chin and jaw protection and a dark visor – totally hid his face. In his left hand he carried another wooden box with a handle on top. This box was about eighteen inches long and a foot high. The man wore heavy leather gloves.

''ore 'ees?' Tom's voice was burdened with so much dread he could barely get the sounds out of his throat.

'More bees? No.' The man shook his head, hefting the box slightly. 'Snakes this time. Vipers.'

'*What?*'

The man repeated himself. 'I said, "Vipers." It's a terribly misunderstood species of snake.'

He moved forward and placed the wooden box flush against the chain-link fence, reached down, and lifted the side that was closest to the fence straight up and away from the box.

Ten seconds later, a glistening head about the size of a small egg emerged from the shadows and extended through one of the galvanized diamonds in the mesh of the fence.

'It's about fear, Tom. Do you get it yet?'

Tom was incredulous. He couldn't take his eyes off the box and the snake that was emerging from the darkness. ''i'ers?' he asked. 'That's a 'i'er?'

'Yes, Tom. Vipers. That's a viper.'

'Hel'! Hel'!' He scrambled to his feet and backed away, dragging the sleeping bag with him across the enclosure.

'No one's going to help you, Tom. Do you know what that's like? Not to have anyone help you when you're afraid? To have someone know that you're afraid and be in a position to help you but refuse you help? Can you imagine what that is like, Tom? You know, I bet you can.'

'Hel'! Hel'!' Tom's voice cracked as he screamed. His parched throat couldn't generate the volume that his lungs were demanding.

'You don't have to wonder what it's like to be stalked anymore, Tom. The vipers are stalking you now.'

The snake surged forward so that about a foot of its body extended out of the wooden box. There it stilled, its sleek head frozen in space about ten inches above the dirt.

The man said, 'He hasn't eaten in well over a week.'

'*Hel'!*'

A second head emerged from the box, protruding through a different diamond in the mesh.

'Neither has that one,' said the man, who turned and walked back toward the forest. He paused and said, 'Remember, Tom. It's about fear. It's all about fear. *Feel the fear.*'

Just then a prison door slammed in the middle of the Colorado wilderness.

34

One of the two snakes had slithered about halfway across the enclosure toward Tom when he came to the sudden realization that the man in the beekeeper's suit and the motorcycle helmet wasn't Detective Prehost.

Why would Prehost want to teach him lessons about fear?

In Tom's experience, Prehost's motivations had no heuristic undertones. Prehost's scheme was devoid of pretense. He simply wanted Tom poisoned to death in the execution chamber at the Colorado State Penitentiary. He wouldn't bother to engage in theater to torment Tom about the meaning of fear.

So, Tom wondered, if the man in the motorcycle helmet wasn't Fred Prehost, who the hell was he?

While Tom desperately pondered the identity of his captor, the second snake cleared the fence and stretched down to the dry earth. The dark natural camouflage of the two vipers failed to disguise them in the pale dust of Colorado's high country. As the snakes slithered across the open space in the fenced-in pen, they were as visible to Tom as shark fins in a swimming pool.

Tom tried to remember what he'd read you were supposed to do if you confronted a snake.

Run or not run?

Stay still or back away?

Act big or act small?

He couldn't remember. At that moment he wasn't sure he could remember how to tie his shoes. If he had shoes. 'Hel' 'ee,' he whispered. 'Oh God, 'ease hel' 'ee.'

He wondered if he could use the electricity in the fence against the snakes. But how?

The second of the two vipers to exit the box began making up for lost time. Edging forward, it overtook the first snake and seemed to be on a direct line for where Tom stood in the corner. He took two sideways steps toward the west.

The physician in Tom Clone noticed that he wasn't sweating at all, and he began to wonder about heatstroke. He was oddly comforted by a sudden thought: Growing delirious from heatstroke might be preferable to whatever these snakes might do to him.

That's what he was thinking about when he heard the rattle.

He growled, 'Rattlesnakes! These are rattlesnakes! I thought you said they were 'i'ers!'

The amplified voice responded, *'Most people don't know that rattlesnakes are part of the viper family. But they are. Technically, these two are western diamondback rattlesnakes.*

Native to this region, but never seen at this altitude unless someone like me gives them a lift. One real cold night up here and these guys will be toast. Or ice, as the case may be. But I didn't actually mislead you, rest assured that these are indeed vipers.' He paused. 'Would you have preferred a pair of puff adders or a couple of copperheads instead? I can oblige, I assure you.'

Tom couldn't take his eyes off the black-brown ropes slithering in his direction. He cried, 'They'll kill 'e!'

'Well, obviously we'll have to wait and see about that. They're certainly capable of it. These western diamondbacks aren't the most aggressive of the vipers, but neither are they the most docile. They're quite venomous, though; you absolutely wouldn't want to be bitten by one. They have fangs from hell – a true marvel of bioengineering. Bye now, Tom.'

'No! No!'

'I'll check back in a while and see how things turned out. Remember the lesson: It's all about fear.'

A cell door slammed in the distance.

Tom felt his stomach roil. He doubled over in dry heaves.

35

Ira lived in a tract home half a mile from the Boulder Turnpike in the nondescript suburban landscape where Arvada became Westminster became Broomfield. In the years that they had known each other, Kelda had never asked him in which town he actually lived, because she couldn't see how it really mattered to anyone but the mailman, the tax collector, and maybe the guy who drove the UPS truck. For everybody else, 'Denver's western suburbs' sufficed.

Given that almost all the streets around Ira's house had the exact same name – Dudley – distinguished only by different suffixes: Parkway, Lane, Way, Street, Place, Circle – Kelda found it amazing that anyone ever found a specific address in Ira's neighborhood. She knew how to get there. That was all that was important to her.

The ride to Ira's house took her fifteen minutes after she dropped Maria off at work on North Federal. Ira's home was the one on the cul-de-sac with the siding that was painted the darkest shade of putty permitted by the covenants of the homeowners' association. The distinctive waffle-batter-with-too-much-vanilla color – as opposed to the predominant sky-on-a-hazy-day color – was the only way Kelda was able to identify Ira's dwelling from a distance. Once she was close enough to the house, she could confirm it was indeed Ira's by spotting the menagerie of animal sculptures that he'd hidden amongst the shrubs and bushes of the otherwise association-approved landscaping. Her favorite statue was the brass baboon that peeked out from behind the rose of Sharon by the front door.

Ira had told her once that if any of his neighbors complained, he would be forced to remove the sculptures. Apparently, they were a violation of an association covenant that was intended to protect the burg against an invasion of lawn jockeys and pink flamingos. She'd had to break the news to him that not even the FBI could do anything about the covenant.

During her rare evening visits to Ira's house – they both preferred her place in the disappearing open country around Lafayette – she usually saw children playing on the wide asphalt course at the fat end of the cul-de-sac. But on that scorching weekday afternoon the neighborhood looked more like a modern ghost town. Not a single car was parked along the curb, not even an air-conditioning repair truck or a plumber unplugging a stopped-up drain. The lawn sprinklers were all off, the garage doors were all closed, and the miniblinds and curtains were all pulled to ward off the summer sun. The kids, she figured, must all be away at camp. The lawn service companies must have been busy on another block.

She pulled into Ira's driveway and walked to his door as though she were expected. She didn't bother to knock. Instead, she slipped her key into the lock and let herself inside. The air-conditioning in the house was off and the air inside was still and warm.

'Ira,' she called in a sardonic honey-I'm-home voice. 'Ira, it's Kelda. Are you here?'

She knew he wasn't.

She continued to the back of the house. The kitchen had the model-home quality of a room that wasn't accustomed to use. She couldn't recall ever seeing Ira prepare food there. In the center of the island counter was a tape recorder. On it was a yellow sticky note that read 'Kelda.'

She sat on a stool adjacent to the island and hit the button marked 'play.' As she touched the button, she said, 'Hi, Ira,' and was almost surprised at how pleasant her greeting sounded.

She wondered how he would word it, what tone he would take.

She didn't wonder what the message was going to say.

Ira's voice was as casual as it always was. '*Hi, babe,*' he started. '*Knowing you, I'm guessing that it didn't take long for you to figure out what was going on and that it's Wednesday morning that you're listening to this. It doesn't really matter. Maybe you were even quicker than I thought you'd be. It doesn't make any difference. If you're listening to this, I'm gone, and if I'm gone, you won't find me until I'm done. Don't even waste your energy looking.*'

Kelda said, 'Actually, I'm a little slow catching up with you, Ira. I think maybe it's the drugs.'

Ira didn't wait for her to finish her thought. *'I don't know whether it's fair or not – even whether it's warranted or not – but I've lost faith in your commitment to our . . . plan. I've been keeping an eye on you since our boy got free, and it seems that you've been keeping some things from me. Sooo, I've decided to accelerate things a bit. Okay, I've accelerated things a lot. You and I never exactly agreed about the delay you wanted before we got things started . . . Hey, what can I say? I changed the plans. Your doubts aren't my doubts.'*

Kelda heard the sound of a ringing phone emerge from the recorder. Ira responded by saying 'Damn' and shutting off the machine.

A second or two later the recording continued and he said, *'Where was I? Oh yeah.*

'Anyway, babe, I'm off on our adventure and obviously I'm . . . flying solo. I won't muck it up, I promise. Look around, everything's been sanitized. And this way your hands stay clean. That's good, right? You know that I love you, Kelda. Go ice your legs, babe, put on a fresh patch, and pray for the monsoons.'

She hit 'stop,' then 'rewind,' and a few moments later, 'eject.' She plucked the tape from the machine, placed it in her purse, poured some water into the ficus by the back door, checked to make sure the parakeets, Oliver and Lee, had seeds and water, and headed back toward the front of the house. She stopped just before she reached the door, and stepped into the tiny room by the entryway that the developer of the neighborhood generously referred to in his marketing materials as 'an executive study.' The two big aquariums inside the room were empty. She bent at the waist so that she could be sure that the snakes hadn't burrowed deep beneath the shredded newspaper in their glass homes.

They hadn't.

No surprise.

She ran down the stairs to the unfinished basement. It was as empty as it had been the day Ira had moved in. All the equipment was gone.

As she climbed the stairs back up to the first floor, she realized that her feet were on fire. The sharp needles she usually walked on by this time of almost every day had become so fiery hot they felt as if they were glowing. The pain of their sharpness was indistinguishable from the pain of their heat. She closed her eyes and tried to breathe through the pain.

It didn't help.

She locked the front door of Ira's house with the key when she left. Once in the car she phoned Tom Clone's grandfather's number again. She didn't expect an answer and she didn't get one.

She was at a loss.

Gary Cross, her first supervising agent in the Denver Field Office, had told her that there was only one thing to do when she reached a dead end during an investigation.

'What?' she'd asked.

'Something else,' he'd replied.

She stared at Maria's cell phone and tried to decide what exactly that something else might be. In the meantime, she searched her shoulder bag for her stash of Percocet.

36

L unch for psychotherapists is a moveable feast. What that means in reality is that it is usually moved until midafternoon.

Midday appointments are a coveted commodity for most clinical mental health professionals. Few working people are able to steal forty-five minutes from their workday once or twice a week for an appointment with a therapist, so 'meeting over lunch' is a common solution to the dilemma. On some days those 'lunch' appointments begin as early as eleven and end as late as two.

That's why I was walking out the door of my building at a few minutes after two o'clock to get something to eat.

I was halfway down Walnut to Ninth when I heard a female voice call my name. Not 'Dr. Gregory,' but 'Alan, Alan.' I looked over at the sound.

The woman in the car who was calling for me was Kelda James. She lowered her sunglasses and leaned toward the open window so that I could see her face. 'Do you have a second?' she asked.

'Do we have an appointment?' I replied, suddenly flustered by the possibility that I really wasn't actually free for lunch, but that I had another scheduled appointment that I'd forgotten to record.

'No, no. But can we talk for a second?'

I was almost broadsided by a young man – he definitely wasn't a kid – on a skateboard who zoomed past me before he disappeared around the corner onto Ninth. I stepped off the sidewalk onto the street and leaned down toward the window of Kelda's car.

'Thank you,' she said.

'Is this an emergency?' I asked. Translation: *Is this more important than me eating lunch?*

She nodded. 'Yes, I'm afraid it is.'

'Go on.'

'I'm not sure I know how to ask this but . . . I need to know if you know where I can find Tom Clone.'

I pressed my tongue against my teeth for a moment before I untangled my mouth enough to say, 'What?' I admit that my first thought was to uncomplicate my afternoon and simply say, 'No.'

Kelda repeated, 'Do you know where I can find Tom Clone?'

If I said I couldn't respond, I would be acknowledging that Tom was my patient. That was the trap that Sam Purdy had set for me with the exact same question. If I said I didn't know where he was, I was coming perilously close to flouting Tom's confidentiality.

'Kelda, I'm . . .' I watched a huge tractor-trailer fail to

317

complete the turn from Ninth onto Walnut. Traffic in both directions was totally blockaded by the truck's trailer, which extended across the width of Ninth. 'What are you asking me? You want to know if I know where someone you referred to me for psychotherapy is right now?'

'This isn't just my curiosity, Alan. This is an emergency. A serious emergency.'

I shaded my eyes against the afternoon sun. 'Are you asking this question as my patient or as an FBI agent?' Unlike Kelda, I *was* just being curious with my question. It made no difference to me whether Kelda was acting personally or professionally. My hands were tied with the same ethical twine regardless of the hat she was wearing while she asked the question.

'I don't know.'

I thought she looked quite despairing.

'But it's serious?'

She nodded.

'Then go ahead and park your car. I'll meet you back at my office in a minute or two.'

She sighed – I interpreted it as frustration, not relief – and said, 'Thank you.'

It's a long story,' she said. She hadn't even settled onto the chair. Her shoulder bag was still clutched in her hand. I suspected that she wasn't convinced that I was really going to insist that she explain what was going on.

I sat and crossed my legs. 'I have another patient at three,' I replied evenly. 'You should probably get started telling your long story.'

My curiosity and my concern for Tom Clone had almost eclipsed my hunger. Almost.

'I shouldn't spend the time' – I could tell she almost said 'waste the time' – 'telling you all this. I wish you would trust me that it would be better for Tom if you would just tell me what I need to know. Then I could go do whatever it is I can do to . . . help him.'

'Sorry, Kelda, but we're going to have to do this my way. Why don't you sit down? There are very limited circumstances that permit me to divulge privileged information.'

She fell heavily onto the chair. The shoulder bag clunked to the floor as though it were stuffed with a shot put. The fingertips of her left hand almost immediately began kneading her quad. 'I think Tom's in danger,' she said.

'Go on,' I said. I was thinking that my cast felt heavy.

CHAPTER

37

'*Tom? Where did the snakes go?*' The voice blew out of the speaker with an uncertain timbre.

'O'er there.' Tom's heart didn't even leap at the sound of his captor's voice. He pointed in the direction of the line of lodgepole pines south of the enclosure. He was standing within six inches of the fence on the north side of his prison. 'I think they got hot. They needed the shade.'

'*That happens with snakes. They're too hot; they're too cold. Who knows, they may be back, right? Tonight for instance. Who knows? It may be too cold in there for them, and they'll have to come looking for warmth. Like from you, or from your sleeping bag. Or – maybe – you in your sleeping bag.*'

'Yes,' Tom agreed. In the hour or so since the man had first opened the box and the two vipers had edged through the diamond links of the fence, Tom had decided that he was much more worried about the snakes than he was about the bees. Much more worried.

'When you fall asleep tonight I may just throw a few lame mice in there with you. They like mice. The vipers do. I don't want them to get too hungry.'

"i'ers. 'ice,' Tom repeated numbly. "'lease don't. No la'e 'ice. I think I already know all a'out 'ear.'

'You do? That's terrific. I'd love to hear, so please tell me what you know about fear. No, no, no. Instead tell me why . . . tell me why it's important that you know all about fear.'

Tom didn't know. "'Cause it's i'ortant.'

'Duh. Good guess. Why is it important?'

"'Cause . . . 'cause. . . uh . . .'

'Think about girls you've known, Tom? Does that help?'
'Huh?'

'Dingdong. Ring a bell, Tom? Girls, girls, girls. Hello.'

Tom was tired. He was hot. He was dehydrated. His brain was almost fried from fear. His adrenals were parched from depositing gallons of hormones into his bloodstream. He had enough histamines in his system from the bee stings to thwart the effects of a tanker-truckload of Benadryl. No matter how hard he was trying, he couldn't manage to fire the synapses that were necessary to help him figure out why the hell some guy was imprisoning him in the mountains and what some girl from his past had to do with the bees and the vipers.

'Girls? Girls I dated?'

'Think, Tom. Think about girls you've dated. Any blond girls? Real pretty, beautiful even. Why are we here today, Tom?'

'To learn a'out 'ear.'

'Very good.'

Tom said, 'Girls. 'ear. They go together.' He wasn't sure where the thought had come from, but he knew it was right. He suddenly felt like an A student.

'Oh yes, some girls know about fear. Some girls know about fear the way that bees know about honey.'

''ees,' Tom said. His pulse raced at the word.

The man suddenly appeared through the trees from the west. Once again he was wearing the motorcycle helmet with the visor. On this approach he was dragging a huge canvas bundle behind him through the forest. The bundle was so heavy that the man needed both hands to get it over the rough spots on the forest floor.

'What is that?' Tom asked. He waited for the big sack to move on its own and for a mountain lion or a black bear to pop out of the bag like a crazed stripper emerging from a cake at some old-time bachelor party.

The man didn't answer. He let go of the bundle and disappeared back into the woods. A minute or so later, he returned, dragging another canvas bundle. He left it beside the first and immediately took long strides toward the fence. Once again he threw a half-liter bottle of water over the fence. Tom hopped out of the way, not even trying to catch it.

He shifted his eyes from the bottle to the canvas sacks and back again. 'What's in those 'ags?' A tremor caused his voice to twang.

'These?' The man's voice was oddly hollow behind the dark visor. 'Growing a little wary, Tom? Paranoia setting in? These are just supplies I need for the lessons. The fear lessons.'

''ear lessons.' He stepped back a solitary step. After

looking over his shoulder to see how close he was to the chain-link, he stepped back once more. 'I know a'out 'ear. No 'ore lessons. 'lease.'

'Drink, Tom. It's just water in the bottle, I promise. If you don't want it, just throw it back over. I don't want to litter.'

Tom leaned down and lifted the bottle from the dust. He examined the bottle to make certain the seal was intact.

The man made a *tsk, tsk, tsk* sound behind the dark visor. 'You going to drink it or send it out for a lab analysis?'

Tom unscrewed the cap. He smelled the contents before he raised it to his lips. He drained the entire bottle. He wanted more.

'Thank you,' he said.

The man tossed a sealed foil bag over the fence. Tom examined it without lifting it. He had no idea what it was. As soon as he was done with the examination he returned his eyes to the two canvas sacks.

The man said, 'It's high-energy food, Tom. A new thing called energy gel. High in carbs and proteins. Rip a corner off the bag and just suck it down. Don't worry, it goes down good.'

Tom read the small print on the bag for a few seconds, then did as his captor instructed.

'I need you hydrated and nourished,' the man explained. 'The lessons aren't over. There's always more to learn about fear.'

'Girls,' Tom said.

'Yes,' the man agreed. 'Girls. Specifically, a girl.'

Just then Tom thought he began to get it.

'Oh shit,' he said. His adrenals cramped and squeezed and dumped their remaining bounty, and within seconds Tom knew all over again exactly what fear was.

'Is it Joan?' he whimpered. The question roared in his head but little sound escaped his swollen lips.

'What?' the man said. 'I can't hear you, Tom.'

CHAPTER

38

Kelda opened her mouth with so much reluctance that for a moment I felt not like a psychologist but like a dentist brandishing a gleaming hypodermic full of Novocain. She said, 'Jones's journal? The one I told you about that was with the things we picked up in Maui?'

'Yes,' I said.

'A few years ago, I got a chance to read it.'

'Yes,' I said. I thought, *I bet it wasn't pretty.*

'Someone was after her. That's really why she went to Hawaii. To get away from him.'

A pan-phobic woman writing in her diary about someone being after her, I thought. *Now there's a surprise.* My frustration was only exceeded by my fatigue and hunger. I waited about ten seconds before I said, 'The Cliffs Notes version won't suffice, Kelda. I need to know what's going on before I can decide how to help you.'

She looked away, then back at me. 'Okay. A guy she

started dating after I left for Australia threatened her. And then he followed her to Hawaii when she moved. According to her journal his name was Tom Clone.'

Oh boy.

'She had just started seeing him when the news media began to link him with the murder of Ivy Campbell.'

I thought, *I bet that's when she got spooked. Really spooked.*

Kelda continued. 'For whatever reason, Jones was convinced that she was going to be his next victim. She felt . . . threatened. A week or two later, she got the offer to go join the co-op in Paia, and she went. For her to do that – to get on a plane by herself and go to Hawaii – she must have been seriously frightened.'

'But he found her there?'

'Yes. She wasn't sure how he found her. But he did. He followed her over to Maui.'

'This is all in her journal?'

'Yes, it is. And he told her that she made him want to dance.'

Tom had used the phrase with me once, describing Ivy. Or had it been describing Kelda? I wasn't sure, though I was sure it wasn't a coincidence that I was hearing it now from her. I said, 'He did? That's important?'

'To me it is.'

'Go on.'

'What?'

I waited. Godot never came.

Finally, I said, 'And you think that he killed her? That Tom Clone pushed Jones off that cliff?'

'I go back and forth on that, actually. Some nights, I'm

lying awake and I think he literally pushed her. Other nights, I think he just went there and scared her to death. That he figuratively pushed her. Either way . . .'

Some reality testing seemed in order. Gently, I asked, 'Why, Kelda? Why would he do that?'

'She broke up with him. She left him. Just like what happened with Ivy Campbell.'

I thought that it had been Tom who had broken up with Ivy, not the other way around. But I knew that arguing the facts with Kelda wasn't the correct therapeutic move. This conversation wasn't about facts. I said, 'That's it? She broke up with him?' I wanted Kelda to hear the fragility of the motive for murder she was proposing.

'Yes.'

'And you think he went to Hawaii to . . .?' I let my uncasted hand float to express the lethal void at the end of the sentence. 'And . . . you hold him responsible for her death?'

'That's not important.'

It's not? But I nodded, processing her denial.

'It is quite a coincidence,' I said.

'What?'

'That all these years later, you turn out to be instrumental in getting him off death row for the first murder. The same guy who threatened your friend.'

'Yes,' she agreed. Her eyes never wavered from mine. 'It is quite a coincidence.'

'Where do I come in?' I suspected that the answer was that I was supposed to be willing to be played for the fool. One of the many nice things about my friend Sam Purdy was that Sam never pretended to be squeezing my ass

327

while he tried to pick my pocket. He just went right for my wallet.

Kelda wasn't being quite so straightforward. She was enticing me with the story about Tom Clone and Jones's diary. That was hot breath in my ear. All she actually wanted to do was to rifle my files.

'What do you mean?'

'You referred Tom to me, Kelda. Why? If you hold him responsible for your friend's death, why would you do that?'

'I was half asleep when he asked for a name. I've regretted it ever since. I regret it right now, I guarantee you that.'

'And you think it's that simple? You were half asleep so you gave him my name?'

'Yes,' she said. Her tone had become defiant. My impression was that she wasn't particularly eager to entertain any alternative hypotheses, although I had come up with two or three without breaking a sweat.

I tried a gentle confrontation. 'I think you wanted me in the middle of this, whatever it is.'

'Why would I do that?'

I didn't know what to say, so I said nothing. I'm not always wise enough to do that.

'You want to know how you come in now, Alan? You can tell me whether you know where I can find him. That's where you come in.'

'Is he in danger?' I asked. If she told me he was, and I decided the threat was serious and imminent, all the rules about confidentiality changed. I assumed that Kelda, a law enforcement officer – albeit a federal one – knew that. I was eager to hear her response to my question, but tried not to show it.

'Let's just say I'm worried about him. Very worried. Will that suffice?'

'Worried personally or professionally?'

'Let's just say . . . worried.'

For the first time in days I felt a dull ache in my humerus. I curled my fingers around the end of the cast, but that didn't change the pain.

She shook her head in frustration and said, 'You're not going to tell me, are you? I'm just wasting my time here.'

'You're assuming I know something, Kelda. All this visit has assured me of is that I know much less than just about everybody else.'

'That's what this is about? You're upset because everybody hasn't shared their secrets with you? How petty.'

Was that what it was all about? I hoped not. I said, 'I'm sorry if you see it that way.'

She squeezed her eyes shut. I watched the muscles tighten in her jaw. Wearily, she demanded, 'Just tell me. Where is he?'

Almost involuntarily I shook my head. I asked, 'How's your pain right now, Kelda?'

She said, 'Fuck you,' and stood to leave.

39

K elda stood on the sidewalk outside Dr. Gregory's office for a moment, feeling disoriented. She didn't immediately recognize the keys that she held in her hand; she couldn't even remember what kind of car she was driving.

Her dead end had just become a brick wall.

'Something else,' she said aloud. 'Something else. What is my "something else"?'

Behind her she heard someone say her name.

With a name like Kelda, she didn't even entertain the possibility that the person might be talking to someone besides her.

CHAPTER

40

I sat immobile on my chair, staring at the door she'd left open, half expecting her to return.

She didn't.

I walked out to the waiting room and stood at the front window, my good hand in my trousers pocket, my casted arm hanging at its constantly useless angle. Kelda was standing on the sidewalk. A man in a gray business suit was walking toward her. His lips were moving.

Concerned that she would spot me spying on her, I stepped back from the window. I sat at my desk for a few seconds, stood right back up, walked to the rear window, and immediately returned to the desk. I picked up the phone and punched in Sam Purdy's number at the police department, expecting to hear the greeting from his voicemail. Instead, I listened as he said, 'This is Purdy.'

'Sam, it's Alan. Hi.'

'Hi, Alan.'

'Listen, I only have a minute between patients, but I was wondering something. Have you found Tom Clone?'

'No,' he said. I thought that there was some incongruous levity attached to the solitary word.

'No sign of the Vespa?'

Again Sam's voice carried a little lilt as he said, 'Turns out that there're Vespas all over town. Did you know that? Some new trendoid thing that's going on in Boulder. I see them all the time now that I know what they are. I just didn't know what those whiny little things were called.'

'Yeah, I've heard they're getting popular. But any sign of the grandfather's Vespa in particular? The red one?'

'No. No sign of it. Don't get me wrong, we're looking, but finding Tom Clone and the Vespa are not the most important things the Boulder Police Department is doing right now. Basically, that case is an unsolved assault on the elderly. It's not a nice thing, but it's not the end of the world from a law enforcement perspective. You know what I mean? We have rapes, we have unsolved murders, we have—'

'Yeah, yeah. I understand. Life goes on.'

After a few seconds of silence, my friend asked, 'Have you heard from Tom Clone, Alan?'

'Sorry, Sam.'

'Sorry you can't tell me? Or sorry you haven't heard from him?'

'Take your pick. I'm sorry about a lot of things these days.'

'You know, you don't sound too good.' His voice had softened. 'You want to tell me what's going on?'

'Nothing . . . nothing. I was just curious about your progress with the investigation. Thought I'd call and see how everything was going.'

'Middle of the afternoon and you just have this undeniable urge to know where Clone is? You really want to think your public servants are goofy enough to believe that? That's what I'm supposed to believe?'

'Yes, Sam. That's exactly what I would like you to believe.'

I heard him sigh before he said, 'You know, I might actually be tempted to go along with you if you were the first person to call me this afternoon trying to find Tom Clone. But since you aren't, I'm a little more suspicious than usual.'

'Who else called?'

He laughed. 'You think I'm going to tell you that? Though it probably doesn't matter whether I do or I don't. I think you already know the answer.'

Kelda, I thought. *God, she called Sam trying to find Tom. What the hell is going on?*

Sam said, 'If you have another minute or two before your next victim shows up, maybe we could talk a little more about that Fed you never seem to want to talk about. Remember her? The one I told you about who alibied Clone? We could do that. After we have that conversation, I fervently believe that both of us would feel better.'

I didn't know what to say.

'Alan, you still there? I don't hear you. Are we breaking up? Are you on a cell phone or something?'

'I'm, uh . . . I'm, uh . . . Oh shit, Sam. I don't know what the hell I am.'

He chuckled. 'Why don't you call me sometime when you're in a better mood,' he said, and he hung up the phone.

I wanted to hit redial and tell Sam about Jones and Paia and Kelda and the fact that everybody seemed to want to know where Tom Clone was.

I wanted to but I couldn't.

Right at that moment I hated the work I did.

CHAPTER

41

Politically, Colorado is a bastion of western conservatism. As a result, the vast majority of Coloradans view the decidedly less-than-conservative city of Boulder either as an amusing curiosity or, less benignly, as an irritating oddity. For many of the state's residents, Boulder is too idiosyncratic, too idealistic, too liberal, too pretty, too different, and too weird.

And, ironically enough, that is almost exactly how the majority of Boulder residents view the little town of Ward.

Although it is within the high western boundary of Boulder County – barely, some would point out – Ward, Colorado, attracts a different breed of residents than most of the county's mountain towns. Many people have been lured to Ward over the years by its laissez-faire reputation, its spectacular but isolated location high in the eastern shadows of the Continental Divide, and by its defiant municipal independence. Although many have been lured to attempt to live in Ward, the process of natural selection routinely whittles down the population to a manageable number. The rigors associated with spending Rocky Mountain winters in an infrastructurally challenged, socioeconomically marginal community at an elevation well in excess of nine thousand feet rapidly separate the hardy from the foolhardy.

The combination of isolation and altitude ensures that for nine months a year life isn't easy in Ward, but its residents tend to be the kind of people who would find life intolerable almost anyplace else.

Founded in 1860 by Calvin Ward, who was drawn to the area by its rich veins of minerals, the town has endured the collapse of its mining backbone, the evaporation of its brief status as a tourist mecca, the departure of its only railroad, and two devastating fires, which some locals still argue were actually arsons instigated by envious folk from down the road in Central City. The Ward that has survived these trials is an anachronistic village that is still housed in many of the frame or stone buildings that somehow escaped the last of the big fires at the end of the nineteenth century.

Remove a few of the newer structures, cut down some utility poles, and cart away the rusting hulks of a few hundred abandoned motorized vehicles of all descriptions, and it wouldn't take much else to make Ward appear something as it did a hundred years earlier. The mine tailings that sit above town look just as they did in photos from the 1890s, a series of unbroken rust-colored waves frozen in ominous time above the village.

Ward is a town where self-sufficiency and independence are prized and a generous dose of tolerance isn't questioned; it's assumed.

If the town of Ward were the type of place that cared to have a motto – which it isn't – its motto might well be 'Leave Us Fucking Alone.'

Living in Park County fifty miles due south of Boulder County, Fred Prehost was accustomed to mountain people, but after five minutes in Ward he knew he wasn't in Park County anymore. The few people who were walking the town's streets appeared to consist primarily of refugees from the original Woodstock or extras from some post-apocalyptic movie that nobody ever saw twice. Human residents seemed to be outnumbered by canine residents by at least two to one, and the canines appeared to be much better fed than the *Homo sapiens*.

As his car was circled by a pack of four dogs, Prehost was thinking that, apparently, in Ward, obeying leash laws was considered optional.

'Hey, Hoppy,' he said. 'Any ideas?'

The two friends were sitting in the front seat of Prehost's old Suburban, which, other than being a bit too well cared for, actually looked right at home on the streets of Ward.

'We need to talk to some people, I guess, find that car I saw them in. My best advice would be for us to forget that we're cops. One, this isn't our county. Two, I figure the folks that I'm looking at around here' – Hoppy gestured with a nod at an obese, bald man with a snake tattoo curling up around his ear and an old poncho over his shoulders – 'are dispositionally more likely to be fond of strangers than they are to be fond of strangers who are cops.'

Prehost snorted. 'You think Boulder County has ever sent a building inspector to this place? I mean, like, ever? Look at these buildings. That one there is half 1950s Greyhound bus, half God-knows-what. I don't think there's a section in the building code that covers that.'

'Got me, Fred.'

'But this is where you lost Clone, you're sure? Right here? You know that much?'

'Yeah, the guy in the green Pathfinder flagged him down on North Broadway in Boulder. They talked for a few minutes and then they came right up here in the Pathfinder without stopping.'

'And they took Left Hand Canyon, not Boulder Canyon?' Fred Prehost knew all this already but he had the detective disease that made him want to hear everything two or three times, even when he was talking to another detective.

'That's right.'

'Go on.'

'Like I said, I was worried that they'd figure out I was following them, so when they pulled into town I was giving them some space – I was maybe a quarter mile behind. When I chugged into town the Pathfinder had vanished. I looked for them for a while, and when I couldn't find them, I went back down the hill and waited back at his grandfather's house in Boulder, but Clone never came back down. He may not be here anymore, but this is the last place I saw them.'

'And the motorbike is where he left it? You actually checked that? You're not just assuming?'

'It's still parked at the Mental Health Center on Iris. Right where he left it.'

Prehost had run the plates on the green Pathfinder himself. A couple of phone calls revealed that the tags had been stolen from a new Hyundai Santa Fe that was parked nights in an apartment building lot in Arvada and days in the huge lot of the MCI service center in Glendale. Other than the fact that the owner of the truck felt he needed stolen tags, the information wasn't helpful at all: Plate picking would have been a piece of cake in either location.

'So we need to find somebody who can tell us who around here might have a nice green Pathfinder,' Prehost said.

'Yep.'

'We do it together or separate?'

'Us? Separate. Definitely separate. We don't want to look like cops, and we don't want to look like queers,' said Hoppy.

'What's our cover?'

'Don't look at me.'

Prehost scratched his chin for a moment. 'What about we say we were visiting relatives in Nederland and somebody in a Cadillac – no, even better, make that a Mercedes – so somebody in a big black Mercedes hit our car – no, no, no, somebody in a big black Mercedes hit our *dog* – and we think the guy in this Pathfinder saw the whole thing and may be able to be a witness for us, and somebody in Nederland said that they thought they recognized the Pathfinder and that they thought that the guy who owned it lived somewhere near Ward. How about that?'

'I think you're a genius, Fred. You just come up with that right now? What kind of dog?'

'A Lab, everybody loves Labs. Or maybe a golden retriever. What do you think?'

'Lab. Did the dog die in the accident?'

'Hell no. You ruin the story if you have the dog die. People get morose, then they don't want to talk to you. Our dog's in the hospital; he needs surgery to walk again. It's going to be expensive, some experimental thing that has to be done by specialists at the veterinary school in Fort Collins. We need to find the guy in the Pathfinder so we can make sure the guy in the Mercedes pays through the nose so our dog isn't crippled for the rest of his life.'

'Is it your dog or my dog?'

'Let's make it your dog, Hoppy. You're better at looking miserable than me. You head that way.' Prehost pointed through the windshield. 'I'll do the other side of the street. I want to know what Clone and this guy with the stolen tags are up to. Maybe we'll find them in a meth lab or something. That would be sweet. With the slightest bit of luck, we'll have Clone back in jail by dinnertime.'

Hoppy pushed his door open and began to climb out. Then he stopped. 'What's his name? My dog?'

Prehost was already thinking about something else. He said, 'What? Oh. D.P. His name is D.P.'

'Huh? T.P.? Toilet Paper?'

'No, D.P. – Death Penalty. The dog's name is D.P.'

Hoppy laughed. 'Gotcha.'

*

340

Fifteen minutes later, Fred Prehost found Hoppy standing at something vaguely resembling a counter at the Ward General Store having a cup of coffee with an earth-mother type. For a moment, Prehost thought that the woman was somebody he'd busted in Cripple Creek for tipping over slot machines, but memory told him that woman was a size-ten felon, and this one was at least a sixteen.

'This building's original, Fred. Did you know that? It's been a general store just like this for over a hundred and forty years. Survived all the fires. This is Clara, by the way.'

Prehost pretended he was tipping the hat he wasn't wearing. 'Hello, Clara. Nice to meet you.'

Clara smiled. 'Coffee? Fresh a few minutes ago. We roast the beans ourselves. Best in town.' She laughed heartily and pointed to a gorgeous old roaster in the corner of the store. 'Store' was a generous assessment of the establishment. A few shelves harboring a sparse collection of foodstuffs separated the part of the structure where things were sold from the part where people lived. Or hung out. To Prehost, it wasn't at all a clear demarcation.

'No, thank you, I'll pass.'

Hoppy said, 'It turns out that Clara has a Lab, too, though hers is one of those golden ones, not a black one like old D.P. And she knows the car we're looking for, even knows the guy who drives it to see him, but doesn't know where he lives. She thinks he's just up here occasionally, isn't really a local, but that we should keep asking. She's sure someone in town will know where to find him.'

'Well, Clara, you do know what you're talking about. The guy down at the — what is that down there a little ways? Is that a junkyard? Anyway, the guy with the hair that's all—'

'Lootie,' Clara supplied. 'With the cornrows.'

'Yeah, that's his name. Lootie. Anyway, Lootie knew the vehicle right away. He gave me pretty good directions to the cabin this guy's been fixing up, says the man's real pleasant.'

Clara nodded and said, 'He is a pleasant man.' She snapped her stubby fingers. 'What *is* his name?'

'Oliver. Lootie said he calls himself Oliver.'

'I'll remember that now. Next time I see him I'll remember to call him Oliver. Like the book, *Oliver Twist*. Or the movie. My memory is trouble, especially with names. I do okay with faces, but names . . .' Clara shook her head, smiled, and added, 'You ask me, I think it was all the acid I took.'

After they thanked Clara for her hospitality, Hoppy carried his coffee and a couple of muffins back to the Suburban. As he settled onto his seat, he asked, 'So where are we going?'

'That way,' Prehost responded. He pointed up the hill to the west before he looked down at his little pocket notebook. 'We head up something Lootie called the Brainard Lake Road. He said we should go out Morning Star to Chatham and we'll run into the Brainard Lake Road. When we get near Left Hand Creek apparently it all gets complicated. But I got it all written down.'

'You act like you know this place.'

'Ward? Hardly.' He was quiet for a moment. 'But I do get the feeling that being a cop here would be like shooting ducks in a pond. I bet the half of the town that's not using right now still has adequate blood levels of illegal substances in their bodies from the sixties and seventies. Local cops would just have to line everybody up on Main Street or whatever the hell they call it and hand out urine cups. The rest would be up to the guys with the test tubes and the white coats.'

'Clara?' Hoppy said.

'Clara, indeed.'

'This guy Lootie seem to have all his brain cells?'

'Mostly. Lootie seemed all right. Actually, if you get past his looks and the smell from his rotting teeth, he's the sort of guy you'd like to have a beer with. I think the directions he gave me will get us to Oliver's cabin. In fact, I smell Mr. Clone already. Ten dollars says that this Oliver guy is somebody that Clone knows from inside and what they're working up here is a meth lab or an ecstasy dump.'

'I like my money too much to take that bet. Your instincts are good on this shit, Fred.'

'What time you have?'

Hoppy checked his watch. 'Almost five. Do we have enough time before it gets dark?'

Prehost said, 'Sure, plenty. I like approaching at dusk anyway. Reminds me of my infantry training. Ducks in a pond,' he repeated softly.

'I s'ell gas,' Tom said.

'You do? You sell gas? You work in a gas station? I thought you'd be able to get a better job than that,' the man said absently. His words were muffled by the helmet and visor.

'No! I don't sell gas, I s'ell gas.' Tom was looking all around, pivoting on one foot, trying to identify the source of the odor.

'You smell gas? Natural gas?'

'No, no. Gasoline. I s'ell gasoline. Don't you s'ell it? Where is it? What are you doing?'

The man unfolded the sides of one of the canvas bags to reveal an old Coleman cooler. The cooler was dark blue with a white plastic top.

The man stood and faced Tom. 'The smell is coming from in here, Tom.'

'What is that?'

'Here, see for yourself.'

The man flipped off the lid of the cooler, reached inside, and removed an orb about the size of a softball. Small tubes stuck off the sides. The man raised the device and held it up so that Tom could see it.

'What is it?'

'It's a latex glove, Tom. Filled with my own little recipe for napalm. You know napalm, Tom?'

'What?' Tom was incredulous. His mouth hung open and his eyes grew wide. 'Na'al'? Why?' he cried. But he knew why.

'Fear, Tom. Remember, it's all about fear. You afraid of fire?'

Tom's voice cracked as he whined, 'Every'ody is a'raid o'ire. Don't 'urn 'e. 'lease!'

The man underhanded the orb over the fence. The latex ball hit the dirt about ten feet from Tom and imploded upon impact. A green transparent jell splashed up and out from the wrist hole, which had blown open as soon as the glove hit the ground. 'Watch,' the man said.

The man lit an entire book of matches and placed it in a small metal basket at the end of a telescoping aluminum pole that Tom recognized as a device for retrieving golf balls from water hazards. Once he pushed the basket through the fence, the man extended the pole until the basket hovered two feet above the splash of napalm.

'No!' Tom wailed. He turned, ran to the far corner of the enclosure, crouched, and raised his hands to his face.

The man tipped the basket over and the book of flaming matches fluttered toward the stained soil. A huge *whoosh* of flames jumped from the ground and engulfed the matchbook before gravity could help it complete its descent toward the fuel.

Tom yelped.

The fire settled. The blue-yellow flames licked across the ground like slithering insects.

The man reached into the cooler and grabbed two more puffy surgical gloves. One by one he tossed them over the fence. Each imploded upon impact. Each was closer to Tom than the first.

Tom called out, 'Let's talk a'out girls and 'ear.'

The man was retracting the aluminum pole. 'You want to talk about girls and fear? Now? Because you're afraid of fire?'

Tom nodded dramatically.

The man paused and faced Tom.

'Fear kills, doesn't it, Tom?'

Desperate, Tom tried frantically to guess what it was that the man wanted to hear. 'I guess it can. Yes, 'ear can kill. Are you going to kill 'e?'

The man didn't answer. He shook his head. Tom couldn't tell whether it was an expression of disdain or denial.

Finally, the man said, 'Did it kill any girls, Tom? Or did you?'

'What?' Tom said.

'Well?' the man's voice taunted.

'*What?*'

'After you killed Ivy, Tom, was another girl next?'

'*What?*'

The man readied another book of matches. Before he set it afire, he paused and retrieved two more little napalm bombs and tossed them toward Tom. One bomblet hit six feet from him, splashing gel onto his feet.

The man returned his attention to the flaming matches in the basket of the telescoping pole.

'I didn't kill I'y. I' innocent. The DNA! The DNA! You 'ust ha'e heard a'out the DNA.'

The man stopped what he was doing. His voice flattened as he said, 'Heard about it? Have I heard about it? You know whose blood was on that knife, Tom? The one that the FBI agent found?'

'No. Who?'

The man lit the matches. He placed the little ball of fire in the basket at the end of the pole.

The sun completed its drop behind the Continental Divide, and thunder exploded in the western sky.

A few fat drops of rain plopped and cratered on the dust inside the enclosure.

The man raised his hands and looked up toward the sky. 'So are you a lucky man, Tom? Are the monsoons coming today? No reason to be afraid of fire in a thunderstorm, is there?'

More thunder clapped; lightning snapped a bolt of fire a second or two later. For an instant, the lightning was so bright that it muted the brilliance of the flames from the napalm.

Tom squirmed and said, ''e? Lucky?'

The man inserted the basket through the fence. He lit the puddle of napalm closest to Tom. A breeze picked up the flames and immediately blew them to the other pool of fuel.

Tom hurried to brush dirt into the jell on his feet as he watched black-brown smoke snake upward.

The flames jumped to a puddle of napalm even closer to Tom.

The man readied a couple of more bombs to throw over the fence. He said, 'If I hit you with one of these, it's not going to be pretty. But I'm going to try.'

All around Tom, the dirt looked as if it was covered with flaming Sterno.

'*God!*' he implored. '*God?*'

43

'Bill,' Kelda said.

Bill Graves stood on the sidewalk outside Dr. Gregory's office with his hands in the pockets of his suit trousers. His thin lips were in a flat line but she thought a hint of triumph flickered in his eyes.

'How did you find me? Are you on your Harley? Is that how I missed you?' Kelda asked.

'No, I'm not on my bike. It wasn't hard finding you, Kelda. I followed you all the way from downtown.' His voice was warm, almost teasing. 'You're not as clever as you think. You almost spotted me when you stopped at that house on the west side to get that crappy little car that you're driving, but after that it's been a breeze to stay with you.'

'Why?'

His eyes narrowed a little. 'Because I like you, Kelda. And because I think you may be wading into something that's a shade deeper than you thought it was.'

Because I like you. Kelda's mind flashed on the empty picture frame on her colleague's desk.

'And what I'm wading into is your business, Bill?'

'I think it might be.'

'Once more, why?'

'Once more, because I like you. But also – and this is a guess – I think the situation you're in has something to do with Clone and that knife we found. That makes it my business.'

Above Bill's head an immense thunderhead was crowning the peaks of the Divide. She didn't even consider the possibility that it would blow down and cool the Front Range. This was one of those summers where the storms only taunted and teased.

'Can we talk, Kelda?'

'I don't think that's a good idea.'

'But whatever you're up to is?'

'You're a nice guy, Bill. You don't really want to know what's going on. Trust me, you don't want a piece of this.'

'You telling me that because you like me, too?'

She said, 'Maybe.'

'Was that Bureau work you were doing in there?' He nodded toward the building she'd just exited. 'Or did you have an appointment with a shrink?'

The pain flared in her legs. She closed her eyes for a second, then turned and walked away from her colleague. After two steps she stopped and looked back over her shoulder. 'I can lose you. Don't bother to try to follow me.'

'Are you trying to be a hero again, Kelda? Is this – whatever the hell you're doing – is this about that little girl?'

She spun and faced him. 'Rosa Alija? Is that the little girl you're talking about?' Her words popped from her lips and she regretted the intensity.

'You have to move on. It's been a long time, Kelda.'

'Since what? Since I saved her life? Since I put three slugs into the chest of a monster? You think I want to do that again? Is that what you're saying? Is that what you think of me?'

'You know what people say, Kelda. In the Bureau. People talk, you know that.'

'No. What? What do people say in the Bureau?' She knew what other agents thought and she knew what they said behind her back. But she discovered that she didn't want to believe that Bill thought it, too.

'It must be hard being a hero, and then . . . not . . . being a hero. You and I chase numbers. It's not too glamorous. It has to be hard for you after—'

Tears filled her eyes. 'I don't know what I'm doing today, Bill. But I can promise you that it has nothing to do with being a hero.'

CHAPTER

44

Hoppy was in charge of the arsenal.

While Prehost drove up the Brainard Lake Road toward Oliver's cabin, Hoppy checked both their handguns and loaded Prehost's twelve-gauge shotgun with buckshot. Hoppy already knew that the little pistol in his ankle holster was ready to go. It always was.

Hoppy asked, 'How does this go down? If we're going to do this on our own, we have to get him back to Park County, right?'

'We'll see. Depending on what we find, it may be better just to turn things over to Boulder County. If we decide to take it back home, we'll do something with the green Pathfinder. We'll make it look like we followed it down the Peak to Peak Highway and then back home. Then we'll make sure that's where everything will go down.'

'What about this Oliver guy?'

Prehost didn't hesitate. 'Depends what his involvement is. I doubt if he'll make the trip south. But we'll have to see.'

Following Lootie's directions, Prehost didn't make a single wrong turn on the way to the little log cabin on the hillside above Left Hand Creek. The green Pathfinder was parked twenty feet from the front door.

Prehost stopped his Suburban. 'Here we go, Hoppy.'

'You want the shotgun?'

'Put it on the seat so we can reach it easily. We'll say hello first. But let's take a look inside that car before we do.'

Hoppy approached the Pathfinder with the barrel of his handgun pointing skyward. 'Some supplies in the back, Fred. Boxes and shit. I don't see any weapons or anything.'

Thunder shook the sky. First a sharp crack, but the rumble that followed was long and low. Raindrops dotted the dusty metal on the hood of the green Pathfinder.

Prehost said, 'Good. Pop the hood.'

'Doors are locked.'

Prehost walked over to the driver's door and slammed the butt of his handgun through the glass. 'Not anymore. Pop the hood.'

Hoppy did.

As thunder roared and echoed off the mountains, Prehost yanked at some wires in the engine compartment, eased the hood of the Pathfinder shut, then took long strides toward the cabin. He didn't hesitate at the door. With his handgun at waist height he walked right into the cabin. Hoppy stayed a few steps behind.

A fancy little red enamel woodstove dominated the single room. On one side was a full-size bed in an iron frame, and a rocking chair. On the other side was an oak table with two chairs, a hot plate, and a small microwave.

'Guy's a neat freak,' Prehost said as he lowered his gun.

Hoppy poked his head in the door. 'This ain't no meth lab, Fred.'

'Nope, it's not. But there might be another building someplace where they keep the equipment, you know? Damn stuff stinks. What's this?' He kicked at a heavy canvas suit that was folded on the floor near the door. A helmet with a mesh front topped the pile.

Hoppy took two steps into the cabin and focused his attention on the canvas suit. He said, 'I don't know.'

Prehost said, 'Where do you think our two guys are?'

A fresh burst of lightning lit the inside of the cabin, and thunder boomed off the log walls. Both men glanced toward the windows.

Hoppy shook his head. 'We could wait for them. Darkness might be our friend. You know they'll be back by dark, right? Maybe even sooner if this thunderstorm sticks around. I wouldn't want to be outside up here in a lightning storm like this.'

'I would think that's the case. But let's take a closer look outside again first. Make sure our friends don't have another way out of here.'

'Wait, Fred. What's this?' Hoppy walked over to a small portable television that sat on the oak table.

'It's a TV, Hoppy. You don't have one at home?'

'Fred, it has a cable attached to the back. There's no cable up here. You're telling me that this Oliver guy went to the trouble of installing a satellite dish just to feed this crappy little nine-inch set?'

Prehost stepped back and waved his hand at the TV. He said, 'Wait, wait, wait. This isn't from a satellite dish. There's no receiver here. Those dishes require that you have a receiver. You know, to process the signal. You see a receiver?'

'Fred, screw the receiver. There's no power here. This cabin doesn't even have electricity. This TV must be running on batteries or a generator or something. Something's fishy.'

'Did you see a generator outside? There has to be a generator for the TV and the microwave.'

'No, I didn't see a generator.'

'Solar?'

'Did you see panels on the roof? I didn't.'

Hoppy lifted the thin black cable from the TV and tracked it out the nearest window. Even in the dying light of dusk he could tell that the cable snaked along the dusty path that disappeared into the pine woods behind the cabin to the north. He cringed as a bolt of lightning flashed on the Divide.

Prehost looked over Hoppy's shoulder and said, 'I think this might be some kind of closed-circuit feed, Hoppy. That's why there's no receiver.'

'What the hell?'

Prehost said, 'Turn it on, Hoppy. Turn on that set.'

Hoppy moved to the front of the television and pushed the tiny button marked 'Power.'

An image flickered to life on the screen. Hoppy said, 'This thing must be using batteries. Has to be.'

The two cops immediately lowered themselves onto the wooden chairs that were beside the table and leaned toward the little appliance while they tried to make sense of what they were seeing on the TV. The colors of the image were muted to tinted grays and pastels.

'What is that? Is that a fence? What's that fence for? Is that like a corral or something?' Hoppy asked.

'No, I don't think so. That's a person outside there, closest to the camera, with his back to us. He's wearing like a . . . helmet or something. And over there, see, that's a person inside crouching on the far side, inside the fence. See that, right there. That's a person.'

'Is that Clone?'

'Which one?'

'Inside.'

'I can't tell,' Prehost said. 'Maybe.'

'Me neither. But I think it might be.'

'Whoa! What was that flash? Turn up the sound.'

The screen momentarily went almost totally white before the flash narrowed to a spot that was close to the human who was crouching inside the fence.

Hoppy asked, 'Was that lightning that did that, Fred? What made the TV do that?' He kept his fingertip pressed to the 'Volume A' button, but he heard nothing come from the speaker of the TV set.

'No, I don't think so, Hoppy.'

'It looks like fire.'

'Is this live? What are we watching?' asked Fred.

'I can think of one good way to find out.' Hoppy stood from the table and moved toward the door.

Prehost watched the screen as the guy outside the

enclosure underhanded something over the fence. Whatever he threw landed within feet of the person inside the enclosure and seemed to deflate. Prehost said, 'Wait! Look!'

'You go ahead. I'm going to follow that cable, Fred, see where it goes. This is too weird for me.'

Prehost watched until another flash turned the screen white. He wasted a moment trying to figure out what he had just seen before he took off after Hoppy. Once he was outside he stopped at the Suburban to grab the shotgun.

Hoppy already had it. Fred snagged his big flashlight out of the backseat and jogged out behind the cabin to find the cable so he could follow his partner into the woods.

Rain had started falling steadily. Prehost decided it was a really shitty time for the arrival of the monsoons.

Kelda waited until Bill Graves got in his car and drove away before she returned to Maria Alija's car. Graves's words echoed in her head. '*Are you trying to be a hero again, Kelda?*'

Maybe I am, she thought as she recalled how it all started.

It was that the-shock-is-wearing-off-and-I've-never-been-so-tired-in-my-life week after the jetliners crashed into the buildings in New York City and Washington, D.C.

She was with Ira for the first time since that morning. He was sitting on the sofa in Kelda's living room, and she was on the floor, her legs resting on a carefully arranged array of bags of frozen peas. She'd worked almost nonstop for over a week as part of a task force of FBI accounting specialists that was trying to follow the money trail the hijackers had left behind.

She considered it the equivalent of tracking scat.

After a week of relentless activity and almost no sleep, the pain in her lower legs was close to intolerable. She silently compared it to the suffering of strangers in New York and Washington, knew that her pain was nothing, and shifted her weight on the peas.

Ira shook a copy of the *Denver Post* at her and said, 'No, no! It's too good for him.'

'What is?' Kelda said. Her attention was focused on CNN. Jeff Greenberg was talking to Gary Hart. She still wasn't sure why.

'Bush said he wants bin Laden dead or alive. That's too good for him. Killing him is too easy a way out for him after what he did to us. Putting him on trial or putting him in jail? What good does that do?'

'What?' She lowered the volume on the television. Jeff Greenberg's lips kept moving. 'I'm sorry. What?'

He repeated his argument.

She reached out and caressed the long muscles of his calf. 'I know,' she said. 'I know.'

Ira didn't want to be comforted. 'No, Kelda. Don't put me off about this. I mean it.'

She turned her head to face him. 'Okay. I believe you mean it. But we don't even know where bin Laden is yet.'

Ira dropped the paper onto his lap. His eyes were bleak. 'We can't do anything about him, can we? Can we even find him?' She knew he was asking her the questions as an FBI agent, not as a girlfriend.

'I don't know,' she said. 'It's not easy.' On the screen across the room, a wall in a firehouse in New York City was covered with photographs of young men holding small children, of young women hugging their families. Even without any commentary, Kelda knew that the pictures were of those who had never made it home from the World Trade Center.

She started to weep.

What about Tom Clone?' Ira whispered a couple of hours later as he lay beside her in bed.

'What about him?' Kelda said.

'Is "dead or alive" good enough for him?'

She didn't reply.

'He terrorized Joan,' Ira argued. 'What did we do? All we did was put him in prison. Whatever happened to "an eye for an eye"? Where's the retribution? Where's the justice?'

When she replied, she spoke into the darkness. He was taking her someplace she didn't want to go, and her voice was as tired as she was. 'He's on death row, Ira. He's eventually going to die for what he did to Ivy Campbell.'

'Is that enough? He thinks we don't even know about Joan.'

She counted to three. 'He can only die once no matter how many women he killed.'

'He terrorized her. Imagine her fear at the end. When he was stalking her. When she was on that cliff. Imagine what she felt. He'll die not even knowing that he's being punished for what he did to Joan. He'll die not knowing what she felt when she died.'

Kelda thought about Jones. About that moment on the cliff in Maui.

Ira pulled himself up on his elbows. 'Wouldn't you like a week alone in a room with bin Laden?'

What? 'Yeah. Of course I would. I'd take an hour alone with him. Hell, give me ten minutes.'

'I can't give you that. I wish to God I could. But maybe I can get you ten minutes alone in a room with Tom Clone. We could force-feed him some of the agony that Joan felt. We could force-feed him some of Joan's fear. Wouldn't you like that?'

'Ira, what on earth are you talking about?'

'I'm not sure,' he said. 'But I think I have an idea.'

She swung her legs to the floor. 'I have to pee.'

Ira called after her as she crossed the room. 'We could get even, Kelda. We could get even. How many times can people say that they really, really got even?'

The next morning, Kelda was up and ready to leave the house before dawn. She had dreamed about Jones. Jones was the woman in the chasing pictures. In Kelda's dreams the paintings came to life and Jones was the one running, running, running.

Kelda shook Ira awake before she left. He'd been sleeping on his back and he woke up without moving. Only his open eyelids betrayed the fact that he'd abandoned his dreams.

'What would I have to do?' she asked him, her lips inches from his. She could taste his sour breath.

His heart rate quickened. 'All you have to do is get into the property room in Park County and get some of Ivy Campbell's blood. A piece of the clothing she was wearing the day she was killed, something like that. I don't need much. Some, a scrap, but it has to have her blood on it. There was lots of blood. We only need a little. We'll do it together.'

She thought about the implications of his words. She thought about her dreams the night before. About Jones's nightmare on the cliff's edge. 'I can do that,' she said.

'I know you can,' he said.

He kissed her. 'I'll do the lab work. That's my thing. But we'll do the time alone in the room with Clone together.'

'I'll get my ten minutes?'

'Minimum.'

She stared into his eyes trying to detect bravado or hesitation or doubt. 'Once I go to Park County and . . . you know, there won't be any turning back, Ira.'

'No turning back, Kelda.'

She pulled the covers from his naked body and straddled him. He reached below her skirt but didn't take his eyes from her face.

Kelda literally jumped when her cell phone rang. She took her hands from the wheel of Maria Alija's car, fumbled for her phone, not Maria's, and checked the number on the screen. The call had originated from a Boulder exchange, and although the number seemed vaguely familiar she wasn't sure who it was.

'Hello,' she said.

A male voice said, 'I'm looking for an FBI agent named James. Is she at this number?'

She recognized the voice. 'Hello, Detective Purdy. You've found her.'

'I figured that. I've also found a red Vespa. You interested in taking a look at it with us?'

'Absolutely. Yes, yes. Where are you?'

'You know Boulder?'

'Well enough.'

'I'm in the parking lot of the Mental Health Center at Iris and Broadway. Know where that is?'

'I know where Iris is and I know where Broadway is. The Mental Health Center is right on the corner?'

'Yeah. Northeast corner. Red brick building. One story. You'll see us. We're the ones with the police cruisers and the yellow crimescene tape.'

She closed her eyes and shook her head at his sarcasm before she regained her composure and said, 'It turns out that I'm in Boulder right now, Detective. I'll be there within minutes.'

'Why am I not surprised to hear that you're in town? You're where exactly? Like the vicinity of Walnut Street maybe? Up by the Mall?'

She thought, *How the hell does he know that?* 'Ten minutes, Detective Purdy. Ten minutes.'

CHAPTER

46

Prehost caught up with Hoppy about a hundred feet into the woods. Hoppy was standing still, straddling the black cable that led from the log cabin window. A second cable, bright yellow, and fatter than the video feed, came from the other direction and disappeared into the boarded-up entrance of an old mine. Thick timbers that were deeply creviced from a century of exposure to the elements outlined the mine entrance. From somewhere deep inside the mine, they could hear a muted, rhythmic rumble.

The rain was still falling in intermittent fat drops. Occasional thunder shook the trees.

Hoppy whispered, 'Fred, that there's a power cable.' He pointed at the entrance to the mine. 'And that's a generator running inside there, I bet. He has the entrance insulated for sound.'

Prehost nodded. 'Let's go. I want to see what the hell is going on with that fence.'

Hoppy moved the shotgun into his right hand and stepped back. 'You first, Fred. This one's yours.'

They walked another hundred feet into the aspen trees and lodgepole pines before they saw an eruption of flames through the trees and heard someone wail, 'I know a'out 'ear! I know a'out 'ear! No 'ire! No 'ore 'ire!'

'Then tell me about the girl.'

'I didn't kill any girl. I didn't. You ha'e to 'elieve 'e!'

'I know who killed the girl, Tom.'

Hoppy whispered, 'What the hell is he talking about? He knows who killed what girl?'

Prehost looked back and glared at him while he raised an index finger to his lips. He mouthed, 'Quiet, we may learn something.'

'He knows who killed what girl? What's he saying, Fred?'

'Shut up.'

The light was more dusk than day but Prehost could see the man with the motorcycle helmet standing between the forest and the fence. On the far side of the enclosure another man crouched in the corner.

A crack of lightning lit the sky all around them. The person in the motorcycle helmet spun at the rumble from the storm, then dropped to his hands and knees.

Hoppy hissed, 'Shit, he saw us.'

Prehost shook his head. 'Stay still.'

The rain accelerated. The drops grew smaller and dozens were multiplied by thousands. Around them the aspen leaves flickered from their impact. In the enclosure, the dirt began to turn dark.

The person in the helmet continued to stare into the forest.

His voice as quiet as he could make it, Hoppy told his partner, 'He has something in his hand.'

'Shhh.'

Inside the enclosure, the flames that had erupted moments before became smaller, mostly licking the ground.

'Watch it, Fred,' Hoppy whispered. 'He has something in his hand.'

The person in the helmet suddenly underhanded whatever he was holding in his hand. The object hit a spindly aspen tree twenty feet or so in front of the Park County cops and immediately burst apart.

Both men dropped to the ground.

Seconds passed and Hoppy felt a bitter tingle in his nose. He said, 'Shit. That's gas. Run, Fred, run.'

As they scrambled to their feet they could see that the person in the helmet was trying to light matches in the rain.

The two cops sprinted in opposite directions.

Prehost yelled, 'Police! Drop your weapons! Raise your hands!'

From the enclosure came the unbelieving cry of a reply. ''olice? 'olice? Really? 'olice?'

The person in the helmet stopped fumbling with the matches. Instead, he reached down and grabbed something out of a cooler on the ground. He spotted Hoppy running away through the woods and immediately threw the object at him.

Hoppy saw the projectile coming and flung himself to the wet earth of the forest floor. He pulled the shotgun close to his body and covered his head with his other arm. When he thought it was safe to look up again, he discovered that his face was fifteen inches from the onyx eyes of a pissed-off snake.

CHAPTER

47

Purdy's life was tucked into his trousers and his shield wallet hung open on his overtaxed belt. He had the end of the earpiece of a pair of cheap reading glasses stuck between his teeth while he was leaning over and staring at the red Vespa as though he were deciding how best to cook it.

Kelda had never actually met Sam Purdy, but she intuitively picked him out of the cluster of people at the scene. She flashed her FBI identification to a patrol officer so that he would let her get close enough to Purdy to say 'Detective Purdy? I'm Special Agent Kelda James.'

He turned his head to look at her. At seeing how pretty she was in person, he mumbled, 'Figures.'

'Excuse me?' she said.

He pulled the glasses from between his teeth. 'Nothing. Nice to meet you. This look like the Vespa?'

'It does.'

He turned his attention back to the red scooter. 'Do you know these things don't even need real license plates? When they have these whiny little 50cc engines they're not even considered motorcycles. The state just gives them that little sticker right there.' He pointed at the rear fender. 'See it? That thing. A square inch, maybe. If you didn't know to look for it, you'd miss it for sure.'

'Yes,' she said. She was wondering what his act was all about and was not even considering the possibility that it wasn't an act. She was determined to remain his audience and not become his foil.

Purdy went on. 'So, I was wondering, was your friend using the services of the . . . you know, county?' He tilted his head in the direction of the red brick building that housed the Boulder County Mental Health Center.

The sky to the west was dark gray and lightning was jumping off the high peaks between Boulder and the Divide. From Boulder and its vantage so close to the mountains, approaching thunderstorms sometimes appeared suddenly as the huge wave of an approaching airborne tsunami. This was one of those times. The blustery air out in front of the storm smelled of rain.

'Was Tom Clone a client of the Mental Health Center? Not that I know of.'

'So why was he here?'

She made a perplexed face for his benefit but her concentration was focused on the puzzle of how Ira had managed to get Tom off the Vespa and into his Pathfinder. She guessed that Ira had used her as bait.

To Purdy, she said, 'Clone was looking for work. Maybe he was here trying to get some kind of job. Have you talked to the people inside the building? He may have filled out an application.'

Purdy smiled just enough to let her know that he'd recognized her joust. He tapped his watch. 'It's a little late in the day, unfortunately. The Human Resources people are gone for the day. The staff people that are still in there after hours are the, um, clinical types.' He tucked his lower lip so that it disappeared below his mustache. 'You ever try to get help with an investigation from a shrink, Agent James? It's not pretty. It's just not pretty.'

She noticed that he was managing to maintain the smile in his eyes.

'I take it that nobody saw Tom drive it here? And that nobody recognizes the Vespa as his?'

'That's right. Nobody but you.'

A profound clap of thunder echoed off the mountains. Purdy didn't react to it, but he stepped around to the front end of the scooter and spread an open palm over the Vespa as though he were a magician who was about to levitate it one-handed. 'Want to make a guess where this was seen last? I mean before today?'

She almost cursed aloud at his question and her best guess about the answer, but managed to say, 'No. Why don't you just tell me where it was?' She knew he was going to tell her that it had been outside Dr. Gregory's office.

He did. 'It was on Walnut Street. Just west of Ninth. Do you know the neighborhood? It's mixed residential and offices. Nice, but a little too close to Canyon Boulevard for my taste.'

Yes, Gregory's office. What was she supposed to say next? Her eyes jumped to a bolt of lightning that seemed to elevate from the hogbacks on the western edge of town. 'I think it's finally going to rain,' she said.

Purdy looked toward the mountains. His eyes registered surprise, as though he hadn't noticed the approaching thunderstorm before. He nodded and said, 'Yep, it's that time of year. Monsoon season. So why do you think this Vespa was on Walnut Street?'

'How would I know?'

'Just thought you might.'

'When was it seen there?' she asked. She didn't really think Purdy would answer her.

He did. 'Day before yesterday.'

'Who was driving it on Walnut Street?'

'Your friend.'

Ah, she thought, *here it comes*. 'Maybe he had business over there.'

'Business? Like an appointment? That kind of business?'

'Sure. Like an appointment.'

'Yeah, that's it. Maybe he was buying life insurance. Or setting up a blind trust with a tax attorney or something.'

'Cut the crap, please, Detective. I don't know what Tom was doing over there. I don't keep his Day-Timer. I barely know him.'

'Bullshit. You know him better than you're letting on. And you know exactly what he was doing there. But that's okay. Because I do, too – I know what he was doing there. I know all about his appointment on Walnut Street. I just wanted to see how we were doing on the honesty scale, here. You and me. Local cop and federal agent. *Mano a womano*.'

She was speechless.

Rain started pelting the ground. A patrol officer was standing ready to cover the Vespa with a tarp.

Purdy indicated the officer should go ahead and drape the scooter, then he wrinkled his nose and looked at Kelda. 'Have you seen Clone or talked to Clone since he was last seen on this scooter the day before yesterday?'

'No, I haven't.'

'In case you're wondering – on that honesty scale I was talking about, we're not doing too well,' he said, while he rubbed his temples with his fingertips. 'This is giving me a headache. You got any Tylenol or anything? I noticed you were limping.'

To herself, she said, 'Shit.'

She hoped that her lips hadn't moved.

CHAPTER

48

Hoppy thought, *So that's what that sound is.*
The snake was coiled up on a rock for warmth, but its rattle had begun clattering and the snake had raised its head in ominous alert. To Hoppy the viper's eyes looked like charred grains of rice.

He was wondering if there were rules that prescribed what he was supposed to do in his current predicament.

Do I move or do I not move?

If I move, do I go fast or do I go slow?

Hoppy slid his finger onto the trigger of the shotgun. The plan he was formulating in his head was simple: Get to his feet as fast as he could and shoot the damn snake to smithereens with buckshot. He told himself he'd do it on the count of three. His eyes frozen on the snake, he silently counted, 'One . . . two . . .'

The snake moved first. It was a quick little jerk of its head. Off to the right, maybe an inch. That was it.

Hoppy never got to 'three.' He didn't pop to his feet. Once his eyes registered the movement of the snake his finger squeezed the trigger on the shotgun.

The flash from the barrel was as bright as lightning and the roar many times louder than any thunder he'd ever heard. He was so startled by the noise and the light and what the recoil had done to his elbow and by the intense stinging he felt on his scalp that he momentarily forgot all about the snake.

Then, a second or two later, he remembered, and he scrambled backward and leaped to his feet. He managed to get the barrel of the gun aimed directly at the rock where the snake was coiled.

About eight inches of snake remained on the rock. The beady black eyes were gone but the rattle end was intact. Rain was pelting the bare stone.

Hoppy thought the rattle was silent but he couldn't be sure because he really couldn't hear a thing. His ears hadn't recovered from the decibel concussion of the shotgun blast. The sharp pain on top of his head had him truly concerned that the snake might have sunk his fangs into his flesh before the buckshot turned the reptile into ground chuck.

He called out, 'Fred! Fred!' having temporarily forgotten about the man in the motorcycle helmet with the little balloons full of God-knows-what, not to mention that guy inside the fence with the speech impediment.

The rain, so intense for a few minutes, had eased to something that only a generous meteorologist would call a drizzle. A thin ribbon of dark blue and orange sky lit the tops of the Divide.

The only person that Fred Prehost could spot was his buddy, Hoppy, who was standing in a small clearing in the woods pointing his shotgun at a rock. Prehost couldn't see the guy in the motorcycle helmet, and he couldn't see the guy who was in the enclosure.

He still couldn't figure out who the hell Hoppy had decided needed shooting.

Prehost hissed, 'Hoppy, get down! Hoppy! Get down!' But Hoppy wasn't responding.

Prehost crawled closer. From twenty feet away, he said, 'Down! Get down! Jesus.'

Nothing.

Prehost threw a small rock at his friend's feet. As the stone hit his boot, Hoppy spun with the shotgun ready. Prehost waved his hands and said, 'It's me. It's me.' But he was thinking, *Shit, he's going to shoot me*.

Finally, Hoppy recognized his friend and lowered the barrel of the gun. Fred made a dramatic motion with both hands, urging him to get down; Hoppy lowered himself to a crouch.

In a voice that was at least a couple of measures too loud, he declared, 'I shot a snake.'

'You what?'

Hoppy saw Fred's lips move but didn't hear him. He shook his head and said, 'It was a rattlesnake.'

'Up here? No way, buddy.'

Hoppy pointed at his ear with his free hand and shook his head. He said, 'I can't hear you. My ears.'

From the direction of the enclosure, Prehost heard, ''olice? Hel'! 'olice? Hel'! Hel'!'

Prehost held a hand up to Hoppy.

'Hel'! Hel'!'

Hoppy said, 'I heard that.'

Fred said, 'Let's go. Careful. We don't know where the other guy is.'

Hoppy said, 'Okay.' The two men made their way the last few yards through the woods.

Prehost said, 'Cover me.' When his friend didn't respond, he added, 'You hear that?'

Hoppy nodded and raised his shotgun again. 'I got you.'

Prehost checked the woods in all directions before he approached the enclosure. He barely recognized the man inside the fence. 'Clone? Is that you?'

'Yes! Yes!'

'Who did this? Who put you in here?'

'A guy. 'ear! 'ear! It's all a'out 'ear and so'e girl.'

Prehost had no idea what Clone was talking about. He stepped closer to the pen. 'What? There's no gate? Can you climb out? Do you think you can climb the fence?'

Tom yelped, 'Don't touch the 'ence! Don't touch the 'ence! It's electric. You'll get a shock!'

'Oh,' Prehost replied and withdrew his hand. He walked to the corner of the enclosure and examined the connection where the cable from the mineshaft was wired to the steel of the fence. He turned back to Hoppy. 'We okay, here? You watching the woods?'

Hoppy gave him the thumbs-up. Prehost grabbed the orange cable with his left hand and with a single hard pull yanked it free of the fence. He raised the loose cable in the air and shook it. 'It's not going to shock you anymore, Clone. Can you climb out now?'

'I think so.'

'Then do it. Wait a second. First, where did he go? The helmet guy?'

Clone pointed back in the direction of the cabin. 'That way. He ran down that way.'

'You know who he is?'

He said, 'No. No. I don't. I think I saw hi' yesterday in 'oulder, 'ut I don't re'e'er anything until I woke u' u' here.'

'Why is he doing this?'

Tom said, ''ear. It's all a'out 'ear. And so'e girl.'

Prehost said, 'Ears?'

Tom Clone groaned.

Hoppy stepped forward. 'Fred, we should leave Clone here while we find the guy. He'll get in the way if he comes with us. He's safe inside there. We don't want to lose him.'

Prehost said, 'You're right.' He turned to Tom. 'Change of plans. I want you to stay here for a few minutes while we round that other guy up. I want to talk to him and find out what he knows about who killed the girl. We'll be back for you real soon.'

Tom screamed, 'No! No!'

Prehost lowered the orange power cable and touched the frayed end to the wiring that was still attached to the fence post. Fiery sparks lit the dusk as the electrical connection bridged the wires. 'Yes, yes, I'm afraid,' Prehost said. 'I wouldn't touch that fence if I were you.'

'No!'

'Don't worry, we'll be back. You sit tight.' Prehost turned to Hoppy. 'Are you getting your hearing back?'

'Little by little, Fred.'

'What are those marks on your head?'

Hoppy's dirty fingertips grazed the skin near his hairline. 'I'm thinking maybe he got me. The snake. How long will the poison take, Fred? Do you know how long it takes?'

'A rattlesnake, huh? You say you shot a rattlesnake?'

'I did. It's back there. I'll show you the rattles.'

'No way, Hoppy. Not up here. I think you're seeing things. Those are blast burns on your head from the shotgun. It looks like you almost blew your own damn head off trying to kill that imaginary rattlesnake.'

Fifty feet away Tom Clone listened to the whole exchange with his mouth hanging open in exasperation. Finally, his voice swollen with defeat, he interjected, *"i'er . . .* It was a 'i'er.'

'Huh? Hyper?'

"i'er! 'lease don't 'orget a'out 'e. 'lease.'

Prehost stopped and faced the man in the enclosure. 'Forget about you, Tom? All I can say is watch what you wish for. Didn't your momma ever teach you that? Watch what you wish for.'

49

Lauren had the afternoon off from work at the district attorney's office. After the conclusion of Grace's afternoon nap, my two girls were planning on coming downtown to run some errands before we all met for dinner. The gray light streaming in my office windows and the sounds of distant crackling thunder indicated that a thunderhead seemed to be descending on Boulder from the mountains, so the plans were subject to change. I stepped into the backyard of the building through the French door on the south side of my office to get a closer look at the approaching storm. Although the eastern skies were cobalt, the western view was nothing but gray waves undulating above the inert mass of the mountains.

Something was blowing in off the Divide and it was blowing in fast.

I stepped back inside and phoned Lauren on her cell.

'Hi, sweetie,' I said after she answered. 'How are my girls?'

'We're good. It looks like we're finally going to get some rain. Did you see this storm?'

'I sure did. Where are you two?'

'Nordstrom. I'm waiting to pay for some things for Grace. Are you done already?'

Nordstrom meant Flatiron Crossing, a shopping mecca east of Boulder. The new mall made me crazy. When I got within a mile of it, my blood pressure went crazy, my pulse raced, and whatever patience I possessed evaporated. The allure of Nordstrom's baby department aside, shopping excursions to suburban malls were Lauren's exclusive domain, one that I always thought she embraced with a little too much enthusiasm.

I said, 'Yeah, I am. My last patient canceled. You want to change plans and just have dinner at home? That way you and Grace don't have to drive all the way back into town in the weather.'

'Will you cook?'

'Cook? I'll make sure there's food on the table. I'm thinking takeout.'

'Can you kill fifteen or twenty minutes?' she asked. 'Let's see how the storm develops. I think I'd still like to go out to dinner. So would Grace.'

'You have enough energy?' My question was a small curtsy to Lauren's multiple sclerosis. An afternoon of shopping was often more than enough to do her in for the rest of the day.

'So far, so good.'

'Then, sure, I can stay busy here for a little while. Why don't you call me back when you decide what you want to do?'

'Grace says she loves you.'

'Sure she does. Tell her I love her and her mother, too.'

I busied myself with patient charts, making some fresh case notations in terms that were as obscure as I could manage, caught up on some filing that dated back months, and I waited for the phone to ring.

Diane poked her head in the doorway to say good night. I told her that I'd lock up the building.

After a half hour passed and the return call didn't come, I moved to the window. The storm was fierce overhead but clearing skies to the west told me that this wasn't the advance guard of the summer monsoons. It was a routine Rocky Mountain afternoon thunderstorm cell that would pass into the plains within minutes. Tomorrow the relentless summer heat would be back.

My pager vibrated on my hip. I pulled it from its holster and saw a number I didn't recognize.

I punched in the number I used to retrieve my voicemail. The most recent message played first.

A frantic voice spoke. 'Doctor Gregory? This is To' Clone? Can you hel'e? 'lease? I was kidna'ed and 'ut inside a 'ence and so'eone is trying to kill 'e. 'ear lessons! 'ear lessons! Call 'e 'ack right away. Hurry, 'lease. I need hel'!' He left the same number that was on the screen of my pager.

'Tom?' I said aloud. 'What the hell?'

The number that he'd left was busy. I waited for half a minute and tried again. Still busy. I paced the office for another thirty seconds, then tried one more time. The phone rang twice before someone answered.

'Tom?' I said.

A sonorous male voice, not Tom's, replied calmly, 'Just a second. Your friend is right here. You hold on.'

Tom answered by saying, 'Dr. Gregory? Hel'e.'

I was using my therapist's demeanor, but it felt an odd fit for the circumstances, given Tom's obvious alarm. 'Sure, Tom. I'll do whatever I can to help you. Where are you right now?'

'In the 'ountains.' Away from the phone, I heard him say, 'Where a' I, 'oca?' A second later, he spoke to me again. 'I' near Ward. It's in the 'ountains. You know where that is? Indian 'eaks.'

'Yes,' I said. 'I know where Ward is. Do you need an ambulance? I can send an ambulance.'

'No!'

'Then you need to call the police, Tom. They'll help you. Whatever trouble you're in, they'll help.'

'No!' he barked. 'No 'olice. I didn't do anything. Nothing. So'eone kidna'ed 'e to teach 'e 'ear lessons! You ha'e to co'e and get 'e, 'ut you can't call the 'olice! They're the ones trying to kill 'e. Will you co'e get 'e?'

He sounded as desperate as anyone I'd ever spoken with. 'Yes, Tom. I'll come get you. Can someone there give me directions?'

'Yes. Here's 'oca.'

'Oka? His name is Oka?'

'No! 'oca. Here he is.'

The deep voice returned to the phone. 'This is Boca. Your friend's a mess. It's pitiful. I'd hurry if I were you.'

'What's wrong with his voice? Why can't he talk?'

'He's been stung all over his body by bees. His face, and inside his mouth. He smells like gasoline and he keeps talking about vipers and napalm and electric fences. And fear? He goes on and on about fear, and fear lessons. He looks like he's been through a damn war. I've been to one or two, so I know how people look after they've been in the shit.'

Bees and snakes and napalm? I didn't know whether Tom needed a trauma surgeon or an IM injection of Haldol. 'Are you in a position to drive him someplace?'

'My truck is in town being repaired. I hit an elk down near Allenspark. All I have is my mountain bike.'

I suspected there was a story there. I didn't have time for it, though.

'How do I get to you?'

When he was done dictating directions, I repeated what I'd written down. He made one correction. I said, 'Boca, could you ask Tom something for me?'

'Shoot.'

'Ask him if he's ever been to Hawaii.'

'What?'

'I know it sounds strange. Just please ask him if he's ever been to Hawaii.'

I could hear Boca repeat my question to Tom and I could hear Tom say, 'Wha'? No.'

I said, 'I heard him. Never?'

Boca said, 'Never?'

Tom said, 'Ne'er. I'e ne'er 'een to Hawaii.'

Tom had no reason to lie. None. Given the stress he was under he couldn't possibly have guessed why I was asking the question. Even if he had, my clinical intuition was that he wouldn't be able to lie with such facility in those circumstances. I said, 'Thanks, Boca.'

Ten seconds after I hung up, while I was contemplating what it meant that Tom Clone had never flown across the Pacific to Hawaii, my private line rang. Lauren said, 'It's me. Grace is cranky. We're going to head home after all. We'll see you there, okay? You'll pick something up for dinner?'

'Change of plans. I have an emergency brewing with one of my patients. It looks like I have to make a house call. Sorry.'

'You're kidding?' She wasn't happy.

'I wish I was. It's up in the mountains. I could be late.'

'A house call? Really? You make house calls?'

'In rare circumstances, I guess I do. Give Grace a kiss. I love you guys. I'll call when I know what's going on.'

CHAPTER
50

Prehost and Hoppy were walking side by side down the trail that led back to the cabin. Prehost said, 'I say he went to the car and when he discovered he couldn't drive it, he took off down that road on foot. He's probably trying to make it back to Ward so he can catch a ride out of here. Somebody in that crazy town will help him no matter what he's done.'

Hoppy replied, 'Sounds possible, Fred. But I think we should do a quick check on that boarded-up mine first. It would be his first place to hide. He may have thought we were right on his tail. Maybe he didn't try to make it all the way back to the car or the cabin. He probably thinks we don't know about the mine.'

'Maybe.'

'We have to be careful, though. He could have guns or God-knows-what stashed in there.'

Prehost chuckled. 'Or maybe another rattlesnake.'

Hoppy didn't respond.

The rain had stopped and the night held a chill. Prehost said, 'Bet the summers are even shorter up here than they are in Park County. Don't you think?'

'This doesn't feel like summer to me. What do you think, Fred? Should we check the mine?'

'Yeah, okay, we'll take a quick look at the mine.'

'Yeah. A quick look.'

Prehost said, 'Who the hell is this Oliver guy? What the hell was he doing back there with that . . . that . . . thing where he had Clone? What was that, like a, I don't know, a corral? What was that?'

Hoppy answered just as they reached the clearing that led to the mine entrance. 'Got me. More like a prison camp, I think. How you want to do this?'

'Can we pull that door off?'

Hoppy tugged lightly at it. 'Yeah, it'll come right off. It's not bolted or anything like that. It's just there for soundproofing, I think.'

'Well, let's do that, first.' Prehost held up the flashlight so his friend could see better. 'Then we'll see what we have inside there.'

The door on the shaft entrance was just a sheet of plywood lined on both sides with rigid foam insulation. It wasn't even secured to the entrance; it just rested against the opening. Prehost tossed it aside by himself. The insistent throb of the generator seemed to roar from the cave.

Prehost peered into the opening. 'He's not in there, Hoppy. Let's go.'

'Damn it, Fred, we're here. Let me at least look. It'll just take a minute. Give me the flashlight.'

Prehost handed the light to Hoppy, who lowered his head and stepped into the rough framed opening that led to the mine. 'Be quick, Hoppy; that mine has to be full of carbon monoxide from that generator. And he ain't in there. I'm damn near sure of it. We're losing time.'

The darkness inside the mine swallowed Hoppy after three or four steps. Seconds later, Prehost couldn't even see the glow from the beam from his partner's flashlight. He cursed softly.

A minute or so later, he saw the flashlight beam reemerge from the darkness, and seconds later, he spotted Hoppy. He was breathing with his mouth open, like a dog on a hot day. He gasped for ten or fifteen seconds, unable to speak. Finally, he managed to say, 'You gotta see this.'

'He's in there?'

Hoppy nodded. He rested the shotgun across his knees and leaned over it, wheezing. 'You gotta see it.'

Prehost said, 'I don't like caves and shit. How far in is it? Do I really have to go in there and see what you found?'

'It's no big deal getting in. Thirty feet in there's like a room. You can walk the whole way, just have to bend over. But you have to see what he had going, Fred. You have to.'

'Did he shoot himself?'

Hoppy shrugged. 'Couldn't tell.'

'Blood?'

'It's a mess. But you have to see the setup. What he had planned inside that mine.'

'Meth lab?'

'I don't know. Maybe you'll know what all that stuff is.'

'Shit. Show me the way.'

Hoppy leaned the shotgun against the mineshaft door,

took a noisy breath of clean air, and stooped low to reenter the cave. Prehost was a step behind him. The smell of gasoline exhaust in the narrow tunnel was as thick as fog.

After eight or nine feet the shaft took a forty-five-degree turn to the right. The timbers that supported the tunnel were as rotten as tomatoes still on the vine after the first freeze. Prehost said, 'I hate this shit, Hoppy.'

'Not too much farther, Fred. The generator's in a little alcove right ahead. Five more feet. His body's right past it.'

Sure enough, the generator was roaring exactly where Hoppy said it would be. He warned, 'Stay on the right side for the next few feet. It's a low ceiling on the left.'

Prehost said, 'I really hate this shit, Hoppy.' But he stayed right, just as he was told.

Seconds later, Hoppy turned and flashed the beam of the light above Prehost's head. 'Okay, you can stand up now, Fred. There's headroom here.'

Prehost felt queasy and a fierce headache was burning up the back of his neck. He figured he was already starting to suffer from the first signs of carbon monoxide poisoning. 'Let's hurry, Hoppy. We're going to die in here. This is poison we're sucking.'

Hoppy said, 'You're half right. One of us is going to die in here. I'm real sorry, Fred.'

Prehost said, 'What?' just as he spotted the little pistol in his friend's left hand.

'If Oliver really knows who killed the girl, I just can't risk you ever finding out. I'm so sorry, Fred.'

'Hoppy, what the hell—'

The little gun made a huge roar in the cave. Prehost took a hasty step back as though he'd concluded that the bullet from the gun was a punch he could absorb better from a distance. His brain registered the earth disappearing from beneath his back foot before it noted the slug that had pierced the firm flesh of his upper abdomen. His last words as he disappeared into the void of a deep vertical shaft were a surprised 'Oh shit, Hoppy.'

Hoppy watched Prehost disappear into the mineshaft and counted to two before he heard the dull punctuation of a thud.

He retraced his steps to the opening of the mine. Once outside, he stumbled forward into a somersault and came up gasping for air, tears in his eyes.

Aloud he said, 'I'm so sorry, Fred.'

After a minute he raised himself to his feet and looked down the trail toward the cabin. Then he looked in the other direction back toward the fenced pen that imprisoned Tom Clone. Hoppy wasn't sure which way to go. Finally, he said, 'Oliver, I'll get you later. Hel-lo, Tom.'

Hoppy took half a dozen steps toward the trail before he remembered the shotgun that he'd leaned next to the entrance to the mine.

He spun and returned to grab the gun. To his amazement, he saw that it was gone.

'Damn,' he said. 'Damn.' He aimed the flashlight into the woods all around him but saw no one lurking. He carefully checked his service weapon and reloaded a round into the pistol from his ankle holster before he trotted down the trail to the enclosure.

He could tell before he'd even made it out of the woods that the fenced pen was empty.

Tom Clone was gone.

A closer examination revealed that the orange power cable was separated by almost a foot from the wiring that led to the fence post. Clone had somehow managed to sever the connection that Prehost had reset, and then he had scaled the fence to freedom.

Tom Clone was gone.

The shotgun was gone.

Oliver was gone.

Fred Prehost, Hoppy's only ally, was long gone.

Hoppy stepped back into the woods to reconsider his plan.

At least, he reassured himself, the damn rattlesnake was dead.

He allowed himself the comfort of that thought for a few seconds before he realized that he should have asked Fred Prehost for the keys to the Suburban before he sent him to the bottom of the mineshaft.

That was an oversight, for sure.

PART FOUR

A Step into Darkness

The section of Boulder Canyon Road that is closest to town is a curvy two-lane wonder of engineering that hugs the irregular contour of Boulder Creek as the river carries snowmelt from the highest reaches of the Rockies down the Front Range toward the plains. Even within a few hundred yards of town, the deepest parts of the canyon are perpetually bathed in the shadows of imposing vertical rock walls. Depending on the season, the canyon draws hordes of hikers, bikers, picnickers, rock climbers, ice climbers, and sightseers from the city.

On a typical summer evening, the cars cruising Boulder Canyon Road are most likely to be driven by residents commuting home to the mountain towns up the hill, or gamblers heading farther south up to the high-country gaming meccas in Blackhawk and Central City.

As she climbed the unfamiliar road out of Boulder, Kelda was keenly monitoring the cars that lined up behind her, wary about being followed. The pavement was still wet from the thunderstorm, and she was driving cautiously, unsure of the handling of Maria Alija's car, and hoping her slow speed would bring any potential tails into sight of her rearview mirror. As she passed the Red Lion Inn she spotted two cars lined up behind her: a big SUV with headlights as bright as lasers and, behind it, a four-door sedan. She guessed it was a Mitsubishi something, but she wasn't really sure.

She counted a single passenger in the SUV, and no passengers in the sedan. Within minutes a third car – she thought it was a Lexus sports car – joined the parade up the hill. Kelda kept her pace moderate – fast enough to get her to the top of the canyon as soon as possible, slow enough to keep the traffic lining up behind her. The Lexus driver wasn't satisfied with Kelda's pace, however; she blew past all three vehicles in front of her on a straight-away so short that the double yellow line never broke into dashes.

Twenty uneventful minutes later, after completing a climb to eight thousand feet above sea level, Kelda approached Barker Reservoir near Nederland, the funky little town that guards the top of Boulder Canyon. A third and fourth car had joined the uphill procession, but darkness kept Kelda from identifying makes or models. She assumed that the lights of Nederland would allow her to gather all the information she needed to know about the cars behind her.

The big SUV that had been tailgating her since Boulder pulled into the parking lot of a restaurant in Nederland. Moments later, both of the unidentified cars at the rear of the pack headed south on Highway 72. Only the sedan that Kelda thought was a Mitsubishi stayed with her after she turned north toward the town of Ward. The car kept a steady position about a hundred yards behind her. If this was a tail, she decided, whoever was doing it should be involuntarily retired from law enforcement.

She was thinking it was Bill Graves. And she was thinking that he wanted her to know he was there.

Little traffic impeded her progress toward Ward. Nighttime traffic north of Nederland on 72 is typically light. But then, so is daytime traffic. She fumbled to review the map on the seat beside her and almost missed her turn onto Chief Street, finally braking hard to manage the left-hand turn that seemed to lead directly into the wilderness between Ward and the Continental Divide.

She thought there was a fifty-fifty chance that the sedan would stay right behind her.

It did.

Kelda said, 'Damn you, Bill. This is none of your business.'

As she cleared a bend and was temporarily invisible to the driver of the sedan, she floored Maria's car and sped through a second turn and a third, finally putting the car into a skid that left it sideways across the narrow lane. She hopped out of the car and ran, crouching in a ditch at the side of the road, most of her body shielded by a big boulder. Her Sig Sauer was in her hand, light as a feather.

What if it isn't Bill?

Seconds later a different car – not the sedan that had been following her – skidded to a stop. The driver stepped into the darkness. It was a man in gray pants. He hesitated, apparently befuddled at the sight of the empty car with the open driver's door blocking the road in front of him.

Kelda couldn't identify the man in the darkness. Everything about his silhouette said Bill Graves, with one exception: The man's left hand was empty. Bill Graves would never walk into an obvious ambush without his weapon.

Unless, she scolded herself, he knew that it was Kelda who had set the trap. Which, if he was following her, he did know.

She pulled herself from the drainage ditch and crept behind the man as he slowly approached Maria's car. Three feet from his back she hissed, 'On your knees.'

The man dropped to his knees as though he were a Catholic who'd just recognized he was standing in front of the Pope.

'Now lie down, on your face. Leave your hands where I can see them,' she ordered.

He did.

She saw the red cast and said, 'Oh no.'

Alan Gregory said, 'God, I hoped it was you. Can I get up now?'

52

After leaving Sam Purdy and the red Vespa at the Boulder County Mental Health Center, Kelda had stopped at the Ideal Market on North Broadway to get something to eat while she pondered what 'something else' she was going to do next. She sipped at a bottle of iced green tea and took tasteless bites of a turkey sandwich on wheat while sitting in Maria Alija's car in the grocery store lot. The car was facing south and the sky above the Flatirons was dark but clear. The brief storm was history.

Her phone chirped in her shoulder bag.

The number she saw on the tiny screen shocked her. Just in case someone else was using his phone, she answered, 'Kelda James.'

His voice a tense whisper, Ira said, 'It's me, babe. I think I've really screwed things up. Some guys showed up with guns and shit and I had to run, and I think he got out. Got away.'

'Who? Who got out?'

'You know. The guy. Our ten-minutes guy. He got out.'

'Out of . . . the room?'

'Yes. Out of the room. Things are a mess and I need your help, Kelda. I really need your help.'

'What do you need?' She felt surprisingly calm. Her heart was lingering on the fact that both Ira and Tom Clone were alive.

'Come get me,' Ira pleaded.

'Where are you?'

'Up near Ward, on the Peak to Peak. I have a cabin up there I never told you about.'

'That's the room where you were . . .' She swallowed. 'You know . . . alone with him?'

'Yes. That's the room. It's close to the room. The room is actually outside. It's complicated, Kelda.'

'But you're at your cabin?'

'No, no. I'm in the woods. I'm afraid they're watching the cabin. I'm sure they're watching the cabin. They disabled my car.'

'Who were the two guys with the guns?'

'I don't know. They just showed up behind me and a minute later one of them started shooting.'

'Did they see you?'

'Not my face. But they saw my cabin, and my car.'

'And the car?'

'Dead.'

'The . . . guy? He got away?'

'I'm pretty sure he did. Either that or the other two guys who showed up have him. That's possible. I don't know.'

'Does the guy know who you are?'

'No. I've been careful.'

Yeah, right, she thought. 'What do they look like? The two guys with the guns?'

'I barely saw them. It was getting dark and it was raining. Everything happened real fast. White guys. Not young.'

'Cops?'

'I don't know. Maybe.'

'Did they identify themselves as police officers, Ira?'

Kelda noted hesitation before he said, 'No.'

'No?'

'No.'

She immediately reasoned that if the two guys were cops, Ira wouldn't tell her. He'd be worried that she would be even more reluctant to get further involved in his predicament.

'Ira, tell me something. Did you have anything to do with what happened to . . . the guy's grandfather?'

She felt Ira's second hesitation like a flash of agony up her legs.

'He walked in on me. I didn't mean to . . .'

'Ira, tell me how to find you.'

'I didn't want to hurt the old guy. You believe me?'

'Tell me how to find you.'

'Do you know how to get to Brainard Lake? It's in the Indian Peaks above the Peak to Peak.'

'I've been there once, I think. Camping.'

'Well, you have to get to Ward, first. Then here's what I need you to do.' He gave her directions and concluded with, 'You have your gun?'

'You know I do. Ira, you need to do something for me, too.'

'Anything.'

'While I'm on my way up there, you need to figure out what comes next, okay? I don't know what you've done. So, you need to decide the next step.'

'I can do that. You know I can. I love you, babe.'

She folded the phone and pulled out her *Pierson Guides* atlas. A quick glance at the map told her she could take either Left Hand Canyon or Boulder Canyon up the mountains to Ward. Left Hand was more direct and probably had less traffic. But she knew the Boulder Canyon road.

Kelda had never taken the road up Left Hand and she didn't trust Maria's car, so she pulled left on Broadway in the direction of Canyon Boulevard and the entrance to Boulder Canyon.

She was stopped at a red light at Pine Street when her phone rang a second time. She figured it was Ira calling again and answered without checking the ID screen.

A frantic voice said, 'Kelda, it's 'e! To'. Hel' 'e! 'lease hel' 'e! Can you hel' 'e?'

After I confessed to Lauren that I was making a house call, I fumbled with my files, dropped my car keys, and then momentarily couldn't find my cell phone in the clutter on my desk. The cherry red cast on my arm seemed to be mocking me, and I dreaded the prospect of trying to drive the curves of Boulder Canyon with one hand. *Two hands and my new Mini – sure.* The prospect brought a smile. Briefly.

It's only a block from my office on Walnut Street to Canyon Boulevard. Nine blocks past downtown the boulevard narrows to two lanes and quickly begins to adopt the contour of the curvy, steep mountain passage that is Boulder Canyon. Just before I reached the mouth of the canyon, I reconsidered my impulsive plan. I turned off onto Pearl Street so I could make a phone call. In the best of circumstances, I'm not the most coordinated human being in the Western Hemisphere. With the cast on my arm, the odds of my successfully juggling a cell phone while driving with my knees through Boulder Canyon were on the low side. Anyway, the cell reception in the confines of the canyon was miserable.

'Diane,' I said after the call clicked through. 'It's Alan.' Diane Estevez wasn't just a wonderful friend and a good business partner. She was a heck of a clinical psychologist. I valued her counsel.

'You're breaking up,' she whined.

On the negative side, she wasn't always the most patient person I knew.

'I'm not surprised. I'm up at Eben Fine Park. I need some advice.'

'Sure, here's some advice: Don't try to make cell phone calls from mountain canyons. It doesn't work.'

'Thanks. This is serious, okay? I need some consultation from you. You have a second?'

'I'm busy trying to decide what kind of takeout I want Raoul to pick up for dinner. What's up?'

'A patient just called me and said that he's been hurt by . . . some people . . . you know, injured – that kind of hurt – and he says that he's still in danger from them and he wants me to come get him. He's up in the mountains, way up in the mountains, like near Ward. A guy who's helping him confirms that he's in bad shape. The thing is that my patient's telling me that some of the people who are after him are the police, so I can't call the cops for help.'

'How the hell do you get in situations like this, Alan? I swear, I don't know anyone else—'

'Diane, that's not helpful. Please be helpful. I know you have it in you.'

'Is he paranoid?'

'Fearful. Let's say fearful. But he has some reasons to be fearful. His circumstances are very unusual.'

'Psychological reasons? Or practical reasons?'

'Both.'

She made an I-don't-believe-what-I'm-hearing kind of noise before she asked, 'Does he have any reason to try to get you mixed up in something crazy? Think about this one before you answer.'

I hesitated. 'Kind of.'

I could hear her mumble, 'Shit.' After an audible exhale she asked, 'Is he in imminent danger?'

'All the evidence I have says yes, he probably is.'

'Why can't this guy who's helping him take him someplace safe?'

'He doesn't have a car.'

'You want advice? Here's advice: Call the police. Don't go up there. Don't do it, Alan. The presence of imminent danger gives you the freedom to do what you need to do regarding confidentiality.'

'That's what I thought you'd say.'

'You're not going to listen to me, are you? You have a baby, Alan. Alan! Don't even—'

'I'm thinking.'

'You're breaking up on me. Don't go. I swear I'll—'

A burned-out therapist, one who didn't care, would have eagerly heeded Diane's caution.

I didn't want to be that therapist, the one who didn't care.

Each recent morning as I climbed out of bed, I'd been more and more terrified of being that therapist.

The connection to Diane was crappy, but not so crappy that I couldn't have continued the conversation. I closed the phone anyway. Seconds later, I reopened it and speed-dialed Sam Purdy at home.

His wife heard something in my tone and handed the phone immediately to Sam.

'Yeah,' he said.

'I found Tom Clone, Sam. Or he found me.'

His voice flat as a good pool table, he replied, 'Cool. The good news is that you win the scavenger hunt; the bad news is that the prize fund is empty. Why are you calling me? You want to gloat? You know you're not going to tell me where Clone is. But do tell him this for me when you see him, would you? If he wants his little motorbike back, he's probably going to have to come down and fill out some paperwork. Tell him it should take about a week.'

'Sam, I'm calling because I need your help with something . . . goofy.' 'Goofy' was Sam's Minnesota word. It seemed apropos to the current situation.

It took me a couple of minutes to explain about Tom Clone's phone call from Boca's cabin. Sam was especially interested in the part about the fear lessons and the bees and the snakes and the napalm. He asked quite a few questions that I couldn't answer to his satisfaction.

One of them was 'And he's absolutely sure cops are involved in this torture?'

'He says he's sure that the two guys who showed up at the end identified themselves as police.'

'What do you think?'

Sam, I knew, was asking me about the quality of Tom's thinking. 'Some Park County cops have been hounding him since he got out of prison, Sam. You know, over the Campbell murder.'

'Why don't I know about this?'

'Clone didn't report it to anyone. Considering the circumstances, he didn't think anybody would believe him. He was really trying to keep a low profile with law enforcement.'

'He reported it to you, though, right?'

'Yes.'

'And in your wisdom, you decided to keep it to yourself?'

'Sam, please.'

'Do you believe Clone? Come on. I need something to work with. You're serving me nothing here.'

'Some of what he said, yes, I believe him.'

'And this guy he's with right now in Ward? He sounded legit?'

'Yeah. He was coherent, well-spoken. He implied that he had been in the military. I'd say he's reliable. He said that it looked to him like Tom had been worked over by someone or something.'

'Yeah?'

'Clone's apparently covered with bee stings and smells like gasoline. I can tell you from my brief conversation with him that he can barely talk. He apparently has bee stings on his lips and inside his mouth.'

'Shit. You said he's in Ward, right? You ever been to Ward, Alan? It's like a rest stop on a road trip to Mars.'

'Yeah, I've been to Ward. Last time I was there, I actually found it kind of charming.'

'You wouldn't find it charming if you were a cop,' he scoffed. 'Where are you right now?'

405

'Eben Fine Park. Apparently I'm about to make a rest stop on a road trip to Mars.'

'And you're going to take Boulder Canyon?'

'I was.'

'Don't be a fool. Take Lee Hill to Left Hand. Less aggravation, less traffic. Save you ten minutes, easy.'

'I'm already at the mouth of Boulder Canyon, Sam.'

'I don't care. You'll be behind all the commuters in Boulder Canyon. With your luck you'll get stuck behind a propane truck, or even worse a septic truck, the entire way up the hill. You don't want that. I know; I've done it. Cut across town on Ninth. You'll be glad you did.'

'I'll think about it.'

'You want me to come with you, don't you?' Sam asked me. It wasn't really a question, more like an accusation.

'Yes. I'd be grateful.'

'Ward's out of my jurisdiction, Alan. Way out of my jurisdiction. I can't just sit tall in the saddle and ride right into town with my six-guns blazing.'

I had no time to savor the image Sam was painting for me. 'Just call the sheriff and tell him that you're following a lead in the assault on Clone's grandfather. He'll give you permission to talk to anybody you want in Ward and you know it. He probably won't even insist on sending a deputy along to babysit you.'

He harrumphed.

'The best part is that it's not even a lie.'

'If your wife wasn't an assistant DA, you wouldn't know any of this, would you? You're not that smart, you know.'

He was begging for a wise-ass retort. I declined.

Sam said, 'I need ten minutes here. I want to lay my

eyes on my kid and he's not home from his baseball game yet, but he's due back soon. I'll pick you up in what, fifteen minutes, maybe twenty. Or even better, you can just stop here on your way to Lee Hill. You'll come right by me.'

I couldn't shake the intensity of Tom Clone's desperation from my imagination. 'I'm going to head up there now, Sam. I'll meet you in Ward. That'll give me a few minutes to prepare Tom for your arrival. You got something to write with? I want to give you the directions to Boca's cabin.'

'The guy's name is Boca? What kind of name is that? What's his last name?'

'You want to run his name, don't you?'

'Of course I do. I run just about everybody's name. It's a hobby of mine. '

'I don't have his last name, just Boca. He lives in Ward, Sam, remember.'

'Right, I forgot. I should just go to NCIC and run "Boca in Ward." That should work real well. What is "Boca"? What kind of name is that?'

'I don't know. I think it's Spanish for "mouth."'

'Mouth? Who calls themselves Mouth?'

'Sam, you want the directions?'

'Listen, I won't be long here,' Sam said when I'd given him the route to Boca's cabin. 'Simon's due home any minute from his baseball game. I'd rather you wait for me or come by here and get me. You know if you go up there by yourself, you're going to—'

'I'm going to what, Sam?'

'You know, Alan.'

'What?'

407

'You're going to get in trouble. People will get shot. Bombs will go off. Plagues will start. Something. It's a karma thing with you.'

I couldn't argue with him. My track record where mayhem was concerned wasn't exemplary. 'To be honest, Sam, I'd rather not go at all, but I think I have to. It's the right thing to do. I'll see you in Ward.'

'I didn't think you'd wait for me.'

'You're a good man for doing this, Sam Purdy.'

'No,' he said. 'What I am is a moron.'

I took Sam's advice and backtracked across town on Ninth Street, passing within a couple of blocks of Sam's house. I was tempted to stop, but I didn't.

As he predicted, there was almost no traffic as I climbed on Lee Hill Road. Thirty minutes and three thousand plus feet of altitude later, Kelda James ordered me to my knees.

CHAPTER
54

After she lowered her gun and permitted me to get up from the ground, I followed Kelda's car as she drove the final few minutes to Boca's cabin, which was near Left Hand Creek down an unmarked dirt lane off the main road to Brainard Lake.

Neither Kelda nor I was driving a vehicle suitable for maneuvering up the steep, rutted, rock-pitted passage that Boca probably called his 'driveway,' so we parked at the bottom and hiked the last fifty yards or so up to the cabin. Although the trees at this altitude tended to be stunted by the arid, harsh climate, the pine forest was surprisingly thick, the sky was frosted with stars, and the air was so clean it tingled. I thought, *This must be why people live up here*. As we neared the front door of the neat frame cabin, my lungs were aching from the brief climb, as though my body was intent on reminding me that the difference between the east and west boundaries of Boulder County was, vertically at least, over a half a mile.

Kelda wasn't as winded as I was. But I thought she was limping. Between gasping inhalations I asked, 'How are your legs?'

She shook her head, opened her mouth to speak, and then allowed her lips to close back together. After a quick breath, she said, 'My legs hurt. It doesn't mean I'm going to sit down. It doesn't mean I'm going to go home. They hurt. They usually hurt. Let's go get Tom.'

'Okay,' I said, digesting her animosity. I was closest to the cabin, so I pounded on the door with the side of my fist.

A stunningly handsome black man answered the door. His upper cheeks were peppered with faint freckles, and his dark eyes expressed an inner warmth that seemed to surround him with a glow. He held out his hand and said, 'Hello, I'm Boca. Won't you please come in? You must be the doctor.' He looked past me out the door. 'And you must be the FBI agent. Tom told me about both of you.'

Kelda said, 'Nice to meet you.' Something about him – his beauty? his eyes? his manner? – had softened her like room temperature softens butter.

I added, 'It's a pleasure. We're very grateful for all you've done to help Tom.' I took the man's right hand with my left. He glanced briefly at my cast. My breathing was almost back to normal.

'I didn't do anything but offer a man in need some courtesy. May I see some identification from the two of you? Please don't be offended.'

Kelda's FBI badge was a better statement than my

driver's license but both sufficed. Boca required reading glasses to check the fine print. The glasses were hung on a chain around his thick neck. After he was satisfied with our ID, he said, 'Thank you. But I'm afraid Tom's gone.'

It was Kelda who said, 'What?' It was part exclamation, part resignation. She hadn't expected this part of her evening to go smoothly.

Boca fingered the graying hair on the side of his head and spent a moment examining Kelda and me as though he was trying to decide whether he could really trust us. Although he'd invited us into his cabin, he hadn't removed his significant mass from the doorway. 'A man came to my door about five minutes ago. When I stepped outside to speak with the gentleman, Tom decided it was a good idea to go out the back window.'

'Did the man introduce himself?'

'No, he did not.'

'Tell me about him, please. Everything you remember.' Kelda did the talking.

When Boca responded, each word was measured and intonated gorgeously, as though he'd memorized lines. 'He was a thin man with new blue jeans and a plain gray sweatshirt. He was quite dirty.' He paused. 'And he had frog eyes.'

'Frog eyes?'

'They stuck out, bulged. The way frogs' eyes do. And, oh yes' – with the 'oh yes' his voice moved momentarily from tenor to baritone – 'he had powder burns on his head.'

Kelda's head tilted a fraction of an inch before she asked, 'Where exactly?' I couldn't understand why the precise location was important.

411

Boca spread his big hand a few inches into the hairline above his forehead and dragged his fingers over his temple and right ear. 'This area, ma'am.'

'Why do you think they were powder burns?' she pressed.

'Because they were. And because I could still smell it on him. The residue from the gunpowder. I have a nose for it.'

Kelda said, 'Can you describe him? The man at the door? Was he a strong man? With biceps like . . . like that firewood there?' She pointed at the trim pile of aspen logs stacked a few feet from the cabin. Each white-barked log was six to eight inches in diameter.

'No. He was not a strong man. Quite the opposite.'

'Was he tall? Thin?'

'Yes, but not as tall as the doctor.' He nodded slightly in my direction.

'His hair? Long, short? What?'

'Short. Combed over.'

I was acutely aware that Kelda was asking questions that indicated that she had suspects in mind. How was that possible? What had Tom told her during their conversation that he hadn't told me?

'Did he introduce himself?' Kelda asked Boca.

'No. He merely said he was lost and he asked to use my telephone. He was trying to look past me into the cabin.'

'Was he armed?'

Boca reached behind him and removed something from the back pocket of his trousers. He held it flat across his palm. His hand was so large that the gun in it looked like a toy. 'He was carrying this on his ankle. It made me uncomfortable, so I removed it from him.'

Kelda said, 'You took it from him? Just like that?'

'I know some martial arts, ma'am. What I did was, I encouraged him to lose his balance. From that point on, the removal of the weapon was not particularly difficult. As I said, he was not a strong man.'

'May I take the gun from you? Do you mind?'

'I wish you would.'

She lifted the gun from his hand, checked to see that it was loaded, and placed it in her shoulder bag.

'Where is this man now?'

'After I removed his weapon, he wriggled away from me and ran back into the woods. I suspect that he never really wished to use my phone.'

'What about Tom? Was he armed?'

Boca stared hard at her before he answered, as though he was looking for something specific in her eyes. Some assurance. Something. Finally, he said, 'He has a shotgun with him, ma'am.'

'Boca?' I asked. 'We'd like to know everything Tom said to you. Will you spend a few minutes going over that?'

Kelda said, 'I've got to find Tom. I can't be late for this.' She faced Boca. 'I'm in a borrowed car and I don't have my equipment. Do you have a flashlight I could borrow?'

I wanted to ask what she meant by that, what she meant when she said she couldn't be late.

But Boca said, 'Yes, ma'am.' And Kelda took the flashlight and went silently into the night.

Before Kelda disappeared into the woods behind the cabin, she called back at me, admonishing me not to call anyone for help.

When I opened my mouth to argue with her, she said, 'There are things going on that you don't know anything about.'

The understatement almost made me laugh.

Boca's home was a single room. An alcove on the far side functioned as a bathroom; an expensive-looking high-tech toilet was visible through a hanging curtain. The entire wall adjacent to the entry door was covered with books. Mostly paperbacks. Not one appeared unread. A lamp by the bed was the sole illumination in the space.

Boca took a minute to tend a fire in a stove in the corner before he said, 'Please have a seat.'

I took a chair at an oak table. Boca sat on the edge of his bed. The bed was neatly made. I don't know why I found that odd, but I did. If I lived halfway to heaven all by myself, I didn't think I'd make my bed.

I think he saw me looking at the lamp by the bed. 'I have solar panels on the roof. And I have a gasoline generator for backup electricity. I read a lot. I listen to jazz. Besides that, I have little use for power. There is ample wood for heat.'

'It's beautiful up here,' I said.

'Yes,' Boca said. 'You broke your arm?'

'I tripped over my dog. I can be a klutz.'

His eyes softened. 'You're a psychologist, right? That's what Tom said.'

'Yes, sir, I am. I'm a clinical psychologist.'

He leaned forward and rested his elbows on his knees. 'Is Tom . . . you know, unbalanced? Is that why he's—'

I didn't want him to ask me something I couldn't reveal about Tom. Before he could finish his thought, I interrupted and said, 'Tom told you . . . what he's been through?'

'Kind of. I knew some things already. I read newspapers when I'm in town. He told me some other things.'

'Well, he's been through a lot. And when you've been through the kind of trauma that he's been through, well, it tends to take its toll on people.'

My words seemed to strike my host almost like a physical blow. After he regained his composure he slowly rolled up the sleeves on his shirt. First the left, then the right. As the cuff of his right sleeve reached his elbow, I saw a tattoo that he'd uncovered on his dark skin. The art was simple. In inch-tall black letters it read 'IX-XI.' From the bottom of each Roman numeral flowed a bright red tear.

A focused pressure formed in my chest, as though a dense weight were tugging on my heart. I swallowed and nodded once, my eyes glued to the rippling forearm of this dignified man who, without saying a thing, had just whispered volumes about a chapter in the life he'd lived.

I said, 'You're new in Colorado, Boca?'

He almost smiled as he said, 'Yes. Yes, sir, I am. Less than a year. I once lived in . . . on the East Coast.'

I recalled his story about disarming the man at the door and guessed, 'Policeman?'

He shook his head.

'Firefighter?'

He nodded.

I thought, *Oh my God.*

Boca didn't travel two-thirds of the way across the

country to live by himself nearly nine thousand feet above sea level so that a stranger could pepper him with questions about the reason for his exile. That's what I told myself, anyway. Call it intuition.

I said, 'Tom's not crazy, Boca. He's trying to adjust to some monumental events. I imagine after what he's been through the past few days that he'll have some more adjusting to do.'

Boca shifted his weight back, resting his hands on the mattress. 'You're not sure about him, though, are you?'

'I don't know exactly what you're asking.' I knew what he was asking. I just didn't want him to be asking it.

Boca didn't deign to dance with me. I was getting the impression that if he ever knew the steps to the prevarication dance, he'd forgotten them before the dust settled in September 2001. He said, 'You're not convinced that he didn't kill that girl. That's what you're not sure about.'

I wanted to ask, *Which girl is that? The one in Park County or the one in Maui that her friend calls Jones?* But I didn't. I still knew the steps to the prevarication dance. I knew them well. So I danced with him. 'I can't talk about that, I'm sorry. Confidentiality. I'm sure you understand.'

But Boca's suspicion was right. Despite his assertion that he'd never been to Hawaii, I wasn't at all sure about Tom Clone. Kelda's disclosures that afternoon about Jones's journal and her fears about Tom Clone had haunted me since I'd heard them. Sam Purdy's suspicions had aggravated my own. My doubts about Tom, which had germinated shortly after I'd first met him, had spent the past few hours growing with the alacrity of Jack's beanstalk.

'With all due respect, Doctor, Tom needs your help. Your own doubts aside.'

'I know he does.' I did know that Tom needed my help. In my heart, though, I wasn't certain that the sentiment I expressed to Boca was as sincere as my words.

Boca said, 'People . . . sometimes have to do things even when they're not sure. For the sake of humanity, sometimes we must reach out a hand. Sometimes we all must step into the darkness. The step may lead nowhere, but sometimes we all must take it.'

My breathing stopped. 'Thank you,' I said.

'Yes,' he replied.

He scratched absently at his forearm.

I considered the possibility that Boca was inviting me to comment further on his tattoo, and maybe, maybe, to hear about one time that he'd reached out a hand and stepped into the darkness, but I decided that in the absence of a more direct summons from him, the best thing I could do was to move on.

Some distant thunder echoed through the Indian Peaks.

I said, 'We get monsoons each summer. Did you know that? Sometimes people who are new to Colorado don't know about the monsoons.'

He raised his eyebrows. 'Monsoons? Like in India? It rains all the time, that kind of monsoon?'

'Not all the time, but it rains. Every July the storms come up from the Gulf of Mexico and the Gulf of California. I thought for a while that the storm that passed through here earlier this evening was the start of the monsoons. It's been dry on the Front Range so far this summer.'

'Monsoons?' he mused. 'Everybody's been warning me about winter. I didn't know about the monsoons.'

'You don't have to worry about the monsoons unless you're a farmer. Too few are bad. Too many are bad. Hail is bad. The lightning can be a problem up here. But for most of us they come and they go. They're just summer storms. They just . . . are.'

He was staring into the blackness beyond his window as though he half expected to see the monsoons coming over the Divide right that minute.

'So do you have neighbors up here, Boca?'

He looked at me with some suspicion. I thought he was puzzled by my small talk.

'The closest cabin is almost a half mile away. A guy comes up on weekends and works on it. Other than that, his cabin's empty. Next closest neighbor is a quarter mile past him.' He smiled. 'May I offer you some tea? It will just take a moment. The stove's hot.'

'No, thank you. Do you know the guy who's fixing up the cabin?'

'No, sir, I do not. He's a young man who drives a green SUV that he washes frequently. People in town tell me that his name is Oliver. He and I have not spoken. Not once.'

'Did Tom say anything else while you were waiting for us to get up here? Anything that would help us understand what we should do next?'

'The older I get, the fewer truths I know. But one truth I know well is the face of fear. When he walked in my door,

Tom had that face.' Boca's voice moved again from tenor to baritone. 'His eyes were hooded with dread. His words sang the song of disbelief. His spirit sagged under the burden of despair.'

He was reciting something, I thought. Some stanzas from some anthem he'd read or written once after a personal sojourn in hell. I thought I knew the hell. At least I knew it the way I knew about things like Tora Bora and the Gaza Strip.

I'd seen it on television.

When he went on, it was as though he could hear my thoughts. 'Tom was a man who'd walked halfway to hell and he wasn't sure yet whether or not he was going to make it back out.'

'That bad?'

'He kept saying that he spent the last few days getting fear lessons.'

'Fear lessons?'

'Yes, sir. Have you had fear lessons yet in this life? Tom had his lessons right on this mountain. I could see it in his face. And the good Lord knows I've had mine.'

'I don't know . . . what you mean.'

'You will. When the time for your fear lesson comes, you'll know it.'

A sharp *craaaack* punctured the night.

I jumped. Boca didn't. But his eyes filled with tears.

He said, 'I'm afraid that was a gunshot.'

'Shotgun?' I asked.

'I'd say a handgun.'

He stood and walked to the corner of the large room.

I noted that he was as far as possible from the door.

I said, 'I'm going to go check on Kelda and Tom.'

'If you don't mind, I'm going to stay here.' He reached into a drawer and pulled something out. A whistle. He handed it to me. 'Blow that once or twice and I'll call nine-one-one. I'm sorry but it's the best I can do.'

He'd said, *When the time for your fear lesson comes, you'll know it.*

As I closed the door behind me, I had an inkling.

CHAPTER

55

The thunderstorm that passed earlier in the evening had temporarily transformed the mountain air from arid to almost humid. I felt a chill as I stepped away from Boca's cabin.

I allowed my eyes a moment to adjust to the blackness and my ears to adjust to the silence. Since the shot had fractured my illusion of safety, I hadn't heard another sound from outside. Not a call for help, not a whelp of pain, not labored breath, or careless footsteps.

I could hear my own heart beating. I could also hear Diane's admonition: '*You have a baby, Alan. Don't go!*'

The alternative? Not going.

Not going meant allowing my two patients – Kelda and Tom – to survive this puzzle on their own. My job, I reminded myself, was to help them survive *after* they'd survived this trial. Or the next trial. Or the one after that.

What had Diane said? The goal isn't to help patients get

better, but rather to help them get better equipped. How did this fit?

I didn't know.

I was tempted to go back to my car and wait for Sam Purdy to arrive. I fingered the whistle. A single blow and a fraction of an hour later some fine deputies of the Boulder County Sheriff's Office would descend on these woods.

But Tom Clone didn't trust them.

And Kelda James had been clear that she didn't want them around.

Who did I trust?

Not Tom, not Kelda. My gut said I could rely on Boca. But if push came to shove – and push was perilously close to coming to shove – I was planning to trust the Boulder County Sheriff.

I clambered down the steep driveway and listened some more for some indication of where anybody might be.

The roar of a second gunshot splintered the night. Almost simultaneously, I thought I heard the distinctive ping of a slug impacting rock. My breath snagged in my chest.

Fear lesson, I thought. *Is this my time?*

It was. Boca was right. I knew.

Without another moment of hesitation I raised the whistle to my lips. I blew.

The second I stopped, a tattered voice called out, 'Who's there?'

Tom Clone was still alive.

Wishing I had Boca on my flank, I moved in the direction of his voice.

It was my step into the darkness.

56

The burning in Kelda's lower legs was so intense that she could no longer tell if the sensation was one of searing heat or freezing cold, and the bones in her legs felt as though someone had been pinging them with a ball-peen hammer. The two Percocets she'd swallowed on the way up Boulder Canyon had had about as much impact on her pain as a couple of M&M's.

She was trying to maneuver down the dirt road near Left Hand Creek without using the flashlight that Boca had given her. She stopped every few steps to listen for a sound to guide her.

She desperately wanted to escape the darkness, to flick on the flashlight, but she knew that the beam of precious light would act as a magnet for the black hole at the end of the barrel of every gun in the forest. She attempted to quell her fears by trying to decide whom she hoped to find first.

Tom? She absolutely had to find Tom, but she was worried about what he knew. What had he figured out on his own? What had Ira told him?

Ira? Oh, Ira. Baby. What would she do when she found Ira? Even the brief conversation with Boca left her concerned that Ira hadn't covered his trail well. The trail to Ira would lead back to her.

That trail would destroy her.

And the guy who'd come to the door of Boca's cabin? She thought he was one of the Park County cops who had tried to roust Tom and her on their way from the penitentiary. But where was the other one? The one with the big arms and the attitude? Prehost? Where was Prehost?

Kelda figured that when she stumbled on one of the cops, she'd find the other. Despite the fact that Boca had managed to get the backup gun from one of them, she figured they were still pretty well armed.

The first sound that alerted her was the snap of a twig. She flattened herself into a ditch by the dirt path.

Deer? Bear? Lion?

She wished. She knew she wasn't that lucky.

The second sound was a man groaning as though he'd been punched high in the gut.

Kelda held her gun steady, pointed into the night in the direction of the groan. The Sig weighed as much as a watermelon.

Five seconds passed. Ten. Her legs throbbed. She imagined a bed of frozen peas.

A sudden wail rapidly swelled into a scream as a person

sprinted from the evergreen forest onto the road about thirty yards in front of her. Kelda's brain was trying to make sense of the noise and the shadows and the silhouettes.

The runner seemed to be turning toward her.

A breathless voice came from the shadows. 'Stop, damn it! I'll fucking shoot you. I will.'

The voice wasn't Ira's. And she didn't think it was Tom's. She thought she recognized it, though; it was the voice from the burgundy Toyota pickup that had followed her home to Lafayette two weeks before.

The voice of the man who had said, 'Evening, darlin'.'

Now she figured that it was one of the Park County cops – probably the one called Hoppy – or somebody else who was up here that she didn't even know about.

The charcoal silhouette on the trail froze. From the silhouette came the plea, 'Okay, okay. Don't shoot.'

Kelda knew it was Ira. And she knew from his voice that Ira was scared to death.

On her hands and knees, she edged closer to him. She stopped abruptly as a second figure emerged at the very edge of the forest and said, 'Don't fucking move! Got it?'

Kelda thought that was the 'Evening, darlin'' cop.

'Okay, okay. Don't shoot.' Ira's dread chilled her.

'Who are you?'

The cop was scared, too.

Ira hesitated before he said, 'Oliver Lee.'

Kelda recognized the name – Oliver and Lee were Ira's parakeets.

'What the hell were you doing back there? With Clone and that fence? What was that?'

'Just a prank. A thing. You know.'

'Do I sound like I fucking know? What kind of prank thing?'

'You know, we were . . . getting even.'

'Who's "we"?'

'Me. Not we. Me.'

'You said "we."'

'I meant me.'

'Getting even for what?'

'Something Clone did before he went to prison. An old . . . grudge. That kind of thing. Come on, let me go. Let me go. I won't do it again. I got even. But now I'm all done. Let me go.'

'Where's my shotgun?'

Ira said, 'I don't know.'

'You don't have it?'

'No.'

'You lying?'

'No.'

Kelda could see enough of his silhouette to know that Ira was holding out his hands to show that he didn't have the gun. She wondered how the cop had managed to lose both his shotgun and his backup gun in the same evening. She also wondered where the cop's partner was.

'Keep your hands out like that.'

Kelda thought that the cop was trying to sound as if he was in control, but all he was succeeding in doing was showing how frightened he was.

Ira kept his hands out.

The cop asked, 'What'd he do? Clone? What do you want revenge for?'

'He killed a girl.'

'Yeah, he was in prison for that. What's your grudge? What are you getting even for?'

Ira said, 'He killed another girl. Someone . . . I knew.'

Kelda worried how far Ira was willing to go with the story. The disclosures he'd made so far wouldn't allow the cop to figure out who he really was. But if he offered much more . . . She mouthed, 'Be careful, baby. Be careful.'

She was, she guessed, twenty yards from Ira, twenty-five from the Park County cop. She considered moving closer but decided not to risk being discovered.

'No shit? He killed another girl?' the cop asked.

Kelda noted that the man's tone had changed. Ira's revelation about another murder interested him.

'Yes, a few weeks after Ivy Campbell was murdered.'

'What?' the cop asked. To Kelda's ear, the question was a defiant 'Are you crazy?' kind of 'What?'

Ira explained, 'Clone was dating her, the other girl. She was living in Denver when she broke up with him. He threatened her, then he followed her to Hawaii, and . . . he killed her there.'

The cop was silent for ten seconds. Finally, he said, 'No, he didn't. He didn't go to Hawaii and kill any girl. You're wrong, you don't know what the hell you're talking about.'

'He did,' Ira said.

Kelda thought she heard the slightest fissure emerge in Ira's voice.

'Then why haven't I heard about this? Where's your evidence? What do you have?' the cop asked.

'Her journal. He was, like, stalking her. It says he was going to come to Hawaii to kill her. Then it says that she saw him there. And then . . . then she was dead.'

'He cut her throat?'

'No, no. He, he . . .'

Kelda thought, *Don't Ira! Don't!*

'He didn't cut her throat.'

The 'Evening, darlin'' cop thought about something for almost half a minute before he said, 'You're saying he killed her in Hawaii?'

Ira said, 'Yes, yes.'

The man grew silent again. When he broke his silence, his tone was even more skeptical than before. He asked, 'And this was when?'

'Just after Ivy Campbell was killed in Park County. Like I said, a few weeks. Nineteen days later to be precise. That's all, just nineteen days.'

The cop laughed. 'You don't know what the hell you're talking about. You got the wrong guy. Clone didn't do it. He didn't kill any girl in Hawaii. Are you making all this up for me?'

It was Ira's turn to say, 'What?' Kelda could tell that he was befuddled. It was easy for her to tell because she was, too.

The cop said, 'We were watching Clone the whole time after Ivy Campbell was killed in Park County. He was our prime guy from almost the beginning. He'd been dating her, he lied to us about being up there, his fingerprints were places they shouldn't have been. From day two on, we were watching him. We might have lost him for a few hours here and there, or left him alone while he was at work, or asleep, but we never lost him long enough for him to get on a plane and fly to Hawaii and kill some girl. How long was he supposed to be there? In Hawaii.'

'A few days, three or four. Less than a week.'

'No way,' the cop said. He laughed some more. 'You've been torturing the wrong asshole.'

Kelda almost gasped for air. She hadn't even realized she was holding her breath.

'No! He did it. He killed her,' Ira sputtered.

The 'Evening, darlin'' cop kept laughing.

We've been torturing the wrong asshole? Kelda thought. *Is that really possible? Ira?*

'Sorry,' the cop said. 'You're full of shit. You set all this up for the wrong guy. You're as pitiful as he is.'

Kelda wanted to yell, 'No way, no . . . way!' Instead she struggled to still her heart as she listened to Ira's reply.

'No, it's true. It is. I've seen the investigation from the Park County detectives. The file they put together. There's nothing in there about anybody following Clone around during those first few weeks. He had time to go to Hawaii. He even had time off from work during the few days he was gone. I read the file. I read the whole . . . thing. I checked the timeline myself. He did it. He did.'

Kelda thought, *Oh shit. Careful, Ira, careful. Don't fall into his trap. Don't go there. Don't reveal too much.*

She wished she knew where the second cop was. If she knew where the guy with the big arms was, it would really increase her options on how to intervene if Ira started revealing too much, which it appeared he was about to do.

The cop asked, 'How did you get a chance to read it? The murder book? How did you get ahold of it? That's not public information. You can't just walk in the door and get a copy of the murder book.'

Ira's breathing changed. He stammered, 'Somebody showed it to me.'

'Somebody?'

'A friend from . . . there.'

'Park County?'

'Yeah.'

'Well, I'm from there. Park County. In fact, I'm the one who followed Clone about half the time between the murder and the day we arrested him. There wasn't a twenty-four-hour period during the weeks before he was arrested that I didn't lay my own eyes on Clone. He didn't take any trips to any island paradise while I was watching him, I promise you that.'

'You're wrong. That's not . . . It's not in the . . . the . . . file. There's nothing in the file about anybody following him. I read it. I checked all the dates. He had time off. He was free.'

'You're right about one thing. There's nothing in the file. Because maybe I didn't put it in the file. Maybe I did it on my own because I wanted to catch the creep . . . that bad.'

We've been torturing the wrong asshole? Kelda thought, once again.

Ira tried to mount an offensive. He said, 'Why are you here? Tonight? Why are you up here? What do you want with me?'

'We're not up here for you.'

Kelda noted that he'd said 'We.'

Ira again. 'Then what do you want with Clone?'

Kelda thought, *Good, Ira. Keep thinking. Keep thinking. Keep the pressure on him. Make him talk.*

'We're cops. He's a perp. Beyond that, you'll never know the answer, asshole.'

Ira said, 'You're wrong. You don't know what Clone did. I know what he did.'

The cop exploded in rage. '*I'm* wrong? *I'm* wrong? You little fuck, you don't know who the hell you're messing with. I'm going to make you so sorry—'

Her vision had adjusted a little more to the darkness and, with the cop's outburst, she registered a flurry of movement on the edge of the woods.

Ira must have noticed the movement, too.

Suddenly, the silhouette that was Ira disappeared in a blur.

Across from where Ira had been, the muzzle blast of a handgun flared in the darkness on the forest edge. The sound of footsteps followed, sparking yet another fiery blast from the handgun.

The footsteps stopped.

Behind her, from the direction of Boca's cabin, Kelda heard the rattling shrill of a whistle.

Seconds later her cell phone chirped.

Damn!

She dove into the forest and tried to find the phone so she could quiet the thing. Another shot ripped through the darkness.

This one was aimed at her.

She hunched behind a tree and got the phone to her ear. 'What?'

Ira whispered, 'I heard the phone ring. I know you're here, babe. And I really, really need your help.'

CHAPTER

57

She took a deep breath and yelled, 'I'm a special agent of the FBI! Everybody drop your weapons! Everybody!' .

The sharp crack of a semiautomatic weapon answered her command. At the same instant a slug buried itself in the soft soil a yard from her legs. She hunkered even closer to the tree.

The Park County cop knew she was FBI. He was shooting at her anyway.

Why?

From somewhere in the woods, not close, not too far away, Tom Clone called, 'Kelda?'

Kelda heard Ira yell, 'I'm really exposed out here,' an instant before another shot flared from the handgun.

Ira's words and the clap from the handgun were followed a second or two later by Tom Clone's distinctive slur. 'You're the 'ear lessons guy! You're the 'ear lessons guy!'

That earned another shot from the handgun.

The disproportionate roar of a shotgun blast swallowed the handgun's echo.

In the silence that followed, Kelda heard the characteristic hiss of a gasping exhale.

Whose?

She didn't know.

She felt almost paralyzed by fear.

Who had guns? Who was shooting?

Who were the good guys? Whom could she trust?

The darkness had surrounded her and doubt was eating away at her soul. She turned her head toward the dirt road and thought, *Is that Death Row?*

CHAPTER

58

While I heard the shots from the handgun, I was crouching low, picking my footfalls carefully, trying to progress through the woods in the direction of Tom's voice. Each time a gunshot sounded, I froze. But when the reverberations of the shotgun blast bounced off the mountainside, I fell hard to the earth, pushing my cheek into the soil. A mini-landslide of dirt slid inside my cast.

In the silence that followed I could hear my own blood rushing in my ears, and the breeze sluicing through the pines, but nothing else.

Tom's last call before the boom of the shotgun had been, 'You're the 'ear lessons guy!'

Fear lessons.

What had Boca said? When the time comes for the fear lessons, I'll know it?

The time had come.

When the series of gunshots sliced through the darkness the way a machete slices through flesh, I knew it.

After an eternity, a voice said, 'I'm standing up and going into the middle of this road here. Don't shoot anymore. I'm dropping my weapon.'

I couldn't see him, had no way to know whether he was doing what he said he was doing. And I had no way to know who he was.

After twenty more seconds, Kelda said, 'Tom? Are you there?'

In front of me, I guessed maybe twenty or thirty yards, Tom Clone, breathless, replied, 'Yes.'

Then she said, 'Anybody else here?'

No one else responded.

Kelda said, 'I'm a special agent of the FBI and I'm not dropping my weapon. I want everybody on that dirt road. You have ten seconds. You got it?'

Tom said yes. The other male voice echoed the word.

I could hear someone – Tom? – creeping into the woods. He was brushing branches and crushing twigs as he made his way to the road.

Fingers closed over my ankle and someone cautioned, 'Shhh. Not a sound.'

My heart felt as though it instantly doubled in size.

I snarled, 'Damn you, Sam.'

His lips so close to my ear that I could feel his breath, he said, 'Sorry I'm late. Simon's game went long. This thing here? This is the goofiest thing I've ever heard. How long you been here?'

'Maybe ten minutes,' I whispered. 'I think somebody was just shot.'

'Yeah, the shotgun. I got that. You stay right here, understand? I'm feeling like my services are needed.'

59

S am called my name another ten minutes later.
I'd been watching flashlight beams crisscrossing in the woods in the distance. I hiked toward them.

I was almost close enough to Sam to begin to question him about what had happened when the *thwap-thwap-thwap* of an approaching helicopter drowned out every other sound that the night was manufacturing in the Indian Peaks.

Sam waved me closer with one hand while with the other he painted light patterns in the sky with the flashlight. I thought that he was providing guidance to the helicopter pilot who was hovering above.

Kelda stood in a caricature of catatonia on a narrow dirt lane about ten yards from Sam. She was holding a flashlight, too. The beam in her hand was locked in place at her feet, highlighting the torso of a man I didn't recognize. Sprawled on his side, legs splayed, he too was still. Crimson shadows of blood darkened his neck and face.

Kelda wasn't tending to him.

To me, that meant that he was dead.

I wanted to ask someone who he was. How he had died. Who had killed him. And why. But the helicopter rotors insisted on my silence.

I kept walking closer to Sam until I saw another man.

He was sitting against the base of an aspen tree, his arms circled around the trunk behind him. Another step and I could see that his wrists were shackled with a plastic band. His head was bowed.

Suddenly, a beam of light burst from the helicopter with an intensity that felt obscene, illuminating the tiny piece of the forest where I stood.

That's when I spotted Tom. Or someone who I guessed was Tom.

He was curled in a ball on the forest floor about five feet away from Sam.

He looked like a pile of rags that had been dumped in the woods.

No, more accurately, he looked like a pile of rags that a passing motorist had used to cover, unsuccessfully, the carcass of some roadkill that had been dumped in the woods.

I said, 'Sam? Is Tom dead?'

I stepped closer to them both.

The helicopter rotors answered, '*Thwap-thwap-thwap.*'

The obscene light slid away and the helicopter disappeared over the ridge near Boca's cabin.

'Sam,' I repeated. 'Is that Tom Clone? Is he okay?' I was ducking clumsily beneath the low branch of an aspen tree.

'The Flight for Life chopper is for him. He'll be okay, I think. Stop right there, Alan. I don't want you any closer for now. Do you understand?'

Sam's voice told me he wasn't kidding.

I stopped, and then I took a step back for good measure. 'Who's the guy in the road?' I asked.

'No ID on him. Best I can piece together so far, he's the guy who was torturing Mr. Clone.'

'And the guy cuffed to the tree? He shot the guy on the road?'

'The guy cuffed to the tree says he's a Park County sheriff's deputy, if you can believe it.'

'Why did he shoot the guy on the road?'

'He didn't. Clone shot him. Clone had the shotgun.'

I glanced at Kelda. She still hadn't moved. Not a muscle.

I barely reacted to Sam's recitation. Apparently, I was all out of adrenaline; I felt bone tired.

I'd stepped into the darkness and found fear.

Had I accomplished anything else?

Boca had said that sometimes the step into the darkness leads nowhere.

That, I decided, was the step I took. The one that led nowhere.

PART FIVE

Seeking Higher Ground

CHAPTER

60

The Boulder County Sheriff's investigators completed the first round of questioning with Kelda and me at about the same time, about ten minutes before midnight.

I could hear her a few steps behind me as I trudged back up the hill toward Boca's cabin and my car.

'Can we meet?' she asked slightly breathlessly. Her catatonia had disappeared along with the helicopter that had ferried Tom Clone down the Front Range to a hospital in Boulder.

'Sure,' I said into the blackness. 'Call my office tomorrow. We'll work out a time.' My mind was elsewhere – the reverberation of the shotgun blast continued to echo and the darkness continued to shroud my vision – and I was tired. I told myself that I would have been more gracious to her if I weren't so tired.

She came abreast of me and touched my arm. 'What about now, Alan? Right now?'

'It's the middle of the night, Kelda.'

'I know what time it is. I think we should talk about . . .
what happened here. I think there are some things that . . .
you should be aware of. Things you didn't see down there.
It could change things for you . . . tomorrow.'

'Change things how?'

She looked behind her. 'Not here, Alan.'

'It can't wait?'

'I don't think it should. I think you need to know
everything that happened up here tonight.'

*Bees and snakes and napalm. Fear lessons, darkness.
Shotguns and death*, I mused.

'That's funny,' I said. 'I was just thinking that maybe it
would be better if I never knew what happened up here
tonight.'

'You don't mean that.'

I did mean that, but I said, 'You obviously have
someplace in mind. What are you thinking?'

'I was thinking, I don't know, that Boca might loan us
his cabin for a short while. We could talk there.'

I shook my head. 'Boca's been dragged into enough. I
don't want to intrude on him again. He moved up here to
get away from . . . situations like this. From people like us.'

'How about a restaurant in Nederland?'

At that hour, all that would be open would be a bar, and
Nederland's bars were a little too notorious for my taste.
'It's not appropriate for us to meet in a restaurant.'

I expected her to argue with me. She didn't. It was
apparent that she had a long string of options prepared.
'Then how about your office? Say, half an hour, forty
minutes?'

'You're sure that this can't wait?'

'I'm not going to have any free time tomorrow and I don't think you are either. I think we should do it now. If the sheriff calls for another interview before we get a chance to talk . . .' She let the thought hang provocatively.

'What if he does?'

'You should hear what I have to say before you talk to him again. That's all.'

'You want to influence what I say to the sheriff?'

'Not at all. I want to talk about some things we both experienced tonight. Tell you my impressions.'

'This makes it sound like this meeting you want will be therapy?'

'Yes. Therapy.'

I took three more steps. 'Okay. My office. I guess I'll see you in Boulder, then.'

I don't know whether it was a function of the hour or her casual dress or what we'd just been through up near Ward, but Kelda kicked off her shoes in my office and positioned herself on the sofa as though she were curling up to watch TV at home. Her fingertips immediately found a quad muscle to knead.

I waited. Although for some reason I wasn't as tired as I'd been an hour earlier, I would have much preferred at that moment to be inhaling the aroma of my little girl as I kissed her good night on the way to join my wife in bed.

Kelda wasn't looking at me when she finally began. 'Could Jones really have made it all up? All that stuff she'd written in her journal about Tom following her to Hawaii?'

Given the events of the evening, and the prologue Kelda had offered up near Boca's cabin, I'd expected something more profound.

I considered how a clinical psychologist at the top of his game might respond to her question. Whatever the proper response might have been, I'm sure mine wasn't it. I answered, 'I don't think she exactly made it up, Kelda. Jones wasn't well. You know that. After she heard that the guy she'd been dating was a suspect in almost beheading a girl who was not that different from her in age, appearance, circumstances—'

She finished my thought, 'That's when her paranoia took over.'

I leaned forward, closing the distance between us by a third, and made my voice soft. 'Yes, that's probably when her paranoia took over. Looking back, it seems as though she may have developed a delusion that was centered on Tom Clone, or he conveniently stepped into one that she was developing anyway. Given her predisposition to paranoia, given the absence of her primary emotional support – you – given what she was hearing in the news about Ivy Campbell's murder, given some tension that may have existed in her relationship with Tom – all the pieces were in place for her to suffer some deterioration in her emotional balance, which was precarious at best, anyway.

'I think it's a safe assumption that her reality testing was quite impaired at the end. Once she got to Hawaii, probably even before she left, she began to see Tom Clone where he wasn't, and she totally convinced herself that he was after her. So . . . to answer your question, no, Jones didn't make it up. I'm sure she believed that Tom was after her. Remember the paintings. The chasing pictures. Her fears – the danger she felt – were her reality.' I added firmly, 'But that doesn't mean that any of it actually happened.'

'She was sweet, Alan. If you could get past her fears, she had a terrific heart underneath.'

'I don't doubt that, Kelda. Jones had an illness. Not a nice illness. The fears weren't real. But Jones was.'

She smiled faintly at me, as though she was grateful that I wasn't going to ask her to give up her love for her friend.

Although I still hadn't heard anything that convinced me that this emergency session was necessary, I reminded myself to be patient. I decided to try to plant a seed even though I didn't expect to see anything sprout from it anytime soon. 'I'm thinking that Jones wasn't the first girl that you tried to rescue, Kelda.'

'What?'

I allowed a few seconds to drip away before I responded. 'So much of what we've talked about since you first came into my office has to do with Jones and with Rosa Alija. In a way, your life has been very much consumed with your efforts to save those two people, and the consequences of those efforts.'

I expected her to brush me off. She didn't.

'I . . . um. I . . .' She looked away from me.

'Go on, Kelda,' I said.

She wrinkled her nose in an expression I'd not seen before. She said, 'I've never told you much about . . . growing up.'

Here we go, I thought. *Here we go.* 'No, you haven't. You haven't spoken about your family much at all.'

'You've guessed, though, haven't you? Do you already know?'

'Do I know what happened when you were growing up? No, I don't. I don't have any idea. Have I imagined that something did happen? Yes, I have. We all have history.'

She grew silent and stayed quiet for a length of time that stretched into minutes. Her hands stilled and she ceased massaging her legs. It was by far the longest period of contemplation – or escape? – that I'd witnessed since I started seeing her for psychotherapy.

If you had asked me to bet, I would have bet that Kelda was going to take a protective stroll away from any examination of her past. I would have bet that her defenses would rise to protect her like her gun rising from her holster. A quick-draw.

I would have bet wrong.

'We had a tree house,' she said. 'My little sister and I. My dad built it for us. A really, really special tree house. With a shingled roof and curtains and rugs. We loved it. It was our favorite place.

'I could climb all the way from my bedroom window, out onto the roof, down some long limbs, and into the tree house. Sometimes I'd sneak up on my sister and scare her when she was there by herself. One time.'

Kelda didn't pause after she said 'One time.'

She stopped.

I did the therapist's equivalent of putting a hand on her back and shoving. 'Go on,' I said.

She took a long, slow breath to steel herself. 'One time,

one night, when I was eleven and she was eight, I went out my window after dinner and snuck up on her and I found her in the tree house with the boy who lived two doors down from us.' She closed her eyes. 'You know the rest.'

'No, I don't.'

'Her shorts were down. He was touching her. That's the rest.'

'No. It's not.'

She opened her eyes. The glare was incendiary. I fought an impulse to pull away from her fury.

She swallowed once and went on. 'I pushed him out the door. He fell, and landed on his neck. That's it.'

'You saved her?'

'Are you kidding? I was too late to save her. I'm always too late. But I punished him. He hasn't taken a step since that day. Not one.'

Clarity. A little girl molested by a neighbor. A culprit punished.

Clarity?

Hardly.

'That's not all, though, is it?' I asked.

'What?'

'The fall paralyzed him. But that wasn't all, was it?'

'No, that wasn't all. He had brain damage, too. He couldn't talk. He couldn't communicate.'

The fire had left her eyes and Kelda's voice was cold.

I stated the obvious. Often it was the most important part of my job. 'Which meant that he couldn't tell you why he did it. He couldn't tell you what made him tick.'

'No. He couldn't.'

'And that left you feeling . . . what?' I asked.

Her nostrils flared just a tiny bit. 'So,' she said flatly, 'Tom Clone didn't have anything to do with Jones's death.'

The change in direction was so abrupt that I felt as though I'd just been subjected to inhumane *g* forces. I managed to say, 'No. It appears he didn't. You changed the subject, Kelda.'

'Did I? That leaves—'

My phone rang in my pocket. I guessed it was Lauren wondering where the hell I was, so, despite the poignancy of the therapeutic moment, I took my attention away from Kelda and glanced at the caller ID on my cell. I was wrong about the identity of the caller. 'I'm sorry to interrupt, but, given the circumstances, I should get this,' I told Kelda.

'I understand.'

I stood, moved behind my desk, and turned my back on Kelda. I considered walking out into the hallway to take the call but didn't want to leave Kelda alone in the office with my phone logs and files. I said, 'Hi.'

Sam said, 'You knew it was me, didn't you? I hate caller ID. Listen, there's something I thought you'd want to know. This Park County cop we have up here? He's a guy named Bonnet, George Bonnet, calls himself Hoppy for some reason. Thing is, after sitting quiet for almost three hours, he just confessed to killing Ivy Campbell.'

I opened my mouth, closed it, and finally managed to say, 'You're kidding, right?'

'No, I'm not. One of the sheriff's guys leaned on him a little – not hard. Well, not too hard – and he just started talking. Then he led us all to this mineshaft and showed us where he killed his friend – another Park County cop named – just a second – named Prehost. Says he shot Prehost and let his body go down an old mineshaft. It's going to be a bitch to recover.'

'He killed his friend, too?'

'Yeah. Apparently the two of them had been following Clone, trying to get the focus of the old murder case back on him and then, then . . . well, then something totally screwy happened up here. There's some weird prison fence thing out in the forest and Tom Clone was trying to tell everybody he was kidnapped and attacked by bees and snakes and shit. Goofiest thing I've ever seen in my life.' He paused. 'Well, almost.'

'But you're sure about Ivy Campbell's murder?'

'I'm sure Bonnet confessed, if that's what you're asking. I heard it myself. Is it legit? Who the hell knows? But this cop says he did it. I can't come up with a reason why he'd confess if it wasn't true.'

'Was the other cop part of it?'

'Hoppy says not. He says the other cop thought Clone was guilty of the old murder the whole time. Hoppy killed him because he was afraid that the guy who was torturing Tom might say something that would let his partner figure out that Hoppy was involved in Ivy's murder.'

'Wow.'

Sam's voice changed a little. 'You don't know anything about any of this, do you, Alan?'

I was grateful that the answer was that I didn't.

I said, 'Just what I heard from Boca at the cabin. Just what I heard from Boca. The same stuff you've probably heard about the kidnapping and the fence thing and the fear lessons. The bees and snakes. And the gasoline. There

451

was something about gasoline. I told you that earlier on the phone. Remember?'

I looked over my shoulder at Kelda. Her attention to my conversation was rapt. She mouthed, 'What?'

A minute too late, I walked out into the hall and closed the door behind me.

Sam said, 'Boca's great. I like Boca. Yeah, we got all that, the gas part, too – found a cooler full of some napalm stuff out by this fenced-in pen. Had to get the HazMat guys out of bed to deal with it. But you don't know anything about this guy Hoppy and the Campbell girl? That's news to you, right?'

'Absolutely.'

'Hoppy says the guy who was shot up here had been babbling about some old murder in Hawaii. You know anything about that?'

'A murder in Hawaii?' I managed. In a split second I spied the trapdoor that was hidden in a dark corner of Sam's question. Without much hesitation, I lifted the lid and slithered into the blackness. By uttering a few additional words – 'I don't know anything about a murder in Hawaii' – I pulled the door shut over my head.

'No?'

'No.'

I know about a girl who died at the base of a cliff near Paia. But no murder. No. The girl I know about jumped. Or maybe she fell. But no murder. No. 'What was Hoppy's motive?'

'He says Ivy offended him in a bar. He says she "disrespected" him in a bar the night before. He followed her to where she was staying and then went back out there the next day and demanded an apology from her. He says he was drunk, that he used to have a problem with alcohol. She responded by disrespecting him again. Things deteriorated from there, apparently.'

'That's it? Jesus.'

'This Hoppy guy was assisting on the murder investigation from day one. He made sure that Clone was framed like a picture in a museum. He was in a perfect position to do it.'

'I guess.'

One more time, Sam asked, 'Is there anything you want to add, Alan? This Hawaii thing, maybe? You don't know anything about it, you're sure? Last chance. I have to go.'

'Nothing. Nothing. I don't know anything about any murder in Hawaii. Not a thing.'

He was silent. His silence felt like a big fat hand shoving me insistently in the back. I was glad he couldn't see my face. I said, 'Thanks for calling. Thanks for everything you've done tonight.'

'If you decide you know something, you have my cell number, right?'

What did he think I knew? Worse, what did he know I knew? 'Yes, I know the number. But I don't know anything.'

He hung up. I folded the phone, returned to my office, and sat back down. Kelda didn't appear to have moved.

Kelda said, 'What's going on?'

I tried to remember where we'd left off. 'You had just changed the subject. You'd been talking about your sister and the tree house and then you said that Tom didn't have anything to do with Jones's death.'

'That was Purdy, wasn't it? What did he just tell you?'

When totally off balance, I tend to fall back on the rules. It's not one of my more endearing traits. I said, 'This is therapy, Kelda. I don't discuss my personal phone conversations in therapy.'

She didn't hesitate. She said, 'You're joking, right?'

'No. I'm serious.'

'Then you're fired.'

'What?'

'You're fired. You're not my therapist anymore. So what did Purdy just tell you? Answer me or I'll go get my phone and find out for myself. You know that if I have someone call the Boulder Sheriff, they'll tell us what's going on.'

I was too tired to care about the rules. 'Hoppy Bonnet? The Park County cop? He just confessed to murdering Ivy Campbell.'

She blinked twice as though she had to translate my words from English before she could process them. Then she gasped and her hand flew to her mouth. After fifteen seconds or so, she started to weep.

'Can I start therapy again?' she asked.

With that as a prelude, I definitely wanted to hear whatever she was planning to say next. Cynical? Sure. Was it the right clinical course to jump back and forth into a therapeutic relationship, given the events of the night? Probably not, but I didn't think about it long enough to come to a thoughtful conclusion. I was too determined to hear what was going to come next.

I said, 'Yes.'

'Right now? We're in therapy again? This is confidential?'

'Yes.'

She said, 'I planted the knife that got Tom Clone out of prison. It wasn't the real murder weapon.'

'You . . .'

'The man who was killed up there tonight is Ira Winslett. Ira is Jones's brother. He and I planted the knife that got Clone freed from prison.'

My mouth hung open.

'I came up with a ruse to get into the property room in Park County, and I stole a section of her bloody clothing out of evidence. Ira doctored the knife with the blood that was dried on the clothes. We hid the knife, and then I went and pretended to find it.'

I actually said, 'I'm speechless.' I was that incredulous.

'Once our lab determined that some of the blood on the knife wasn't Tom Clone's, I anonymously let the attorney who was handling Tom's appeals know that the anomaly had shown up. That got everything going. He contacted the Bureau; the courts took another look at the case . . . It all took some time, but we got Tom out of prison.'

'Why, Kelda? Why did you do it?'

'Ira and I wanted to get him out of jail so we could punish him for what he did to Jones.'

'Punish him? He was on death row, for Christ's sake.' I didn't feel I had to add, *For a crime it turns out he didn't commit.* So I didn't.

'He was on death row for what he did to Ivy Campbell. We wanted time alone with him for what he did to Jones.'

'Oh my God,' I said as I finally comprehended what Kelda and Jones's brother had been doing.

'Yeah,' she agreed. 'Oh my God.'

'That's what the thing was with the fence and the fear lessons and the snakes and the bees and—'

'Yes, yes, yes. But that was all Ira. He cut me out of all the planning a while ago. He didn't trust me anymore. Maybe he never really trusted me. Maybe he just needed me to get Tom out of prison. Right now, I don't know what to think.'

'That's why you've been frantically looking for Tom? Because you knew that Ira had him? And you guessed what he was going to do to him? No, you didn't guess, you knew?'

She nodded and wiped away a tear that had migrated to her chin.

'That's why you referred Tom to me, isn't it?'

She cocked her head and looked at me. 'What do you mean?'

'You wanted me to stop you. To interfere with this . . . this plot you were cooking up with Ira.'

'No. No. Giving him your name that day . . . it was just a . . . brain cramp. That's all.'

'I don't think so. Think about it, Kelda. You wanted me in the middle of this. You must have wanted me to stop you.'

'No,' she said.

'You were dating Tom, Kelda.'

I watched her try to chase the thought away. 'That was . . . I don't know . . . tactical.'

'How?'

'At first, I wanted to know how he was most vulnerable. How to get to him . . . most effectively. That's what I told myself, anyway. But then . . . I don't know. I started to want to know what made him tick, to understand how he could have done what he did to Ivy Campbell and to Jones. I wanted to find his weak spot, the way he found theirs.' She shifted on the sofa, crossing her legs beneath her. 'But after a while . . . the last couple of times . . . I wasn't so sure at all why I was spending time with him. Something had changed.'

I said, 'This time, you wanted to know him before you pushed him out of the tree house?'

'Maybe that's it. I don't know. I've thought about it that way. I just don't know.'

'Prisons take different forms, don't they, Kelda?'

'What do you mean?'

'The kid you pushed out of the tree house? He's in one, isn't he?'

'Yes, he is.'

'Are you in a prison, too, Kelda?' I asked.

'Are you?' she shot back, after half a heartbeat's delay.

I considered pressing her further, upping the ante. Instead, I asked, 'Tom was being tortured, wasn't he?' The t-word was Sam's, but it seemed to fit. 'Jones's brother took him up to Ward to imprison him and to torture him?'

'I never used that word. But, yes,' she said, 'that was his plan. Our plan. We wanted ten minutes alone in a room with Clone. That's what we called it. "Alone in a room."'

'Ten minutes?'

'Metaphorically.'

'You got Tom Clone out of prison to torture him, Kelda?'

'We wanted him to know what she felt. What she wrote about in her journal. Her agony. Her terror. We wanted him to know what anguish he caused her. We wanted him to know it, to *feel* it.'

'Revenge?' My incredulousness had hardly abated.

'Retaliation. Revenge. Retribution. Vengeance. I've found lots of words for it since it all started. But they were all just different ways of saying that we were teaching him a lesson, we were getting even. It's all been about getting some satisfaction, Alan. I never felt any satisfaction after saving Rosa, because the way it ended was too easy for the guy who molested her. I didn't want that to happen again. So that's what it's been about for me. I wanted some satisfaction.'

'Did you feel satisfaction after you pushed the boy from the tree house?'

She glared at me. 'At least he knew my sister's helplessness, didn't he? After that, he knew exactly what vulnerability was. Didn't he? Didn't he?'

I didn't know what to say. *Of course he did.*

Kelda wasn't burdened by any doubts. 'He got what was coming to him. And I got satisfaction.'

I repeated the last word silently before I opened my mouth to speak. But words to describe my feeling were as elusive as the summer monsoons.

Kelda leaned forward. 'Oh, don't be so naïve – think about it, Alan. Think about September 11. If you offered the families of the people who died that day ten minutes alone in a room with bin Laden, you don't think they'd take it? What about the Oklahoma City victims and McVeigh? Of course they'd go for it. All of them. In a New York second. Well, Ira and I decided to take our ten minutes. We saw a way to do it and we were going to get our time alone with Clone.'

'Fear? The "fear lessons"? This is what the fear lessons

were about? You were making him as frightened as she was?'

'I wanted him to stand on the edge of that cliff with Jones and feel the thrust of a hand on his back. I wanted him to feel what that boy felt after he fell from the tree house. I wanted that second or two he spent in the air before his neck snapped to last for infinity.'

'The boy didn't fall from that tree house, Kelda. You pushed him. Not to punish him, but to save your sister.'

'Whatever.'

'Tom Clone didn't kill anybody, Kelda,' I said. My outrage was barely in check. 'He didn't kill Ivy Campbell and he didn't have anything to do with Jones's death. Nothing.'

I could see the muscles in her jaws tighten into ropes.

'We didn't know that. Yes, we manufactured the evidence that got him out, Ira and I, but we were working under the assumption that he really had killed Ivy Campbell. The system said he did it. A jury said he did it. The evidence said he did it.

'And we were absolutely sure that he killed Jones. Her journal made that as clear as day.'

I wanted to scream at her. I settled for packing my words in ice. 'Tom Clone has never been to Hawaii, Kelda. Never.'

She swallowed. 'He hasn't? You're sure about that?' I could tell that she wasn't truly surprised by my revelation. The tenor of her questions told me she had already come to the conclusion that Tom had never followed Jones to Hawaii.

'Yes, I'm sure. I asked him on the phone earlier tonight. After you told me about what you read in Jones's journal,

459

I had Boca ask him if he'd ever been there. I didn't tell him why I was asking. I just asked him if he'd ever been. Well, he said he hadn't. I don't think he even knows that Jones moved to Maui.

'He didn't have anything to do with what happened in Paia. Nothing at all. Jones fell off that cliff. Or she jumped. Or someone else pushed her. But Tom Clone didn't do it.'

She looked away from me. 'You have to believe that I didn't know that before tonight. I didn't know . . . that he didn't kill Jones.'

'He didn't kill anyone.' I made sure that I laded my voice with as much irony as it could bear when I added, 'Until tonight, anyway.'

'Ira and I thought what we were doing was right. That our crusade was just. We were sure . . .' Her voice trailed off.

I half expected a knock on the door. A loud knock, pounding fists. A sheriff with a warrant for her arrest.

I asked, 'Are you going to get away with this, Kelda?'

'I'm not sure. It depends on what Ira said before he was killed. There's no evidence down here. If Ira was careful up there . . . maybe. Nobody can even tie Tom to Jones's death. Without doing that, why would they look for Ira or me? Nobody knows what we were planning but you.'

The weight of the knowledge that I was the keeper of the secrets plastered me to my chair. I could barely fill my lungs, the burden on my heart felt so great.

'Now it turns out that we got Tom out of prison for all the wrong reasons, but I'm beginning to think that maybe it was the right thing to do after all. Is that possible? That the right thing happened? If Ira and I hadn't gotten Tom out of prison, he'd still be on death row, right? He'd be scheduled to die in Cañon City. No matter what Ira did to him up there, it's better than that, isn't it? It's better than Tom dying from a lethal injection, right?'

I chewed her words reluctantly and tried to swallow the rationalization even though I knew that every bit of it was rotten. My capacity for empathy deserted me and I thought, *How am I supposed to feel right now?*

Before I could get too far lost in that egocentric miasma, Kelda said, 'I can't believe what I did to Tom. And . . . I can't believe that Ira is dead. He was my lover. I never told you that. Maybe you guessed. It doesn't matter. Now he's dead and there's a hole right here' – she thumped a fist between her breasts – 'where he used to be. I don't know what to think anymore.' Her voice sharpened. 'What am I supposed to feel, Alan? Tell me, please. I'm . . . lost. Now that this is over, what am I supposed to feel?'

A single word emerged in my head.

Satisfaction?

Only a few lights were on in the Denver Field Office. A solitary special agent was on night shift handling the after-hours FBI phone duty. When Kelda stepped off the elevator and said hello to the agent at the phones, a new guy she barely recognized, he told her that the shift, thus far, had been slow.

'Hope it stays that way,' Kelda said.

One of the lines rang just then and the agent brought his hands together like an altar boy in prayer before he reached for the receiver. Although she thought she'd seen a flicker of recognition in his eyes, he didn't say a thing to her about the events in Ward the night before.

Were she planning on staying with the FBI, she would have remembered him for his discretion.

Kelda made her way to her desk and began packing her things into a couple of cardboard file boxes. She expected to collect the few personal items she kept at work and to be back in the elevator in ten minutes.

She almost made it.

As she was completing a final search of the drawers of the desk, someone approached her from behind so silently she didn't hear his footfalls until the last few steps.

Without turning to face him, she said, 'You need to change whatever it is you use on your hair, Bill. It precedes you like a toxic wave.'

'Thanks for the tip, Kelda. I've been wondering why I've been striking out with so many women. I had been worried that it's a character flaw. It's nice to know it's merely a question of bad hair gel. My favorite problems in life are the ones that can be solved for less than five bucks.'

'Hint: Spend more than five bucks. It will probably smell better. How did you know I'd be here?'

'After what happened last night up in the mountains with Clone and those Park County cops, I bugged the SAC all day today. He handed me a bunch of bullshit before he finally admitted that you were going on leave, but he wouldn't tell me why.

'Knowing you, I figured that you'd try to sneak out of here without saying good-bye to anyone. I told Carter at the desk that I'd owe him one if he'd give me a heads-up if you showed your face while he was covering the phones. I was killing time down at Panzano when he called. Great *fritto misto*. The bartender is keeping a couple of seats warm at the bar for me. Why don't you come on down? I'll buy us a bottle of Barolo.'

Kelda glanced at the empty section in the hinged frame on Bill's desk.

'I don't think so, Bill.'

'Come on, finish packing up. I'll help you carry that stuff to your car. Then we'll go have some wine.'

She said, 'Your calamari will already be cold by the time we get back to the restaurant.' She didn't really want to put him off; she merely wanted to gauge his persistence.

'I suspect they'll fry some up fresh if we ask them to. I just got my tax refund check. Come on, I'm celebrating.'

She lowered herself to her desk chair, thinking that it would be the last time she would sit in the Denver Field Office, and she allowed her eyes to close. Her legs didn't hurt, and for an extended moment, she wondered why. Finally, she opened her eyes and looked up at Bill Graves.

'What?' he asked. 'What's that face?'

'Is your cousin really the governor of Kansas? Tell me the truth. No bullshit this time.'

He didn't smile. He said, 'We've known each other for a long time, Kelda. We're colleagues. We're friends. We wouldn't lie to each other, would we?'

She tasted his words for irony, but couldn't quite decide.

The *fritto misto* was terrific, as advertised, and the wine that Bill picked was so supple and rich that Kelda thought that if red grapes could actually bleed, they would bleed this Barolo.

Bill held his wineglass in front of his face and looked at Kelda through the tannic legs that rippled down from the rim on the inside of the glass. 'You know somebody set us up,' he said.

'What?'

'That knife we found up in the mountains? Somebody

set us up. If it wasn't the real murder weapon – and the Park County cop who now says he killed that girl is telling everybody that it wasn't – then somebody set us up to find what we found.'

'Yes?' She focused on spearing a ring of calamari.

'Doesn't that piss you off?'

She didn't trust that she could make her face a good enough mask, so she poked the squid into her mouth before she gazed at the surface of the wine in her glass. She could see a distorted reflection of Bill Graves in the mahogany surface of the wine. Finally, she said, 'I guess.'

'Why would somebody do that?'

'Somebody wanted him off death row, I suppose. You know as well as I do how many fanatics there are out there about . . . capital punishment.'

'Why us, though? Why the Bureau? Why didn't they just use the local cops as their patsies?'

'Does it matter? They didn't do it to us personally, Bill. We were just somebody's tools.'

'I know that. I'm wondering why someone would conspire to get him out of jail. That's what I don't get.'

'Maybe it was somebody who knew that he was innocent. That's why they did it. Whatever the reason, it appears that . . . justice was done. If we hadn't retrieved that knife, Clone would have been executed for a crime he didn't commit. So we did a good thing, right?'

'I know, I know. But who would've known that for sure? The real murderer. Nobody else. And I can't see that Park County cop they arrested arranging this whole charade. It doesn't add up. What would be in it for him?'

She leaned in close to him, hoping to dissuade his

interest in the topic. 'Why do people do half the shit they do, Bill?'

'You know, I really thought Clone did it,' Bill said, ignoring her subtle flirtation. 'I thought he killed Ivy Campbell. Eighty percent of the people on death row were convicted on less evidence than there is against Clone.'

'I did, too,' Kelda replied, sitting back again. 'I thought he did it.'

'Right from the start, I had reservations about what we did to help Clone get out of the penitentiary. I know we were just doing our jobs – you and me – but given the evidence against the guy, I wasn't sure he should be free. No, that's not true. The truth is that I *was* sure he *shouldn't* be set free.'

She speared a tiny scallop, dipped it in some fiery red sauce, lifted it to her mouth, and took a long sip of wine before she said, 'I had doubts, too. About getting him out.' She thought that the words were one hundred percent honest, and because they were she liked the feel of them as they slid across the contour of her lips.

'So why were you up there last night?'

'In Ward?'

'Yes, in Ward.'

'Clone called me and asked for help. He sounded desperate. That's why I went. He didn't know where else to turn.'

'Why didn't you get some backup?'

She thought that Bill was trying to sound nonchalant, nonjudgmental. She liked him for that. She knew some of her colleagues would have blasted her with, 'What the hell were you thinking going up there alone?'

'He thought that there were some cops involved in

whatever it was that was going on. He asked me not to call anybody, said it would only make things worse. I went along with him.'

After a moment spent digesting her rationale, Bill asked, 'Why didn't you get Bureau help?'

'Maybe I should have,' she replied. But she knew that Bill's question was ripe with subtext. What he really wanted to know is why she didn't call *him*. 'He didn't call me until after you and I talked in Boulder, Bill. I didn't shut you out. If I'd known what was going to go down, I would have called you.'

The last lie wasn't necessary. She immediately regretted it.

To her, he seemed to be processing her words as though he were checking the addition on a column of figures. After a few minutes, he said, 'Clone was being tortured up there. That's what I hear.'

'I didn't see that part. It was dark when I got to Ward, and everybody was already running around the forest. I didn't actually see Tom up close until he was being loaded into the chopper. But I can tell you that he looked awful. I believe that something terrible happened to him up there. Maybe torture.'

She thought of Ira's vipers and his bees and the laboratory in his basement.

Bill said, 'Well, I hear he was being tortured. That's what the local cops are telling the SAC.'

'Bill, I really don't want to talk about this. Is that okay? Do you mind? The wine's nice. Let's enjoy it.'

'No,' he said, his voice suddenly stern. 'House wine is nice. This bottle of Barolo is as lovely as you are.'

She forced a smile in reply.

'What are you going to do, Kelda? Now that you're gone from the Bureau.'

'It's only a leave of absence. I've had some health problems. I need to get some things with my health . . . under control. I don't think I'll make any decisions until I make some progress on that.'

'You want to tell me about the health problems?'

She eyed him for a while, deciding.

'I've had problems with my legs for a long time, but it's been unclear what's been going on. Just this morning I got word that an MRI I had last week shows a little lesion on my spinal column. The radiologist thinks that could explain a lot of my problems. My neurologist was pretty surprised by the news.'

'Why?'

'I think he was beginning to believe that it was all in my head. And I think I was beginning to agree with him.'

'A lesion? That sounds like it could be serious.'

'That's exactly what I said to my doctor.'

'Well, is it? Serious?'

'He says he doesn't know yet. He wants to do more tests to see what it really is. You know how it goes with doctors.'

'You'll keep me informed?'

'Maybe.'

He shook his head gently. 'It's not just a leave. You know it isn't. You won't be coming back to work.'

She raised an eyebrow. 'You're so sure?'

'I have radar for some things. It's the way I knew that Cynthia was screwing her boss. This is one of the things I have radar for.'

'I'm not screwing my boss, Bill.'

He found something funny in whatever image he conjured of the SAC and Kelda romantically entwined. 'Thank God for that, Kelda. But you are sneaking out the back door. Whether you admit it to yourself or not, you're leaving. There'll be somebody fresh at your desk next week. Some frigging new guy.'

She was tempted to argue with him. Didn't. Tacitly granting his point, she said, 'I like forensic accounting, and I'm pretty good at it. I think I can find some work if I need to.'

'I suspect you can,' he said, pouring some fresh wine into his empty glass. 'And you'll probably make enough to afford to drink this stuff whenever you want.'

'It'd be nice to make some money for a change.'

He looked into his wine as he asked. 'Are you still going to see him, Kelda?'

She stopped breathing. She was thinking, *I can't see Ira anymore, he's dead.* Her grief had almost erupted through her façade when she realized that Bill wasn't talking about Ira at all.

'Tom Clone?' she asked. 'You mean date him?'

'I guess that's what I mean.'

'I don't know. We haven't talked. You know, since . . .' She thought about Tom for a few seconds and repeated, 'I don't know.'

'But you were dating him? That's what that was that you two were doing?'

'I don't even know that for sure. Maybe. It was just one of those things. We went out. I didn't let myself think about what it meant. I was more curious than interested, if that makes any sense. It didn't feel romantic. I felt that I needed to be with him for some other reason. There was a connection to him because of . . . the knife . . . and everything. And I wanted to understand him. That was part of it. What he'd been through, you know? I was curious.'

'Like with Rosa?' he said. 'That kind of connection? The way you still see her sometimes?'

The irony and innocence of the question almost caused Kelda to lose her balance on the stool. 'Yes,' she managed. 'Kind of like that. But maybe it was more like the way that I always wished I'd had a chance to get inside the head of the guy who kidnapped her. To know evil like that. I didn't know what it was going to be with Tom, what I was going to discover about him. But I had to look, you know? Like at a traffic accident?' She liked the sound of the rationale. 'Yeah, more like that.'

They sat in silence until Bill said, 'In my head, Kelda – and this is just me – this right here' – he waved an index finger between her stool and his – 'right now, is my first date since I kicked Cynthia out of the house. I thought you should know that I feel that way, so there's no confusion. I haven't felt I could trust anybody since she did what she did to me.'

Kelda almost blurted, 'And you trust *me*?'

She didn't.

But she thought it was likely that Bill Graves was about to make the same mistake with her that he'd made with Cynthia. The poor guy still didn't know whom he could trust. Just the slightest encouragement on her part, she figured, and she and Bill would be done talking about Tom Clone for a while.

She looked away long enough to consider the likelihood that Dr. Gregory would tell her that accepting Bill's advances might be a repetition of the pattern with Ira, and man after man before him. What had Alan said? That her romantic relationships always seemed to mix business with pleasure? Yes, that she chose boyfriends because of something they could do for her.

But Dr. Gregory's comments made no more sense to her then than they had when he'd first uttered them.

Yeah, she thought. *Even if he's right, what's so wrong with that?*

Forcing a smile onto her face, she looked up and touched Bill's hand. She felt a sudden camaraderie with him. It surprised her. Warmth flushed her skin, and she knew she couldn't blame it on the wine.

Not totally, anyway.

CHAPTER

62

I'd cleared my schedule and had a day free of patients. It seemed like the right thing to do.

First thing that morning, in return for a promised turn behind the wheel, the orthopedist who was treating my broken arm fitted me with a new cast that he thought would allow me to drive my still-virgin Mini. He had me sit in a plastic chair in his casting room with my arm extended at just the right angle, and then he proceeded to fit the fiberglass and plaster onto my hand in such a way that we both thought I could grasp an imaginary gearshift.

It was amazing what difference a little geometry made. As I drove home to Spanish Hills in my old car, I felt like a new man.

My very first spin in the reincarnated Mini was a solitary jaunt over the route of the famed Morgul Bismarck bicycle-racing course in the eastern side of the county, not far from my house. My arm ached from the effort when I was done, but the drive was worth every second of discomfort.

Lauren was working only until noon and we were planning to meet for lunch. She was surprised when I called and said that I would pick her up at the district attorney's office instead of meeting her at a downtown restaurant. She was shocked to see me pull up at the front doors of the Justice Center in the red and white Mini.

'New cast,' I said, lifting my color-coordinated arm.

A big smile on her face, she asked, 'How is it?' She was talking about the car, not the cast.

'I'll show you. Get in.'

The thing purred like a big cat as I motored north on Broadway before pulling up Lee Hill Road into the deep cavern behind one of the many hogbacks that line the long center stretch of Colorado's Front Range. Omit the previous forty-eight hours and I couldn't recall the last time I had been up Left Hand in a car, though I'd probably done the climb a dozen times on my bike in the past couple of years, so I knew the road with the intimacy of a cyclist. I skipped the bypass to Olde Stage and stayed on Lee Hill all the way up to Left Hand Canyon, where I turned west to go even farther into the mountains.

Halfway up the climb Lauren said, 'So are we eating or just motoring?'

I said, 'Eating, eventually. Motoring, definitely. Other things, too.'

'Other things?'

'Indeed.'

'What about Grace?'

473

'Viv will stay with her until we get home. I offered her twenty bucks on top of the extra hours she'll get. She thought about it for a second or two before she said yes.'

'So do you like your car?'

'Watch.'

With a short thrust of my casted arm, I downshifted. The little box on wheels hopped to attention and I maneuvered it through the curving canyons as though it had already memorized every turn.

Ten minutes later, high in the Rockies, at the very top of Left Hand Canyon, we approached the anachronistic town of Ward. I said, 'This is where it all happened the other night.'

Lauren was still angry about the danger I'd put myself in for Tom Clone. But she nodded because she already knew that this is where it had all happened.

I slowed to a crawl to allow a trio of dogs to cross the road. None of the dogs' gene pools had been contaminated with an AKC specimen in many generations.

She said, 'You needed to come back, didn't you?'

I said, 'Yes,' but I didn't say more.

A turn to the south on the other side of Ward would have brought us down the Peak to Peak toward Nederland, Barker Reservoir, and the upper reaches of Boulder Canyon. But I pulled north instead, leaving the little town of Ward behind us before I cut off onto the washboard dirt track of Gold Lake Road and meandered a few miles to the entrance to the remote Gold Lake Resort.

'What's this?' my wife asked.

'A little treat for us. A thank-you for the car. A thank-you for being you. An apology for how . . . distracted I've been.'

She gazed out at the pristine meadows and the pine and aspen forests that were spread in the wilderness below the Divide before her eyes settled on the log cabins clustered on a gentle hillside. 'I didn't even know this place was here.'

'Good. Then it will be a surprise for you. It was once a camp for affluent girls from St. Louis. Now it's something else.'

'Affluent girls,' she repeated absently. I watched her eyes and could tell she was transfixed by the reflection of Sawtooth Mountain in the still waters of Gold Lake. 'Something else indeed,' she said.

Twenty minutes later, after we changed out of our clothes in one of the resort's tepees, we were sitting in a stone-lined hot pool on the uncluttered banks of Gold Lake. The summer wonder of the Indian Peaks Wilderness towered above us to the west, the cold face of Longs Peak's glaciers dominating the sky to the north. As sublime as the setting was, I knew our stay in the pool would be brief; Lauren's MS severely reduced her tolerance to hot water.

'Can I break the mood?' I asked.

'Only if you really, really have to.'

'What's going to happen to Tom Clone? Did you hear anything at the office this morning?' I'd called Tom a few times at Community Hospital, but the police weren't permitting him to receive calls, at least not from the likes of me.

Lauren's eyes were closed, the water lapping at the skin of her throat and steam enveloping her dark hair. 'Physically, he's going to be okay. I heard that he'll be ready to leave the hospital today, and nobody in the office seems to think he'll be arrested when he gets out. Given everything we know about what happened up there that night – I guess it's up *here* that night, isn't it? – I don't think he's going to be charged with any crimes. Unless the sheriff's investigators develop something new, what we have so far would never stand up to a jury. You've read the *Camera*, Alan; public sentiment is definitely to set Tom Clone free. He's done thirteen years already for a crime he didn't commit. Nobody wants to see him go back to prison for whatever part he played in whatever the hell happened two nights ago. Call the shooting self-defense, call it whatever you want, but, after what he went through up here, I think he's going to walk out of that hospital something resembling a free man. For once in his life everybody seems to want to grant him the benefit of the doubt.'

'So he really gets to start from square one? A new life. A clean slate.'

'In theory. But after what he's been through, he's probably starting from square minus four or five. He'll have his grandfather to lean on, though. I heard this morning that he's doing better, is out of the ICU.'

'That makes me happy.'

She opened her violet eyes wide and looked at me. She said, 'Show me where everything happened.'

My new cast high in the air, I floated to the other side of the pool and pointed west and slightly south toward the Continental Divide, in the direction of the lodgepole and aspen forests that surround Brainard Lake.

'Right over there,' I said. 'No more than a couple of miles from here. Just a little bit west and south of Ward.'

'This side of the Peak to Peak or the other side?'

'The other side.'

She floated over beside me and seemed to stare directly at the spot in the wilderness where I was pretty sure Boca's cabin stood. Below the surface of the pool, her hand found the soft skin adjacent to my navel.

She said, 'Are you going to keep seeing him for therapy?' Although I'd never said a word to Lauren about treating Tom Clone, events had made it crystal clear exactly who had been the recipient of my house call.

I didn't answer right away, trying to conjure an ethically appropriate way to respond. Finally, I said, 'Usually when a patient wants to continue in therapy, it's fine with me, too.'

'And there's no reason to think that this case would be unusual?'

I almost laughed at the thought that this case wasn't unusual. But I said, 'No. There's no reason to think that.'

'I'm glad,' she said. 'I'm sure he needs you.'

I didn't know how to respond to that. Didn't know whether to tell her about the bricklayer who was afraid he'd grown to despise the bricks. Nor did I want to admit to her my own failure to grant Tom the benefit of the doubt.

She said, 'Just don't do it again, okay? Something stupid like the other night? Just don't do it.'

I'd already prepared my defense. 'I want Grace to know the difference between right and wrong. I want her to know that people matter. Given the work we do, you and me, sometimes . . . we're going to need to be part of the lesson.'

'Well, I want Grace to know her father.'

'Okay,' I said. I'd been trumped. I knew that if Lauren and I debated this fifty times, I would win exactly none of the contests.

Zero.

I cupped some water in my good hand and watched it slip through the cracks between my fingers. 'I can't argue with you. I don't know that what I did was right. It's like justice. Just when you think you have a good way to hold on to it, it leaks out someplace and flows away.'

'Welcome to my world,' Lauren said. 'You balance yourself on top of the fence. You look in both directions and eventually you pick a side, and you jump off. That's it. I'm sure you did what you thought was best. And that's all you can do.' She rested her fingers on my cast. 'I just need to know that you'll always, *always*, consider Grace and me high in your equation.'

I nodded as I lofted some more water and watched it spill away. But I wasn't satisfied. 'Aren't there times when you think you know better, though? Times when you think that the justice you could create would be better than the justice the system dishes out?'

'Of course there are those times,' Lauren said. 'Frequently.'

'Then what do you do?'

'I let the system work.'

'Even when you know it's inadequate?'

'Sure. But it's inadequate almost by definition. Ultimately, by choosing to live in a civilized world, we trump any sense of ultimate justice. Truly satisfying justice – where the punishment really, really fits the crime – would demand that we do things that civilized societies can't risk doing. It's just the way it is. The system is imperfect.'

I cupped one more handful of water. It took a second or two longer, but it, too, dripped away. Lauren seemed so at peace with the imperfections.

'Hey, when's lunch?' she asked. I figured she'd spotted the log cabin splendor of Alice's Restaurant in the main lodge when we checked in.

'I left my watch in the tepee. Half an hour or so is what I would guess. You have a facial scheduled after that. And then a foot massage in another one of the tepees.'

My wife adored foot massages. 'Really? A foot massage in a tepee?'

'Really.'

'What are you going to do while I get my massage?'

'I thought I'd go for a hike. Or maybe see exactly how hard it is to paddle a canoe with one arm in a cast.'

She smirked. 'There, that's the answer to your question: That's what justice is like – paddling a canoe with one arm in a cast. But we still have half an hour or so before lunch?'

I nodded.

'That should be enough time,' she said.

'For what?'

I felt her fingers move south.

Every muscle in her body stilled for a moment as she said, 'We all go through bad times.'

'And usually we survive them?' I asked.

'Yes,' she said. 'We do.'